The Masters of Mystery

The Masters of Mystery

Collected and introduced by
MARTIN RADCLIFFE

First Published in Great Britain in 2004
by The Do-Not Press Ltd
16 The Woodlands, London SE13 6TY

Collection and editorial content copyright © Martin Radcliffe 2004

British Library Cataloguing in Publication Data
A catalogue record for this book is available from
the British Library.

Trade paperback: ISBN 1-904-316-23-9
Casebound edition: ISBN 1-904-316-22-0

1 3 5 7 9 10 8 6 4 2

Printed and bound in Great Britain

www.thedonotpress.com

CONTENTS

Contents

SOURCES

'The Mystery of Marie Roget' by Edgar Allen Poe comes from *Tales*, edited by Evert A Duyckninck (New York, Wiley & Putnam, 1845).

'The Murdered Cousin' by J S Le Fanu is taken from *Ghost Stories and Tales of Mystery* (London, William S Orr & Co, 1851).

The Biter Bit' by Wilkie Collins appeared in *Atlantic Monthly*, April 1858.

'Hunted Down' by Charles Dickens first appeared over three instalments in the *New York Ledger* from 20th August to 3rd September 1859.

'The Stolen White Elephant' by Mark Twain is taken from *The Stolen White Elephant and Other Detective Stories* (Boston, James R Osgood and Co, 1882)

'Jerry Stokes' by Grant Allen appeared in *The Strand*, September 1891.

'The Adventure of the Copper Beeches' by Sir Arthur Conan Doyle first appeared in *The Strand*, June 1892.

'Cheating the Gallows' by Israel Zangwill was first published in *The Idler*, February 1893.

'The Great Pegram Mystery' by 'Luke Sharp' (Robert Barr) is taken from *The Face and the Mask* (New York, Stokes, 1895)

'The Accusing Shadow' by Harry Blyth first appeared in *The Halfpenny Marvel*, 3rd October, 1894.

'The Ripening Rubies' by Max Pemberton appeared in *Jewel Mysteries I Have Known* (London, Ward, Lock & Bowden, 1894).

'The Case of Laker Absconded' by Arthur Morrison is taken from *Chronicles of Martin Hewitt* (London, Ward, Lock & Bowden, 1894).

'The Azteck Opal' by Rodrigues Ottolengui originally appeared in the *Idler*, April 1895.

'The Problem of Dead Wood Hall' by by Dick Donovan (JE Muddock) comes from *Riddles Read*, 1896.

'The Purple Emperor' by Robert W Chambers comes from *The Mystery of Choice* (New York, D Appleton and Company, 1897).

'The Duchess of Wiltshire's Diamonds' by Guy Boothby first appeared in *Pearson's Magazine*, January to July 1897.

'Gentlemen and Players' by EW Hornung first appeared in *Cassell's*, August 1898.

'The Mysterious Death of the Underground Railway' by Baroness Orczy was first published in the *Royal Magazine*, July 1901.

Sources

'The Secret of the Fox Hunter' by William Le Queux is taken from *Secrets of the Foreign Office* (London, Hutchinson, 1903).

'The Submarine Boat' by Clifford Ashdown was first published in *Cassell's*, September 1903.

'A Solution of the Algiers Mystery' by Arnold Bennett was originally published in *The Windsor* magazine, September 1905.

'The Problem of Cell 13' by Jacques Futrelle was first published in *The Best American*, December 1906.

'The Mysterious Railway Passenger' by Maurice Leblanc is taken from from *The Exploits of Arsene Lupin*, translated by Alexander Teixera de Mattos (London, Ward, 1907).

This version of 'A Christmas Mystery' by William J Locke is taken from *Tales of Far-Away* (1923).

'The Wrong Shape' by GK Chesterton first appeared in *The Storyteller*, January 1911.

'The Tragedy at Brookbend Cottage' by Ernest Bramah comes from *Max Carrados*, (London, Methuen, 1914).

'The Case of the White Footprints' by R Austin Freeman comes from *A Century of Detective Stories* (London, Hutchinson & Co, 1921).

INTRODUCTION

THE ORIGINS OF CRIME AND MYSTERY FICTION

It is generally agreed that Edgar Allan Poe's 'The Murders in the Rue Morgue', written in 1841, is the first real crime story. But Poe didn't write in a vacuum: criminal behaviour has long been a dominant subject of literature of all kinds and Poe was subject to all manner of influences. When looking back at the history of crime fiction, Dorothy L Sayers suggests we can travel as far back as the *Aeneid* and stories from the Apocrypha; and, in his introduction to *Great Detective Stories* (1927), Willard Huntington Wright puts forward ancient Persian and Sanskrit texts, Herodotus's story of King Rhampsinitus's treasure house (written in 500 BC), and Chaucer's 'The Tale of the Nun's Priest' among others. When it comes to the first crime novel, candidates include Defoe's *Moll Flanders* (1722), Fielding's *Jonathan Wild* (1725), and Voltaire's *Zadig* (1747).

Traditionally 'mystery stories' dealt with the unknown and in the Middle Ages they included religious, mythical and folk tales, gradually evolving and separating into two distinct strands: tales of the supernatural and puzzles. The first strand took in the Gothic tradition, heralded in 1765 by Horace Walpole's *Castle of Otranto*, and which transformed via Mary Shelley's *Frankenstein* (1818), Bram Stoker's *Dracula* (1897) and short stories by the likes of Algernon Blackwood, HP Lovecraft and Lord Dunsany into the work of modern writers such as Anne Rice, Stephen King and JP Rowling.

Writing both supernatural and puzzle mysteries – often in the same story – Prussian-born author, painter and composer E(rnst) T(heodor) A(madeus) Hoffmann (1776-1822) was a huge influence on later writers in the mystery field. His work was adapted for influential operas and ballets, including 'The Nutcracker' and Offenbach's 'The Tales of Hoffmann'. At their best – as collected in *Nachstücke* (*Hoffmann's Strange Stories*, 1817) and *Die Serapionsbrüder* (*The Serapion Brethren*, 1819-21) – they were stories in which the sinister and fanciful inveigled their way into everyday life. His best known 'mystery' story, 'Das Fräulein von Scuderi' (1819), in which a respected goldsmith turns to nocturnal crime, is a strong candidate for the first crime story and there is no doubt that Hoffmann influenced many English-speaking writers, including Edgar Allan Poe

(1809-49), whose own supernatural tales mirrored Hoffmann's work twenty years later.

Rightly or wrong, Poe is generally regarded as the father of both the mystery and of the detective story, although it is clear that he wasn't working entirely alone. Another of his early influences and one that helped him shape the subsequent course of the detective story were the highly embroidered *Memoirs of Vidocq* (1829), supposedly written by Eugène François Vidocq (1775-1857). Vidocq was a criminal who joined the security police of the Paris Sûreté as an informer and worked his way up to become the unpopular but very effective head of the detective bureau. An uneducated man, he is said to have been a good guesser – relying on what later detectives would call 'hunches' – and his memoirs, ghost-written by a hack called LFL Héritier de l'ain, are at pains to depict him as a master of disguise and as a serious analytical detective. It is said that Vidocq only authorised half of the four volumes that appeared under his name. The memoirs were republished in Baltimore in 1834 and so it is likely that Poe had access to them.

Poe's 'Murders in the Rue Morgue' (1841) is widely accepted as the first wholly fictional story to be actually written *about* crime and to feature a proper detective. Despite its slightly unsatisfactory conclusion – the murderer turns out to be an escaped orangutan – 'Murders in the Rue Morgue' features as its detective the eccentric but brilliant Chevalier C Auguste Dupin, and includes a suitably bewildered sidekick who narrates the story and acts as foil to the great sleuth's genius. Other facets that were to survive and flourish in the genre in later years include Dupin's scientific approach to collecting and analysing clues and the inclusion of a surprising denouement – all of which was new and groundbreaking at the time.

There had been earlier sleuths in all but name – William Godwin's *Caleb Williams* (1794) has two people suspected of a murder which is subsequently solved by an amateur detective, for example – but Poe's Dupin is regarded as the first professional fictional detective. Although there are undoubted similarities between Dupin and Vidocq that go beyond just location and nationality, there is no doubt that Poe created his own character his own way. Where Vidocq was self-educated and working class, Dupin was a cultured and urbane chevalier. As Poe has Dupin say in 'Murders in the Rue Morgue':

'The Parisian police, so much extolled for *acumen*, are cunning, but no more. There is no method in their proceedings, beyond the method of the moment... The results attained by them are not unfrequently surprising, but, for the most part, are brought about by simple diligence and activity. When these qualities are unavailing, their schemes fail. Vidocq, for example, was a good guesser and a persevering man. But, without educated thought, he erred continually by the very intensity of his investigations. He impaired his vision by holding the object too close. He might see, perhaps, one or two points with unusual clearness, but in so doing he, necessarily, lost sight of the matter as a whole. Thus there is such a thing as being too profound. Truth is not always in a well. In fact, as regards the more important knowledge, I do believe that she is invariably superficial. The depth lies in the valleys where we seek her, and not upon the mountaintops where she is found.'

Dupin appears in three stories: 'Murders in the Rue Morgue', 'The Murder of Marie Roget' (1842) and 'The Purloined Letter' (1845). He solves the first by reasoning that, as the crime was inhuman, then the perpetrator would also not be human. This was the first example in fiction of the phenomenon known as the 'locked room mystery', in which a crime takes place inside a seemingly impregnable room from which the perpetrator could not possibly escape. The second story – and the one included here – mirrored the events of the real life case of Mary Rogers, a young woman murdered in mysterious circumstances in New Jersey in July 1841, transposing the fictional case to Paris. Dupin 'solves' the case merely by extracting clues from contemporary newspaper articles. 'The Purloined Letter' sees Dupin earn a hefty reward for pointing out that the obvious place to discover a letter (purloined or otherwise) is in a letter-rack. Simple, but groundbreaking in the 1840s.

Two other Poe stories that have exercised an immense influence are 'The Gold Bug' (1843) and 'Thou Art The Man' (1850). In the first a code must be deciphered before buried pirate treasure can be unearthed; and in the second we have a murderer who lays a trail of misleading clues. This introduced the standard device of subsequent detective fiction, the 'least likely suspect'.

Catherine Crowe's *Adventures of Susan Hopley, or Circumstantial Evidence* (1841), which was published several months before 'Murders in the Rue Morgue', has been suggested as the first detective novel. At the time Crowe was a hugely-selling and influential author and – so the argument goes – it is inconceivable that Poe would not have at least heard of the book. Poe may well have been influenced but that does not alter the fact that Dupin is a professional with no personal involvement in the crimes he is investigating, whereas Susan Hopley is an amateur (a maid), and is only spurred into solving crimes to right wrongs and to clear her family name.

Also predating Poe were the three volumes of *Richmond: or, Scenes in the Life of a Bow Street Officer*, which appeared in 1827. Published anonymously and centred around the fictional (though supposedly real-life) exploits of one Tom Richmond, it was a collection of stories that can lay claim to being one of the very first examples of a 'police procedural'. As was the custom at the time, Richmond took rewards from those he helped, operating more as a 'private' detective than his equivalents would have done even a few years later. Although by no means a pre-Holmsean detective, Richmond followed clues, questioned witnesses and grilled suspects in order to unearth wrongdoers. His more serious cases included child murder, grave-robbing, smuggling and counterfeiting.

Coinciding with the growth of this kind of 'mystery' story was the tradition of romanticising or fictionalising episodes from the life of real persons. This can be traced back to stories surrounding folk legends such as Robin Hood, Fulk fitzWarin and William Wallace, and to the 'real life' crime stories portrayed in the *Newgate Calendar*, which first appeared in 1773. The Newgate stories, named after the infamous London gaol, often utilised plots lifted from the calendar of executions. They were moral tales, intended chiefly as entertainment but also warning of the dangers of sinking into criminality. These expanded into what became known as the 'Newgate Novel', a phenomenon which peaked in the 1830s. Taking the likes of Defoe's *Moll Flanders* and Fielding's *Jonathan Wild* as literary precedents, authors like William Harrison Ainsworth (1805-82) and Edward Bulwer Lytton (1803-73) took real life cases and adapted them to appeal to a wide, if not always discerning, readership.

Dismissed by Sir Walter Scott in his diaries as 'a copyist', Ainsworth had huge successes with *Rookwood* (1834), which featured a cameo appearance from Dick Turpin and later with *Jack Sheppard* (1839), which told the story of the little-known highwayman and prison escapee of the 1720s. Bulwer Lytton – best known today for persuading Dickens to change the ending of *Great Expectations* – was a Liberal Member of Parliament and a reformer, which led him to portray the lead character of his novel *Paul Clifford* (1830) as a victim of circumstance. His subsequent works took a similar position.

Published between 1837 and 1839, *Oliver Twist* by Charles Dickens, was a reaction to the sympathetic treatment many of the Newgate Novels gave their protagonists. Spurred on by his own observations of the squalor and degradation of early Victorian London and by his less than happy experiences as a child-worker, Dickens sought to redress the balance, whilst at the same time aiming for a higher literary standard. He was horrified when the critics declared his work a Newgate Novel and compared it to *Jack Sheppard*, which – to add insult to injury – went on to outsell his own book by a huge margin.

William Makepiece Thackeray made no bones about his hatred of the genre and his satirical anti-Newgate novel, *Catherine* (1839), based on the life and death of husband-killer Catherine Hayes, offered a realistic view of what was in effect a terrible crime and its consequences – she was executed by being burnt alive at the stake. Unfortunately the reading public missed the satire and the novel was panned by critics.

In the outside world, real life developments in policing were providing structure for future detective and crime writers. In Paris the Sûreté had been founded by Vidocq in 1810 and, using a system of spies and informers, within seven years he and his dozen assistants were jailing 800 criminals a year. In 1829, Sir Robert Peel's Police Act created the Metropolitan force in London, to be followed in 1844 by its New York equivalent. A specialist detective division was established in London in 1842 and Boston was the first American city to follow suit four years later. The popular view of the police on both sides of the Atlantic was hardly flattering. They were perceived to be of low intelligence, bullying and with a tendency to manufacture evidence to fit the most likely suspect. The glamorous image of the intelligent detective battling evil was to come later and was largely due to the exploits of fictionalised crime-fighters.

In the USA policing was fragmentary and, outside of the big cities, often enforced by corrupt local bodies, if at all. Under pressure from influential businessmen, states brought in laws giving companies the power to create their own private police forces. The Coal and Iron Police of Pennsylvania was one such company police force that became notorious for its ruthless suppression of dissidents and unionisers. Individuals and companies were able to pursue criminals across county and state borders, making them privately-run forerunners of the FBI and giving rise to the notion of the 'private detective'.

Angus Reach is an all but forgotten name in British mystery

fiction, but his *Clement Lorimer: or, The Book with the Iron Clasps* (published in serial form from 1848) predates the 'Sensation' novels – as thrillers were then called – that dominated literary output a decade or more later. The book features mind-controlling drugs, characters who are 'doubles' of each other and a gambler who wants to fix a horse race. It could almost be the synopsis of a modern movie.

In March 1853 the first part of Charles Dickens' *Bleak House* was published and 'Inspector Bucket of the Detective' became the first police detective to appear in an English language novel. Although not a leading character, Bucket is well employed, working on three distinct cases throughout the book. Based largely on Dickens' friend, Inspector Field, it was a sympathetic portrayal, showing the policeman as eager to help, keen-eyed and – like many of his fictional successors – a master of disguise. In order to serve a warrant, Bucket disguises himself as a physician: '...a very respectable old gentleman, with grey hair, wearing spectacles, and dressed in a black spenser and gaiters and a broad-brimmed hat, and carrying a large gold-headed cane... When we had all arrived here, the physician stopped, and taking off his hat, appeared to vanish by magic, and to leave another and quite a different man in his place.' One particular aspect of the policeman's role that fascinated Dickens and one that was highly relevant in the class-obsessed Victorian era, was the power a lower class constable held over upper class people, as can be seen especially well in the clash between Bucket and Sir Leicester Dedlock.

Dickens' 'On Duty With Inspector Field' appeared in 1851 and was a straightforward record of a night spent shadowing the 'guardian genius of the British Museum'. It portrayed Field not only as a fiery opponent of lawbreakers but as a friend to the honest poor. Fictional police memoirs, supposedly written by genuine officers, suddenly became in vogue. The best known is 'Recollections of a Policeman', which appeared in *Chambers' Edinburgh Review* from 1849 and was collected into a volume published in New York in 1852 and in London four years later as *Waters: Recollections of a Detective Police-Officer*. As was often the case with 'memoirs' from this time, 'Waters' was not a policeman at all but a hack-writer called William Russell.

Another early detective novelist in all but name was Mary Elizabeth Braddon (1835-1915), a leading author of 'Sensation' novels. In her début, *The Trail of the Serpent* (1861), the main character is wrongfully convicted of murder, and his friends turn to amateur detection in order to clear his name and bring the real culprit to justice. *The Trail of the Serpent*, also known as *Three Times Dead*, contains two firsts of crime fiction: a disabled detective and a child detective. They are Peters – who cannot speak and communicates by sign language – and his adopted son, 'Sloshy', a boy trained from birth in the fine art of detection. Later the same year the serialisation of *Lady Audley's Secret* began, in which the secret of the title was as much a part of the mystery as the central disappearance of George Talboys. *Eleanor's Victory* (1863) features an early amateur female detective very fond of reading novels: 'Perhaps she formed her ideas of life from the numerous novels she had read, in which the villain was always confounded in the last chapter, however triumphant he might be through two volumes and three-quarters of successful iniquity.'

Although the London police did not employ female detectives until 1927, the idea of women investigating crime was in full swing by the mid-1860s. The anonymous *Revelations of a Lady Detective* (usually attributed to WS Hayward) and Andrew Forester's *The Female Detective* were both published in 1864. Another woman writer with a place in the evolution of the crime and detective story is Mrs Henry Wood, whose second novel, *East Lynne* (1861), contains a murder story as a sub-plot. But the most influential of these 'novels with secrets', as Kathleen Tillotson describes them, was *The Woman in White* (1859-60) by Wilkie Collins (1824-89).

The Woman in White was an immediate bestseller. Told through eye-witness accounts and carefully plotted, its story centres around the female of the title who, it turns out, has escaped from a mental hospital after being incarcerated because of knowledge she possessed about the rich, powerful and very nasty Sir Percival Glyde. Glyde is engaged to be married to Laura Percival, a young woman with a large amount of money, and Laura's half-sister Marian acts as the novel's amateur detective.

The Wilkie Collins story included in this collection was first published anonymously in the April 1858 issue of the *Atlantic Monthly* as 'Who is the Thief? (Extracted from the correspondence of the London police)', and later as 'The Biter Bit'. Like *The Woman in White*, the story is told through first person accounts and, as Michael Cox points out in his introduction to *Victorian Tales of Mystery and Detection* (1992): 'Its humorous intent does not diminish its importance, containing as it does elements such as false clues, procedural details, and the "Most Unlikely Person" formula that were to become the stock-in-trade of so many later writers.'

TS Eliot famously said that *The Moonstone* is the first, longest, and best of English detective novels'. Sadly, none of these statements – except maybe the last – is true. Regarded as Wilkie Collins' masterpiece and published in 1868, *The Moonstone* is an elaborate mystery in which police detective Sergeant Cuff (said to be based on Inspector Jonathan Whicher, a colleague of Dickens' friend Inspector Field), solves the theft of the jewel of the title. It stands out from the crowd of 'Sensation' novels for its suspenseful narrative and lack of convoluted sub-plots. But both Angus Reach's *Clement Lorimer: or, The Book with the Iron Clasps* (published in serial form from 1848) and *The Notting Hill Mystery* (1863) by Charles Felix pre-date it. Nevertheless, in *Wilkie Collins – An Illustrated Guide* (OUP, 1998), Andrew Gasson points out that *The Moonstone* contains many elements that were to be regularly used in later mystery stories, including: a country house robbery, an 'inside job', a 'celebrated policeman with a touch of amiable eccentricity', a bungling local constabulary, false suspects, 'the least likely suspect', a rudimentary 'locked room' murder, a reconstruction of the crime, and a final twist in the plot.

It has been suggested that had Dickens not died before he'd finished *The Mystery of Edwin Drood* (1870), he would have provided a template for all future detective novels and overshadowed his friend, Wilkie Collins. In the six completed instalments (of the projected twelve), Dickens set up John Jasper, cathedral choirmaster and opium addict, as the obvious villain and introduced Dick Datchery, maybe a detective but in any case a man in disguise. The real mystery has become what Dickens meant to happen in the final six instalments. Several writers have come up with endings, but none of them have any sense of authenticity. It has even been put forward that Dickens knew he was in poor health and that the book was never meant to be finished. To support this view they point to a motif of incomplete items within the novel, including Rosa's portrait and Durdle's house.

The Detective story was not only evolving in Britain, all around the world authors were exploring the new genre. In America Anna Katharine Green (1846-1935) wrote several detective novels, the best of which was *The Leavenworth Case, A Lawyer's Story* (1878), which is notable for offering the first 'body in the library' and a diagram of the murder scene. Across the English Channel, Emile Gaboriau (1833-73) had written *L'Affaire Lerouge* (1866), which was translated into English as *The Widow Lerouge* (Boston, 1873) and *The Lerouge Case* (London, 1885). It introduced an amateur detective called 'Tirauclaire', who possessed a skill of deducing facts from the merest clues left at the crime scene. His apprentice was a young policeman called Lecoq, who became the hero in three of Gaboriau's detective novels. Lecoq was obviously influenced by Dupin and François Vidocq, but his powers of deduction appear to have been Gaboriau's own invention. He became hugely popular in France, the UK and USA and proved a huge influence on other authors.

British-born New Zealand barrister Fergus W Hume (1859-1932) set his *The Mystery of a Hansom Cab: A Story of Melbourne Social Life* in Australia, self-published it then sold the rights for a £50 flat fee, and watched as it became the runaway bestseller of the Victorian era, shifting over half a million copies in his lifetime. It is a simple story: a man is discovered in a hansom cab, dead from chloroform poisoning and detective Samuel Gorby of the Melbourne City Police is called in to investigate. Although he wrote 139 other novels, Hume never repeated the success of his début. To make it worse, he made no bones about money being his motivation for picking up a pen: 'I enquired of a leading Melbourne bookseller what style of book he sold most of. He replied that the detective stories of Gaboriau had a large sale; and as, at this time, I had never even heard of this author, I bought all his works – eleven or thereabouts – and read them carefully. The style of these stories attracted me, and I determined to write a book of the same class; containing a mystery, a murder, and a description of low life in Melbourne.'

Then came Sherlock Holmes. The first novel, *A Study in Scarlet*, was published in *Beeton's Christmas Annual* in 1887, followed three years later by *The Sign of Four*. Few realised it, but under-employed Dr Arthur Conan Doyle, a Southsea GP, had created the world's most-enduring and popular fictional detective. But it was not until the short stories appeared, published in *The Strand* from July 1891 ('A Scandal in Bohemia') and illustrated by Sidney Paget, that the phenomenon really began.

On top of the oft-recorded influence of Dr Joseph Bell (one of Doyle's tutors at Edinburgh University) on the methods and mannerisms of Holmes, it is clear that Doyle had read Poe, for the Dupin and Holmes stories have much in common. Here were two very brilliant but idiosyncratic detectives, accompanied by admiring but less accomplished friend-narrators; their cases are puzzles, culminating in surprising final solutions. It is also very possible that Holmes' powers of deduction were helped by input from Gaboriau's Monsieur Lecoq.

By December 1893, after 22 short stories and two novels, Conan Doyle decided that enough was enough and did away with his creation at the Reichenbach Falls in 'The Final Problem'. The world mourned: City workers wore black armbands, *The Strand* suffered a huge decline in subscriptions, Conan Doyle received hundreds of abusive letters and was constantly under pressure to bring back his most loved creation. Determined to get on with his more spiritually-rewarding historical fiction, Doyle relented by submitting a 'posthumous' case – *The Hound of the Baskervilles* (serialised in *The Strand* from August 1901) – but finally capitulated and brought his detective back to life in 'The Adventure of the Empty House' (1902). In all, Doyle wrote four Sherlock Holmes novels and 56 short stories and triggered an explosion in detective fiction.

Forget the limp and largely unoriginal 1920s and '30s, the closing decade of the 19th Century was the true Golden Age of Crime Fiction, and dozens of detectives débuted in novels and in magazine short stories. Founded by *Tit Bits* proprietor George Newnes in January 1891, *The Strand* led the way but was by no means alone, competing with the likes of *Pearson's*, *Harmsworth's*, *Cassell's*, *The Windsor Magazine* and dozens more for a seemingly never-ending supply of short crime fiction. Among the best of the post-Holmesians were Arthur Morrison's Martin Hewitt, Baroness Orczy's 'Old Man in the Corner' and Lady Molly of Scotland Yard, MP Shiel's Prince Zaleski, R Austin Freeman's Dr John Thorndyke, Robert Barr's Eugène Valmont, Jacques Futrelle's 'Thinking Machine', Ernest Bramah's Max Carrados, Guy Boothby's Dr Nikola, GK Chesterton's Father Brown and the various characters of Mrs LT Meade.

Created by Scottish newspaperman Harry Blyth in December 1893, Sexton (originally Frank) Blake was a deliberate attempt to cash in on the 'death' of Holmes. Although Blyth died in poverty in 1898, Blake – like Conan Doyle's creation – went on to 'live' to the present day and his exploits were written by over 200 different writers. Others – EW Hornung's Raffles and GK Chesterton's Father Brown being obvious examples – went on to enjoy a similar longevity, but none would ever eclipse Sherlock Holmes.

The stories in this collection represent the best and the most influential from an era when crime writing was exciting, fresh and – above all – new. There were no rules to follow and authors were allowed a free hand – within the usual restraints of propriety, of course – to let their creative juices flow.

The results speak quite eloquently for themselves.

Martin Radcliffe
Cambridge, October 2004

SHORT BIOGRAPHICAL NOTES ON AUTHORS

Includes only those authors not covered in detail in the Introduction. Listed in the order of their appearance in this anthology.

JS (Joseph Sheridan) Le Fanu (1814-72) was born into a wealthy Huguenot family in Dublin and is remembered mainly for his Gothic novels *The House by the Churchyard* (1863) and *Uncle Silas* (1864), of which 'The Murdered Cousin' is an early shortened version.

Mark Twain (Samuel Langhorne Clements, 1835-1910) was one of America's most popular nineteenth century authors and humorists, credited with introducing colloquial speech into American fiction. He deserted from the Confederate Army, worked as a printer, prospector and riverboat pilot, travelling all over the USA before settling down to write. He wrote several mysteries, including *The Tragedy of Pudd'head Wilson* (1884) and the novelette, *A Double-Barrelled Detective Story* (1902). The story here (from 1882) is a parody of both the genre and of police detectives.

Grant Allen (Charles Grant Blairfindie Allen, 1848-99) was born in Kingston, Ontario, the son of an Irish clergyman. Allen was educated in the USA, France and England, finishing at Merton College, Oxford. Aside being from a prolific novelist (29) and short story writer he was a teacher, evolutionist and populariser of science. In March 1891 'Jerry Stokes' was the first crime fiction to appear in *The Strand* magazine.

Israel Zangwill (1864-1926) was born in London of Russian-Jewish parents and he was to become a renowned chronicler of immigrant life in London's East End. *The Big Bow Mystery* (1892) was his only crime novel but contains one of the very first – and most accomplished – 'locked room' puzzles.

Robert Barr (1850-1912) was Scottish-born and best known for creating Eugène Valmont.The Sherlock Holmes pastiche collected here was published under the appalling pen-name of Luke Sharp.

Harry Blyth (1850-1898) – using the pseudonym 'Hal Meredith' –was the creator of Sexton Blake and his French partner, Eugène Valmont – who works alone in the story here. Blyth always insisted that his son came up with the name 'Sexton Blake', the publishers said otherwise. Blyth sold the copyright and all rights to the characters to Associated Press, publishers of the *Halfpenny Marvel* for just £9 9s.

Max Pemberton (1863-1950) was an editor of *Chums* and *Cassell's* magazines and later a director of Northcliffe Newspapers. *Jewel Mysteries I Have Known* (of which 'The Ripening Rubies' was the stand-out story) was a loose collection of short fiction with any kind of jewellery theme. Pemberton went on to found the London School of Journalism, write over 60 novels and countless short stories (some of them quite good); he was knighted in 1928.

Arthur Morrison (1863-1945) was a fine author and a wonderful chronicler of the East End of London in books such as *Tales of Mean Streets* and *The Hole in the Wall*. But it is for his Martin Hewitt stories – including 'The Case of Laker, Absconded' – that mystery fans will remember him. As a part-time constable during World War I, he reported the first Zeppelin raid on London in May 1915.

Rodrigues Orrolengui (1861-1937) was an American writer and dentist of Sephardic descent who pioneered the use of x-rays in dentistry. 'The Azteck Opal' was the second of three completed Barnes and Mitchel stories.

Dick Donovan was the pseudonym adopted by Joyce Emmerson (Preston-) Muddock (1842-1934) for 297 detective and mystery stories and 28 novels written between 1889 and 1922. His fictional detective predated Holmes and, for a brief time, was as popular.

Robert W(illiam) Chambers (1865-1933) is the American-born author of for *The King in Yellow*, a collection of supernatural and 'French' stories, as well as a canon of science-fiction comedies, 'society novels' and historical romances.

Guy (Newell) Boothby (1867-1905) was a native of Adelaide, where he worked as secretary to the mayor. He turned to full-time writing in 1894 and moved to England. He wrote 56 novels and around 90 short stories. His most successful creation was Dr Nikola, arch-criminal and vivisectionist.

E(rnest) W Hornung (1866-1921) was married to Conan Doyle's sister, Connie. He worked as a teacher and as a clerk before turning to writing full-time. He wrote several novels (some of them set in Australia, where he lived for two years) but none approached the success of AJ Raffles, gentleman-crook and 'amateur cracksman'.

Baroness Orczy (1865-1947) is famous for creating the Scarlet Pimpernel but she began by writing detective fiction. The Old Man in the Corner, who appears in 'The Mysterious Death on the Underground Railway', featured in a series of twelve British movies filmed from 1924, and Lady Molly is widely regarded as the best of the early female detectives.

William Le Queux (1864-1927) was a prolific British author who fancied himself an amateur spy and friend of the crowned heads of Europe. He wrote two books in the late 19th century concerning the invasion of Britain by foreign powers and a wealth of espionage and fantasy thrillers. Early in his life he found himself broke and discouraged in Paris and was encouraged in his writing by Emile Zola.

Clifford Ashdown (see R Austin Freeman, below)

Arnold Bennett (1867-1931) was born in the Staffordshire Potteries area of central England and is best known for his writing about the 'Five Towns' and the Clayhanger family.

Jacques Futrelle (1875-1912) was an American journalist, crime writer and theatrical manager. Professor Van Dusen, the 'Thinking Machine', who appears in 'The Problem of Cell 13', was his best-known creation. Futrelle died on the Titanic, after first ensuring that his wife took a place on one of the ship's few lifeboats.

Maurice Leblanc (1864-1941) was the prolific French author and journalist, creator of Arsène Lupin, gentleman-thief turned detective. Lupin met his rival Sherlock Holmes in 'Arsène Lupin Versus Holmlock Shears' (1908) and (of course) outwitted the Englishman.

William J Locke (1863-1930) was a prolific author, best known for his romantic and adventure novels: *Idols*, *Derelicts*, *Simon The Jester* and *The Beloved Vagabond*.

G(ilbert) K(eith) Chesterton (1874-1936) began life as an illustrator and his drawings appeared in books by his friend, Hilaire Belloc. He is best remembered for his Father Brown stories, which were published from September 1910. 'The Wrong Shape' was the fifth.

Ernest Bramah (Smith) (1869-42) first came into print with the charmingly titled *English Farming and Why I Turned it up* (1894). He created two series detectives, the Chinese philosopher Kai Lung and the blind Mac Carrados.

R(ichard) Austin Freeman (1862-1943) worked as a doctor and administrator in the Gold Coast (now Ghana) until 1904 when he caught blackwater fever and returned to London. He wrote scientific-based detective fiction from around 1902, occasionally with Dr James Pitcairn (1860-1936), using the pseudonym Clifford Ashdown and the series character Romney Pringle. His best-known detective was Dr John Thorndyke, a pathologist (often aided by his friend Dr Jervis), who first appeared in the 1907 novel, *The Red Thumb Mark*.

EDGAR ALLEN POE

The Mystery of Marie Roget
A Sequel to 'The Murder in the Rue Morgue'

<small>INTRODUCTION</small>

*Es giebt eine Reihe idealischer Begebenheiten, die der Wirklichkeit
parallel läuft. Selten fallen sie zusammen. Menschen und Zufälle
modificiren gewöhnlich die idealische Begebenheit, so dass sie unvollkommen erscheint, und ihre Folgen gleichfalls unvollkommen sind.
So bei der Reformation; statt des Protestantismus kam das
Lutherthum hervor.* (There are ideal series of events which run parallel with the real ones. They rarely coincide. Men and circumstances
generally modify the ideal train of events, so that it seems imperfect,
and its consequences are equally imperfect. Thus with the
Reformation; instead of Protestantism came Lutheranism.) – Novalis
(the nom de plume of Van Hardenberg), *Morale Ansichten.*

Upon the original publication of 'Marie Roget', the footnotes now
appended were considered unnecessary; but the lapse of several years
since the tragedy upon which the tale is based, renders it expedient to
give them, and also to say a few words in explanation of the general
design. A young girl, Mary Cecilia Rogers, was murdered in the vicinity of New York; and although her death occasioned an intense and
long-enduring excitement, the mystery attending it had remained
unsolved at the period when the present paper was written and published (November, 1842). Herein, under pretence of relating the fate
of a Parisian grisette, the author has followed, in minute detail, the
essential, while merely paralleling the inessential, facts of the real
murder of Mary Rogers. Thus all argument founded upon the fiction
is applicable to the truth: and the investigation of the truth was the
object.

The 'Mystery of Marie Roget' was composed at a distance from
the scene of the atrocity, and with no other means of investigation
than the newspapers afforded. Thus much escaped the writer of
which he could have availed himself had he been upon the spot and
visited the localities. It may not be improper to record, nevertheless,
that the confessions of two persons (one of them the Madame Deluc

of the narrative), made, at different periods, long subsequent to the publication, confirmed, in full, not only the general conclusion, but absolutely all the chief hypothetical details by which that conclusion was attained.

THERE ARE few persons, even among the calmest thinkers, who have not occasionally been startled into a vague yet thrilling half-credence in the supernatural, by coincidences of so seemingly marvellous a character that, as mere coincidences, the intellect has been unable to receive them. Such sentiments – for the half-credences of which I speak have never the full force of thought – such sentiments are seldom thoroughly stifled unless by reference to the doctrine of chance, or, as it is technically termed, the Calculus of Probabilities. Now this Calculus is, in its essence, purely mathematical; and thus we have the anomaly of the most rigidly exact in science applied to the shadow and spirituality of the most intangible in speculation.

The extraordinary details which I am now called upon to make public, will be found to form, as regards sequence of time, the primary branch of a series of scarcely intelligible coincidences, whose secondary or concluding branch will be recognised by all readers in the late murder of MARY CECILIA ROGERS, at New York.

When, in an article entitled 'The Murders in the Rue Morgue', I endeavoured, about a year ago, to depict some very remarkable features in the mental character of my friend, the Chevalier C Auguste Dupin, it did not occur to me that I should ever resume the subject. This depicting of character constituted my design; and this design was thoroughly fulfilled in the wild train of circumstances brought to instance Dupin's idiosyncrasy. I might have adduced other examples, but I should have proven no more. Late events, however, in their surprising development, have startled me into some further details, which will carry with them the air of extorted confession. Hearing what I have lately heard, it would be indeed strange should I remain silent in regard to what I both heard and saw so long ago.

Upon the winding up of the tragedy involved in the deaths of Madame L'Espanaye and her daughter, the Chevalier dismissed the affair at once from his attention, and relapsed into his old habits of moody reverie. Prone, at all times, to abstraction, I readily fell in with his humour; and continuing to occupy our chambers in the Faubourg Saint Germain, we gave the Future to the winds, and slumbered tranquilly in the Present, weaving the dull world around us into dreams.

But these dreams were not altogether uninterrupted. It may

readily be supposed that the part played by my friend, in the drama at the Rue Morgue had not failed of its impression upon the fancies of the Parisian police. With its emissaries, the name of Dupin had grown into a household word. The simple character of those inductions by which he had disentangled the mystery never having been explained even to the Prefect, or to any other individual than myself, of course it is not surprising that the affair was regarded as little less than miraculous, or that the Chevalier's analytical abilities acquired for him the credit of intuition. His frankness would have led him to disabuse every inquirer of such prejudice; but his indolent humour forbade all further agitation of a topic whose interest to himself had long ceased. It thus happened that he found himself the cynosure of the political eyes; and the cases were not few in which attempt was made to engage his services at the Prefecture. One of the most remarkable instances was that of the murder of a young girl named Marie Roget.

This event occurred about two years after the atrocity in the Rue Morgue. Marie, whose Christian and family name will at once arrest attention from their resemblance to those of the unfortunate 'cigar-girl' was the only daughter of the widow Estelle Roget. The father had died during the child's infancy, and from the period of his death, until within eighteen months before the assassination which forms the subject of our narrative, the mother and daughter had dwelt together in the Rue Pavee Saint Andree[1]; Madame there keeping a pension, assisted by Marie. Affairs went on thus until the latter had attained her twenty-second year, when her great beauty attracted the notice of a perfumer, who occupied one of the shops in the basement of the Palais Royal, and whose custom lay, chiefly among the desperate adventurers infesting that neighbourhood. Monsieur Le Blanc[2] was not unaware of the advantages to be derived from the attendance of the fair Marie in his perfumery; and his liberal proposals were accepted eagerly by the girl, although with somewhat more of hesitation by Madame.

The anticipations of the shopkeeper were realised, and his rooms soon became notorious through the charms of the sprightly grisette. She had been in his employ about a year, when her admirers were thrown into confusion by her sudden disappearance from the shop. Monsieur Le Blanc was unable to account for her absence, and Madame Roget was distracted with anxiety and terror. The public

[1] Nassau Street
[2] Anderson

papers immediately took up the theme, and the police were upon the point of making serious investigations, when, one fine morning, after the lapse of a week, Marie, in good health, but with a somewhat sad-dened air, made her reappearance at her usual counter in the per-fumery. All inquiry, except that of a private character, was of course, immediately hushed. Monsieur Le Blanc professed total ignorance, as before. Marie, with Madame, replied to all questions, that the last week had been spent at the house of a relation in the country. Thus the affair died away, and was generally forgotten; for the girl, ostensi-bly to relieve herself from the impertinence of curiosity soon bade a final adieu to the perfumer, and sought the shelter of her mother's residence in the Rue Pavee Saint Andree.

It was about five months after this return home, that her friends were alarmed by her sudden disappearance for the second time. Three days elapsed, and nothing was heard of her. On the fourth her corpse was found floating in the Seine[1] near the shore which is oppo-site the Quartier of the Rue Saint Andre, and at a point not very far distant from the secluded neighbourhood of the Barriere du Roule.[2]

The atrocity of this murder (for it was at once evident that murder had been committed), the youth and beauty of the victim, and, above all her previous notoriety, conspired to produce intense excitement in the minds of the sensitive Parisians. I can call to mind no similar occurrence producing so general and so intense an effect. For several weeks, in the discussion of this one absorbing theme, even the momentous political topics of the day were forgotten. The Prefect made unusual exertions; and the powers of the whole Parisian police were, of course, tasked to the utmost extent.

Upon the first discovery of the corpse, it was not supposed that the murderer would be able to elude, for more than a very brief period, the inquisition which was immediately set on foot. It was not until the expiration of a week that it was deemed necessary to offer a reward; and even then this reward was limited to a thousand francs. In the meantime the investigation proceeded with vigour, if not always with judgement, and numerous individuals were examined to no purpose; while, owing to the continual absence of all clew to the mystery, the popular excitement greatly increased. At the end of the tenth day it was thought advisable to double the sum originally pro-posed; and, at length, the second week having elapsed without leading to any discoveries, and the prejudice which always exists in

[1] The Hudson
[2] Weehawken

Paris against the Police having given vent to itself in several serious emeutes, the Prefect took it upon himself to offer the sum of twenty thousand francs 'for the conviction of the assassin,' or, if more than one should prove to have been implicated, 'for the conviction of any one of the assassins.' In the proclamation setting forth this reward, a full pardon was promised to any accomplice who should come forward in evidence against his fellow; and to the whole was appended, wherever it appeared, the private placard of a committee of citizens, offering ten thousand francs, in addition to the amount proposed by the Prefecture. The entire reward thus stood at no less than thirty thousand francs, which will be regarded as an extraordinary sum when we consider the humble condition of the girl, and the great frequency, in large cities, of such atrocities as the one described.

No one doubted now that the mystery of this murder would be immediately brought to light. But although, in one or two instances, arrests were made which promised elucidation, yet nothing was elicited which could implicate the parties suspected; and they were discharged forthwith. Strange as it may appear, the third week from the discovery of the body had passed, and passed without any light being thrown upon the subject, before even a rumour of the events which had so agitated the public mind reached the ears of Dupin and myself. Engaged in researches which had absorbed our whole attention, it had been nearly a month since either of us had gone abroad, or received a visitor, or more than glanced at the leading political articles in one of the daily papers. The first intelligence of the murder was brought us by G—, in person. He called upon us early in the afternoon of the thirteenth of July, 18—, and remained with us until late in the night. He had been piqued by the failure of all his endeavours to ferret out the assassins. His reputation – so he said with a peculiarly Parisian air – was at stake. Even his honour was concerned. The eyes of the public were upon him; and there was really no sacrifice which he would not be willing to make for the development of the mystery. He concluded a somewhat droll speech with a compliment upon what he was pleased to term the tact of Dupin, and made him a direct and certainly a liberal proposition, the precise nature of which I do not feel myself at liberty to disclose, but which has no bearing upon the proper subject of my narrative.

The compliment my friend rebutted as best he could, but the proposition he accepted at once, although its advantages were altogether provisional. This point being settled, the Prefect broke forth at once into explanations of his own views, interspersing them with long comments upon the evidence; of which latter we were not yet in possession. He discoursed much and, beyond doubt, learnedly; while I hazarded an occasional suggestion as the night wore drowsily away. Dupin, sitting steadily in his accustomed armchair, was the embodiment of respectful attention. He wore spectacles, during the whole interview; and an occasional glance beneath their green glasses sufficed to convince me that he slept not the less soundly, because silently, throughout the seven or eight leaden-footed hours which immediately preceded the departure of the Prefect.

In the morning, I procured, at the Prefecture, a full report of all the evidence elicited, and, at the various newspaper offices, a copy of every paper in which, from first to last, had been published any decisive information in regard to this sad affair. Freed from all that was positively disproved, this mass of information stood thus:

Marie Roget left the residence of her mother, in the Rue Pavee St Andree, about nine o'clock in the morning of Sunday, June the twenty second, 18—. In going out, she gave notice to a Monsieur Jacques St Eustache[1], and to him only, of her intention to spend the day with an aunt, who resided in the Rue des Dromes. The Rue des Dromes is a short and narrow but populous thoroughfare, not far from the banks of the river, and at a distance of some two miles, in the most direct course possible, from the pension of Madame Roget. St Eustache was the accepted suitor of Marie, and lodged, as well as took his meals, at the pension. He was to have gone for his betrothed at dusk, and to have escorted her home. In the afternoon, however, it came on to rain heavily; and, supposing that she would remain all night at her aunt's (as she had done under similar circumstances before), he did not think it necessary to keep his promise. As night drew on, Madame Roget (who was an infirm old lady, seventy years of age) was heard to express a fear 'that she should never see Marie again'; but this observation attracted little attention at the time.

On Monday it was ascertained that the girl had not been to the Rue des Dromes; and when the day elapsed without tidings of her, a tardy search was instituted at several points in the city and its environs. It was not, however, until the fourth day from the period of her disappearance that any thing satisfactory was ascertained respecting her. On this day (Wednesday, the twenty-fifth of June) a Monsieur Beauvais,[2] who, with a friend, had been making inquiries for Marie near the Barriere du Roule, on the shore of the Seine which is opposite the Rue Pavee St Andree, was informed that a corpse had just

[1] Payne
[2] Crommelin

been towed ashore by some fishermen, who had found it floating in the river. Upon seeing the body, Beauvais, after some hesitation, identified it as that of the perfumery-girl. His friend recognised it more promptly.

The face was suffused with dark blood, some of which issued from the mouth. No foam was seen, as in the case of the merely drowned. There was no discolouration in the cellular tissue. About the throat were bruises and impressions of fingers. The arms were bent over on the chest, and were rigid. The right hand was clenched; the left partially open. On the left wrist were two circular excoriations, apparently the effect of ropes, or of a rope in more than one volution. A part of the right wrist, also, was much chafed, as well as the back throughout its extent, but more especially at the shoulder-blades. In bringing the body to the shore the fishermen had attached to it a rope, but none of the excorations had been effected by this. The flesh of the neck was much swollen. There were no cuts apparent, or bruises which appeared the effect of blows. A piece of lace was found tied so tightly around the neck as to be hidden from sight; it was completely buried in the flesh, and was fastened by a knot which lay just under the left ear. This alone would have sufficed to produce death. The medical testimony spoke confidently of the virtuous character of the deceased. She had been subjected, it said, to brutal violence. The corpse was in such condition when found, that there could have been no difficulty in its recognition by friends.

The dress was much torn and otherwise disordered. In the outer garment, a slip, about a foot wide, had been torn upward from the bottom hem to the waist, but not torn off. It was wound three times around the waist, and secured by a sort of hitch in the back. The dress immediately beneath the frock was of fine muslin; and from this a slip eighteen inches wide had been torn entirely out-torn very evenly and with great care. It was found around her neck, fitting loosely, and secured with a hard knot. Over this muslin slip and the slip of lace the strings of a bonnet were attached, the bonnet being appended. The knot by which the strings of the bonnet were fastened was not a lady's, but a slip or sailors knot.

After the recognition of the corpse, it was not, as usual, taken to the Morgue (this formality being superfluous), but hastily interred not far from the spot at which it was brought ashore. Through the exertions of Beauvais, the matter was industriously hushed up, as far as possible; and several days had elapsed before any public emotion resulted. A weekly paper[1], however, at length took up the theme; the corpse was disinterred, and a re-examination instituted; but nothing was elicited beyond what has been already noted. The clothes, however, were now submitted to the mother and friends of the deceased, and fully identified as those worn by the girl upon leaving home.

Meantime, the excitement increased hourly. Several individuals were arrested and discharged. St Eustache fell especially under suspicion; and he failed, at first, to give an intelligible account of his whereabouts during the Sunday on which Marie left home. Subsequently, however, he submitted to Monsieur G——, affidavits, accounting satisfactorily for every hour of the day in question. As time passed and no discovery ensued, a thousand contradictory rumours were circulated and journalists busied themselves in suggestions. Among these, the one which attracted the most notice, was the idea that Marie Roget still lived – that the corpse found in the Seine was that of some other unfortunate. It will be proper that I submit to the reader some passages which embody the suggestion alluded to. These passages are literal translations from *L'Etoile*[1], a paper conducted, in general, with much ability.

'Mademoiselle Roget left her mother's house on Sunday morning, June the twenty-second, 18——, with the ostensible purpose of going to see her aunt, or some other connection, in the Rue des Dromes. From that hour, nobody is proved to have seen her. There is no trace or tidings of her at all... There has no person, whatever, come forward, so far, who saw her at all in that day, after she left her mother's door... Now, though we have no evidence that Marie Roget was in the land of the living after nine o'clock on Sunday, June the twenty-second, we have proof that, up to that hour, she was alive. On Wednesday noon, at twelve, a female body was discovered afloat on the shore of the Barriere du Roule. This was, even if we presume that Marie Roget was thrown into the river within three hours after she left her mother's house, only three days from the time she left her home – three days to an hour. But it is folly to suppose that the murder, if murder was committed on her body, could have been consummated soon enough to have enabled her murderers to throw the body into the river before midnight. Those who are guilty of such horrid crimes choose darkness rather than light... Thus we see that if the body found in the river was that of Marie Roget it could only have been in the water two and a half days, or three at the outside. All experience has shown that drowned bodies, or bodies thrown into the water immediately after death by violence, require from six to ten days for sufficient decomposition to take place to bring them to the top of the water. Even where a cannon is fired over a corpse, and it rises before at least five or six days' immersion, it sinks again, if left alone. Now, we ask, what was there in this case to cause a departure from the ordinary course of nature?... If the body had been kept in its mangled state on shore until Tuesday night some trace would be found in shore of the murderers. It is a doubtful point, also, whether the body would be so soon afloat, even were it thrown in after having been dead two days. And, furthermore, it is exceedingly improbable that any villains who had committed such a murder as is here supposed, would have thrown the body in without weight to sink it, when such a precaution could have so easily been taken.'

The editor here proceeds to argue that the body must have been in the water 'not three days merely, but, at least, five times three days,' because it was so far decomposed that Beauvais had great difficulty in recognising it. This latter point, however, was fully disproved. I continue the translation:

'What, then, are the facts on which M Beauvais says that he had no doubt the body was that of Marie Roget? He ripped up the gown sleeve, and says he found marks which satisfied him of the identity. The public generally supposed those marks to have consisted of some description of scars. He rubbed the arm and found hair upon it – something as indefinite, we think, as can readily be imagined – as little conclusive as finding an arm in the sleeve. M Beauvais did not return that night, but sent word to Madame Roget, at seven o'clock, on Wednesday evening, that an investigation was still in progress respecting her daughter. If we allow that Madame Roget, from her age and grief, could not go over (which is allowing a great deal), there certainly must have been someone who would have thought it worth while to go over and attend the investigation, if they thought the body was that of Marie. Nobody went over. There was nothing said or heard about the matter in the Rue Pavee St Andree, that reached even the occupants of the same building. M St Eustache, the lover and intended husband of Marie, who boarded in her mother's house, deposes that he did not hear of the discovery of the body of his intended until the next morning, when M Beauvais came into his chamber and told him of it. For an item of news like this, it strikes us it was very coolly received.'

In this way the journal endeavoured to create the impression of an apathy on the part of the relatives of Marie, inconsistent with the supposition that these relatives believed the corpse to be hers. Its insinuations amount to this: – that Marie, with the connivance of her friends, had absented herself from the city for reasons involving a charge against her chastity; and that these friends upon the discovery of a corpse in the Seine, somewhat resembling that of the girl, had availed themselves of the opportunity to impress the public with the belief of her death. But *L'Etoile* was again overhasty. It was distinctly proved that no apathy, such as was imagined, existed; that the old lady was exceedingly feeble, and so agitated as to be unable to attend to any duty; that St Eustache, so far from receiving the news coolly, was distracted with grief, and bore himself so frantically, that M Beauvais prevailed upon a friend and relative to take charge of him, and prevent his attending the examination at the disinterment. Moreover, although it was stated by *L'Etoile*, that the corpse was reinterred at the public expense – that an advantageous offer of private sepulture was absolutely declined by the family – and that no member of the family attended the ceremonial: – although, I say, all this was asserted by *L'Etoile* in furtherance of the impression it designed to convey – yet all this was satisfactorily disproved. In a subsequent number of the paper, an attempt was made to throw suspicion upon Beauvais himself. The editor says:

'Now, then, a change comes over the matter. We are told that, on one occasion, while a Madame B— was at Madame Roget's house, M Beauvais, who was going out, told her that a gendarme was expected there, and that she, Madame B., must not say any thing to the gendarme until he returned, but let the matter be for him... In the present posture of affairs, M Beauvais appears to have the whole matter locked up in his head. A single step cannot be taken without M Beauvais, for, go which way you will you run against him... For some reason he determined that nobody shall have anything to do with the proceedings but himself, and he has elbowed the male relatives out of the way, according to their representations, in a very singular manner. He seems to have been very much averse to permitting the relatives to see the body.'

By the following fact, some colour was given to the suspicion thus thrown upon Beauvais. A visitor at his office, a few days prior to the girl's disappearance, and during the absence of its occupant, had observed a rose in the keyhole of the door, and the name 'Marie' inscribed upon a slate which hung near at hand.

The general impression, so far as we were enabled to glean it from the newspapers, seemed to be, that Marie had been the victim of a gang of desperadoes – that by these she had been borne across the river, maltreated, and murdered. *Le Commerciel*[1], however, a print of extensive influence, was earnest in combating this popular idea. I quote a passage or two from its columns:

'We are persuaded that pursuit has hitherto been on a false scent, so far as it has been directed to the Barriere du Roule. It is impossible that a person so well known to thousands as this young woman was, should have passed three blocks without someone having seen her; and anyone who saw her would have remembered it, for she interested all who knew her. It was when the streets were full of people, when she went out… It is impossible that she could have gone to the Barriere du Roule, or to the Rue des Dromes, without being recognised by a dozen persons; yet no one has come forward who saw her outside of her mother's door, and there is no evidence, except the testimony concerning her expressed intentions, that she did go out at all. Her gown was torn, bound round her, and tied; and by that the body was carried as a bundle. If the murder had been committed at the Barriere du Roule, there would have been no necessity for any such arrangement. The fact that the body was found floating near the Barriere, is no proof as to where it was thrown into the water… A piece of one of the unfortunate girl's petticoats, two feet long and one foot wide, was torn out and tied under her chin around the back of her head, probably to prevent screams. This was done by fellows who had no pocket-handkerchief.'

A day or two before the Prefect called upon us, however, some important information reached the police, which seemed to overthrow, at least, the chief portion of *Le Commerciel*'s argument. Two small boys, sons of a Madame Deluc, while roaming among the woods near the Barriere du Roule, chanced to penetrate a close thicket, within which were three or four large stones, forming a kind of seat with a back and footstool. On the upper stone lay a white petticoat; on the second, a silk scarf. A parasol, gloves, and a pocket-handkerchief were also here found. The handkerchief bore the name 'Marie Roget'. Fragments of dress were discovered on the brambles around. The earth was trampled, the bushes were broken, and there was every evidence of a struggle. Between the thicket and the river, the fences were found taken down, and the ground bore evidence of some heavy burden having been dragged along it.

[1] *The New York Journal of Commerce*

A weekly paper, *Le Soleil*[1], had the following comments upon this discovery – comments which merely echoed the sentiment of the whole Parisian press:

'The things had all evidently been there at least three or four weeks; they were all mildewed down hard with the action of the rain, and stuck together from mildew. The grass had grown around and over some of them. The silk on the parasol was strong, but the threads of it were run together within. The upper part, where it had been doubled and folded, was all mildewed and rotten, and tore on its being opened... The pieces of her frock torn out by the bushes were about three inches wide and six inches long. One part was the hem of the frock, and it had been mended; the other piece was part of the skirt, not the hem. They looked like strips torn off, and were on the thorn bush, about a foot from the ground... There can be no doubt, therefore, that the spot of this appalling outrage has been discovered.'

Consequent upon this discovery, new evidence appeared. Madame Deluc testified that she keeps a roadside inn not far from the bank of the river, opposite the Barriere du Roule. The neighbourhood is secluded – particularly so. It is the usual Sunday resort of black-guards from the city, who cross the river in boats. About three o'clock, in the afternoon of the Sunday in question, a young girl arrived at the inn, accompanied by a young man of dark complexion. The two remained here for some time. On their departure, they took the road to some thick woods in the vicinity. Madame Deluc's atten-tion was called to the dress worn by the girl, on account of its resem-blance to one worn by a deceased relative. A scarf was particularly noticed. Soon after the departure of the couple, a gang of miscreants made their appearance, behaved boisterously, ate and drank without making payment, followed in the route of the young man and girl, returned to the inn about dusk, and re-crossed the river as if in great haste.

It was soon after dark, upon this same evening, that Madame Deluc, as well as her eldest son, heard the screams of a female in the vicinity of the inn. The screams were violent but brief. Madame D recognised not only the scarf which was found in the thicket, but the dress which was discovered upon the corpse. An omnibus-driver, Valence[1], now also testified that he saw Marie Roget cross a ferry on the Seine, on the Sunday in question, in company with a young man of dark complexion. He, Valence, knew Marie, and could not be mis-taken in her identity. The articles found in the thicket were fully iden-

[1] *Philadelphia Saturday Evening Post*, edited by C I Peterson, Esq.

tified by the relatives of Marie.

The items of evidence and information thus collected by myself, from the newspapers, at the suggestion of Dupin, embraced only one more point – but this was a point of seemingly vast consequence. It appears that, immediately after the discovery of the clothes as above described, the lifeless or nearly lifeless body of St Eustache, Marie's betrothed, was found in the vicinity of what all now supposed the scene of the outrage. A phial labelled 'laudanum', and emptied, was found near him. His breath gave evidence of the poison. He died without speaking. Upon his person was found a letter, briefly stating his love for Marie, with his design of self-destruction.

'I need scarcely tell you,' said Dupin, as he finished the perusal of my notes, 'that this is a far more intricate case than that of the Rue Morgue; from which it differs in one important respect. This is an ordinary, although an atrocious, instance of crime. There is nothing peculiarly outré about it. You will observe that, for this reason, the mystery has been considered easy, when, for this reason, it should have been considered difficult, of solution. Thus, at first, it was thought unnecessary to offer a reward. The myrmidons of G— were able at once to comprehend how and why such an atrocity might have been committed. They could picture to their imaginations a mode – many modes – and a motive – many motives; and because it was not impossible that either of these numerous modes or motives could have been the actual one, they have taken it for granted that one of them must. But the ease with which these variable fancies were entertained, and the very plausibility which each assumed, should have been understood as indicative rather of the difficulties than of the facilities which must attend elucidation. I have before observed that it is by prominences above the plane of the ordinary, that reason feels her way, if at all, in her search for the true, and that the proper question in cases such as this, is not so much "what has occurred?" as "what has occurred that has never occurred before?" In the investigations at the house of Madame L'Espanaye[2], the agents of G— were discouraged and confounded by that very unusualness which, to a properly regulated intellect, would have afforded the surest omen of success; while this same intellect might have been plunged in despair at the ordinary character of all that met the eye in the case of the perfumery girl, and yet told of nothing but easy triumph to the functionaries of the Prefecture.

[1] Adam
[2] See 'Murders in the Rue Morgue'

'In the case of Madame L'Espanaye and her daughter, there was, even at the beginning of our investigation, no doubt that murder had been committed. The idea of suicide was excluded at once. Here, too, we are freed, at the commencement, from all supposition of self-murder. The body found at the Barriere du Roule was found under such circumstances as to leave us no room for embarrassment upon this important point. But it has been suggested that the corpse discovered is not that of the Marie Roget for the conviction of whose assassin, or assassins, the reward is offered, and respecting whom, solely, our agreement has been arranged with the Prefect. We both know this gentleman well. It will not do to trust him too far. If, dating our inquiries from the body found, and then tracing a murderer, we yet discover this body to be that of some other individual than Marie; or if, starting from the living Marie, we find her, yet find her unassassinated – in either case we lose our labour; since it is Monsieur G— with whom we have to deal. For our own purpose, therefore, if not for the purpose of justice, it is indispensable that our first step should be the determination of the identity of the corpse with the Marie Roget who is missing.

'With the public the arguments of *L'Etoile* have had weight; and that the journal itself is convinced of their importance would appear from the manner in which it commences one of its essays upon the subject: "Several of the morning papers of the day," it says, "speak of the conclusive article in Monday's *Etoile*". To me, this article appears conclusive of little beyond the zeal of its inditer. We should bear in mind that, in general, it is the object of our newspapers rather to create a sensation – to make a point – than to further the cause of truth. The latter end is only pursued when it seems coincident with the former. The print which merely falls in with ordinary opinion (however well founded this opinion may be) earns for itself no credit with the mob. The mass of the people regard as profound only him who suggests pungent contradictions of the general idea. In ratiocination, not less than in literature, it is the epigram which is the most immediately and the most universally appreciated. In both, it is of the lowest order of merit.

'What I mean to say is, that it is the mingled epigram and melodrama of the idea, that Marie Roget still lives, rather than any true plausibility in this idea, which have suggested it to *L'Etoile*, and secured it a favourable reception with the public. Let us examine the heads of this journal's argument, endeavouring to avoid the incoherence with which it is originally set forth.

'The first aim of the writer is to show, from the brevity of the interval between Marie's disappearance and the finding of the floating corpse, that this corpse cannot be that of Marie. The reduction of this interval to its smallest possible dimension, becomes thus, at once, an object with the reasoner. In the rash pursuit of this object, he rushes into mere assumption at the outset. "It is folly to suppose," he says, "that the murder, if murder was committed on her body, could have been consummated soon enough to have enabled her murderers to throw the body into the river before midnight." We demand at once, and very naturally, why? Why is it folly to suppose that the murder was committed within five minutes after the girl's quitting her mother's house? Why is it folly to suppose that the murder was committed at any given period of the day? There have been assassinations at all hours. But, had the murder taken place at any moment between nine o'clock in the morning of Sunday and a quarter before midnight, there would still have been time enough "to throw the body into the river before midnight". This assumption, then, amounts precisely to this – that the murder was not committed on Sunday at all – and, if we allow *L'Etoile* to assume this, we may permit it any liberties whatever. The paragraph beginning "It is folly to suppose that the murder, etc," however it appears as printed in *L'Etoile*, may be imagined to have existed actually thus in the brain of its inditer: "It is folly to suppose that the murder, if murder was committed on the body, could have been committed soon enough to have enabled her murderers to throw the body into the river before midnight; it is folly, we say, to suppose all this, and to suppose at the same time, (as we are resolved to suppose), that the body was not thrown in until after midnight" – a sentence sufficiently inconsequential in itself, but not so utterly preposterous as the one printed.

'Were it my purpose,' continued Dupin, 'merely to make out a case against this passage of *L'Etoile*'s argument, I might safely leave it where it is. It is not, however, with *L'Etoile* that we have to do, but with truth. The sentence in question has but one meaning, as it stands; and this meaning I have fairly stated, but it is material that we go behind the mere words, for an idea which these words have obviously intended, and failed to convey. It was the design of the journalists to say that at whatever period of the day or night of Sunday this murder was committed, it was improbable that the assassins would have ventured to bear the corpse to the river before midnight. And herein lies, really, the assumption of which I complain. It is assumed that the murder was committed at such a position, and under such circumstances, that the bearing it to the river became necessary. Now, the assassination might have taken place upon the river's brink, or on the river itself; and, thus, the throwing the corpse in the water might have been resorted to at any period of the day or night, as the most obvious and most immediate mode of disposal. You will understand that I suggest nothing here as probable, or as coincident with my own opinion. My design, so far, has no reference to the facts of the case. I wish merely to caution you against the whole tone of *L'Etoile*'s suggestion, by calling your attention to its ex-parte character at the outset.

'Having prescribed thus a limit to suit its own preconceived notions; having assumed that, if this were the body of Marie, it could have been in the water but a very brief time, the journal goes on to say:

All experience has shown that drowned bodies, or bodies thrown into the water immediately after death by violence, require from six to ten days for sufficient decomposition to take place to bring them to the top of the water. Even when a cannon is fired over a corpse, and it rises before at least five or six days' immersion, it sinks again if let alone.

'These assertions have been tacitly received by every paper in Paris, with the exception of *Le Moniteur*[1]. This latter print endeavours to combat that portion of the paragraph which has reference to "drowned bodies" only, by citing some five or six instances in which the bodies of individuals known to be drowned were found floating after the lapse of less time than is insisted upon by *L'Etoile*. But there is something excessively unphilosophical in the attempt, on the part of *Le Moniteur*, to rebut the general assertion of *L'Etoile*, by a citation of particular instances militating against that assertion. Had it been possible to adduce fifty instead of five examples of bodies found floating at the end of two or three days, these fifty examples could still have been properly regarded only as exceptions to *L'Etoile*'s rule, until such time as the rule itself should be confuted. Admitting the rule, (and this *Le Moniteur* does not deny, insisting merely upon its exceptions,) the argument of *L'Etoile* is suffered to remain in full force; for this argument does not pretend to involve more than a question of the probability of the body having risen to the surface in less than three days; and this probability will be in favour of *L'Etoile*'s position until the instances so childishly adduced shall be sufficient in number to establish an antagonistical rule.

[1] *The New York Times Commercial Advertiser*, Edited by Colonel Stone

'You will see at once that all argument upon this head should be urged, if at all, against the rule itself; and for this end we must examine the rationale of the rule. Now the human body, in general is neither much lighter nor much heavier than the water of the Seine; that is to say, the specific gravity of the human body, in its natural condition, is about equal to the bulk of fresh water which it displaces. The bodies of fat and fleshy persons, with small bones, and of women generally, are lighter than those of the lean and large-boned, and of men; and the specific gravity of the water of a river is somewhat influenced by the presence of the tide from the sea. But, leaving this tide out of the question, it may be said that very few human bodies will sink at all, even in fresh water, of their own accord. Almost anyone, falling into a river, will be enabled to float, if he suffer the specific gravity of the water fairly to be adduced in comparison with his own – that is to say, if he suffer his whole person to be immersed, with as little exception as possible. The proper position for one who cannot swim, is the upright position of the walker on land, with the head thrown fully back, and immersed; the mouth and nostrils alone remaining above the surface. Thus circumstanced; we shall find that we float without difficulty and without exertion. It is evident, however, that the gravities of the body, and of the bulk of water displaced, are very nicely balanced, and that a trifle will cause either to preponderate. An arm, for instance, uplifted from the water, and thus deprived of its support, is an additional weight sufficient to immerse the whole head, while the accidental aid of the smallest piece of timber will enable us to elevate the head so as to look about. Now, in the struggles of one unused to swimming, the arms are invariably thrown upward, while an attempt is made to keep the head in its usual perpendicular position. The result is the immersion of the mouth and nostrils, and the inception, during efforts to breathe while beneath the surface, of water into the lungs. Much is also received into the stomach, and the whole body becomes heavier by the difference between the weight of the air originally distending these cavities, and that of the fluid which now fills them. This difference is sufficient to cause the body to sink, as a general rule; but is insufficient in the case of individuals with small bones and an abnormal quantity of flaccid or fatty matter. Such individuals float even after drowning.

'The corpse, being supposed at the bottom of the river, will there remain until, by some means, its specific gravity again becomes less than that of the bulk of water which it displaces. This effect is brought about by decomposition, or otherwise. The result of decomposition is the generation of gas, distending the cellular tissues and all the cavities, and giving the puffed appearance which is so horrible. When this distension has so far progressed that the bulk of the corpse is materially increased without a corresponding increase of mass or weight, its specific gravity becomes less than that of the water displaced, and it forthwith makes its appearance at the surface. But decomposition is modified by innumerable circumstances – is hastened or retarded by innumerable agencies; for example, by the heat or cold of the season, by the mineral impregnation or purity of the water, by its depth or shallowness, by its currency or stagnation, by the temperament of the body, by its infection or freedom from disease before death. Thus it is evident that we can assign no period, with anything like accuracy, at which the corpse shall rise through decomposition. Under certain conditions this result would be brought about within an hour, under others it might not take place at all. There are chemical infusions by which the animal frame can be preserved forever from corruption; the Bi-chloride of Mercury is one. But, apart from decomposition, there may be, and very usually is, a generation of gas within the stomach, from the acetous fermentation of vegetable matter (or within other cavities from other causes), sufficient to induce a distension which will bring the body to the surface. The effect produced by the firing of a cannon is that of simple vibration. This may either loosen the corpse from the soft mud or ooze in which it is imbedded, thus permitting it to rise when other agencies have already prepared it for so doing, or it may overcome the tenacity of some putrescent portions of the cellular tissue, allowing the cavities to distend under the influence of the gas.

'Having thus before us the whole philosophy of this subject, we can easily test by it the assertions of *L'Etoile*. "All experience shows," says this paper, "that drowned bodies, or bodies thrown into the water immediately after death by violence, require from six to ten days for sufficient decomposition to take place to bring them to the top of the water. Even when a cannon is fired over a corpse, and it rises before at least five or six days' immersion, it sinks again if let alone."

'The whole of this paragraph must now appear a tissue of inconsequence and incoherence. All experience does not show that "drowned bodies" require from six to ten days for sufficient decomposition to take place to bring them to the surface. Both science and experience show that the period of their rising is, and necessarily must be, indeterminate. If, moreover, a body has risen to the surface through firing of cannon, it will not "sink again if let alone", until decomposition has so far progressed as to permit the escape of the generated gas. But I wish to call your attention to the distinction which is made between "drowned bodies", and "bodies thrown into the water immediately after death by violence". Although the writer admits the distinction, he yet includes them all in the same category. I have shown how it is that the body of a drowning man becomes specifically heavier than its bulk of water, and that he would not sink at all, except for the struggle by which he elevates his arms above the surface, and his gasps for breath while beneath the surface – gasps which supply by water the place of the original air in the lungs. But these struggles and these gasps would not occur in the body "thrown into the water immediately after death by violence". Thus, in the latter instance, the body, as a general rule, would not sink at all – a fact of which *L'Etoile* is evidently ignorant. When decomposition had proceeded to a very great extent – when the flesh had in a great measure left the bones – then, indeed, but not till then, should we lose sight of the corpse.

'And now what are we to make of the argument, that the body found could not be that of Marie Roget, because, three days only having elapsed, this body was found floating? If drowned, being a woman, she might never have sunk; or, having sunk, might have reappeared in twenty-four hours or less. But no one supposes her to have been drowned; and, dying before being thrown into the river, she might have been found floating at any period afterwards whatever.

'"But," says *L'Etoile*, "if the body had been kept in its mangled state on shore until Tuesday night, some trace would be found on shore of the murderers". Here it is at first difficult to perceive the intention of the reasoner. He means to anticipate what he imagines would be an objection to his theory – viz: that the body was kept on shore two days, suffering rapid decomposition – more rapid than if immersed in water. He supposes that, had this been the case, it might have appeared at the surface on the Wednesday, and thinks that only under such circumstances it could so have appeared. He is accordingly in haste to show that it was not kept on shore; for, if so, "some trace would be found on shore of the murderers". I presume you smile at the sequitur. You cannot be made to see how the mere duration of the corpse on the shore could operate to multiply traces of the assassins. Nor can I.

'"And furthermore it is exceedingly improbable," continues our journal, 'that any villains who had committed such a murder as is here supposed, would have thrown the body in without weight to sink it, when such a precaution could have so easily been taken". Observe, here, the laughable confusion of thought! No one – not even *L'Etoile* – disputes the murder committed on the body found. The marks of violence are too obvious. It is our reasoner's object merely to show that this body is not Marie's. He wishes to prove that Marie is not assassinated – not that the corpse was not. Yet his observation proves only the latter point. Here is a corpse without weight attached. Murderers, casting it in, would not have failed to attach a weight. Therefore it was not thrown in by murderers. This is all which is proved, if any thing is. The question of identity is not even approached, and *L'Etoile* has been at great pains merely to gainsay now what it has admitted only a moment before. "We are perfectly convinced," it says, "that the body found was that of a murdered female".

'Nor is this the sole instance, even in this division of the subject, where our reasoner unwittingly reasons against himself. His evident object I have already said, is to reduce, as much as possible, the interval between Marie's disappearance and the finding of the corpse. Yet we find him urging the point that no person saw the girl from the moment of her leaving her mother's house. "We have no evidence," he says, "that Marie Roget was in the land of the living after nine o'clock on Sunday, June the twenty-second." As his argument is obviously an *ex-parte* one, he should, at least, have left this matter out of sight; for had anyone been known to see Marie, say on Monday, or on Tuesday, the interval in question would have been much reduced, and, by his own ratiocination, the probability much diminished of the corpse being that of the grisette. It is, nevertheless, amusing to observe that *L'Etoile* insists upon its point in the full belief of its furthering its general argument.

'Reperuse now that portion of this argument which has reference to the identification of the corpse by Beauvais. In regard to the hair upon the arm, *L'Etoile* has been obviously disingenuous. M Beauvais, not being an idiot, could never have urged in identification of the corpse, simply hair upon its arm. No arm is without hair. The generality of the expression of *L'Etoile* is a mere perversion of the witness' phraseology. He must have spoken of some peculiarity in this hair. It must have been a peculiarity of colour, of quantity, of length, or of situation.

'Her foot, says the journal, was small – so are thousands of feet.

Her garter is no proof whatever – nor is her shoe – for shoes and garters are sold in packages. The same may be said of the flowers in her hat. One thing upon which M Beauvais strongly insists is, that the clasp on the garter found had been set back to take it in. This amounts to nothing; for most women find it proper to take a pair of garters home and, fit them to the size of the limbs they are to encircle, rather than to try them in the store where they purchase.' Here it is difficult to suppose the reasoner in earnest. Had M Beauvais, in his search for the body of Marie, discovered a corpse corresponding in general size and appearance to the missing girl, he would have been warranted (without reference to the question of habiliment at all) in forming an opinion that his search had been successful. If, in addition to the point of general size and contour, he had found upon the arm a peculiar hairy appearance which he had observed upon the living Marie, his opinion might have been justly strengthened; and the increase of positiveness might well have been in the ratio of the peculiarity, or unusualness, of the hairy mark. If, the feet of Marie being small, those of the corpse were also small, the increase of probability that the body was that of Marie would not be an increase in a ratio merely arithmetical, but in one highly geometrical, or accumulative. Add to all this shoes such as she had been known to wear upon the day of her disappearance, and, although these shoes may be "sold in packages", you so far augment the probability as to verge upon the certain. What, of itself, would be no evidence of identity, becomes through its corroborative position, proof most sure. Give us, then, flowers in the hat corresponding to those worn by the missing girl, and we seek for nothing farther. If only one flower, we seek for nothing farther – what then if two or three, or more? Each successive one is multiple evidence – proof not added to proof, but multiplied by hundreds or thousands. Let us now discover, upon the deceased, garters such as the living used, and it is almost folly to proceed. But these garters are found to be tightened, by the setting back of a clasp, in just such a manner as her own had been tightened by Marie shortly previous to her leaving home. It is now madness or hypocrisy to doubt. What *L'Etoile* says in respect to this abbreviation of the garter's being an unusual occurrence, shows nothing beyond its own pertinacity in error. The elastic nature of the clasp-garter is self-demonstration of the unusualness of the abbreviation. What is made to adjust itself, must of necessity require foreign adjustment but rarely. It must have been by an accident, in its strictest sense, that these garters of Marie needed the tightening described. They alone would have amply established her identity. But it is not that the corpse was found to have the garters of the missing girl, or found to have her shoes, or her bonnet, or the flowers of her bonnet, or her feet, or a peculiar mark upon the arm, or her general size and appearance – it is that the corpse had each and all collectively. Could it be proved that the editor of *L'Etoile* really entertained a doubt, under the circumstances, there would be no need, in his case, of a commission de lunatico inquirendo. He has thought it sagacious to echo the small talk of the lawyers, who, for the most part, content themselves with echoing the rectangular precepts of the courts. I would here observe that very much of what is rejected as evidence by a court, is the best of evidence to the intellect. For the court, guiding itself by the general principles of evidence – the recognised and booked principles – is averse from swerving at particular instances. And this steadfast adherence to principle, with rigourous disregard of the conflicting exception, is a sure mode of attaining the maximum of attainable truth, in any long sequence of time. The practice, in mass, is therefore philosophical; but it is not the less certain that it engenders vast individual error.[1]

'In respect to the insinuations levelled at Beauvais, you will be willing to dismiss them in a breath. You have already fathomed the true character of this good gentleman. He is a busybody, with much of romance and little of wit. Any one so constituted will readily so conduct himself, upon occasion of real excitement, as to render himself liable to suspicion on the part of the over-acute, or the ill-disposed. M Beauvais (as it appears from your notes) had some personal interviews with the editor of *L'Etoile*, and offended him by venturing an opinion that the corpse, notwithstanding the theory of the editor, was, in sober fact, that of Marie. "He persists," says the paper, "in asserting the corpse to be that of Marie, but cannot give a circumstance, in addition to those which we have commented upon, to make others believe." Now, without readverting to the fact that stronger evidence "to make others believe", could never have been adduced, it may be remarked that a man may very well be understood to believe, in a case of this kind, without the ability to advance a single reason

[1] 'A theory based on the qualities of an object, will prevent its being unfolded according to its objects; and he who arranges topics in reference to their causes, will cease to value them according to their results. Thus the jurisprudence of every nation will show that, when law becomes a science and a system, it ceases to be justice. The errors into which a blind devotion to principles of classification has led the common law, will be seen by observing how often the legislature has been obliged to come forward to restore the equity its scheme had lost.'- Landor.

for the belief of a second party. Nothing is more vague than impressions of individual identity. Each man recognises his neighbour, yet there are few instances in which anyone is prepared to give a reason for his recognition. The editor of *L'Etoile* had no right to be offended at M Beauvais' unreasoning belief.

'The suspicious circumstances which invest him, will be found to tally much better with my hypothesis of romantic busy-bodyism, than with the reasoner's suggestion of guilt. Once adopting the more charitable interpretation, we shall find no difficulty in comprehending the rose in the keyhole; the "Marie" upon the slate; the "elbowing the male relatives out of the way"; the "aversion to permitting them to see the body"; the caution given to Madame B—, that she must hold no conversation with the gendarme until his return (Beauvais); and, lastly, his apparent determination "that nobody should have any thing to do with the proceedings except himself". It seems to be unquestionable that Beauvais was a suitor of Marie's; that she coquetted with him; and that he was ambitious of being thought to enjoy her fullest intimacy and confidence. I shall say nothing more upon this point; and, as the evidence fully rebuts the assertion of *L'Etoile*, touching the matter of apathy on the part of the mother and other relatives – an apathy inconsistent with the supposition of their believing the corpse to be that of the perfumery-girl – we shall now proceed as if the question of identity were settled to our perfect satisfaction.'

'And what,' I here demanded, 'do you think of the opinions of *Le Commerciel*?'

'That in spirit, they are far more worthy of attention than any which have been promulgated upon the subject. The deductions from the premises are philosophical and acute; but the premises, in two instances, at least, are founded in imperfect observation. *Le Commerciel* wishes to intimate that Marie was seized by some gang of low ruffians not far from her mother's door. "It is impossible," it urges, "that a person so well known to thousands as this young woman was, should have passed three blocks without someone having seen her." This is the idea of a man long resident in Paris – a public man – and one whose walks to and fro in the city have been mostly limited to the vicinity of the public offices. He is aware that he seldom passes so far as a dozen blocks from his own bureau, without being recognised and accosted. And, knowing the extent of his personal acquaintance with others, and of others with him, he compares his notoriety with that of the perfumery-girl, finds no great difference between them, and reaches at once the conclusion that she, in her walks, would be equally liable to recognition with himself in his. This could only be the case were her walks of the same unvarying, methodical character, and within the same species of limited region as are his own. He passes to and fro, at regular intervals, within a confined periphery, abounding in individuals who are led to observation of his person through interest in the kindred nature of his occupation with their own. But the walks of Marie may, in general, be supposed discursive. In this particular instance, it will be understood as most probable, that she proceeded upon a route of more than average diversity from her accustomed ones. The parallel which we imagine to have existed in the mind of *Le Commerciel* would only be sustained in the event of the two individuals traversing the whole city. In this case, granting the personal acquaintances to be equal, the chances would be also equal that an equal number of personal encounters would be made. For my own part, I should hold it not only as possible, but as very far more probable, that Marie might have proceeded, at any given period, by any one of the many routes between her own residence and that of her aunt, without meeting a single individual whom she knew, or by whom she was known. In viewing this question in its full and proper light, we must hold steadily in mind the great disproportion between the personal acquaintances of even the most noted individual in Paris, and the entire population of Paris itself.

'But whatever force there may still appear to be in the suggestion of *Le Commerciel*, will be much diminished when we take into consideration the hour at which the girl went abroad. "It was when the streets were full of people," says *Le Commerciel*, "that she went out." But not so. It was at nine o'clock in the morning. Now at nine o'clock of every morning in the week, with the exception of Sunday, the streets of the city are, it is true, thronged with people. At nine on Sunday, the populace are chiefly within doors preparing for church. No observing person can have failed to notice the peculiarly deserted air of the town, from about eight until ten on the morning of every Sabbath. Between ten and eleven the streets are thronged, but not at so early a period as that designated.

'There is another point at which there seems a deficiency of observation on the part of *Le Commerciel*. "A piece," it says, "of one of the unfortunate girl's petticoats, two feet long, and one foot wide, was torn out and tied under her chin, and around the back of her head, probably to prevent screams. This was done by fellows who had no pocket-handkerchiefs." Whether this idea is or is not well founded, we will endeavour to see hereafter, but by "fellows who have no pocket-handkerchiefs", the editor intends the lowest class of ruffians. These, however, are the very description of people who will always be found to have handkerchiefs even when destitute of shirts. You must have had occasion to observe how absolutely indispensable, of late years, to the thorough blackguard, has become the pocket-handkerchief.'

'And what are we to think,' I asked, 'of the article in *Le Soleil*?'

'That it is a vast pity its inditer was not born a parrot – in which case he would have been the most illustrious parrot of his race. He has merely repeated the individual items of the already published opinion; collecting them, with a laudable industry, from this paper and from that. "The things had all evidently been there," he says, "at least three or four weeks, and there can be no doubt that the spot of this appalling outrage has been discovered." The facts here restated by *Le Soleil*, are very far indeed from removing my own doubts upon this subject, and we will examine them more particularly hereafter in connection with another division of the theme.

'At present we must occupy ourselves with other investigations. You cannot fail to have remarked the extreme laxity of the examination of the corpse. To be sure, the question of identity was readily determined, or should have been; but there were other points to be ascertained. Had the body been in any respect despoiled? Had the deceased any articles of jewellery about her person upon leaving home? If so, had she any when found? These are important questions utterly untouched by the evidence; and there are others of equal moment, which have met with no attention. We must endeavour to satisfy ourselves by personal inquiry. The case of St Eustache must be re-examined. I have no suspicion of this person; but let us proceed methodically. We will ascertain beyond a doubt the validity of the affidavits in regard to his whereabouts on the Sunday. Affidavits of this character are readily made matter of mystification. Should there be nothing wrong here, however, we will dismiss St Eustache from our investigations. His suicide, however, corroborative of suspicion, were there found to be deceit in the affidavits, is, without such deceit, in no respect an unaccountable circumstance, or one which need cause us to deflect from the line of ordinary analysis.

'In that which I now propose, we will discard the interior points of this tragedy, and concentrate our attention upon its outskirts. Not the least usual error in investigations such as this is the limiting of

inquiry to the immediate, with total disregard of the collateral or circumstantial events. It is the malpractice of the courts to confine evidence and discussion to the bounds of apparent relevancy. Yet
experience has shown, and a true philosophy will always show, that a
vast, perhaps the larger, portion of truth arises from the seemingly
irrelevant. It is through the spirit of this principle, if not precisely
through its letter, that modern science has resolved to calculate upon
the unforeseen. But perhaps you do not comprehend me. The history
of human knowledge has so uninterruptedly shown that to collateral,
or incidental, or accidental events we are indebted for the most
numerous and most valuable discoveries, that it has at length become
necessary, in any prospective view of improvement, to make not only
large, but the largest, allowances for inventions that shall arise by
chance, and quite out of the range of ordinary expectation. It is no
longer philosophical to base upon what has been a vision of what is
to be. Accident is admitted as a portion of the substructure. We make
chance a matter of absolute calculation. We subject the unlooked for
and unimagined to the mathematical formulae of the schools.

'I repeat that it is no more than fact that the larger portion of all
truth has sprung from the collateral; and it is but in accordance with
the spirit of the principle involved in this fact that I would divert
inquiry, in the present case, from the trodden and hitherto unfruitful
ground of the event itself to the contemporary circumstances which
surround it. While you ascertain the validity of the affidavits, I will
examine the newspapers more generally than you have as yet done.
So far, we have only reconnoitred the field of investigation; but it will
be strange, indeed, if a comprehensive survey, such as I propose, of
the public prints will not afford us some minute points which shall
establish a direction for inquiry.'

In pursuance of Dupin's suggestion, I made scrupulous examination of the affair of the affidavits. The result was a firm conviction of
their validity, and of the consequent innocence of St Eustache. In the
meantime my friend occupied himself, with what seemed to me a
minuteness altogether objectless, in a scrutiny of the various newspaper files. At the end of a week he placed before me the following
extracts:

'About three years and a half ago, a disturbance very similar to
the present was caused by the disappearance of this same Marie
Roget from the parfumerie of Monsieur Le Blanc, in the Palais Royal.
At the end of a week, however, she reappeared at her customary
comptoir, as well as ever, with the exception of a slight paleness not

altogether usual. It was given out by Monsieur Le Blanc and her mother that she had merely been on a visit to some friend in the country; and the affair was speedily hushed up. We presume that the present absence is a freak of the same nature, and that, at the expiration of a week or, perhaps, of a month, we shall have her among us again.'– *Evening Paper*, Monday, June 23.[1]

'An evening journal of yesterday refers to a former mysterious disappearance of Mademoiselle Roget. It is well known that, during the week of her absence from Le Blanc's parfumerie, she was in the company of a young naval officer much noted for his debaucheries. A quarrel, it is supposed, providentially, led to her return home. We have the name of the Lothario in question, who is at present stationed in Paris, but for obvious reasons forbear to make it public.' – *Le Mercure*, Tuesday Morning, June 24.[2]

'An outrage of the most atrocious character was perpetrated near this city the day before yesterday. A gentleman, with his wife and daughter, engaged, about dusk, the services of six young men, who were idly rowing a boat to and fro near the banks of the Seine, to convey him across the river. Upon reaching the opposite shore the three passengers stepped out, and had proceeded so far as to be beyond the view of the boat, when the daughter discovered that she had left in it her parasol. She returned for it, was seized by the gang, carried out into the stream, gagged, brutally treated, and finally taken to the shore at a point not far from that at which she had originally entered the boat with her parents. The villains have escaped for the time, but the police are upon their trail, and some of them will soon be taken.' – *Morning Paper*, June 25.[3]

'We have received one or two communications, the object of which is to fasten the crime of the late atrocity upon Mennais;[4] but as this gentleman has been fully exonerated by a legal inquiry, and as the arguments of our several correspondents appear to be more zealous than profound, we do not think it advisable to make them public.'– *Morning Paper*, June 28.[5]

'We have received several forcibly written communications, apparently from various sources, and which go far to render it a matter of certainty that the unfortunate Marie Roget has become a victim of

---

[1] *New York Express*
[2] *New York Herald*
[3] *New York Courier and Inquirer*
[4] *Mennais was one of the parties originally arrested, but discharged through total lack of evidence.*
[5] *Ibid.*

one of the numerous bands of blackguards which infest the vicinity of the city upon Sunday. Our own opinion is decidedly in favour of this supposition. We shall endeavour to make room for some of these arguments hereafter.' – *Evening Paper*, Tuesday, June 31.[1]

'On Monday, one of the bargemen connected with the revenue service saw an empty boat floating down the Seine. Sails were lying in the bottom of the boat. The bargeman towed it under the barge office. The next morning it was taken from thence without the knowledge of any of the officers. The rudder is now at the barge office.'– *Le Diligence*, Thursday, June 26.[2]

Upon reading these various extracts, they not only seemed to me irrelevant, but I could perceive no mode in which any one of them could be brought to bear upon the matter in hand. I waited for some explanation from Dupin.

'It is not my present design,' he said, 'to dwell upon the first and second of these extracts. I have copied them chiefly to show you the extreme remissness of the police, who, as far as I can understand from the Prefect, have not troubled themselves, in any respect, with an examination of the naval officer alluded to. Yet it is mere folly to say that between the first and second disappearance of Marie there is no supposable connection. Let us admit the first elopement to have resulted in a quarrel between the lovers, and the return home of the betrayed. We are now prepared to view a second elopement (if we know that an elopement has again taken place) as indicating a renewal of the betrayer's advances, rather than as the result of new proposals by a second individual – we are prepared to regard it as a "making up" of the old amour, rather than as the commencement of a new one. The chances are ten to one, that he who had once eloped with Marie would again propose an elopement, rather than that she to whom proposals of an elopement had been made by one individual, should have them made to her by another. And here let me call your attention to the fact, that the time elapsing between the first ascertained and the second supposed elopement is a few months more than the general period of the cruises of our men-of-war. Had the lover been interrupted in his first villainy by the necessity of departure to sea, and had he seized the first moment of his return to renew the base designs not yet altogether accomplished – or not yet altogether accomplished by him? Of all these things we know nothing.

'You will say, however, that, in the second instance, there was no elopement as imagined. Certainly not – but are we prepared to say that there was not the frustrated design? Beyond St Eustache, and perhaps Beauvais, we find no recognised, no open, no honourable suitors of Marie. Of none other is there any thing said. Who, then, is the secret lover, of whom the relatives (at least most of them) know nothing, but whom Marie meets upon the morning of Sunday, and who is so deeply in her confidence, that she hesitates not to remain with him until the shades of the evening descend, amid the solitary groves of the Barriere du Roule? Who is that secret lover, I ask, of whom, at least, most of the relatives know nothing? And what means the singular prophecy of Madam Roget on the morning of Marie's departure? – "I fear that I shall never see Marie again".

'But if we cannot imagine Madame Roget privy to the design of elopement, may we not at least suppose this design entertained by the girl? Upon quitting home, she gave it to be understood that she was about to visit her aunt in the Rue des Dromes, and St Eustache was requested to call for her at dark. Now, at first glance, this fact strongly militates against my suggestion; but let us reflect. That she did meet some companion, and proceed with him across the river, reaching the Barriere du Roule at so late an hour as three o'clock in the afternoon, is known. But in consenting so to accompany this individual, (for whatever purpose – to her mother known or unknown,) she must have thought of her expressed intention when leaving home, and of the surprise and suspicion aroused in the bosom of her affianced suitor, St Eustache, when, calling for her, at the hour appointed, in the Rue des Dromes, he should find that she had not been there, and when, moreover, upon returning to the pension with this alarming intelligence, he should become aware of her continued absence from home. She must have thought of these things, I say. She must have foreseen the chagrin of St Eustache, the suspicion of all. She could not have thought of returning to brave this suspicion; but the suspicion becomes a point of trivial importance to her, if we suppose her not intending to return.

'We may imagine her thinking thus – "I am to meet a certain person for the purpose of elopement, or for certain other purposes known only to myself. It is necessary that there be no chance of interruption – there must be sufficient time given us to elude pursuit – I will give it to be understood that I shall visit and spend the day with my aunt at the Rue des Dromes – I will tell St Eustache not to call for me until dark – in this way, my absence from home for the longest possible period, without causing suspicion or anxiety, will be

accounted for, and I shall gain more time than in any other manner. If
I bid St Eustache call for me at dark, he will be sure not to call before;
but if I wholly neglect to bid him call, my time for escape will be
diminished, since it will be expected that I return the earlier, and my
absence will the sooner excite anxiety. Now, if it were my design to
return at all – if I had in contemplation merely a stroll with the individual in question – it would not be my policy to bid St Eustache call;
for, calling, he will be sure to ascertain that I have played him false –
a fact of which I might keep him forever in ignorance, by leaving
home without notifying him of my intention, by returning before
dark, and by then stating that I had been to visit my aunt in the Rue
des Dromes. But, as it is my design never to return – or not for some
weeks – or not until certain concealments are effected – the gaining of
time is the only point about which I need give myself any concern."

'You have observed, in your notes, that the most general opinion
in relation to this sad affair is, and was from the first, that the girl had
been the victim of a gang of blackguards. Now, the popular opinion,
under certain conditions, is not to be disregarded. When arising of
itself – when manifesting itself in a strictly spontaneous manner – we
should look upon it as analogous with that intuition which is the
idiosyncrasy of the individual man of genius. In ninety-nine cases
from the hundred I would abide by its decision. But it is important
that we find no palpable traces of suggestion. The opinion must be
rigourously the public's own, and the distinction is often exceedingly
difficult to perceive and to maintain. In the present instance, it
appears to me that this "public opinion", in respect to a gang, has
been superinduced by the collateral event which is detailed in the
third of my extracts. All Paris is excited by the discovered corpse of
Marie, a girl young, beautiful, and notorious. This corpse is found,
bearing marks of violence, and floating in the river. But it is now
made known that, at the very period, or about the very period, in
which it is supposed that the girl was assassinated, an outrage similar
in nature to that endured by the deceased, although less in extent,
was perpetrated by a gang of young ruffians, upon the person of a
second young female. Is it wonderful that the one known atrocity
should influence the popular judgement in regard to the other
unknown? This judgement awaited direction, and the known outrage
seemed so opportunely to afford it! Marie, too, was found in the
river; and upon this very river was this known outrage committed.
The connection of the two events had about it so much of the palpable, that the true wonder would have been a failure of the populace to

appreciate and to seize it. But, in fact, the one atrocity, known to be so committed, is, if any thing, evidence that the other, committed at a time nearly coincident, was not so committed. It would have been a miracle indeed, if, while a gang of ruffians were perpetrating, at a given locality, a most unheard-of wrong, there should have been another similar gang, in a similar locality, in the same city, under the same circumstances, with the same means and appliances, engaged in a wrong of precisely the same aspect, at precisely the same period of time! Yet in what, if not in this marvellous train of coincidence, does the accidentally suggested opinion of the populace call upon us to believe?

'Before proceeding farther, let us consider the supposed scene of the assassination, in the thicket at the Barriere du Roule. This thicket, although dense, was in the close vicinity of a public road. Within were three or four large stones, forming a kind of seat with a back and a footstool. On the upper stone was discovered a white petticoat; on the second, a silk scarf. A parasol, gloves, and a pocket-handkerchief were also here found. The handkerchief bore the name "Marie Roget". Fragments of dress were seen on the branches around. The earth was trampled, the bushes were broken, and there was every evidence of a violent struggle.

'Notwithstanding the acclamation with which the discovery of this thicket was received by the press, and the unanimity with which it was supposed to indicate the precise scene of the outrage, it must be admitted that there was some very good reason for doubt. That it was the scene, I may or I may not believe – but there was excellent reason for doubt. Had the true scene been, as *Le Commerciel* suggested, in the neighbourhood of the Rue Pavee St Andree, the perpetrators of the crime, supposing them still resident in Paris, would naturally have been stricken with terror at the public attention thus acutely directed into the proper channel; and, in certain classes of minds, there would have arisen, at once, a sense of the necessity of some exertion to re-divert this attention. And thus, the thicket of the Barriere du Roule having been already suspected, the idea of placing the articles where they were found, might have been naturally entertained. There is no real evidence, although *Le Soleil* so supposes, that the articles discovered had been more than a very few days in the thicket; while there is much circumstantial proof that they could not have remained there, without attracting attention, during the twenty days elapsing between the fatal Sunday and the afternoon upon which they were found by the boys. "They were all mildewed down hard," says *Le*

Soleil, adopting the opinions of its predecessors, "with the action of the rain and stuck together from mildew. The grass had grown around and over some of them. The silk of the parasol was strong, but the threads of it were run together within. The upper part, where it had been doubled and folded, was all mildewed and rotten, and tore on being opened." In respect to the grass having "grown around and over some of them", it is obvious that the fact could only have been ascertained from the words, and thus from the recollections, of two small boys; for these boys removed the articles and took them home before they had been seen by a third party. But the grass will grow, especially in warm and damp weather (such as was that of the period of the murder), as much as two or three inches in a single day. A parasol lying upon a newly turfed ground, might, in a single week, be entirely concealed from sight by the upspringing grass. And touching that mildew upon which the editor of *Le Soleil* so pertinaciously insists, that he employs the word no less than three times in the brief paragraph just quoted, is he really unaware of the nature of this mildew? Is he to be told that it is one of the many classes of fungus, of which the most ordinary feature is its upspringing and decadence within twenty-four hours?

'Thus we see, at a glance, that what has been most triumphantly adduced in support of the idea that the articles had been "for at least three or four weeks" in the thicket, is most absurdly null as regards any evidence of that fact. On the other hand, it is exceedingly difficult to believe that these articles could have remained in the thicket specified for a longer period than a single week – for a longer period than from one Sunday to the next. Those who know any thing of the vicinity of Paris, know the extreme difficulty of finding seclusion, unless at a great distance from its suburbs. Such a thing as an unexplored or even an infrequently visited recess, amid its woods or groves, is not for a moment to be imagined. Let anyone who, being at heart a lover of nature, is yet chained by duty to the dust and heat of this great metropolis – let any such one attempt, even during the weekdays, to slake his thirst for solitude amid the scenes of natural loveliness which immediately surround us. At every second step, he will find the growing charm dispelled by the voice and personal intrusion of some ruffian or party of carousing blackguards. He will seek privacy amid the densest foliage, all in vain. Here are the very nooks where the unwashed most abound – here are the temples most desecrate. With sickness of the heart the wanderer will flee back to the polluted Paris as to a less odious because less incongruous sink of pollution. But if the vicinity of the city is so beset during the working days of the week, how much more so on the Sabbath! It is now especially that, released from the claims of labour, or deprived of the customary opportunities of crime, the town blackguard seeks the precincts of the town, not through love of the rural, which in his heart he despises, but by way of escape from the restraints and conventionalities of society. He desires less the fresh air and the green trees, than the utter license of the country. Here, at the roadside inn, or beneath the foliage of the woods, he indulges unchecked by any eye except those of his boon companions, in all the mad excess of a counterfeit hilarity – the joint offspring of liberty and of rum. I say nothing more than what must be obvious to every dispassionate observer, when I repeat that the circumstance of the articles in question having remained undiscovered, for a longer period than from one Sunday to another, in any thicket in the immediate neighbourhood of Paris, is to be looked upon as little less than miraculous.

'But there are not wanting other grounds for the suspicion that the articles were placed in the thicket with the view of diverting attention from the real scene of the outrage. And first, let me direct your notice to the date of the discovery of the articles. Collate this with the date of the fifth extract made by myself from the newspapers. You will find that the discovery followed, almost immediately, the urgent communications sent to the evening paper. These communications, although various, and apparently from various sources, tended all to the same point – *viz*, the directing of attention to a gang as the perpetrators of the outrage, and to the neighbourhood of the Barriere du Roule as its scene. Now, here, of course, the suspicion is not that, in consequence of these communications, or of the public attention by them directed, the articles were found by the boys; but the suspicion might and may well have been, that the articles were not before found by the boys, for the reason that the articles had not before been in the thicket; having been deposited there only at so late a period as at the date, or shortly prior to the date of the communications, by the guilty authors of these communications themselves.

'This thicket was a singular – an exceedingly singular one. It was unusually dense. Within its naturally walled enclosure were three extraordinary stones, forming a seat with a back and a footstool. And this thicket, so full of art, was in the immediate vicinity, within a few rods, of the dwelling of Madame Deluc, whose boys were in the habit of closely examining the shrubberies about them in search of the bark of the sassafras. Would it be a rash wager – a wager of one thousand to one – that a day never passed over the heads of these boys without finding at least one of them ensconced in the umbrageous hall, and enthroned upon its natural throne? Those who would hesitate at such a wager, have either never been boys themselves, or have forgotten the boyish nature. I repeat – it is exceedingly hard to comprehend how the articles could have remained in this thicket undiscovered, for a longer period than one or two days; and that thus there is good ground for suspicion, in spite of the dogmatic ignorance of *Le Soleil*, that they were, at a comparatively late date, deposited where found.

'But there are still other and stronger reasons for believing them so deposited, than any which I have as yet urged. And, now, let me beg your notice to the highly artificial arrangement of the articles. On the upper stone lay a white petticoat; on the second, a silk scarf; scattered around, were a parasol, gloves, and a pocket-handkerchief bearing the name "Marie Roget". Here is just such an arrangement as would naturally be made by a not over-acute person wishing to dispose the articles naturally. But it is by no means a really natural arrangement. I should rather have looked to see the things all lying on the ground and trampled under foot. In the narrow limits of that bower, it would have been scarcely possible that the petticoat and scarf should have retained a position upon the stones, when subjected to the brushing to and fro of many struggling persons. "There was evidence," it is said, "of a struggle; and the earth was trampled, the bushes were broken," – but the petticoat and the scarf are found deposited as if upon shelves. "The pieces of the frock torn out by the bushes were about three inches wide and six inches long. One part was the hem of the frock and it had been mended. They looked like strips torn off." Here, inadvertently, *Le Soleil* has employed an exceedingly suspicious phrase. The pieces, as described, do indeed look like strips torn off; but purposely and by hand. It is one of the rarest of accidents that a piece is "torn off", from any garment such as is now in question, by the agency of a thorn. From the very nature of such fabrics, a thorn or nail becoming tangled in them, tears them rectangularly – divides them into two longitudinal rents, at right angles with each other, and meeting at an apex where the thorn enters – but it is scarcely possible to conceive the piece "torn off". I never so knew it, nor did you. To tear a piece off from such fabric, two distinct forces, in different directions, will be, in almost every case, required. If there be two edges to the fabric – if, for example, it be a pocket-handkerchief, and it is desired to tear from it a slip, then, and then only, will the one force serve the purpose. But in the present case the question is of a dress, presenting but one edge. To tear a piece from the interior, where no edge is presented, could only be effected by a miracle through the agency of thorns, and no one thorn could accomplish it. But, even where an edge is presented, two thorns will be necessary, operating, the one in two distinct directions, and the other in one. And this in the supposition that the edge is unhemmed. If hemmed, the matter is nearly out of the question. We thus see the numerous and great obstacles in the way of pieces being "torn off" through the simple agency of "thorns"; yet we are required to believe not only that one piece but that many have been so torn. "And one part," too, "was the hem of the frock"! Another piece was "part of the skirt, not the hem," – that is to say, was torn completely out, through the agency of thorns, from the unedged interior of the dress! These, I say, are things which one may well be pardoned for disbelieving; yet, taken collectedly, they form, perhaps, less of reasonable ground for suspicion, than the one startling circumstance of the articles having been left in this thicket at all, by any murderers who had enough precaution to think of removing the corpse. You will not have apprehended me rightly, however, if you suppose it my design to deny this thicket as the scene of the outrage. There might have been a wrong here, or more possibly, an accident at Madame Deluc's. But, in fact, this is a point of minor importance. We are not engaged in an attempt to discover the scene, but to produce the perpetrators of the murder. What I have adduced, notwithstanding the minuteness with which I have adduced it, has been with the view, first, to show the folly of the positive and headlong assertions of *Le Soleil*, but secondly and chiefly, to bring you, by the most natural route, to a further contemplation of the doubt whether this assassination has, or has not, been the work of a gang.

'We will resume this question by mere allusion to the revolting details of the surgeon examined at the inquest. It is only necessary to say that his published inferences, in regard to the number of the ruffians, have been properly ridiculed as unjust and totally baseless, by all the reputable anatomists of Paris. Not that the matter might not have been as inferred, but that there was no ground for the inference: was there not much for another?

'Let us reflect now upon "the traces of a struggle"; let me ask what these traces have been supposed to demonstrate. A gang. But do they not rather demonstrate the absence of a gang? What struggle could have taken place – what struggle so violent and so enduring as to have left its "traces" in all directions – between a weak and defenceless girl and a gang of ruffians imagined? The silent grasp of a few rough arms and all would have been over. The victim must have been absolutely passive at their will. You will here bear in mind that the arguments urged against the thicket as the scene, are applicable, in chief part, only against it as the scene of an outrage committed by more than a single individual. If we imagine but one violator, we can conceive, and thus only conceive, the struggle of so violent and so obstinate a nature as to have left the "traces" apparent.

'And again. I have already mentioned the suspicion to be excited by the fact that the articles in question were suffered to remain at all in the thicket where discovered. It seems almost impossible that these evidences of guilt should have been accidentally left where found. There was sufficient presence of mind (it is supposed) to remove the corpse, and yet a more positive evidence than the corpse itself (whose features might have been quickly obliterated by decay), is allowed to lie conspicuously in the scene of the outrage – I allude to the handkerchief with the name of the deceased. If this was accident, it was not the accident of a gang. We can imagine it only the accident of an individual. Let us see. An individual has committed the murder. He is alone with the ghost of the departed. He is appalled by what lies motionless before him. The fury of his passion is over, and there is abundant room in his heart for the natural awe of the deed. His is none of that confidence which the presence of numbers inevitably inspires. He is alone with the dead. He trembles and is bewildered. Yet there is a necessity for disposing of the corpse. He bears it to the river, and leaves behind him the other evidences of his guilt; for it is difficult, if not impossible to carry all the burden at once, and it will be easy to return for what is left. But in his toilsome journey to the water his fears redouble within him. The sounds of life encompass his path. A dozen times he hears or fancies he hears the step of an observer. Even the very lights from the city bewilder him. Yet, in time, and by long and frequent pauses of deep agony, he reaches the river's brink, and disposes of his ghastly charge – perhaps through the medium of a boat. But now what treasure does the world hold – what threat of vengeance could it hold out – which would have power to urge the return of that lonely murderer over that toilsome and perilous path, to the thicket and its blood-chilling recollections? He returns not, let the consequences be what they may. He could not return if he would. His sole thought is immediate escape. He turns his back forever upon those dreadful shrubberies, and flees as from the wrath to come.

'But how with a gang? Their number would have inspired them with confidence; if, indeed, confidence is ever wanting in the breast of the arrant blackguard; and of arrant blackguards alone are the supposed gangs ever constituted. Their number, I say, would have prevented the bewildering and unreasoning terror which I have imagined to paralyse the single man. Could we suppose an oversight in one, or two, or three, this oversight would have been remedied by a fourth. They would have left nothing behind them; for their number would have enabled them to carry all at once. There would have been no need of return.

'Consider now the circumstance that, in the outer garment of the corpse when found: "a slip, about a foot wide, had been torn upward from the bottom hem to the waist, wound three times around the waist, and secured by a sort of hitch in the back". This was done with the obvious design of affording a handle by which to carry the body. But would any number of men have dreamed of resorting to such an expedient? To three or four, the limbs of the corpse would have afforded not only a sufficient, but the best possible, hold. The device is that of a single individual; and this brings us to the fact that "between the thicket and the river, the rails of the fences were found taken down, and the ground bore evident traces of some heavy burden having been dragged along it"! But would a number of men have put themselves to the superfluous trouble of taking down a fence, for the purpose of dragging through it a corpse which they might have lifted over any fence in an instant? Would a number of men have so dragged a corpse at all as to have left evident traces of the dragging?

'And here we must refer to an observation of *Le Commerciel*; an observation upon which I have already, in some measure, commented. "A piece," says this journal, "of one of the unfortunate girl's petticoats was torn out and tied under her chin, and around the back of her head, probably to prevent screams. This was done by fellows who had no pocket-handkerchiefs."

'I have before suggested that a genuine blackguard is never without a pocket-handkerchief. But it is not to this fact that I now especially advert. That it was not through want of a handkerchief for the purpose imagined by *Le Commerciel* that this bandage was employed, is rendered apparent by the handkerchief left in the thicket; and that the object was not "to prevent screams" appears, also, from the bandage having been employed in preference to what would so much better have answered the purpose. But the language of the evidence speaks of the strip in question as "found around the neck, fitting loosely, and secured with a hard knot". These words are sufficiently vague, but differ materially from those of *Le Commerciel*. The slip was eighteen inches wide, and therefore, although of muslin, would form a strong band when folded or rumpled longitudinally. And thus rumpled it was discovered. My inference is this. The solitary murderer, having borne the corpse for some distance (whether from the thicket or elsewhere) by means of the bandage hitched around its middle, found the weight, in this mode of procedure, too much for his strength. He resolved to drag the burden – the evidence goes to show that it was dragged. With this object in view, it became necessary to attach something like a rope to one of the extremities. It could be best attached about the neck, where the head would prevent it slipping off. And now the murderer bethought him, unquestionably, of the bandage about the loins. He would have used this, but for its volution about the corpse, the hitch which embarrassed it, and the reflection that it had not been "torn off from the garment". It was easier to tear a new slip from the petticoat. He tore it, made it fast about the neck, and so dragged his victim to the brink of the river. That this "bandage", only attainable with trouble and delay, and but imperfectly answering its purpose – that this bandage was employed at all, demonstrates that the necessity for its employment sprang from circumstances arising at a period when the handkerchief was no longer attainable – that is to say, arising, as we have imagined, after quitting the thicket (if the thicket it was), and on the road between the thicket and the river.

'But the evidence, you will say, of Madame Deluc(!) points especially to the presence of a gang in the vicinity of the thicket, at or about the epoch of the murder. This I grant. I doubt if there were not a dozen gangs, such as described by Madame Deluc, in and about the vicinity of the Barriere du Roule at or about the period of this tragedy. But the gang which has drawn upon itself the pointed animadversion, although the somewhat tardy and very suspicious evidence, of Madame Deluc, is the only gang which is represented by that honest and scrupulous old lady as having eaten her cakes and swallowed her brandy, without putting themselves to the trouble of making her payment. *Et hinc illae irae*?

'But what is the precise evidence of Madame Deluc? "A gang of miscreants made their appearance, behaved boisterously, ate and drank without making payment, followed in the route of the young man and the girl, returned to the inn about dusk, and re-crossed the river as if in great haste."

'Now this "great haste" very possibly seemed greater haste in the eyes of Madame Deluc, since she dwelt lingeringly and lamentingly upon her violated cakes and ale – cakes and ale for which she might still have entertained a faint hope of compensation. Why, otherwise, since it was about dusk, should she make a point of the haste? It is no cause for wonder, surely, that even a gang of blackguards should make haste to get home when a wide river is to be crossed in small boats, when storm impends, and when night approaches.

'I say approaches, for the night had not yet arrived. It was only about dusk that the indecent haste of these "miscreants" offended the sober eyes of Madame Deluc. But we are told that it was upon this very evening that Madame Deluc, as well as her eldest son, "heard the screams of a female in the vicinity of the inn". And in what words does Madame Deluc designate the period of the evening at which these screams were heard? "It was soon after dark," she says. But "soon after dark" is, at least, dark; and "about dusk" is as certainly daylight. Thus it is abundantly clear that the gang quitted the Barriere da Roule prior to the screams overheard(?) by Madame Deluc. And although, in all the many reports of the evidence, the relative expressions in question are distinctly and invariably employed just as I have employed them in this conversation with yourself, no notice whatever of the gross discrepancy has, as yet, been taken by any of the public journals, or by any of the myrmidons of police.

'I shall add but one to the arguments against a gang, but this one has, to my own understanding at least, a weight altogether irresistible. Under the circumstances of large reward offered, and full pardon to any king's evidence, it is not to be imagined, for a moment, that some member of a gang of low ruffians, or of any body of men would not long ago have betrayed his accomplices. Each one of a gang, so placed, is not so much greedy of reward, or anxious for escape, as fearful of betrayal. He betrays eagerly and early that he may not himself be betrayed. That the secret has not been divulged is the very best of proof that it is, in fact, a secret. The horrors of this dark deed are known only to one, or two, living human beings, and to God.

'Let us sum up now the meagre yet certain fruits of our long analysis. We have attained the idea either of a fatal accident under the roof of Madame Deluc, or of a murder perpetrated, in the thicket at the Barriere du Roule, by a lover, or at least by an intimate and secret associate of the deceased. This associate is of swarthy complexion. This complexion, the "hitch" in the bandage, and the "sailor's knot"

with which the bonnet-ribbon is tied, point to a seaman. His companionship with the deceased, a gay but not an abject young girl, desig-
nates him as above the grade of the common sailor. Here the
well-written and urgent communications to the journals are much in
the way of corroboration. The circumstance of the first elopement as
mentioned by *Le Mercurie*, tends to blend the idea of this seaman
with that of that "naval officer" who is first known to have led the
unfortunate into crime.

'And here, most fitly, comes the consideration of the continued
absence of him of the dark complexion. Let me pause to observe that
the complexion of this man is dark and swarthy; it was no common
swarthiness which constituted the sole point of remembrance, both as
regards Valence and Madame Deluc. But why is this man absent?
Was he murdered by the gang? If so, why are there only traces of the
assassinated girl? The scene of the two outrages will naturally be supposed identical. And where is his corpse? The assassins would most
probably have disposed of both in the same way. But it may be said
that this man lives, and is deterred from making himself known,
through dread of being charged with the murder. This consideration
might be supposed to operate upon him now – at late period – since it
has been given in evidence that he was seen with Marie – but it would
have had no force at the period of the deed. The first impulse of an
innocent man would have been to announce the outrage, and to aid
in identifying the ruffians. This, policy would have suggested. He had
been seen with the girl. He had crossed the river with her in an open
ferryboat. The denouncing of the assassins would have appeared,
even to an idiot, the surest and sole means of relieving himself from
suspicion. We cannot suppose him, on the night of the fatal Sunday,
both innocent himself and incognisant of an outrage committed. Yet
only under such circumstances is it possible to imagine that he would
have failed, if alive, in the denouncement of the assassins.

'And what means are ours of attaining the truth? We shall find
these means multiplying and gathering distinctness as we proceed.
Let us sift to the bottom this affair of the first elopement. Let us know
the full history of "the officer", with his present circumstances, and
his whereabouts at the precise period of the murder. Let us carefully
compare with each other the various communications sent to the
evening paper, in which the object was to inculpate a gang. This
done, let us compare these communications, both as regards style and
MS, with those sent to the morning paper, at a previous period, and
insisting so vehemently upon the guilt of Mennais. And, all this done,

let us again compare these various communications with the known MSS of the officer. Let us endeavour to ascertain, by repeated questionings of Madame Deluc and her boys, as well as of the omnibus-driver, Valence, something more of the personal appearance and bearing of the "man of dark complexion". Queries, skilfully directed will not fail to elicit, from some of these parties, information on this particular point (or upon others) – information which the parties themselves may not even be aware of possessing. And let us now trace the boat picked up by the bargeman on the morning of Monday the twenty-third of June, and which was removed from the barge-office, without the cognisance of the officer in attendance, and without the rudder, at some period prior to the discovery of the corpse. With a proper caution and perseverance we shall infallibly trace this boat; for not only can the bargeman who picked it up identify it, but the rudder is at hand. The rudder of a sail boat would not have been abandoned, without inquiry, by one altogether at ease in heart. And here let me pause to insinuate a question. There was no advertisement of the picking up of this boat. It was silently taken to the barge-office and as silently removed. But its owner or employer – how happened he, at so early a period as Tuesday morning, to be informed, without the agency of advertisement, of the locality of the boat taken up on Monday, unless we imagine some connection with the navy – some personal permanent connexion leading to cognisance of its minute interests – its petty local news?

'In speaking of the lonely assassin dragging his burden to the shore, I have already suggested the probability of his availing himself of a boat. Now we are to understand that Marie Roget was precipitated from a boat. This would naturally have been the case. The corpse could not have been trusted to the shallow waters of the shore. The peculiar marks on the back and shoulders of the victim tell of the bottom ribs of a boat. That the body was found without weight is also corroborative of the idea. If thrown from the shore a weight would have been attached. We can only account for its absence by supposing the murderer to have neglected the precaution of supplying himself with it before pushing off. In the act of consigning the corpse to the water, he would unquestionably have noticed his oversight; but then no remedy would have been at hand. Any risk would have been preferred to a return to that accursed shore. Having rid himself of his ghastly charge, the murderer would have hastened to the city. There, at some obscure wharf, he would have leaped on land. But the boat – would he have secured it? He would have been in too great haste for such things as securing a boat. Moreover, in fastening it to the wharf, he would have felt as if securing evidence against himself. His natural thought would have been to cast from him, as far as possible, all that had held connection with his crime. He would not only have fled from the wharf, but he would not have permitted the boat to remain. Assuredly he would have cast it adrift. Let us pursue our fancies. In the morning, the wretch is stricken with unutterable horror at finding that the boat has been picked up and detained at a locality which he is in the daily habit of frequenting – at a locality, perhaps, which his duty compels him to frequent. The next night, without daring to ask for the rudder, he removes it. Now where is that rudderless boat? Let it be one of our first purposes to discover. With the first glimpse we obtain of it, the dawn of our success shall begin. This boat shall guide us, with a rapidity which will surprise even ourselves, to him who employed it in the midnight of the fatal Sabbath. Corroboration will rise upon corroboration, and the murderer will be traced.'

(For reasons which we shall not specify, but which to many readers will appear obvious, we have taken the liberty of here omitting, from the MSS placed in our hands, such portion as details the following up of the apparently slight clew obtained by Dupin. We feel it advisable only to state, in brief, that the result desired was brought to pass; and that the Prefect fulfilled punctually, although with reluctance, the terms of his compact with the Chevalier. Mr Poe's article concludes with the following words. – Eds.[1])

It will be understood that I speak of coincidences and no more. What I have said above upon this topic must suffice. In my own heart there dwells no faith in praeter-nature. That Nature and its God are two, no man who thinks will deny. That the latter, creating the former, can, at will, control or modify it, is also unquestionable. I say 'at will'; for the question is of will, and not, as the insanity of logic has assumed, of power. It is not that the Deity cannot modify his laws, but that we insult him in imagining a possible necessity for modification. In their origin these laws were fashioned to embrace all contingencies which could lie in the Future. With God all is Now.

I repeat, then, that I speak of these things only as of coincidences. And further: in what I relate it will be seen that between the fate of the unhappy Mary Cecilia Rogers, so far as that fate is known, and the fate of one Marie Roget up to a certain epoch in her history, there has existed a parallel in the contemplation of whose wonderful exactitude the reason becomes embarrassed. I say all this will be seen. But

[1] Of the magazine in which the article was originally published.

let it not for a moment be supposed that, in proceeding with the sad narrative of Marie from the epoch just mentioned, and in tracing to its denouement the mystery which enshrouded her, it is my covert design to hint at an extension of the parallel, or even to suggest that the measures adopted in Paris for the discovery of the assassin of a grisette, or measures founded in any similar ratiocination would produce any similar result.

For, in respect to the latter branch of the supposition, it should be considered that the most trifling variation in the facts of the two cases might give rise to the most important miscalculations, by diverting thoroughly the two courses of events; very much as, in arithmetic, an error which, in its own individuality, may be inappreciable, produces, at length, by dint of multiplication at all points of the process, a result enormously at variance with truth. And, in regard to the former branch, we must not fail to hold in view that the very Calculus of Probabilities to which I have referred, forbids all idea of the extension of the parallel – forbids it with a positiveness strong and decided just in proportion as this parallel has already been long-drawn and exact. This is one of those anomalous propositions which, seemingly appealing to thought altogether apart from the mathematical, is yet one which only the mathematician can fully entertain. Nothing, for example, is more difficult than to convince the merely general reader that the fact of sixes having been thrown twice in succession by a player at dice, is sufficient cause for betting the largest odds that sixes will not be thrown in the third attempt. A suggestion to this effect is usually rejected by the intellect at once. It does not appear that the two throws which have been completed, and which lie now absolutely in the Past, can have influence upon the throw which exists only in the Future. The chance for throwing sixes seems to be precisely as it was at any ordinary time – that is to say, subject only to the influence of the various other throws which may be made by the dice. And this is a reflection which appears so exceedingly obvious that attempts to controvert it are received more frequently with a derisive smile than with any thing like respectful attention. The error here involved – a gross error redolent of mischief – I cannot pretend to expose within the limits assigned me at present; and with the philosophical it needs no exposure. It may be sufficient here to say that it forms one of an infinite series of mistakes which arise in the path of Reason through her propensity for seeking truth in detail.

JS LE FANU

The Murdered Cousin

And they lay wait for their own blood: they lurk privily for their own lives.
    So are the ways of every one that is greedy for gain; which taketh away the
life of the owner thereof.

THIS STORY of the Irish peerage is written, as nearly as possible, in the very words in which it was related by its 'heroine', the late Countess D—, and is therefore told in the first person.

MY MOTHER died when I was an infant, and of her I have no recollection, even the faintest. By her death my education was left solely to the direction of my surviving parent. He entered upon his task with a stern appreciation of the responsibility thus cast upon him. My religious instruction was prosecuted with an almost exaggerated anxiety; and I had, of course, the best masters to perfect me in all those accomplishments which my station and wealth might seem to require. My father was what is called an oddity, and his treatment of me, though uniformly kind, was governed less by affection and tenderness, than by a high and unbending sense of duty. Indeed I seldom saw or spoke to him except at mealtimes, and then, though gentle, he was usually reserved and gloomy. His leisure hours, which were many, were passed either in his study or in solitary walks; in short, he seemed to take no further interest in my happiness or improvement, than a conscientious regard to the discharge of his own duty would seem to impose.

Shortly before my birth an event occurred which had contributed much to induce and to confirm my father's unsocial habits; it was the fact that a suspicion of *murder* had fallen upon his younger brother, though not sufficiently definite to lead to any public proceedings, yet strong enough to ruin him in public opinion. This disgraceful and dreadful doubt cast upon the family name, my father felt deeply and bitterly, and not the less so that he himself was thoroughly convinced of his brother's innocence. The sincerity and strength of this conviction he shortly afterwards proved in a manner which produced the catastrophe of my story.

Before, however, I enter upon my immediate adventures, I ought to relate the circumstances which had awakened that suspicion to which I have referred, inasmuch as they are in themselves somewhat curious, and in their effects most intimately connected with my own after-history.

My uncle, Sir Arthur Tyrrell, was a gay and extravagant man, and, among other vices, was ruinously addicted to gaming. This unfortunate propensity, even after his fortune had suffered so severely as to render retrenchment imperative, nevertheless continued to engross him, nearly to the exclusion of every other pursuit. He was, however, a proud, or rather a vain man, and could not bear to make the diminution of his income a matter of triumph to those with whom he had hitherto competed; and the consequence was, that he frequented no longer the expensive haunts of his dissipation, and retired from the gay world, leaving his coterie to discover his reasons as best they might. He did not, however, forego his favourite vice, for though he could not worship his great divinity in those costly temples where he was formerly wont to take his place, yet he found it very possible to bring about him a sufficient number of the votaries of chance to answer all his ends. The consequence was, that Carrick-leigh, which was the name of my uncle's residence, was never without one or more of such visitors as I have described. It happened that upon one occasion he was visited by one Hugh Tisdall, a gentleman of loose, and, indeed, low habits, but of considerable wealth, and who had, in early youth, travelled with my uncle upon the Continent. The period of this visit was winter, and, consequently, the house was nearly deserted excepting by its ordinary inmates; it was, therefore, highly acceptable, particularly as my uncle was aware that his visitor's tastes accorded exactly with his own.

Both parties seemed determined to avail themselves of their mutual suitability during the brief stay which Mr Tisdall had promised; the consequence was, that they shut themselves up in Sir Arthur's private room for nearly all the day and the greater part of the night, during the space of almost a week, at the end of which the servant having one morning, as usual, knocked at Mr Tisdall's bedroom door repeatedly, received no answer, and, upon attempting to enter, found that it was locked. This appeared suspicious, and the inmates of the house having been alarmed, the door was forced open, and, on proceeding to the bed, they found the body of the occupant perfectly lifeless, and hanging halfway out, the head downwards, and near the floor. One deep wound had been inflicted upon the temple, apparently with some blunt instrument, which had penetrated the brain, and another blow, less effective – probably the first aimed – had grazed his head, removing some of his scalp. The door had been double locked upon the *inside*, evidence of which the key still lay where it had been placed in the lock. The window, though not secured on the interior, was closed; a circumstance not a little puzzling, as it afforded the only other mode of escape from the room. It looked out, too, upon a kind of courtyard, round which the old buildings stood, formerly accessible by a narrow doorway and passage lying in the oldest side of the quadrangle, but which had since been built up, so as to preclude all ingress or egress; the room was also upon the second storey, and the height of the window considerable; in addition to all which the stone window-sill was much too narrow to allow anyone's standing upon it when the window was closed. Near the bed were found a pair of razors belonging to the murdered man, one of them upon the ground, and both of them open. The weapon which inflicted the mortal wound was not to be found in the room, nor were any footprints or other traces of the murderer discoverable. At the suggestion of Sir Arthur himself, the coroner was instantly summoned to attend, and an inquest was held. Nothing, however, in any degree conclusive was elicited. The walls, ceiling, and floor of the room were carefully examined, in order to ascertain whether they contained a trapdoor or other concealed mode of entrance, but no such thing appeared. Such was the minuteness of investigation employed, that, although the grate had contained a large fire during the night, they proceeded to examine even the very chimney, in order to discover whether escape by it were possible. But this attempt, too, was fruitless, for the chimney, built in the old fashion, rose to a perfectly perpendicular line from the hearth, to a height of nearly fourteen feet above the roof, affording in its interior scarcely the possibility of ascent, the flue being smoothly plastered, and sloping towards the top like an inverted funnel; promising, too, even if the summit were attained, owing to its great height, but a precarious descent upon the sharp and steep-ridged roof; the ashes, too, which lay in the grate, and the soot, as far as it could be seen, were undisturbed, a circumstance almost conclusive upon the point.

Sir Arthur was, of course, examined. His evidence was given with clearness and unreserve, which seemed calculated to silence all suspicion. He stated that, up to the day and night immediately preceding the catastrophe, he had lost to a heavy amount, but that, at their last sitting, he had not only won back his original loss, but upwards of

£4,000 in addition; in evidence of which he produced an acknowl-
edgement of debt to that amount in the handwriting of the deceased,
bearing date the night of the catastrophe. He had mentioned the circumstance to Lady Tyrrell, and in presence of some of his domestics;
which statement was supported by *their* respective evidence. One of
the jury shrewdly observed, that the circumstance of Mr Tisdall's
having sustained so heavy a loss might have suggested to some ill-
minded persons, accidentally hearing it, the plan of robbing him,
after having murdered him in such a manner as might make it appear
that he had committed suicide; a supposition which was strongly supported by the razors having been found thus displaced and removed
from their case. Two persons had probably been engaged in the
attempt, one watching by the sleeping man, and ready to strike him in
case of his awakening suddenly, while the other was procuring the
razors and employed in inflicting the fatal gash, so as to make it
appear to have been the act of the murdered man himself. It was said
that while the juror was making this suggestion Sir Arthur changed
colour. There was nothing, however, like legal evidence to implicate
him, and the consequence was that the verdict was found against a
person or persons unknown, and for some time the matter was suffered to rest, until, after about five months, my father received a letter
from a person signing himself Andrew Collis, and representing
himself to be the cousin of the deceased. This letter stated that his
brother, Sir Arthur, was likely to incur not merely suspicion but personal risk, unless he could account for certain circumstances connected with the recent murder, and contained a copy of a letter
written by the deceased, and dated the very day upon the night of
which the murder had been perpetrated. Tisdall's letter contained,
among a great deal of other matter, the passages which follow:

> I have had sharp work with Sir Arthur: he tried some of his stale
> tricks, but soon found that *I* was Yorkshire, too; it would not do –
> you understand me. We went to the work like good ones, head, heart,
> and soul; and in fact, since I came here, I have lost no time. I am
> rather fagged, but I am sure to be well paid for my hardship; I never
> want sleep so long as I can have the music of a dice-box, and where-
> withal to pay the piper. As I told you, he tried some of his queer turns,
> but I foiled him like a man, and, in return, gave him more than he
> could relish of the genuine *dead knowledge*. In short, I have plucked
> the old baronet as never baronet was plucked before; I have scarce left
> him the stump of a quill. I have got promissory notes in his hand to
> the amount of —; if you like round numbers, say five-and-twenty

thousand pounds, safely deposited in my portable strong box, alias, double-clasped pocket-book. I leave this ruinous old rat-hole early on tomorrow, for two reasons: first, I do not want to play with Sir Arthur deeper than I think his security would warrant; and, secondly, because I am safer a hundred miles away from Sir Arthur than in the house with him. Look you, my worthy, I tell you this between ourselves – I may be wrong – but, by —, I am sure as that I am now living, that Sir A— attempted to poison me last night. So much for old friendship on both sides. When I won the last stake, a heavy one enough, my friend leant his forehead upon his hands, and you'll laugh when I tell you that his head literally smoked like a hot dumpling. I do not know whether his agitation was produced by the plan which he had against me, or by his having lost so heavily; though it must be allowed that he had reason to be a little funked, whichever way his thoughts went; but he pulled the bell, and ordered two bottles of Champagne. While the fellow was bringing them, he wrote a promissory note to the full amount, which he signed, and, as the man came in with the bottles and glasses, he desired him to be off. He filled a glass for me, and, while he thought my eyes were off, for I was putting up his note at the time, he dropped something slyly into it, no doubt to sweeten it; but I saw it all, and, when he handed it to me, I said, with an emphasis which he might easily understand, 'There is some sediment in it, I'll not drink it.' 'Is there?' said he, and at the same time snatched it from my hand and threw it into the fire. What do you think of that? Have I not a tender bird in hand? Win or lose, I will not play beyond five thousand tonight, and tomorrow sees me safe out of the reach of Sir Arthur's Champagne.

Of the authenticity of this document, I never heard my father express a doubt; and I am satisfied that, owing to his strong conviction in favour of his brother, he would not have admitted it without sufficient inquiry, inasmuch as it tended to confirm the suspicions which already existed to his prejudice. Now, the only point in this letter which made strongly against my uncle, was the mention of the 'double-clasped pocketbook', as the receptacle of the papers likely to involve him, for this pocketbook was not forthcoming, nor anywhere to be found, nor had any papers referring to his gaming transactions been discovered upon the dead man.

But whatever might have been the original intention of this man, Collis, neither my uncle nor my father ever heard more of him; he published the letter, however, in Faulkner's newspaper, which was shortly afterwards made the vehicle of a much more mysterious attack. The passage in that journal to which I allude, appeared about four years afterwards, and while the fatal occurrence was still fresh in public recollection. It commenced by a rambling preface, stating that 'a *certain person* whom *certain* persons thought to be dead, was not so, but living, and in full possession of his memory, and moreover, ready and able to make *great* delinquents tremble': it then went on to describe the murder, without, however, mentioning names; and in doing so, it entered into minute and circumstantial particulars of which none but an *eyewitness* could have been possessed, and by implications almost too unequivocal to be regarded in the light of insinuation, to involve the '*titled gambler*' in the guilt of the transaction.

My father at once urged Sir Arthur to proceed against the paper in an action of libel, but he would not hear of it, nor consent to my father's taking any legal steps whatever in the matter. My father, however, wrote in a threatening tone to Faulkner, demanding a surrender of the author of the obnoxious article; the answer to this application is still in my possession, and is penned in an apologetic tone: it states that the manuscript had been handed in, paid for, and inserted as an advertisement, without sufficient enquiry, or any knowledge as to whom it referred. No step, however, was taken to clear my uncle's character in the judgement of the public; and, as he immediately sold a small property, the application of the proceeds of which were known to none, he was said to have disposed of it to enable himself to buy off the threatened information; however the truth might have been, it is certain that no charges respecting the mysterious murder were afterwards publicly made against my uncle, and, as far as external disturbances were concerned, he enjoyed henceforward perfect security and quiet.

A deep and lasting impression, however, had been made upon the public mind, and Sir Arthur Tyrrell was no longer visited or noticed by the gentry of the county, whose attentions he had hitherto received. He accordingly affected to despise those courtesies which he no longer enjoyed, and shunned even that society which he might have commanded. This is all that I need recapitulate of my uncle's history, and I now recur to my own.

Although my father had never, within my recollection, visited, or been visited by my uncle, each being of unsocial, procrastinating, and indolent habits, and their respective residences being very far apart – the one lying in the county of Galway, the other in that of Cork – he was strongly attached to his brother, and evinced his affection by an active correspondence, and by deeply and proudly resenting that neglect which had branded Sir Arthur as unfit to mix in society.

When I was about eighteen years of age, my father, whose health had been gradually declining, died, leaving me in heart wretched and desolate, and, owing to his habitual seclusion, with few acquaintances, and almost no friends. The provisions of his will were curious, and when I was sufficiently come to myself to listen to, or comprehend them, surprised me not a little: all his vast property was left to me, and to the heirs of my body, for ever; and, in default of such heirs, it was to go after my death to my uncle, Sir Arthur, without any entail.

At the same time, the will appointed him my guardian, desiring that I might be received within his house, and reside with his family, and under his care, during the term of my minority; and in consideration of the increased expense consequent upon such an arrangement, a handsome allowance was allotted to him during the term of my proposed residence. The object of this last provision I at once understood; my father desired, by making it the direct apparent interest of Sir Arthur that I should die without issue, while at the same time he placed my person wholly in his power, to prove to the world how great and unshaken was his confidence in his brother's innocence and honour. It was a strange, perhaps an idle scheme, but as I had been always brought up in the habit of considering my uncle as a deeply injured man, and had been taught, almost as a part of my religion, to regard him as the very soul of honour, I felt no further uneasiness respecting the arrangement than that likely to affect a shy and timid girl at the immediate prospect of taking up her abode for the first time in her life among strangers. Previous to leaving my home, which I felt I should do with a heavy heart, I received a most tender and affectionate letter from my uncle, calculated, if anything could do so, to remove the bitterness of parting from scenes familiar and dear from my earliest childhood, and in some degree to reconcile me to the measure. It was upon a fine autumn day that I approached the old domain of Carrictdeigh. I shall not soon forget the impression of sadness and of gloom which all that I saw produced upon my mind; the sunbeams were falling with a rich and melancholy lustre upon the fine old trees, which stood in lordly groups, casting their long sweeping shadows over rock and sward; there was an air of neglect and decay about the spot, which amounted almost to desolation, and mournfully increased as we approached the building itself, near which the ground had been originally more artificially and carefully cultivated than elsewhere, and where consequently neglect more immediately and strikingly betrayed itself.

As we proceeded, the road wound near the beds of what had been formerly two fishponds, which were now nothing more than stagnant swamps, overgrown with rank weeds, and here and there encroached upon by the straggling underwood; the avenue itself was much broken; and in many places the stones were almost concealed by grass and nettles; the loose stone walls which had here and there intersected the broad park, were, in many places, broken down, so as no longer to answer their original purpose as fences; piers were now and then to be seen, but the gates were gone; and to add to the general air of dilapidation, some huge trunks were lying scattered through the venerable old trees, either the work of the winter storms, or perhaps the victims of some extensive but desultory scheme of denudation, which the projector had not capital or perseverance to carry into full effect.

After the carriage had travelled a full mile of this avenue, we reached the summit of a rather abrupt eminence, one of the many which added to the picturesqueness, if not to the convenience of this rude approach; from the top of this ridge the grey walls of Carrick-leigh were visible, rising at a small distance in front, and darkened by the hoary wood which crowded around them; it was a quadrangular building of considerable extent, and the front, where the great entrance was placed, lay towards us, and bore unequivocal marks of antiquity; the timeworn, solemn aspect of the old building, the ruinous and deserted appearance of the whole place, and the associations which connected it with a dark page in the history of my family, combined to depress spirits already predisposed for the reception of sombre and dejecting impressions. When the carriage drew up in the grass-grown courtyard before the hall-door, two lazy-looking men, whose appearance well accorded with that of the place which they tenanted, alarmed by the obstreperous barking of a great chained dog, ran out from some half-ruinous outhouses, and took charge of the horses; the hall-door stood open, and I entered a gloomy and imperfectly lighted apartment, and found no one within it. However, I had not long to wait in this awkward predicament, for before my luggage had been deposited in the house, indeed before I had well removed my cloak and other muffles, so as to enable me to look around, a young girl ran lightly into the hall, and kissing me heartily and somewhat boisterously exclaimed, 'My dear cousin, my dear Margaret – I am so delighted – so out of breath, we did not expect you till ten o'clock; my father is somewhere about the place, he must be close at hand. James – Corney – run out and tell your master; my brother is seldom at home, at least at any reasonable hour; you must be so tired – so fatigued – let me show you to your room; see that Lady Margaret's luggage is all brought up; you must lie down and rest yourself. Deborah, bring some coffee – up these stairs; we are so delighted to see you – you cannot think how lonely I have been; how steep these stairs are, are not they? I am so glad you are come – I could hardly bring myself to believe that you were really coming; how good of you, dear Lady Margaret.' There was real good nature and delight in my cousin's greeting, and a kind of constitutional confidence of manner which placed me at once at ease, and made me feel immediately upon terms of intimacy with her. The room into which she ushered me, although partaking in the general air of decay which pervaded the mansion and all about it, had, nevertheless, been fitted up with evident attention to comfort, and even with some dingy attempt at luxury; but what pleased me most was that it opened, by a second door, upon a lobby which communicated with my fair cousin's apartment; a circumstance which divested the room, in my eyes, of the air of solitude and sadness which would otherwise have characterised it, to a degree almost painful to one so depressed and agitated as I was.

After such arrangements as I found necessary were completed, we both went down to the parlour, a large wainscotted room, hung round with grim old portraits, and, as I was not sorry to see, containing, in its ample grate, a large and cheerful fire. Here my cousin had leisure to talk more at her ease; and from her I learned something of the manners and the habits of the two remaining members of her family, whom I had not yet seen. On my arrival I had known nothing of the family among whom I was come to reside, except that it consisted of three individuals, my uncle, and his son and daughter, Lady Tyrrell having been long dead; in addition to this very scanty stock of information, I shortly learned from my communicative companion, that my uncle was, as I had suspected, completely retired in his habits, and besides that, having been, so far back as she could well recollect, always rather strict, as reformed rakes frequently become, he had latterly been growing more gloomily and sternly religious than heretofore. Her account of her brother was far less favourable, though she did not say anything directly to his disadvantage. From all that I could gather from her, I was led to suppose that he was a specimen of the idle, coarse-mannered, profligate 'squirearchy' – a result which might naturally have followed from the circumstance of his being, as it were, outlawed from society, and driven for companionship to grades below his own – enjoying, too, the dangerous prerogative of spending a good deal of money. However, you may easily suppose that I found nothing in my cousin's communication fully to bear me out in so very decided a conclusion.

I awaited the arrival of my uncle, which was every moment to be expected, with feelings half of alarm, half of curiosity – a sensation which I have often since experienced, though to a less degree, when upon the point of standing for the first time in the presence of one of whom I have long been in the habit of hearing or thinking with interest. It was, therefore, with some little perturbation that I heard, first a slight bustle at the outer door, then a slow step traverse the hall, and finally witnessed the door open, and my uncle enter the room. He was a striking looking man; from peculiarities both of person and of dress, the whole effect of his appearance amounted to extreme singularity. He was tall, and when young his figure must have been strikingly elegant; as it was, however, its effect was marred by a very decided stoop; his dress was of a sober colour, and in fashion anterior to any thing which I could remember. It was, however, handsome, and by no means carelessly put on; but what completed the singularity of his appearance was his uncut, white hair, which hung in long, but not at all neglected curls, even so far as his shoulders, and which combined with his regularly classic features, and fine dark eyes, to bestow upon him an air of venerable dignity and pride, which I have seldom seen equalled elsewhere. I rose as he entered, and met him about the middle of the room; he kissed my cheek and both my hands, saying:

'You are most welcome, dear child, as welcome as the command of this poor place and all that it contains can make you. I am rejoiced to see you – truly rejoiced. I trust that you are not much fatigued; pray be seated again.' He led me to my chair, and continued, 'I am glad to perceive you have made acquaintance with Emily already; I see, in your being thus brought together, the foundation of a lasting friendship. You are both innocent, and both young. God bless you – God bless you, and make you all that I could wish.'

He raised his eyes, and remained for a few moments silent, as if in secret prayer. I felt that it was impossible that this man, with feelings manifestly so tender, could be the wretch that public opinion had represented him to be. I was more than ever convinced of his innocence. His manners were, or appeared to me, most fascinating. I know not how the lights of experience might have altered this estimate. But I was then very young, and I beheld in him a perfect mingling of the courtesy of polished life with the gentlest and most genial virtues of the heart. A feeling of affection and respect towards him began to spring up within me, the more earnest that I remembered how sorely he had suffered in fortune and how cruelly in fame. My uncle having given me fully to understand that I was most welcome, and might command whatever was his own, pressed me to take some supper; and on my refusing, he observed that, before bidding me Goodnight, he had one duty further to perform, one in which he was convinced I would cheerfully acquiesce. He then proceeded to read a chapter from the Bible; after which he took his leave with the same affectionate kindness with which he had greeted me, having repeated his desire that I should consider everything in his house as altogether at my disposal. It is needless to say how much I was pleased with my uncle – it was impossible to avoid being so; and I could not help saying to myself, if such a man as this is not safe from the assaults of slander, who is? I felt much happier than I had done since my father's death, and enjoyed that night the first refreshing sleep which had visited me since that calamity. My curiosity respecting my male cousin did not long remain unsatisfied; he appeared upon the next day at dinner. His manners, though not so coarse as I had expected, were exceedingly disagreeable; there was an assurance and a forwardness for which I was not prepared; there was less of the vulgarity of manner, and almost more of that of the mind, than I had anticipated. I felt quite uncomfortable in his presence; there was just that confidence in his look and tone, which would read encouragement even in mere toleration; and I felt more disgusted and annoyed at the coarse and extravagant compliments which he was pleased from time to time to pay me, than perhaps the extent of the atrocity might fully have warranted. It was, however, one consolation that he did not often appear, being much engrossed by pursuits about which I neither knew nor cared anything; but when he did, his attentions, either with a view to his amusement, or to some more serious object, were so obviously and perseveringly directed to me, that young and inexperienced as I was, even I could not be ignorant of their significance. I felt more provoked by this odious persecution than I can express, and discouraged him with so much vigour, that I did not stop even at rudeness to convince him that his assiduities were unwelcome; but all in vain.

This had gone on for nearly a twelvemonth, to my infinite annoyance, when one day, as I was sitting at some needlework with my companion, Emily, as was my habit, in the parlour, the door opened, and my cousin Edward entered the room. There was something, I thought, odd in his manner, a kind of struggle between shame and impudence, a kind of flurry and ambiguity, which made him appear, if possible, more than ordinarily disagreeable.

'Your servant, ladies,' he said, seating himself at the same time; 'sorry to spoil your tête-à-tête; but never mind, I'll only take Emily's place for a minute or two, and then we part for a while, fair cousin. Emily, my father wants you in the corner turret; no shilly, shally, he's in a hurry.' She hesitated. 'Be off – tramp, march, I say,' he exclaimed, in a tone which the poor girl dared not disobey.

She left the room, and Edward followed her to the door. He stood there for a minute or two, as if reflecting what he should say, perhaps satisfying himself that no one was within hearing in the hall. At length he turned about, having closed the door, as if carelessly, with his foot, and advancing slowly, in deep thought, he took his seat at the side of the table opposite to mine. There was a brief interval of silence, after which he said:

'I imagine that you have a shrewd suspicion of the object of my early visit; but I suppose I must go into particulars. Must I?'

'I have no conception,' I replied, 'what your object may be.'

'Well, well,' said he becoming more at his ease as he proceeded, 'it may be told in a few words. You know that it is totally impossible, quite out of the question, that an offhand young fellow like me, and a good-looking girl like yourself, could meet continually as you and I have done, without an attachment – a liking growing up on one side or other; in short, I think I have let you know as plainly as if I spoke it, that I have been in love with you, almost from the first time I saw you.' He paused, but I was too much horrified to speak. He interpreted my silence favourably. 'I can tell you,' he continued, I'm reckoned rather hard to please, and very hard to *hit*. I can't say when I was taken with a girl before, so you see fortune reserved me—'

Here the odious wretch actually put his arm round my waist: the action at once restored me to utterance, and with the most indignant vehemence I released myself from his hold, and at the same time said:

'I *have*, sir, of course, perceived your most disagreeable attentions; they have long been a source of great annoyance to me; and you must be aware that I have marked my disapprobation, my disgust, as unequivocally as I possibly could, without actual indelicacy.'

I paused, almost out of breath from the rapidity with which I had spoken; and without giving him time to renew the conversation, I hastily quitted the room, leaving him in a paroxysm of rage and mortification. As I ascended the stairs, I heard him open the parlour-door with violence, and take two or three rapid strides in the direction in which I was moving. I was now much frightened, and ran the whole way until I reached my room, and having locked the door, I listened breathlessly, but heard no sound. This relieved me for the present; but so much had I been overcome by the agitation and annoyance attendant upon the scene which I had just passed through, that when my cousin Emily knocked at the door, I was weeping in great agitation. You will readily conceive my distress, when you reflect upon my strong dislike to my cousin Edward, combined with my youth and extreme inexperience. Any proposal of such a nature must have agitated me; but that it should come from the man whom, of all others, I instinctively most loathed and abhorred, and to whom I had, as clearly as manner could do it, expressed the state of my feelings, was almost too annoying to be borne; it was a calamity, too, in which I could not claim the sympathy of my cousin Emily, which had always been extended to me in my minor grievances. Still I hoped that it might not be unattended with good; for I thought that one inevitable and most welcome consequence would result from this painful *éclaircissement*, in the discontinuance of my cousin's odious persecution.

When I arose next morning, it was with the fervent hope that I might never again behold his face, or even hear his name; but such a consummation, though devoutly to be wished, was hardly likely to occur. The painful impressions of yesterday were too vivid to be at once erased; and I could not help feeling some dim foreboding of coming annoyance and evil. To expect on my cousin's part anything like delicacy or consideration for me, was out of the question. I saw that he had set his heart upon my property, and that he was not likely easily to forego such a prize, possessing what might have been considered opportunities and facilities almost to compel my compliance. I now keenly felt the unreasonableness of my father's conduct in placing me to reside with a family, with all the members of which, with one exception, he was wholly unacquainted, and I bitterly felt the helplessness of my situation. I determined, however, in the event of my cousin's persevering in his addresses, to lay all the particulars before my uncle, although he had never, in kindness or intimacy, gone a step beyond our first interview, and to throw myself upon his hospitality and his sense of honour for protection against a repetition of such annoyances.

My cousin's conduct may appear to have been an inadequate cause for such serious uneasiness; but my alarm was awakened neither by his acts nor by words, but entirely by his manner, which was strange and even intimidating. At the beginning of our yesterday's interview, there was a sort of bullying swagger in his air, which, towards the end, gave place to something bordering upon the brutal vehemence of an undisguised ruffian, a transition which had tempted me into a belief that he might seek, even forcibly, to extort from me a consent to his wishes, or by means still more horrible, of which I scarcely dared to trust myself to think, to possess himself of my property.

I was early next day summoned to attend my uncle in his private room, which lay in a comer turret of the old building; and thither I accordingly went, wondering all the way what this unusual measure might prelude. When I entered the room, he did not rise in his usual courteous way to greet me, but simply pointed to a chair opposite to his own; this boded nothing agreeable. I sat down, however, silently waiting until he should open the conversation.

'Lady Margaret,' at length he said, in a tone of greater sternness than I thought him capable of using, 'I have hitherto spoken to you as a friend, but I have not forgotten that l am also your guardian, and that my authority as such gives me a right to control your conduct. I shall put a question to you, and I expect and will demand a plain, direct answer. Have I rightly been informed that you have contemptuously rejected the suit and hand of my son Edward?'

I stammered forth with a good deal of trepidation:

'I believe, that is, I have, sir, rejected my cousin's proposals; and my coldness and discouragement might have convinced him that I had determined to do so.'

'Madame,' replied he, with suppressed, but, as it appeared to me, intense anger, 'I have lived long enough to know that *coldness* and *discouragement*, and such terms, form the common cant of a worthless coquette. You know to the full, as well as I, that *coldness* and *discouragement* may be so exhibited as to convince their object that he is neither distasteful nor indifferent to the person who wears that manner. You know, too, none better, that an affected neglect, when skilfully managed, is amongst the most formidable of the allurements which artful beauty can employ. I tell you, madame, that having, without one word spoken in discouragement, permitted my son's most marked attentions for a twelvemonth or more, you have no *right* to dismiss him with no further explanation than demurely telling him that you had always looked coldly upon him, and neither your wealth nor *your ladyship* (there was an emphasis of scorn on the word which would have become Sir Giles Overreach himself) can warrant you in treating with contempt the affectionate regard of an honest heart.'

I was too much shocked at this undisguised attempt to bully me into an acquiescence in the interested and unprincipled plan for their own aggrandisement, which I now perceived my uncle and his son had deliberately formed, at once to find strength or collectedness to frame an answer to what he had said. At length I replied, with a firmness that surprised myself:

'In all that you have just now said, sir, you have grossly misstated my conduct and motives. Your information must have been most incorrect, as far as it regards my conduct towards my cousin; my manner towards him could have conveyed nothing but dislike; and if anything could have added to the strong aversion which I have long felt towards him, it would be his attempting thus to frighten me into a marriage which he knows to be revolting to me, and which is sought by him only as a means for securing to himself whatever property is mine.'

As I said this, I fixed my eyes upon those of my uncle, but he was too old in the world's ways to falter beneath the gaze of more searching eyes than mine; he simply said:

'Are you acquainted with the provisions of your father's will?'

I answered in the affirmative; and he continued: 'Then you must be aware that if my son Edward were, which God forbid, the unprincipled, reckless man, the ruffian you pretend to think him' – (here be spoke very slowly, as if he intended that every word which escaped him should be registered in my memory, while at the same time the expression of his countenance underwent a gradual but horrible change, and the eyes which he fixed upon me became so darkly vivid, that I almost lost sight of everything else) – 'if he were what you have described him, do you think, child, he would have found no shorter way than marriage to gain his ends? A single blow, an outrage not a degree worse than you insinuate, would transfer your property to us!!'

I stood staring at him for many minutes after he had ceased to speak, fascinated by the terrible, serpent-like gaze, until he continued with a welcome change of countenance:

'I will not speak again to you, upon this topic, until one month has passed. You shall have time to consider the relative advantages of the two courses which are open to you. I should be sorry to hurry you to a decision. I am satisfied with having stated my feelings upon the subject, and pointed out to you the path of duty. Remember this day month; not one word sooner.'

He then rose, and I left the room, much agitated and exhausted.

This interview, all the circumstances attending it, but most particularly the formidable expression of my uncle's countenance while he talked, though hypothetically, of *murder*, combined to arouse all my worst suspicions of him. I dreaded to look upon the face that had so recently worn the appalling livery of guilt and malignity. I regarded it with the mingled fear and loathing with which one looks upon an object which has tortured them in a nightmare.

In a few days after the interview, the particulars of which I have just detailed, I found a note upon my toilet-table, and on opening it I read as follows:

My Dear Lady Margaret,
    You will be, perhaps, surprised to see a strange face in your room today. I have dismissed your Irish maid, and secured a French one to wait upon you; a step rendered necessary by my proposing shortly to visit the Continent with all my family.
Your faithful guardian,
ARTHUR TYRELL.

On enquiry, I found that my faithful attendant was actually gone, and far on her way to the town of Galway; and in her stead there appeared a tall, raw-boned, ill-looking, elderly Frenchwoman, whose sullen and presuming manners seemed to imply that her vocation had never before been that of a lady's-maid. I could not help regarding her as a creature of my uncle's, and therefore to be dreaded, even had she been in no other way suspicious.

Days and weeks passed away without any, even a momentary doubt upon my part, as to the course to be pursued by me. The allotted period had at length elapsed; the day arrived upon which I was to communicate my decision to my uncle. Although my resolution had never for a moment wavered, I could not shake off the dread of the approaching colloquy; and my heart sank within me as I heard the expected summons. I had not seen my cousin Edward since the occurrence of the grand *éclaircissement*; he must have studiously avoided me; I suppose from policy, it could not have been from delicacy. I was prepared for a terrific burst of fury from my uncle, as soon as I should make known my determination; and I not unreasonably feared that some act of violence or of intimidation would next be resorted to. Filled with these dreary forebodings, I fearfully opened the study door, and the next minute I stood in my uncle's presence. He received me with a courtesy which I dreaded, as arguing a favourable anticipation respecting the answer which I was to give; and after some slight delay he began by saying:

'It will be a relief to both of us, I believe, to bring this conversation as soon as possible to an issue. You will excuse me, then, my dear niece, for speaking with a bluntness which, under other circumstances, would be unpardonable. You have, I am certain, given the subject of our last interview fair and serious consideration; and I trust that you are now prepared with candour to lay your answer before me. A few words will suffice; we perfectly understand one another.'

He paused; and I, though feeling that I stood upon a mine which might in an instant explode, nevertheless answered with perfect composure: 'I must now, sir, make the same reply which I did upon the last occasion, and I reiterate the declaration which I then made, that I never can nor will, while life and reason remain, consent to a union with my cousin Edward.'

This announcement wrought no apparent change in Sir Arthur, except that he became deadly, almost lividly pale. He seemed lost in dark thought for a minute, and then, with a slight effort, said, 'You have answered me honestly and directly; and you say your resolution is unchangeable; well, would it had been otherwise – would it had been otherwise – but be it as it is; I am satisfied.'

He gave me his hand – it was cold and damp as death; under an assumed calmness, it was evident that he was fearfully agitated. He continued to hold my hand with an almost painful pressure, while, as if unconsciously, seeming to forget my presence, he muttered, 'Strange, strange, strange, indeed! fatuity, helpless fatuity!' there was here a long pause. 'Madness *indeed* to strain a cable that is rotten to the very heart; it must break – and then – all goes.' There was again a pause of some minutes, after which, suddenly changing his voice and manner to one of wakeful alacrity, he exclaimed, 'Margaret, my son Edward shall plague you no more. He leaves this country tomorrow for France; he shall speak no more upon this subject – never, never more; whatever events depended upon your answer must now take their own course; but as for this fruitless proposal, it has been tried enough; it can be repeated no more.'

At these words he coldly suffered my hand to drop, as if to express his total abandonment of all his projected schemes of alliance; and certainly the action, with the accompanying words, produced upon my mind a more solemn and depressing effect than I believed possible to have been caused by the course which I had determined to pursue; it struck upon my heart with an awe and heaviness which *will* accompany the accomplishment of an important and irrevocable act, even though no doubt or scruple remains to make it possible that the agent should wish it undone.

'Well,' said my uncle, after a little time, 'we now cease to speak upon this topic, never to resume it again. Remember you shall have no further uneasiness from Edward; he leaves Ireland for France tomorrow; this will be a relief to you; may I depend upon your honour that no word touching the subject of this interview shall ever escape you?' I gave him the desired assurance; he said, 'It is well; I am satisfied; we have nothing more, I believe, to say upon either side, and my presence must be a restraint upon you, I shall therefore bid you farewell.' I then left the apartment, scarcely knowing what to think of the strange interview which had just taken place.

On the next day my uncle took occasion to tell me that Edward had actually sailed, if his intention had not been prevented by adverse winds or weather; and two days after he actually produced a letter from his son, written, as it said, *on board*, and despatched while the ship was getting under way. This was a great satisfaction to me, and as being likely to prove so, it was no doubt communicated to me by Sir Arthur.

During all this trying period I had found infinite consolation in the society and sympathy of my dear cousin Emily. I never, in afterlife, formed a friendship so close, so fervent, and upon which, in all its progress, I could look back with feelings of such unalloyed pleasure, upon whose termination I must ever dwell with so deep, so yet unembittered a sorrow. In cheerful converse with her I soon recovered my spirits considerably, and passed my time agreeably enough, although still in the utmost seclusion. Matters went on smoothly enough, although I could not help sometimes feeling a momentary, but horrible uncertainty respecting my uncle's character; which was not altogether unwarranted by the circumstances of the two trying interviews, the particulars of which I have just detailed. The unpleasant impression which these conferences were calculated to leave upon my mind was fast wearing away, when there occurred a circumstance, slight indeed in itself, but calculated irrepressibly to awaken all my worst suspicions, and to overwhelm me again with anxiety and terror.

I had one day left the house with my cousin Emily, in order to take a ramble of considerable length, for the purpose of sketching some favourite views, and we had walked about half a mile when I perceived that we had forgotten our drawing materials, the absence of which would have defeated the object of our walk. Laughing at our own thoughtlessness, we returned to the house, and leaving Emily outside, I ran upstairs to procure the drawing-books and pencils which lay in my bedroom. As I ran up the stairs, I was met by the tall, ill-looking Frenchwoman, evidently a good deal flurried; '*Que veut Madame?*' said she, with a more decided effort to be polite, than I had ever known her make before. 'No, no – no matter,' said I, hastily running by her in the direction of my room. '*Madame,*' cried she, in a high key, '*restez ici s'il vous plait, votre chambre n'est pas faite.*' I continued to move on without heeding her. She was some way behind me, and feeling that she could not otherwise prevent my entrance, for I was now upon the very lobby, she made a desperate attempt to seize hold of my person; she succeeded in grasping the end of my shawl, which she drew from my shoulders, but slipping at the same time upon the polished oak floor, she fell at full length upon the boards. A little frightened as well as angry at the rudeness of this strange woman, I hastily pushed open the door of my room, at which I now stood, in order to escape from her; but great was my amazement on entering to find the apartment preoccupied. The window was open, and beside it stood two male figures; they appeared to be examining the fastenings of the casement, and their backs were turned towards the door. One of them was my uncle; they both had turned on my entrance, as if startled; the stranger was booted and cloaked, and wore a heavy, broad-leafed hat over his brows; he turned but for a moment, and averted his face; but I had seen enough to convince me that he was no other than my cousin Edward. My uncle had some iron instrument in his hand, which he hastily concealed behind his back; and coming towards me, said something as if in an explanatory tone; but I was too much shocked and confounded to understand what it might be. He said something about '*repairs* – window-frames – cold, and safety'. I did not wait, however, to ask or to receive explanations, but hastily left the room. As I went down stairs I thought I heard the voice of the Frenchwoman in all the shrill volubility of excuse, and others uttering suppressed but vehement imprecations, or what seemed to me to be such.

I joined my cousin Emily quite out of breath. I need not say that my head was too full of other things to think much of drawing that day. I imparted to her frankly the cause of my alarms, but, at the same time, as gently as I could; and with tears she promised vigilance, devotion, and love. I never had reason for a moment to repent the unreserved confidence which I then reposed in her. She was no less surprised than I at the unexpected appearance of Edward, whose departure for France neither of us had for a moment doubted, but which was now proved by his actual presence to be nothing more than an imposture practised, I feared, for no good end. The situation in which I had found my uncle had very nearly removed all my doubts as to his designs; I magnified suspicions into certainties, and dreaded night after night that I should be murdered in my bed. The nervousness produced by sleepless nights and days of anxious fears increased the horrors of my situation to such a degree, that I at length wrote a letter to a Mr Jefferies, an old and faithful friend of my father's, and perfectly acquainted with all his affairs, praying him, for God's sake, to relieve me from my present terrible situation, and communicating without reserve the nature and grounds of my suspicions. This letter I kept sealed and directed for two or three days always about my person, for discovery would have been ruinous, in expectation of an opportunity, which might be safely trusted, of having it placed in the post office; as neither Emily nor I were permitted to pass beyond the precincts of the demesne itself, which was surrounded by high walls formed of dry stone, the difficulty of procuring such an opportunity was greatly enhanced.

At this time Emily had a short conversation with her father, which she reported to me instantly. After some indifferent matter, he had asked her whether she and I were upon good terms, and whether I was unreserved in my disposition. She answered in the affirmative; and he then enquired whether I had been much surprised to find him in my chamber on the other day. She answered that I had been both surprised and amused. 'And what did she think of George Wilson's appearance?' 'Who?' enquired she. 'Oh! the architect,' he answered, 'who is to contract for the repairs of the house; he is accounted a handsome fellow.' 'She could not see his face,' said Emily, 'and she was in such a hurry to escape that she scarcely observed him.' Sir Arthur appeared satisfied, and the conversation ended.

This slight conversation, repeated accurately to me by Emily, had the effect of confirming, if indeed any thing was required to do so, all that I had before believed as to Edward's actual presence; and I naturally became, if possible, more anxious than ever to dispatch the letter to Mr Jefferies. An opportunity at length occurred. As Emily and I were walking one day near the gate of the demesne, a lad from the village happened to be passing down the avenue from the house; the spot was secluded, and as this person was not connected by service with those whose observation I dreaded, I committed the letter to his keeping, with strict injunctions that he should put it, without delay, into the receiver of the town post office; at the same time I added a suitable gratuity, and the man having made many protestations of punctuality, was soon out of sight. He was hardly gone when I began to doubt my discretion in having trusted him; but I had no better or safer means of despatching the letter, and I was not warranted in suspecting him of such wanton dishonesty as a disposition to tamper with it; but I could not be quite satisfied of its safety until I had received an answer, which could not arrive for a few days. Before I did, however, an event occurred which a little surprised me. I was sitting in my bedroom early in the day, reading by myself, when I heard a knock at the door. 'Come in,' said I, and my uncle entered the room. 'Will you excuse me,' said he, 'I sought you in the parlour, and thence I have come here. I desired to say a word to you. I trust that you have hitherto found my conduct to you such as that of a guardian towards his ward should be.' I dared not withhold my assent. 'And,' he continued, 'I trust that you have not found me harsh or unjust, and that you have perceived, my dear niece, that I have sought to make this poor place as agreeable to you as may be?' I assented again; and he put his hand in his pocket, whence he drew a folded paper, and dashing it upon the table with startling emphasis he said, 'Did you write that letter?' The sudden and fearful alteration of his voice, manner, and face, but more than all, the unexpected production of my letter to Mr Jefferies, which I at once recognised, so confounded and terrified me, that I felt almost choking. I could not utter a word. 'Did you write that letter?' he repeated, with slow and intense emphasis. 'You did, liar and hypocrite. You dared to write that foul and infamous libel; but it shall be your last. Men will universally believe you mad, if I choose to call for an inquiry. I can make you appear so. The suspicions expressed in this letter, are the hallucinations and alarms of a moping lunatic. I have defeated your first attempt, madam; and by the holy God, if ever you make another, chains, darkness, and the keeper's whip shall be your portion.' With these astounding words he left the room, leaving me almost fainting.

I was now almost reduced to despair; my last cast had failed; I had no course left but that of escaping secretly from the castle, and placing myself under the protection of the nearest magistrate. I felt if this were not done, and speedily, that I should be *murdered*. No one, from mere description, can have an idea of the unmitigated horror of my situation; a helpless, weak, inexperienced girl, placed under the power, and wholly at the mercy of evil men, and feeling that I had it not in my power to escape for one moment from the malignant influences under which I was probably doómed to fall; with a consciousness, too, that if violence, if murder were designed, no human being would be near to aid me; my dying shriek would be lost in void space.

I had seen Edward but once during his visit, and as I did not meet him again, I began to think that he must have taken his departure; a conviction which was to a certain degree satisfactory, as I regarded his absence as indicating the removal of immediate danger. Emily also arrived circuitously at the same conclusion, and not without good grounds, for she managed indirectly to learn that Edward's black horse had actually been for a day and part of a night in the castle stables, just at the time of her brother's supposed visit. The horse had gone, and as she argued, the rider must have departed with it.

This point being so far settled, I felt a little less uncomfortable; when being one day alone in my bedroom, I happened to look out from the window, and to my unutterable horror, I beheld peering through an opposite casement, my cousin Edward's face. Had I seen the evil one himself in bodily shape, I could not have experienced a more sickening revulsion. I was too much appalled to move at once from the window, but I did so soon enough to avoid his eye. He was looking fixedly down into the narrow quadrangle upon which the window opened. I shrunk back unperceived, to pass the rest of the day in terror and despair. I went to my room early that night, but I was too miserable to sleep.

At about twelve o'clock, feeling very nervous, I determined to call my cousin Emily, who slept, you will remember, in the next room, which communicated with mine by a second door. By this private entrance I found my way into her chamber, and without difficulty persuaded her to return to my room and sleep with me. We accordingly lay down together, she undressed, and I with my clothes on, for I was every moment walking up and down the room, and felt too nervous and miserable to think of rest or comfort. Emily was soon fast asleep, and I lay awake, fervently longing for the first pale gleam of morning, and reckoning every stroke of the old clock with an impatience which made every hour appear like six.

It must have been about one o'clock when I thought I heard a slight noise at the partition door between Emily's room and mine, as if caused by somebody's turning the key in the lock. I held my breath, and the same sound was repeated at the second door of my room, that which opened upon the lobby; the sound was here distinctly caused by the revolution of the bolt in the lock, and it was followed by a slight pressure upon the door itself, as if to ascertain the security of the lock. The person, whoever it might be, was probably satisfied, for I heard the old boards of the lobby creak and strain, as if under the weight of somebody moving cautiously over them. My sense of heating became unnaturally, almost painfully acute. I suppose the imagination added distinctness to sounds vague in themselves. I thought that I could actually hear the breathing of the person who was slowly returning along the lobby.

At the head of the staircase there appeared to occur a pause; and I could distinctly hear two or three sentences hastily whispered; the steps then descended the stairs with apparently less caution. I ventured to walk quickly and lightly to the lobby door, and attempted to open it; it was indeed fast locked upon the outside, as was also the other. I now felt that the dreadful hour was come; but one desperate expedient remained – it was to awaken Emily, and by our united strength, to attempt to force the partition door, which was slighter than the other, and through this to pass to the lower part of the house, whence it might be possible to escape to the grounds, and so to the village. I returned to the bedside, and shook Emily, but in vain; nothing that I could do availed to produce from her more than a few incoherent words; it was a deathlike sleep. She had certainly drunk of some narcotic, as, probably, had I also, in spite of all the caution with which I had examined every thing presented to us to eat or drink. I now attempted, with as little noise as possible, to force first one door, then the other; but all in vain. I believe no strength could have affected my object, for both doors opened inwards. I therefore collected whatever movables I could carry thither, and piled them against the doors, so as to assist me in whatever attempts I should make to resist the entrance of those without. I then returned to the bed and endeavoured again, but fruitlessly, to awaken my cousin. It was not sleep, it was torpor, lethargy, death. I knelt down and prayed with an agony of earnestness; and then seating myself upon the bed, I awaited my fate with a kind of terrible tranquillity.

I heard a faint clanking sound from the narrow court which I have already mentioned, as if caused by the scraping of some iron instrument against stones or rubbish. I at first determined not to disturb the

calmness which I now experienced, by uselessly watching the proceedings of those who sought my life; but as the sounds continued,
the horrible curiosity which I felt overcame every other emotion, and
I determined, at all hazards, to gratify it. I, therefore, crawled upon
my knees to the window, so as to let the smallest possible portion of
my head appear above the sill.

The moon was shining with an uncertain radiance upon the
antique grey buildings, and obliquely upon the narrow court beneath;
one side of it was therefore clearly illuminated, while the other was
lost in obscurity, the sharp outlines of the old gables, with their
nodding clusters of ivy, being at first alone visible. Whoever or whatever occasioned the noise which had excited my curiosity, was concealed under the shadow of the dark side of the quadrangle. I placed
my hand over my eyes to shade them from the moonlight, which was
so bright as to be almost dazzling, and, peering into the darkness, I
first dimly, but afterwards gradually, almost with full distinctness,
beheld the form of a man engaged in digging what appeared to be a
rude hole close under the wall. Some implements, probably a shovel
and pickaxe, lay beside him, and to these he every now and then
applied himself as the nature of the ground required. He pursued his
task rapidly, and with as little noise as possible. 'So,' thought I, as
shovelful after shovelful, the dislodged rubbish mounted into a heap,
'they are digging the grave in which, before two hours pass, I must lie,
a cold, mangled corpse. I am *theirs* – I cannot escape.' I felt as if my
reason was leaving me. I started to my feet, and in mere despair I
applied myself again to each of the two doors alternately. I strained
every nerve and sinew, but I might as well have attempted, with my
single strength, to force the building itself from its foundations. I
threw myself madly upon the ground, and clasped my hands over my
eyes as if to shut out the horrible images which crowded upon me.

The paroxysm passed away. I prayed once more with the bitter,
agonised fervour of one who feels that the hour of death is present
and inevitable. When I arose, I went once more to the window and
looked out, just in time to see a shadowy figure glide stealthily along
the wall. The task was finished. The catastrophe of the tragedy must
soon be accomplished. I determined now to defend my life to the last;
and that I might be able to do so with some effect, I searched the
room for something which might serve as a weapon; but either
through accident, or else in anticipation of such a possibility, everything which might have been made available for such a purpose has
been removed.

I must then die tamely and without an effort to defend myself. A thought suddenly struck me; might it not be possible to escape through the door, which the assassin must open in order to enter the room? I resolved to make the attempt. I felt assured that the door through which ingress to the room would be effected was that which opened upon the lobby. It was the more direct way, besides being, for obvious reasons, less liable to interruption than the other. I resolved, then, to place myself behind a projection of the wall, the shadow would serve fully to conceal me, and when the door should be opened, and before they should have discovered the identity of the occupant of the bed, to creep noiselessly from the room, and then to trust to Providence for escape. In order to facilitate this scheme, I removed all the lumber which I had heaped against the door; and I had nearly completed my arrangements, when I perceived the room suddenly darkened, by the close approach of some shadowy object to the window. On turning my eyes in that direction, I observed at the top of the casement, as if suspended from above, first the feet, then the legs, then the body, and at length the whole figure of a man present itself. It was Edward Tyrrell. He appeared to be guiding his descent so as to bring his feet upon the centre of the stone block which occupied the lower part of the window; and having secured his footing upon this, he kneeled down and began to gaze into the room. As the moon was gleaming into the chamber, and the bed-curtains were drawn, he was able to distinguish the bed itself and its contents. He appeared satisfied with his scrutiny, for he looked up and made a sign with his hand. He then applied his hands to the window-frame, which must have been ingeniously contrived for the purpose, for with apparently no resistance the whole frame, containing casement and all, slipped from its position in the wall, and was by him lowered into the room. The cold night wind waved the bed-curtains, and he paused for a moment; all was still again, and he stepped in upon the floor of the room. He held in his hand what appeared to be a steel instrument, shaped something like a long hammer. This he held rather behind him, while, with three long, tip-toe strides, he brought himself to the bedside. I felt that the discovery must now be made, and held my breath in momentary expectation of the execration in which he would vent his surprise and disappointment. I closed my eyes; there was a pause, but it was a short one. I heard two dull blows, given in rapid succession; a quivering sigh, and the long-drawn, heavy breathing of the sleeper was for ever suspended. I unclosed my eyes, and saw the murderer fling the quilt across the head of his victim; he then, with the instrument of death still in his hand, proceeded to the lobby-door, upon which he tapped sharply twice or thrice. A quick step was then heard approaching, and a voice whispered something from without. Edward answered, with a kind of shuddering chuckle, 'Her ladyship is past complaining; unlock the door, in the devil's name, unless you're afraid to come in, and help me to lift her out of the window.' The key was turned in the lock, the door opened, and my uncle entered the room. I have told you already that I had placed myself under the shade of a projection of the wall, close to the door. I had instinctively shrunk down cowering towards the ground on the entrance of Edward through the window. When my uncle entered the room, he and his son both stood so very close to me that his hand was every moment upon the point of touching my face. I held my breath, and remained motionless as death.

'You had no interruption from the next room?' said my uncle.

'No,' was the brief reply.

'Secure the jewels, Ned; the French harpy must not lay her claws upon them. You're a steady hand, by God; not much blood – eh?'

'Not twenty drops,' replied his son, 'and those on the quilt.'

'I'm glad it's over,' whispered my uncle again; 'we must lift the – the *thing* through the window, and lay the rubbish over it.'

They then turned to the bedside, and, winding the bedclothes round the body, carried it between them slowly to the window, and exchanging a few brief words with someone below, they shoved it over the windowsill, and I heard it fall heavily on the ground underneath.

'I'll take the jewels,' said my uncle; 'there are two caskets in the lower drawer.'

He proceeded, with an accuracy which, had I been more at ease, would have furnished me with matter of astonishment, to lay his hand upon the very spot where my jewels lay; and having possessed himself of them, he called to his son:

'Is the rope made fast above?'

'I'm no fool; to be sure it is,' replied he.

They then lowered themselves from the window; and I rose lightly and cautiously, scarcely daring to breathe, from my place of concealment, and was creeping towards the door, when I heard my uncle's voice, in a sharp whisper, exclaim, 'Get up again; God damn you, you've forgot to lock the room door'; and I perceived, by the straining of the rope which hung from above, that the mandate was instantly obeyed. Not a second was to be lost. I passed through the door, which was only closed, and moved as rapidly as I could, consistently with stillness, along the lobby. Before I had gone many yards, I heard the door through which I had just passed roughly locked on the inside. I glided down the stairs in terror, lest, at every corner, I should meet the murderer or one of his accomplices. I reached the hall, and listened, for a moment, to ascertain whether all was silent around. No sound was audible; the parlour windows opened on the park, and through one of them I might, I thought, easily effect my escape. Accordingly, I hastily entered; but, to my consternation, a candle was burning in the room, and by its light I saw a figure seated at the dinner-table, upon which lay glasses, bottles, and the other accompaniments of a drinking party. Two or three chairs were placed about the table, irregularly, as if hastily abandoned by their occupants. A single glance satisfied me that the figure was that of my French attendant. She was fast asleep, having, probably, drank deeply. There was something malignant and ghastly in the calmness of this bad woman's features, dimly illuminated as they were by the flickering blaze of the candle. A knife lay upon the table, and the terrible thought struck me – 'Should I kill this sleeping accomplice in the guilt of the murderer, and thus secure my retreat?' Nothing could be easier; it was but to draw the blade across her throat, the work of a second.

An instant's pause, however, corrected me. 'No,' thought I, 'the God who has conducted me thus far through the valley of the shadow of death, will not abandon me now. I will fall into their hands, or I will escape hence, but it shall be free from the stain of blood; His will be done.' I felt a confidence arising from this reflection, an assurance of protection which I cannot describe. There were no other means of escape, so I advanced, with a firm step and collected mind, to the window. I noiselessly withdrew the bars, and unclosed the shutters; I pushed open the casement, and without waiting to look behind me, I ran with my utmost speed, scarcely feeling the ground beneath me, down the avenue, taking care to keep upon the grass which bordered it.

I did not for a moment slacken my speed, and I had now gained the central point between the park-gate and the mansion-house. Here the avenue made a wider circuit, and in order to avoid delay, I directed my way across the smooth sward round which the carriage-way wound, intending, at the opposite side of the level, at a point which I distinguished by a group of old birch trees, to enter again upon the beaten track, which was from thence tolerably direct to the gate. I had, with my utmost speed, got about half way across this broad flat, when the rapid tramp of a horse's hoofs struck upon my ear. My heart swelled in my bosom, as though I would smother. The clattering of galloping hoofs approached; I was pursued; they were now upon the sward on which I was running; there was not a bush or a bramble to shelter me; and, as if to render escape altogether desperate, the moon, which had hitherto been obscured, at this moment shone forth with a broad, clear light, which made every object distinctly visible. The sounds were now close behind me. I felt my knees bending under me, with the sensation which unnerves one in a dream. I reeled, I stumbled, I fell; and at the same instant the cause of my alarm wheeled past me at full gallop. It was one of the young fillies which pastured loose about the park, whose frolics had thus all but maddened me with terror. I scrambled to my feet, and rushed on with weak but rapid steps, my sportive companion still galloping round and round me with many a frisk and fling, until, at length, more dead than alive, I reached the avenue-gate, and crossed the stile, I scarce knew how. I ran through the village, in which all was silent as the grave, until my progress was arrested by the hoarse voice of a sentinel, who cried 'Who goes there?' I felt that I was now safe. I turned in the direction of the voice, and fell fainting at the soldier's feet. When I came to myself, I was sitting in a miserable hovel, surrounded by strange faces, all bespeaking curiosity and compassion. Many soldiers were in it also; indeed, as I afterwards found, it was employed as a guardroom by a detachment of troops quartered for that night in the town. In a few words I informed their officer of the circumstances which had occurred, describing also the appearance of the persons engaged in the murder; and he, without further loss of time than was necessary to procure the attendance of a magistrate, proceeded to the mansion-house of Carrickleigh, taking with him a party of his men. But the villains had discovered their mistake, and had effected their escape before the arrival of the military.

The Frenchwoman was, however, arrested in the neighbourhood upon the next day. She was tried and condemned at the ensuing assizes; and previous to her execution confessed that '*she had a hand in making Hugh Tisdall's bed*'. She had been a housekeeper in the castle at the time, and a *chère amie* of my uncle's. She was, in reality, able to speak English like a native, but had exclusively used the French language, I suppose to facilitate her designs. She died the same hardened wretch she had lived, confessing her crimes only, as she alleged, that her doing so might involve Sir Arthur Tyrrell, the great author of her guilt and misery, and whom she now regarded with unmitigated detestation.

With the particulars of Sir Arthur's and his son's escape, as far as they are known, you are acquainted. You are also in possession of their after fate; the terrible, the tremendous retribution which, after long delays of many years, finally overtook and crushed them. Wonderful and inscrutable are the dealings of God with his creatures!

Deep and fervent as must always be my gratitude to heaven for my deliverance, effected by a chain of providential occurrences, the failing of a single link of which must have ensured my destruction, it was long before I could look back upon it with other feelings than those of bitterness, almost of agony. The only being that had ever really loved me, my nearest and dearest friend, ever ready to sympathise, to counsel, and to assist; the gayest, the gentlest, the warmest heart; the only creature on earth that cared for me; *her* life had been the price of my deliverance; and I then uttered the wish, which no event of my long and sorrowful life has taught me to recall, that she had been spared, and that, in her stead, *I* were mouldering in the grave, forgotten, and at rest.

WILKIE COLLINS

The Biter Bit

Extracted from the correspondence of the London Police

FROM CHIEF INSPECTOR THEAKSTONE, OF THE
DETECTIVE POLICE,
TO SERGEANT BULMER OF THE SAME FORCE
LONDON, 4th July, 18—.

SERGEANT BULMER, – This is to inform you that you are wanted to assist in looking up a case of importance, which will require all the attention of an experienced member of the force. The matter of the robbery on which you are now engaged, you will please to shift over to the young man who brings you this letter. You will tell him all the circumstances of the case, just as they stand; you will put him up to the progress you have made (if any) towards detecting the person or persons by whom the money has been stolen; and you will leave him to make the best he can of the matter now in your hands. He is to have the whole responsibility of the case, and the whole credit of his success, if he brings it to a proper issue.

So much for the orders that I am desired to communicate to you.

A word in your ear, next, about this new man who is to take your place. His name is Matthew Sharpin; and he is to have the chance given him of dashing into our office at a jump – supposing he turns out strong enough to take it. You will naturally ask me how he comes by this privilege. I can only tell you that he has some uncommonly strong interest to back him in certain high quarters which you and I had better not mention except under our breaths. He has been a lawyer's clerk; and he is wonderfully conceited in his opinion of himself, as well as mean and underhand to look at. According to his own account, he leaves his old trade, and joins ours, of his own free will and preference. You will no more believe that than I do. My notion is, that he has managed to ferret out some private information in connexion with the affairs of one of his master's clients, which makes him rather an awkward customer to keep in the office for the future, and which, at the same time, gives him hold enough over his employer to make it dangerous to drive him into a corner by turning

him away. I think that giving him this unheard-of chance among us, is, in plain words, pretty much like giving him hush-money to keep him quiet. However that may be, Mr Matthew Sharpin is to have the case now in your hands; and if he succeeds with it, he pokes his ugly nose into our office, as sure as fate. I put you up to this, Sergeant, so that you may not stand in your own light by giving the new man any cause to complain of you at headquarters, and remain yours,
Francis Theakstone.

FROM Mr MATTHEW SHARPIN
TO CHIEF INSPECTOR THEAKSTONE
LONDON, 5th July, 18—.

DEAR SIR, – Having now been favoured with the necessary instructions from Sergeant Bulmer, I beg to remind you of certain directions which I have received, relating to the report of my future proceedings which I am to prepare for examination at headquarters.

The object of my writing, and of your examining what I have written, before you send it in to the higher authorities, is, I am informed, to give me, as an untried hand, the benefit of your advice, in case I want it (which I venture to think I shall not) at any stage of my proceedings. As the extraordinary circumstances of the case on which I am now engaged, make it impossible for me to absent myself from the place where the robbery was committed, until I have made some progress towards discovering the thief, I am necessarily precluded from consulting you personally. Hence the necessity of my writing down the various details, which might, perhaps, be better communicated by word of mouth. This, if I am not mistaken, is the position in which we are now placed. I state my own impressions on the subject, in writing, in order that we may clearly understand each other at the outset; and have the honour to remain, your obedient servant,
Matthew Sharpin

FROM CHIEF INSPECTOR THEAKSTONE
TO Mr MATTHEW SHARPIN
LONDON, 5th July, 18—.

SIR, – You have begun by wasting time, ink, and paper. We both of us perfectly well knew the position we stood in towards each other, when I sent you with my letter to Sergeant Bulmer. There was not the least need to repeat it in writing. Be so good as to employ your pen, in future, on the business actually in hand.

You have now three separate matters on which to write to me. First, You have to draw up a statement of your instructions received from Sergeant Bulmer, in order to show us that nothing has escaped your memory, and that you are thoroughly acquainted with all the circumstances of the case which has been entrusted to you. Secondly, You are to inform me what it is you propose to do. Thirdly, You are to report every inch of your progress (if you make any) from day to day, and, if need be, from hour to hour as well. This is your duty. As to what my duty may be, when I want you to remind me of it, I will write and tell you so. In the meantime, I remain, yours,
Francis Theakstone

FROM Mr MATTHEW SHARPIN
TO CHIEF INSPECTOR THEAKSTONE
LONDON, 6th July, 18—.

SIR, – You are rather an elderly person, and, as such, naturally inclined to be a little jealous of men like me, who are in the prime of their lives and their faculties. Under these circumstances, it is my duty to be considerate towards you, and not to bear too hardly on your small failings. I decline, therefore, altogether, to take offence at the tone of your letter; I give you the full benefit of the natural generosity of my nature; I sponge the very existence of your surly communication out of my memory – in short, Chief Inspector Theakstone, I forgive you, and proceed to business.

My first duty is to draw up a full statement of the instructions I have received from Sergeant Bulmer. Here they are at your service, according to my version of them.

At number 13, Rutherford Street, Soho, there is a stationer's shop. It is kept by one Mr Yatman. He is a married man, but has no family. Besides Mr and Mrs Yatman, the other inmates in the house are a young single man named Jay, who lodges in the front room on the second floor – a shopman, who sleeps in one of the attics, – and a servant-of-all-work, whose bed is in the back-kitchen. Once a week a charwoman comes for a few hours in the morning only, to help this servant. These are all the persons who, on ordinary occasions, have means of access to the interior of the house, placed, as a matter of course, at their disposal.

Mr Yatman has been in business for many years, carrying on his affairs prosperously enough to realise a handsome independence for a person in his position. Unfortunately for himself, he endeavoured to increase the amount of his property by speculating. He ventured boldly in his investments, luck went against him, and rather less than two years ago he found himself a poor man again. All that was saved out of the wreck of his property was the sum of two hundred pounds.

Although Mr Yatman did his best to meet his altered circumstances, by giving up many of the luxuries and comforts to which he and his wife had been accustomed, he found it impossible to retrench so far as to allow of putting by any money from the income produced by his shop. The business has been declining of late years – the cheap advertising stationers having done it injury with the public. Consequently, up to the last week the only surplus property possessed by Mr Yatman consisted of the two hundred pounds which had been recovered from the wreck of his fortune. This sum was placed as a deposit in a joint-stock bank of the highest possible character.

Eight days ago, Mr Yatman and his lodger, Mr Jay, held a conversation on the subject of the commercial difficulties which are hampering trade in all directions at the present time. Mr Jay (who lives by supplying the newspapers with short paragraphs relating to accidents, offences, and brief records of remarkable occurrences in general – who is, in short, what they call a penny-a-liner) told his landlord that he had been in the city that day, and had heard unfavourable rumours on the subject of the joint-stock banks. The rumours to which he alluded had already reached the ears of Mr Yatman from other quarters; and the confirmation of them by his lodger had such an effect on his mind – predisposed as it was to alarm by the experience of his former losses – that he resolved to go at once to the bank and withdraw his deposit.

It was then getting on towards the end of the afternoon; and he arrived just in time to receive his money before the bank closed.

He received the deposit in bank-notes of the following amounts; – one fifty-pound note, three twenty-pound notes, six ten-pound notes, and six five-pound notes. His object in drawing the money in this form was to have it ready to lay out immediately in trifling loans, on good security, among the small tradespeople of his district, some of whom are sorely pressed for the very means of existence at the present time. Investments of this kind seemed to Mr Yatman to be the most safe and the most profitable on which he could now venture.

He brought the money back in an envelope placed in his breast-pocket; and asked his shopman, on getting home, to look for a small flat tin cash-box, which had not been used for years, and which, as Mr Yatman remembered it, was exactly of the right size to hold the bank-notes. For some time the cash-box was searched for in vain. Mr

Yatman called to his wife to know if she had any idea where it was. The question was overheard by the servant-of-all-work, who was taking up the tea-tray at the time, and by Mr Jay, who was coming downstairs on his way out to the theatre. Ultimately the cash-box was found by the shopman. Mr Yatman placed the bank-notes in it, secured them by a padlock, and put the box in his coat-pocket. It stuck out of the coat-pocket a very little, but enough to be seen. Mr Yatman remained at home, upstairs, all the evening. No visitors called. At eleven o'clock he went to bed, and put the cash-box along with his clothes, on a chair by the bedside.

When he and his wife woke the next morning, the box was gone. Payment of the notes was immediately stopped at the bank of England; but no news of the money has been heard of since that time.

So far, the circumstances of the case are perfectly clear. They point unmistakably to the conclusion that the robbery must have been committed by some person living in the house. Suspicion falls, therefore, upon the servant-of-all-work, upon the shopman, and upon Mr Jay. The two first knew that the cash-box was being inquired for by their master, but did not know what it was he wanted to put into it. They would assume, of course, that it was money. They both had opportunities (the servant, when she took away the tea, and the shopman, when he came, after shutting up, to give the keys of the till to his master) of seeing the cash-box in Mr Yatman's pocket, and of inferring naturally, from its position there, that he intended to take it into his bedroom with him at night.

Mr Jay, on the other hand, had been told, during the afternoon's conversation on the subject of joint-stock banks, that his landlord had a deposit of two hundred pounds in one of them. He also knew that Mr Yatman left him with the intention of drawing that money out; and he heard the inquiry for the cash-box, afterwards, when he was coming downstairs. He must, therefore, have inferred that the money was in the house, and that the cash-box was the receptacle intended to contain it. That he could have had any idea, however, of the place in which Mr Yatman intended to keep it for the night, is impossible, seeing that he went out before the box was found, and did not return till his landlord was in bed. Consequently, if he committed the robbery, he must have gone into the bedroom purely on speculation.

Speaking of the bedroom reminds me of the necessity of noticing the situation of it in the house, and the means that exist of gaining easy access to it at any hour of the night.

The room in question is the back-room on the first floor. In consequence of Mrs Yatman's constitutional nervousness on the subject of fire (which makes her apprehend being burnt alive in her room, in case of accident, by the hampering of the lock if the key is turned in it) her husband has never been accustomed to lock the bedroom door. Both he and his wife are, by their own admission, heavy sleepers. Consequently the risk to be run by any evil-disposed persons wishing to plunder the bedroom, was of the most trifling kind. They could enter the room by merely turning the handle of the door; and if they moved with ordinary caution, there was no fear of their waking the sleepers inside. This fact is of importance. It strengthens our conviction that the money must have been taken by one of the inmates of the house, because it tends to show that the robbery, in this case, might have been committed by persons not possessed of the superior vigilance and cunning of the experienced thief.

Such are the circumstances, as they were related to Sergeant Bulmer, when he was first called in to discover the guilty parties, and, if possible, to recover the lost bank-notes. The strictest inquiry which he could institute, failed of producing the smallest fragment of evidence against any of the persons on whom suspicion naturally fell. Their language and behaviour, on being informed of the robbery, was perfectly consistent with the language and behaviour of innocent people. Sergeant Bulmer felt from the first that this was a case for private inquiry and secret observation. He began by recommending Mr and Mrs Yatman to affect a feeling of perfect confidence in the innocence of the persons living under their roof; and he then opened the campaign by employing himself in following the goings and comings, and in discovering the friends, the habits, and the secrets of the maid-of-all-work.

Three days and nights of exertion on his own part, and on that of others competent to assist his investigations, were enough to satisfy him that there was no sound cause for suspicion against the girl.

He next practised the same precaution in relation to the shopman. There was more difficulty and uncertainty in privately clearing up this person's character without his knowledge, but the obstacles were at last smoothed away with tolerable success; and though there is not the same amount of certainty, in this case, which there was in that of the girl, there is still fair reason for supposing that the shopman has had nothing to do with the robbery of the cash-box.

As a necessary consequence of these proceedings, the range of suspicion now becomes limited to the lodger, Mr Jay.

When I presented your letter of introduction to Sergeant Bulmer, he had already made some inquiries on the subject of this young man. The result, so far, has not been at all favourable. Mr Jay's habits are irregular; he frequents public houses, and seems to be familiarly acquainted with a great many dissolute characters; he is in debt to most of the tradespeople whom he employs; he has not paid his rent to Mr Yatman for the last month; yesterday evening he came home excited by liquor, and last week he was seen talking to a prize-fighter. In short, though Mr Jay does call himself a journalist, in virtue of his penny-a-line contributions to the newspapers, he is a young man of low tastes, vulgar manners, and bad habits. Nothing has yet been discovered in relation to him, which redounds to his credit in the smallest degree.

I have now reported, down to the very last details, all the particulars communicated to me by Sergeant Bulmer. I believe you will not find an omission anywhere; and I think you will admit, though you are prejudiced against me, that a clearer statement of facts was never laid before you than the statement I have now made. My next duty is to tell you what I propose to do, now that the case is confided to my hands.

In the first place, it is clearly my business to take up the case at the point where Sergeant Bulmer has left it. On his authority, I am justified in assuming that I have no need to trouble myself about the maid-of-all-work and the shopman. Their characters are now to be considered as cleared up. What remains to be privately investigated is the question of the guilt or innocence of Mr Jay. Before we give up the notes for lost, we must make sure, if we can, that he knows nothing about them.

This is the plan that I have adopted, with the full approval of Mr and Mrs Yatman, for discovering whether Mr Jay is or is not the person who has stolen the cash-box:

I propose, to-day, to present myself at the house in the character of a young man who is looking for lodgings. The back-room on the second floor will be shown to me as the room to let; and I shall establish myself there tonight, as a person from the country who has come to London to look for a situation in a respectable shop or office.

By this means I shall be living next to the room occupied by Mr Jay. The partition between us is mere lath and plaster. I shall make a small hole in it, near the cornice, through which I can see what Mr Jay does in his room, and hear every word that is said when any friend happens to call on him. Whenever he is at home, I shall be at my post of observation. Whenever he goes out, I shall be after him. By employing these means of watching him, I believe I may look forward to the discovery of his secret – if he knows anything about the lost bank-notes – as to a dead certainty.

What you may think of my plan of observation I cannot undertake to say. It appears to me to unite the invaluable merits of boldness and simplicity. Fortified by this conviction, I close the present communication with feelings of the most sanguine description in regard to the future, and remain your obedient servant,
Matthew Sharpin

FROM THE SAME
TO THE SAME
7th July.

SIR, – As you have not honoured me with any answer to my last communication, I assume that, in spite of your prejudices against me, it has produced the favourable impression on your mind which I ventured to anticipate. Gratified beyond measure by the token of approval which your eloquent silence conveys to me, I proceed to report the progress that has been made in the course of the last twenty-four hours.

I am now comfortably established next door to Mr Jay; and I am delighted to say that I have two holes in the partition, instead of one. My natural sense of humour has led me into the pardonable extravagance of giving them appropriate names. One I call my peep-hole, and the other my pipe-hole. The name of the first explains itself; the name of the second refers to a small tin pipe, or tube, inserted in the hole, and twisted so that the mouth of it comes close to my ear, while I am standing at my post of observation. Thus, while I am looking at Mr Jay through my peep-hole, I can hear every word that may be spoken in his room through my pipe-hole.

Perfect candour – a virtue which I have possessed from my childhood – compels me to acknowledge, before I go any further, that the ingenious notion of adding a pipe-hole to my proposed peep-hole originated with Mrs Yatman. This lady – a most intelligent and accomplished person, simple, and yet distinguished, in her manners – has entered into all my little plans with an enthusiasm and intelligence which I cannot too highly praise. Mr Yatman is so cast down by his loss, that he is quite incapable of affording me any assistance. Mrs Yatman, who is evidently most tenderly attached to him, feels her husband's sad condition of mind even more acutely than she feels the loss of the money; and is mainly stimulated to exertion by her desire to assist in raising him from the miserable state of prostration into which he has now fallen.

'The money, Mr Sharpin,' she said to me yesterday evening, with tears in her eyes, 'the money may be regained by rigid economy and strict attention to business. It is my husband's wretched state of mind that makes me so anxious for the discovery of the thief. I may be wrong, but I felt hopeful of success as soon as you entered the house; and I believe, if the wretch who has robbed us is to be found, you are the man to discover him.' I accepted this gratifying compliment in the spirit in which it was offered – firmly believing that I shall be found, sooner or later, to have thoroughly deserved it.

Let me now return to business; that is to say, to my peep-hole and my pipe-hole.

I have enjoyed some hours of calm observation of Mr Jay. Though rarely at home, as I understand from Mrs Yatman, on ordinary occasions, he has been indoors the whole of this day. That is suspicious, to begin with. I have to report, further, that he rose at a late hour this morning (always a bad sign in a young man), and that he lost a great deal of time, after he was up, in yawning and complaining to himself of headache. Like other debauched characters, he ate little or nothing for breakfast. His next proceeding was to smoke a pipe – a dirty clay pipe, which a gentleman would have been ashamed to put between his lips. When he had done smoking, he took out pen, ink, and paper, and sat down to write with a groan – whether of remorse for having taken the bank-notes, or of disgust at the task before him, I am unable to say. After writing a few lines (too far away from my peep-hole to give me a chance of reading over his shoulder), he leaned back in his chair, and amused himself by humming the tunes of certain popular songs.

Whether these do, or do not, represent secret signals by which he communicates with his accomplices remains to be seen. After he had amused himself for some time by humming, he got up and began to walk about the room, occasionally stopping to add a sentence to the paper on his desk. Before long, he went to a locked cupboard and opened it. I strained my eyes eagerly, in expectation of making a discovery. I saw him take something carefully out of the cupboard – he turned round – and it was only a pint bottle of brandy! Having drunk some of the liquor, this extremely indolent reprobate lay down on his bed again, and in five minutes was fast asleep.

After hearing him snoring for at least two hours, I was recalled to my peep-hole by a knock at his door. He jumped up and opened it with suspicious activity.

A very small boy, with a very dirty face, walked in, said, 'Please, sir, they're waiting for you,' sat down on a chair, with his legs a long way from the ground, and instantly fell asleep! Mr Jay swore an oath, tied a wet towel round his head, and going back to his paper, began to cover it with writing as fast as his fingers could move the pen. Occasionally getting up to dip the towel in water and tie it on again, he continued at this employment for nearly three hours; then folded up the leaves of writing, woke the boy, and gave them to him, with this remarkable expression – 'Now, then, young sleepyhead, quick – march! If you see the governor, tell him to have the money ready when I call for it.' The boy grinned, and disappeared. I was sorely tempted to follow 'sleepy-head', but, on reflection, considered it safest still to keep my eye on the proceedings of Mr Jay.

In half an hour's time, he put on his hat and walked out. Of course, I put on my hat and walked out also. As I went downstairs, I passed Mrs Yatman going up. The lady has been kind enough to undertake, by previous arrangement between us, to search Mr Jay's room, while he is out of the way, and while I am necessarily engaged in the pleasing duty of following him wherever he goes. On the occasion to which I now refer, he walked straight to the nearest tavern, and ordered a couple of mutton chops for his dinner. I placed myself in the next box to him, and ordered a couple of mutton chops for my dinner. Before I had been in the room a minute, a young man of highly suspicious manners and appearance, sitting at a table opposite, took his glass of porter in his hand and joined Mr Jay. I pretended to be reading the newspaper, and listened, as in duty bound, with all my might.

'Jack has been here inquiring after you,' says the young man.

'Did he leave any message?' asks Mr Jay.

'Yes,' says the other. 'He told me, if I met with you, to say that he wished very particularly to see you tonight; and that he would give you a look-in, at Rutherfold Street, at seven o'clock.'

'All right,' says Mr Jay. 'I'll get back in time to see him.'

Upon this, the suspicious-looking young man finished his porter, and saying that he was rather in a hurry, took leave of his friend (perhaps I should not be wrong if I said his accomplice) and left the room.

At twenty-five minutes and a half past six – in these serious cases it is important to be particular about time – Mr Jay finished his chops and paid his bill. At twenty-six minutes and three-quarters I finished my chops and paid mine. In ten minutes more I was inside the house in Rutherford Street, and was received by Mrs Yatman in the passage. That charming woman's face exhibited an expression of melancholy and disappointment which it quite grieved me to see.

'I am afraid, Ma'am,' says I, 'that you have not hit on any little criminating discovery in the lodger's room?'

She shook her head and sighed. It was a soft, languid, fluttering sigh; – and, upon my life, it quite upset me. For the moment I forgot business, and burned with envy of Mr Yatman.

'Don't despair, Ma'am,' I said, with an insinuating mildness which seemed to touch her. 'I have heard a mysterious conversation – I know of a guilty appointment – and I expect great things from my peep-hole and my pipe-hole tonight. Pray, don't be alarmed, but I think we are on the brink of a discovery.'

Here my enthusiastic devotion to business got the better of my tender feelings. I looked – winked – nodded – left her.

When I got back to my observatory, I found Mr Jay digesting his mutton chops in an armchair, with his pipe in his mouth. On his table were two tumblers, a jug of water, and the pint bottle of brandy. It was then close upon seven o'clock. As the hour struck, the person described as 'Jack' walked in.

He looked agitated – I am happy to say he looked violently agitated. The cheerful glow of anticipated success diffused itself (to use a strong expression) all over me, from head to foot. With breathless interest I looked through my peep-hole, and saw the visitor – the 'Jack' of this delightful case – sit down, facing me, at the opposite side of the table to Mr Jay. Making allowance for the difference in expression which their countenances just now happened to exhibit, these two abandoned villains were so much alike in other respects as to lead at once to the conclusion that they were brothers. Jack was the cleaner man and the better dressed of the two. I admit that, at the outset. It is, perhaps, one of my failings to push justice and impartiality to their utmost limits. I am no Pharisee; and where Vice has its redeeming point, I say, let Vice have its due – yes, yes, by all manner of means, let Vice have its due.

'What's the matter now, Jack?' says Mr Jay.

'Can't you see it in my face?' says Jack.

'My dear fellow, delays are dangerous. Let us have done with suspense, and risk it the day after tomorrow.'

'So soon as that?' cried Mr Jay, looking very much astonished.

'Well, I'm ready, if you are. But, I say, Jack, is Somebody Else ready too? Are you quite sure of that?'

He smiled as he spoke – a frightful smile – and laid a very strong emphasis on those two words, 'Somebody Else'. There is evidently a third ruffian, a nameless desperado, concerned in the business.

'Meet us tomorrow,' says Jack, 'and judge for yourself. Be in the Regent's Park at eleven in the morning, and look out for us at the turning that leads to the Avenue Road.'

'I'll be there,' says Mr Jay. 'Have a drop of brandy and water? What are you getting up for? You're not going already?'

'Yes, I am,' says Jack. 'The fact is, I'm so excited and agitated that I can't sit still anywhere for five minutes together. Ridiculous as it may appear to you, I'm in a perpetual state of nervous flutter. I can't, for the life of me, help fearing that we shall be found out. I fancy that every man who looks twice at me in the street is a spy—'

At those words, I thought my legs would have given way under me. Nothing but strength of mind kept me at my peep-hole – nothing else, I give you my word of honour.

'Stuff and nonsense!' cried Mr Jay, with all the effrontery of a veteran in crime. 'We have kept the secret up to this time, and we will manage cleverly to the end. Have a drop of brandy and water, and you will feel as certain about it as I do.'

Jack steadily refused the brandy and water, and steadily persisted in taking his leave.

'I must try if I can't walk it off,' he said. 'Remember tomorrow morning – eleven o'clock, Avenue Road side of the Regent's Park.'

With those words he went out. His hardened relative laughed desperately, and resumed the dirty clay pipe.

I sat down on the side of my bed, actually quivering with excitement.

It is clear to me that no attempt has yet been made to change the stolen bank-notes; and I may add that Sergeant Bulmer was of that opinion also, when he left the case in my hands. What is the natural conclusion to draw from the conversation which I have just set down? Evidently, that the confederates meet tomorrow to take their respective shares in the stolen money, and to decide on the safest means of getting the notes changed the day after. Mr Jay is, beyond a doubt, the leading criminal in this business, and he will probably run the chief risk – that of changing the fifty-pound note. I shall, therefore, still make it my business to follow him – attending at the Regent's Park tomorrow, and doing my best to hear what is said there. If another appointment is made for the day after, I shall, of course, go to it. In the meantime, I shall want the immediate assistance of two competent persons (supposing the rascals separate after their meeting) to follow the two minor criminals. It is only fair to add, that, if the rogues all retire together, I shall probably keep my subordinates in reserve. Being naturally ambitious, I desire, if possible, to have the whole credit of discovering this robbery to myself.

8th July.

I have to acknowledge, with thanks, the speedy arrival of my two subordinates – men of very average abilities, I am afraid; but, fortunately, I shall always be on the spot to direct them.

My first business this morning was, necessarily, to prevent mistakes by accounting to Mr and Mrs Yatman for the presence of two strangers on the scene. Mr Yatman (between ourselves, a poor feeble man) only shook his head and groaned. Mrs Yatman (that superior woman) favoured me with a charming look of intelligence.

'Oh, Mr Sharpin!' she said, 'I am so sorry to see those two men! Your sending for their assistance looks as if you were beginning to be doubtful of success.'

I privately winked at her (she is very good in allowing me to do so without taking offence), and told her, in my facetious way, that she laboured under a slight mistake.

'It is because I am sure of success, Ma'am, that I send for them. I am determined to recover the money, not for my own sake only, but for Mr Yatman's sake – and for yours.'

I laid a considerable amount of stress on those last three words. She said, 'Oh, Mr Sharpin!' again – and blushed of a heavenly red – and looked down at her work. I could go to the world's end with that woman, if Mr Yatman would only die.

I sent off the two subordinates to wait, until I wanted them, at the Avenue Road gate of the Regent's Park. Half an hour afterwards I was following the same direction myself, at the heels of Mr Jay.

The two confederates were punctual to the appointed time, I blush to record it, but it is nevertheless necessary to state, that the third rogue – the nameless desperado of my report, or if you prefer it, the mysterious 'Somebody Else' of the conversation between the two brothers – is a Woman! and, what is worse, a young woman! and what is more lamentable still, a nice-looking woman! I have long resisted a growing conviction, that, wherever there is mischief in this world, an individual of the fair sex is inevitably certain to be mixed up in it. After the experience of this morning, I can struggle against that sad conclusion no longer. – I give up the sex – excepting Mrs Yatman, I give up the sex.

The man named 'Jack' offered the woman his arm. Mr Jay placed himself on the other side of her. The three then walked away slowly among the trees. I followed them at a respectful distance. My two subordinates, at a respectful distance also, followed me.

It was, I deeply regret to say, impossible to get near enough to them to overhear their conversation, without running too great a risk of being discovered. I could only infer from their gestures and actions that they were all three talking with extraordinary earnestness on some subject which deeply interested them. After having been engaged in this way a full quarter of an hour, they suddenly turned round to retrace their steps. My presence of mind did not forsake me in this emergency. I signed to the two subordinates to walk on carelessly and pass them, while I myself slipped dexterously behind a tree. As they came by me, I heard 'Jack' address these words to Mr Jay: —

'Let us say half-past ten tomorrow morning. And mind you come in a cab. We had better not risk taking one in this neighbourhood.'

Mr Jay made some brief reply, which I could not overhear. They walked back to the place at which they had met, shaking hands there with an audacious cordiality which it quite sickened me to see. They then separated. I followed Mr Jay. My subordinates paid the same delicate attention to the other two.

Instead of taking me back to Rutherford Street, Mr Jay led me to the Strand. He stopped at a dingy, disreputable-looking house, which, according to the inscription over the door, was a newspaper office, but which, in my judgment, had all the external appearance of a place devoted to the reception of stolen goods.

After remaining inside for a few minutes, he came out, whistling, with his finger and thumb in his waistcoat pocket. A less discreet man than myself would have arrested him on the spot. I remembered the necessity of catching the two confederates, and the importance of not interfering with the appointment that had been made for the next morning. Such coolness as this, under trying circumstances, is rarely to be found, I should imagine, in a young beginner, whose reputation as a detective policeman is still to make.

From the house of suspicious appearance, Mr Jay betook himself to a cigar-divan, and read the magazines over a cheroot. I sat at a table near him, and read the magazines likewise over a cheroot. From the divan he strolled to the tavern and had his chops. I strolled to the tavern and had my chops. When he had done, he went back to his lodging. When I had done, I went back to mine. He was overcome with drowsiness early in the evening, and went to bed. As soon as I heard him snoring, I was overcome with drowsiness, and went to bed also.

Early in the morning my two subordinates came to make their report. They had seen the man named 'Jack' leave the woman near the gate of an apparently respectable villa-residence, not far from the Regent's Park. Left to himself, he took a turning to the right, which led to a sort of suburban street, principally inhabited by shopkeepers. He stopped at the private door of one of the houses, and let himself in with his own key – looking about him as he opened the door, and staring suspiciously at my men as they lounged along on the opposite side of the way. These were all the particulars which the subordinates had to communicate. I kept them in my room to attend on me, if needful, and mounted to my peep-hole to have a look at Mr Jay.

He was occupied in dressing himself, and was taking extraordinary pains to destroy all traces of the natural slovenliness of his appearance. This was precisely what I expected. A vagabond like Mr Jay knows the importance of giving himself a respectable look when he is going to run the risk of changing a stolen bank-note. At five minutes past ten o'clock, he had given the last brush to his shabby hat and the last scouring with bread-crumb to his dirty gloves. At ten minutes past ten he was in the street, on his way to the nearest cab-stand, and I and my subordinates were close on his heels.

He took a cab, and we took a cab. I had not overheard them appoint a place of meeting, when following them in the Park on the previous day; but I soon found that we were proceeding in the old direction of the Avenue Road gate.

The cab in which Mr Jay was riding turned into the Park slowly. We stopped outside, to avoid exciting suspicion. I got out to follow the cab on foot. Just as I did so, I saw it stop, and detected the two confederates approaching it from among the trees. They got in, and the cab was turned about directly. I ran back to my own cab, and told the driver to let them pass him, and then to follow as before.

The man obeyed my directions, but so clumsily as to excite their suspicions. We had been driving after them about three minutes (returning along the road by which we had advanced) when I looked out of the window to see how far they might be ahead of us. As I did this, I saw two hats popped out of the windows of their cab, and two faces looking back at me. I sank into my place in a cold sweat; the expression is coarse, but no other form of words can describe my condition at that trying moment.

'We are found out!' I said faintly to my two subordinates. They stared at me in astonishment. My feelings changed instantly from the depth of despair to the height of indignation.

'It is the cabman's fault. Get out, one of you,' I said, with dignity – 'get out and punch his head.'

Instead of following my directions (I should wish this act of dis-obedience to be reported at headquarters) they both looked out of the window. Before I could pull them back, they both sat down again. Before I could express my just indignation, they both grinned, and said to me, 'Please to look out, sir!'

I did look out. The thieves' cab had stopped.

Where?

At a church door!!!

What effect this discovery might have had upon the ordinary run of men, I don't know. Being of a strong religious turn myself, it filled me with horror. I have often read of the unprincipled cunning of criminal persons; but I never before heard of three thieves attempting to double on their pursuers by entering a church! The sacrilegious audacity of that proceeding is, I should think, unparalleled in the annals of crime.

I checked my grinning subordinates by a frown. It was easy to see what was passing in their superficial minds. If I had not been able to look below the surface, I might, on observing two nicely-dressed men and one nicely-dressed woman enter a church before eleven in the morning on a week day, have come to the same hasty conclusion at which my inferiors had evidently arrived. As it was, appearances had no power to impose on me. I got out, and, followed by one of my men, entered the church. The other man I sent round to watch the vestry door. You may catch a weasel asleep – but not your humble servant, Matthew Sharpin!

We stole up the gallery stairs, diverged to the organ loft and peered through the curtains in front. There they were all three, sitting in a pew below – yes, incredible as it may appear, sitting in a pew below!

Before I could determine what to do, a clergyman made his appearance in full canonicals, from the vestry door, followed by a clerk. My brain whirled, and my eyesight grew dim. Dark remem-brances of robberies committed in vestries floated through my mind. I trembled for the excellent man in full canonicals – I even trembled for the clerk.

The clergyman placed himself inside the altar rails. The three desperadoes approached him. He opened his book, and began to read. What? – you will ask.

I answer, without the slightest hesitation, the first lines of the Marriage Service.

My subordinate had the audacity to look at me, and then to stuff his pocket-handkerchief into his mouth. I scorned to pay any attention to him. After I had discovered that the man 'Jack' was the bridegroom, and that the man Jay acted the part of father, and gave away the bride, I left the church, followed by my man, and joined the other subordinate outside the vestry door. Some people in my position would now have felt rather crestfallen, and would have begun to think that they had made a very foolish mistake. Not the faintest misgiving of any kind troubled me. I did not feel in the slightest degree depreciated in my own estimation. And even now, after a lapse of three hours, my mind remains, I am happy to say, in the same calm and hopeful condition.

As soon as I and my subordinates were assembled together outside the church, I intimated my intention of still following the other cab, in spite of what had occurred. My reason for deciding on this course will appear presently. The two subordinates were astonished at my resolution. One of them had the impertinence to say to me:

'If you please, sir, who is it that we are after? A man who has stolen money, or a man who has stolen a wife?'

The other low person encouraged him by laughing. Both have deserved an official reprimand; and both, I sincerely trust, will be sure to get it.

When the marriage ceremony was over, the three got into their cab; and once more our vehicle (neatly hidden round the corner of the church, so that they could not suspect it to be near them) started to follow theirs.

We traced them to the terminus of the South-Western Railway. The newly-married couple took tickets for Richmond – paying their fare with a half-sovereign, and so depriving me of the pleasure of arresting them, which I should certainly have done, if they had offered a bank-note. They parted from Mr Jay, saying, 'Remember the address – 14 Babylon Terrace. You dine with us tomorrow week.' Mr Jay accepted the invitation, and added, jocosely, that he was going home at once to get off his clean clothes, and to be comfortable and dirty again for the rest of the day. I have to report that I saw him home safely, and that he is comfortable and dirty again (to use his own disgraceful language) at the present moment.

Here the affair rests, having by this time reached what I may call its first stage.

I know very well what persons of hasty judgment will be inclined to say of my proceedings thus far. They will assert that I have been deceiving myself all through, in the most absurd way; they will declare that the suspicious conversations which I have reported, referred solely to the difficulties and dangers of successfully carrying out a runaway match; and they will appeal to the scene in the church, as offering undeniable proof of the correctness of their assertions. So let it be. I dispute nothing up to this point. But I ask a question, out of the depths of my own sagacity as a man of the world, which the bitterest of my enemies will not, I think, find it particularly easy to answer.

Granted the fact of the marriage, what proof does it afford me of the innocence of the three persons concerned in that clandestine transaction? It gives me none. On the contrary, it strengthens my suspicions against Mr Jay and his confederates, because it suggests a distinct motive for their stealing the money. A gentleman who is going to spend his honeymoon at Richmond wants money; and a gentleman who is in debt to all his tradespeople wants money. Is this an unjustifiable imputation of bad motives? In the name of outraged morality, I deny it. These men have combined together, and have stolen a woman. Why should they not combine together, and steal a cashbox? I take my stand on the logic of rigid virtue; and I defy all the sophistry of vice to move me an inch out of my position.

Speaking of virtue, I may add that I have put this view of the case to Mr and Mrs Yatman. That accomplished and charming woman found it difficult, at first, to follow the close chain of my reasoning. I am free to confess that she shook her head, and shed tears, and joined her husband in premature lamentation over the loss of the two hundred pounds. But a little careful explanation on my part, and a little attentive listening on hers, ultimately changed her opinion. She now agrees with me, that there is nothing in this unexpected circumstance of the clandestine marriage which absolutely tends to divert suspicion from Mr Jay, or Mr 'Jack', or the runaway lady. 'Audacious hussy' was the term my fair friend used in speaking of her, but let that pass. It is more to the purpose to record that Mrs Yatman has not lost confidence in me and that Mr Yatman promises to follow her example, and do his best to look hopefully for future results.

I have now, in the new turn that circumstances have taken, to await advice from your office. I pause for fresh orders with all the composure of a man who has got two strings to his bow. When I traced the three confederates from the church door to the railway terminus, I had two motives for doing so. First, I followed them as a matter of official business, believing them still to have been guilty of the robbery. Secondly, I followed them as a matter of private speculation, with a view of discovering the place of refuge to which the runaway couple intended to retreat, and of making my information a marketable commodity to offer to the young lady's family and friends. Thus, whatever happens, I may congratulate myself beforehand on not having wasted my time. If the office approves of my conduct, I have my plan ready for further proceedings. If the office blames me, I shall take myself off, with my marketable information, to the genteel villa-residence in the neighbourhood of the Regent's Park. Any way, the affair puts money into my pocket, and does credit to my penetration as an uncommonly sharp man.

I have only one word more to add, and it is this: If any individual ventures to assert that Mr Jay and his confederates are innocent of all share in the stealing of the cash-box, I, in return, defy that individual – though he may even be Chief Inspector Theakstone himself – to tell me who has committed the robbery at Rutherford Street, Soho.

I have the honour to be,

Your very obedient servant,

Matthew Sharpin

FROM CHIEF INSPECTOR THEAKSTONE
TO SERGEANT BULMER
BIRMINGHAM, 9th July.

SERGEANT BULMER, – That empty-headed puppy, Mr Matthew Sharpin, has made a mess of the case at Rutherford Street, exactly as I expected he would. Business keeps me in this town; so I write to you to set the matter straight. I enclose, with this, the pages of feeble scribble-scrabble which the creature, Sharpin, calls a report. Look them over; and when you have made your way through all the gabble, I think you will agree with me that the conceited booby has looked for the thief in every direction but the right one. You can lay your hand on the guilty person in five minutes, now. Settle the case at once; forward your report to me at this place; and tell Mr Sharpin that he is suspended till further notice. Yours,

Francis Theakstone

FROM SERGEANT BULMER
TO CHIEF INSPECTOR THEAKSTONE
LONDON, 10th July.

INSPECTOR THEAKSTONE, Your letter and enclosure came safe to hand. Wise men, they say, may always learn something, even from a fool. By the time I had got through Sharpin's maundering report of his own folly, I saw my way clear enough to the end of the Rutherford Street case, just as you thought I should. In half an hour's time I was at the house. The first person I saw there was Mr Sharpin himself.

'Have you come to help me?' says he.

'Not exactly,' says I. 'I've come to tell you that you are suspended till further notice.'

'Very good,' says he, not taken down, by so much as a single peg, in his own estimation, 'I thought you would be jealous of me. It's very natural; and I don't blame you. Walk in, pray, and make yourself at home. I'm off to do a little detective business on my own account, in the neighbourhood of the Regent's Park. Ta-ta, sergeant, ta-ta!'

With those words he took himself out of the way – which was exactly what I wanted him to do.

As soon as the maid-servant had shut the door, I told her to inform her master that I wanted to say a word to him in private. She showed me into the parlour behind the shop; and there was Mr Yatman, all alone, reading the newspaper.

'About this matter of the robbery, sir,' says I.

He cut me short, peevishly enough – being naturally a poor, weak, womanish sort of man. 'Yes, yes, I know,' says he. 'You have come to tell me that your wonderfully clever man, who has bored holes in my second-floor partition, has made a mistake, and is off the scent of the scoundrel who has stolen my money.'

'Yes, sir,' says I. 'That is one of the things I came to tell you. But I have got something else to say, besides that.'

'Can you tell me who the thief is?' says he, more pettish than ever.

'Yes, sir,' says I, 'I think I can.'

He put down the newspaper, and began to look rather anxious and frightened.

'Not my shopman?' says he. 'I hope, for the man's own sake, it's not my shopman.'

'Guess again, sir,' says I.

'That idle slut, the maid?' says he.

'She is idle, sir,' says I, 'and she is also a slut; my first inquiries about her proved as much as that. But she's not the thief.'

'Then in the name of heaven, who is?' says he.

'Will you please to prepare yourself for a very disagreeable surprise, sir?' says I. 'And in case you lose your temper, will you excuse my remarking that I am the stronger man of the two, and that, if you allow yourself to lay hands on me, I may unintentionally hurt you, in pure self-defence?'

He turned as pale as ashes, and pushed his chair two or three feet away from me.

'You have asked me to tell you, sir, who has taken your money,' I went on. 'If you insist on my giving you an answer—'

'I do insist,' he said, faintly. 'Who has taken it?'

'Your wife has taken it,' I said very quietly, and very positively at the same time.

He jumped out of the chair as if I had put a knife into him, and struck his fist on the table, so heavily that the wood cracked again.

'Steady, sir,' says I. 'Flying into a passion won't help you to the truth.'

'It's a lie!' says he, with another smack of his fist on the table – 'a base, vile, infamous lie! How dare you—'

He stopped, and fell back into the chair again, looked about him in a bewildered way, and ended by bursting out crying.

'When your better sense comes back to you, sir,' says I, 'I am sure you will be gentleman enough to make an apology for the language you have just used. In the meantime, please to listen, if you can, to a word of explanation. Mr Sharpin has sent in a report to our inspector, of the most irregular and ridiculous kind; setting down, not only all his own foolish doings and sayings, but the doings and sayings of Mrs Yatman as well. In most cases, such a document would have been fit for the waste-paper basket; but, in this particular case, it so happens that Mr Sharpin's budget of nonsense leads to a certain conclusion, which the simpleton of a writer has been quite innocent of suspecting from the beginning to the end. Of that conclusion I am so sure, that I will forfeit my place, if it does not turn out that Mrs Yatman has been practising upon the folly and conceit of this young man, and that she has tried to shield herself from discovery by purposely encouraging him to suspect the wrong persons. I tell you that confidently; and I will even go further. I will undertake to give a decided opinion as to why Mrs Yatman took the money, and what she has done with it, or with a part of it. Nobody can look at that lady, sir, without being struck by the great taste and beauty of her dress—'

As I said those last words, the poor man seemed to find his powers of speech again. He cut me short directly, as haughtily as if he had been a duke instead of a stationer.

'Try some other means of justifying your vile calumny against my wife,' says he. 'Her milliner's bill for the past year, is on my file of receipted accounts at this moment.'

'Excuse me, sir,' says I, 'but that proves nothing. Milliners, I must tell you, have a certain rascally custom which comes within the daily experience of our office. A married lady who wishes it, can keep two accounts at her dressmaker's; one is the account which her husband sees and pays; the other is the private account, which contains all the extravagant items, and which the wife pays secretly, by instalments, whenever she can. According to our usual experience, these instalments are mostly squeezed out of the housekeeping money. In your case, I suspect no instalments have been paid; proceedings have been threatened; Mrs Yatman, knowing your altered circumstances, has felt herself driven into a corner; and she has paid her private account out of your cash-box.'

'I won't believe it,' says he. 'Every word you speak is an abominable insult to me and to my wife.'

'Are you man enough, sir,' says I, taking him up short, in order to save time and words, 'to get that receipted bill you spoke of just now off the file, and come with me at once to the milliner's shop where Mrs Yatman deals?'

He turned red in the face at that, got the bill directly, and put on his hat. I took out of my pocket-book the list containing the numbers of the lost notes, and we left the house together immediately.

Arrived at the milliner's (one of the expensive West-end houses, as I expected), I asked for a private interview, on important business, with the mistress of the concern. It was not the first time that she and I had met over the same delicate investigation. The moment she set eyes on me, she sent for her husband. I mentioned who Mr Yatman was, and what we wanted.

'This is strictly private?' inquires her husband. I nodded my head.

'And confidential?' says the wife. I nodded again.

'Do you see any objection, dear, to obliging the sergeant with a sight of the books?' says the husband.

'None in the world, love, if you approve of it,' says the wife.

All this while poor Mr Yatman sat looking the picture of astonishment and distress, quite out of place at our polite conference. The books were brought – and one minute's look at the pages in which

Mrs Yatman's name figured was enough, and more than enough, to prove the truth of every word I had spoken.

There, in one book, was the husband's account, which Mr Yatman had settled. And there, in the other, was the private account, crossed off also; the date of settlement being the very day after the loss of the cash-box. This said private account amounted to the sum of a hundred and seventy-five pounds, odd shillings; and it extended over a period of three years. Not a single instalment had been paid on it. Under the last line was an entry to this effect: 'Written to for the third time, June 23rd.' I pointed to it, and asked the milliner if that meant 'last June'. Yes, it did mean last June; and she now deeply regretted to say that it had been accompanied by a threat of legal proceedings.

'I thought you gave good customers more than three years' credit?' says I.

The milliner looks at Mr Yatman, and whispers to me – 'Not when a lady's husband gets into difficulties.'

She pointed to the account as she spoke. The entries after the time when Mr Yatman's circumstances became involved were just as extravagant, for a person in his wife's situation, as the entries for the year before that period. If the lady had economised in other things, she had certainly not economised in the matter of dress.

There was nothing left now but to examine the cash-book, for form's sake. The money had been paid in notes, the amounts and numbers of which exactly tallied with the figures set down in my list.

After that, I thought it best to get Mr Yatman out of the house immediately. He was in such a pitiable condition, that I called a cab and accompanied him home in it. At first he cried and raved like a child: but I soon quieted him – and I must add, to his credit, that he made me a most handsome apology for his language, as the cab drew up at his house door. In return, I tried to give him some advice about how to set matters right, for the future, with his wife. He paid very little attention to me, and went upstairs muttering to himself about a separation. Whether Mrs Yatman will come cleverly out of the scrape or not, seems doubtful. I should say, myself, that she will go into screeching hysterics, and so frighten the poor man into forgiving her. But this is no business of ours. So far as we are concerned, the case is now at an end; and the present report may come to a conclusion along with it.

I remain, accordingly, yours to command,
THOMAS BULMER.

PS – I have to add, that, on leaving Rutherford Street, I met Mr Matthew Sharpin coming to pack up his things.

'Only think!' says he, rubbing his hands in great spirits, 'I've been to the genteel villa-residence; and the moment I mentioned my business, they kicked me out directly. There were two witnesses of the assault; and it's worth a hundred pounds to me, if it's worth a farthing.'

'I wish you joy of your luck,' says I.

'Thank you,' says he. 'When may I pay you the same compliment on finding the thief?'

'Whenever you like,' says I, 'for the thief is found.'

'Just what I expected,' says he. 'I've done all the work; and now you cut in, and claim all the credit – Mr Jay of course?'

'No,' says I.

'Who is it then?' says he.

'Ask Mrs Yatman,' says I. 'She's waiting to tell you.'

'All right! I'd much rather hear it from that charming woman than from you,' says he, and goes into the house in a mighty hurry.

What do you think of that, Inspector Theakstone? Would you like to stand in Mr Sharpin's shoes? I shouldn't, I can promise you!

FROM CHIEF INSPECTOR THEAKSTONE TO Mr MATTHEW SHARPIN

12th July.

SIR, – Sergeant Bulmer has already told you to consider yourself suspended until further notice. I have now authority to add, that your services as a member of the Detective Police are positively declined. You will please to take this letter as notifying officially your dismissal from the force.

I may inform you, privately, that your rejection is not intended to cast any reflections on your character. It merely implies that you are not quite sharp enough for our purpose. If we are to have a new recruit among us, we should infinitely prefer Mrs Yatman.

Your obedient servant,

Francis Theakstone

NOTE ON THE PRECEDING CORRESPONDENCE, ADDED BY Mr THEAKSTONE

The Inspector is not in a position to append any explanations of importance to the last of the letters. It has been discovered that Mr Matthew Sharpin left the house in Rutherford Street five minutes after his interview outside of it with Sergeant Bulmer – his manner expressing the liveliest emotions of terror and astonishment, and his left cheek displaying a bright patch of red, which might have been the result of a slap on the face from a female hand. He was also heard, by the shopman at Rutherford Street, to use a very shocking expression in reference to Mrs Yatman; and was seen to clench his fist vindictively, as he ran round the corner of the street. Nothing more has been heard of him; and it is conjectured that he has left London with the intention of offering his valuable services to the provincial police.

On the interesting domestic subject of Mr and Mrs Yatman still less is known. It has, however, been positively ascertained that the medical attendant of the family was sent for in a great hurry, on the day when Mr Yatman returned from the milliner's shop. The neighbouring chemist received, soon afterwards, a prescription of a soothing nature to make up for Mrs Yatman. The day after, Mr Yatman purchased some smelling-salts at the shop, and afterwards appeared at the circulating library to ask for a novel, descriptive of high life, that would amuse an invalid lady. It has been inferred from these circumstances that he has not thought it desirable to carry out his threat of separating himself from his wife – at least in the present (presumed) condition of that lady's sensitive nervous system.

CHARLES DICKENS

Hunted Down
I.

MOST OF us see some romances in life. In my capacity as Chief Manager of a Life Assurance Office, I think I have within the last thirty years seen more romances than the generality of men, however unpromising the opportunity may, at first sight, seem.

As I have retired, and live at my ease, I possess the means that I used to want, of considering what I have seen, at leisure. My experiences have a more remarkable aspect, so reviewed, than they had when they were in progress. I have come home from the Play now, and can recall the scenes of the Drama upon which the curtain has fallen, free from the glare, bewilderment, and bustle of the Theatre.

Let me recall one of these Romances of the real world.

There is nothing truer than physiognomy, taken in connection with manner. The art of reading that book of which Eternal Wisdom obliges every human creature to present his or her own page with the individual character written on it, is a difficult one, perhaps, and is little studied. It may require some natural aptitude, and it must require (for everything does) some patience and some pains. That these are not usually given to it – that numbers of people accept a few stock commonplace expressions of the face as the whole list of characteristics, and neither seek nor know the refinements that are truest – that You, for instance, give a great deal of time and attention to the reading of music, Greek, Latin, French, Italian, Hebrew, if you please, and do not qualify yourself to read the face of the master or mistress looking over your shoulder teaching it to you – I assume to be five hundred times more probable than improbable. Perhaps a little self-sufficiency may be at the bottom of this; facial expression requires no study from you, you think; it comes by nature to you to know enough about it, and you are not to be taken in.

I confess, for my part, that I *have* been taken in, over and over again. I have been taken in by acquaintances, and I have been taken in (of course) by friends; far oftener by friends than by any other class of persons. How came I to be so deceived? Had I quite misread their faces?

No. Believe me, my first impression of those people, founded on face and manner alone, was invariably true. My mistake was in suffering them to come nearer to me and explain themselves away.

II.

The partition which separated my own office from our general outer office in the City was of thick plate-glass. I could see through it what passed in the outer office, without hearing a word. I had it put up in place of a wall that had been there for years – ever since the house was built. It is no matter whether I did or did not make the change in order that I might derive my first impression of strangers, who came to us on business, from their faces alone, without being influenced by anything they said.

Enough to mention that I turned my glass partition to that account, and that a Life Assurance Office is at all times exposed to be practised upon by the most crafty and cruel of the human race.

It was through my glass partition that I first saw the gentleman whose story I am going to tell.

He had come in without my observing it, and had put his hat and umbrella on the broad counter, and was bending over it to take some papers from one of the clerks. He was about forty or so, dark, exceedingly well dressed in black – being in mourning – and the hand he extended with a polite air, had a particularly well-fitting black-kid glove upon it. His hair, which was elaborately brushed and oiled, was parted straight up the middle; and he presented this parting to the clerk, exactly (to my thinking) as if he had said, in so many words: 'You must take me, if you please, my friend, just as I show myself. Come straight up here, follow the gravel path, keep off the grass, I allow no trespassing.'

I conceived a very great aversion to that man the moment I thus saw him.

He had asked for some of our printed forms, and the clerk was giving them to him and explaining them. An obliged and agreeable smile was on his face, and his eyes met those of the clerk with a sprightly look. (I have known a vast quantity of nonsense talked about bad men not looking you in the face. Don't trust that conventional idea. Dishonesty will stare honesty out of countenance, any day in the week, if there is anything to be got by it.)

I saw, in the corner of his eyelash, that he became aware of my looking at him. Immediately he turned the parting in his hair toward the glass partition, as if he said to me with a sweet smile, 'Straight up here, if you please. Off the grass!'

In a few moments he had put on his hat and taken up his umbrella, and was gone.

I beckoned the clerk into my room, and asked, 'Who was that?'

He had the gentleman's card in his hand. 'Mr Julius Slinkton, Middle Temple.'

'A barrister, Mr Adams?'

'I think not, sir.'

'I should have thought him a clergyman, but for his having no Reverend here,' said I.

'Probably, from his appearance,' Mr Adams replied, 'he is reading for orders.'

I should mention that he wore a dainty white cravat, and dainty linen altogether.

'What did he want, Mr Adams?'

'Merely a form of proposal, sir, and form of reference.'

'Recommended here? Did he say?'

'Yes, he said he was recommended here by a friend of yours. He noticed you, but said that as he had not the pleasure of your personal acquaintance he would not trouble you.'

'Did he know my name?'

'Oh yes, sir! He said, 'There *is* Mr Sampson, I see!"'

'A well-spoken gentleman, apparently?'

'Remarkably so, sir.'

'Insinuating manners, apparently?'

'Very much so, indeed, sir.'

'Hah!' said I. 'I want nothing at present, Mr Adams.'

Within a fortnight of that day I went to dine with a friend of mine, a merchant, a man of taste, who buys pictures and books, and the first man I saw among the company was Mr Julius Slinkton.

There he was, standing before the fire, with good large eyes and an open expression of face; but still (I thought) requiring everybody to come at him by the prepared way he offered, and by no other.

I noticed him ask my friend to introduce him to Mr Sampson, and my friend did so. Mr Slinkton was very happy to see me. Not too happy; there was no overdoing of the matter; happy in a thoroughly well-bred, perfectly unmeaning way.

'I thought you had met,' our host observed.

'No,' said Mr Slinkton. 'I did look in at Mr Sampson's office, on your recommendation; but I really did not feel justified in troubling Mr Sampson himself, on a point in the everyday, routine of an ordinary clerk.'

I said I should have been glad to show him any attention on our friend's introduction.

'I am sure of that,' said he, 'and am much obliged. At another time, perhaps, I may be less delicate. Only, however, if I have real business; for I know, Mr Sampson, how precious business time is, and what a vast number of impertinent people there are in the world.'

I acknowledged his consideration with a slight bow. 'You were thinking,' said I, 'of effecting a policy on your life.'

'Oh dear no! I am afraid I am not so prudent as you pay me the compliment of supposing me to be, Mr Sampson. I merely inquired for a friend. But you know what friends are in such matters. Nothing may ever come of it. I have the greatest reluctance to trouble men of business with inquiries for friends, knowing the probabilities to be a thousand to one that the friends will never follow them up. People are so fickle, so selfish, so inconsiderate. Don't you, in your business, find them so every day, Mr Sampson?'

I was going to give a qualified answer; but he turned his smooth, white parting on me with its 'Straight up here, if you please!' and I answered, 'Yes.'

'I hear, Mr Sampson,' he resumed presently, for our friend had a new cook, and dinner was not so punctual as usual, 'that your profession has recently suffered a great loss.'

'In money?' said I.

He laughed at my ready association of loss with money, and replied, 'No, in talent and vigour.'

Not at once following out his allusion, I considered for a moment. '*Has* it sustained a loss of that kind?' said I. 'I was not aware of it.'

'Understand me, Mr Sampson. I don't imagine that you have retired. It is not so bad as that. But Mr Meltham—'

'Oh, to be sure!' said I. 'Yes! Mr Meltham, the young actuary of the "Inestimable".'

'Just so,' he returned in a consoling way.

'He is a great loss. He was at once the most profound, the most original, and the most energetic man I have ever known connected with Life Assurance.'

I spoke strongly; for I had a high esteem and admiration for Meltham; and my gentleman had indefinitely conveyed to me some suspicion that he wanted to sneer at him. He recalled me to my guard by presenting that trim pathway up his head, with its internal 'Not on the grass, if you please – the gravel'.

'You knew him, Mr Slinkton.'

'Only by reputation. To have known him as an acquaintance or as a friend, is an honour I should have sought if he had remained in society, though I might never have had the good fortune to attain it, being a man of far inferior mark. He was scarcely above thirty, I suppose?'

'About thirty.'

'Ah!' he sighed in his former consoling way. 'What creatures we are! To break up, Mr Sampson, and become incapable of business at that time of life! – Any reason assigned for the melancholy fact?'

('Humph!' thought I, as I looked at him. 'But I *won't* go up the track, and I *will* go on the grass.')

'What reason have you heard assigned, Mr Slinkton?' I asked, point-blank.

'Most likely a false one. You know what Rumour is, Mr Sampson. I never repeat what I hear; it is the only way of paring the nails and shaving the head of Rumour. But when *you* ask me what reason I have heard assigned for Mr Meltham's passing away from among men, it is another thing. I am not gratifying idle gossip then. I was told, Mr Sampson, that Mr Meltham had relinquished all his avocations and all his prospects, because he was, in fact, broken-hearted. A disappointed attachment I heard – though it hardly seems probable, in the case of a man so distinguished and so attractive.'

'Attractions and distinctions are no armour against death,' said I.

'Oh, she died? Pray pardon me. I did not hear that. That, indeed, makes it very, very sad. Poor Mr Meltham! She died? Ah, dear me! Lamentable, lamentable!'

I still thought his pity was not quite genuine, and I still suspected an unaccountable sneer under all this, until he said, as we were parted, like the other knots of talkers, by the announcement of dinner:

'Mr Sampson, you are surprised to see me so moved on behalf of a man whom I have never known. I am not so disinterested as you may suppose. I have suffered, and recently too, from death myself. I have lost one of two charming nieces, who were my constant companions. She died young – barely three-and-twenty; and even her remaining sister is far from strong. The world is a grave!'

He said this with deep feeling, and I felt reproached for the coldness of my manner. Coldness and distrust had been engendered in me, I knew, by my bad experiences; they were not natural to me; and I often thought how much I had lost in life, losing trustfulness, and how little I had gained, gaining hard caution.

This state of mind being habitual to me, I troubled myself more about this conversation than I might have troubled myself about a greater matter. I listened to his talk at dinner, and observed how readily other men responded to it, and with what a graceful instinct he adapted his subjects to the knowledge and habits of those he talked with. As, in talking with me, he had easily started the subject I might be supposed to understand best, and to be the most interested in, so, in talking with others, he guided himself by the same rule. The company was of a varied character; but he was not at fault, that I could discover, with any member of it. He knew just as much of each man's pursuit as made him agreeable to that man in reference to it, and just as little as made it natural in him to seek modestly for information when the theme was broached.

As he talked and talked – but really not too much, for the rest of us seemed to force it upon him – I became quite angry with myself.

I took his face to pieces in my mind, like a watch, and examined it in detail. I could not say much against any of his features separately; I could say even less against them when they were put together. 'Then is it not monstrous,' I asked myself, 'that because a man happens to part his hair straight up the middle of his head, I should permit myself to suspect, and even to detest him?'

(I may stop to remark that this was no proof of my sense. An observer of men who finds himself steadily repelled by some apparently trifling thing in a stranger is right to give it great weight. It may be the clue to the whole mystery. A hair or two will show where a lion is hidden. A very little key will open a very heavy door.)

I took my part in the conversation with him after a time, and we got on remarkably well. In the drawing-room I asked the host how long he had known Mr Slinkton. He answered, not many months; he had met him at the house of a celebrated painter then present, who had known him well when he was travelling with his nieces in Italy for their health. His plans in life being broken by the death of one of them, he was reading with the intention of going back to college as a matter of form, taking his degree, and going into orders. I could not but argue with myself that here was the true explanation of his interest in poor Meltham, and that I had been almost brutal in my distrust on that simple head.

III.

On the very next day but one I was sitting behind my glass partition, as before, when he came into the outer office, as before. The moment

I saw him again without hearing him, I hated him worse than ever.

It was only for a moment that I had this opportunity; for he waved his tight-fitting black glove the instant I looked at him, and came straight in.

'Mr Sampson, good-day! I presume, you see, upon your kind permission to intrude upon you. I don't keep my word in being justified by business, for my business here – if I may so abuse the word – is of the slightest nature.'

I asked, was it anything I could assist him in?

'I thank you, no. I merely called to inquire outside whether my dilatory friend had been so false to himself as to be practical and sensible. But, of course, he has done nothing. I gave him your papers with my own hand, and he was hot upon the intention, but of course he has done nothing. Apart from the general human disinclination to do anything that ought to be done, I dare say there is a specially about assuring one's life. You find it like will-making. People are so superstitious, and take it for granted they will die soon afterwards.'

'Up here, if you please; straight up here, Mr Sampson. Neither to the right nor to the left.' I almost fancied I could hear him breathe the words as he sat smiling at me, with that intolerable parting exactly opposite the bridge of my nose.

'There is such a feeling sometimes, no doubt,' I replied; 'but I don't think it obtains to any great extent.'

'Well,' said he, with a shrug and a smile, 'I wish some good angel would influence my friend in the right direction. I rashly promised his mother and sister in Norfolk to see it done, and he promised them that he would do it. But I suppose he never will.'

He spoke for a minute or two on indifferent topics, and went away.

I had scarcely unlocked the drawers of my writing-table next morning, when he reappeared. I noticed that he came straight to the door in the glass partition, and did not pause a single moment outside.

'Can you spare me two minutes, my dear Mr Sampson?'

'By all means.'

'Much obliged,' laying his hat and umbrella on the table; 'I came early, not to interrupt you. The fact is, I am taken by surprise in reference to this proposal my friend has made.'

'Has he made one?' said I.

'Ye-es,' he answered, deliberately looking at me; and then a bright idea seemed to strike him – 'or he only tells me he has. Perhaps that may be a new way of evading the matter. By Jupiter, I never thought of that!'

Mr Adams was opening the morning's letters in the outer office.

'What is the name, Mr Slinkton?' I asked.

'Beckwith.'

I looked out at the door and requested Mr Adams, if there were a proposal in that name, to bring it in. He had already laid it out of his hand on the counter. It was easily selected from the rest, and he gave it me. Alfred Beckwith. Proposal to effect a policy with us for two thousand pounds. Dated yesterday.

'From the Middle Temple, I see, Mr Slinkton.'

'Yes. He lives on the same staircase with me; his door is opposite. I never thought he would make me his reference though.'

'It seems natural enough that he should.'

'Quite so, Mr Sampson; but I never thought of it. Let me see.'

He took the printed paper from his pocket. 'How am I to answer all these questions?'

'According to the truth, of course,' said I.

'Oh, of course!' he answered, looking up from the paper with a smile; 'I meant they were so many. But you do right to be particular. It stands to reason that you must be particular. Will you allow me to use your pen and ink?'

'Certainly.'

'And your desk?'

'Certainly.'

He had been hovering about between his hat and his umbrella for a place to write on. He now sat down in my chair, at my blotting-paper and inkstand, with the long walk up his head in accurate perspective before me, as I stood with my back to the fire.

Before answering each question he ran over it aloud, and discussed it. How long had he known Mr Alfred Beckwith? That he had to calculate by years upon his fingers. What were his habits? No difficulty about them; temperate in the last degree, and took a little too much exercise, if anything. All the answers were satisfactory. When he had written them all, he looked them over, and finally signed them in a very pretty hand. He supposed he had now done with the business. I told him he was not likely to be troubled any farther. Should he leave the papers there? If he pleased. Much obliged. Good-morning.

I had had one other visitor before him; not at the office, but at my own house. That visitor had come to my bedside when it was not yet daylight, and had been seen by no one else but by my faithful confidential servant.

A second reference paper (for we required always two) was sent down into Norfolk, and was duly received back by post. This, likewise, was satisfactorily answered in every respect. Our forms were all complied with; we accepted the proposal, and the premium for one year was paid.

IV.

For six or seven months I saw no more of Mr Slinkton. He called once at my house, but I was not at home; and he once asked me to dine with him in the Temple, but I was engaged. His friend's assurance was effected in March. Late in September or early in October I was down at Scarborough for a breath of sea-air, where I met him on the beach. It was a hot evening; he came toward me with his hat in his hand; and there was the walk I had felt so strongly disinclined to take in perfect order again, exactly in front of the bridge of my nose.

He was not alone, but had a young lady on his arm.

She was dressed in mourning, and I looked at her with great interest. She had the appearance of being extremely delicate, and her face was remarkably pale and melancholy; but she was very pretty. He introduced her as his niece, Miss Niner.

'Are you strolling, Mr Sampson? Is it possible you can be idle?'

It *was* possible, and I *was* strolling.

'Shall we stroll together?'

'With pleasure.'

The young lady walked between us, and we walked on the cool sea sand, in the direction of Filey.

'There have been wheels here,' said Mr Slinkton. 'And now I look again, the wheels of a hand-carriage! Margaret, my love, your shadow without doubt!'

'Miss Niner's shadow?' I repeated, looking down at it on the sand.

'Not that one,' Mr Slinkton returned, laughing. 'Margaret, my dear, tell Mr Sampson.'

'Indeed,' said the young lady, turning to me, 'there is nothing to tell – except that I constantly see the same invalid old gentleman at all times, wherever I go. I have mentioned it to my uncle, and he calls the gentleman my shadow.'

'Does he live in Scarborough?' I asked.

'He is staying here.'

'Do you live in Scarborough?'

'No, I am staying here. My uncle has placed me with a family here, for my health.'

'And your shadow?' said I, smiling.

'My shadow,' she answered, smiling too, 'is – like myself – not very robust, I fear; for I lose my shadow sometimes, as my shadow loses me at other times. We both seem liable to confinement to the house. I have not seen my shadow for days and days; but it does oddly happen, occasionally, that wherever I go, for many days together, this gentleman goes. We have come together in the most unfrequented nooks on this shore.'

'Is this he?' said I, pointing before us.

The wheels had swept down to the water's edge, and described a great loop on the sand in turning. Bringing the loop back towards us, and spinning it out as it came, was a hand-carriage, drawn by a man.

'Yes,' said Miss Niner, 'this really is my shadow, uncle.'

As the carriage approached us and we approached the carriage, I saw within it an old man, whose head was sunk on his breast, and who was enveloped in a variety of wrappers. He was drawn by a very quiet but very keen-looking man, with iron-gray hair, who was slightly lame.

They had passed us, when the carriage stopped, and the old gentleman within, putting out his arm, called to me by my name. I went back, and was absent from Mr Slinkton and his niece for about five minutes.

When I rejoined them, Mr Slinkton was the first to speak. Indeed, he said to me in a raised voice before I came up with him:

'It is well you have not been longer, or my niece might have died of curiosity to know who her shadow is, Mr Sampson.'

'An old East India Director,' said I. 'An intimate friend of our friend's, at whose house I first had the pleasure of meeting you. A certain Major Banks. You have heard of him?'

'Never.'

'Very rich, Miss Niner; but very old, and very crippled. An amiable man, sensible – much interested in you. He has just been expatiating on the affection that he has observed to exist between you and your uncle.'

Mr Slinkton was holding his hat again, and he passed his hand up the straight walk, as if he himself went up it serenely, after me.

'Mr Sampson,' he said, tenderly pressing his niece's arm in his, 'our affection was always a strong one, for we have had but few near ties. We have still fewer now. We have associations to bring us together, that are not of this world, Margaret.'

'Dear uncle!' murmured the young lady, and turned her face aside to hide her tears.

'My niece and I have such remembrances and regrets in common, Mr Sampson,' he feelingly pursued, 'that it would be strange indeed if the relations between us were cold or indifferent. If I remember a conversation we once had together, you will understand the reference I make. Cheer up, dear Margaret. Don't droop, don't droop. My Margaret! I cannot bear to see you droop!'

The poor young lady was very much affected, but controlled herself.

His feelings, too, were very acute. In a word, he found himself under such great need of a restorative, that he presently went away, to take a bath of sea-water, leaving the young lady and me sitting by a point of rock, and probably presuming – but that you will say was a pardonable indulgence in a luxury – that she would praise him with all her heart.

She did, poor thing! With all her confiding heart, she praised him to me, for his care of her dead sister, and for his untiring devotion in her last illness. The sister had wasted away very slowly, and wild and terrible fantasies had come over her toward the end, but he had never been impatient with her, or at a loss; had always been gentle, watchful, and self-possessed. The sister had known him, as she had known him, to be the best of men, the kindest of men, and yet a man of such admirable strength of character, as to be a very tower for the support of their weak natures while their poor lives endured.

'I shall leave him, Mr Sampson, very soon,' said the young lady; 'I know my life is drawing to an end; and when I am gone, I hope he will marry and be happy. I am sure he has lived single so long, only for my sake, and for my poor, poor sister's.'

The little hand-carriage had made another great loop on the damp sand, and was coming back again, gradually spinning out a slim figure of eight, half a mile long.

'Young lady,' said I, looking around, laying my hand upon her arm, and speaking in a low voice, 'time presses. You hear the gentle murmur of that sea?'

She looked at me with the utmost wonder and alarm, saying, 'Yes!'

'And you know what a voice is in it when the storm comes?'

'Yes!'

'You see how quiet and peaceful it lies before us, and you know what an awful sight of power without pity it might be, this very night!'

'Yes!'

'But if you had never heard or seen it, or heard of it in its cruelty, could you believe that it beats every inanimate thing in its way to pieces, without mercy, and destroys life without remorse?'

'You terrify me, sir, by these questions!'

'To save you, young lady, to save you! For God's sake, collect your strength and collect your firmness! If you were here alone, and hemmed in by the rising tide on the flow to fifty feet above your head, you could not be in greater danger than the danger you are now to be saved from.'

The figure on the sand was spun out, and straggled off into a crooked little jerk that ended at the cliff very near us.

'As I am, before Heaven and the Judge of all mankind, your friend, and your dead sister's friend, I solemnly entreat you, Miss Niner, without one moment's loss of time, to come to this gentleman with me!'

If the little carriage had been less near to us, I doubt if I could have got her away; but it was so near that we were there before she had recovered the hurry of being urged from the rock. I did not remain there with her two minutes. Certainly within five, I had the inexpressible satisfaction of seeing her – from the point we had sat on, and to which I had returned – half supported and half carried up some rude steps notched in the cliff, by the figure of an active man. With that figure beside her, I knew she was safe anywhere.

I sat alone on the rock, awaiting Mr Slinkton's return. The twilight was deepening and the shadows were heavy, when he came round the point, with his hat hanging at his buttonhole, smoothing his wet hair with one of his hands, and picking out the old path with the other and a pocket-comb.

'My niece not here, Mr Sampson?' he said, looking about.

'Miss Niner seemed to feel a chill in the air after the sun was down, and has gone home.'

He looked surprised, as though she were not accustomed to do anything without him; even to originate so slight a proceeding.

'I persuaded Miss Niner,' I explained.

'Ah!' said he. 'She is easily persuaded – for her good. Thank you, Mr Sampson; she is better within doors. The bathing-place was farther than I thought, to say the truth.'

'Miss Niner is very delicate,' I observed.

He shook his head and drew a deep sigh. 'Very, very, very. You may recollect my saying so. The time that has since intervened has not strengthened her. The gloomy shadow that fell upon her sister so early in life seems, in my anxious eyes, to gather over her, ever darker, ever darker. Dear Margaret, dear Margaret! But we must hope.'

The hand-carriage was spinning away before us at a most indecorous pace for an invalid vehicle, and was making most irregular curves upon the sand. Mr Slinkton, noticing it after he had put his handkerchief to his eyes, said; 'If I may judge from appearances, your friend will be upset, Mr Sampson.'

'It looks probable, certainly,' said I.

'The servant must be drunk.'

'The servants of old gentlemen will get drunk sometimes,' said I.

'The major draws very light, Mr Sampson.'

'The major does draw light,' said I.

By this time the carriage, much to my relief, was lost in the darkness. We walked on for a little, side by side over the sand, in silence. After a short while he said, in a voice still affected by the emotion that his niece's state of health had awakened in him, 'Do you stay here long, Mr Sampson?'

'Why, no. I am going away tonight.'

'So soon? But business always holds you in request. Men like Mr Sampson are too important to others, to be spared to their own need of relaxation and enjoyment.'

'I don't know about that,' said I. 'However, I am going back.'

'To London?'

'To London.'

'I shall be there too, soon after you.'

I knew that as well as he did. But I did not tell him so. Any more than I told him what defensive weapon my right hand rested on in my pocket, as I walked by his side. Any more than I told him why I did not walk on the sea side of him with the night closing in.

We left the beach, and our ways diverged. We exchanged Good-night, and had parted indeed, when he said, returning, 'Mr Sampson, *may* I ask? Poor Meltham, whom we spoke of – dead yet?'

'Not when I last heard of him; but too broken a man to live long, and hopelessly lost to his old calling.'

'Dear, dear, dear!' said he, with great feeling. 'Sad, sad, sad! The world is a grave!' And so went his way.

It was not his fault if the world were not a grave; but I did not call that observation after him, any more than I had mentioned those other things just now enumerated. He went his way, and I went mine with all expedition. This happened, as I have said, either at the end of September or beginning of October. The next time I saw him, and the last time, was late in November.

V.

I had a very particular engagement to breakfast in the Temple. It was a bitter north-easterly morning, and the sleet and slush lay inches deep in the streets. I could get no conveyance, and was soon wet to the knees; but I should have been true to that appointment, though I had to wade to it up to my neck in the same impediments.

The appointment took me to some chambers in the Temple. They were at the top of a lonely corner house overlooking the river. The name, *Mr Alfred Beckwith*, was painted on the outer door. On the door opposite, on the same landing, the name *Mr Julius Slinkton*.

The doors of both sets of chambers stood open, so that anything said aloud in one set could be heard in the other.

I had never been in those chambers before. They were dismal, close, unwholesome, and oppressive; the furniture, originally good, and not yet old, was faded and dirty – the rooms were in great disorder; there was a strong prevailing smell of opium, brandy, and tobacco; the grate and fire-irons were splashed all over with unsightly blotches of rust; and on a sofa by the fire, in the room where breakfast had been prepared, lay the host, Mr Beckwith, a man with all the appearances of the worst kind of drunkard, very far advanced upon his shameful way to death.

'Slinkton is not come yet,' said this creature, staggering up when I went in; 'I'll call him. Halloa! Julius Caesar! Come and drink!' As he hoarsely roared this out, he beat the poker and tongs together in a mad way, as if that were his usual manner of summoning his associate.

The voice of Mr Slinkton was heard through the clatter from the opposite side of the staircase, and he came in. He had not expected the pleasure of meeting me. I have seen several artful men brought to a stand, but I never saw a man so aghast as he was when his eyes rested on mine.

'Julius Caesar,' cried Beckwith, staggering between us, 'Mist' Sampson! Mist' Sampson, Julius Caesar! Julius, Mist' Sampson, is the friend of my soul. Julius keeps me plied with liquor, morning, noon, and night. Julius is a real benefactor. Julius threw the tea and coffee out of window when I used to have any. Julius empties all the water-jugs of their contents, and fills 'em with spirits. Julius winds me up and keeps me going. – Boil the brandy, Julius!'

There was a rusty and furred saucepan in the ashes – the ashes looked like the accumulation of weeks – and Beckwith, rolling and staggering between us as if he were going to plunge headlong into the fire, got the saucepan out, and tried to force it into Slinkton's hand.

'Boil the brandy, Julius Caesar! Come! Do your usual office. Boil the brandy!'

He became so fierce in his gesticulations with the saucepan, that I expected to see him lay open Slinkton's head with it. I therefore put out my hand to check him. He reeled back to the sofa, and sat there panting, shaking, and red-eyed, in his rags of dressing-gown, looking at us both. I noticed then that there was nothing to drink on the table but brandy, and nothing to eat but salted herrings, and a hot, sickly, highly-peppered stew.

'At all events, Mr Sampson,' said Slinkton, offering me the smooth gravel path for the last time, 'I thank you for interfering between me and this unfortunate man's violence. However you came here, Mr Sampson, or with whatever motive you came here, at least I thank you for that.'

'Boil the brandy,' muttered Beckwith.

Without gratifying his desire to know how I came there, I said, quietly, 'How is your niece, Mr Slinkton?'

He looked hard at me, and I looked hard at him.

'I am sorry to say, Mr Sampson, that my niece has proved treacherous and ungrateful to her best friend. She left me without a word of notice or explanation. She was misled, no doubt, by some designing rascal. Perhaps you may have heard of it.'

'I did hear that she was misled by a designing rascal. In fact, I have proof of it.'

'Are you sure of that?' said he.

'Quite.'

'Boil the brandy,' muttered Beckwith. 'Company to breakfast, Julius Caesar. Do your usual office – provide the usual breakfast, dinner, tea, and supper. Boil the brandy!'

The eyes of Slinkton looked from him to me, and he said, after a moment's consideration, 'Mr Sampson, you are a man of the world, and so am I. I will be plain with you.'

'Oh no, you won't,' said I, shaking my head.

'I tell you, sir, I will be plain with you.'

'And I tell you you will not,' said I. 'I know all about you. *You* plain with anyone? Nonsense, nonsense!'

'I plainly tell you, Mr Sampson,' he went on, with a manner almost composed, 'that I understand your object. You want to save your funds, and escape from your liabilities; these are old tricks of trade with you office gentlemen. But you will not do it, sir; you will not succeed. You have not an easy adversary to play against, when you play against me. We shall have to inquire, in due time, when and how Mr Beckwith fell into his present habits. With that remark, sir, I put this poor creature, and his incoherent wanderings of speech, aside, and wish you a good morning and a better case next time.'

While he was saying this, Beckwith had filled a half-pint glass with brandy. At this moment, he threw the brandy at his face, and threw the glass after it. Slinkton put his hands up, half blinded with the spirit, and cut with the glass across the forehead. At the sound of the breakage, a fourth person came into the room, closed the door, and stood at it; he was a very quiet but very keen-looking man, with iron-gray hair, and slightly lame.

Slinkton pulled out his handkerchief, assuaged the pain in his smarting eyes, and dabbled the blood on his forehead. He was a long time about it, and I saw that in the doing of it, a tremendous change came over him, occasioned by the change in Beckwith – who ceased to pant and tremble, sat upright, and never took his eyes off him. I never in my life saw a face in which abhorrence and determination were so forcibly painted as in Beckwith's then.

'Look at me, you villain,' said Beckwith, 'and see me as I really am. I took these rooms, to make them a trap for you. I came into them as a drunkard, to bait the trap for you. You fell into the trap, and you will never leave it alive. On the morning when you last went to Mr Sampson's office, I had seen him first Your plot has been known to both of us, all along, and you have been counter-plotted all along. What? Having been cajoled into putting that prize of two thousand pounds in your power, I was to be done to death with brandy, and, brandy not proving quick enough, with something quicker? Have I never seen you, when you thought my senses gone, pouring from your little bottle into my glass? Why, you murderer and forger, alone here with you in the dead of night, as I have so often been, I have had my hand upon the trigger of a pistol, twenty times, to blow your brains out!'

This sudden starting up of the thing that he had supposed to be his imbecile victim into a determined man, with a settled resolution to hunt him down and be the death of him, mercilessly expressed from head to foot, was, in the first shock, too much for him. Without any figure of speech, he staggered under it. But there is no greater mistake than to suppose that a man who is a calculating criminal, is, in any phase of his guilt, otherwise than true to himself, and perfectly consistent with his whole character. Such a man commits murder, and murder is the natural culmination of his course; such a man has to outface murder, and will do it with hardihood and effrontery. It is a sort of fashion to express surprise that any notorious criminal, having such crime upon his conscience, can so brave it out. Do you think that if he had it on his conscience at all, or had a conscience to have it upon, he would ever have committed the crime?

Perfectly consistent with himself, as I believe all such monsters to be, this Slinkton recovered himself, and showed a defiance that was sufficiently cold and quiet. He was white, he was haggard, he was changed; but only as a sharper who had played for a great stake and had been outwitted and had lost the game.

'Listen to me, you villain,' said Beckwith, 'and let every word you hear me say be a stab in your wicked heart. When I took these rooms, to throw myself in your way and lead you on to the scheme that I knew my appearance and supposed character and habits would suggest to such a devil, how did I know that? Because you were no stranger to me. I knew you well. And I knew you to be the cruel wretch who, for so much money, had killed one innocent girl while she trusted him implicitly, and who was by inches killing another.'

Slinkton took out a snuffbox, took a pinch of snuff, and laughed.

'But see here,' said Beckwith, never looking away, never raising his voice, never relaxing his face, never unclenching his hand.

'See what a dull wolf you have been, after all! The infatuated drunkard who never drank a fiftieth part of the liquor you plied him with, but poured it away, here, there, everywhere – almost before your eyes; who bought over the fellow you set to watch him and to ply him, by outbidding you in his bribe, before he had been at his work three days – with whom you have observed no caution, yet who was so bent on ridding the earth of you as a wild beast, that he would have defeated you if you had been ever so prudent – that drunkard whom you have, many a time, left on the floor of this room, and who has even let you go out of it, alive and undeceived, when you have turned him over with your foot – has, almost as often, on the same night, within an hour, within a few minutes, watched you awake, had his hand at your pillow when you were asleep, turned over your papers, taken samples from your bottles and packets of powder, changed their contents, rifled every secret of your life!'

He had had another pinch of snuff in his hand, but had gradually let it drop from between his fingers to the floor; where he now smoothed it out with his foot, looking down at it the while.

'That drunkard,' said Beckwith, 'who had free access to your rooms at all times, that he might drink the strong drinks that you left in his way and be the sooner ended, holding no more terms with you than he would hold with a tiger, has had his master-key for all your locks, his test for all your poisons, his clue to your cipher-writing. He can tell you, as well as you can tell him, how long it took to complete that deed, what doses there were, what intervals, what signs of gradual decay upon mind and body; what distempered fancies were produced, what observable changes, what physical pain.

He can tell you, as well as you can tell him, that all this was recorded day by day, as a lesson of experience for future service.

He can tell you, better than you can tell him, where that journal is at this moment.'

Slinkton stopped the action of his foot, and looked at Beckwith.

'No,' said the latter, as if answering a question from him. 'Not in the drawer of the writing-desk that opens with a spring; it is not there, and it never will be there again.'

'Then you are a thief!' said Slinkton.

Without any change whatever in the inflexible purpose, which it was quite terrific even to me to contemplate, and from the power of which I had always felt convinced it was impossible for this wretch to escape, Beckwith returned, 'And I am your niece's shadow, too.'

With an imprecation Slinkton put his hand to his head, tore out some hair, and flung it to the ground. It was the end of the smooth walk; he destroyed it in the action, and it will soon be seen that his use for it was past.

Beckwith went on: 'Whenever you left here, I left here. Although I understood that you found it necessary to pause in the completion of that purpose, to avert suspicion, still I watched you close, with the poor confiding girl. When I had the diary, and could read it word by word – it was only about the night before your last visit to Scarborough – you remember the night? you slept with a small flat vial tied to your wrist – I sent to Mr Sampson, who was kept out of view. This is Mr Sampson's trusty servant standing by the door. We three saved your niece among us.'

Slinkton looked at us all, took an uncertain step or two from the place where he had stood, returned to it, and glanced about him in a very curious way – as one of the meaner reptiles might, looking for a hole to hide in. I noticed at the same time, that a singular change took place in the figure of the man – as if it collapsed within his clothes, and they consequently became ill-shaped and ill-fitting.

'You shall know,' said Beckwith, 'for I hope the knowledge will be bitter and terrible to you, why you have been pursued by one man, and why, when the whole interest that Mr Sampson represents would have expended any money in hunting you down, you have been tracked to death at a single individual's charge. I hear you have had the name of Meltham on your lips sometimes?'

I saw, in addition to those other changes, a sudden stoppage come upon his breathing.

'When you sent the sweet girl whom you murdered (you know with what artfully made-out surroundings and probabilities you sent her) to Meltham's office, before taking her abroad to originate the transaction that doomed her to the grave, it fell to Meltham's lot to see her and to speak with her. It did not fall to his lot to save her, though I know he would freely give his own life to have done it. He admired her; I would say he loved her deeply, if I thought it possible that you could understand the word. When she was sacrificed, he was thoroughly assured of your guilt. Having lost her, he had but one object left in life, and that was to avenge her and destroy you.'

I saw the villain's nostrils rise and fall convulsively; but I saw no moving at his mouth.

'That man Meltham,' Beckwith steadily pursued, 'was as absolutely certain that you could never elude him in this world, if he devoted himself to your destruction with his utmost fidelity and earnestness, and if he divided the sacred duty with no other duty in life, as he was certain that in achieving it he would be a poor instrument in the hands of Providence, and would do well before Heaven in striking you out from among living men. I am that man, and I thank God that I have done my work!'

If Slinkton had been running for his life from swift-footed savages, a dozen miles, he could not have shown more emphatic signs of being oppressed at heart and labouring for breath, than he showed now, when he looked at the pursuer who had so relentlessly hunted him down.

'You never saw me under my right name before; you see me under my right name now. You shall see me once again in the body, when you are tried for your life. You shall see me once again in the spirit, when the cord is round your neck, and the crowd are crying against you!'

When Meltham had spoken these last words, the miscreant suddenly turned away his face, and seemed to strike his mouth with his open hand. At the same instant, the room was filled with a new and powerful odour, and, almost at the same instant, he broke into a crooked run, leap, start – I have no name for the spasm – and fell, with a dull weight that shook the heavy old doors and windows in their frames.

That was the fitting end of him.

When we saw that he was dead, we drew away from the room, and Meltham, giving me his hand, said, with a weary air, 'I have no more work on earth, my friend. But I shall see her again elsewhere.'

It was in vain that I tried to rally him. He might have saved her, he said; he had not saved her, and he reproached himself; he had lost her, and he was broken-hearted.

'The purpose that sustained me is over, Sampson, and there is nothing now to hold me to life. I am not fit for life; I am weak and spiritless; I have no hope and no object; my day is done.'

In truth, I could hardly have believed that the broken man who then spoke to me was the man who had so strongly and so differently impressed me when his purpose was before him. I used such entreaties with him, as I could; but he still said, and always said, in a patient, undemonstrative way – nothing could avail him – he was broken-hearted.

He died early in the next spring. He was buried by the side of the poor young lady for whom he had cherished those tender and unhappy regrets; and he left all he had to her sister. She lived to be a happy wife and mother; she married my sister's son, who succeeded poor Meltham; she is living now, and her children ride about the garden on my walking-stick when I go to see her.

MARK TWAIN

The Stolen White Elephant

THE FOLLOWING curious history was related to me by a chance
railway acquaintance. He was a gentleman more than seventy years
of age, and his thoroughly good and gentle face and earnest and
sincere manner imprinted the unmistakable stamp of truth upon
every statement which fell from his lips. He said:

You know in what reverence the royal white elephant of Siam is
held by the people of that country. You know it is sacred to kings,
only kings may possess it, and that it is, indeed, in a measure even
superior to kings, since it receives not merely honour but worship.
Very well; five years ago, when the troubles concerning the frontier
line arose between Great Britain and Siam, it was presently manifest
that Siam had been in the wrong. Therefore every reparation was
quickly made, and the British representative stated that he was satisfied and the past should be forgotten. This greatly relieved the King of
Siam, and partly as a token of gratitude, partly also, perhaps, to wipe
out any little remaining vestige of unpleasantness which England
might feel toward him, he wished to send the Queen a present – the
sole sure way of propitiating an enemy, according to Oriental ideas.
This present ought not only to be a royal one, but transcendently
royal. Wherefore, what offering could be so meet as that of a white
elephant? My position in the Indian civil service was such that I was
deemed peculiarly worthy of the honour of conveying the present to
her Majesty. A ship was fitted out for me and my servants and the
officers and attendants of the elephant, and in due time I arrived in
New York harbour and placed my royal charge in admirable quarters
in Jersey City. It was necessary to remain awhile in order to recruit,
the animal's health before resuming the voyage.

All went well during a fortnight – then my calamities began. The
white elephant was stolen! I was called up at dead of night and
informed of this fearful misfortune. For some moments I was beside
myself with terror and anxiety; I was helpless. Then I grew calmer
and collected my faculties. I soon saw my course – for, indeed, there
was but the one course for an intelligent man to pursue. Late as it
was, I flew to New York and got a policeman to conduct me to the

headquarters of the detective force. Fortunately I arrived in time, though the chief of the force, the celebrated Inspector Blunt was just on the point of leaving for his home. He was a man of middle size and compact frame, and when he was thinking deeply he had a way of knitting his brows and tapping his forehead reflectively with his finger, which impressed you at once with the conviction that you stood in the presence of a person of no common order. The very sight of him gave me confidence and made me hopeful.

I stated my errand. It did not flurry him in the least; it had no more visible effect upon his iron self-possession than if I had told him somebody had stolen my dog. He motioned me to a seat, and said, calmly:

'Allow me to think a moment, please.'

So saying, he sat down at his office table and leaned his head upon his hand. Several clerks were at work at the other end of the room; the scratching of their pens was all the sound I heard during the next six or seven minutes. Meantime the inspector sat there, buried in thought.

Finally he raised his head, and there was that in the firm lines of his face which showed me that his brain had done its work and his plan was made. Said he – and his voice was low and impressive:

'This is no ordinary case. Every step must be warily taken; each step must be made sure before the next is ventured. And secrecy must be observed – secrecy profound and absolute. Speak to no one about the matter, not even the reporters. I will take care of them; I will see that they get only what it may suit my ends to let them know.' He touched a bell; a youth appeared. 'Alaric, tell the reporters to remain for the present.' The boy retired. 'Now let us proceed to business – and systematically. Nothing can be accomplished in this trade of mine without strict and minute method.'

He took a pen and some paper. 'Now – name of the elephant?'

'Hassan Ben Ali Ben Selim Abdallah Mohammed Moist Alhammal Jamsetjejeebhoy Dhuleep Sultan Ebu Bhudpoor.'

'Very well. Given name?'

'Jumbo.'

'Very well. Place of birth?'

'The capital city of Siam.'

'Parents living?'

'No – dead.'

'Had they any other issue besides this one?'

'None. He was an only child.'

'Very well. These matters are sufficient under that head. Now please describe the elephant, and leave out no particular, however insignificant – that is, insignificant from your point of view. To me in my profession there are no insignificant particulars; they do not exist.'

I described, he wrote. When I was done, he said:

'Now listen. If I have made any mistakes, correct me.'

He read as follows:

'Height, 19 feet; length from apex of forehead insertion of tail, 26 feet; length of trunk, 16 feet; length of tail, 6 feet; total length, including trunk, and tail, 48 feet; length of tusks, 9´ feet; ears keeping with these dimensions; footprint resembles the mark left when one upends a barrel in the snow; the colour of the elephant, a dull white; has a hole the size of a plate in each ear for the insertion of jewellery and possesses the habit in a remarkable degree of squirting water upon spectators and of maltreating with his trunk not only such persons as he is acquainted with, but even entire strangers; limps slightly with his right hind leg, and has a small scar in his left armpit caused by a former boil; had on, when stolen, a castle containing seats for fifteen persons, and a gold-cloth saddle-blanket the size of an ordinary carpet.'

There were no mistakes. The inspector touched the bell, handed the description to Alaric, and said:

'Have fifty thousand copies of this printed at once and mailed to every detective office and pawnbroker's shop on the continent.' Alaric retired. 'There – so far, so good. Next, I must have a photograph of the property.'

I gave him one. He examined it critically, and said:

'It must do, since we can do no better; but he has his trunk curled up and tucked into his mouth. That is unfortunate, and is calculated to mislead, for of course he does not usually have it in that position.'

He touched his bell.

'Alaric, have 50,000 copies of this photograph made the first thing in the morning, and mail them with the descriptive circulars.'

Alaric retired to execute his orders. The inspector said:

'It will be necessary to offer a reward, of course. Now as to the amount?'

'What sum would you suggest?'

'To begin with, I should say, well, $25,000. It is an intricate and difficult business; there are a thousand avenues of escape and opportunities of concealment. These thieves have friends and pals everywhere.'

'Bless me, do you know who they are?'

The wary face, practised in concealing the thoughts and feelings within, gave me no token, nor yet the replying words, so quietly uttered:

'Never mind about that. I may, and I may not. We generally gather a pretty shrewd inkling of who our man is by the manner of his work and the size of the game he goes after. We are not dealing with a pickpocket or a hall thief now, make up your mind to that. This property was not "lifted" by a novice. But, as I was saying, considering the amount of travel which will have to be done, and the diligence with which the thieves will cover up their traces as they move along, twenty-five thousand may be too small a sum to offer, yet I think it worth while to start with that.'

So we determined upon that figure as a beginning. Then this man, whom nothing escaped which could by any possibility be made to serve as a clue, said:

'There are cases in detective history to show that criminals have been detected through peculiarities, in their appetites. Now, what does this elephant eat, and how much?'

'Well, as to what he eats – he will eat anything. He will eat a man, he will eat a Bible – he will eat anything between a man and a Bible.'

'Good, very good, indeed, but too general. Details are necessary – details are the only valuable things in our trade. Very well – as to men. At one meal – or, if you prefer, during one day – how man men will he eat, if fresh?'

'He would not care whether they were fresh or not; at a single meal he would eat five ordinary men.'

'Very good; five men; we will put that down. What nationalities would he prefer?'

'He is indifferent about nationalities. He prefers acquaintances, but is not prejudiced against strangers.'

'Very good. Now, as to Bibles. How many Bibles would he eat at a meal?'

'He would eat an entire edition.'

'It is hardly succinct enough. Do you mean the ordinary octavo, or the family illustrated?'

'I think he would be indifferent to illustrations that is, I think he would not value illustrations above simple letterpress.'

'No, you do not get my idea. I refer to bulk. The ordinary octavo Bible weighs about two pound and a half, while the great quarto with the illustrations weighs ten or twelve. How many Dore Bibles would he eat at a meal?'

'If you knew this elephant, you could not ask. He would take what they had.'

'Well, put it in dollars and cents, then. We must get at it somehow. The Dore costs $100 a copy, Russia leather, bevelled.'

'He would require about $50,000 worth – say an edition of five hundred copies.'

'Now that is more exact. I will put that down. Very well; he likes men and Bibles; so far, so good. What else will he eat? I want particulars.'

'He will leave Bibles to eat bricks, he will leave bricks to eat bottles, he will leave bottles to eat clothing, he will leave clothing to eat cats, he will leave cats to eat oysters, he will leave oysters to eat ham, he will leave ham to eat sugar, he will leave sugar to eat pie, he will leave pie to eat potatoes, he will leave potatoes to eat bran; he will leave bran to eat hay, he will leave hay to eat oats, he will leave oats to eat rice, for he was mainly raised on it. There is nothing whatever that he will not eat but European butter, and he would eat that if he could taste it.'

'Very good. General quantity at a meal – say about...'

'Well, anywhere from a quarter to half a ton.'

'And he drinks...'

'Everything that is fluid. Milk, water, whisky, molasses, castor oil, camphene, carbolic acid – it is no use to go into particulars; whatever fluid occurs to you set it down. He will drink anything that is fluid, except European coffee.'

'Very good. As to quantity?'

'Put it down five to fifteen barrels – his thirst varies; his other appetites do not.'

'These things are unusual. They ought to furnish quite good clues toward tracing him.'

He touched the bell.

'Alaric; summon Captain Burns.'

Burns appeared. Inspector Blunt unfolded the whole matter to him, detail by detail. Then he said in the clear, decisive tones of a man whose plans are clearly defined in his head and who is accustomed to command:

'Captain Burns, detail Detectives Jones, Davis, Halsey, Bates, and Hackett to shadow the elephant.'

'Yes, sir.'

'Detail Detectives Moses, Dakin, Murphy, Rogers, Tupper, Higgins, and Bartholomew to shadow the thieves.'

'Yes, sir.'

'Place a strong guard – a guard of thirty picked men, with a relief of thirty – over the place from whence the elephant was stolen, to keep strict watch there night and day, and allow none to approach – except reporters – without written authority from me.'

'Yes, sir.'

'Place detectives in plain clothes in the railway, steamship, and ferry depots, and upon all roadways leading out of Jersey City, with orders to search all suspicious persons.'

'Yes, sir.'

'Furnish all these men with photograph and accompanying description of the elephant, and instruct them to search all trains and outgoing ferryboats and other vessels.'

'Yes, sir.'

'If the elephant should be found, let him be seized, and the information forwarded to me by telegraph.'

'Yes, sir.'

'Let me be informed at once if any clues should be found: footprints of the animal, or anything of that kind.'

'Yes, sir.'

'Get an order commanding the harbour police to patrol the frontages vigilantly.'

'Yes, sir.'

'Despatch detectives in plain clothes over all the railways, north as far as Canada, west as far as Ohio, south as far as Washington.'

'Yes, sir.'

'Place experts in all the telegraph offices to listen in to all messages; and let them require that all cipher despatches be interpreted to them.'

'Yes, sir.'

'Let all these things be done with the utmost's secrecy – mind, the most impenetrable secrecy.'

'Yes, sir.'

'Report to me promptly at the usual hour.'

'Yes, sir.'

'Go!'

'Yes, sir.'

He was gone.

Inspector Blunt was silent and thoughtful a moment, while the fire in his eye cooled down and faded out. Then he turned to me and said in a placid voice:

'I am not given to boasting, it is not my habit; but – we shall find the elephant.'

I shook him warmly by the hand and thanked him; and I felt my thanks, too. The more I had seen of the man the more I liked him and the more I admired him and marvelled over the mysterious wonders of his profession.

Then we parted for the night, and I went home with a far happier heart than I had carried with me to his office.

II.

Next morning it was all in the newspapers, in the minutest detail. It even had additions – consisting of Detective This, Detective That, and Detective The Other's 'Theory' as to how the robbery was done, who the robbers were, and whither they had flown with their booty. There were eleven of these theories, and they covered all the possibilities; and this single fact shows what independent thinkers detectives are. No two theories were alike, or even much resembled each other, save in one striking particular, and in that one all the other eleven theories were absolutely agreed. That was, that although the rear of my building was torn out and the only door remained locked, the elephant had not been removed through the rent, but by some other (undiscovered) outlet.

All agreed that the robbers had made that rent only to mislead the detectives. That never would have occurred to me or to any other layman, perhaps, but it had not deceived the detectives for a moment. Thus, what I had supposed was the only thing that had no mystery about it was in fact the very thing I had gone furthest astray in. The eleven theories all named the supposed robbers, but no two named the same robbers; the total number of suspected persons was thirty-seven. The various newspaper accounts all closed with the most important opinion of all – that of Chief Inspector Blunt. A portion of this statement read as follows:

The Chief knows who the two principals are, namely, 'Brick' Daffy and 'Red' McFadden. Ten days before the robbery was achieved he was already aware that it was to be attempted, and had quietly proceeded to shadow these two noted villains; but unfortunately on the night in question their track was lost, and before it could be found again the bird was flown – that is, the elephant.

Daffy and McFadden are the boldest scoundrels in the profession; the Chief has reasons for believing that they are the men who stole the stove out of the detective headquarters on a bitter night last winter – in consequence of which the Chief and every detective present were in the hands of the physicians before morning, some with frozen feet, others with frozen fingers, ears, and other members.

When I read the first half of that I was more astonished than ever at the wonderful sagacity of this strange man. He not only saw everything in the present with a clear eye, but even the future could not be hidden from him. I was soon at his office, and said I could not help wishing he had had those men arrested, and so prevented the trouble and loss; but his reply was simple and unanswerable:

'It is not our province to prevent crime, but to punish it. We cannot punish it until it is committed.'

I remarked that the secrecy with which we had begun had been marred by the newspapers; not only all our facts but all our plans and purposes had been revealed; even all the suspected persons had been named; these would doubtless disguise themselves now, or go into hiding.

'Let them. They will find that when I am ready for them my hand will descend upon them, in their secret places, as unerringly as the hand of fate. As to the newspapers, we must keep in with them. Fame, reputation, constant public mention – these are the detective's bread and butter. He must publish his facts, else he will be supposed to have none; he must publish his theory, for nothing is so strange or striking as a detective's theory, or brings him so much wonderful respect; we must publish our plans, for these the journals insist upon having, and we could not deny them without offending. We must constantly show the public what we are doing, or they will believe we are doing nothing.

It is much pleasanter to have a newspaper say, 'Inspector Blunt's ingenious and extraordinary theory is as follows,' than to have it say some harsh thing, or, worse still, some sarcastic one.'

'I see the force of what you say. But I noticed that in one part of your remarks in the papers this morning you refused to reveal your opinion upon a certain minor point.'

'Yes, we always do that; it has a good effect. Besides, I had not formed any opinion on that point, anyway.'

I deposited a considerable sum of money with the inspector, to meet current expenses, and sat down to wait for news. We were expecting the telegrams to begin to arrive at any moment now. Meantime I reread the newspapers and also our descriptive circular, and observed that our $25,000 reward seemed to be offered only to detectives. I said I thought it ought to be offered to anybody who would catch the elephant. The inspector said:

'It is the detectives who will find the elephant; hence the reward will go to the right place. If other people found the animal, it would only be by watching the detectives and taking advantage of clues and indications stolen from them, and that would entitle the detectives to the reward, after all. The proper office of a reward is to stimulate the men who deliver up their time and their trained sagacities to this sort of work, and not to confer benefits upon chance citizens who stumble upon a capture without having earned the benefits by their own merits and labours.'

This was reasonable enough, certainly. Now the telegraphic machine in the corner began to click, and the following despatch was the result:

> FLOWER STATION, NY, 7.30 AM.
>
> Have got a clue. Found a succession of deep tracks across a farm near here. Followed them two miles east without result; think elephant went west. Shall now shadow him in that direction.
>
> DARLEY, Detective.

'Darley's one of the best men on the force,' said the inspector. 'We shall hear from him again before long.'

Telegram number two came:

> BARKER'S, NJ, 7.40 AM.
>
> Just arrived. Glass factory broken open here during night, and eight hundred bottles taken. Only water in large quantity near here is five miles distant. Shall strike for there. Elephant will be thirsty. Bottles were empty.
>
> DARLEY, Detective.

'That promises well, too,' said the inspector.

I told you the creature's appetites would not be bad clues.'

Telegram number three:

> TAYLORVILLE, LI, 8.15 AM.
>
> A haystack near here disappeared during night. Probably eaten. Have got a clue, and am off.
>
> HUBBARD, Detective.

'How he does move around!' said the inspector. 'I knew we had a difficult job on hand, but we shall catch him yet.'

> FLOWER STATION, NY, 9 AM.
>
> Shadowed the tracks three miles westward. Large, deep, and ragged.
>
> Have just met a farmer who says they are not elephant-tracks.
> Says they are holes where he dug up saplings for shade-trees

when ground was frozen last winter. Give me orders how to proceed.

DARLEY, Detective.

'Aha! a confederate of the thieves! The thing, grows warm,' said the inspector.

He dictated the following telegram to Darley:

Arrest the man and force him to name his pals. Continue to follow the tracks to the Pacific, if necessary. Chief BLUNT.

Next telegram:

CONEY POINT, PA., 8.45 AM.

Gas office broken open here during night and three month's unpaid gas bills taken. Have got a clue and am away.

MURPHY, Detective.

'Heavens!' said the inspector; 'would he eat gas bills?'

'Through ignorance – yes; but they cannot support life. At least, unassisted.'

Now came this exciting telegram:

IRONVILLE, NY, 9.30 AM.

Just arrived. This village in consternation. Elephant passed through here at five this morning. Some say he went east some say west, some north, some south – but all say they did not wait to notice, particularly. He killed a horse; have secured a piece of it for a clue. Killed it with his trunk; from style of blow, think he struck it left-handed. From position in which horse lies, think elephant travelled northward along line Berkley Railway. Has four and a half hours' start, but I move on his track at once.

HAWES, Detective

I uttered exclamations of joy. The inspector was as self-contained as a graven image. He calmly touched his bell.

'Alaric, send Captain Burns here.'

Burns appeared.

'How many men are ready for instant orders?'

'Ninety-six, sir.'

'Send them north at once. Let them concentrate along the line of the Berkley road north of Ironville.'

'Yes, sir.'

'Let them conduct their movements with the utmost secrecy. As fast as others are at liberty, hold them for orders.'

'Yes, sir.'

'Go!'

'Yes, sir.'

Presently came another telegram:

SAGE CORNERS, NY, 10.30.

Just arrived. Elephant passed through here at 8.15. All escaped from the town but a policeman. Apparently elephant did not strike at policeman, but at the lamppost. Got both. I have secured a portion of the policeman as clue.

STUMM, Detective.

'So the elephant has turned westward,' said the inspector. 'However, he will not escape, for my men are scattered all over that region.'

The next telegram said:

GLOVER'S, 11.15

Just arrived. Village deserted, except sick and aged. Elephant passed through three-quarters of an hour ago. The anti-temperance mass-meeting was in session; he put his trunk in at a window and washed it out with water from cistern. Some swallowed it - since dead; several drowned.

Detectives Cross and O'Shaughnessy were passing through town, but going south - so missed elephant. Whole region for many miles around in terror - people flying from their homes. Wherever they turn they meet elephant, and many are killed.

BRANT, Detective.

I could have shed tears, this havoc so distressed me. But the inspector only said:

'You see – we are closing in on him. He feels our presence; he has turned eastward again.'

Yet further troublous news was in store for us. The telegraph brought this:

HOGANSPORT, 12.19.

Just arrived. Elephant passed through half an hour ago, creating wildest fright and excitement. Elephant raged around streets; two plumbers going by, killed one - other escaped. Regret general.

O'FLAHERTY, Detective.

'Now he is right in the midst of my men,' said the inspector. 'Nothing can save him.'

A succession of telegrams came from detectives who were scattered through New Jersey and Pennsylvania, and who were following clues consisting of ravaged barns, factories, and Sunday-school libraries, with high hopes-hopes amounting to certainties, indeed.

The inspector said:

'I wish I could communicate with them and order them north, but that is impossible. A detective only visits a telegraph office to send his report; then he is off again, and you don't know where to put your hand on him.'

Now came this despatch:

BRIDGEPORT, CT, 12.15.

Barnum offers rate of $4,000 a year for exclusive privilege of using elephant as travelling advertising medium from now till detectives find him. Wants to paste circus-posters on him. Desires immediate answer.

BOGGS, Detective.

'That is perfectly absurd!' I exclaimed.

'Of course it is,' said the inspector. 'Evidently Mr Barnum, who thinks he is so sharp, does not know me – but I know him.'

Then he dictated this answer to the despatch:

Mr Barnum's offer declined. Make it $7,000 or nothing.

Chief BLUNT.

'There. We shall not have to wait long for an answer. Mr Barnum is not at home; he is in the telegraph office – it is his way when he has business on hand. Inside of three—'

Done. – PT BARNUM.

So interrupted the clicking telegraphic instrument. Before I could make a comment upon this extraordinary episode, the following despatch carried my thoughts into another and very distressing channel:

BOLIVIA, NY, 12.50.

Elephant arrived here from the south and passed through toward the forest at 11.50, dispersing a funeral on the way, and diminishing the mourners by two. Citizens fired some small cannonballs into him, and they fled. Detective Burke and I arrived ten minutes later, from the north, but mistook some excavations for footprints, and so lost a good deal of time; but at last we struck the right trail and followed it to the woods. We then got down on our hands and knees and continued to keep a sharp eye on the track, and so shadowed it into the brush. Burke was in advance. Unfortunately the animal had stopped to rest; therefore, Burke having his head down, intent upon the track, butted up against the elephant's hind legs before he was aware of his vicinity. Burke instantly arose to his feet, seized the tail, and exclaimed joyfully,

'I claim the re—' but got no further, for a single blow of
the huge trunk laid the brave fellow's fragments low in
death. I fled rearward, and the elephant turned and shadowed
me to the edge of the wood, making tremendous speed, and I
should inevitably have been lost, but that the remains of the
funeral providentially intervened again and diverted his
attention. I have just learned that nothing of that funeral
is now left; but this is no loss, for there is abundance of
material for another. Meantime, the elephant has disappeared
again.

MULROONEY, Detective.

We heard no news except from the diligent and confident detectives scattered about New Jersey, Pennsylvania, Delaware, and Vir-
ginia – who were all following fresh and encouraging clues – until
shortly after 2PM, when this telegram came:

BAXTER CENTRE, 2.15.

Elephant been here, plastered over with circus-bills, and
broke up a revival, striking down and damaging many who were
on the point of entering upon a better life. Citizens penned
him up and established a guard. When Detective Brown and I
arrived, some time after, we entered enclosure and proceeded
to identify elephant by photograph and description. All masks
tallied exactly except one, which we could not see – the
boil-scar under armpit. To make sure, Brown crept under to
look, and was immediately brained – that is, head crushed and
destroyed, though nothing issued from debris. All fled, so did
elephant, striking right and left with much effect. He
escaped, but left bold blood-track from cannon-wounds.
Rediscovery certain. He broke southward, through a dense
forest.

BRENT, Detective.

That was the last telegram. At nightfall a fog shut down which
was so dense that objects but three feet away could not be discerned.
This lasted all night. The ferryboats and even the omnibuses had to
stop running.

III.

Next morning the papers were as full of detective theories as before;
they had all our tragic facts in detail also, and a great many more
which they had received from their telegraphic correspondents.
Column after column was occupied, a third of its way down, with

glaring headlines, which it made my heart sick to read. Their general tone was like this:

THE WHITE ELEPHANT AT LARGE! HE MOVES UPON HIS FATAL MARCH WHOLE VILLAGES DESERTED BY THEIR FRIGHT-STRICKEN OCCUPANTS! PALE TERROR GOES BEFORE HIM, DEATH AND DEVASTA-TION FOLLOW AFTER! AFTER THESE, THE DETEC-TIVES! BARNS DESTROYED, FACTORIES GUTTED, HARVESTS DEVOURED, PUBLIC ASSEMBLAGES DIS-PERSED, ACCOMPANIED BY SCENES OF CARNAGE IMPOSSIBLE TO DESCRIBE! THEORIES OF THIRTY-FOUR OF THE MOST DISTINGUISHED DETECTIVES ON THE FORCES! THEORY OF CHIEF BLUNT!

'There!' said Inspector Blunt, almost betrayed into excitement, 'this is magnificent! This is the greatest windfall that any detective organisation ever had. The fame of it will travel to the ends of the earth, and endure to the end of time, and my name with it.'

But there was no joy for me. I felt as if I had committed all those red crimes, and that the elephant was only my irresponsible agent. And how the list had grown! In one place he had 'interfered with an election and killed five repeaters'. He had followed this act with the destruction of two poor fellows, named O'Donohue and McFlanni-gan, who had 'found a refuge in the home of the oppressed of all lands only the day before, and were in the act of exercising for the first time the noble right of American citizens at the polls, when stricken down by the relentless hand of the Scourge of Siam'. In another, he had 'found a crazy sensation-preacher preparing his next season's heroic attacks on the dance, the theatre, and other things which can't strike back, and had stepped on him'. And in still another place he had 'killed a lightning-rod agent'.

And so the list went on, growing redder and redder, and more and more heartbreaking. Sixty persons had been killed, and two hundred and forty wounded. All the accounts bore just testimony to the activ-ity and devotion of the detectives, and all closed with the remark that 'three hundred thousand citizen; and four detectives saw the dread creature, and two of the latter he destroyed.'

I dreaded to hear the telegraphic instrument begin to click again.

By and by the messages began to pour in, but I was happily disap-pointed in they nature. It was soon apparent that all trace of the ele-phant was lost. The fog had enabled him to search out a good hiding-place unobserved. Telegrams from the most absurdly distant points reported that a dim vast mass had been glimpsed there through the fog at such and such an hour, and was 'undoubtedly the elephant.' This dim vast mass had been glimpsed in New Haven, in New Jersey, in Pennsylvania, in interior New York, in Brooklyn, and even in the city of New York itself! But in all cases the dim vast mass had vanished quickly and left no trace.

Every detective of the large force scattered over this huge extent of country sent his hourly report, and each and every one of them had a clue, and was shadowing something, and was hot upon the heels of it.

But the day passed without other result.

The next day the same.

The next just the same.

The newspaper reports began to grow monotonous with facts that amounted to nothing, clues which led to nothing, and theories which had nearly exhausted the elements which surprise and delight and dazzle.

By advice of the inspector I doubled the reward.

Four more dull days followed. Then came a bitter blow to the poor, hardworking detectives – the journalists declined to print their theories, and coldly said, 'Give us a rest.'

Two weeks after the elephant's disappearance I raised the reward to $75,000 by the inspector's advice. It was a great sum, but I felt that I would rather sacrifice my whole private fortune than lose my credit with my government. Now that the detectives were in adversity, the newspapers turned upon them, and began to fling the most stinging sarcasms at them. This gave the minstrels an idea, and they dressed themselves as detectives and hunted the elephant on the stage in the most extravagant way. The caricaturists made pictures of detectives scanning the country with spyglasses, while the elephant, at their backs, stole apples out of their pockets. And they made all sorts of ridiculous pictures of the detective badge – you have seen that badge printed in gold on the back of detective novels, no doubt it is a wide-staring eye, with the legend: 'WE NEVER SLEEP.' When detectives called for a drink, the would-be facetious barkeeper resurrected an obsolete form of expression and said, 'Will you have an eye-opener?'

All the air was thick with sarcasms.

But there was one man who moved calm, untouched, unaffected, through it all. It was that heart of oak, the Chief inspector. His brave eye never drooped, his serene confidence never wavered. He always said:

'Let them rail on; he laughs best who laughs last.'

My admiration for the man grew into a species of worship. I was at his side always. His office had become an unpleasant place to me, and now became daily more and more so. Yet if he could endure it I meant to do so also – at least, as long as I could. So I came regularly, and stayed – the only outsider who seemed to be capable of it. Everybody wondered how I could; and often it seemed to me that I must desert, but at such times I looked into that calm and apparently unconscious face, and held my ground.

About three weeks after the elephant's disappearance I was about to say, one morning, that I should have to strike my colours and retire, when the great detective arrested the thought by proposing one more superb and masterly move.

This was to compromise with the robbers. The fertility of this man's invention exceeded anything I have ever seen, and I have had a wide intercourse with the world's finest minds. He said he was confident he could compromise for $100,000 and recover the elephant. I said I believed I could scrape the amount together, but what would become of the poor detectives who had worked so faithfully? He said:

'In compromises they always get half.'

This removed my only objection. So the inspector wrote two notes, in this form:

DEAR MADAM, - Your husband can make a large sum of money (and be entirely protected from the law) by making an immediate, appointment with me. Chief BLUNT.

He sent one of these by his confidential messenger to the 'reputed wife' of Brick Duffy, and the other to the reputed wife of Red McFadden.

Within the hour these offensive answers came:

YE OWLD FOOL: brick Duffys bin ded 2 yere. BRIDGET MAHONEY.

CHIEF BAT, - Red McFadden is hung and in heving 18 month. Any Ass but a detective know that. MARY O'HOOLIGAN.

'I had long suspected these facts,' said the inspector; 'this testimony proves the unerring accuracy of my instinct.'

The moment one resource failed him he was ready with another. He immediately wrote an advertisement for the morning papers, and I kept a copy of it:

A. – xWhlv. 242 ht. Tjnd-fz328wmlg. Ozpo, – 2 m! 2m!. M! ogw.

He said that if the thief was alive this would bring him to the usual rendezvous. He further explained that the usual rendezvous was a glare where all business affairs between detectives and criminals were conducted. This meeting would take place at twelve the next night.

We could do nothing till then, and I lost no time in getting out of the office, and was grateful indeed for the privilege.

At eleven the next night I brought $100,000 in banknotes and put them into the Chief's hands, and shortly afterward he took his leave, with the brave old undimmed confidence in his eye.

An almost intolerable hour dragged to a close; then I heard his welcome tread, and rose gasping and tottered to meet him. How his fine eyes flamed with triumph! He said:

'We've compromised! The jokers will sing a different tune tomorrow! Follow me!'

He took a lighted candle and strode down into the vast vaulted basement where sixty detectives always slept, and where a score were now playing cards to while the time. I followed close after him. He walked swiftly down to the dim and remote end of the place, and just as I succumbed to the pangs of suffocation and was swooning away he stumbled and fell over the outlying members of a mighty object, and I heard him exclaim as he went down:

'Our noble profession is vindicated. Here is your elephant!'

I was carried to the office above and restored with carbolic acid. The whole detective force swarmed in, and such another season of triumphant rejoicing ensued as I had never witnessed before. The reporters were called, baskets of champagne were opened, toasts were drunk, the handshakings and congratulations were continuous and enthusiastic.

Naturally the Chief was the hero of the hour, and his happiness was so complete and had been so patiently and worthily and bravely won that it made me happy to see it, though I stood there a homeless beggar, my priceless charge dead, and my position in my country's service lost to me through what would always seem my fatally careless execution of a great trust. Many an eloquent eye testified its deep admiration for the Chief, and many a detective's voice murmured, 'Look at him – just the king of the profession; only give him a clue, it's all he wants, and there ain't anything hid that he can't find.' The dividing of the $50,000 made great pleasure; when it was finished the Chief made a little speech while he put his share in his pocket, in which he said, 'Enjoy it, boys, for you've earned it; and, more than that, you've earned for the detective profession undying fame.'

A telegram arrived, which read:

MONROE, MICH, 10 PM.

First time I've struck a telegraph office in over three weeks. Have followed those footprints, horseback, through the woods, a thousand miles to here, and they get stronger and bigger and fresher every day. Don't worry - inside of another week I'll have the elephant. This is dead sure.

DARLEY, Detective.

The Chief ordered three cheers for 'Darley, one of the finest minds on the force,' and then commanded that he be telegraphed to come home and receive his share of the reward.

So ended that marvellous episode of the stolen elephant. The newspapers were pleasant with praises once more, the next day, with one contemptible exception. This sheet said, 'Great is the detective! He may be a little slow in finding a little thing like a mislaid elephant he may hunt him all day and sleep with his rotting carcass all night for three weeks, but he will find him at last if he can get the man who mislaid him to show him the place!'

Poor Hassan was lost to me forever. The cannon shots had wounded him fatally, he had crept to that unfriendly place in the fog, and there, surrounded by his enemies and in constant danger of detection, he had wasted away with hunger and suffering till death gave him peace.

The compromise cost me $100,000; my detective expenses were $42,000 more; I never applied for a place again under my government; I am a ruined man and a wanderer on the earth but my admiration for that man, whom I believe to be the greatest detective the world has ever produced, remains undimmed to this day, and will so remain unto the end.

GRANT ALLEN

Jerry Stokes

JERRY STOKES was a member of Her Majesty's civil service. To put it more plainly, he was the provincial hangman. Not a man in all Canada, he used to boast with pardonable professional pride, had turned off as many famous murderers as he had. He was a pillar of the constitution, was Jerry Stokes. He represented the Executive. And he wasn't ashamed of his office, either. Quite on the contrary, zeal for his vocation shone visible in his face. He called it a useful, a respectable, and a necessary calling. If it were not for him and his utensils, he loved to say to the gaping crowd that stood him treat in the saloons, no man's life would be safe for a day in the province. He was a practical philanthropist in his way, a public benefactor. It is not good that foul crime should stalk unpunished through the land; and he, Jerry Stokes, was there to prevent it. He was the chosen instrument for its salutary repression:

Executions performed with punctuality and despatch; for terms, apply to Jeremiah Stokes, Port Hope, Ontario.

Not that philanthropy was the most salient characteristic in Jerry's outer man. He was a short and thickset person, very burly and dogged looking; he had a massive, square head, and a powerful jaw, and a coarse bull neck, and a pair of stout arms, acquired in the lumber trade, but forcibly suggestive of a prize-fighter's occupation. Except on the subject of the Executive, he was a taciturn soul; he had nothing to say, and he said it briefly. Silence, stolidity, and a marked capacity for the absorption of liquids without detriment to his centre of gravity, physical or mental, were the leading traits in Mr Stokes' character. Those who knew him well, however, affirmed that Jerry was 'a straight man'; and though the security was perhaps a trifle doubtful, 'a straight man' nevertheless he was generally considered by all who had the misfortune to require his services.

It was a principle with Jerry never to attend a trial for murder. This showed his natural delicacy of feeling. Etiquette, I believe, forbids an undertaker to make kind inquiries at the door of a dying person. It is feared the object of his visits might be misunderstood; he might be considered to act from interested motives. A similar and equally creditable scruple restrained Jerry Stokes from putting in an appearance at a court of justice when a capital charge was under investigation. People might think, he said, he was on the lookout for a job. Nay, more; his presence might even interfere with the administration of justice; for if the jury had happened to spot him in the body of the hall, it would naturally prejudice them in the prisoner's favour. To prevent such a misfortune – which would of course, incidentally, be bad for trade – Mr Stokes denied himself the congenial pleasure of following out in detail the cases on which he might in the end be called upon to operate – except through the medium of the public press. He was a kind-hearted man, his friends averred; and he knew that his presence in court might be distasteful to the prisoner and the prisoner's relations. Though, to say the truth, in thus absenting himself, Mr Stokes was exercising considerable self-denial; for to a hangman, even more than to all the rest of the world, a good first-class murder case is replete with plot interest.

Every man, however, is guilty at some time or other in his life of a breach of principle; and once, though only once, in his professional experience, Jerry Stokes, like the rest of us, gave way to temptation. To err is human; Jerry erred by attending a capital trial in Kingston courthouse. The case was one that aroused immense attention at the time in the Dominion. A young lawyer at Napanee, it was said, had poisoned his wife to inherit her money, and public feeling ran fierce and strong against him. From the very first, this dead set of public opinion brought out Jerry Stokes' sympathy in the prisoner's favour. The crowd had tried to mob Ogilvy – that was the man's name – on his way from his house to jail, and again on his journey from Napanee to Kingston assizes. Men shook their fists angrily in the face of the accused; women surged around with deep cries, and strove to tear him to pieces. The police with difficulty prevented the swaying mass from lynching him on the spot. Jerry Stokes, who was present, looked on at these irregular proceedings with a disapproving eye. Most unconstitutional, to dismember a culprit by main force, without form of trial, instead of handing him over in due course of law to be properly turned off by the appointed officer!

So when the trial came, Jerry Stokes, in defiance of established etiquette, took his stand in court, and watched the progress of the case with profound interest.

The public recognised him, and nudged one another, well pleased. Farmers had driven in with their wagons from the townships. All

Ontario was agog. People stared at Jerry, and then at the prisoner. 'Stokes is looking out for him!' they chuckled in their satisfaction. 'He's got no chance. He'll never get off. The hangman's in waiting!'

The suspected man took his place in the dock. Jerry Stokes glanced across at him – rubbed his eyes – thought it curious. 'Well, I never saw a murderer like him in my born days afore,' Jerry philosophised to himself. 'I've turned off square dozens of 'em in my time, in the province; and I know their looks. But hanged if I've ever come across a murderer like this one, any way!'

'Richard Ogilvy, stand up; are you guilty or not guilty?' asked the clerk of assigns.

And the prisoner, leaning forward, in a very low voice, but clear and distinct, answered out, 'Not guilty!'

He was a tall and delicate palefaced man, with thoughtful grey eyes and a high white forehead. But to Jerry Stokes' experienced gaze all that counted for nothing. He knew his patients well enough to know there are murderers and murderers, the refined and educated as well as the coarse and brutal. Why, he'd turned off square dozens of them, and both sorts, too, equally. No; it wasn't that and he couldn't say what it was but as Richard Ogilvy answered 'Not guilty' that morning a thrill ran cold down the hangman's back. He was sure it was true: he felt intuitively certain of it.

From that moment forth, Jerry followed the evidence with the closest interest. He leaned forward in his place, and drank it all in anxiously. People who sat near him remarked that his conduct was disgusting. He was thirsting for a conviction. It was ghastly to see the hangman so intent upon his prey. He seemed to hang on the lips of the witness for the prosecution.

But Jerry himself sat on, all unconscious of their criticism. For the very first time in his life, he forgot his trade. He remembered only that a human soul was at stake that day, and that in one glimpse of intuition he had seen its innocence.

Counsel for the Crown piled up a cumulative case, very strong and conclusive against the man Ogilvy. They showed that the prisoner had lived on bad terms with his wife – though through whose fault they had lived so, whether his or hers, wasn't very apparent. They showed that scenes had lately occurred between them. They showed that Ogilvy had bought poison at a chemist's in Kingston on the usual plea, 'to get rid of the rats'. They showed that Mrs Ogilvy had died of such poison. Their principal witness was the Napanee doctor, a man named Wade, who attended the deceased in her fatal illness. This doctor was intelligent, and frank, and straightforward; he gave his evidence in the most admirable style – evidence that told dead against the prisoner in every way. At the close of the case for the Crown, the game was up; everybody in court said all was finished: impossible for Ogilvy to rebut such a mass of damning evidence.

Everybody in court – except Jerry Stokes. And Jerry Stokes went home – for it was a two days' trial – much concerned in soul about Richard Ogilvy.

It was something new for Jerry Stokes, this disinterested interest in an accused criminal; and it took hold of him with all the binding and compelling force of a novel emotion. He wrestled and strained with it. All night long he lay awake, and tossed and turned on his bed, and thought of Richard Ogilvy's pale white face, as he stood there, a picture of mute agony, in the courthouse. Strange thoughts surged up thick in Jerry Stokes' soul, that had surged up in no other soul among all those actively hostile spectators. The silent suffering in the man's grey eyes had stirred him deeply. A thousand times over, Jerry said to himself, as he tossed and turned, 'That man never done it'. Now and again he dozed off, and awoke with a start, and each time he woke he found himself muttering in his sleep, with all the profound force of unreasoned conviction, 'He never done it! He never done it!'

Next morning, as soon as the court was open, Jerry Stokes was in his place again, craning his bull neck eagerly. All day long he craned that bull neck and listened. The public was scandalised now. Jerry Stokes in court! He ought to have kept away! This was really atrocious!

Evidence for the defence hung fire sadly. To say the truth, Ogilvy's counsel had no defence at all to offer, except an assurance that he didn't do it. They confined themselves to suggesting a possible alternative here, and a possible alternative there. Mrs Ogilvy might have taken the rat poison by mistake; or this person might have given it her somehow unawares, or that person might have had some unknown grudge against her. Jerry Stokes sat and listened with a sickening heart. The man in the dock was innocent, he felt sure; but the case – why, the case was going dead against him.

Slowly, as he listened, an idea began to break in upon Jerry Stokes' mind. Ideas didn't often come his way. He was a thick-headed man, little given to theories, and he didn't know even now it was a theory he was forming. He only knew this was the way the case impressed him.

The prisoner at the bar had never done it. But there had been scenes in his house, scenes brought about by Mrs Ogilvy's conduct. Mrs Ogilvy, he felt confident from the evidence he heard, had been given to drink – perhaps to other things; and the prisoner, for his child's sake (he had one little girl of three years old), was anxious to screen his wife's shame from the public. So he had suggested but little in this direction to his counsel. The scenes, however, were not of his making, and he certainly never meant to poison the woman. Jerry Stokes watched him closely as each witness stood up and told his tale, and he was confident of so much. That twitching of the lips was no murderer's trick. It was the plain emotion of an honest man who sees the circumstances unaccountably turning against him.

There was another person in court who watched the case almost as closely as Jerry himself, and that person was the doctor who attended Mrs Ogilvy and made the post mortem. His steely grey eyes were fixed with a frank stare on each witness as he detailed his story; and from time to time he gave a little satisfied gasp, when anything went obviously against the prisoner's chances. Jerry was too much occupied, however, for the most part, in watching the man in the dock to have any time left for watching the doctor. Once only he raised his eyes and caught the other's. It was at a critical moment. A witness for the defence, under severe cross-examination, had just admitted a most damaging fact that told hard against Ogilvy. Then the doctor smiled. It was a sinister smile, a smile of malice, a smile of mute triumph. No one else noticed it. But Jerry Stokes, looking up, observed it with a start. A shade passed over his square face like a sudden cloud. He knew that smile well. It was a typical murderer's.

'Mind you,' Jerry said to himself, as he watched the smile die away, 'I don't pretend to be as smart a chap as all these crack lawyer fellows, but I'm a straight man in my way, and I know my business. If that doctor ain't got a murderer's face on his front, my name isn't Jeremiah Stokes; that's the long and the short of it.'

He looked hard at the prisoner, he looked hard at the doctor. The longer and harder he looked, the more he was sure of it. He was an expert in murderers, and he knew his men. Ogilvy hadn't done it; Ogilvy couldn't do it; the doctor might; the doctor was, at any rate, a potential murderer. Not that Jerry put it to himself quite so fine as that; he contented himself with saying in his own dialect, 'The doctor was one of 'em.'

Evidence, however, went all against the prisoner, and the judge, to Jerry's immense surprise, summed up upon nothing except the evidence. Nobody in court, indeed, seemed to think of anything else.

Jerry rubbed his eyes once more. He couldn't understand it. Why, they were going to hang the man on nothing at all but the paltry evidence! Professional as he was, it surprised him to find a man could swing on so little! To think that our lives should depend on such a thread! Just the gossip of nurses and the tittle-tattle of a doctor with a smile like a murderer's!

At last the jury retired to consider their verdict. But they were not gone long. The case, said everybody, was as clear as daylight. In the public opinion it was a foregone conclusion. Jerry stood aghast at that. What! Hang a man merely because they thought he'd done it! And with a face like his! Why, it was sheer injustice!

The jury returned. The prisoner stood in the dock, now pale and hopeless. Only one man in court seemed to feel the slightest interest in the delivery of the verdict. And that one man was the public hangman. Everybody else knew precisely how the case would go. But Jerry Stokes still refused to believe any jury in Canada could perpetrate such an act of flagrant injustice.

'Gentlemen of the jury, do you find the prisoner, Richard Ogilvy, guilty or not guilty of wilful murder?'

There was a slight rhetorical pause. Then the answer rang out, in quietly solemn tones: 'We find him guilty. That is the verdict of all of us.'

Jerry Stokes held his breath. This was appalling, awful! The man was innocent. But by virtue of his office he would have to hang him!

If anybody had told Jerry Stokes the week before that he possessed an ample, unexhausted fund of natural enthusiasm, Jerry Stokes would have looked upon him as only fit for Hatwood Asylum. He was a solid, stolid, thick-headed man, was Jerry, who honestly believed in the importance of his office, and hanged men as respectably as he would have slaughtered oxen. But that incredible verdict, as it seemed to him, begot in him suddenly a fierce outburst of zeal which was all the more violent because of its utter novelty. For the first time in his life he woke up to the enthusiasm of humanity. You'll often find it so in very phlegmatic men; it takes a great deal to stir their stagnant depths; but let them once be aroused, and the storm is terrible, the fire within them burns bright with a warmth and light which astonishes everybody. For days the look on Richard Ogilvy's face, when he heard that false verdict returned against him, haunted the hangman's brain every hour of the twenty-four. He lay awake on his bed and shuddered to think of it. Come what might, that man must never be hanged. And, please heaven, Jerry added, they should never hang him.

The sentence, Canadian fashion, was for six clear weeks. And at the end of that time, unless anything should turn up meanwhile to prevent it, it would be Jerry's duty to hang the man he believed to be innocent.

For all those years, Jerry had stolidly and soberly hanged whomever he was bid, taking it for granted the law was always in the right, and that the men on whom he operated were invariably malefactors. But now, a great horror possessed his soul. The revulsion was terrible. This one gross miscarriage of justice, as it seemed to him, raised doubts at the same time in his startled soul as to the rightfulness of all his previous hangings. Had he been in the habit of doing innocent men to death for years? Was the law, then, always so painfully fallible? Could it go wrong in all the dignity of its unsullied ermine? Jerry could hang the guilty without one pang of remorse. But to hang the innocent! – he drew himself up; that was altogether a different matter.

Yet what could he do? A petition? Impossible! Never within his memory could Jerry recollect so perfect a unanimity of public opinion in favour of a sentence. A petition was useless. Not a soul would sign it. Everybody was satisfied. Let Ogilvy swing! The very women would have lynched the man if they could have caught him at the first. And now that he was to be hanged, they were heartily glad of it.

Still there is nothing to spur a man on in a hopeless cause like the feeling that you stand alone and unaided. Jerry Stokes saw all the world was for hanging Ogilvy with the strange and solitary exception of the public hangman. And what did the public hangman's opinion count in such a case? As Jerry Stokes well knew, rather less than nothing.

Day after day wore away, and the papers were full of 'the convict Ogilvy'. Would he confess, or would he not? That was now the question. Every second night the Toronto papers had a special edition with a 'Rumoured Confession of the Napanee Murderer,' and every second morning they had a telegram direct from Kingston jail to contradict it. Not a doubt seemed to remain with anybody as to the convict's guilt. But the papers reiterated daily the same familiar phrase, 'Ogilvy persists to the end in maintaining his innocence.'

Jerry had read these words a hundred times before, about other prisoners, with a gentle smile of cynical incredulity; he read them now with blank amazement and horror at the callousness of a world which could hang an innocent man without appeal or inquiry.

Time ran on, and the eve of the execution arrived at last. Something must be done: and Jerry did it. That night he sat long in his room by himself, in the unwonted throes of literary composition. He was writing a letter, a letter of unusual length and surprising earnestness.

It cost him dear, that epistle; with his dictionary by his side, he stopped many times to think, and bit his penholder to the fibre. But he wrote nonetheless with fiery indignation, and in a fever of moral zeal that positively astonished himself. Then he copied it out clean on a separate sheet, and folded the letter when done, with a prayer in his heart. It was a prayer for mercy on a condemned criminal – by the public hangman.

After that he stuck a stamp on with trembling fingers, and posted it himself at the post office.

All that night long Jerry lay awake and thought about the execution. As a rule, executions troubled his rest very little. But then, he had never before had to hang an innocent man at least he hoped not though his faith in the law had received a severe shock, and he trembled to think now what judicial murders he might have helped in his time unconsciously to consummate.

Next morning early, at the appointed hour, Jerry Stokes presented himself at Kingston jail. The sheriff was there, and the chaplain, and the prisoner. Ogilvy looked at him hard with a shrinking look of horror. Jerry had seen that look, too, a hundred times before, and disregarded it utterly: it was only the natural objection of a condemned criminal to the constitutional officer appointed to operate on him. But this time it cut the man to the very quick. That an innocent fellow creature should regard him like that was indeed unendurable, especially when he, the public hangman, was the only soul on earth who believed in his innocence!

The chaplain stood forward and read the usual prayers. The condemned man repeated them after him in a faltering voice. As he finished, the sheriff turned with a grave face to Jerry. 'Do your duty,' he said. And Jerry stared at him stolidly.

'Sheriff,' he began at last, after a very long pause, bracing himself up for an effort, 'I've done my duty all my life till this, and I'll do it now. There ain't going to be no execution at all here this morning!'

The sheriff gazed at him astonished.

'What do you mean, Stokes?' he asked, taken aback at this sudden turn. 'No reprieve has come. The prisoner is to be hanged without fail today in accordance with his sentence. It says so in the warrant: 'wherein fail not at your peril.'"

Jerry looked round him with an air of expectation. 'No reprieve hasn't come yet,' he answered, in a stolid way, 'but I'm expecting one presently. I've done my duty all my life, sheriff, I tell you, and I'll do it now. I ain't a-going to hang this man at all because I know he's innocent!'

The prisoner gasped, and turned round to him in amazement. 'Yes, I'm innocent!' he said slowly, looking him over from head to foot, 'but you – how do you know it?'

'I know it by your face,' Jerry answered sturdily, 'and I know by the other one's face it was him that did it.'

The sheriff looked on in puzzled wonderment. This was a hitch in the proceedings he had never expected. 'Your conduct is most irregular, Stokes,' he said at last, stroking his chin in his embarrassment; 'most irregular and disconcerting. If you had a conscientious scruple against hanging the prisoner, you should have told us before. Then we might have arranged for some other executioner to serve in your place. As it is, the delay is most unseemly and painful: especially for the prisoner. Your action can only cause him unnecessary suspense. Sooner or later this morning, somebody must hang him.'

But Jerry only looked back at him with an approving nod. The sheriff had supplied him, all inarticulate that he was, with suitable speech. 'Ah, that's just it, don't you see,' he made answer promptly, 'it's a conscientious scruple. That's why I won't hang him. No man can't be expected to go agin his conscience. I never hanged an innocent man yet – leastways not to my knowledge; and s'help me heaven, I won't hang one now, not for the Queen nor for nobody!'

The sheriff paused. The sheriff deliberated. 'What on earth am I to do?' he exclaimed, in despair. 'If you won't hang him, how on earth at this hour can I secure a substitute?'

Jerry stared at him stolidly once more, after his wont. 'If I don't hang him,' he answered, with the air of one who knows his ground well, 'it's your business to do it with your own hands. 'Wherein fail not at your peril.' And I give you warning beforehand, sheriff, if you do hang him – why, you'll have to remember all your life long that you helped to get rid of an innocent man, when the common hangman refused to execute him!'

To such a pitch of indignation was he roused by events that he said it plump out, just so, 'the common hangman.' Rather than let his last appeal lack aught of effectiveness in the cause of justice, he consented so to endorse the public condemnation of his own respectable, useful, and necessary calling!

There was a pause of a few minutes, during which the sheriff once more halted and hesitated; the prisoner looked around with a pale and terrified air; and Jerry kept his eye fixed hard on the gate, like one who really expects a reprieve or a pardon.

'Then you absolutely refuse?' the sheriff asked at last, in a despairing sort of way.

'I absolutely refuse,' Jerry answered, in a very decided tone. But it was clear he was beginning to grow anxious and nervous.

'In that case,' the sheriff replied, turning round to the jailer, 'I must put off this execution for half an hour, till I can get someone else to come in and assist me.'

Hardly had he spoken the words, however, when a policeman appeared at the door of the courtyard, and in a very hurried voice asked eagerly to be admitted. His manner was that of a man who brings important news. 'The execution's not over, sir?' he said, turning to the sheriff with a very scared face. 'Well, thank heaven for that! Dr Wade's outside, and he says, for God's sake, he must speak at once with you.'

The sheriff hesitated. He hardly knew what to do. 'Bring him in,' he said at last, after a solemn pause. 'He may have something to tell us that will help us out of this difficulty.'

The condemned man, thus momentarily respited on the very brink of the grave, stood by with a terrible look of awed suspense upon his bloodless face. But Jerry Stokes' lips bore an expression of quiet triumph. He had succeeded in his attempt, then. He had brought his man to book. That was something to be proud of. Alone he had done it! He had saved the innocent and exposed the guilty!

As they stood there and pondered, each man in silence, on his own private thoughts, the policeman returned, bringing with him the doctor whose evidence had weighed most against Ogilvy at the trial. Jerry Stokes started to see the marvellous alteration in the fellow's face. He was pale and haggard; his lips were parched; and his eyes had a sunken and hollow look with remorse and horror. Cold sweat stood on his brow. His mouth twitched horribly. It was clear he had just passed through a terrible crisis.

He turned first to Jerry. His lips were bloodless, and trembled as he spoke; his throat was dry; but in a husky voice he still managed to deliver himself of the speech that haunted him. 'Your letter did it,' he said slowly, fixing his eyes on the hangman. 'I couldn't stand that. It broke me down utterly. All night long I lay awake and knew I had sent him to the gallows in my place. It was terrible – terrible! But I wouldn't give way: I'd made up my mind, and I meant to pull through with it. Then the morning came – the morning of the execution, and with it your letter. Till that moment I thought nobody knew but myself. I wasn't even suspected. When I saw you knew, I could stand it no longer. You said: 'If you let this innocent man swing in your place, I, the common hangman, will refuse to execute him. If he dies, I'll avenge him. I'll hound you to your grave. I'll follow up clues till I've brought your crime home to you. Don't commit two murders instead of one. It'll do you no good, and be worse in the end for you.' When I read those words – those terrible words! – from the common hangman, 'Ah, heaven!' I thought, 'I need try to conceal it no longer.' All's up now. I've come to confess. Thank heaven I'm in time! Sheriff, let this man go. It was I who poisoned her!'

There was a dead silence again for several seconds. Jerry Stokes was the first of them all to break it. 'I knew it,' he said solemnly. 'I was sure of it. I could have sworn to it.'

'And I am sure of it, too,' the condemned man put in, with tremulous lips. 'I was sure it was he; but how on earth could I prove it?'

The sheriff looked about him at all three in turn. 'Well,' he said deliberately, with a sigh of relief, 'I must telegraph for instructions to Ottawa immediately. Prisoner, you are not reprieved; but under these peculiar circumstances, as Dr Wade makes a voluntary confession of having committed the crime himself, I defer the execution for the present on my own responsibility. Jailer, I remit Mr Ogilvy to the cells till further instructions arrive from the Viceroy. Policeman, take charge of Dr Wade, who gives himself into custody for the murder of Mrs Ogilvy. Stokes, perhaps you did right after all. Ten minutes' delay made all the difference. If you'd consented to hang the prisoner at first, this confession might only have come after all was over.'

The doctor turned to Jerry, with the wan ghost of a grim smile upon his worn and pallid face. The marks of a great struggle were still visible in every line. 'And you won't be balked of your fee, after all,' he added, with a ghastly effort at cynical calmness, 'for you'll have me to hang before you have seen the end of this business.'

But Jerry shook his head. 'I ain't so sure about that,' he said, scratching his thick, bullet poll, and holding his great square neck a little on one side. 'I ain't so sure of my trade as I used to be once, sheriff and gentlemen. I always used to hold it was a useful, a respectable, and a necessary trade, and of benefit to the community.

But I've began to doubt it. If the law can string up an innocent man like this, and no appeal, except for the exertions of the public executioner, why, I've began to doubt the expediency, so to speak, of capital punishment. I ain't so certain as I was about the usefulness of hanging. Dr Wade, I think somebody else may have the turning of you off. Mr Ogilvy, I'm glad, sir, it was me that had the hanging of you. An unscrupulous man might ha' gone for his fee. I couldn't do that: I gone for justice. Give me your hand, sir. Thank you. You needn't be ashamed of shaking hands once in a way with a public functionary – especially when it's for the last time in his official career. Sheriff, I've had enough of this 'ere work for life. I go back to the lumbering trade. I resign my appointment.'

It was a great speech for Jerry – an oratorical effort. But a prouder or happier man there wasn't in Kingston that day than Jeremiah Stokes, late public executioner.

SIR ARTHUR CONAN DOYLE

The Adventure of the Copper Beeches

'TO THE man who loves art for its own sake,' remarked Sherlock Holmes, tossing aside the advertisement sheet of the *Daily Telegraph*, 'it is frequently in its least important and lowliest manifestations that the keenest pleasure is to be derived. It is pleasant to me to observe, Watson, that you have so far grasped this truth that in these little records of our cases which you have been good enough to draw up, and, I am bound to say, occasionally to embellish, you have given prominence not so much to the many *causes celebres* and sensational trials in which I have figured but rather to those incidents which may have been trivial in themselves, but which have given room for those faculties of deduction and of logical synthesis which I have made my special province.'

'And yet,' said I, smiling, 'I cannot quite hold myself absolved from the charge of sensationalism which has been urged against my records.'

'You have erred, perhaps,' he observed, taking up a glowing cinder with the tongs and lighting with it the long cherry-wood pipe which was wont to replace his clay when he was in a disputatious rather than a meditative mood, 'you have erred perhaps in attempting to put colour and life into each of your statements instead of confining yourself to the task of placing upon record that severe reasoning from cause to effect which is really the only notable feature about the thing.'

'It seems to me that I have done you full justice in the matter,' I remarked with some coldness, for I was repelled by the egotism which I had more than once observed to be a strong factor in my friend's singular character.

'No, it is not selfishness or conceit,' said he, answering, as was his wont, my thoughts rather than my words. 'If I claim full justice for my art, it is because it is an impersonal thing – a thing beyond myself. Crime is common. Logic is rare. Therefore it is upon the logic rather than upon the crime that you should dwell. You have degraded what should have been a course of lectures into a series of tales.'

It was a cold morning of the early spring, and we sat after breakfast on either side of a cheery fire in the old room at Baker Street. A thick fog rolled down between the lines of dun-coloured houses, and the opposing windows loomed like dark, shapeless blurs through the heavy yellow wreaths. Our gas was lit and shone on the white cloth and glimmer of china and metal, for the table had not been cleared yet. Sherlock Holmes had been silent all the morning, dipping continuously into the advertisement columns of a succession of papers until at last, having apparently given up his search, he had emerged in no very sweet temper to lecture me upon my literary shortcomings.

'At the same time,' he remarked after a pause, during which he had sat puffing at his long pipe and gazing down into the fire, 'you can hardly be open to a charge of sensationalism, for out of these cases which you have been so kind as to interest yourself in, a fair proportion do not treat of crime, in its legal sense, at all. The small matter in which I endeavoured to help the King of Bohemia, the singular experience of Miss Mary Sutherland, the problem connected with the man with the twisted lip, and the incident of the noble bachelor, were all matters which are outside the pale of the law. But in avoiding the sensational, I fear that you may have bordered on the trivial.'

'The end may have been so,' I answered, 'but the methods I hold to have been novel and of interest.'

'Pshaw, my dear fellow, what do the public, the great unobservant public, who could hardly tell a weaver by his tooth or a compositor by his left thumb, care about the finer shades of analysis and deduction! But, indeed, if you are trivial, I cannot blame you, for the days of the great cases are past. Man, or at least criminal man, has lost all enterprise and originality. As to my own little practice, it seems to be degenerating into an agency for recovering lost lead pencils and giving advice to young ladies from boarding-schools. I think that I have touched bottom at last, however. This note I had this morning marks my zero-point, I fancy. Read it!' He tossed a crumpled letter across to me.

It was dated from Montague Place upon the preceding evening, and ran thus:

DEAR MR HOLMES:

I am very anxious to consult you as to whether I should or should not accept a situation which has been offered to me as governess. I shall call at half-past ten tomorrow if I do not inconvenience you.

Yours faithfully,
VIOLET HUNTER.

'Do you know the young lady?' I asked.

'Not I.'

'It is half-past ten now.'

'Yes, and I have no doubt that is her ring.'

'It may turn out to be of more interest than you think. You remember that the affair of the blue carbuncle, which appeared to be a mere whim at first, developed into a serious investigation. It may be so in this case, also.'

'Well, let us hope so. But our doubts will very soon be solved, for here, unless I am much mistaken, is the person in question.'

As he spoke the door opened and a young lady entered the room. She was plainly but neatly dressed, with a bright, quick face, freckled like a plover's egg, and with the brisk manner of a woman who has had her own way to make in the world.

'You will excuse my troubling you, I am sure,' said she, as my companion rose to greet her, 'but I have had a very strange experience, and as I have no parents or relations of any sort from whom I could ask advice, I thought that perhaps you would be kind enough to tell me what I should do.'

'Pray take a seat, Miss Hunter. I shall be happy to do anything that I can to serve you.'

I could see that Holmes was favourably impressed by the manner and speech of his new client. He looked her over in his searching fashion, and then composed himself, with his lids drooping and his fingertips together, to listen to her story.

'I have been a governess for five years,' said she, 'in the family of Colonel Spence Munro, but two months ago the colonel received an appointment at Halifax, in Nova Scotia, and took his children over to America with him, so that I found myself without a situation. I advertised, and I answered advertisements, but without success. At last the little money which I had saved began to run short, and I was at my wit's end as to what I should do.

'There is a well-known agency for governesses in the West End called Westaway's, and there I used to call about once a week in order to see whether anything had turned up which might suit me. Westaway was the name of the founder of the business, but it is really managed by Miss Stoper. She sits in her own little office, and the ladies who are seeking employment wait in an anteroom, and are then shown in one by one, when she consults her ledgers and sees whether she has anything which would suit them.

'Well, when I called last week I was shown into the little office as usual, but I found that Miss Stoper was not alone. A prodigiously stout man with a very smiling face and a great heavy chin which rolled down in fold upon fold over his throat sat at her elbow with a pair of glasses on his nose, looking very earnestly at the ladies who entered. As I came in he gave quite a jump in his chair and turned quickly to Miss Stoper.

'"That will do," said he; "I could not ask for anything better. Capital! Capital!" He seemed quite enthusiastic and rubbed his hands together in the most genial fashion. He was such a comfort-able-looking man that it was quite a pleasure to look at him.

'"You are looking for a situation, miss?" he asked.

'"Yes, sir."

'"As governess?"

'"Yes, sir."

'"And what salary do you ask?"

'"I had £4 a month in my last place with Colonel Spence Munro."

'"Oh, tut, tut! Sweating – rank sweating!" he cried, throwing his fat hands out into the air like a man who is in a boiling passion. "How could anyone offer so pitiful a sum to a lady with such attrac-tions and accomplishments?"

'"My accomplishments, sir, may be less than you imagine," said I. "A little French, a little German, music, and drawing—"

'"Tut, tut!" he cried. "This is all quite beside the question. The point is, have you or have you not the bearing and deportment of a lady? There it is in a nutshell. If you have not, you are not fined for the rearing of a child who may some day play a considerable part in the history of the country. But if you have why, then, how could any gentleman ask you to condescend to accept anything under the three figures? Your salary with me, madam, would commence at £100 a year."

'You may imagine, Mr Holmes, that to me, destitute as I was, such an offer seemed almost too good to be true. The gentleman, however, seeing perhaps the look of incredulity upon my face, opened a pocketbook and took out a note.

'"It is also my custom," said he, smiling in the most pleasant fashion until his eyes were just two little shining slits amid the white creases of his face, "to advance to my young ladies half their salary beforehand, so that they may meet any little expenses of their journey and their wardrobe."

'It seemed to me that I had never met so fascinating and so thoughtful a man. As I was already in debt to my tradesmen, the advance was a great convenience, and yet there was something unnatural about the whole transaction which made me wish to know a little more before I quite committed myself.

'"May I ask where you live, sir?" said I.

'"Hampshire. Charming rural place. The Copper Beeches, five miles on the far side of Winchester. It is the most lovely country, my dear young lady, and the dearest old country-house."

'"And my duties, sir? I should be glad to know what they would be."

'"One child – one dear little romper just six years old. Oh, if you could see him killing cockroaches with a slipper! Smack! smack! smack! Three gone before you could wink!" He leaned back in his chair and laughed his eyes into his head again.

'I was a little startled at the nature of the child's amusement, but the father's laughter made me think that perhaps he was joking.

'"My sole duties, then," I asked, "are to take charge of a single child?"

'"No, no, not the sole, not the sole, my dear young lady," he cried. "Your duty would be, as I am sure your good sense would suggest, to obey any little commands my wife might give, provided always that they were such commands as a lady might with propriety obey. You see no difficulty, heh?"

'"I should be happy to make myself useful."

'"Quite so. In dress now, for example. We are faddy people, you know – faddy but kind-hearted. If you were asked to wear any dress which we might give you, you would not object to our little whim. Heh?"

'"No," said I, considerably astonished at his words.

'"Or to sit here, or sit there, that would not be offensive to you?"

'"Oh, no."

'"Or to cut your hair quite short before you come to us?"

'I could hardly believe my ears. As you may observe, Mr Holmes, my hair is somewhat luxuriant, and of a rather peculiar tint of chestnut. It has been considered artistic. I could not dream of sacrificing it in this offhand fashion.

'"I am afraid that that is quite impossible," said I. He had been watching me eagerly out of his small eyes, and I could see a shadow pass over his face as I spoke.

'"I am afraid that it is quite essential," said he. "It is a little fancy of my wife's, and ladies' fancies, you know, madam, ladies' fancies must be consulted. And so you won't cut your hair?"

'"No, sir, I really could not," I answered firmly.

'"Ah, very well; then that quite settles the matter. It is a pity, because in other respects you would really have done very nicely. In that case, Miss Stoper, I had best inspect a few more of your young ladies."

'The manageress had sat all this while busy with her papers without a word to either of us, but she glanced at me now with so much annoyance upon her face that I could not help suspecting that she had lost a handsome commission through my refusal.

'"Do you desire your name to be kept upon the books?" she asked.

'"If you please, Miss Stoper."

'"Well, really, it seems rather useless, since you refuse the most excellent offers in this fashion," said she sharply. "You can hardly expect us to exert ourselves to find another such opening for you. Good-day to you, Miss Hunter." She struck a gong upon the table, and I was shown out by the page.

'Well, Mr Holmes, when I got back to my lodgings and found little enough in the cupboard, and two or three bills upon the table. I began to ask myself whether I had not done a very foolish thing. After all, if these people had strange fads and expected obedience on the most extraordinary matters, they were at least ready to pay for their eccentricity. Very few governesses in England are getting £100 a year. Besides, what use was my hair to me? Many people are improved by wearing it short and perhaps I should be among the number. Next day I was inclined to think that I had made a mistake, and by the day after I was sure of it. I had almost overcome my pride so far as to go back to the agency and inquire whether the place was still open when I received this letter from the gentleman himself. I have it here and I will read it to you:

'The Copper Beeches, near Winchester.

'DEAR MISS HUNTER:

'Miss Stoper has very kindly given me your address, and I write from here to ask you whether you have reconsidered your decision. My wife is very anxious that you should come, for she has been much attracted by my description of you. We are willing to give £30 a quarter, or £120 a year, so as to recompense you for any little inconvenience which our fads may cause you. They are not very exacting, after all. My wife is fond of a particular shade of electric blue and would like you to wear such a dress indoors in the morning. You need not, however, go to the expense of purchasing one, as we have one belonging to my dear daughter Alice (now in Philadelphia), which would, I should think, fit you very well. Then, as to sitting here or there, or amusing yourself in any manner indicated, that need cause you no inconvenience. As regards your hair, it is no doubt a pity, especially as I could not help remarking its beauty during our short interview, but I am afraid that I must remain firm upon this point, and I only hope that the increased salary may recompense you for the loss. Your duties, as far as the child is concerned, are very light. Now do try to come, and I shall meet you with the dogcart at Winchester. Let me know your train.

'Yours faithfully,
'JEPHRO RUCASTLE.

'That is the letter which I have just received, Mr Holmes, and my mind is made up that I will accept it. I thought, however, that before taking the final step I should like to submit the whole matter to your consideration.'

'Well, Miss Hunter, if your mind is made up, that settles the question,' said Holmes, smiling.

'But you would not advise me to refuse?'

'I confess that it is not the situation which I should like to see a sister of mine apply for.'

'What is the meaning of it all, Mr Holmes?'

'Ah, I have no data. I cannot tell. Perhaps you have yourself formed some opinion?'

'Well, there seems to me to be only one possible solution. Mr Rucastle seemed to be a very kind, good-natured man. Is it not possible that his wife is a lunatic, that he desires to keep the matter quiet for fear she should be taken to an asylum, and that he humours her fancies in every way in order to prevent an outbreak?'

'That is a possible solution – in fact, as matters stand, it is the most probable one. But in any case it does not seem to be a nice household for a young lady.'

'But the money, Mr Holmes, the money!'

'Well, yes, of course the pay is good – too good. That is what makes me uneasy. Why should they give you £120 a year, when they could have their pick for £40? There must be some strong reason behind.'

'I thought that if I told you the circumstances you would understand afterwards if I wanted your help. I should feel so much stronger if I felt that you were at the back of me.'

'Oh, you may carry that feeling away with you. I assure you that your little problem promises to be the most interesting which has come my way for some months. There is something distinctly novel about some of the features. If you should find yourself in doubt or in danger—'

'Danger! What danger do you foresee?'

Holmes shook his head gravely. 'It would cease to be a danger if we could define it,' said he. 'But at any time, day or night, a telegram would bring me down to your help.'

'That is enough.' She rose briskly from her chair with the anxiety all swept from her face. 'I shall go down to Hampshire quite easy in my mind now. I shall write to Mr Rucastle at once, sacrifice my poor hair tonight, and start for Winchester tomorrow.' With a few grateful words to Holmes she bade us both Goodnight and bustled off upon her way.

'At least,' said I as we heard her quick, firm steps descending the stairs, 'she seems to be a young lady who is very well able to take care of herself.'

'And she would need to be,' said Holmes gravely. 'I am much mistaken if we do not hear from her before many days are past.'

It was not very long before my friend's prediction was fulfilled. A fortnight went by, during which I frequently found my thoughts turning in her direction and wondering what strange side-alley of human experience this lonely woman had strayed into. The unusual salary, the curious conditions, the light duties, all pointed to something abnormal, though whether a fad or a plot, or whether the man were a philanthropist or a villain, it was quite beyond my powers to determine. As to Holmes, I observed that he sat frequently for half an hour on end, with knitted brows and an abstracted air, but he swept the matter away with a wave of his hand when I mentioned it. 'Data! data! data!' he cried impatiently. 'I can't make bricks without clay.' And yet he would always wind up by muttering that no sister of his should ever have accepted such a situation.

The telegram which we eventually received came late one night just as I was thinking of turning in and Holmes was settling down to one of those all-night chemical researches which he frequently indulged in, when I would leave him stooping over a retort and a test-tube at night and find him in the same position when I came down to breakfast in the morning. He opened the yellow envelope, and then, glancing at the message, threw it across to me.

'Just look up the trains in Bradshaw,' said he, and turned back to his chemical studies.

The summons was a brief and urgent one.

Please be at the Black Swan Hotel at Winchester at midday tomorrow [it said]. Do come! I am at my wit's end.

HUNTER.

'Will you come with me?' asked Holmes, glancing up.

'I should wish to.'

'Just look it up, then.'

'There is a train at half-past nine,' said I, glancing over my Bradshaw. 'It is due at Winchester at 11:30.'

'That will do very nicely. Then perhaps I had better postpone my analysis of the acetones, as we may need to be at our best in the morning.'

By eleven o'clock the next day we were well upon our way to the old English capital. Holmes had been buried in the morning papers all the way down, but after we had passed the Hampshire border he threw them down and began to admire the scenery. It was an ideal spring day, a light blue sky, flecked with little fleecy white clouds drifting across from west to east. The sun was shining very brightly, and yet there was an exhilarating nip in the air, which set an edge to a man's energy. All over the countryside, away to the rolling hills around Aldershot, the little red and grey roofs of the farm-steadings peeped out from amid the light green of the new foliage.

'Are they not fresh and beautiful?' I cried with all the enthusiasm of a man fresh from the fogs of Baker Street.

But Holmes shook his head gravely.

'Do you know, Watson,' said he, 'that it is one of the curses of a mind with a turn like mine that I must look at everything with reference to my own special subject. You look at these scattered houses, and you are impressed by their beauty. I look at them, and the only thought which comes to me is a feeling of their isolation and of the impunity with which crime may be committed there.'

'Good heavens!' I cried. 'Who would associate crime with these dear old homesteads?'

'They always fill me with a certain horror. It is my belief, Watson, founded upon my experience, that the lowest and vilest alleys in London do not present a more dreadful record of sin than does the smiling and beautiful countryside.'

'You horrify me!'

'But the reason is very obvious. The pressure of public opinion can do in the town what the law cannot accomplish. There is no lane so vile that the scream of a tortured child, or the thud of a drunkard's blow, does not beget sympathy and indignation among the neighbours, and then the whole machinery of justice is ever so close that a word of complaint can set it going, and there is but a step between the crime and the dock. But look at these lonely houses, each in its own fields, filled for the most part with poor ignorant folk who know little of the law. Think of the deeds of hellish cruelty, the hidden wickedness which may go on, year in, year out, in such places, and none the wiser. Had this lady who appeals to us for help gone to live in Winchester, I should never have had a fear for her. It is the five miles of country which makes the danger. Still, it is clear that she is not personally threatened.'

'No. If she can come to Winchester to meet us she can get away.'

'Quite so. She has her freedom.'

'What can be the matter, then? Can you suggest no explanation?'

'I have devised seven separate explanations, each of which would cover the facts as far as we know them. But which of these is correct can only be determined by the fresh information which we shall no doubt find waiting for us. Well, there is the tower of the cathedral, and we shall soon learn all that Miss Hunter has to tell.'

The Black Swan is an inn of repute in the High Street, at no distance from the station, and there we found the young lady waiting for us. She had engaged a sitting-room, and our lunch awaited us upon the table.

'I am so delighted that you have come,' she said earnestly. 'It is so very kind of you both; but indeed I do not know what I should do. Your advice will be altogether invaluable to me.'

'Pray tell us what has happened to you.'

'I will do so, and I must be quick, for I have promised Mr Rucastle to be back before three. I got his leave to come into town this morning, though he little knew for what purpose.'

'Let us have everything in its due order.' Holmes thrust his long thin legs out towards the fire and composed himself to listen.

'In the first place, I may say that I have met, on the whole, with no actual ill-treatment from Mr and Mrs Rucastle. It is only fair to them to say that. But I cannot understand them, and I am not easy in my mind about them.'

'What can you not understand?'

'Their reasons for their conduct. But you shall have it all just as it occurred. When I came down, Mr Rucastle met me here and drove me in his dogcart to the Copper Beeches. It is, as he said, beautifully situated, but it is not beautiful in itself, for it is a large square block of a house, whitewashed, but all stained and streaked with damp and bad weather. There are grounds round it, woods on three sides, and on the fourth a field which slopes down to the Southampton high-road, which curves past about a hundred yards from the front door. This ground in front belongs to the house, but the woods all round are part of Lord Southerton's preserves. A clump of copper beeches immediately in front of the hall door has given its name to the place.

'I was driven over by my employer, who was as amiable as ever, and was introduced by him that evening to his wife and the child. There was no truth, Mr Holmes, in the conjecture which seemed to us to be probable in your rooms at Baker Street. Mrs Rucastle is not mad. I found her to be a silent, pale-faced woman, much younger than her husband, not more than thirty, I should think, while he can hardly be less than forty-five. From their conversation I have gathered that they have been married about seven years, that he was a widower, and that his only child by the first wife was the daughter who has gone to Philadelphia. Mr Rucastle told me in private that the reason why she had left them was that she had an unreasoning aversion to her stepmother. As the daughter could not have been less than twenty, I can quite imagine that her position must have been uncomfortable with her father's young wife.

'Mrs Rucastle seemed to me to be colourless in mind as well as in feature. She impressed me neither favourably nor the reverse. She was a nonentity. It was easy to see that she was passionately devoted both to her husband and to her little son. Her light grey eyes wandered continually from one to the other, noting every little want and forestalling it if possible. He was kind to her also in his bluff, boisterous fashion, and on the whole they seemed to be a happy couple. And yet she had some secret sorrow, this woman. She would often be lost in deep thought, with the saddest look upon her face. More than once I have surprised her in tears. I have thought sometimes that it was the disposition of her child which weighed upon her mind, for I have never met so utterly spoiled and so ill-natured a little creature. He is small for his age, with a head which is quite disproportionately large. His whole life appears to be spent in an alternation between savage fits of passion and gloomy intervals of sulking. Giving pain to any creature weaker than himself seems to be his one idea of amusement, and he shows quite remarkable talent in planning the capture of mice, little birds, and insects. But I would rather not talk about the creature, Mr Holmes, and, indeed, he has little to do with my story.'

'I am glad of all details,' remarked my friend, 'whether they seem to you to be relevant or not.'

'I shall try not to miss anything of importance. The one unpleasant thing about the house, which struck me at once, was the appearance and conduct of the servants. There are only two, a man and his wife. Toller, for that is his name, is a rough, uncouth man, with grizzled hair and whiskers, and a perpetual smell of drink. Twice since I have been with them he has been quite drunk, and yet Mr Rucastle seemed to take no notice of it. His wife is a very tall and strong woman with a sour face, as silent as Mrs Rucastle and much less amiable. They are a most unpleasant couple, but fortunately I spend most of my time in the nursery and my own room, which are next to each other in one corner of the building.

'For two days after my arrival at the Copper Beeches my life was very quiet; on the third, Mrs Rucastle came down just after breakfast and whispered something to her husband.

'"Oh, yes," said he, turning to me, "we are very much obliged to you, Miss Hunter, for falling in with our whims so far as to cut your hair. I assure you that it has not detracted in the tiniest iota from your appearance. We shall now see how the electric-blue dress will become you. You will find it laid out upon the bed in your room, and if you would be so good as to put it on we should both be extremely obliged."

'The dress which I found waiting for me was of a peculiar shade of blue. It was of excellent material, a sort of beige, but it bore unmistakable signs of having been worn before. It could not have been a better fit if I had been measured for it. Both Mr and Mrs Rucastle expressed a delight at the look of it, which seemed quite exaggerated in its vehemence. They were waiting for me in the drawing-room, which is a very large room, stretching along the entire front of the house, with three long windows reaching down to the floor. A chair had been placed close to the central window, with its back turned towards it. In this I was asked to sit, and then Mr Rucastle, walking up and down on the other side of the room, began to tell me a series of the funniest stories that I have ever listened to. You cannot imagine how comical he was, and I laughed until I was quite weary. Mrs Rucastle, however, who has evidently no sense of humour, never so much as smiled, but sat with her hands in her lap, and a sad, anxious look upon her face. After an hour or so, Mr Rucastle suddenly remarked that it was time to commence the duties of the day, and that I might change my dress and go to little Edward in the nursery.

'Two days later this same performance was gone through under exactly similar circumstances. Again I changed my dress, again I sat in the window, and again I laughed very heartily at the funny stories of which my employer had an immense repertoire, and which he told inimitably. Then he handed me a yellowbacked novel, and moving my chair a little sideways, that my own shadow might not fall upon the page, he begged me to read aloud to him. I read for about ten minutes, beginning in the heart of a chapter, and then suddenly, in the middle of a sentence, he ordered me to cease and to change my dress.

'You can easily imagine, Mr Holmes, how curious I became as to what the meaning of this extraordinary performance could possibly be. They were always very careful, I observed, to turn my face away from the window, so that I became consumed with the desire to see what was going on behind my back. At first it seemed to be impossible, but I soon devised a means. My hand-mirror had been broken, so a happy thought seized me, and I concealed a piece of the glass in my handkerchief. On the next occasion, in the midst of my laughter, I put my handkerchief up to my eyes, and was able with a little management to see all that there was behind me. I confess that I was disappointed. There was nothing. At least that was my first impression. At the second glance, however, I perceived that there was a man standing in the Southampton Road, a small bearded man in a grey suit, who seemed to be looking in my direction. The road is an important highway, and there are usually people there. This man, however, was leaning against the railings which bordered our field and was looking earnestly up. I lowered my handkerchief and glanced at Mrs Rucastle to find her eyes fixed upon me with a most searching gaze. She said nothing, but I am convinced that she had divined that I had a mirror in my hand and had seen what was behind me. She rose at once.

'"Jephro," said she, "there is an impertinent fellow upon the road there who stares up at Miss Hunter."

'"No friend of yours, Miss Hunter?" he asked.

'"No, I know no one in these parts."

'"Dear me! How very impertinent! Kindly turn round and motion to him to go away."

'"Surely it would be better to take no notice."

'"No, no, we should have him loitering here always. Kindly turn round and wave him away like that."

'I did as I was told, and at the same instant Mrs Rucastle drew down the blind. That was a week ago, and from that time I have not sat again in the window, nor have I worn the blue dress, nor seen the man in the road.'

'Pray continue,' said Holmes. 'Your narrative promises to be a most interesting one.'

'You will find it rather disconnected, I fear, and there may prove to be little relation between the different incidents of which I speak. On the very first day that I was at the Copper Beeches, Mr Rucastle took me to a small outhouse which stands near the kitchen door. As we approached it I heard the sharp rattling of a chain, and the sound as of a large animal moving about.

'"Look in here!" said Mr Rucastle, showing me a slit between two planks. "Is he not a beauty?"

'I looked through and was conscious of two glowing eyes, and of a vague figure huddled up in the darkness.

'"Don't be frightened," said my employer, laughing at the start which I had given. "It's only Carlo, my mastiff. I call him mine, but really old Toller, my groom, is the only man who can do anything with him. We feed him once a day, and not too much then, so that he is always as keen as mustard. Toller lets him loose every night, and God help the trespasser whom he lays his fangs upon. For goodness' sake don't you ever on any pretext set your foot over the threshold at night, for it's as much as your life is worth."

'The warning was no idle one, for two nights later I happened to look out of my bedroom window about two o'clock in the morning. It was a beautiful moonlight night, and the lawn in front of the house was silvered over and almost as bright as day. I was standing, rapt in the peaceful beauty of the scene, when I was aware that something was moving under the shadow of the copper beeches. As it emerged into the moonshine I saw what it was. It was a giant dog, as large as a calf, tawny tinted, with hanging jowl, black muzzle, and huge projecting bones. It walked slowly across the lawn and vanished into the shadow upon the other side. That dreadful sentinel sent a chill to my heart which I do not think that any burglar could have done.

'And now I have a very strange experience to tell you. I had, as you know, cut off my hair in London, and I had placed it in a great coil at the bottom of my trunk. One evening, after the child was in bed, I began to amuse myself by examining the furniture of my room and by rearranging my own little things. There was an old chest of drawers in the room, the two upper ones empty and open, the lower one locked. I had filled the first two with my linen, and as I had still much to pack away I was naturally annoyed at not having the use of the third drawer. It struck me that it might have been fastened by a mere oversight, so I took out my bunch of keys and tried to open it. The very first key fitted to perfection, and I drew the drawer open. There was only one thing in it, but I am sure that you would never guess what it was. It was my coil of hair.

'I took it up and examined it. It was of the same peculiar tint, and the same thickness. But then the impossibility of the thing obtruded itself upon me. How could my hair have been locked in the drawer? With trembling hands I undid my trunk, turned out the contents, and drew from the bottom my own hair. I laid the two tresses together, and I assure you that they were identical. Was it not extraordinary? Puzzle as I would, I could make nothing at all of what it meant. I returned the strange hair to the drawer, and I said nothing of the matter to the Rucastles as I felt that I had put myself in the wrong by opening a drawer which they had locked.

'I am naturally observant, as you may have remarked, Mr Holmes, and I soon had a pretty good plan of the whole house in my head. There was one wing, however, which appeared not to be inhabited at all. A door which faced that which led into the quarters of the Tollers opened into this suite, but it was invariably locked. One day, however, as I ascended the stair, I met Mr Rucastle coming out through this door, his keys in his hand, and a look on his face which made him a very different person to the round, jovial man to whom I was accustomed. His cheeks were red, his brow was all crinkled with anger, and the veins stood out at his temples with passion. He locked the door and hurried past me without a word or a look.

'This aroused my curiosity, so when I went out for a walk in the grounds with my charge, I strolled round to the side from which I could see the windows of this part of the house. There were four of them in a row, three of which were simply dirty, while the fourth was shuttered up. They were evidently all deserted. As I strolled up and down, glancing at them occasionally, Mr Rucastle came out to me, looking as merry and jovial as ever.

'"Ah!" said he, "you must not think me rude if I passed you without a word, my dear young lady. I was preoccupied with business matters."

'I assured him that I was not offended. "By the way," said I, "you seem to have quite a suite of spare rooms up there, and one of them has the shutters up."

'He looked surprised and, as it seemed to me, a little startled at my remark.

'"Photography is one of my hobbies," said he. "I have made my dark room up there. But, dear me! what an observant young lady we have come upon. Who would have believed it? Who would have ever believed it?" He spoke in a jesting tone, but there was no jest in his eyes as he looked at me. I read suspicion there and annoyance, but no jest.

'Well, Mr Holmes, from the moment that I understood that there was something about that suite of rooms which I was not to know, I was all on fire to go over them. It was not mere curiosity, though I have my share of that. It was more a feeling of duty – a feeling that some good might come from my penetrating to this place. They talk of woman's instinct; perhaps it was woman's instinct which gave me that feeling. At any rate, it was there, and I was keenly on the lookout for any chance to pass the forbidden door.

'It was only yesterday that the chance came. I may tell you that, besides Mr Rucastle, both Toller and his wife find something to do in these deserted rooms, and I once saw him carrying a large black linen bag with him through the door. Recently he has been drinking hard, and yesterday evening he was very drunk; and when I came upstairs there was the key in the door. I have no doubt at all that he had left it there. Mr and Mrs Rucastle were both downstairs, and the child was with them, so that I had an admirable opportunity. I turned the key gently in the lock, opened the door, and slipped through.

'There was a little passage in front of me, unpapered and uncarpeted, which turned at a right angle at the farther end. Round this corner were three doors in a line, the first and third of which were open. They each led into an empty room, dusty and cheerless, with two windows in the one and one in the other, so thick with dirt that the evening light glimmered dimly through them. The centre door was closed, and across the outside of it had been fastened one of the broad bars of an iron bed, padlocked at one end to a ring in the wall, and fastened at the other with stout cord. The door itself was locked as well, and the key was not there. This barricaded door corresponded clearly with the shuttered window outside, and yet I could see by the glimmer from beneath it that the room was not in darkness. Evidently there was a skylight which let in light from above. As I stood in the passage gazing at the sinister door and wondering what secret it might veil, I suddenly heard the sound of steps within the room and saw a shadow pass backward and forward against the little slit of dim light which shone out from under the door. A mad, unrea-soning terror rose up in me at the sight, Mr Holmes. My overstrung nerves failed me suddenly, and I turned and ran – ran as though some dreadful hand were behind me clutching at the skirt of my dress. I rushed down the passage, through the door, and straight into the arms of Mr Rucastle, who was waiting outside.

'"So," said he, smiling, "it was you, then. I thought that it must be when I saw the door open."

'"Oh, I am so frightened!" I panted.

'"My dear young lady! my dear young lady!" – you cannot think how caressing and soothing his manner was – "and what has fright-ened you, my dear young lady?"

'But his voice was just a little too coaxing. He overdid it. I was keenly on my guard against him.

'"I was foolish enough to go into the empty wing," I answered. "But it is so lonely and eerie in this dim light that I was frightened and ran out again. Oh, it is so dreadfully still in there!"

'"Only that?" said he, looking at me keenly.

'"Why, what did you think?" I asked.

'"Why do you think that I lock this door?"

'"I am sure that I do not know."

'"It is to keep people out who have no business there. Do you see?" He was still smiling in the most amiable manner.

'"I am sure if I had known—"

'"Well, then, you know now. And if you ever put your foot over that threshold again" – here in an instant the smile hardened into a grin of rage, and he glared down at me with the face of a demon – "I'll throw you to the mastiff."

'I was so terrified that I do not know what I did. I suppose that I must have rushed past him into my room. I remember nothing until I found myself lying on my bed trembling all over. Then I thought of you, Mr Holmes. I could not live there longer without some advice. I was frightened of the house, of the man of the woman, of the ser-vants, even of the child. They were all horrible to me. If I could only bring you down all would be well. Of course I might have fled from the house, but my curiosity was almost as strong as my fears. My mind was soon made up. I would send you a wire. I put on my hat and cloak, went down to the office, which is about half a mile from the house, and then returned, feeling very much easier. A horrible doubt came into my mind as I approached the door lest the dog might be loose, but I remembered that Toller had drunk himself into a state of insensibility that evening, and I knew that he was the only one in the household who had any influence with the savage creature, or who would venture to set him free. I slipped in in safety and lay awake half the night in my joy at the thought of seeing you. I had no difficulty in getting leave to come into Winchester this morning, but I must be back before three o'clock, for Mr and Mrs Rucastle are going on a visit, and will be away all the evening, so that I must look after the child. Now I have told you all my adventures, Mr Holmes, and I should be very glad if you could tell me what it all means, and, above all, what I should do.'

Holmes and I had listened spellbound to this extraordinary story. My friend rose now and paced up and down the room, his hands in his pockets, and an expression of the most profound gravity upon his face.

'Is Toller still drunk?' he asked.

'Yes. I heard his wife tell Mrs Rucastle that she could do nothing with him.'

'That is well. And the Rucastles go out tonight?'

'Yes.'

'Is there a cellar with a good strong lock?'

'Yes, the wine-cellar.'

'You seem to me to have acted all through this matter like a very brave and sensible girl, Miss Hunter. Do you think that you could perform one more feat? I should not ask it of you if I did not think you a quite exceptional woman.'

'I will try. What is it?'

'We shall be at the Copper Beeches by seven o'clock, my friend and I. The Rucastles will be gone by that time, and Toller will, we hope, be incapable. There only remains Mrs Toller, who might give the alarm. If you could send her into the cellar on some errand, and then turn the key upon her, you would facilitate matters immensely.'

'I will do it.'

'Excellent! We shall then look thoroughly into the affair. Of course there is only one feasible explanation. You have been brought there to personate someone, and the real person is imprisoned in this chamber. That is obvious. As to who this prisoner is, I have no doubt that it is the daughter, Miss Alice Rucastle, if I remember right, who was said to have gone to America. You were chosen, doubtless, as resembling her in height, figure, and the colour of your hair. Hers had been cut off, very possibly in some illness through which she has passed, and so, of course, yours had to be sacrificed also. By a curious

chance you came upon her tresses. The man in the road was undoubtedly some friend of hers – possibly her fiancé – and no doubt, as you
wore the girl's dress and were so like her, he was convinced from
your laughter, whenever he saw you, and afterwards from your
gesture, that Miss Rucastle was perfectly happy, and that she no
longer desired his attentions. The dog is let loose at night to prevent
him from endeavouring to communicate with her. So much is fairly
clear. The most serious point in the case is the disposition of the
child.'

'What on earth has that to do with it?' I ejaculated.

'My dear Watson, you as a medical man are continually gaining
light as to the tendencies of a child by the study of the parents. Don't
you see that the converse is equally valid. I have frequently gained my
first real insight into the character of parents by studying their children. This child's disposition is abnormally cruel, merely for cruelty's
sake, and whether he derives this from his smiling father, as I should
suspect, or from his mother, it bodes evil for the poor girl who is in
their power.'

'I am sure that you are right, Mr Holmes,' cried our client. 'A
thousand things come back to me which make me certain that you
have hit it. Oh, let us lose not an instant in bringing help to this poor
creature.'

'We must be circumspect, for we are dealing with a very cunning
man. We can do nothing until seven o'clock. At that hour we shall be
with you, and it will not be long before we solve the mystery.'

We were as good as our word, for it was just seven when we
reached the Copper Beeches, having put up our trap at a wayside
public house. The group of trees, with their dark leaves shining like
burnished metal in the light of the setting sun, were sufficient to mark
the house even had Miss Hunter not been standing smiling on the
doorstep.

'Have you managed it?' asked Holmes.

A loud thudding noise came from somewhere downstairs. 'That is
Mrs Toller in the cellar,' said she. 'Her husband lies snoring on the
kitchen rug. Here are his keys, which are the duplicates of Mr Rucastle's.'

'You have done well indeed!' cried Holmes with enthusiasm.
'Now lead the way, and we shall soon see the end of this black business.'

We passed up the stair, unlocked the door, followed on down a
passage, and found ourselves in front of the barricade which Miss

Hunter had described. Holmes cut the cord and removed the transverse bar. Then he tried the various keys in the lock, but without success. No sound came from within, and at the silence Holmes's face clouded over.

'I trust that we are not too late,' said he. 'I think, Miss Hunter, that we had better go in without you. Now, Watson, put your shoulder to it, and we shall see whether we cannot make our way in.'

It was an old rickety door and gave at once before our united strength. Together we rushed into the room. It was empty. There was no furniture save a little pallet bed, a small table, and a basketful of linen. The skylight above was open, and the prisoner gone.

'There has been some villainy here,' said Holmes; 'this beauty has guessed Miss Hunter's intentions and has carried his victim off.'

'But how?'

'Through the skylight. We shall soon see how he managed it.' He swung himself up onto the roof. 'Ah, yes,' he cried, 'here's the end of a long light ladder against the eaves. That is how he did it.'

'But it is impossible,' said Miss Hunter; 'the ladder was not there when the Rucastles went away.'

'He has come back and done it. I tell you that he is a clever and dangerous man. I should not be very much surprised if this were he whose step I hear now upon the stair. I think, Watson, that it would be as well for you to have your pistol ready.'

The words were hardly out of his mouth before a man appeared at the door of the room, a very fat and burly man, with a heavy stick in his hand. Miss Hunter screamed and shrunk against the wall at the sight of him, but Sherlock Holmes sprang forward and confronted him.

'You villain!' said he, 'where's your daughter?'

The fat man cast his eyes round, and then up at the open skylight.

'It is for me to ask you that,' he shrieked, 'you thieves! Spies and thieves! I have caught you, have I? You are in my power. I'll serve you!' He turned and clattered down the stairs as hard as he could go.

'He's gone for the dog!' cried Miss Hunter.

'I have my revolver,' said I.

'Better close the front door,' cried Holmes, and we all rushed down the stairs together. We had hardly reached the hall when we heard the baying of a hound, and then a scream of agony, with a horrible worrying sound which it was dreadful to listen to. An elderly man with a red face and shaking limbs came staggering out at a side door.

'My God!' he cried. 'Someone has loosed the dog. It's not been fed for two days. Quick, quick, or it'll be too late!'

Holmes and I rushed out and round the angle of the house, with Toller hurrying behind us. There was the huge famished brute, its black muzzle buried in Rucastle's throat, while he writhed and screamed upon the ground. Running up, I blew its brains out, and it fell over with its keen white teeth still meeting in the great creases of his neck. With much labour we separated them and carried him, living but horribly mangled, into the house. We laid him upon the drawing-room sofa, and having dispatched the sobered Toller to bear the news to his wife, I did what I could to relieve his pain. We were all assembled round him when the door opened, and a tall, gaunt woman entered the room.

'Mrs Toller!' cried Miss Hunter.

'Yes, miss. Mr Rucastle let me out when he came back before he went up to you. Ah, miss, it is a pity you didn't let me know what you were planning, for I would have told you that your pains were wasted.'

'Ha!' said Holmes, looking keenly at her. 'It is clear that Mrs Toller knows more about this matter than anyone else.'

'Yes, sir, I do, and I am ready enough to tell what I know.'

'Then, pray, sit down, and let us hear it for there are several points on which I must confess that I am still in the dark.'

'I will soon make it clear to you,' said she; 'and I'd have done so before now if I could ha' got out from the cellar. If there's police-court business over this, you'll remember that I was the one that stood your friend, and that I was Miss Alice's friend too.

'She was never happy at home, Miss Alice wasn't, from the time that her father married again. She was slighted like and had no say in anything, but it never really became bad for her until after she met Mr Fowler at a friend's house. As well as I could learn, Miss Alice had rights of her own by will, but she was so quiet and patient, she was, that she never said a word about them but just left everything in Mr Rucastle's hands. He knew he was safe with her; but when there was a chance of a husband coming forward, who would ask for all that the law would give him, then her father thought it time to put a stop on it. He wanted her to sign a paper, so that whether she married or not, he could use her money. When she wouldn't do it, he kept on worrying her until she got brain-fever, and for six weeks was at death's door. Then she got better at last, all worn to a shadow, and with her beautiful hair cut off; but that didn't make no change in her young man, and he stuck to her as true as man could be.'

'Ah,' said Holmes, 'I think that what you have been good enough to tell us makes the matter fairly clear, and that I can deduce all that remains. Mr Rucastle then, I presume, took to this system of imprisonment?'

'Yes, sir.'

'And brought Miss Hunter down from London in order to get rid of the disagreeable persistence of Mr Fowler.'

'That was it, sir.'

'But Mr Fowler being a persevering man, as a good seaman should be, blockaded the house, and having met you succeeded by certain arguments, metallic or otherwise, in convincing you that your interests were the same as his.'

'Mr Fowler was a very kind-spoken, freehanded gentleman,' said Mrs Toller serenely.

'And in this way he managed that your good man should have no want of drink, and that a ladder should be ready at the moment when your master had gone out.'

'You have it, sir, just as it happened.'

'I am sure we owe you an apology, Mrs Toller,' said Holmes, 'for you have certainly cleared up everything which puzzled us. And here comes the country surgeon and Mrs Rucastle, so I think. Watson, that we had best escort Miss Hunter back to Winchester, as it seems to me that our *locus standi* now is rather a questionable one.'

And thus was solved the mystery of the sinister house with the copper beeches in front of the door. Mr Rucastle survived, but was always a broken man, kept alive solely through the care of his devoted wife. They still live with their old servants, who probably know so much of Rucastle's past life that he finds it difficult to part from them. Mr Fowler and Miss Rucastle were married, by special license, in Southampton the day after their flight, and he is now the holder of a government appointment in the island of Mauritius. As to Miss Violet Hunter, my friend Holmes, rather to my disappointment, manifested no further interest in her when once she had ceased to be the centre of one of his problems, and she is now the head of a private school at Walsall, where I believe that she has met with considerable success.

ISRAEL ZANGWILL

Cheating the Gallows

THEY SAY that a union of opposites makes the happiest marriage, and perhaps it is on the same principle that men who chum together are always so oddly assorted. You shall find a man of letters sharing diggings with an auctioneer, and a medical student pigging with a stockbroker's clerk. Perhaps each thus escapes the temptation to talk 'shop' in his hours of leisure, while he supplements his own experience of life by his companion's.

There could not be an odder couple than Tom Peters and Everard G Roxdal – the contrast began with their names, and ran through the entire chapter. They had a bedroom and a sitting-room in common, but it would not be easy to find what else. To his landlady, worthy Mrs Seacon, Tom Peters's profession was a little vague, but everybody knew that Roxdal was the manager of the City and Suburban Bank, and it puzzled her to think why a bank manager should live with such a seedy-looking person, who smoked clay pipes and sipped whiskey and water all the evening when he was at home. For Roxdal was as spruce and erect as his fellow lodger was round-shouldered and shabby, he never smoked, and he confined himself to a small glass of claret at dinner.

It is possible to live with a man and see very little of him. Where each of the partners lives his own life in his own way, with his own circle of friends and external amusements, days may go by without the men having five minutes together. Perhaps this explains why these partnerships jog along so much more peaceably than marriages, where the chain is drawn so much more tightly and galls the wedded rather than links them. Diverse, however, as were the hours and habits of Peters and Roxdal, they often breakfasted together, and they agreed in one thing – they never stayed out at night. For the rest, Peters sought his diversions in the company of journalists, and frequented debating rooms, where he propounded the most iconoclastic views; while Roxdal had highly respectable houses open to him in the suburbs and was, in fact, engaged to be married to Clara Newell, the charming daughter of a retired corn merchant, a widower with no other child.

Clara naturally took up a good deal of Roxdal's time, and he often dressed to go to the play with her, while Peters stayed at home in a faded dressing-gown and loose slippers. Mrs Seacon liked to see gentlemen about the house in evening dress, and made comparisons not favourable to Peters. And this in spite of the fact that he gave her infinitely less trouble than the younger man. It was Peters who first took the apartments, and it was characteristic of his easy-going temperament that he was so openly and naively delighted with the view of the Thames obtainable from the bedroom window, that Mrs Seacon was emboldened to ask twenty-five per cent more than she had intended. She soon returned to her normal terms, however, when his friend Roxdal called the next day to inspect the rooms, and overwhelmed her with a demonstration of their numerous shortcomings. He pointed out that their being on the ground floor was not an advantage, but a disadvantage, since they were nearer the noises of the street – in fact, the house being a corner one, the noises of two streets. Roxdal continued to exhibit the same finicking temperament in the petty details of the menage. His shirt fronts were never sufficiently starched, nor his boots sufficiently polished. Tom Peters, having no regard for rigid linen, was always good-tempered and satisfied, and never acquired the respect of his landlady. He wore blue-check shirts and loose ties even on Sundays. It is true he did not go to church, but slept on till Roxdal returned from morning service, and even then it was difficult to get him out of bed, or to make him hurry up his toilette operations. Often the midday meal would be smoking on the table while Peters would still be smoking in the bed, and Roxdal, with his head thrust through the folding doors that separated the bedroom from the sitting-room, would be adjuring the sluggard to arise and shake off his slumbers, and threatening to sit down without him, lest the dinner be spoiled. In revenge, Tom was usually up first on weekdays, sometimes at such unearthly hours that Polly had not yet removed the boots from outside the bedroom door, and would bawl down to the kitchen for his shaving water. For Tom, lazy and indolent as he was, shaved with the unfailing regularity of a man to whom shaving has become an instinct. If he had not kept fairly regular hours, Mrs Seacon would have set him down as an actor, so clean shaven was he. Roxdal did not shave. He wore a full beard, and being a fine figure of a man to boot, no uneasy investor could look upon him without being reassured as to the stability of the bank he managed so successfully. And thus the two men lived in an economical comradeship, all the firmer, perhaps, for their incongruities.

*

It was on a Sunday afternoon in the middle of October, ten days after Roxdal had settled in his new rooms, that Clara Newell paid her first visit to him there. She enjoyed a good deal of liberty, and did not mind accepting his invitation to tea. The corn merchant, himself indifferently educated, had an exaggerated sense of the value of culture, and so Clara, who had artistic tastes without much actual talent, had gone in for painting, and might be seen, in pretty smocks, copying pictures in the Museum. At one time it looked as if she might be reduced to working seriously at her art, for Satan, who still finds mischief for idle hands to do, had persuaded her father to embark the fruits of years of toil in bubble companies. However, things turned out not so bad as they might have been; a little was saved from the wreck, and the appearance of a suitor, in the person of Everard G Roxdal, insured her a future of competence, if not of the luxury she had been entitled to expect. She had a good deal of affection for Everard, who was unmistakably a clever man, as well as a good-looking one. The prospect seemed fair and cloudless. Nothing presaged the terrible storm that was about to break over these two lives. Nothing had ever for a moment come to vex their mutual contentment, till this Sunday afternoon. The October sky, blue and sunny, with an Indian summer sultriness, seemed an exact image of her life, with its aftermath of a happiness that had once seemed blighted.

Everard had always been so attentive, so solicitous, that she was as much surprised as chagrined to find that he had apparently forgotten the appointment. Hearing her astonished interrogation of Polly in the passage, Tom shambled from the sitting-room in his loose slippers and his blue-check shirt, with his eternal clay pipe in his mouth, and informed her that Roxdal had gone out suddenly.

'G-g-one out,' stammered poor Clara, all confused. 'But he asked me to come to tea.'

'Oh, you're Miss Newell, I suppose,' said Tom.

'Yes, I am Miss Newell.'

'He has told me a great deal about you, but I wasn't able honestly to congratulate him on his choice till now.'

Clara blushed uneasily under the compliment, and under the ardour of his admiring gaze. Instinctively she distrusted the man. The very first tones of his deep bass voice gave her a peculiar shudder. And then his impoliteness in smoking that vile clay was so gratuitous.

'Oh, then you must be Mr Peters,' she said in return. 'He has often spoken to me of you.'

'Ah!' said Tom, laughingly, 'I suppose he's told you all my vices. That accounts for your not being surprised at my Sunday attire.'

She smiled a little, showing a row of pearly teeth. 'Everard ascribes to you all the virtues,' she said.

'Now that's what I call a friend!' he cried, ecstatically. 'But won't you come in? He must be back in a moment. He surely would not break an appointment with *you*.' The admiration latent in the accentuation of the last pronoun was almost offensive to her.

She shook her head. She had a just grievance against Everard, and would punish him by going away indignantly.

'Do let *me* give you a cup of tea,' Tom pleaded. 'You must be awfully thirsty in this sultry weather. There! I will make a bargain with you! If you will come in now, I promise to clear out the moment Everard returns, and not spoil your tête-à-tête.' But Clara was obstinate; she did not at all relish this man's society, and besides, she was not going to throw away her grievance against Everard. 'I know Everard will slang me dreadfully when he comes in if I let you go,' Tom urged. 'Tell me at least where he can find you.'

'I am going to take the bus at Charing Cross, and I'm going straight home,' Clara announced determinedly. She put up her parasol, and went up the street into the Strand. A cold shadow seemed to have fallen over all things. But just as she was getting into the bus, a hansom dashed down Trafalgar Square, and a well-known voice hailed her. The hansom stopped, and Everard got out.

'I'm so glad you're a bit late,' he said. 'I was called out unexpectedly, and have been trying to rush back in time. You wouldn't have found me if you had been punctual. But I thought,' he added, laughing, 'I could rely on you as a woman.'

'I was punctual,' Clara said angrily. 'I was not getting out of this bus, as you seem to imagine, but into it, and was going home.'

'My darling!' he cried remorsefully. 'A thousand apologies.' The regret on his handsome face soothed her. He took the rose he was wearing in the buttonhole of his fashionably-cut coat and gave it to her.

'Why were you so cruel?' he murmured, as she nestled against him in the hansom. 'Think of my despair if I had come home to hear you had come and gone. Why didn't you wait a few moments?'

A shudder traversed her frame. 'Not with that man, Peters!' she murmured.

'Not with that man, Peters!' he echoed sharply. 'What is the matter with Peters?'

'I don't know,' she said. 'I don't like him.'

'Clara,' he said, half sternly, half cajolingly, 'I thought you were above these feminine weaknesses. You are punctual, strive also to be reasonable. Tom is my best friend. There is nothing Tom would not do for me, or I for Tom. You must like him, Clara; you must, if only for my sake.'

'I'll try,' Clara promised, and then he kissed her in gratitude and broad daylight.

'You'll be very nice to him at tea, won't you?' he said anxiously. 'I shouldn't like you two to be bad friends.'

'I don't want to be bad friends,' Clara protested; 'only the moment I saw him a strange repulsion and mistrust came over me.'

'You are quite wrong about him – quite wrong,' he assured her earnestly. 'When you know him better, you'll find him the best of fellows. Oh, I know,' he said suddenly, 'I suppose he was very untidy, and you women go so much by appearances!'

'Not at all,' Clara retorted. ''Tis you men who go by appearances.'

'Yes, you do. That's why you care for me,' he said, smiling.

She assured him it wasn't, that she didn't care for him only because he plumed himself, but he smiled on. His smile died away, however, when he entered his rooms and found Tom nowhere.

'I dare say you've made him run about hunting for me,' he grumbled unhappily.

'Perhaps he knew I'd come back, and went away to leave us together,' she answered. 'He said he would when you came.'

'And yet you say you don't like him!'

She smiled reassuringly. Inwardly, however, she felt pleased at the man's absence.

If Clara Newell could have seen Tom Peters carrying on with Polly in the passage, she might have felt justified in her prejudice against him. It must be confessed, though, that Everard also carried on with Polly. Alas! it is to be feared that men are much of a muchness where women are concerned; shabby men and smart men, bank managers and journalists, bachelors and semi-detached bachelors. Perhaps it was a mistake after all to say the chums had nothing patently in common. Everard, I am afraid, kissed Polly rather more often than Clara, and although it was because he respected her less, the reason would perhaps not have been sufficiently consoling to his affianced wife. For Polly was pretty, especially on alternate Sunday afternoons, and when at 10pm she returned from her outings, she was generally met in the passage by one or the other of the men. Polly liked to receive the homage of real gentlemen, and set her white cap at all indifferently. Thus, just before Clara knocked on that memorable Sunday afternoon, Polly, being confined to the house by the unwritten code regulating the lives of servants, was amusing herself by flirting with Peters.

'You *are* fond of me a little bit,' the graceless Tom whispered, 'aren't you?'

'You know I am, sir,' Polly replied.

'You don't care for anyone else in the house?'

'Oh, no sir, and never let anyone kiss me but you. I wonder how it is, sir?' Polly replied ingenuously.

'Give me another,' Tom answered.

She gave him another, and tripped to the door to answer Clara's knock.

And that very evening, when Clara was gone and Tom still out, Polly turned without the faintest atom of scrupulosity, or even jealousy, to the more fascinating Roxdal, and accepted his amorous advances. If it would seem at first sight that Everard had less excuse for such frivolity than his friend; perhaps the seriousness he showed in this interview may throw a different light upon the complex character of the man.

'You're quite sure you don't care for anyone but me?' he asked earnestly.

'Of course not, sir!' Polly replied indignantly. 'How could I?'

'But you care for that soldier I saw you out with last Sunday?'

'Oh, no sir, he's only my young man,' she said apologetically.

'Would you give him up?' he asked suddenly.

Polly's pretty face took a look of terror. 'I couldn't, sir! He'd kill me. He's such a jealous brute, you've no idea.'

'Yes, but suppose I took you away from here?' he whispered eagerly. 'Some place where he couldn't find you – South America, Africa, somewhere thousands of miles away.'

'Oh, sir, you frighten me!' whispered Polly, cowering before his ardent eyes, which shone in the dimly-lit passage.

'Would you come with me?' he entreated. She did not answer; she shook herself free and ran into the kitchen, trembling with a vague fear.

*

One morning, earlier than his earliest hour of demanding shaving water, Tom rang the bell violently and asked the alarmed Polly what had become of Mr Roxdal.

'How should I know, sir?' she gasped. 'Ain't he been in, sir?'

'Apparently not,' Tom answered anxiously. 'He never remains out. We have been here for weeks now, and I can't recall a single night he hasn't been home before twelve. I can't make it out.' All inquiries proved futile. Mrs Seacon reminded him of the thick fog that had come on suddenly the night before.

'What fog?' asked Tom.

'Lord! didn't you notice it, sir?'

'No, I came in early, smoked, read, and went to bed about eleven. I never thought of looking out of the window.'

'It began about ten,' said Mrs Seacon, 'and got thicker and thicker. I couldn't see the lights of the river from my bedroom. The poor gentleman has been and gone and walked into the water.' She began to whimper.

'Nonsense, nonsense,' said Tom, though his expression belied his words. 'At the worst I should think he couldn't find his way home, and couldn't get a cab, so put up for the night at some hotel. I dare say it will be all right.' He began to whistle as if in restored cheerfulness. At eight o'clock there came a letter for Roxdal, marked *Immediate*, but as he did not turn up for breakfast, Tom went round personally to the City and Suburban Bank. He waited half an hour there, but the manager did not make his appearance. Then he left the letter with the cashier and went away.

That afternoon it was all over London that the manager of the City and Suburban had disappeared, and that many thousands of pounds in gold and notes had disappeared with him.

Scotland Yard opened the letter marked *Immediate*, and noted that there had been a delay in its delivery, for the address had been obscure, and an official alteration had been made. It was written in a feminine hand and said: 'On second thought I cannot accompany you. Do not try to see me again. Forget me. I shall never forget you.'

There was no signature.

Clara Newell, distracted, disclaimed all knowledge of this letter. Polly deposed that the fugitive had proposed flight to her, and the routes to Africa and South America were especially watched.

Yet months passed without result. Tom Peters went about overwhelmed with grief and astonishment. The police took possession of all the missing man's effects.

Gradually the hue and cry dwindled, and died.

'At last we meet!' cried Tom Peters, his face lighting up in joy. 'How *are* you, dear Miss Newell?'

Clara greeted him coldly. Her face had an abiding pallor now. Her lover's flight and shame had prostrated her for weeks. Her soul was the arena of contending instincts. Alone of all the world she still believed in Everard's innocence, felt that there was something more than met the eye, divined some devilish mystery behind it all. And yet that damning letter from the anonymous lady shook her sadly. Then, too, there was the deposition of Polly. When she heard Peters's voice accosting her, all her old repugnance resurged. It flashed upon her that this man – Roxdal's boon companion – must know far more than he had told to the police. She remembered how Everard had spoken of him, with what affection and confidence! Was it likely he was utterly ignorant of Everard's movements?

Mastering her repugnance, she held out her hand. It might be well to keep in touch with him; he was possibly the clue to the mystery. She noticed he was dressed a shade more trimly, and was smoking a meerschaum. He walked along at her side, making no offer to put his pipe out.

'You have not heard from Everard?' he asked. She flushed.

'Do you think I'm an accessory after the fact?' she cried.

'No, no,' he said soothingly. 'Pardon me, I was thinking he might have written – giving no exact address, of course. Men do sometimes dare to write thus to women. But, of course, he knows you too well – you would have told the police.'

'Certainly,' she exclaimed, indignantly. 'Even if he is innocent he must face the charge.'

'Do you still entertain the possibility of his innocence?'

'I do,' she said boldly, and looked him full in the face. His eyelids drooped with a quiver. 'Don't you?'

'I have hoped against hope,' he replied, in a voice faltering with emotion. 'Poor old Everard! But I am afraid there is no room for doubt. Oh, this wicked curse of money – tempting the noblest and the best of us.'

The weeks rolled on. Gradually she found herself seeing more and more of Tom Peters, and gradually, strange to say, he grew less repulsive. From the talks they had together, she began to see that there was really no reason to put faith in Everard; his criminality, his faithlessness, were too flagrant. Gradually she grew ashamed of her early mistrust of Peters; remorse bred esteem, and esteem ultimately ripened into feelings so warm that when Tom gave freer vent to the love that had been visible to Clara from the first, she did not repulse him.

It is only in books that love lives forever. Clara, so her father thought, showed herself a sensible girl in plucking out an unworthy affection and casting it from her heart. He invited the new suitor to his house, and took to him at once. Roxdal's somewhat supercilious manner had always jarred upon the unsophisticated corn merchant. With Tom the old man got on much better. While evidently quite as well informed and cultured as his whilom friend, Tom knew how to impart his superior knowledge with the accent on the knowledge rather than on the superiority, while he had the air of gaining much information in return. Those who are most conscious of the defects in early education are most resentful of other people sharing their consciousness. Moreover, Tom's *bonhomie* was far more to the old fellow's liking than the studied politeness of his predecessor, so that on the whole Tom made more of a conquest of the father than of the daughter. Nevertheless, Clara was by no means unresponsive to Tom's affection, and when, after one of his visits to the house, the old man kissed her fondly and spoke of the happy turn things had taken, and how, for the second time in their lives, things had mended when they seemed at their blackest, her heart swelled with a gush of gratitude and joy, and she fell sobbing into her father's arms.

Tom calculated that he made a clear five hundred a year by occasional journalism, besides possessing some profitable investments which he had inherited from his mother, so that there was no reason for delaying the marriage. It was fixed for May Day, and the honeymoon was to be spent in Italy.

But Clara was not destined to happiness. From the moment she had promised herself to her first love's friend, old memories began to rise up and reproach her. Strange thoughts stirred in the depths of her soul, and in the silent watches of the night she seemed to hear Everard's voice, charged with grief and upbraiding. Her uneasiness increased as her wedding day drew near. One night, after a pleasant afternoon spent in being rowed by Tom among the upper reaches of the Thames, she retired full of vague forebodings. And she dreamed a terrible dream. The dripping figure of Everard stood by her bedside, staring at her with ghastly eyes. Had he been drowned on the passage to his land of exile? Frozen with horror, she put the question.

'I have never left England!' the vision answered.

Her tongue clove to the roof of her mouth.

'Never left England?' she repeated, in tones which did not seem to be hers.

The wraith's stony eyes stared on.

'Where have you been?' she asked in her dream.

'Very near you.'

'There has been foul play then!' she shrieked.

The phantom shook its head in doleful assent.

'I knew it!' she shrieked. 'Tom Peters – Tom Peters has done away with you. Is it not he? Speak!'

'Yes, it is he – Tom Peters – whom I loved more than all the world.'

Even in the terrible oppression of the dream she could not resist saying, woman-like: 'Did I not warn you against him?'

The phantom made no reply.

'But what was the motive?' she asked at length.

'Love of gold – and you. And you are giving yourself to him,' it said sternly.

'No, no, Everard! I will not! I swear it! Forgive me!' The spirit shook its head.

'You love him. Women are false – as false as men.'

She strove to protest again, but her tongue refused to speak.

'If you marry him, I shall always be with you! Beware!'

The dripping figure vanished as suddenly as it came, and Clara awoke in a cold perspiration. Oh, it was horrible! The man she had learned to love was the murderer of the man she had learned to forget! How her original prejudice had been justified! Distracted, shaken to her depths, she would not take counsel even of her father, but informed the police of her suspicions. A raid was made on Tom s rooms, and lo! the stolen notes were found.

Tom was arrested. Attention was now concentrated on the corpses washed up by the river. It was not long before the body of Roxdal came to shore, the face distorted beyond recognition by long immersion, but the clothes patently his, a pocketbook in the breast-pocket removing the last doubt. Mrs Seacon and Polly and Clara Newell all identified the body. Both juries returned a verdict of murder against Tom Peters, the recital of Clara's dream producing a unique impression in the court and throughout the country. The theory of the prosecution was that Roxdal had brought home the money, whether to fly alone or to divide it, or even for some innocent purpose, as Clara believed; that Peters determined to have it all, that he had gone out for a walk with the deceased, and had pushed him into the river, and that he was further impelled to the crime by his love for Clara Newell, as was evident from his subsequent relations with her. The judge put on the black cap. Tom Peters was duly hanged by the neck till he was dead.

BRIEF RESUMÉ OF THE CULPRIT'S CONFESSION

When you all read this I shall be dead and laughing at you. I have been hanged for my own murder. I am Everard G Roxdal. I am also Tom Peters. *We two were one!*

When I was a young man my moustache and beard wouldn't come. I bought false ones to improve my appearance. One day, after I had become manager of the City and Suburban Bank, I took off my beard and moustache at home; and then the thought crossed my mind that nobody would know me without them. I was another man. Instantly it flashed upon me that if I ran away from the Bank, that other man could be left in London, while the police were scouring the world for a non-existent fugitive.

But this was only the crude germ of the idea. Slowly I matured my plan. The man who was going to be left in London must be known to a circle of acquaintances beforehand. It would be easy enough to masquerade in the evenings in my beardless condition, with other disguises of dress and voice. But this was not brilliant enough. *I conceived the idea of living with him!*

We shared rooms at Mrs Seacon's. It was a great strain, but it was only for a few weeks. I had trick clothes in my bedroom like those of quick-change artists; in a moment I could pass from Roxdal to Peters and from Peters to Roxdal. Polly had to clean two pairs of boots each morning, cook two dinners, and so on. She and Mrs Seacon saw one or the other of us nearly every moment; it never dawned upon them that *they never saw both of us together!*

At meals I would not be interrupted, ate off two plates, and conversed with my friend in loud tones. At other times we dined at different hours. On Sundays one was supposed to be asleep when the other was in church. There is no landlady in the world to whom the idea would have occurred than one man was troubling himself to be two (and to pay for two, including washing).

I worked up the idea of Roxdal's flight, asked Polly to go with me, manufactured that feminine letter that arrived on the morning of my disappearance. As Tom Peters I mixed with a journalistic set. I had another room where I kept the gold and notes till I mistakenly thought the thing had blown over. Unfortunately, returning from the other room on the night of my disappearance with Roxdal's clothes in a bundle I intended to drop into the river, the bundle was stolen from me in the fog, and the man into whose possession it ultimately came appears to have committed suicide.

What, perhaps, ruined me was my desire to keep Clara's love, and to transfer it to the survivor. Everard told her I was the best of fellows. Once married to her, I would not have had anything to fear. Even if she had discovered the trick, a wife cannot give evidence against her husband, and often does not want to. I made none of the usual slips, but no man can guard against a girl's nightmare after a day up the river and a supper at the Star and Garter. I might have told the judge he was an ass, but then I should have had penal servitude for bank robbery, and that sentence would have been a great deal worse than death.

The only thing that puzzles me, though, is whether the law has committed murder or I have committed suicide.

ROBERT BARR

The Great Pegram Mystery

(with apologies to Dr Conan Doyle, and our mutual and lamented
friend the late Sherlock Holmes)

I DROPPED in on my friend, Sherlaw Kombs, to hear what he had to
say about the Pegram mystery, as it had come to be called in the
newspapers. I found him playing the violin with a look of sweet peace
and serenity on his face, which I never noticed on the countenances of
those within hearing distance. I knew this expression of seraphic calm
indicated that Kombs had been deeply annoyed about something.
Such, indeed, proved to be the case, for one of the morning papers
had contained an article, eulogising the alertness and general competence of Scotland Yard.

So great was Sherlaw Kombs's contempt for Scotland Yard that
he never would visit Scotland during his vacations, nor would he ever
admit that a Scotchman was fit for anything but export.

He generously put away his violin, for he had a sincere liking for
me, and greeted me with his usual kindness.

'I have come,' I began, plunging at once into the matter on my
mind, 'to hear what you think of the great Pegram mystery.'

'I haven't heard of it,' he said quietly, just as if all London were
not talking of that very thing. Kombs was curiously ignorant on some
subjects, and abnormally learned on others. I found, for instance,
that political discussion with him was impossible, because he did not
know who Salisbury and Gladstone were. This made his friendship a
great boon.

'The Pegram mystery has baffled even Gregory, of Scotland Yard.'

'I can well believe it,' said my friend, calmly. 'Perpetual motion, or
squaring the circle, would baffle Gregory. He's an infant, is Gregory.'

This was one of the things I always liked about Kombs. There was
no professional jealousy in him, such as characterises so many other
men.

He filled his pipe, threw himself into his deep-seated armchair,
placed his feet on the mantel, and clasped his hands behind his head.

'Tell me about it,' he said simply.

'Old Barrie Kipson,' I began, 'was a stockbroker in the City. He
lived in Pegram, and it was his custom to—'

'*Come in*!' shouted Kombs, without changing his position, but with a suddenness that startled me. I had heard no knock.

'Excuse me,' said my friend, laughing, 'my invitation to enter was a trifle premature. I was really so interested in your recital that I spoke before I thought, which a detective should never do. The fact is, a man will be here in a moment who will tell me all about this crime, and so you will be spared further effort in that line.'

'Ah, you have an appointment. In that case I will not intrude,' I said, rising.

'Sit down; I have no appointment. I did not know until I spoke that he was coming.'

I gazed at him in amazement. Accustomed as I was to his extraordinary talents, the man was a perpetual surprise to me. He continued to smoke quietly, but evidently enjoyed my consternation.

'I see you are surprised. It is really too simple to talk about, but from my position opposite the mirror, I can see the reflection of objects in the street. A man stopped, looked at one of my cards, and then glanced across the street. I recognised my card, because as you know, they are all in scarlet. If, as you say, London is talking of this mystery, it naturally follows that he will talk of it, and the chances are he wished to consult me about it. Anyone can see that, besides there is always – Come in!' There was a rap at the door this time.

A stranger entered. Sherlaw Kombs did not change his lounging attitude.

'I wish to see Mr Sherlaw Kombs, the detective,' said the stranger, coming within the range of the smoker's vision.

'This is Mr Kombs,' I remarked at last, as my friend smoked quietly, and seemed half-asleep.

'Allow me to introduce myself,' continued the stranger, fumbling for a card.

'There is no need. You are a journalist,' said Kombs.

'Ah,' said the stranger, somewhat taken aback, 'you know me, then.'

'Never saw or heard of you in my life before.'

'Then how in the world—'

'Nothing simpler. You write for an evening paper. You have written an article slating the book of a friend. He will feel badly about it, and you will condole with him. He will never know who stabbed him unless I tell him.'

'The devil!' cried the journalist, sinking into a chair and mopping his brow, while his face became livid.

'Yes,' drawled Kombs, 'it is a devil of a shame that such things are done. But what would you? as we say in France.'

When the journalist had recovered his second wind he pulled himself together somewhat. 'Would you object to telling me how you know these particulars about a man you say you have never seen?'

'I rarely talk about these things,' said Kombs with great composure. 'But as the cultivation of the habit of observation may help you in your profession, and thus in a remote degree benefit me by making your paper less deadly dull, I will tell you. Your first and second fingers are smeared with ink, which shows that you write a great deal. This smeared class embraces two sub-classes, clerks or accountants, and journalists. Clerks have to be neat in their work. The ink-smear is slight in their case. Your fingers are badly and carelessly smeared; therefore, you are a journalist. You have an evening paper in your pocket. Anyone might have any evening paper, but yours is a Special Edition, which will not be on the streets for half-an-hour yet. You must have obtained it before you left the office, and to do this you must be on the staff. A book-notice is marked with a blue pencil. A journalist always despises every article in his own paper not written by himself; therefore, you wrote the article you have marked, and doubtless are about to send it to the author of the book referred to. Your paper makes a speciality of abusing all books not written by some member of its own staff. That the author is a friend of yours, I merely surmised. It is all a trivial example of ordinary observation.'

'Really, Mr Kombs, you are the most wonderful man on earth. You are the equal of Gregory, by Jove, you are.'

A frown marred the brow of my friend as he placed his pipe on the sideboard and drew his self-cocking six-shooter.

'Do you mean to insult me, sir?'

'I do not – I – I assure you. You are fit to take charge of Scotland Yard tomorrow. I am in earnest, indeed I am, sir.'

'Then Heaven help you,' cried Kombs, slowly raising his right arm.

I sprang between them.

'Don't shoot!' I cried. 'You will spoil the carpet. Besides Sherlaw, don't you see the man means well. He actually thinks it is a compliment!'

'Perhaps you are right,' remarked the detective, flinging his revolver carelessly beside his pipe, much to the relief of the third party. Then, turning to the journalist, he said, with his customary bland courtesy:

'You wanted to see me, I think you said. What can I do for you Mr Wilber Scribbings?'

The journalist started.

'How do you know my name?' he gasped.

Kombs waved his hand impatiently.

'Look inside your hat if you doubt your own name.'

I then noticed for the first time that the name was plainly to be seen inside the top-hat Scribbings held upside down in his hands.

'You have heard, of course, of the Pegram mystery—'

'Tush,' cried the detective; 'do not, I beg of you, call it a mystery. There is no such thing. Life would become more tolerable if there ever was a mystery. Nothing is original. Everything has been done before. What about the Pegram affair?'

'The Pegram – ah – case has baffled everyone. The *Evening Blade* wishes you to investigate, so that it may publish the result. It will pay you well. Will you accept the commission?'

'Possibly. Tell me about the case.'

'I thought everybody knew the particulars. Mr Barrie Kipson lived at Pegram. He carried a first-class season ticket between the terminus and that station. It was his custom to leave for Pegram on the 5.30 train each evening. Some weeks ago, Mr Kipson was brought down by the influenza. On his first visit to the City after his recovery, he drew something like £300 in notes, and left the office at his usual hour to catch the 5.30. He was never seen again alive, as far as the public have been able to learn. He was found at Brewster in a first-class compartment on the Scotch Express, which does not stop between London and Brewster. There was a bullet in his head, and his money was gone, pointing plainly to murder and robbery.'

'And where is the mystery, may I ask?'

'There are several unexplainable things about the case. First, how came he on the Scotch Express, which leaves at six, and does not stop of Pegram? Second, the ticket examiners at the terminus would have turned him out if he showed his season ticket; and all the tickets sold for the Scotch Express on the 21st are accounted for. Third, how could the murderer have escaped? Fourth, the passengers in the two compartments on each side of the one where the body was found heard no scuffle and no shot fired.'

'Are you sure the Scotch Express on the 21st did not stop between London and Brewster?'

'Now that you mention the fact, it did. It was stopped by signal just outside of Pegram. There was a few moments' pause, when the line was reported clear, and it went on again. This frequently happens, as there is a branch line beyond Pegram.'

Mr Sherlaw Kombs pondered for a few moments, smoking his pipe silently.

'I presume you wish the solution in time for tomorrow's paper?'

'Bless my soul, no. The editor thought if you evolved a theory in a month you would do well.'

'My dear sir, I do not deal with theories, but with facts. If you can make it convenient to call here tomorrow at 8am. I will give you the full particulars early enough for the first edition. There is no sense in taking up much time over so simple an affair as the Pegram case. Good afternoon, sir.'

Mr Scribbings was too much astonished to return the greeting. He left in a speechless condition, and I saw him go up the street with his hat still in his hand.

Sherlaw Kombs relapsed into his old lounging attitude, with his hands clasped behind his head. The smoke came from his lips in quick puffs at first, then at longer intervals. I saw he was coming to a conclusion, so I said nothing.

Finally he spoke in his most dreamy manner. 'I do not wish to seem to be rushing things at all, Whatson, but I am going out tonight on the Scotch Express. Would you care to accompany me?'

'Bless me!' I cried, glancing at the clock, 'you haven't time, it is after five now.'

'Ample time, Whatson – ample,' he murmured, without changing his position. 'I give myself a minute and a half to change slippers and dressing-gown for boots and coat, three seconds for hat, twenty-five seconds to the street, forty-two seconds waiting for a hansom, and then seven at the terminus before the express starts. I shall be glad of your company.'

I was only too happy to have the privilege of going with him. It was most interesting to watch the workings of so inscrutable a mind. As we drove under the lofty iron roof of the terminus I noticed a look of annoyance pass over his face.

'We are fifteen seconds ahead of our time,' he remarked, looking at the big clock. 'I dislike having a miscalculation of that sort occur.'

The great Scotch Express stood ready for its long journey. The detective tapped one of the guards on the shoulder.

'You have heard of the so-called Pegram mystery, I presume?'

'Certainly, sir. It happened on this very train, sir.'

'Really? Is the same carriage still on the train?'

'Well, yes, sir, it is,' replied the guard, lowering his voice, 'but of course, sir, we have to keep very quiet about it. People wouldn't travel in it, else, sir.'

'Doubtless. Do you happen to know if anybody occupies the compartment in which the body was found?'

'A lady and gentleman, sir; I put 'em in myself, sir.'

'Would you further oblige me,' said the detective, deftly slipping half-a-sovereign into the hand of the guard, 'by going to the window and informing them in an offhand casual sort of way that the tragedy took place in that compartment?'

'Certainly, sir.'

We followed the guard, and the moment he had imparted his news there was a suppressed scream in the carriage. Instantly a lady came out, followed by a florid-faced gentleman, who scowled at the guard. We entered the now empty compartment, and Kombs said:

'We would like to be alone here until we reach Brewster.'

'I'll see to that, sir,' answered the guard, locking the door.

When the official moved away, I asked my friend what he expected to find in the carriage that would cast any light on the case.

'Nothing,' was his brief reply.

'Then why do you come?'

'Merely to corroborate the conclusions I have already arrived at.'

'And may I ask what those conclusions are?'

'Certainly,' replied the detective, with a touch of lassitude in his voice. 'I beg to call your attention, first, to the fact that this train stands between two platforms, and can be entered from either side. Any man familiar with the station for years would be aware of that fact. This shows how Mr Kipson entered the train just before it started.'

'But the door on this side is locked,' I objected, trying it.

'Of course. But every season ticket-holder carries a key. This accounts for the guard not seeing him, and for the absence of a ticket. Now let me give you some information about the influenza. The patient's temperature rises several degrees above normal, and he has a fever. When the malady has run its course, the temperature falls to three-quarters of a degree below normal. These facts are unknown to you, I imagine, because you are a doctor.'

I admitted such was the case.

'Well, the consequence of this fall in temperature is that the convalescent's mind turns toward thoughts of suicide. Then is the time he should be watched by his friends. Then was the time Mr Barrie

Kipson's friends did not watch him. You remember the 21st, of course. No? It was a most depressing day. Fog all around and mud under foot. Very good. He resolves on suicide. He wishes to be unidentified, if possible but forgets his season ticket. My experience is that a man about to commit a crime always forgets something.'

'But how do you account for the disappearance of the money?'

'The money has nothing to do with the matter. If he was a deep man, and knew the stupidness of Scotland Yard, he probably sent the notes to an enemy. If not, they may have been given to a friend. Nothing is more calculated to prepare the mind for self-destruction than the prospect of a night ride on the Scotch Express, and the view from the windows of the train as it passes through the northern part of London is particularly conducive to thoughts of annihilation.'

'What became of the weapon?'

'That is just the point on which I wish to satisfy myself. Excuse me for a moment.'

Mr Sherlaw Kombs drew down the window on the right hand side, and examined the top of the casing minutely with a magnifying glass. Presently he heaved a sigh of relief, and drew up the sash.

'Just as I expected,' he remarked, speaking more to himself than to me. 'There is a slight dent on the top of the window-frame. It is of such a nature as to be made only by the trigger of a pistol falling from the nerveless hand of a suicide. He intended to throw the weapon far out of the window, but had not the strength. It might have fallen into the carriage. As a matter of fact, it bounced away from the line and lies among the grass about ten feet six inches from the outside rail. The only question that now remains is where the deed was committed, and the exact present position of the pistol reckoned in miles from London, but that, fortunately, is too simple to even need explanation.'

'Great heavens, Sherlaw!' I cried. 'How can you call that simple? It seems to me impossible to compute.'

We were now flying over Northern London, and the great detective leaned back with every sign of ennui, closing his eyes. At last he spoke wearily:

'It is really too elementary, Whatson, but I am always willing to oblige a friend. I shall be relieved, however, when you are able to work out the ABC of detection for yourself, although I shall never object to helping you with the words of more than three syllables. Having made up his mind to commit suicide, Kipson naturally intended to do it before he reached Brewster, because tickets are again examined at that point. When the train began to stop at the signal near Pegram, he came to the false conclusion that it was stopping at Brewster. The fact that the shot was not heard is accounted for by the screech of the air-brake, added to the noise of the train. Probably the whistle was also sounding at the same moment. The train being a fast express would stop as near the signal as possible. The air-brake will stop a train in twice its own length. Call it three times in this case. Very well. At three times the length of this train from the signal-post towards London, deducting half the length of the train, as this carriage is in the middle, you will find the pistol.'

'Wonderful! ' I exclaimed.

'Commonplace,' he murmured.

At this moment the whistle sounded shrilly, and we felt the grind of the air-brakes.

'The Pegram signal again,' cried Kombs, with something almost like enthusiasm. 'This is indeed luck. We will get out here, Whatson, and test the matter.'

As the train stopped, we got out on the right-hand side of the line. The engine stood panting impatiently under the red light, which changed to green as I looked at it. As the train moved on with increasing speed, the detective counted the carriages, and noted down the number. It was now dark, with the thin crescent of the moon hanging in the western sky throwing a weird half-light on the shining metals. The rear lamps of the train disappeared around a curve, and the signal stood at baleful red again. The black magic of the lonesome night in that strange place impressed me, but the detective was a most practical man. He placed his back against the signal-post, and paced up the line with even strides, counting his steps. I walked along the permanent way beside him silently. At last he stopped, and took a tape-line from his pocket. He ran it out until the ten feet six inches were unrolled, scanning the figures in the wan light of the new moon. Giving me the end, he placed his knuckles on the metals, motioning me to proceed down the embankment. I stretched out the line, and then sank my hand in the damp grass to mark the spot.

'Good God!' I cried, aghast, 'what is this?'

'It is the pistol,' said Kombs quietly.

It was!!

Journalistic London will not soon forget the sensation that was caused by the record of the investigations of Sherlaw Kombs, as printed at length in the next day's *Evening Blade*. Would that my story ended here. Alas! Kombs contemptuously turned over the pistol to Scotland Yard. The meddlesome officials, actuated, as I always hold, by jealousy, found the name of the seller upon it. They investigated. The seller testified that it had never been in the possession of Mr Kipson, as far as he knew. It was sold to a man whose description tallied with that of a criminal long watched by the police. He was arrested, and turned Queen's Evidence in the hope of hanging his pal. It seemed that Mr Kipson, who was a gloomy, taciturn man, and usually came home in a compartment by himself, thus escaping observation, had been murdered in the lane leading to his house. After robbing him, the miscreants turned their thoughts towards the disposal of the body – a subject that always occupies a first-class criminal mind before the deed is done. They agreed to place it on the line, and have it mangled by the Scotch Express, then nearly due. Before they got the body halfway up the embankment the express came along and stopped. The guard got out and walked along the other side to speak with the engineer. The thought of putting the body into an empty first-class carriage instantly occurred to the murderers. They opened the door with the deceased's key. It is supposed that the pistol dropped when they were hoisting the body in the carriage.

The Queen's Evidence dodge didn't work, and Scotland Yard ignobly insulted my friend Sherlaw Kombs by sending him a pass to see the villains hanged.

HARRY BLYTH

The Accusing Shadow

'AH, YES, my friend, success in our profession has its joys, but when one becomes my age, and has seen as much as I have of tragedy and evilness, fraud and generosity, dark plottings, and the grimmest of humour, repose offers delights which, in my younger years, were undreamed of by me. So it comes that now I say gladly, let my good partner, Sexton Blake, take the rewards and the honours, while I sit peacefully under my vine, and cultivate my garden.'

'In other words, Jules Gervaise, the most astute of cosmopolitan detectives, the expertest unraveller of mysteries, and the most profound of observers, will cease to be a terror to evil-doers, and those who seek his sage counsel and quick action will seek in vain.'

'That, my dear Saul Lynn, is precisely my determination. Unfortunately I have not quite settled where my vine shall grow, or in which particular part of Europe I shall raise my cabbages. Like most men who are at home in any part of the world. I have had no real home anywhere, so I have a wide choice before me.'

These two men – Jules Gervaise, of Paris, thin, wiry, alert, and wonderfully keen-eyed, and Saul Lynn, a stout, florid man, with rubicund, unwrinkled face, and short white hair, which stood up like bristles on a short brush – sat together in the latter's dining-room in a small comfortable house in the neighbourhood of Kennington Oval.

It was a heavy, gloomy afternoon, in the dreariest autumn London had known for some years, which is a great deal to allow; and both men regarded the fire which glowed in the grate with encouraging appreciation.

'In a few days I shall be pretty much in the same position as yourself, said Mr Lynn. 'When my dear daughter Daisy is married, I shall stand alone in the world, without chick or child. Two lone men might do worse than rent a house between them.'

'Indeed, yes,' replied Gervaise, without enthusiasm. 'Although we have not seen much of one another, our acquaintanceship dates from some years back. But, tell me, my friend, is your daughter's prospected union satisfactory to you both, and especially to her?'

'Bless me, yes! It is a most desirable match from every point of view. George Roach is older than Daisy, that is true, but he is a steady, generous man, wonderfully well off, and devoted to her. What more can any parent desire?'

'And the young lady returns his affection?'

'Of course. There had been some foolish flirtation between her and a young fellow named Rupert Peel, one of Mr Roach's clerks; but it was nothing worth speaking about, and when Mr Roach himself appeared on the scene, Rupert very properly ceased his visits. A worthy young man he is, but, unfortunately, poor.

'This Mr Roach has been a very great friend to you, I suppose?'

'He literally saved me from ruin. Nothing but misfortune dogged me during all my business efforts in the City. But for the generous offices of Mr Roach, I should not now have a roof over my head, and my name would be stained with a very unsatisfactory bankruptcy. He was my principal creditor, and he proved at the critical moment to be my only friend. He got me out of the tangle. By his help my business was set on its legs again, and now he is soon to become my son-in-law, all indebtedness between us will be wiped out.'

'I see,' said Gervaise drily, shooting a keen glance at his companion. 'Your daughter's wedding will include that rare combination of a love-match enveloping a business necessity.'

Up to this moment the famous criminal investigator had spoken carelessly – lazily; but now his interest was aroused, for he was a man peculiarly solicitous about the happiness of young people. Often had he declared that it gave him more satisfaction to attend a funeral than to witness a marriage which did not promise real happiness to the bride and bridegroom. He came from a country where loveless unions were, alas! too common.

'Not a necessity, my dear Gervaise,' objected Saul Lynn, with a smile. 'Under no circumstances would Mr Roach have pressed his claims against me.'

'Such generous creditors are rare. Is it possible that I may be honoured with an introduction to your future son-in-law?

'Undoubtedly. In the ordinary way you would have seen him this evening, for he gives us a call nearly every night. Yesterday, however, he was summoned hurriedly to Glasgow. He left St Pancras by the night express. We have been expecting a telegram from him all day, announcing his safe arrival in Scotland. He is generally most particular about wiring to Daisy when he is away. He must be terribly busy not to have done so this time. I suppose we shall not hear now until the morning. Hullo! There's a knock at the front door; It's a telegraph boy, I'll be bound! They don't hesitate to give a double rat-tat, with all the confidence of a duke's footman. Dear me! it's Rupert Peel's voice. Something very strange must have happened to bring him here. Daisy has ran to admit him. No doubt the poor child is anxious for news of George Roach.'

Mr Lynn's further reflections were cut short by the entrance of the two young people he had named.

Daisy was a fair, sunny creature, all grace and vivacity, with dazzling hair and bright eyes, in which the detective discerned more affection for her companion, Rupert Peel, than her father had any suspicion of. The young clerk himself was tall, lithe, with deep black locks, and strikingly large and luminous orbs, while his cheeks were peculiar for their perfect whiteness. His was a striking face, darkly handsome, but not altogether an alluring one, until he smiled, when a great light shone in it.

'We are anxious at the office about Mr Roach,' he explained to Saul Lynn. 'We have received a message from his Glasgow friends saying he has not called on them, and desiring to know the reason. We have wired to the manager of the hotel where he always stays, and he has not been there. On the other hand, it is quite certain Mr Roach arrived at St Pancras with his luggage in ample time for the train. It is also plain that while ten through tickets for Glasgow were issued for that express, only nine have been given up. So far this is all we are able to ascertain. I thought it just possible that you might be able to throw some light on this erratic behaviour of our principal. We know that he often thinks more of writing to you that to the office.'

'Indeed, I can give you no assistance. We have been very much surprised and disappointed at receiving no message from him. It's a strange business, Mr Peel. What do you make of it?'

As Mr Saul Lynn put this question, he looked more anxious than anyone there.

Jules Gervaise would have been singularly unobserving had be failed to note how absolutely unconcerned Daisy appeared to be.

'Really, sir, I have no suggestion at all to make,' returned Rupert Peel, 'and our Mr Felix Sark – he is our cashier, and the oldest servant in the firm – says that no doubt our principal changed his mind at the last moment, and, for some good reason, with which his employees have nothing to do. 'Mr Roach is not a baby,' says the cashier, 'and no doubt he is safe enough.' At any rate, it's not our business to tell him when he should communicate with us. He will let us know where he is in good time.'

'I quite agree with Mr Sark,' said Daisy decisively. 'Mr Roach is a well-travelled man, and if any accident had befallen him we should have heard of it. There is no occasion for alarm.'

'I am sure, my dear, I am glad to see you treat the matter so coolly,' said Saul Lynn, regarding his daughter with some displeasure. 'I am sure that something very unusual has occurred to our friend, or he would have written to you. However, I suppose we can do nothing but wait, and see what the morning brings forth.'

Just then someone called to see Mr Lynn on a small matter of business. He went into another room to have his interview with his visitor, and Daisy busied herself in preparing tea, to which Mr Rupert Peel had been invited, so the latter gentleman and Jules Gervaise were left together for a little.

'How are you progressing with your lessons in French, Mr Peel?' the detective asked, as carelessly as possible.

The clerk started slightly, and red spots burned in his white cheeks.

'How did you know I was learning French?'

'That is a simple matter enough. Whenever an Englishman determines to conquer the Parisian accent, he, quite unconsciously, gives a peculiar intonation to his native words, which he never gets in any other way. Yes, my friend, you are studying French, and because you contemplate taking a visit to Paris – Paris, the beautiful! Paris, the gay! Ah, yes!' Gervaise added, with that pathetic touch with which old men, so often tinge their recollections, 'I also have loved my Paris.'

'Your surmises are correct, sir. I have been studying your language. Mr Roach promised me a holiday while he was on his honeymoon, and I have resolved on seeking the distractions of the French capital, in the hope of forgetting there many things it is pain to remember here.'

'There is no forgetting,' declared the detective sagely. 'We cannot bring back a yesterday, because it lives eternally. Though we may not find it at the moment we want it, nevertheless it is stored up in one of those millions of secretive cells which go towards making up what we call brain, mind, memory. Now, be quite free with me, and tell me what you think of this coming wedding. I judge that George Roach is quite an old man – eh?'

'He is forty-eight. Daisy – Miss Lynn – is only nineteen.'

'What a gulf between! Now, had it been yourself, 'Well, sir, to be quite frank with you, I had a true and honest affection for Miss Lynn.

I believe I was not distasteful to her. I should have asked her in marriage from her father, had not Mr Roach informed me, in quite a casual way, that it was in his power to make Mr Lynn a beggar, and drive his daughter into the world to earn her bread. On that hint I ceased my visits. How could I have looked my darling confidently in the face, if she knew it was through me her father was going hungry? My income is small, and though I might have supported Daisy, I could not possibly have kept her father.'

'So,' said the detective, with a pleasant smile, 'if it should turn out that anything very serious has overtaken George Roach, our friend Saul Lynn will be relieved from his oppression, and you may yet be free to marry Daisy?'

'That is true,' said Rupert, with some hesitation, 'but I had never reckoned on my master's death.'

'Bah!' ejaculated Gervaise, 'a lover thinks of everything, and risks his life's happiness on a chance. You are inwardly praying now that George Roach may never be heard of again.'

'It is not in human nature for a man to be anxious for the success of his rival,' was the quiet, and even dignified, declaration of Rupert. 'But,' he added, 'at present there is a reason for supposing that anything at all out of the way has occurred to the gentleman who is so soon to call Daisy his wife.'

'Surely, my young friend, after having your waistcoat washed you have put it on before it 'was properly dry! See how it smokes before the blaze of the fire!'

'Really, sir!' protested the clerk, his white face crimsoning all over, 'your comments are uncommonly personal, and scarcely free from insolence. It is surely my own affair whether I have my waistcoat washed or not.'

'Certainly. But that material is not made to wash. It is two-thirds cotton, and all shoddy. It crinkles up as it dries. You will never be able to wear it again. If you listen to me you will put it into the first convenient fire you can use, and you will be careful to see that it is all consumed. There, there! do not fly into a temper. You will soon want my help and advice. Never forget that the smell of wet blood drying has an unmistakable odour to those who have even once known it.'

'You are a miracle – a wizard!' exclaimed Rupert, gazing aghast at the detective, and swaying before him with his fierce, inward agitation.

'Hush!' cried Gervaise, 'Saul Lynn is coming. I am neither of the things you call me. I am simply *your friend*!'

*

'The fellow who just called on me,' said Mr Lynn, as he re-entered the room, his face more ruddy, and again beaming, 'came from the confectioner's, to arrange about the wedding-breakfast. I shall have a marquee erected in our back garden – indeed, I assure you, Gervaise, I am going to make this marriage quite a stylish thing – absolutely a function. Why, Mr Peel, do you want to leave us so suddenly? I quite understood you were going to remain for tea? Oh! well, if you remember you must go back to the office, I'll not detain you. Business before anything – especially Mr Roach's business. I do hope all is well with him,' he continued fervently, as he followed the clerk to the door, and let him out into the street, with an ill-disguised sigh of relief. 'I don't suppose there is any real cause for anxiety about my future son-in-law. Do you, Gervaise?' added Saul, as he once more returned to the room.

'I cannot tell,' was the grave answer. 'I shall be at St Pancras Station before eight tomorrow morning. The guard who took the Scotch Express out of St Pancras last night will probably be returning from St Enoch to London tonight. If I see him he will be able to tell me whether Mr Roach was among his passengers or not.

'Thank goodness you are so interested in my affairs!' cried Saul Lynn half-incredulously. 'But only an hour ago you declared you had cast all professional work aside. You were sure you would never more busy yourself with the concerns of others. Is the old instinct too strong for you? Must you for ever remain the detective?'

'No, no, my friend,' declared Gervaise gently. 'I hope not. I pray it may not be so. But your daughter is young; she is fair to gaze on. An atmosphere of goodness surrounds her. I should not like to see her stricken down by a great sorrow. Such enquiries as I may make in this affair shall be for Daisy's sake – for her sake only.'

'Of course I know Mr George Roach, sir,' said the guard of the Scotch Express, whom the detective interviewed early on the following morning. 'He has often travelled to Glasgow with me. We know our 'through' passengers, and they know us. I remember quite well seeing that gentleman's portmanteau and handbag, his rug, and his newspapers in the carriage which I had selected for him. I did not miss him until we reached Leicester. When I discovered that he was not in the train I took the gentleman's traps into my own van, and left them in the cloakroom at Glasgow when we arrived there. I thought he had stayed a little too long at Bedford, our first stopping-place, and so had missed us. Bless you, sir, some of our 'regulars' often do that! Under such circumstances a gentleman does not bother much about his luggage, especially by the night train. He knows his things are safe enough in our hands. I did ask a question or two about Mr Roach when I was at Bedford this morning, and when I found he had not got out there I came to one very natural conclusion.'

'And what was that, pray?' asked Gervaise.

'Why, sir, that he did not travel with us. At the last moment something must have happened to make Mr Roach change his mind, and he abandoned our train before it left St Pancras. It's quite plain,' added the guard, 'folks don't disappear out of railway carriages, except in books. If your friend had committed suicide, we should have heard of the body by this time. Take my word for it, sir, he never started by that train at all.'

'My friend,' said Gervaise, as solemnly as though he was reading a funeral oration, 'you are gifted with monumental sense. I am quite sure Mr Roach never did leave London. It is quite refreshing for me to meet with such a piece of living sanity as yourself, but it is odd I should have to go to the guard of a Scotch Express to find it. Ah!' added the detective to himself as he walked very thoughtfully along the Euston Road. 'I am glad I have no Sexton Blake with me. He would inevitably ride a bicycle, plunge into a stream, or stop an engine in full career, before he got to the end of this business. I must do my acrobatic feats in my head, and on the ground. Poor Daisy Lynn! I fear much there are some heavy revelations in store for her.'

Then, as though struck by a sudden thought, he walked into Gower Street Station.

In following closely on Jules Gervaise's heels, in his steps to unravel the desperate mystery which was soon to confront him, we shall find it necessary to omit many touching interviews which he had with Daisy, and also many of his conferences with her less unselfish father. It will be sufficient if we give the salient features of the celebrated detective's investigations.

In that labyrinth of narrow streets, with towering buildings, which lies between Fore Street and Cheapside, where railway vans for ever block the road, and great bales of 'soft' goods monopolize the pavement, might be found the warehouse of George Roach and Co, wholesale dealers in Manchester goods. It appeared to have been accidentally jammed in between two larger buildings, and it wore a constant look of pain, as though suffering from the tightness of the squeeze.

It was one of those dark places where the gas is never extinguished till the last stroke of business has struck, and there was so much hurrying to and fro, and shouting out of marks and figures, that the clerks gave one the idea of being in a perpetual state of altercation.

It was in the midst of this atmosphere, thick with commerce and cotton-dust, that Jules Gervaise soon found himself enquiring for Mr Felix Sark, the firm's cashier and oldest servant.

He proved to be a somewhat meagre individual, but sinewy withal. The bottoms of his trousers showed a marked tendency to creep up to his knees, while his sleeves were absolutely eager to get about his neck.

He had a hairless, parchment-like face, and his eyes might have been of glass for all the expression there was in them.

'No, sir,' he said, in answer to the detective's question, and regarding that worthy gentleman with scant favour, 'we have not received any letter from Mr Roach this morning, but I have no doubt that our principal will communicate with us in his own time. I trust you will tell Mr Saul Lynn what I say. Mr Roach is not a baby, to be tied to the coat-tails of his future father-in-law, and I may assure you, sir, that when he knows that a stranger has been fussing round here about his absence, he will be vastly indignant. Jules Gervaise is, if I do not err, the name of a detective. That is so, eh? Very good, then. I may tell you, sir, that you will not be paid for your meddling by this side. And, as for Mr Saul Lynn, if you expect anything from him I advise you to get it in advance. I have the pleasure of wishing you a very good-morning.'

'Good-day, my friend,' returned Gervaise, smiling blandly on the cashier. 'I look forward with great pleasure to meeting you again.'

As Jules was leaving the place he met Rupert Peel entering it. The young man's face expressed no pleasure at the encounter. With a cold 'Good morning,' he would have passed on.

'There is still no news of Mr Roach,' said the detective, stopping him.

'So I believe,' was the indifferent answer. 'But at present there is no need for alarm,' Peel continued, 'and I am sure the governor will be very cross when he hears that Mr Lynn has engaged you to come down to the warehouse making enquiries about him. Mr Roach is a very passionate man, and such a liberty as he will judge your behaviour to be may be sufficient to make him break off the match.'

'Ah!' said Gervaise, with a dry smack of his lips, fixing the clerk with his keen eyes, 'Don't you think that Death may have already done that?'

'Really, Mr Gervaise, I have not the time nor the inclination to discuss the subject with you.'

He, too, hastened away from the detective, who still smiled blandly.

'I shall get no help there,' he murmured, 'and I am glad it is so. Their aid would be misleading, while their dislike to my interference is significant.'

'It is ridiculous for Mr Sark and young Peel to feel so confident that all is well with George Roach,' declared Saul Lynn, when Gervaise next saw him. 'I am convinced that something very serious has occurred. I know of nothing that would prevent him from writing to Daisy. As he seems never to have gone by that train, the mystery becomes deeper and more alarming. Thank goodness, my dear child does not realize all that his strange silence may mean.'

'I should like you to take me to his home – the place where he lived,' said Gervaise.

'That is easily done. Being a bachelor, he occupied furnished apartments in a good house, situated in Highbury Park. We will go there at once, my dear Gervaise, if you are willing.'

'Mr Roach gave up his rooms more than a week ago,' declared Mrs Ballard, the landlady of the handsome villa at which they called and enquired about the missing man. 'Of course, you know, Mr Lynn, that he has taken a large, old-fashioned house in Canonbury, for your daughter to be mistress of. Well, he has furnished it from cellar to attic, and very beautifully, too, I believe. Latterly he has become nervous lest, as the place is empty, thieves should break into it, and so he determined to sleep there himself.'

'Alone?' asked Gervaise.

'Quite alone.'

'What a remarkable thing to do,' declared Mr Lynn. 'I suppose he said nothing to us for fear of alarming Daisy. Of course, we knew all about the house, and he was very anxious for my daughter to go over it. But the child has a superstitious notion that she must not enter her future home until she does so as its mistress.'

'I presume you found Mr Roach regular in his habits,' asked the detective.

'Most regular,' answered the lady. 'Had he been set by clockwork he could not have gone about his affairs more methodically. No club kept him out till early in the morning, though, of course, since he has been visiting at Mr Lynn's, we have not seen him home so early. I don't think, though, that he was a very happy man, for he used to be subject to long and silent fits of depression. Oh! by the way, Mr Lynn, he left an old scrapbook behind him. It's of no value to anyone but the owner, as the saying is, and not much to him, I should say. Perhaps you'll take it, sir, and give it to Mr Roach when he does make his reappearance?'

'I must enter that house at Canonbury,' said the detective, as he walked away with Saul Lynn.

'Well, so you shall, but I don't see how we can do it today. If George Roach has been sleeping there, he probably has the keys with him. I should not care to break into the place on my own responsibility. I must get some authority from the office before I will do that, so we must wait until tomorrow, at least. The worst part of this business is that no one has any legal right to set the law in motion to find our lost friend.'

The detective returned to Kennington with Mr Lynn, and there he interested himself in examining the pages of the scrapbook.

He found it to consist exclusively of extracts from the public journals, describing the almost innumerable exploits of a notorious adventuress, whose real name was Julia Barretti, but whose aliases were to be counted by the score.

She had been guilty of every variety of fraud, and had suffered various terms of imprisonment, long and short. Her beauty of face and figure was said to rival her deformity of character. She was a complete marvel of grace and wickedness.

Jules Gervaise wondered what peculiar fascination the sordid character of such a creature could have for a steady-going City merchant like Mr George Roach, till his brightened eyes lit on the following paragraph, when all his wonder vanished.

It ran as follows:

THE NOTORIOUS JULIA BARRETTI IN A NEW CHARACTER – In our yesterday's issue we gave the trial of, and sentence passed on, this most expert and dangerous swindler, the more to be feared because of her extreme fascination of manner and appearance. We now learn that three days before her last arrest she had succeeded in luring into matrimony a well-to-do City merchant, named George Roach. The lady's capture by the police brought the honeymoon to an abrupt termination, and Mr Roach is to be congratulated on his escape from the clutches of such a designing harpy. The fact that she has another husband still living has been proved beyond a doubt; so the Court will have no hesitation in releasing the too-confiding City man from his bonds.'

'And that was sixteen years ago!' mused Gervaise. 'It is no wonder that George Roach sometimes looked pensive. This was the skeleton he had in his cupboard. It is more than possible I now hold a clue to the mystery of his disappearance.

When the notion of making a search in the house the missing man had taken in Canonbury was put before Mr Felix Sark, he very promptly, and with great decision, washed his hands of the matter.

'Do as you please, gentlemen,' he said, with a shrug of his lean shoulders, 'but I will be no party to such a desecration of what will yet prove to be my employer's happy and sacred home.'

Rupert Peel also begged to be excused from taking any part in the contemplated proceedings, on the plea that he was sure it was the last thing Mr Roach would care for him to do.

'Of course, Mr Roach has the keys of the house with him,' said Mr Lynn, 'so we shall have to break into it.'

'As for the keys,' answered Felix Sark, with an ugly laugh, 'they are hanging up over Mr Peel's desk.'

'I did not know that,' exclaimed Rupert, with a scared look. 'The master must have put them there before he started for Scotland.'

'If neither of you gentlemen will accompany us yourselves, perhaps there will be no objection to me asking some of the others engaged in the warehouse to do so?'

As Mr Lynn asked this question he took the keys from Rupert Peel's trembling hands, and wondered why that young man looked so faint and ill.

'Do as you please about that,' answered Mr Sark. 'Two of our travellers are on the premises now, and, as a traveller's time always seems to be his own, doubtless they will be glad of the outing. As for me, I have to keep strictly to my time. I am never late coming in nor early in leaving.'

'A very treasure of a cashier,' said Jules Gervaise, with his bland smile.

The gentlemen Mr Sark had alluded to were quite willing to accompany the detective and Saul Lynn to the old Gothic house in Canonbury, which they found to be standing in a goodly piece of ground, well hidden from the roadway by tall, umbrageous trees and rotund shrubs. But neither of the 'bagmen' appeared to merit the disparaging comments of the cashier. One, indeed, was so intent on his business that he carried his account-book with him, and utilized such spare moments as fell to him during the journey in making entries therein, and casting up accounts.

'This place could not be more silent or seemingly more remote were it in the midst of the Black Forest,' said Gervaise. 'My friends!' he cried, with sudden excitement, 'you must, if you please, refrain from mounting these steps leading to the front door. I see, impressed on the green mould which clothes them, the forms of three pairs of boots. These imprints may prove to be of splendid help to us, and they must not be disturbed or confused until we have photographs of them. Stay a few moments here, and I will admit you by the back way.

The detective himself climbed up the left-hand parapet, which ran by the side of the steps to the main entrance. He sat on it while he bent down and turned the key in the lock. Then, having thrown the door open, he sprang into the house, landing on the mat in the hall, never once letting his feet touch the outside stone landing and steps. His desire, born of professional pride, to be the first to enter that house, and to enter alone, was gratified.

He closed the door carefully and struck a light, for the vestibule was in darkness.

Nothing there attracted his attention, save the fact that, when he turned on the burner of the gas pendant, the illuminant issued freely from it, showing that it was not off at the meter. He went into a large room on the left-hand side, mainly because its door was wide open. Here he was sufficiently surprised to see that, though the blinds were drawn down, the shutters had not been closed.

'A man who is afraid of thieves breaking into his place does not leave it so unprotected, especially when he is going on a journey,' reflected the detective, as he lit the gas. 'Ah! what is this? The return half of a double ticket between Paris and London, issued by the tourist agents, Thomas Lock and Co. I will keep it. It should prove a valuable piece of paper. In the grate there are ashes of burned paper – stiff, clayey paper, like the pages of account-books. I will put this little cloth over the fireplace, so that those precious remains may not be blown away. Now I must admit my friends, or they will fancy I am committing crimes myself.'

Making his way to the back of the house, he let his companions in by the tradesmen's entrance, at the side of the building.

'There are evidences of a great struggle having taken place in one of the rooms of the hall,' he said. 'I think it will repay us to examine every part of this house very carefully.'

In the apartment which the detective had first entered there was every proof of a desperate conflict having taken place. Chairs were overturned, some vases broken, the hearthrug heeled up and other unmistakable signs of disorder. There was some blood, too, on the fender, and on the edge of the table. All the other rooms were locked. They opened readily to the keys the detective had with him. In no other part was there any sign of disturbance, or of recent occupation.

'Now, gentlemen, we will see what the basement has to tell us,' said Gervaise.

Every cupboard and cranny was carefully examined, by the detective, at least, but he found nothing which added to his existing knowledge, or which was even suggestive.

Presently they came to a great iron door let into the wall. It evidently guarded a strong-room, built in the house – a place in which former residents had stored their plate and jewels, perchance.

None of the others would have thought it worth while looking into this, but Jules Gervaise did.

'It is odd,' said he, 'that this bunch contains a key for the meanest cupboard in the house; yet the one to open this strong-room is not on the ring. Possibly it is not locked.'

He seized the big knob which stood out in the centre of the ponderous door, and, putting some strength into the attempt, managed to swing it slowly back, disclosing an iron-clad recess, into which the sun streamed through a small, heavily barred window, which looked out from the receptacle on to the bush-covered ground outside.

The four men thronged to the narrow opening, and, looking within, saw, to their horror, the mangled form of a dead man, whose name in life had been George Roach!

Natural it was that this ghastly discovery should produce more effect on Saul Lynn than on any of the others, though each one of them was inexpressibly shocked. But Saul had been the dead man's familiar friend, and, besides, the death of the merchant meant the shattering of Saul's hopes.

The detective was cool and scarcely surprised. His bland countenance was in queer contrast with the blank faces round him.

'Gentlemen,' he said gravely, 'it is not necessary for me to tell you that this is a case of murder – brutal and determined murder!'

'We must lose no time in informing the police!' cried one of the travellers, who was obviously a very excitable man.

'Of course, the police must know of this,' agreed Jules coolly, 'there is no help for it. But, first, I will see what the poor man has left in his pockets. Aha! Here are another set of keys belonging to the house. On this bunch is a key for the door of this strong-room. A significant and suggestive fact.'

'And observe,' said Mr Lynn, 'his rings are on his fingers, his watch and chain are untouched, and now you have found his purse with money in it. So robbery did not prompt this dreadful crime.'

'One may plunder a man, yet not condescend to pick his pockets,' declared Jules. 'Mr Roach's money does not amount to six pounds, all told. It is less than one would expect a man in his position to have with him when he contemplates a journey. There is no cheque-book here. Now, sir,' added Gervaise, to the excitable individual, since you are so anxious to see the police, perhaps you will walk round as far as the station and summon them.'

While Mr Lynn and the other traveller were asking one another, in fearful whispers, who could have done this fell deed, and their other companion set about the errand Jules had suggested to him, the detective very carefully gathered together the ashes he had seen in the grate in the room upstairs. He made a little box of brown paper for them, and this he put inside his hat. After this he busied himself in making a minute examination of the grounds at the back of the house, until the inspector at the station, with two of his men, made his appearance.

To him Jules Gervaise explained what had occurred. Nor did he fail to point out to these gentlemen the importance of not disturbing the footprints he had detected impressed on the green mould which covered the steps leading to the entrance-hall. But, even as he spoke, there came a fierce knocking at the front door, and it was soon seen that three other constables had followed their chief, and had come blundering up the marble ascent, to the utter destruction of those imprints which might have proved of such invaluable help in tracking down the assassin.

'Come,' said Gervaise to Saul Lynn, 'we can do no more good here. I want to return to Mr Roach's warehouse.'

'May Providence help me!' murmured Lynn, 'but this terrible tragedy leaves me a ruined man! I had counted too much on my daughter's marriage. Never was a man so doomed to misfortune as I am.'

'Let me forget how wretchedly selfish you are,' said the detective. 'Your losses are nothing compared with the misery this crime will cause others.'

'It will be a blow to my daughter, of course,' said Lynn, 'but she is young, and will soon get over it, whereas I am old. I need my little comforts, Jules! I need them very much!'

Jules smiled grimly.

'Poor human nature,' he muttered to himself, 'what a ragged thing you are at the core! It savours of madness for me to pursue this case, for I shall not get even the husks of thanks for my pains. But there is poor little Daisy! It would be wicked of me not to put out a hand to save her.'

When Mr Felix Sark heard this distressing news, his face took an expression of such profound consternation and grief that it did not seem possible it could be feigned.

'Gentlemen,' he declared, 'I have dreaded this news all along. It has been my waking fear, and the horror of my dreams. I appeared indifferent to you only because I did not want to have my shocking presentiment realized. Poor Mr Roach! Poor Mr Roach! No better employer ever lived. And then Rupert Peel – a mere boy – so amiable! so well-intentioned! so exact to his time! Think of him! I have loved him as a father might his son! It is too awful to dwell on!'

'What has happened to Rupert Peel?' asked Jules sternly.

'My dear sir, who can possibly have committed this monstrous crime but that most unhappy of young men? Driven insane by love; love and jealousy have done it. Mr Roach had not another enemy in the world, and poor Rupert did not hate him till he took Miss Lynn from him. You don't know how he loved Miss Daisy, sir,' he added, addressing Saul, 'you never would know! I am convinced he would not have survived her wedding-day. But, dear me! how much better for him to have died himself than to have slain his master. Oh! the misery of it! And what a disgrace to our firm!'

'You are quicker than the law will be in your condemnation!' said Gervaise sharply. 'What right have you to say that Rupert Peel is guilty of this murder?'

The old, quiet, sinister look came back to the cashier's face, as he replied:

'What I say to you, gentlemen – as friends taking an interest in my late employer – need not go any further, but I may tell you that since you were here this morning I have discovered in Peel's desk a key which belongs to the door of a safe or strong-room. It is still clammy with the dried blood which stains it. It is a sad piece of evidence against him, but of course, I must not hide it from the police. Would you advise me to do so, Mr Gervaise?'

'Certainly not,' replied Jules; 'but don't forget to tell them that you found it. I think it better for the police to discover such things for themselves. Is Mr Peel here now?'

'No. He went out soon after handing that bunch of keys to you. He has not come back. It is my impression that he never will.'

'I wonder if Sark is right,' said Saul Lynn, in a musing kind of way, as he and the detective elbowed their way through the narrow thoroughfare in which stood the premises of the late George Roach. 'I never thought that Rupert Peel had the pluck to kill a rabbit, much less a man. It's a horrible business altogether.'

'Yes,' answered Gervaise in an abstracted way with the air of a man deeply pondering some problem. 'I want you to go at once to Rupert's house,' he added, with sudden life. 'If you find that he is preparing for flight be sure and make him see me before he takes that step or any other. I will go straight to Kennington, and break the news to Daisy. I will wait there for you. If you do manage to bring Rupert with you, all the better; but I fear that you are already too late – too late!'

'I suppose I must do as you wish,' said Lynn grumblingly, 'but, upon my word, I don't see why I should bother about young Peel.'

By this time they had reached Cheapside, and Jules put an effective stop to any further discussion on the subject by jumping into a passing cab, the driver of which he directed to take him to Saul's house at Kennington, leaving that gentleman to either look up Rupert Peel or follow on as he might choose, or as he best could.

Daisy listened to the horrible story the detective very gently broke to her with blanched cheeks. All its terribleness was reflected in her large, frightened eyes; but her voice was firm and clear, and she displayed no tendency to tears or towards any hysterical symptoms.

'It is very awful! very awful indeed! If it does not quite strike me down, helpless and broken, it is only because I never loved Mr Roach, and I looked with horror towards the day which was to see me his wife. He knew I did not love him. He was well aware that I agreed to marry him to save my father from ruin. This is the truth, my good friend, and it may be told now.'

'It is not news to me, any more than the fact that you do love Rupert Peel.'

'Ah, yes!' sighed the girl, burying her face in her hands. 'And I shall love him to the end of my days, as he will love me.'

'It is odd that he should have relinquished you so readily?'

'Not at all, Mr Gervaise. In the first place, he would not see my father a pauper, and myself reduced to such humble means as he is gaining; and, again, there is some mystery connected with his own father which compels him to say he will not marry anyone until his parent is dead. Ours was a hopeless case, you see, so there was little credit to me in resolving to do my duty to my father, and accept George Roach's offer.'

'Tell me, Daisy, tell me truthfully' – the voice of Jules Gervaise was most convincing and tender as he spoke – 'tell me, without fear or hesitation, whether you think it possible that, driven to frenzy by the thought of the sacrifice you contemplated, made savage and reckless by the prospect of losing you for ever, Rupert Peel can have committed this crime?'

'It is impossible!' she declared, standing up, and elevating her hands to heaven, as though imploring the azure dome beyond the clouds to bear witness to her truth. 'It is absolutely impossible! There does not live a man less likely to spill human blood than Rupert. And yet – and yet!' she cried sinking again on to her chair, 'he knew that if anything did befall George Roach he would be accused of having done the mischief!'

'Did he tell you this?' asked Jules, with a slight start.

'Oh, yes. He told Mr Sark, too, and Mr Sark quite agreed with him. He was very frightened of you, though I did try to persuade him that you would prove his friend.'

'It will be more than he deserves, if I do,' said the detective sharply. 'Ah! here is your father; back at last. You may speak freely, Mr Lynn,' added the detective, as Saul, looking very flurried, entered the room. 'Your daughter knows all about the wretched tragedy.'

'Well,' said Mr Lynn, 'my news is startling enough, but I don't see that it helps us at all. Rupert Peel has undoubtedly made a clean bolt of it. A warrant has already been issued for his apprehension, and the evening papers are all alive with more or less imaginary accounts of the crime. But, what is more extraordinary, Rupert Peel's father lies dead in his house, and his head is battered about pretty much the same as is poor George Roach's.'

'Well, well,' said the imperturbable Jules, 'this is a rare complication. I must go away now. It may be some days ere you see me again. Keep up your heart, little one,' he said to Daisy, 'if your Rupert is innocent he shall not suffer.'

'Never mind Rupert!' cried Saul angrily. 'Where are you going to, Jules?'

'To Paris, my friend. I shall leave by tonight's express. If I am not mistaken, Mr Sark will call on you presently. It may be wise to welcome him.' He nodded to Daisy as he made this remark. 'There!

that short, snappy, half-defiant, half-hesitating knock at the door must be directed by Sark's hand, and by no other.'

The detective's guess proved to be a correct one. The two men passed one another in the hall. Felix Sark was much better pleased to see Jules leave the house than the detective was to observe the cashier entering it.

It will be remembered that the kind-hearted detective had picked up, in the house where the luckless merchant lay murdered, the return portion of a ticket available between the capitals of England and France; and it scarcely need be told that he did not use it on his journey to Paris.

His first care, on his arrival in that city, was to call on the tourist agents who had issued it. As it bore their imprint, and their own number, he was hopeful that Thomas Lock and Company might be able to give him some clue as to the identity of the original purchaser.

'Ah, sir!' cried the clerk, when questioned, 'I have indeed cause for remembering that ticket from us. It was no less celebrated a personage than Madame Ollivier, the magnificence of whose receptions is the wonder and delight of our metropolis. Her superb equipage honoured our office by remaining outside it while she herself paid for the ticket.'

'Tell me,' said Jules, 'is this Madame Ollivier very beautiful?'

'She is incomparable! But, after all, it is not so must her face as the exquisite grace of her manner.'

'And, of course, a Frenchwoman?'

'Ah! Who can tell? I am told she can converse in all languages with equal charm and facility.'

The detective made his way to the offices of the secret police.

'My dear Jules Gervaise, I am delighted to see you,' cried the Chief of the Secret Police, as he grasped our detective's hand with genuine warmth. 'And not the less so because you want information concerning that brilliant but mysterious woman, Madame Ollivier. Our positions are precisely similar. We also are most anxious to learn all we can about the lady, because, though she has succeeded in attracting some of the best people in France, we are convinced she is merely an adventuress. Her residence is the nest of a crowd of conspirators; and there they hatch their nefarious schemes against our Government.

'We want to put an end to these plots,' continued the Chief, 'break up for ever these intrigues, and drive Madame Ollivier out of Paris. Now, Jules, you are the very man for our purpose. By helping us you will gain all the information you desire for yourself. You know quite well that, were we against you, it would be as well for you to return to England at once. It is a bargain, then? Very good. Now let us devise some good scheme that will enable you to enter Madame Ollivier's house this very night as a welcome and unsuspected guest.'

In one of the most fashionable quarters of Paris, standing in its own tastefully arranged grounds, hidden from the gaze of the vulgar by high walls and more lofty trees, stood the ornate building wherein Madame Ollivier had made her sumptuous home.

Here by the lavishness of her hospitality, and the brilliancy of her receptions, she had succeeded in capturing, dazzling, and alluring many of the most renowned men and women of the famous city. On this particular night, carriage after carriage had rolled to her gates, depositing on the rich carpet, which ran to the very gravel, its glittering occupant.

Light streamed from every window, while inside all was colour, movement, and melody. The very air seemed rich with delight and harmony.

But, even when the decorous revelry was at its height, the fascinating hostess, the much-applauded Madame Ollivier, withdrew from the crush of the distinguished guests, and, seating herself in a small, deserted ante-chamber, she sighed wearily. There was that pained expression about her features, too, which told how much relief her feelings would experience could she but let tears loosen the mental strain which made her temples throb.

'Do you think the English lord will come tonight?' she asked a swart, heavy-browed man, who followed her into this retreat.

But for the glamour of his surroundings, and the elegance of his apparel, he might very easily have passed for a common cut-throat, or for one of the meaner kind of brigands who infest Greece.

'He is late, but I do not yet despair of him,' answered Den Lockier. 'Oppression sits on my sister's brow, and the smile has fled from her lips.'

'It is no wonder,' answered Madame Ollivier sharply. 'Unless the big collection is made tonight, all our great schemes fall to the ground, and we must fly from Paris like hunted game, the laughing-stock of those who now drink our wine. Our tradesmen clamour for money, and nothing less than gold will now stop their demands. The day for promises has passed.'

'It is even as you say,' agreed the man, smiling sardonically, 'but the grand collection shall be made tonight. Gold shall replenish our coffers, and then, with our princely fortune, another country shall provide us with grateful ease. All our friends are here, my sister.'

'Except the English nobleman, and his purse is richer than all the others put together.'

'Ah! If I am not mistaken, he has this moment entered the house. Let us approach him. Surely it is he. Though I have never seen him, I could swear that he is the wealthy lord.'

'He is the only stranger we expect here tonight, so no doubt he is the one we have been so anxiously looking for. Welcome, my Lord Sellford, to Paris, and to my poor house,' she added, addressing an elaborately attired old gentleman, who had taken very obvious care to disguise his wrinkles, and to appear young.

'I presume I have the pleasure to address Madame Ollivier,' said he, adjusting his eye-glass, and surveying her with a look of unquali-fied approval. 'Delighted to make the acquaintance of so charming a lady. And this gentleman?'

'My brother.'

'Entirely at your service, my lord,' said the man, with a profound bow.

'That is very good of you, I am sure. I am afraid, madame, I have made a mistake in the night,' continued his lordship, lowering his voice. 'I understood that some trusty friends were to meet here in secret conclave tonight, to decide when the final and decisive blow at existing authority should be struck, but I find your house thronged with merry-makers.'

'Ah!' said madame, smiling sweetly on him, 'many a deep conspiracy has been hatched under the cloak of gay deception. While the music plays and the dance proceeds, our friends meet in a private part of the mansion. The fateful decision will be arrived at while the spies, who are everywhere, have their suspicions lulled by soft sounds and choice wines.'

'It is now the appointed hour,' said Den Lockier. 'If your lordship will condescend to follow me, I will lead the way.'

They passed through many effulgent rooms and strangely silent corridors, till they stood in the grounds, and the revelry within was no more than a low, faint murmur in the air.

*

'So the meeting place is not actually in your own house, madame?' said Lord Sellford, looking about him as well as the darkness would allow.

'It is not in the main building,' answered the lady, 'but it stands in my own grounds. We have to be very careful. Discovery would mean at least ruin to our friends, if not death.'

'Indeed, yes,' added Den Lockier, 'so the sooner we strike the blow the safer it will be for us all. Some of our contrivances are very cunning,' he went on. 'There does not appear to be any outlet from this garden, save through the house we have just left. A high, strong wall surrounds us. But do you see that huge tree which grows against the stonework at the end of the grounds? Its trunk is hollow. Its front bark slides back like a semicircular door. Observe! You see there is room for one person to pass at a time through the tree to an opening in the wall beyond, where steps lead into a building which looks out on to quite another street from the one my sister's house is in.'

'Capital!' chuckled his lordship.

'Yes.' agreed the other man, 'it is rather good. You see we could keep a man imprisoned for years in that building, and he would never be found.'

'Exactly! A most brilliant notion. But surely your friends are of more use to you free than in confinement.'

'Undoubtedly. But I was thinking how we could serve a traitor or a spy. Let me show your lordship the way in, or you may stumble. The light from the lantern shall guide you.'

Having ascended a few steps, the English aristocrat found himself in a long room, hung from floor to ceiling with black velvet. If there were any windows in the place this heavy drapery effectually concealed them. The carpet was also of a deep dark colour, and so thick and soft, that one's feet sank into it as into feathers, and it deadened all sound.

A large oval table stood in the middle of the room, and round this a number of men were gravely seated. At each end was an empty chair, and another one at the side. In the centre of the table stood a large, heavy-looking silver bowl.

'Lord Sellford!' said Madame Ollivier, in a low tone, as she entered the room, and presented his lordship.

The twelve guests rose, and bowed solemnly to the new arrival. He was motioned to take the vacant seat at the side, while madame arranged herself at what was presumably the head of the table; her brother took the chair at the other end, and facing her.

A few minutes passed in absolute and oppressive silence. Then Den Lockier rose, with much dignity, and addressed them in a most impressive manner.

'Gentlemen of the campaign,' said he, 'I need not at this late day recapitulate our aims or our fervent hopes. We are all in accord. The plan of our warfare has been agreed on. My Lord Sellford, who has missed the pleasure of our nightly conferences, has been advised of the progress we have made, and of the determination we have come to. That he approves of our resolves, and is willing to assist our efforts in the most practical way possible, is proved by his presence here now. One cannot, as we all know, initiate a conflict without those golden sinews of war which every nation finds to be of more importance than even its cannon or its soldiery. So, gentlemen, we have met tonight to contribute, each one of us, as much as we individually can towards the furtherance of the campaign we are pledged to. We have each been furnished with a similar envelope. Into that envelope each gentleman will put his contribution, and cast it into the open bowl which is on the table. So no one will know what the other has given. But we are men of honour, and we shall be sure that each one has given to his utmost. Gentlemen, I cast my portion into the bowl, and my heart with it.'

With these words, and with dramatic action, he threw a well-filled envelope into the silver basin.

'My fortune follows my brother's!' cried Madame Ollivier, rising, and drawing from her bosom a packet similar to her brother's. As she dropped it into the receptacle she appeared to be overcome with emotion. With a sudden effort she snatched the diamond bracelet from her wrist, plucked a magnificent spray of precious stones from her hair and a glittering circle of gems from her throat. 'Let them all go!' she exclaimed grandly, dropping them on the top of the little parcel.

A light shone in madame's eyes which lit fires in the hearts of the hitherto impassive conspirators. This, combined with her emotional declamation, made them start to their feet as one man. Each one of them produced his packet.

'Hold!' cried a small, weazened-faced man. 'Hold! I beseech you!' A dead silence followed this intimation. Anxious faces were turned on the speaker.

'Gentlemen,' he continued, with most grave mien, 'I am pained to have to tell you that we are *betrayed*!'

'Betrayed!' repeated the conspirators,' and each one replaced his contribution in his most secret pocket.

'Yes, gentlemen,' continued the little old man, 'betrayed!'

'By whom? By whom?'

Each man now felt stealthily for his revolver, and friend eyed friend with suspicion.

Lord Sellford, the English nobleman, is not with us!' screamed the little gentleman, and every eye was turned on his lordship, who had remained in his seat calm – imperturbable.

'That man who has taken his name, who has adopted his mincing airs, who has personified his lordship to the life, is a spy – a friend of the secret police! His disguise is good, clever, complete! But I see through it. *He is Jules Genvaise, the notorious detective!*'

Each man showed his weapon now, and furious looks were thrown on Jules.

Had Madame Ollivier been struck by a bullet, she could not have sunk into her chair with a more lifeless expression of face or with a keener cry of pain.

'Jules Gervaise, eh?' sneered Den Lockier, showing his teeth. 'Gentlemen, we need not let this incident disturb us. Surely we know what to do with a detective.'

'There is only one fate possible for him,' said madame, in a low tone. 'He must die. If he lives not one of us will be safe. It is a sad necessity,' she added, shedding her bright eyes first on one and then on the other, 'but it is the law of man that one should suffer rather than many.'

'Gentlemen,' said her brother, in his matter-of-fact way, 'a spy has been discovered among us. Our oath compels us to take the life of any of our comrades who prove traitors. Shall we show more mercy to a mere creature of the police? Such a thing cannot be. There are thirteen of you round the table. It is a significant number for a spy. The detective is naturally debarred from voting on the subject of his own funeral. As I hope to have the honour of being his executioner, I, also, will remain passive. As you number a dozen and one, equal voting is impossible. Those who are in favour of the swift "removal" of Jules Gervaise, the detective, will signify their wishes by placing their right hands on the table.'

'I would not condemn him to death to save myself,' said one gentleman, 'but, while he lives, the cause is not safe, and the cause must be above every other consideration.'

Then sixty white fingers showed themselves on the sombre cloth, and, last of all, madame placed her delicate palm on it. So the sentence of execution was pronounced!

'I shall give him such a tap as will render him insensible,' said the self-constituted executioner complacently. 'Then we will weight him with shot, and drop him into the Seine, the close mistress of so many secrets! Bah! It will be but one detective the less, and such rats can be easily spared. I promise you, gentlemen, that Jules Gervaise shall not trouble you again.' The speaker resumed his seat, an acid smile of triumph making his evil face look more revolting than before.

Jules Gervaise – for the so-called Lord Sellford was no other than he – rose quietly to his feet, and addressed that assembly for the first time. Had he been proposing an after-dinner health he could not have been more calm or more at his ease.

'My friends,' said he, 'I perceive that you are gentlemen – too much men of honour to deny to me the privilege which is accorded to the most atrocious criminal in every court of the civilized world and that is the right to say some words in my own defence. If I am to speak at all, it is obvious I must do so before my execution, for you will not be able to hear me afterwards.'

Every face was fixed on the detective's. A grim smile moved their anxious lips, as he uttered this bit of bitter sarcasm.

'It is a long time since I severed my connection with the French police,' he added, 'and I have ceased to take any active interest in the government of France. I have made my home in England, and I have for ever washed my hands of the internal intrigues of Paris. Believe me, gentlemen, I do not know even the name of your society. I am unacquainted with your pass-words, I can only guess at your aims! You may laugh scornfully. You may ask how it comes that I am here if I am no traitor; but still, I will show you that I am your friend, and not your foe. A lucky chance threw me in the way of the true Lord Sellford. It is by his permission that I am here, in his name. It is by his wish that I appear among you to save your fortunes, your persons, maybe your very lives, as I have preserved his!'

'You are here to save us?' many cried at once. 'What mean you?'

Madame gazed at the detective, as though fixed and fascinated by him. Her brothers' face blazed fiercely.

'I am here, gentlemen, to save you from being the dupes of two outrageous swindlers – this so-called Madame Ollivier and her cut-throat brother. That woman,' cried Gervaise, directing his finger at their quivering hostess, his voice growing in volume and scorn as he spoke, 'is not the patriot she pretends to be. She has neither the birth nor the wealth she claims to have, and she is as destitute of truth as she is of either. That woman, I say, who would have decamped with all your fortunes tomorrow morning, and have had you all arrested into the bargain, is no other than the infamous English adventuress Julia Barretti, now wanted for the murder of George Roach at Canonbury, London!'

A low wail came from between madame's parched lips, while her brother hissed defiantly:

'It is a lie – an infamous lie! He will tell you a tale to save his life!'

'It is no lie,' replied Jules firmly, casting an illustrated paper on the table before them. 'There is a picture of Julia Barretti, and a detailed account of many of her crimes. See, gentlemen! See for yourselves that Julia Barretti, the ex-convict, and the grand Madame Ollivier, are one, even to the small mole which shows behind her ear.'

'You are a fiend in your malice!' shouted Den Lockier, livid with passion. 'You libel my sister, and you must die!'

He fired his revolver straight at Jules, but it chanced that the gentleman standing next to the latter bent forward at the critical moment, and he received the bullet in his ear. With a deep groan he sank to the floor.

'Wretch!' cried an aristocratic-looking man on the other side of the table, 'you have killed my dearest friend. Let your own life answer for the deed!'

Very deliberately he shot the villain through the heart – dead.

'For heaven's sake, gentlemen, do not let us lose our senses! Calmness is essential.' The speaker was one whose voice commanded instant attention. 'It is quite plain that Jules Gervaise has told us the truth. We are in a den of thieves, and the sooner we escape from it the better. Our friend still lives. Pray help me to carry him to my carriage, and in my own house he shall have every attention. Den Lockier well deserves his doom. Madame has gone off in a dead swoon. But Jules Gervaise is a clever man, and he will know what to do with the corpse and the unconscious lady. Let us leave them both to him.'

A few minutes later the detective was the only conscious person in that black and mournful room.

'I save them their money and their liberty, and this is their gratitude,' growled Jules, as he gloomily watched the last conspirator disappear behind the arras. 'But if they do not close the opening through the tree, I shall be all right. I have only to make the call, and the police will be here to help me.'

Gervaise ran down the steps, and to his infinite joy found himself in the garden.

In reply to his signal, two men issued from among the shrubs.

'This has been a busy night,' cried one. 'There is not one of us who, is not engaged in shadowing someone. It is a splendid time for us all. Ah! Jules Gervaise, you bring the best of luck with you. But you disappeared like magic. We searched the walls for a secret door, but we never thought of that fraudulent old tree. We will attend to the lady, who is alive, and to the conspirator, who is dead. Come and see his excellency the Chief tomorrow, and discuss matters further. You have done well – very well indeed.'

'Do not let the woman escape,' said Jules.

'You can trust us,' the men laughed.

A little later, Jules turned into his well-aired bed in a near hotel, and slept as soundly as a philosopher should.

The morning came, and Jules Gervaise was closeted with his friend the Chief of the Secret Police.

'The rascal's death is no loss to the world,' said the Chief of the Police smilingly. 'We have the name of each of the conspirators, and can put our hands on them whenever we feel inclined. But they were more dupes than knaves, and as, thanks to you, we have broken up the combination, I do not propose to take any further action in the matter, unless some further indiscretion is committed. But I think they have had a lesson sufficiently sharp to last them a lifetime. As for Madame Ollivier–Julia Barretti, as you will call her – I leave her in your hands, on condition that you take her out of the country. I cannot very well prosecute her; without bringing out the whole pretended conspiracy, and it is not our policy to encourage gossip about political plots. Take her, and, if you can contrive to have her hanged in England, I shall be infinitely obliged to you.'

'You are too kind to me,' declared Gervaise. 'You know I am not invested with any power to arrest her. In charging her with the murder of George Roach, I was but following out one of the theories I have formed concerning that crime. If I succeed in getting her to accompany me to England, it must be by diplomacy.'

'And you are a born diplomat. You will find the lady in the adjoining room. '

Gervaise discovered Julia Barretti, deadly pale, and with such dark rims round her large eyes as suggested that the latter and sleep had been strangers for a long time. Yet she was as calm as though no emotion had ever stirred her dark and secret heart.

'You accuse me of the murder of George Roach, who once called me his wife,' said she, in cold, steady tones to the detective. 'How you obtained any information to warrant you in making such a charge is entirely beyond my comprehension. It is possible that you may be able to make out so strong a case against me that I shall be hanged for the crime; but I tell you, Jules Gervaise, that I am as innocent of spilling that man's blood as you are. My past record has been a bad one, yet I, Julia Barretti, the adventuress, can on occasions speak the truth, and I declare it now!'

'Madame,' answered Jules gravely, 'you were in George Roach's house in Canonbury on the night of this murder.'

'That is true,' she replied quietly, 'but I had no hand in the deed.'

'Then you have but to say who the murderer was to escape from the accusation which now confronts you.'

'Alas! that I cannot do.'

'That is one of those misfortunes which will probably cost you your life.'

For a brief space there was silence between them. The woman appeared to be in deep thought.

Suddenly she said:

'I will tell you my story. You are a clever detective, a shrewd man of the world, surely you will be able to judge clearly whether I speak the truth or not.'

Gervaise motioned to her to proceed.

'A few months back, when I was in London, accident made me acquainted with a young man, named Rupert Peel.'

'Ah!' muttered the detective.

'He took me to be a great lady – a countess at the very least – and he regarded me as a possible wealthy patroness, who would procure for him a lucrative appointment in France, when he had once acquired the language, which he set about learning. You may well ask me why I amused myself with so unimportant a person, but I had discovered that he was in the employ of George Roach, who had once married me, and I was curious to learn all about the doings of that man, often thinking that the information might, some day, prove of pecuniary value to me. Not only did I know when George Roach took that house in Canonbury, but, after much trouble, I persuaded Rupert Peel to "borrow" the keys, and take me all over it. He was very nervous lest it should ever be discovered that he had done this.'

'That fact may possibly account for his confusion when he handed the keys to us,' thought Gervaise.

'My visits to London were occasional ones,' continued Julia Barretti. 'As the day fixed for the marriage of Mr Roach and Daisy Lynn grew nearer and nearer, I became more deeply and more terribly pressed for money. Then, when we were every day threatened with a crisis in our affairs, I resolved to see whether I could not frighten

George Roach into paying me a couple of thousand pounds. In many matters he was a most nervous man, and I judged he would rather part with this money than have me appear before his affianced wife, and relate to her my story. Of course, he could prove that he had been the wronged and injured one, but this would take time; besides, if people considered how easily they could repel a false accusation, there would be an end to blackmailing as a profitable industry altogether. I wrote to George Roach on the day he should have started for Glasgow. In my letter I declared that if he did not meet me at his house in Canonbury at ten o'clock that same night, and agree to my demands, I would, late though it might be, proceed at once to Miss Lynn's residence at Kennington, and expose him. I relied very much on my intimate knowledge of his private affairs, drawn from the well-intentioned Rupert Peel, to add terrors to my threats. My letter was posted so as to reach him in the evening, and, from all I have since gleaned, I judge that it was put into his hand as he was starting for St Pancras Station. Thinking it was some ordinary communication, I believe, he thrust it into his pocket, and did not again think of it until he had taken his place in the railway carriage, and his train was on the point of starting. Then he opened it, and, terrified at the thought of the pain I might cause Miss Lynn, he jumped from the train, and made for Canonbury with all possible haste.'

'So far, I believe, you have not wandered from the truth,' said Gervaise. 'From my point of view, I think it in your favour that you have not attempted to excuse your own wicked part in this bad business.'

'I shall make no attempt to play on your credulity, monsieur. I believe that when Mr Roach reached his house he found someone already in possession of it.'

'Indeed?'

'Yes. I arrived there rather after my time. A light burned in one of the front rooms. I saw a form distinctly shadowed on the blind, but it was not the figure of my husband. I found the front door open, as though Mr Roach, on putting his key into the lock, had heard someone moving about inside, and had made a dash in to secure the trespasser. When I entered the room, Roach stood facing me. Another man faced him. The latter swung a bar of iron over his head to bring down on George's skull, but I, being just behind, was struck by it, and rendered unconscious. How long I remained so I cannot tell. I have a dim recollection of a fierce voice whispering in my ear these words:

'"Do not dare to breathe a word of what you have seen tonight, or

I will take care that you are found guilty of having committed the deed." For a considerable period I remained dazed, and too weak to move. When at last I was able to crawl from that place I did, hoping I should never again be reminded of the fearful experience I had gone through. When I reflected on my past history, on the object of my errand, and, as I remembered that even then he might bear on his slaughtered body the threatening letter I had sent him, I realised how easy it would be to persuade a jury that I had been guilty of bringing about his death. Yes, yes, Jules Gervaise, you, at any rate, will readily understand why I resolved to keep my lips sealed regarding that dark night's work!'

'Well, madame,' said Jules drily, 'if you are innocent of the crime you should not have any difficulty in identifying the assassin, when he is brought before you?'

'Indeed, that I cannot do. When I entered the room his back was towards me, and I was rendered insensible before I could notice even that particularly. But I should know his shadow. The shadow which I saw thrown on the blind of that house at Canonbury is indelibly printed on my brain. I could swear to that shadow, if it ever met my eyes again.'

'Come!' said Gervaise cheerfully, 'that is something. I suppose you are aware that Rupert Peel is at present in prison on suspicion of having committed this murder?'

'I am sorry to hear it,' was the quiet reply. 'He regarded his master with acute bitterness. They were rivals in love. Perhaps Peel did kill him. I could tell you if I saw his shadow.'

This reply was unexpected by the detective. It was a view he was not at all disposed to take.

'Well,' he said sharply, 'will you come with me willingly to England, and help me to prove Rupert Peel innocent or guilty, or do you prefer to go as a prisoner, as which. I candidly confess, you will be of no use to me in establishing the truth of the theory I have formed?'

'I will go with you, and loyally help you as far as I am able. But, remember, I cannot speak to the murderer's tones or to his appearance. I can recognise nothing about him but his shadow.'

'So be it,' said Gervaise. 'I shall not be the first detective who has set out in chase of such airy and insubstantial nothings. We will leave for London tonight.'

'I shall be glad to get from Paris,' was the woman's answer.

*

'I am placing more confidence in you than your previous record warrants,' said Gervaise severely to Julia Barretti, as he left her in a quiet private hotel he had selected for her in the neighbourhood of the central London squares, 'but you know quite well that the Continent is closed to you, and if you manage to slip me here I shall soon find you.'

'I have no desire to break faith with you,' was her cold reply. 'I believe it is not unusual for even criminals to keep their word to detectives.'

'That woman is a born rogue,' Gervaise muttered to himself, as he made his way to Holloway Prison, for he was already armed with a permit to interview Rupert Peel, who was in confinement there. 'She pursues crime as a legitimate profession. What can you do with such people but keep them under lock and key?'

At first, Rupert Peel was somewhat shy of his visitor, who had been working so hard on his behalf, but when Jules Gervaise explained to him who the French lady Rupert had regarded with such awe really was, the young man threw aside all reserve, and spoke quite freely.

'Truly,' said the unhappy young man, 'I cannot suggest to you the name of anyone who is likely to have done this terrible deed. I recognise myself that theoretically I am the one most likely to have been guilty of the murder. And,' he added, 'if the whole truth were known about that woman, what a horribly strong case might be established against both of us! Perhaps the woman did it after all!' he added musingly, 'What a fool I was to have ever taken her into that house!'

'She thinks you may be guilty,' said Jules slowly.

'She is not alone in that opinion,' returned the young man bitterly. 'But, Jules Gervaise, I am an innocent man!'

Rupert spoke with calm, convincing earnestness; and, though the detective made no comment on the young man's declaration, he was not inclined to disbelieve him. All he said was:

'It will be well for you if you can account for every minute of your time on the night on which the murder must have taken place.'

'Ah!' sighed Rupert. 'That sounds an easy thing to do, but it is impossible in my case. The only man who could help me in that way is dead. I mean my father.'

'Tell me about him,' said Jules.

'My life has been a very unhappy one,' said the young man, after a pause. 'My mother died when I was very young, and my father fell into the hands of some low-class betting men. His smooth temper and unsuspicious disposition made him an easy prey to their wiles. To make my painful story short, I will say at once that I have worked all my life to keep him, and to the end I loved him dearly. On the evening when Mr Roach was supposed to have left for Glasgow, my father was brought home sadly injured about the head in some disgraceful racecourse quarrel. Blood still poured profusely from his wounds and, in applying bandages to these cuts, my waistcoat became saturated with the blood. My wardrobe was so scantily furnished that I had to wash this waistcoat that same night, so as to be able to wear it at the office the next day. Now you can understand why I was so upset when you called my attention to the odour of blood which the fire drew out of the half-dried garment. Some days afterwards my father managed to totter out again. He met some of the gang who had previously assaulted him. They once more attacked him, and when he was brought home it was to die. When Mr Roach was murdered, I was nursing my father. But there is no one to prove this but he, and his lips are closed for ever!'

'Your life has been a sad one,' said the sympathetic detective.

'Indeed it has. You see, I could never have married Daisy so long as my father lived.'

'Tell me,' said Jules, with a resumption of his quaint, abrupt way. 'do you ever eat musk lozenges?'

'Never. Why do you ask such an odd question?'

'I will tell you. The key – the key so stained with blood, which fitted the door of the strongroom in which the remains of Mr Roach were found – this key, I say, which was said to have been found in your desk, had still a strong flavour of musk about it when it was shown to me.'

'I cannot account for that at all,' declared Rupert.

'Then I must discover for myself why this was so. Now my time is up, and I must go.'

'What do you think of my case, Mr Jules Gervaise? Will they convict me?'

'Undoubtedly, if you are guilty. If you are innocent, I have already promised to save you, and I will!'

'When I want you I will send for you, and you will come.' Jules had said to Julia Barretti, and she remained in her hotel, waiting for his sign.

For some days the detective disappeared from the resorts where he was usually to be found, and even at his own lodgings scarcely anything was seen of him. Some of his acquaintances had met him in the

City, going in and out of business premises with which it did not seem probable he could have anything in common.

One man declared positively that he had come across Jules Gervaise in the neighbourhood of Hampstead, carrying on his back the outfit of a travelling glazier; and it is certainly a fact that when a rude-mannered boy was brought before the local magistrate, charged with breaking windows belonging to Mr Felix Sark, it was the detective who paid the fine inflicted.

At last Julia Barretti received a communication from Gervaise, and, on the same night, he visited the house of Saul Lynn, and found that gentleman in very much better spirits than might have been looked for.

'Fate is proving most kind to me, after all,' said he. 'It is an extraordinary thing, but Mr Felix Sark has suddenly taken a wonderful fancy to Daisy. To be quite candid with you, Jules, he is anxious to marry her, just as soon as this disagreeable murder business is forgotten. It seems that poor George Roach always left Mr Sark with a power-of-attorney, authorizing him to carry on the business should Mr Roach be taken suddenly ill or detained in some distant part. Sark says it is as good as a will, and that he is quite justified in constituting himself owner of the concern.'

'Mr Sark is a little wrong in his law,' said Gervaise quietly, with an air of indifference. 'Practically no deed survives death, except a man's final testament. But we can let that pass. You make me very tired of human nature, Saul,' the detective added, placidly. 'If you would only hide your selfishness a little, it would be a kindness to your friends. I do not think we shall ever take that house together we once spoke of.'

'And why not?' queried Saul, his red face growing more crimson.

'Because, my friend, there would not be room for me in it. You would want it all.'

'You are a queer fellow, Jules,' said Saul, not in the best of humours. Then, as Daisy came into the room, he left it, suddenly determining that it might be well to buy an evening paper.

'Oh, Mr Gervaise, I am so thankful to see you!' cried the golden-haired little woman. 'I do hope you have brought me good news.'

'Poor little girl! Poor little girl!' said the detective sympathisingly, 'How sorrow has thinned your pretty cheeks. Yes, I hope to have good news for you soon, but not today – not today!'

'I did as you told me,' said Daisy, 'and I was quite civil to Mr Sark after you had gone; but it has been a hard task to keep it up, for I do dislike him so. There! I do believe this is his knock!'

'Let us hope so!' The detective spoke so fervently that Daisy regarded him in a bewildered way.

'You appear to be upset, Mr Sark,' was his comment, as that gentleman joined them.

'Upset? I should think so, indeed!' was the vicious reply. 'And I daresay you would be if a thievish glazier had ransacked your rooms, and broken open your desk and most secret places! Upset is not the word for it, Mr Gervaise! Why, the rascal hires a boy to break glass when he himself finds work slack. He absolutely creates business, which seems to me to consist mainly of robbery. Ah! but I must not forget a little present I have for you, Miss Lynn.'

'What a pretty box!' cried the girl, as she opened the packet he presented her with.

'Musk lozenges,' said Jules reflectively. 'Are you very fond of them, Mr Sark?'

'If I ever buy anything in that way,' was the answer, 'I get musk lozenges from the chemist.'

'They have a remarkably strong scent,' said Jules. 'It clings to everything, even to steel.'

'What are you going to do with the light, Mr Gervaise?' cried Daisy, as she saw the detective lift the lamp from the table.

'I am going to put it on the sideboard, if you don't mind,' he said blandly. 'That is higher than the table, where it hurts my eyes. Now, I am sure that is better. Did you ever see so old a sixpence as this before?' he added, addressing Mr Sark, compelling that gentleman to cross the room between the light and the blind to examine the coin.

Mr Sark saw nothing at all remarkable in the thin piece of silver offered for his inspection. His own private opinion was that Jules Gervaise was afflicted with an eccentricity which perilously bordered on madness. The detective took Felix Sark's contemptuous comments in good part, and very soon after this left the house to join Julia Barretti, who was waiting for him outside.

The little twisted street wherein stood the warehouse of George Roach and Co was made still narrower by the erection of complicated scaffolding outside the murdered man's premises, for they were being repainted, and the brickwork generally was undergoing repairs. The thoroughfare was made impassable by the roadway being denuded of its granite blocks to make way for less noisy ones of wood.

In connection with the new foundation for these a huge cauldron of boiling asphalt stood under the planks, and close to the doorway of the murdered man's busy office. Jules Gervaise observed how the black smoke curled heavenwards from this as he conducted a select party of gentlemen into the presence of Felix Sark, who received them with the sulky inquisitiveness characteristic of him.

'My business, though of a particularly delicate nature from one point of view, cannot be kept private,' said the great detective blandly; 'but, if you prefer it, I will disclose the matter in hand to you in your own room, if you do not care for me to speak openly here.'

'Go on,' said Mr Sark, with an air of indifference, perching himself on a high stool, and looking from one to the other of Jules Gervaise's companions sharply and interrogatively.

'Very good,' said the detective. 'I am here, Mr Sark, to tell you the story of a crime. I will not torture you with suspense, so I will tell you at once that two of these gentlemen come from Scotland Yard. They hold a warrant for your arrest, and they are bent on taking you away with them.'

Mr Sark's face assumed a deeper hue, but he regarded Jules defiantly, and did his utmost to preserve a calm exterior.

'Now, Mr Sark, perhaps you will be so good as to let these gentlemen look at your cash-book for last year?'

'I shall do nothing of the kind,' answered the cashier, with a perceptible start.

'Of course you won't,' said Jules pleasantly, 'because you can't. The cash-book is here.'

The detective rested a large square bag on a bale of goods, and drew out a portly white-bound volume.

'You villain!' cried Sark thoughtlessly. 'It is you, then, who broke into my rooms and stole my goods. You shall suffer for it, you rascal!'

'But,' continued the placid Jules, 'this book is not complete. It wants pages 29 and 30. They are here.'

He now produced the ashes he had taken from the grate of the house at Canonbury. They had been cleverly arranged between two sheets of thin glass, and, by a chemical process, a brilliant red ink followed every trace of writing which was on them, so that each entry in the cash columns could be deciphered with the utmost ease.

'Yes, Mr Sark, they are here; and they show, in your own handwriting, that Messrs Fellow and Mark paid into your hands, on Thursday, the fifth day of May, one hundred and fifteen pounds ten shillings. That's all plain enough, isn't it? Unfortunately for you, Mr

Sark, it chances that Messrs Fellow and Mark paid you five hundred and fifteen pounds ten shillings, and it is for this amount they hold your receipt. You put down in this book the one hundred odd and pocketed four hundred pounds, Mr Sark. Not your first defalcation, by any means, sir.'

By this time the guilty man had turned green and evil-looking, but his composure was perfect.

'The day poor Mr Roach was summoned to Glasgow he chanced to meet Mr Fellow, whom you see before you, ready to corroborate all I say. He mentioned the account, the bulk of which he believed to be still due from that gentleman to him. Your receipt in full was shown to your employer; his suspicions were aroused, and, to your consternation, he took home with him the cash-book containing the fraudulent entry, determined to go carefully through every item in it at the first opportunity. It was the most unfortunate thing George Roach ever did. It signed his death-warrant!

'The agents from whom your master had taken the house at Canonbury had handed you two sets of keys for the premises, but you only gave up one. So, when you fondly fancied Mr Roach was being whirled northward, you entered his house, and commenced to destroy the incriminating cash-book. Naturally enough, you burned the two most damning pages, but you see that even fire refuses to hide your guilt. In the midst of your work, when you were exultant and fearless, who should suddenly appear before you but your too-trusting master himself. A desperate struggle ensued, but finally you killed him – and with this!'

From the detective's bag came a heavy bar of iron.

'You carried away the book and kept it at your lodgings,' continued Jules quietly, 'because, as you had made up your mind to seize this business, you knew it would be useful to you. But why you should have preserved this murderous piece of metal is best known to yourself. The bloodstained key of the strongroom, which you pretended to find in Rupert Peel's desk, came from your own pocket. The flavour of your musk lozenges still clings to it. You were anxious to marry Miss Lynn because you were well aware Mr Roach had bequeathed her, by a legally attested will, which is at present in my possession, every penny he died possessed of. Now, Mr Sark, I think I have brought my story of your crime to a convincing conclusion.'

'It is all an infamous concoction!' cried the wretched man, his eyes blood-red and furtive. He had not yet abandoned all hope; he would escape them yet, if he could. 'It is a malignant series of lies. I am innocent of this crime. If my dear dead master could rise from his grave he would himself declare that to the end I was faithful and true to him.'

'You lie, Felix Sark, you lie!' declared Julia Barretti, coming among them at that moment. 'I saw you strike the fatal blow! The shadow I observed on the blind of the house at Canonbury I saw again last night at Saul Lynn's house in Kennington, and your shadow has condemned you!'

A look of wild terror changed the entire aspect of his face as he gazed at this woman. Had a spectre confronted him he could not have been more staggered.

He stared hopelessly, first to the right then to the left of him. His eyes caught sight of the stairs leading to the rooms above, and he made a dart for them.

'After him!' cried Jules, to the plainclothes men from Scotland Yard. 'He will climb that scaffolding, get on to the roof, and we may miss him altogether. Don't hesitate to follow him wherever he goes!'

The moment Felix reached the upper apartment, he made a plunge for the window, and reached the planks outside.

Taking the detective's advice, one of the young officers dashed through the same opening on to the scaffolding. He was just in time to see the fugitive seize the heavy hanging chain, and then a dreadful thing happened.

It may be presumed that Felix's intention was to reach the street by this means, but he had not observed that it dangled immediately over the great cauldron in which seethed and smoked the boiling pitch.

The murderer's weight brought the chain down with a rasping rush, and he completely disappeared in the molten substance, only to be rescued when life was extinct, and his body most horribly disfigured.

Though there was no question about the guilt of Felix Sark, it took a little time to procure the release of Rupert Peel. It need hardly be said that he married Daisy Peel after a short lapse of time, but it should be mentioned that he now carries on the business of George Roach and Co, as may be seen by anyone who searches for the premises in the street we have described.

Jules Gervaise was very proud of his success in this case, because it made Daisy happy. It brought him such fame, too, that he was compelled to abandon his idea of retiring, until he had, at any rate, solved one more mystery, and about that we may have something to write another day.

MAX PEMBERTON

Ripening Rubies

'THE PLAIN fact is,' said Lady Faber, 'we are entertaining thieves. It positively makes me shudder to look at my own guests, and to think that some of them are criminals.'

We stood together in the conservatory of her house in Portman Square, looking down upon a brilliant ballroom, upon a glow of colour, and the radiance of unnumbered gems. She had taken me aside after the fourth waltz to tell me that her famous belt of rubies had been shorn of one of its finest pendants; and she showed me beyond possibility of dispute that the loss was no accident, but another of those amazing thefts which startled London so frequently during the season of 1893. Nor was hers the only case. Though I had been in her house but an hour, complaints from other sources had reached me. The Countess of Dunholme had lost a crescent brooch of brilliants; Mrs Kenningham-Hardy had missed a spray of pearls and turquoise; Lady Hallingham made mention of an emerald locket which was gone, as she thought, from her necklace; though, as she confessed with a truly feminine doubt, she was not positive that her maid had given it to her. And these misfortunes, being capped by the abstraction of Lady Faber's pendant, compelled me to believe that of all the startling stories of thefts which the season had known the story of this dance would be the most remarkable.

These things and many more came to my mind as I held the mutilated belt in my hand and examined the fracture, while my hostess stood, with an angry flush upon her face, waiting for my verdict. A moment's inspection of the bauble revealed to me at once its exceeding value, and the means whereby a pendant of it had been snatched.

'If you will look closely,' said I, 'you will see that the gold chain here has been cut with a pair of scissors. As we don't know the name of the person who used them, we may describe them as pickpocket's scissors.'

'Which means that I am entertaining a pickpocket,' said she, flushing again at the thought.

'Or a person in possession of a pickpocket's implements,' I suggested.

'How dreadful,' she cried, 'not for myself, though the rubies are very valuable, but for the others. This is the third dance during the week at which people's jewels have been stolen. When will it end?'

'The end of it will come,' said I, 'directly that you, and others with your power to lead, call in the police. It is very evident by this time that some person is socially engaged in a campaign of wholesale robbery. While a silly delicacy forbids us to permit our guests to be suspected or in any way watched, the person we mention may consider himself in a terrestrial paradise, which is very near the seventh heaven of delight. He will continue to rob with impunity, and to offer up his thanks for that generosity of conduct which refuses us a glimpse of his hat, or even an inspection of the boots in which he may place his plunder.'

'You speak very lightly of it,' she interrupted, as I still held her belt in my hands. 'Do you know that my husband values the rubies in each of those pendants at eight hundred pounds?'

'I can quite believe it,' said I; 'some of them are white as these are, I presume; but I want you to describe it for me, and as accurately as your memory will let you.'

'How will that help to its recovery?' she asked, looking at me questioningly.

'Possibly not at all,' I replied; 'but it might be offered for sale at my place, and I should be glad if I had the means of restoring it to you. Stranger things have happened.'

'I believe,' said she sharply, 'you would like to find out the thief yourself.'

'I should not have the smallest objection,' I exclaimed frankly; 'if these robberies continue, no woman in London will wear real stones; and I shall be the loser.'

'I have thought of that,' said she; 'but, you know, you are not to make the slightest attempt to expose any guest in my house; what you do outside is no concern of mine.'

'Exactly,' said I, 'and for the matter of that I am likely to do very little in either case; we are working against clever heads; and if my judgment be correct, there is a whole gang to cope with. But tell me about the rubies.'

'Well,' said she, 'the stolen pendant is in the shape of a rose. The belt, as you know, was brought by Lord Faber from Burmah. Besides the ring of rubies, which each drop has, the missing star includes four yellow stones, which the natives declare are ripening rubies. It is only a superstition, of course; but the gems are full of fire, and as brilliant as diamonds.'

'I know the stones well,' said I; 'the Burmese will sell you rubies of all colours if you will buy them, though the blue variety is nothing more than the sapphire. And how long is it since you missed the pendant?'

'Not ten minutes ago,' she answered.

'Which means that your next partner might be the thief?' I suggested. 'Really, a dance is becoming a capital entertainment.'

'My next partner is my husband,' said she, laughing for the first time, 'and whatever you do, don't say a word to him. He would never forgive me for losing the rubies.'

When she was gone, I, who had come to her dance solely in the hope that a word or a face there would cast light upon the amazing mystery of the season's thefts, went down again where the press was, and stood while the dancers were pursuing the dreary paths of a 'square'. There before me were the hundred types one sees in a London ballroom – types of character and of want of character, of age aping youth, and of youth aping age, of well-dressed women and ill-dressed women, of dandies and of the bored, of fresh girlhood and worn maturity. Mixed in the dazzling *mêlée*, or swaying to the rhythm of a music-hall melody, you saw the lean form of boys; the robust forms of men; the pretty figures of the girls just out; the figures, not so pretty, of the matrons, who, for the sake of the picturesque, should long ago have been in. As the picture changed quickly, and fair faces succeeded to dark faces, and the coquetting eyes of pretty women passed by with a glance to give place to the uninteresting eyes of the dancing men, I asked myself what hope would the astutest spy have of getting a clue to the mysteries in such a room; how could he look for a moment to name one man or one woman who had part or lot in the astounding robberies which were the wonder of the town? Yet I knew that if nothing were done, the sale of jewels in London would come to the lowest ebb the trade had known, and that I, personally, should suffer loss to an extent which I did not care to think about.

I have said often, in jotting down from my book a few of the most interesting cases which have come to my notice, that I am no detective, nor do I pretend to the smallest gift of foresight above my fellow men. Whenever I have busied myself about some trouble it has been from a personal motive which drove me on, or in the hope of serving someone who henceforth should serve me. And never have I brought to my aid other weapon than a certain measure of common sense. In many instances the purest good chance has given to me my only clue;

the merest accident has set me straight when a hundred roads lay before me. I had come to Lady Faber's house hoping that the sight of some stranger, a chance word, or even an impulse might cast light upon the darkness in which we had walked for many weeks. Yet the longer I stayed in the ballroom the more futile did the whole thing seem. Though I knew that a nimble-fingered gentleman might be at my very elbow, that half-a-dozen others might be dancing cheerfully about me in that way of life to which their rascality had called them, I had not so much as a hand-breadth of suspicion; saw no face that was not the face of the dancing ass, or the smart man about town; did not observe a single creature who led me to hazard a question. And so profound at last was my disgust that I elbowed my way from the ballroom in despair; and went again to the conservatory where the palms waved seductively, and the flying corks of the champagne bottles made music harmonious to hear.

There were few people in this room at the moment – old General Sharard, who was never yet known to leave a refreshment table until the supper table was set; the Rev Arthur Mellbank, the curate of St Peter's, sipping tea; a lean youth who ate an ice with the relish of a schoolboy; and the ubiquitous Sibyl Kavanagh, who has been vulgarly described as a garrison hack. She was a woman of many partialities, whom every one saw at every dance, and then asked how she got there – a woman with sufficient personal attraction left to remind you that she was *passée*, and sufficient wit to make an interval tolerable. I, as a rule, had danced once with her, and then avoided both her programme and her chatter; but now that I came suddenly upon her, she cried out with a delicious pretence of artlessness, and ostentatiously made room for me at her side.

'*Do* get me another cup of tea,' she said; 'I've been talking for ten minutes to Colonel Harner, who has just come from the great thirst land, and I've caught it.'

'You'll ruin your nerves,' said I, as I fetched her the cup, 'and you'll miss the next dance.'

'I'll sit it out with you,' she cried gushingly; 'and as for nerves, I haven't got any; I must have shed them with my first teeth. But I want to talk to you – you've heard the news, of course! Isn't it dreadful?'

She said this with a beautiful look of sadness, and for a moment I did not know to what she referred. Then it dawned upon my mind that she had heard of Lady Faber's loss.

'Yes,' said I, 'it's the profoundest mystery I have ever known.'

'And can't you think of any explanation at all?' she asked, as she drank her tea at a draught. 'Isn't it possible to suspect someone just to pass the time?'

'If you can suggest anyone,' said I, 'we will begin with pleasure.'

'Well, there's no one in this room to think of, is there?' she asked with her limpid laugh; 'of course you couldn't search the curate's pockets, unless sermons were missing instead of rubies?'

'This is a case of "sermons in stones",' I replied, 'and a very serious case. I wonder you have escaped with all those pretty brilliants on your sleeves.'

'But I haven't escaped,' she cried; 'why, you're not up to date. Don't you know that I lost a marquise brooch at the Hayes's dance the other evening? I have never heard the last of it from my husband, who will not believe for a minute that I did not lose it in the crowd.'

'And you yourself believe—'

'That it was stolen, of course. I pin my brooches too well to lose them – someone took it in the same cruel way that Lady Faber's rubies have been taken. Isn't it really awful to think that at every party we go to thieves go with us? It's enough to make one emigrate to the shires.'

She fell to the flippant mood again, for nothing could keep her from that; and as there was obviously nothing to be learnt from her, I listened to her chatter sufferingly.

'But we were going to suspect people,' she continued suddenly, 'and we have not done it. As we can't begin with the curate, let's take the slim young man opposite. Hasn't he what Sheridan calls – but there, I mustn't say it; you know – a something disinheriting countenance?'

'He eats too many jam tarts and drinks too much lemonade to be a criminal,' I replied; 'besides, he is not occupied, you'll have to look in the ballroom.'

'I can just see the top of the men's heads,' said she, craning her neck forward in the effort. 'Have you noticed that when a man is dancing, either he stargazes in ecstasy, as though he were in heaven, or looks down to his boots – well, as if it were the other thing?'

'Possibly,' said I; 'but you're not going to constitute yourself a *vehmgericht* from seeing the top of people's heads.'

'Indeed,' she cried, 'that shows how little you know; there is more character in the crown of an old man's head than is dreamt of in your philosophy, as what's-his-name says. Look at that shining roof bobbing up there, for instance; that is the halo of port and honesty – and a difficulty in dancing the polka. Oh! that mine enemy would dance the polka – especially if he were stout.'

'Do you really possess an enemy?' I asked, as she fell into a vulgar burst of laughter at her own humour; but she said:

'Do I possess one? Go and discuss me with the other women – that's what I tell all my partners to do; and they come back and report to me. It's as good as a play!'

'It must be,' said I, 'a complete extravaganza. But your enemy has finished his exercise, and they are going to play a waltz. Shall I take you down?'

'Yes,' she cried, 'and don't forget to discuss me. Oh, these crushes!'

She said this as we came to the press upon the corner of the stairs leading to the ballroom, a corner where she was pushed desperately against the banisters. The vigour of the polka had sent an army of dancers to the conservatory, and for some minutes we could neither descend nor go back; but when the press was somewhat relieved, and she made an effort to progress, her dress caught in a spike of the iron-work, and the top of a panel of silk which went down one side of it was ripped open and left hanging. For a minute she did not notice the mishap; but as the torn panel of silk fell away slightly from the more substantial portion of her dress, I observed, pinned to the inner side of it, a large crescent brooch of diamonds. In the same instant she turned with indescribable quickness, and made good the damage. But her face was scarlet in the flush of its colour; and she looked at me with questioning eyes.

'What a miserable accident,' she said. 'I have spoilt my gown.'

'Have you?' said I sympathetically, 'I hope it was not my clumsiness – but really there doesn't seem much damage done. Did you tear it in front?'

There was need of very great restraint in saying this. Though I stood simply palpitating with amazement, and had to make some show of examining her gown, I knew that even an ill-judged word might undo the whole good of the amazing discovery, and deprive me of that which appeared to be one of the most astounding stories of the year. To put an end to the interview, I asked her laughingly if she would not care to see one of the maids upstairs; and she jumped at the excuse, leaving me upon the landing to watch her hurriedly mounting to the bedroom storey above.

When she was gone, I went back to the conservatory and drank a cup of tea, always the best promoter of clear thought; and for some ten minutes I turned the thing over in my mind. Who was Mrs Sibyl Kavanagh, and why had she sewn a brooch of brilliants to the inside of a panel of her gown – sewn it in a place where it was as safely hid from sight as though buried in the Thames? A child could have given the answer – but a child would have overlooked many things which were vital to the development of the unavoidable conclusion of the discovery. The brooch that I had seen corresponded perfectly with the crescent of which Lady Dunholme was robbed – yet it was a brooch which a hundred women might have possessed; and if I had simply stepped down and told Lady Faber, 'the thief you are entertaining is Mrs Sibyl Kavanagh,' a slander action with damages had trodden upon the heels of the folly. Yet I would have given a hundred pounds to have been allowed full inspection of the whole panel of the woman's dress – and I would have staked an equal sum that there had been found in it the pendant of the ripening rubies; a pendant which seemed to me the one certain clue that would end the series of jewel robberies, and the colossal mystery of the year. Now, however, the woman had gone upstairs to hide in another place whatever she had to hide; and for the time it was unlikely that a sudden searching of her dress would add to my knowledge.

A second cup of tea helped me still further on my path. It made quite clear to me the fact that the woman was the recipient of the stolen jewels, rather than the actual taker of them. She, clearly, could not use the scissors which had severed Lady Faber's pendant from the ruby belt. A skilful man had in all probability done that – but which man, or perhaps men? I had long felt that the season's robberies were the work of many hands. Chance had now marked for me one pair; but it was vastly more important to know the others. The punishment of the woman would scarce stop the widespread conspiracy; the arrest of her for the possession of a crescent brooch, hid suspiciously it is true, but a brooch of a pattern which abounded in every jeweller's shop from Kensington to Temple Bar, would have been consummate lunacy. Of course, I could have taken cab to Scotland Yard, and have told my tale; but with no other support, how far would that have availed me? If the history of the surpassingly strange case were to be written, I knew that I must write it, and lose no moment in the work.

I had now got a sufficient grip upon the whole situation to act decisively, and my first step was to re-enter the ballroom, and take a partner for the next waltz. We had made some turns before I discovered that Mrs Kavanagh was again in the room, dancing with her usual dash, and seemingly in no way moved by the mishap. As we passed in the press, she even smiled at me, saying, 'I've set full sail

again;' and her whole bearing convinced me of her belief that I had
seen nothing.

At the end of my dance my own partner, a pretty little girl in pink,
left me with the remark, 'You're awfully stupid tonight! I ask you if
you've seen *Manon Lescaut*, and the only thing you say is, "The
panel buttons up, I thought so".' This convinced me that it was dangerous to dance again, and I waited in the room only until the supper
was ready, and Mrs Kavanagh passed me, making for the dining-
room, on the arm of General Sharard. I had loitered to see what
jewels she wore upon her dress; and when I had made a note of them,
I slipped from the front door of the house unobserved, and took a
hansom to my place in Bond Street.

At the second ring of the bell my watchman opened the door to
me; and while he stood staring with profound surprise, I walked
straight to one of the jewel cases in which our cheaper jewels are
kept, and took therefrom a spray of diamonds, and hooked it to the
inside of my coat. Then I sent the man up stairs to awaken Abel, and
in five minutes my servant was with me, though he wore only his
trousers and his shirt.

'Abel,' said I, 'there's good news for you. I'm on the path of the
gang we're wanting.'

'Good God, sir!' cried he, 'you don't mean that!'

'Yes,' said I, 'there's a woman named Sibyl Kavanagh in it to
begin with, and she's helped herself to a couple of diamond sprays,
and a pendant of rubies at Lady Faber's tonight. One of the sprays I
know she's got; if I could trace the pendant to her, the case would
begin to look complete.'

'Whew!' he ejaculated, brightening up at the prospect of business.
'I knew there was a woman in it all along – but this one, why, she's a
regular flier, ain't she, sir?'

'We'll find out her history presently. I'm going straight back to
Portman Square now. Follow me in a hansom, and when you get to
the house, wait inside my brougham until I come. But before you do
that, run round to Marlborough Street police-station and ask them if
we can have ten or a dozen men ready to mark a house in Bayswater
some time between this and six o'clock tomorrow morning.'

'You're going to follow her home then?'

'Exactly, and if my wits can find a way I'm going to be her guest
for ten minutes after she quits Lady Faber's. They're sure to let you
have the men either at Marlborough Street or at the Harrow Road
station. This business has been a disgrace to them quite long enough.'

'That's so, sir; King told me yesterday that he'd bury his head in the sand if something didn't turn up soon. You haven't given me the exact address though.'

'Because I haven't got it. I only know that the woman lives somewhere near St Stephen's Church – she sits under, or on, one of the curates there. If you can get her address from her coachman, do so. But go and dress and be in Portman Square at the earliest possible moment.'

It was now very near one o'clock, indeed the hour struck as I passed the chapel in Orchard Street; and when I came into the square I found my own coachman waiting with the brougham at the corner by Baker Street. I told him, before I entered the house, to expect Abel; and not by any chance to draw up at Lady Faber's. Then I made my way quietly to the ballroom and observed Mrs Kavanagh – I will not say dancing, but hurling herself through the last figure of the lancers. It was evident that she did not intend to quit yet awhile; and I left her to get some supper, choosing a seat near to the door of the dining-room, so that anyone passing must be seen by me. To my surprise, I had not been in the room ten minutes when she suddenly appeared in the hall, unattended, and her cloak wrapped round her; but she passed without perceiving me; and I, waiting until I heard the hall door close, went out instantly and got my wraps. Many of the guests had left already, but a few carriages and cabs were in the square, and a linkman seemed busy in the distribution of unlimited potations. It occurred to me that if Abel had not got the woman's address, this man might give it to me, and I put the plain question to him.

'That lady who just left;' said I, 'did she have a carriage or a cab?'

'Oh, you mean Mrs Kevenner,' he answered thickly, 'she's a keb, she is, allus takes a hansom, sir; 192, Westbourne Park; I don't want to ask when I see her, sir.'

'Thank you,' said I, 'she has dropped a piece of jewellery in the hall, and I thought I would drive round and return it to her.'

He looked surprised, at the notion, perhaps, of anyone returning anything found in a London ballroom; but I left him with his astonishment and entered my carriage. There I found Abel crouching down under the front seat, and he met me with a piteous plea that the woman had no coachman, and that he had failed to obtain her address.

'Never mind that,' said I, as we drove off sharply, 'what did they say at the station?'

'They wanted to bring a force of police round, and arrest every

one in the house, sir. I had trouble enough to hold them in, I'm sure.
But I said that we'd sit down and watch if they made any fuss, and
then they gave in. It's agreed now that a dozen men will be at the
Harrow Road station at your call till morning. They've a wonderful
confidence in you, sir.'

'It's a pity they haven't more confidence in themselves – but
anyway, we are in luck. The woman's address is 192, Westbourne
Park, and I seem to remember that it is a square.'

'I'm sure of it,' said he; 'it's a round square in the shape of an
oblong, and one hundred and ninety two is at the side near Durham
something or other; we can watch it easily from the palings.'

After this, ten minutes' drive brought us to the place, and I found
it as he had said, the 'square' being really a triangle. Number one
hundred and ninety-two was a big house, its outer points gone much
to decay, but lighted on its second and third floors; though so far as I
could see, for the blinds of the drawing-room were up, no one was
moving. This did not deter me, however, and, taking my stand with
Abel at the corner where two great trees gave us perfect shelter, we
waited silently for many minutes, to the astonishment of the constable upon the beat, with whom I soon settled; and to his satisfaction.

'Ah,' said he, 'I knew they was rum 'uns all along; they owe fourteen pounds for milk, and their butcher ain't paid; young men going
in all night, too – why, there's one of them there now.'

I looked through the trees at his word, and saw that he was right.
A youth in an opera hat and a black coat was upon the doorstep of
the house; and as the light of a street lamp fell upon his face, I recognised him. He was the boy who had eaten of the jam-tarts so plenti-
fully at Lady Faber's – the youth with whom Sibyl Kavanagh had
pretended to have no acquaintance when she talked to me in the conservatory. And at the sight of him, I knew that the moment had come.

'Abel,' I said, 'it's time you went. Tell the men to bring a short
ladder with them. They'll have to come in by the balcony – but only
when I make a sign. The signal will be the cracking of the glass of that
lamp you can see upon the table there. Did you bring my pistol?'

'Would I forget that?' he asked; 'I brought you two, and look out!
for you may want them.'

'I know that,' said I, 'but I depend upon you. Get back at the earliest possible moment, and don't act until I give the signal. It will mean
that the clue is complete.'

He nodded his head, and disappeared quickly in the direction
where the carriage was; but I went straight up to the house, and

knocked loudly upon the door. To my surprise, it was opened at once by a thick-set man in livery, who did not appear at all astonished to see me.

'They're upstairs, sir, will you go up?' said he.

'Certainly,' said I, taking him at his word. 'Lead the way.'

This request made him hesitate.

'I beg your pardon,' said he, 'I think I have made a mistake – I'll speak to Mrs Kavanagh.'

Before I could answer he had run up the stairs nimbly; but I was quick after him; and when I came upon the landing, I could see into the front drawing-room, where there sat the woman herself, a small and oldish man with long black whiskers, and the youth who had just come into the room. But the back room which gave off from the other with folding-doors, was empty; and there was no light in it. All this I perceived in a momentary glance, for no sooner had the serving-man spoken to the woman, than she pushed the youth out upon the balcony, and came hurriedly to the landing, closing the door behind her.

'Why, Mr Sutton,' she cried, when she saw me, 'this is a surprise; I was just going to bed.'

'I was afraid you would have been already gone,' said I with the simplest smile possible, 'but I found a diamond spray in Lady Faber's hall – just after you had left. The footman said it must be yours, and as I am going out of town tomorrow, I thought I would risk leaving it tonight.'

I handed to her as I spoke the spray of diamonds I had taken from my own showcase in Bond Street; but while she examined it she shot up at me a quick searching glance from her bright eyes, and her thick sensual lips were closed hard upon each other. Yet, in the next instant, she laughed again, and handed me back the jewel.

'I'm indeed very grateful to you,' she exclaimed, 'but I've just put my spray in its case; you want to give me someone else's property.'

'Then it isn't yours?' said I, affecting disappointment. 'I'm really very sorry for having troubled you.'

'It is I that should be sorry for having brought you here,' she cried. 'Won't you have a brandy and seltzer or something before you go?'

'Nothing whatever, thanks,' said I. 'Let me apologise again for having disturbed you – and wish you "Goodnight".'

She held out her hand to me, seemingly much reassured; and as I began to descend the stairs, she re-entered the drawing-room for the purpose, I did not doubt, of getting the man off the balcony. The substantial lackey was then waiting in the hall to open the door for me; but I went down very slowly, for in truth the whole of my plan appeared to have failed; and at that moment I was without the veriest rag of an idea. My object in coming to the house had been to trace, and if possible to lay hands upon the woman's associates, taking her, as I hoped, somewhat by surprise; yet though I had made my chain more complete, vital links were missing; and I stood no nearer to the forging of them. That which I had to ask myself, and to answer in the space of ten seconds, was the question, 'Now, or tomorrow?' – whether I should leave the house without effort, and wait until the gang betrayed itself again; or make some bold stroke which would end the matter there and then. The latter course was the one I chose. The morrow, said I, may find these people in Paris or in Belgium; there never may be such a clue again as that of the ruby pendant – there never may be a similar opportunity of taking at least three of those for whom we had so long hunted. And with this thought a whole plan of action suddenly leaped up in my mind; and I acted upon it, silently and swiftly, and with a readiness which to this day I wonder at.

I now stood at the hall-door, which the lackey held open. One searching look at the man convinced me that my design was a sound one. He was obtuse, patronising – but probably honest. As we faced each other I suddenly took the door-handle from him, and banged the door loudly, remaining in the hall. Then I clapped my pistol to his head (though for this offence I surmise that a judge might have given me a month), and I whispered fiercely to him:

'This house is surrounded by police; if you say a word I'll give you seven years as an accomplice of the woman upstairs, whom we are going to arrest. When she calls out, answer that I'm gone, and then come back to me for instructions. If you do as I tell you, you shall not be charged – otherwise, you go to jail.'

At this speech the poor wretch paled before me, and shook so that I could feel the tremor all down the arm of his which I held.

'I – I won't speak, sir,' he gasped. 'I won't, I do assure you – to think as I should have served such folk.'

'Then hide me, and be quick about it – in this room here, it seems dark. Now run upstairs and say I'm gone.'

I had stepped into a little breakfast-room at the back of the dining-room, and there had gone unhesitatingly under a round table. The place was absolutely dark, and was a vantage ground, since I could see therefrom the whole of the staircase; but before the footman could mount the stairs, the woman came halfway down them, and, looking over the hall, she asked him:

'Is that gentleman gone?'

'Just left, mum,' he replied.

'Then go to bed, and never let me see you admit a stranger like that again.'

She went up again at this, and he turned to me, asking:

'What shall I do now, sir? I'll do anything if you'll speak for me, sir; I've got twenty years' kerecter from Lord Walley; to think as she's a bad 'un – it's hardly creditable.'

'I shall speak for you,' said I, 'if you do exactly what I tell you. Are any more men expected now?'

'Yes, there's two more; the capting and the clergymin, pretty clergymin he must be, too.'

'Never mind that; wait and let them in. Then go upstairs and turn the light out on the staircase as if by accident. After that you can go to bed.'

'Did you say the police was 'ere?' he asked in his hoarse whisper; and I said:

'Yes, they're everywhere, on the roof, and in the street, and on the balcony. If there's the least resistance, the house will swarm with them.'

What he would have said to this I cannot tell, for at that moment there was another knock upon the front door, and he opened it instantly. Two men, one in clerical dress, and one, a very powerful man, in a Newmarket coat, went quickly upstairs, and the butler followed them. A moment later the gas went out on the stairs; and there was no sound but the echo of the talk in the front drawing-room.

The critical moment in my night's work had now come. Taking off my boots, and putting my revolver at the half-cock, I crawled up the stairs with the step of a cat, and entered the back drawing-room. One of the folding doors of this was ajar, so that a false step would probably have cost me my life – and I could not possibly tell if the police were really in the street, or only upon their way. But it was my good luck that the men talked loudly, and seemed actually to be disputing. The first thing I observed on looking through the open door was that the woman had left the four to themselves. Three of them stood about the table whereon the lamp was; the dumpy man with the black whiskers sat in his armchair. But the most pleasing sight of all was that of a large piece of cotton-wool spread upon the table and almost covered with brooches, lockets, and sprays of diamonds; and to my infinite satisfaction I saw Lady Faber's pendant of rubies lying conspicuous even amongst the wealth of jewels which the light showed.

There then was the clue; but how was it to be used? It came to me suddenly that four consummate rogues such as these would not be unarmed. Did I step into the room, they might shoot me at the first sound; and if the police had not come, there would be the end of it. Had opportunity been permitted to me, I would, undoubtedly, have waited five or ten minutes to assure myself that Abel was in the street without. But this was not to be. Even as I debated the point, a candle's light shone upon the staircase; and in another moment Mrs Kavanagh herself stood in the doorway watching me. For one instant she stood, but it served my purpose; and as a scream rose upon her lips, and I felt my heart thudding against my ribs, I threw open the folding doors, and deliberately shot down the glass of the lamp which had cast the aureola of light upon the stolen jewels.

As the glass flew, for my reputation as a pistol shot was not belied in this critical moment, Mrs Kavanagh ran in a wild fit of hysterical screaming to her bedroom above – but the four men turned with loud cries to the door where they had seen me; and as I saw them coming, I prayed that Abel might be there. This thought need not have occurred to me. Scarce had the men taken two steps when the glass of the balcony windows was burst in with a crash, and the whole room seemed to fill with police.

I cannot now remember precisely the sentences which were passed upon the great gang (known to police history as the Westbourne Park gang) of jewel thieves; but the history of that case is curious enough to be worthy of mention. The husband of the woman Kavanagh – he of the black whiskers – was a man of the name of Whyte, formerly a manager in the house of James Thorndike, the Universal Provider near the Tottenham Court Road. Whyte's business had been to provide all things needful for dances; and, though it astonishes me to write it, he had even found dancing men for ladies whose range of acquaintance was narrow. In the course of business, he set up for himself eventually; and as he worked, the bright idea came to him, why not find as guests men who may snap up, in the heat and the security of the dance, such unconsidered trifles as sprays, pendants, and lockets. To this end he married, and his wife being a clever woman who fell in with his idea, she – under the name of Kavanagh – made the acquaintance of a number of youths whose business it was to dance; and eventually wormed herself into many good houses. The trial brought to light the extraordinary fact that no less than twenty-three men and eight women were bound in this amazing conspiracy, and that Kavanagh acted as the buyer of the property they stole, giving them a third of the profits, and swindling them outrageously. He, I believe, is now taking the air at Portland; and the other young men are finding in the exemplary exercise of picking oakum, work for idle hands to do.

As for Mrs Kavanagh, she was dramatic to the end of it; and, as I learnt from King, she insisted on being arrested in bed.

ARTHUR MORRISON

The Case of Laker, Absconded

THERE WERE several of the larger London banks and insurance offices from which Hewitt held a sort of general retainer as detective adviser, in fulfilment of which he was regularly consulted as to the measures to be taken in different cases of fraud, forgery, theft, and so forth, which it might be the misfortune of the particular firms to encounter. The more important and intricate of these cases were placed in his hands entirely, with separate commissions, in the usual way. One of the most important companies of the sort was the General Guarantee Society, an insurance corporation which, among other risks, took those of the integrity of secretaries, clerks, and cashiers. In the case of a cash-box elopement on the part of any person guaranteed by the society, the directors were naturally anxious for a speedy capture of the culprit, and more especially of the booty, before too much of it was spent, in order to lighten the claim upon their funds, and in work of this sort Hewitt was at times engaged, either in general advice and direction or in the actual pursuit of the plunder and the plunderer.

Arriving at his office a little later than usual one morning, Hewitt found an urgent message awaiting him from the General Guarantee Society, requesting his attention to a robbery which had taken place on the previous day. He had gleaned some hint of the case from the morning paper, wherein appeared a short paragraph, which ran thus:

SERIOUS BANK ROBBERY. – In the course of yesterday a clerk employed by Messrs Liddle, Neal & Liddle, the well-known bankers, disappeared, having in his possession a large sum of money, the property of his employers – a sum reported to be rather over £15,000. It would seem that he had been entrusted to collect the money in his capacity of 'walk-clerk' from various other banks and trading concerns during the morning, but failed to return at the usual time. A large number of the notes which he received had been cashed at the Bank of England before suspicion was aroused. We understand that Detective-Inspector Plummer, of Scotland Yard, has the case in hand.

The clerk, whose name was Charles William Laker, had, it appeared from the message, been guaranteed in the usual way by the General Guarantee Society, and Hewitt's presence at the office was at once desired in order that steps might quickly be taken for the man's apprehension and the recovery, at any rate, of as much of the booty as possible.

A smart hansom brought Hewitt to Threadneedle Street in a bare quarter of an hour, and there a few minutes' talk with the manager, Mr Lyster, put him in possession of the main facts of the case, which appeared to be simple. Charles William Laker was twenty-five years of age, and had been in employ of Messrs Liddle, Neal & Liddle for something more than seven years – since he left school, in fact – and until the previous day there had been nothing in his conduct to complain of. His duties as walk-clerk consisted in making a certain round, beginning at about half-past ten each morning. There were a certain number of the more important banks between which and Messrs Liddle, Neal & Liddle there were daily transactions, and a few smaller semi-private banks and merchant firms acting as financial agents with whom there was business intercourse of less importance and regularity; and each of these, as necessary, he visited in turn, collecting cash due on bills and other instruments of a like nature. He carried a wallet, fastened securely to his person by a chain, and this wallet contained the bills and the cash. Usually at the end of his round, when all his bills had been converted into cash, the wallet held very large sums. His work and responsibilities, in fine, were those common to walk-clerks in all banks.

On the day of the robbery he had started out as usual – possibly a little earlier than was customary – and the bills and other securities in his possession represented considerably more than £15,000. It had been ascertained that he had called in the usual way at each establishment on the round, and had transacted his business at the last place by about a quarter-past one, being then, without doubt, in possession of cash to the full value of the bills negotiated. After that, Mr Lyster said, yesterday's report was that nothing more had been heard of him. But this morning there had been a message to the effect that he had been traced out of the country – to Calais, at least it was thought. The directors of the society wished Hewitt to take the case in hand personally and at once, with a view of recovering what was possible from the plunder by way of salvage; also, of course, of finding Laker, for it is an important moral gain to guarantee societies, as an example, if a thief is caught and punished. Therefore Hewitt and Mr

Lyster, as soon as might be, made for Messrs Liddle, Neal & Liddle's, that the investigation might be begun.

The bank premises were quite near – in Leadenhall Street. Having arrived there, Hewitt and Mr Lyster made their way to the firm's private rooms. As they were passing an outer waiting-room, Hewitt noticed two women. One, the elder, in widow's weeds, was sitting with her head bowed in her hand over a small writing-table. Her face was not visible, but her whole attitude was that of a person overcome with unbearable grief; and she sobbed quietly. The other was a young woman of twenty-two or twenty-three. Her thick black veil revealed no more than that her features were small and regular and that her face was pale and drawn. She stood with a hand on the elder woman's shoulder, and she quickly turned her head away as the two men entered.

Mr Neal, one of the partners, received them in his own room. Good morning, Mr Hewitt,' he said, when Mr Lyster had introduced the detective. 'This is a serious business – very. I think I am sorrier for Laker himself than for anybody else, ourselves included – or, at any rate, I am sorrier for his mother. She is waiting now to see Mr Liddle, as soon as he arrives – Mr Liddle has known the family for a long time. Miss Shaw is with her, too, poor girl. She is a governess, or something of that sort, and I believe she and Laker were engaged to be married. It's all very sad.'

'Inspector Plummer, I understand,' Hewitt remarked, 'has the affair in hand, on behalf of the police?'

'Yes,' Mr Neal replied; 'in fact, he's here now, going through the contents of Laker's desk, and so forth; he thinks it possible Laker may have had accomplices. Will you see him?'

'Presently. Inspector Plummer and I are old friends. We met last, I think, in the case of the Stanway cameo, some months ago. But, first, will you tell me how long Laker has been a walk-clerk?'

'Barely four months, although he has been with us altogether seven years. He was promoted to the walk soon after the beginning of the year.'

'Do you know anything of his habits – what he used to do in his spare time, and so forth?'

'Not a great deal. He went in for boating, I believe, though I have heard it whispered that he had one or two more expensive tastes – expensive, that is, for a young man in his position,' Mr Neal explained, with a dignified wave of the hand that he peculiarly affected. He was a stout old gentleman, and the gesture suited him.

'You have had no reason to suspect him of dishonesty before, I take it?'

'Oh, no. He made a wrong return once, I believe, that went for some time undetected, but it turned out, after all, to be a clerical error – mere clerical error.'

'Do you know anything of his associates out of the office?'

'No, how should I? I believe Inspector Plummer has been making inquiries as to that, however, of the other clerks. Here he is, by the bye, I expect. Come in!'

It was Plummer who had knocked, and he came in at Mr Neal's call. He was a middle-sized, small-eyed, impenetrable-looking man, as yet of no great reputation in the force. Some of my readers may remember his connection with that case, so long a public mystery, that I have elsewhere fully set forth and explained under the title of 'The Stanway Cameo Mystery'. Plummer carried his billy-cock hat in one hand and a few papers in the other. He gave Hewitt good-morning, placed his hat on a chair, and spread the papers on the table.

'There's not a great deal here,' he said, 'but one thing's plain – Laker had been betting. See here, and here, and here' – he took a few letters from the bundle in his hand – 'two letters from a bookmaker about settling – wonder he trusted a clerk – several telegrams from tipsters, and a letter from some friend – only signed by initials – asking Laker to put a sovereign on a horse for the friend 'with his own'. I'll keep these, I think. It may be worth while to see that friend, if we can find him. Ah, we often find it's bètting, don't we, Mr Hewitt? Meanwhile, there's no news from France yet.'

'You are sure that is where he is gone?' asked Hewitt.

'Well, I'll tell you what we've done as yet. First, of course, I went round to all the banks. There was nothing to be got from that. The cashiers all knew him by sight, and one was a personal friend of his. He had called as usual, said nothing in particular, cashed his bills in the ordinary way, and finished up at the Eastern Consolidated Bank at about a quarter-past one. So far there was nothing whatever. But I had started two or three men meanwhile making inquiries at the railway stations, and so on. I had scarcely left the Eastern Consolidated when one of them came after me with news. He had tried Palmer's Tourist Office, although that seemed an unlikely place, and there struck the track.'

'Had he been there?'

'Not only had he been there, but he had taken a tourist ticket for

France. It was quite a smart move, in a way. You see it was the sort of
ticket that lets you do pretty well what you like; you have the choice
of two or three different routes to begin with, and you can break your
journey where you please, and make all sorts of variations. So that a
man with a ticket like that, and a few hours' start, could twist about
on some remote branch route, and strike off in another direction altogether, with a new ticket, from some out-of-the-way place, while we
were carefully sorting out and inquiring along the different routes he
might have taken. Not half a bad move for a new hand; but he made
one bad mistake, as new hands always do – as old hands do, in fact,
very often. He was fool enough to give his own name, C Laker!
Although that didn't matter much, as the description was enough to
fix him. There he was, wallet and all, just as he had come from the
Eastern Consolidated Bank. He went straight from there to Palmer's,
by the bye, and probably in a cab. We judge that by the time. He left
the Eastern Consolidated at a quarter-past one, and was at Palmer's
by twenty-five past – ten minutes. The clerk at Palmer's remembered
the time because he was anxious to get out to his lunch, and kept
looking at the clock, expecting another clerk in to relieve him. Laker
didn't take much in the way of luggage, I fancy. We inquired carefully
at the stations, and got the porters to remember the passengers for
whom they had been carrying luggage, but none appeared to have
had any dealings with our man. That, of course, is as one would
expect. He'd take as little as possible with him, and buy what he
wanted on the way, or when he'd reached his hiding-place. Of course,
I wired to Calais (it was a Dover to Calais route ticket) and sent a
couple of smart men off by the 8.15 mail from Charing Cross. I
expect we shall hear from them in the course of the day. I am being
kept in London in view of something expected at headquarters, or I
should have been off myself.'

'That is all, then, up to the present? Have you anything else in
view?'

'That's all I've absolutely ascertained at present. As for what I'm
going to do' – a slight smile curled Plummer's lip – 'well, I shall see.
I've a thing or two in my mind.'

Hewitt smiled slightly himself; he recognised Plummer's touch of
professional jealousy. 'Very well,' he said, rising. 'I'll make an inquiry
or two for myself at once. Perhaps, Mr Neal, you'll allow one of your
clerks to show me the banks, in their regular order, at which Laker
called yesterday. I think I'll begin at the beginning.'

Mr Neal offered to place at Hewitt's disposal anything or

anybody the bank contained, and the conference broke up. As Hewitt, with the clerk, came through the rooms separating Mr Neal's sanctum from the outer office, he fancied he saw the two veiled women leaving by a side door.

The first bank was quite close to Liddle, Neal & Liddle's. There the cashier who had dealt with Laker the day before remembered nothing in particular about the interview. Many other walk-clerks had called during the morning, as they did every morning, and the only circumstances of the visit that he could say anything definite about were those recorded in figures in the books. He did not know Laker's name till Plummer had mentioned it in making inquiries on the previous-afternoon. As far as he could remember, Laker behaved much as usual, though really he did not notice much; he looked chiefly at the bills. He described Laker in a way that corresponded with the photograph that Hewitt had borrowed from the bank; a young man with a brown moustache and ordinary-looking fairly regular face, dressing much as other clerks dressed – tall hat, black cutaway coat, and so on. The numbers of the notes handed over had already been given to Inspector Plummer, and these Hewitt did not trouble about.

The next bank was in Cornhill, and here the cashier was a personal friend of Laker's – at any rate, an acquaintance – and he remembered a little more. Laker's manner had been quite as usual, he said; certainly he did not seem preoccupied or excited in his manner. He spoke for a moment or two – of being on the river on Sunday, and so on – and left in his usual way.

'Can you remember *everything* he said?' Hewitt asked. 'If you can tell me, I should like to know exactly what he did and said to the smallest particular.'

'Well, he saw me a little distance off – I was behind there, at one of the desks – and raised his hand to me, and said, 'How d'ye do?' I came across and took his bills, and dealt with them in the usual way. He had a new umbrella lying on the counter – rather a handsome umbrella – and I made a remark about the handle. He took it up to show me, and told me it was a present he had just received from a friend. It was a gorse-root handle, with two silver bands, one with his monogram, CWL. I said it was a very nice handle, and asked him whether it was fine in his district on Sunday. He said he had been up the river, and it was very fine there. And I think that was all.'

'Thank you. Now about this umbrella. Did he carry it rolled? Can you describe it in detail?'

'Well, I've told you about the handle, and the rest was much as usual, I think; it wasn't rolled – just flapping loosely, you know. It was rather an odd-shaped handle, though. I'll try and sketch it, if you like, as well as I can remember.' He did so, and Hewitt saw in the result, rough indications of a gnarled crook, with one silver band near the end, and another, with the monogram, a few inches down the handle. Hewitt put the sketch in his pocket, and bade the cashier good-day. At the next bank the story was the same as at first – there was nothing remembered but the usual routine. Hewitt and the clerk turned down a narrow paved court, and through into Lombard Street for the next visit. The bank – that of Buller, Clayton, Ladds & Co – was just at the corner at the end of the court, and the imposing stone entrance-porch was being made larger and more imposing still, the way being almost blocked by ladders and scaffold-poles. Here there was only the usual tale, and so on through the whole walk. The cashiers knew Laker only by sight, and that not always very distinctly. The calls of walk-clerks were such matters of routine that little note was taken of the persons of the clerks themselves, who were called by the names of their firms, if they were called by any names at all. Laker had behaved much as usual, so far as the cashiers could remember, and when finally the Eastern Consolidated was left behind, nothing more had been learnt than the chat about Laker's new umbrella.

Hewitt had taken leave of Mr Neal's clerk, and was stepping into a hansom, when he noticed a veiled woman in widow's weeds hailing another hansom a little way behind. He recognised the figure again, and said to the driver:

'Drive fast to Palmer's Tourist Office, but keep your eye on that cab behind, and tell me presently if it is following us.'

The cabman drove off, and after passing one or two turnings, opened the lid above Hewitt's head, and said: 'That there other keb *is* a-follerin' us, sir, an' keepin' about even distance all along.'

'All right; that's what I wanted to know. Palmer's now.'

At Palmer's the clerk who had attended to Laker remembered him very well and described him. He also remembered the wallet, and *thought* he remembered the umbrella – was practically sure of it, in fact, upon reflection. He had no record of the name given, but remembered it distinctly to be Laker. As a matter of fact, names were never asked in such a transaction, but in this case Laker appeared to be ignorant of the usual procedure, as well as in a great hurry, and asked for the ticket and gave his name all in one breath, probably assuming that the name would be required.

Hewitt got back to his cab, and started for Charing Cross. The cabman once more lifted the lid and informed him that the hansom with the veiled woman in it was again following, having waited while Hewitt had visited Palmer's. At Charing Cross Hewitt discharged his cab and walked straight to the lost property office. The man in charge knew him very well, for his business had carried him there frequently before.

'I fancy an umbrella was lost in the station yesterday,' Hewitt said. 'It was a new umbrella, silk, with a gnarled gorse-root handle and two silver bands, something like this sketch. There was a monogram on the lower band – "CWL' were the letters. Has it been brought here?'

'There was two or three yesterday,' the man said; 'let's see.' He took the sketch and retired to a corner of his room. 'Oh, yes – here it is, I think; isn't this it? Do you claim it?'

'Well, not exactly that, but I think I'll take a look at it, if you'll let me. By the way, I see it's rolled up. Was it found like that?'

'No; the chap rolled it up what found it – porter he was. It's a fad of his, rolling up umbrellas close and neat, and he's rather proud of it. He often looks as though he'd like to take a man's umbrella away and roll it up for him when it's a bit clumsy done. Rum fad, eh?'

'Yes; everybody has his little fad, though. Where was this found – close by here?'

'Yes, sir; just there, almost opposite this window, in the little corner.'

'About two o'clock?'

'Ah, about that time, more or less.'

Hewitt took the umbrella up, unfastened the band, and shook the silk out loose. Then he opened it, and as he did so a small scrap of paper fell from inside. Hewitt pounced on it like lightning. Then, after examining the umbrella thoroughly, inside and out, he handed it back to the man, who had not observed the incident of the scrap of paper.

'That will do, thanks,' he said. 'I only wanted to take a peep at it – just a small matter connected with a little case of mine. Good morning.'

He turned suddenly and saw, gazing at him with a terrified expression from a door behind, the face of the woman who had followed him in the cab. The veil was lifted, and he caught but a mere glance of the face ere it was suddenly withdrawn. He stood for a moment to allow the woman time to retreat, and then left the station and walked towards his office, close by.

Scarcely thirty yards along the Strand he met Plummer.

'I'm going to make some much closer inquiries all down the line as far as Dover,' Plummer said. 'They wire from Calais that they have no clue as yet, and I mean to make quite sure, if I can, that Laker hasn't quietly slipped off the line somewhere between here and Dover. There's one very peculiar thing,' Plummer added confidentially. 'Did you see the two women who were waiting to see a member of the firm at Liddle, Neal & Liddle's?'

'Yes. Laker's mother and his *fiancée,* I was told.'

'That's right. Well, do you know that girl – Shaw her name is – has been shadowing me ever since I left the Bank. Of course I spotted it from the beginning – these amateurs don't know how to follow anybody – and, as a matter of fact, she's just inside the jeweller's shop door behind me now, pretending to look at the things in the window. But it's odd, isn't it?'

'Well,' Hewitt replied, 'of course it's not a thing to be neglected. If you'll look very carefully at the corner of Villiers Street, without appearing to stare, I think you will possibly observe some signs of Laker's mother. She's shadowing *me.*'

Plummer looked casually in the direction indicated, and then immediately turned his eyes in another direction.

'I see her,' he said; 'she's just taking a look round the corner. That's a thing not to be ignored. Of course, the Lakers' house is being watched – we set a man on it at once, yesterday. But I'll put someone on now to watch Miss Shaw's place too. I'll telephone through to Liddle's – probably they'll be able to say where it is. And the women themselves must be watched, too. As a matter of fact, I had a notion that Laker wasn't alone in it. And it's just possible, you know, that he has sent an accomplice off with his tourist ticket to lead us a dance while he looks after himself in another direction. Have you done anything?'

'Well,' Hewitt replied, with a faint reproduction of the secretive smile with which Plummer had met an inquiry of his earlier in the morning, 'I've been to the station here, and I've found Laker's umbrella in the lost property office.'

'Oh! Then probably he *has* gone. I'll bear that in mind, and perhaps have a word with the lost property man.'

Plummer made for the station and Hewitt for his office. He mounted the stairs and reached his door just as I myself, who had been disappointed in not finding him in, was leaving. I had called with the idea of taking Hewitt to lunch with me at my club, but he declined lunch. 'I have an important case in hand,' he said. 'Look here, Brett. See this scrap of paper. You know the types of the different newspapers – which is this?' He handed me a small piece of paper. It was part of a cutting containing an advertisement, which had been torn in half.

> oast You 1St Then to-
> 3rd L. No.197 red bl. straight
> time.

'I *think,*' I said, 'this is from the *Daily Chronicle,* judging by the paper. It is plainly from the 'agony column', but all the papers use pretty much the same type for these advertisements, except the *Times*. If it were not torn I could tell you at once, because the *Chronicle* columns are rather narrow.'

'Never mind – I'll send for them all.' He rang, and sent Kerrett for a copy of each morning paper of the previous day. Then he took from a large wardrobe cupboard a decent but well-worn and rather roughened tall hat. Also a coat a little worn and shiny on the collar. He exchanged these for his own hat and coat, and then substituted an old necktie for his own clean white one, and encased his legs in mud-spotted leggings. This done, he produced a very large and thick pocket-book, fastened by a broad elastic band, and said, 'Well, what do you think of this? Will it do for Queen's taxes, or sanitary inspection, or the gas, or the water supply?'

'Very well indeed, I should say,' I replied. 'What's the case?'

'Oh, I'll tell you all about that when it's over – no time now. Oh here you are, Kerrett. By the bye, Kerrett, I'm going out presently by the back way. Wait for about ten minutes or a quarter of an hour after I'm gone, and then just go across the road and speak to that lady in black, with the veil, who is waiting in that little foot-passage opposite. Say Mr Martin Hewitt sends his compliments, and he advises her not to wait, as he has already left his office by another door, and has been gone some little time. That's all; it would be a pity to keep the poor woman waiting all day for nothing. Now the papers. *Daily News, Standard, Telegraph, Chronicle* – yes, here it is, in the *Chronicle*.'

The whole advertisement read thus:

> YOB – HR Shop roast. You 1st Then to-
> night. 02. 2nd top 3rd L. No. 197 red bl.
> straight mon. One at a time.

'What's this,' I asked, 'a cryptogram?'

'I'll see,' Hewitt answered. 'But I won't tell you anything about it till afterwards, so get your lunch. Kerrett, bring the directory.'

This was all I actually saw of this case myself, and I have written the rest in its proper order from Hewitt's information, as I have written some other cases entirely.

To resume at the point where, for the time, I lost sight of the matter. Hewitt left by the back way and stopped an empty cab as it passed. 'Abney Park Cemetery' was his direction to the driver. In little more than twenty minutes the cab was branching off down the Essex Road on its way to Stoke Newington, and in twenty minutes more Hewitt stopped it in Church Street, Stoke Newington. He walked through a street or two, and then down another, the houses of which he scanned carefully as he passed. Opposite one which stood by itself he stopped, and, making a pretence of consulting and arranging his large pocket-book, he took a good look at the house. It was rather larger, neater, and more pretentious than the others in the street, and it had a natty little coach-house just visible up the side entrance. There were red blinds hung with heavy lace in the front windows, and behind one of the blinds Hewitt was able to catch the glint of a heavy gas chandelier.

He stepped briskly up the front steps and knocked sharply at the door. 'Mr Merston?' he asked, pocket-book in hand, when a neat parlourmaid opened the door.

'Yes.'

'Ah!' Hewitt stepped into the hall and pulled off his hat; 'it's only the meter. There's been a great deal of gas running away somewhere here, and I'm just looking to see if the meters are right. Where is it?'

The girl hesitated. 'I'll – I'll ask master,' she said.

'Very well. I don't want to take it away, you know – only to give it a tap or two, and so on.'

The girl retired to the back of the hall, and without taking her eyes off Martin Hewitt, gave his message to some invisible person in a back room, whence came a growling reply of 'All right'.

Hewitt followed the girl to the basement, apparently looking straight before him, but in reality taking in every detail of the place. The gas meter was in a very large lumber cupboard under the kitchen stairs. The girl opened the door and lit a candle. The meter stood on the floor, which was littered with hampers and boxes and odd sheets of brown paper. But a thing that at once arrested Hewitt's attention was a garment of some sort of bright blue cloth, with large brass buttons, which was lying in a tumbled heap in a corner, and appeared to be the only thing in the place that was not covered with dust. Nevertheless, Hewitt took no apparent notice of it, but stooped down and solemnly tapped the meter three times with his pencil, and listened with great gravity, placing his ear to the top. Then he shook his head and tapped again. At length he said:

'It's a bit doubtful. I'll just get you to light the gas in the kitchen a moment. Keep your hand to the burner, and when I call out shut it off *at once*; see?'

The girl turned and entered the kitchen, and Hewitt immediately seized the blue coat – for a coat it was. It had a dull red piping in the seams, and was of the swallowtail pattern livery coat, in fact. He held it for a moment before him, examining its pattern and colour, and then rolled it up and flung it again into the corner.

'Right!' he called to the servant. 'Shut off!'

The girl emerged from the kitchen as he left the cupboard. 'Well,' she asked, 'are you satisfied now?'

'Quite satisfied, thank you,' Hewitt replied.

'Is it all right?' she continued, jerking her hand towards the cupboard.

'Well, no, it isn't; there's something wrong there, and I'm glad I came. You can tell Mr Merston, if you like, that I expect his gas bill will be a good deal less next quarter.' And there was a suspicion of a chuckle in Hewitt's voice as he crossed the hall to leave. For a gas inspector is pleased when he finds at length what he has been searching for.

Things had fallen out better than Hewitt had dared to expect. He saw the key of the whole mystery in that blue coat; for it was the uniform coat of the hall porters at one of the banks that he had visited in the morning, though which one he could not for the moment remember. He entered the nearest post office and despatched a telegram to Plummer, giving certain directions and asking the inspector to meet him; then he hailed the first available cab and hurried towards the City.

At Lombard Street he alighted, and looked in at the door of each bank till he came to Buller, Clayton, Ladds & Co's. This was the bank he wanted. In the other banks the hall porters wore mulberry coats, brick-dust coats, brown coats, and what not, but here, behind the ladders and scaffold poles which obscured the entrance, he could see a man in a blue coat, with dull red piping and brass buttons. He sprang up the steps, pushed open the inner swing door, and finally satisfied himself by a closer view of the coat, to the wearer's astonishment. Then he regained the paved passage at the side, deep in thought. The bank had no windows or doors on the side next to the court, and the two adjoining houses were old and supported in place by wooden shores. Both were empty, and a great board announced that tenders would be received in a month's time for the purchase of the old materials of which they were constructed; also that some part of the site would be let on a long building lease.

Hewitt looked up at the grimy fronts of the old buildings. The windows were crusted thick with dirt – all except the bottom window of the house nearer the bank, which was fairly clean, and seemed to have been quite lately washed. The door, too, of this house was cleaner than that of the other, though the paint was worn. Hewitt reached and fingered a hook driven into the left-hand doorpost about six feet from the ground. It was new, and not at all rusted; also a tiny splinter had been displaced when the hook was driven in, and clean wood showed at the spot.

Having observed these things, Hewitt stepped back and read at the bottom of the big board the name, 'Winsor & Weekes, Surveyors and Auctioneers, Abchurch Lane'. Then he stepped into Lombard Street.

Two hansoms pulled up near the post office, and out of the first stepped Inspector Plummer and another man. This man and the two who alighted from the second hansom were unmistakably plain-clothes constables – their air, gait, and boots proclaimed it.

'What's all this?' demanded Plummer, as Hewitt approached.

'You'll soon see, I think. But, first, have you put the watch on number 197, Hackworth Road?'

'Yes; nobody will get away from there alone.'

'Very good. I am going into Abchurch Lane for a few minutes. Leave your men out here, but just go round into the court by Buller, Clayton & Ladds's, and keep your eye on the first door on the left. I think we'll find something soon. Did you get rid of Miss Shaw?'

'No, she's behind now, and Mrs Laker's with her. They met in the Strand, and came after us in another cab. Rare fun, eh! They think we're pretty green! It's quite handy, too. So long as they keep behind me it saves all trouble of watching *them*.' And Inspector Plummer chuckled and winked.

'Very good. You don't mind keeping your eye on that door, do you? I'll be back very soon,' and with that Hewitt turned off into Abchurch Lane.

At Winsor & Weekes's information was not difficult to obtain. The houses were destined to come down very shortly, but a week or so ago an office and a cellar in one of them was let temporarily to a

Mr Westley. He brought no references; indeed, as he paid a fort-night's rent in advance, he was not asked for any, considering the circumstances of the case. He was opening a London branch for a large firm of cider merchants, he said, and just wanted a rough office and a cool cellar to store samples in for a few weeks till the permanent premises were ready. There was another key, and no doubt the premises might be entered if there were any special need for such a course. Martin Hewitt gave such excellent reasons that Winsor & Weekes's managing clerk immediately produced the key and accompanied Hewitt to the spot.

'I think you'd better have your men handy,' Hewitt remarked to Plummer when they reached the door, and a whistle quickly brought the men over.

The key was inserted in the lock and turned, but the door would not open; the bolt was fastened at the bottom. Hewitt stooped and looked under the door.

'It's a drop bolt,' he said. 'Probably the man who left last let it fall loose, and then banged the door, so that it fell into its place. I must try my best with a wire or a piece of string.'

A wire was brought, and with some manoeuvring Hewitt contrived to pass it round the bolt, and lift it little by little, steadying it with the blade of a pocket-knife. When at length the bolt was raised out of the hole, the knife-blade was slipped under it, and the door swung open.

They entered. The door of the little office just inside stood open, but in the office there was nothing, except a board a couple of feet long in a corner. Hewitt stepped across and lifted this, turning it downward face toward Plummer. On it, in fresh white paint on a black ground, were painted the words

BULLER, CLAYTON, LADDS & CO,
TEMPORARY ENTRANCE.'

Hewitt turned to Winsor & Weekes's clerk and asked, 'The man who took this room called himself Westley, didn't he?'

'Yes.'

'Youngish man, clean-shaven, and well-dressed?'

'Yes, he was.'

'I fancy,' Hewitt said, turning to Plummer, 'I *fancy* an old friend of yours is in this – Mr Sam Gunter.'

'What, the "Hoxton Yob"?'

'I think it's possible he's been Mr Westley for a bit, and somebody else for another bit. But let's come to the cellar.'

Winsor & Weekes's clerk led the way down a steep flight of steps into a dark underground corridor, wherein they lighted their way with many successive matches. Soon the cellar corridor made a turn to the right, and as the party passed the turn, there came from the end of the passage before them a fearful yell.

'Help! help! Open the door! I'm going mad – mad! Oh my God!'

And there was a sound of desperate beating from the inside of the cellar door at the extreme end. The men stopped, startled.

'Come,' said Hewitt, 'more matches!' and he rushed to the door. It was fastened with a bar and padlock.

'Let me out, for God's sake!' came the voice, sick and hoarse, from the inside. 'Let me out!'

'All right!' Hewitt shouted. 'We have come for you. Wait a moment.'

The voice sank into a sort of sobbing croon, and Hewitt tried several keys from his own bunch on the padlock. None fitted. He drew from his pocket the wire he had used for the bolt of the front door, straightened it out, and made a sharp bend at the end.

'Hold a match close,' he ordered shortly, and one of the men obeyed. Three or four attempts were necessary, and several different bendings of the wire were effected, but in the end Hewitt picked the lock, and flung open the door.

From within a ghastly figure fell forward among them fainting, and knocked out the matches.

'Hullo!' cried Plummer. 'Hold up! Who are you?'

'Let's get him up into the open,' said Hewitt. 'He can't tell you who he is for a bit, but I believe he's Laker.'

'Laker! What, here?'

'I think so. Steady up the steps. Don't bump him. He's pretty sore already, I expect.'

Truly the man was a pitiable sight. His hair and face were caked in dust and blood, and his fingernails were torn and bleeding. Water was sent for at once, and brandy.

'Well,' said Plummer hazily, looking first at the unconscious prisoner and then at Hewitt, 'but what about the swag?'

'You'll have to find that yourself,' Hewitt replied. 'I think my share of the case is about finished. I only act for the Guarantee Society, you know, and if Laker's proved innocent—'

'Innocent! How?'

'Well, this is what took place, as near as I can figure it. You'd better undo his collar, I think' – this to the men. 'What I believe has happened is this. There has been a very clever and carefully prepared conspiracy here, and Laker has not been the criminal, but the victim.'

'Been robbed himself you mean? But how? Where?'

'Yesterday morning, before he had been to more than three banks – here, in fact.'

'But then how? You're all wrong. We *know* he made the whole round, and did all the collection. And then Palmer's office, and all, and the umbrella; why—'

The man lay still unconscious. 'Don't raise his head,' Hewitt said. 'And one of you had best fetch a doctor. He's had a terrible shock.' Then turning to Plummer he went on, 'As to *how* they managed the job, I'll tell you what I think. First it struck some very clever person that a deal of money might be got by robbing a walk-clerk from a bank. This clever person was one of a clever gang of thieves – perhaps the Hoxton Row gang, as I think I hinted. Now you know quite as well as I do that such a gang will spend any amount of time over a job that promises a big haul, and that for such a job they can always command the necessary capital. There are many most respectable persons living in good style in the suburbs whose chief business lies in financing such ventures, and taking the chief share of the proceeds. Well, this is their plan, carefully and intelligently carried out. They watch Laker, observe the round he takes, and his habits. They find that there is only one of the clerks with whom he does business that he is much acquainted with, and that this clerk is in a bank which is commonly second in Laker's round. The sharpest man among them – and I don't think there's a man in London could do this as well as young Sam Gunter – studies Laker's dress and habits just as an actor studies a character. They take this office and cellar, as we have seen, *because it is next door to a bank whose front entrance is being altered* – a fact which Laker must know from his daily visits. The smart man – Gunter, let us say, and I have other reasons for believing it to be he – makes up precisely like Laker, false moustache, dress, and everything, and waits here with the rest of the gang. One of the gang is dressed in a blue coat with brass buttons, like a hall-porter in Buller's bank. Do you see?'

'Yes, I think so. It's pretty clear now.'

'A confederate watches at the top of the court, and the moment Laker turns in from Cornhill – having already been, mind, at the only bank where he was so well known that the disguised thief would not have passed muster – as soon as he turns in from Cornhill, I say, a signal is given, and that board' – pointing to that with the white letters – 'is hung on the hook in the doorpost. The sham porter stands beside it, and as Laker approaches says, 'This way in, sir, this morning. The front way's shut for the alterations.' Laker suspecting nothing, and supposing that the firm have made a temporary entrance through the empty house, enters. He is seized when well along the corridor, the board is taken down and the door shut. Probably he is stunned by a blow on the head – see the blood now. They take his wallet and all the cash he has already collected. Gunter takes the wallet and also the umbrella, since it has Laker's initials, and is therefore distinctive. He simply completes the walk in the character of Laker, beginning with Buller, Clayton & Ladds's just round the corner. It is nothing but routine work, which is quickly done, and nobody notices him particularly – it is the bills they examine. Meanwhile this unfortunate fellow is locked up in the cellar here, right at the end of the underground corridor, where he can never make himself heard in the street, and where next him are only the empty cellars of the deserted house next door. The thieves shut the front door and vanish. The rest is plain. Gunter, having completed the round, and bagged some £15,000 or more, spends a few pounds on a tourist ticket at Palmer's as a blind, being careful to give Laker's name. He leaves the umbrella at Charing Cross in a conspicuous place right opposite the lost property office, where it is sure to be seen, and so completes his false trail.'

'Then who are the people at 197 Hackworth Road?'

'The capitalist lives there – the financier, and probably the directing spirit of the whole thing. Merston's the name he goes by there, and I've no doubt he cuts a very imposing figure in chapel every Sunday. He'll be worth picking up – this isn't the first thing he's been in, I'll warrant.'

'But – but what about Laker's mother and Miss Shaw?'

'Well, what? The poor women are nearly out of their minds with terror and shame, that's all, but though they may think Laker a criminal, they'll never desert him. They've been following us about with a feeble, vague sort of hope of being able to baffle us in some way or help him if we caught him, or something, poor things. Did you ever hear of a real woman who'd desert a son or a lover merely because he was a criminal? But here's the doctor. When he's attended to him will you let your men take Laker home? I must hurry and report to the Guarantee Society, I think.'

'But,' said the perplexed Plummer, 'where did you get your clue? You must have had a tip from someone, you know – you can't have done it by clairvoyance. What gave you the tip?'

'The *Daily Chronicle*.'

'The *what*?'

The *Daily Chronicle*. Just take a look at the 'agony column' in yesterday morning's issue, and read the message to 'Yob' – to Gunter, in fact. That's all.'

By this time a cab was waiting in Lombard Street, and two of Plummer's men, under the doctor's directions, carried Laker to it. No sooner, however, were they in the court than the two watching women threw themselves hysterically upon Laker, and it was long before they could be persuaded that he was not being taken to gaol. The mother shrieked aloud, 'My boy – my boy! Don't take him! Oh, don't take him! They've killed my boy! Look at his head – oh, his head!' and wrestled desperately with the men, while Hewitt attempted to soothe her, and promised to allow her to go in the cab with her son if she would only be quiet. The younger woman made no noise, but she held one of Laker's limp hands in both hers.

Hewitt and I dined together that evening, and he gave me a full account of the occurrences which I have here set down. Still, when he was finished I was not able to see clearly by what process of reasoning he had arrived at the conclusions that gave him the key to the mystery, nor did I understand the 'agony column' message, and I said so.

'In the beginning,' Hewitt explained, 'the thing that struck me as curious was the fact that Laker was said to have given his own name at Palmer's in buying his ticket. Now, the first thing the greenest and newest criminal thinks of is changing his name, so that the giving of his own name seemed unlikely to begin with. Still, he *might* have made such a mistake, as Plummer suggested when he said that criminals usually make a mistake somewhere – as they do, in fact. Still, it was the least likely mistake I could think of – especially as he actually didn't wait to be asked for his name, but blurted it out when it wasn't really wanted. And it was conjoined with another rather curious mistake, or what would have been a mistake, if the thief were Laker. Why should he conspicuously display his wallet – such a distinctive article – for the clerk to see and note? Why rather had he not got rid of it before showing himself? Suppose it should be somebody personating Laker? In any case I determined not to be prejudiced by what I had heard of Laker's betting. A man may bet without being a thief.

'But, again, supposing it *were* Laker? Might he not have given his name, and displayed his wallet, and so on, while buying a ticket for France, in order to draw pursuit after himself in that direction while

he made off in another, in another name, and disguised? Each supposition was plausible. And, in either case, it might happen that
whoever was laying this trail would probably lay it a little farther.
Charing Cross was the next point, and there I went. I already had it
from Plummer that Laker had not been recognised there. Perhaps the
trail had been laid in some other manner. Something left behind with
Laker's name on it, perhaps? I at once thought of the umbrella with
his monogram, and, making a long shot, asked for it at the lost property office, as you know. The guess was lucky. In the umbrella, as you
know, I found the scrap of paper. That, I judged, had fallen in from
the hand of the man carrying the umbrella. He had torn the paper in
half in order to fling it away, and one piece had fallen into the loosely
flapping umbrella. It is a thing that will often happen with an
omnibus ticket, as you may have noticed. Also, it was proved that the
umbrella *was* unrolled when found, and rolled immediately after. So
here was a piece of paper dropped by the person who had brought the
umbrella to Charing Cross and left it. I got the whole advertisement,
as you remember, and I studied it. 'Yob' is back-slang for 'boy', and
is often used in nicknames to denote a young smooth-faced thief.
Gunter, the man I suspect, as a matter of fact, is known as the
'Hoxton Yob'. The message, then, was addressed to someone known
by such a nickname. Next, 'HR shop roast'. Now, in thieves' slang, to
'roast' a thing or a person is to watch it or him. They call any place a
shop – notably, a thieves' den. So that this meant that some resort –
perhaps the 'Hoxton Row shop' – was watched. 'You 1st then
tonight' would be clearer, perhaps, when the rest was understood. I
thought a little over the rest, and it struck me that it must be a direction to some other house, since one was warned of as being watched.
Besides, there was the number, 197, and 'red bl.,' which would be
extremely likely to mean 'red blinds', by way of clearly distinguishing
the house. And then the plan of the thing was plain. You have
noticed, probably, that the map of London which accompanies the
Post Office Directory is divided, for convenience of reference, into
numbered squares?'

'Yes. The squares are denoted by letters along the top margin and
figures down the side. So that if you consult the directory, and find a
place marked as being in D 5, for instance, you find vertical division
D, and run your finger down it till it intersects horizontal division 5,
and there you are.'

'Precisely. I got my Post Office Directory, and looked for "O2." It
was in North London, and took in parts of Park Cemetery and Clis-

sold Park; "2nd top" was the next sign. Very well, I counted the
second street intersecting the top of the square counting, in the usual
way, from the left. That was Lordship Road. Then "3rd L". From the
point where Lordship Road crossed the top of the square, I ran my
finger down the road till it came to "3rd L", or, in other words, the
third turning on the left Hackworth Road. So there we were, unless
my guesses were altogether wrong. "Straight mon" probably meant
"straight moniker" – that is to say, the proper name, a thief's real
name, in contradistinction to that he may assume. I turned over the
directory till I found Hackworth Road, and found that No. 197 was
inhabited by a Mr Merston. From the whole thing I judged this, There
was to have been a meeting at the "HR shop", but that was found, at
the last moment, to be watched by the police for some purpose, so that
another appointment was made for this house in the suburbs. "You
1st. Then tonight" the person addressed was to come first, and the
others in the evening. They were to ask for the householder's "straight
moniker" – Mr Merston. And they were to come one at a time.

'Now, then, what was this? What theory would fit it? Suppose this
were a robbery, directed from afar by the advertiser. Suppose, on the
day before the robbery, it was found that the place fixed for division
of spoils were watched. Suppose that the principal thereupon advertised (as had already been agreed in case of emergency) in these terms.
The principal in the actual robbery the "Yob" addressed was to go
first with the booty. The others were to come after, one at a time.
Anyway, the thing was good enough to follow a little further, and I
determined to try number 197 Hackworth Road. I have told you
what I found there, and how it opened my eyes. I went, of course,
merely on chance, to see what I might chance to see. But luck
favoured, and I happened on that coat – brought back rolled up, on
the evening after the robbery, doubtless by the thief who had used it,
and flung carelessly into the handiest cupboard. That was this gang's
mistake.'

'Well, I congratulate you,' I said. 'I hope they'll catch the rascals.'

'I rather think they will, now they know where to look. They can
scarcely miss Merston, anyway. There has been very little to go upon
in this case, but I stuck to the thread, however slight, and it brought
me through. The rest of the case, of course, is Plummer's. It was a
peculiarity of my commission that I could equally well fulfil it by
catching the man with all the plunder, or by proving him innocent.
Having done the latter, my work was at an end, but I left it where
Plummer will be able to finish the job handsomely.'

Plummer did. Sam Gunter, Merston, and one accomplice were
taken – the first and last were well known to the police – and were
identified by Laker. Merston, as Hewitt had suspected, had kept the
lion's share for himself, so that altogether, with what was recovered
from him and the other two, nearly £11,000 was saved for Messrs
Liddle, Neal & Liddle. Merston, when taken, was in the act of
packing up to take a holiday abroad, and there cash his notes, which
were found, neatly packed in separate thousands, in his portmanteau.
As Hewitt had predicted, his gas bill was considerably less next
quarter, for less than half-way through it he began a term in gaol.

As for Laker, he was reinstated, of course, with an increase of
salary by way of compensation for his broken head. He had passed a
terrible twenty-six hours in the cellar, unfed and unheard. Several
times he had become insensible, and again and again he had thrown
himself madly against the door, shouting and tearing at it, till he fell
back exhausted, with broken nails and bleeding fingers. For some
hours before the arrival of his rescuers he had been sitting in a sort of
stupor, from which he was suddenly aroused by the sound of voices
and footsteps. He was in bed for a week, and required a rest of a
month in addition before he could resume his duties. Then he was
quietly lectured by Mr Neal as to betting, and, I believe, dropped that
practice in consequence. I am told that he is 'at the counter' now – a
considerable promotion.

RODRIGUES OTTOLENGUI

The Azteck Opal

'MR MITCHEL,' began Mr Barnes, the detective, after exchanging greetings, 'I have called to see you upon a subject which I am sure will enlist your keenest interest, for several reasons. It relates to a magnificent jewel; it concerns your intimate friends; and it is a problem requiring the most analytical qualities of the mind in its solution.'

'Ah! Then you have solved it?' asked Mr Mitchel.

'I think so. You shall judge. I have today been called in to investigate one of the most singular cases that has fallen in my way. It is one in which the usual detective methods would be utterly valueless. The facts were presented to me, and the solution of the mystery could only be reached by analytical deduction.'

'That is to say, by using your brains?'

'Precisely! Now, you have admitted that you consider yourself more expert in this direction than the ordinary detective. I wish to place you for once in the position of a detective, and then see you prove your ability.

'Early this morning I was summoned, by a messenger, to go aboard of the steam yacht Idler, which lay at anchor in the lower bay.'

'Why, the Idler belongs to my friend Mortimer Gray,' exclaimed Mr Mitchel.

'Yes!' replied Mr Barnes. 'I told you that your friends are interested. I went immediately with the man who had come to my office, and in due season I was aboard of the yacht. Mr Gray received me very politely, and took me to his private room adjoining the cabin. Here he explained to me that he had been off on a cruise for a few weeks, and was approaching the harbour last night, when, in accordance with his plans, a sumptuous dinner was served, as a sort of farewell feast, the party expecting to separate today.'

'What guests were on the yacht?'

'I will tell you everything in order, as the facts were presented to me. Mr Gray enumerated the party as follows. Besides himself and his wife, there were his wife's sister, Mrs Eugene Cortlandt, and her husband, a Wall Street broker. Also, Mr Arthur Livingstone, and his sister, and a Mr Dermett Moore, a young man supposed to be devoting himself to Miss Livingstone.'

'That makes seven persons, three of whom are women. I ought to say, Mr Barnes, that, though Mr Gray is a club friend, I am not personally acquainted with his wife, nor with the others. So I have no advantage over you.'

'I will come at once to the curious incident which made my presence desirable. According to Mr Gray's story, the dinner had proceeded as far as the roast, when suddenly there was a slight shock as the yacht touched, and at the same time the lamps spluttered and then went out, leaving the room totally dark. A second later the vessel righted herself and sped on, so that before any panic ensued, it was evident to all that the danger had passed. The gentlemen begged the ladies to resume their seats, and remain quiet until the lamps were lighted; this, however, the attendants were unable to do, and they were ordered to bring fresh lamps. Thus there was almost total darkness for several minutes.'

'During which, I presume, the person who planned the affair readily consummated his design?'

'So you think that the whole series of events was prearranged? Be that as it may, something did happen in that dark room. The women had started from their seats when the yacht touched, and when they groped their way back in the darkness some of them found the wrong places, as was seen when the fresh lamps were brought. This was considered a good joke, and there was some laughter, which was suddenly checked by an exclamation from Mr Gray, who quickly asked his wife, 'Where is your opal?'

'Her opal?' asked Mr Mitchel, in tones which showed that his greatest interest was now aroused. 'Do you mean, Mr Barnes, that she was wearing the Azteck opal?'

'Oh! You know the gem?'

'I know nearly all gems of great value; but what of this one?'

'Mrs Gray and her sister, Mrs Cortlandt, had both donned *décolleté* costumes for this occasion, and Mrs Gray had worn this opal as a pendant to a thin gold chain which hung round her neck. At Mr Gray's question, all looked towards his wife, and it was noted that the clasp was open, and the opal missing. Of course it was supposed that it had merely fallen to the floor, and a search was immediately instituted. But the opal could not be found.'

'That is certainly a very significant fact,' said Mr Mitchel. 'But was the search thorough?'

'I should say extremely thorough, when we consider it was not conducted by a detective, who is supposed to be an expert in such matters. Mr Gray described to me what was done, and he seems to have taken every precaution. He sent the attendants out of the salon, and he and his guests systematically examined every part of the room.'

'Except the place where the opal really was concealed, you mean.'

'With that exception, of course, since they did not find the jewel. Not satisfied with this search by lamplight, Mr Gray locked the salon, so that no one could enter it during the night, and another investigation was made in the morning.'

'The pockets of the seven persons present were not examined, I presume?'

'No! I asked Mr Gray why this had been omitted, and he said that it was an indignity which he could not possibly show to a guest. As you have asked this question, Mr Mitchel, it is only fair for me to tell you that when I spoke to Mr Gray on the subject he seemed very much confused. Nevertheless, however unwilling he may have been to search those of his guests who are innocent, he emphatically told me that if I had reasonable proof that anyone present had purloined the opal, he wished that individual to be treated as any other thief, without regard to sex or social position.'

'One can scarcely blame him, because that opal was worth a fabulous sum. I have myself offered Gray twenty-five thousand dollars for it, which was refused. This opal is one of the eyes of an Azteck Idol, and if the other could be found, the two would be as interesting as any jewels in the world.'

'That is the story which I was asked to unravel,' continued Mr Barnes, 'and I must now relate to you what steps I have taken towards that end. It appears that, because of the loss of the jewels, no person has left the yacht, although no restraint was placed upon anyone by Mr Gray. All knew, however, that he had sent for a detective, and it was natural that no one should offer to go until formally dismissed by the host. My plan, then, was to have a private interview with each of the seven persons who had been present at the dinner.'

'Then you exempted the attendants from your suspicions?'

'I did. There was but one way by which one of the servants could have stolen the opal, and this was prevented by Mr Gray. It was possible that the opal had fallen on the floor, and, though not found at night, a servant might have discovered and have appropriated it on the following morning, had he been able to enter the salon. But Mr

Gray had locked the doors. No servant, however bold, would have been able to take the opal from the lady's neck.'

'I think your reasoning is good, and we will confine ourselves to the original seven.'

'After my interview with Mr Gray, I asked to have Mrs Gray sent in to me. She came in, and at once I noted that she placed herself on the defensive. Women frequently adopt that manner with a detective. Her story was very brief. The main point was that she was aware of the theft before the lamps were relit. In fact, she felt someone's arms steal around her neck, and knew when the opal was taken. I asked why she had made no outcry, and whether she suspected any special person. To these questions she replied that she supposed it was merely a joke perpetrated in the darkness, and therefore had made no resistance. She would not name anyone as suspected by her, but she was willing to tell me that the arms were bare, as she detected when they touched her neck. I must say here, that although Miss Livingstone's dress was not cut low in the neck, it was, practically, sleeveless; and Mrs Cortlandt's dress had no sleeves at all. One other significant statement made by this lady was that her husband had mentioned to her your offer of twenty-five thousand dollars for the opal, and had urged her to permit him to sell it, but she had refused.'

'So! It was Madam that would not sell. The plot thickens!'

'You will observe, of course, the point about the naked arms of the thief. I therefore sent for Mrs Cortlandt next. She had a curious story to tell. Unlike her sister, she was quite willing to express her suspicions. Indeed, she plainly intimated that she supposed that Mr Gray himself had taken the jewel. I will endeavour to repeat her words:

'"Mr Barnes," said she, "the affair is very simple. Gray is a miserable old skinflint. A Mr Mitchel, a crank who collects gems, offered to buy that opal, and he has been bothering my sister for it ever since. When the lamps went out, he took the opportunity to steal it. I do not think this, I know it. How? Well, on account of the confusion and darkness, I sat in my sister's seat when I returned to the table. This explains his mistake, but he put his arms round my neck, and deliberately felt for the opal. I did not understand his purpose at the time, but now it is very evident."

'"Yes, madam," said I, "but how do you know it was Mr Gray?"

'"Why, I grabbed his hand, and before he could pull it away I felt the large cameo ring on his little finger. Oh! there is no doubt whatever."

'I asked her whether Mr Gray had his sleeves rolled up, and

though she could not understand the purport of the question, she said, 'No'. Next I had Miss Livingstone come in. She is a slight, tremulous young lady, who cries at the slightest provocation. During the interview, brief as it was, it was only by the greatest diplomacy that I avoided a scene of hysterics. She tried very hard to convince me that she knew absolutely nothing. She had not left her seat during the disturbance; of that she was sure. So how could she know anything about it? I asked her to name the one whom she thought might have taken the opal, and at this her agitation reached such a climax that I was obliged to let her go.'

'You gained very little from her I should say.'

'In a case of this kind, Mr Mitchel, where the criminal is surely one of a very few persons, we cannot fail to gain something from each person's story. A significant feature here was that though Miss Livingstone assures us that she did not leave her seat, she was sitting in a different place when the lamps were lighted again.'

'That might mean anything or nothing.'

'Exactly! but we are not deducing values yet. Mr Dermett Moore came to me next, and he is a straightforward, honest man if I ever saw one. He declared that the whole affair was a great mystery to him, and that, while ordinarily he would not care anything about it, he could not but be somewhat interested because he thought that one of the ladies, he would not say which one, suspected him. Mr Livingstone also impressed me favourably in spite of the fact that he did not remove his cigarette from his mouth throughout the whole of my interview with him. He declined to name the person suspected by him, though he admitted that he could do so. He made this significant remark:

'"You are a detective of experience, Mr Barnes, and ought to be able to decide which man amongst us could place his arms around Mrs Gray's neck without causing her to cry out. But if your imagination fails you, suppose you enquire into the financial standing of all of us, and see which one would be most likely to profit by thieving? Ask Mr Cortlandt."'

'Evidently Mr Livingstone knows more than he tells.'

'Yet he told enough for one to guess his suspicions, and to understand the delicacy which prompted him to say no more. He, however, gave me a good point upon which to question Mr Cortlandt. When I asked that gentleman if any of the men happened to be in pecuniary difficulties, he became grave at once. I will give you his answer.

'"Mr Livingstone and Mr Moore are both exceedingly wealthy

men, and I am a millionaire, in very satisfactory business circumstances at present. But I am very sorry to say, that though our host,
Mr Gray, is also a distinctly rich man, he has met with some reverses
recently, and I can conceive that ready money would be useful to him.
But for all that, it is preposterous to believe what your question evidently indicates. None of the persons in this party is a thief, and least
of all could we suspect Mr Gray. I am sure that if he wished his wife's
opal, she would give it to him cheerily. No, Mr Barnes, the opal is in
some crack, or crevice, which we have overlooked. It is lost, not
stolen."

'That ended the interviews with the several persons present, but I
made one or two other enquiries, from which I elicited at least two
significant facts. First, it was Mr Gray himself who had indicated the
course by which the yacht was steered last night, and which ran her
over a sand-bar. Second, someone had nearly emptied the oil from
the lamps, so that they would have burned out in a short time, even
though the yacht had not touched.'

'These, then, are your facts? And from these you have solved the
problem? Well, Mr Barnes, who stole the opal?'

'Mr Mitchel, I have told you all I know, but I wish you to work
out a solution before I reveal my own opinion.'

'I have already done so, Mr Barnes. Here! I will write my suspicion on I bit of paper. So! Now tell me yours, and you shall know
mine afterwards.'

'Why, to my mind it is very simple. Mr Gray, failing to obtain the
opal from his wife by fair means, resorted to a trick. He removed the
oil from the lamps, and charted out a course for his yacht which
would take her over a sand-bar, and when the opportune moment
came he stole the jewel. His actions since then have been merely to
cover his crime, by shrouding the affair with mystery. By insisting
upon a thorough search, and even sending for a detective, he makes it
impossible for those who were present to accuse him hereafter.
Undoubtedly Mr Cortlandt's opinion will be the one generally
adopted. Now what do you think?'

'I think I will go with you at once, and board the yacht Idler.'

'But you have not told me whom you suspect,' said Mr Barnes,
somewhat irritated.

'Oh! That's immaterial,' said Mr Mitchel, calmly preparing for
the street. 'I do not suspect Mr Gray, so if you are correct you will
have shown better ability than I. Come! Let us hurry!'

On their way to the dock, from which they were to take the little steam launch which was waiting to carry the detective back to the yacht, Mr Barnes asked Mr Mitchel the following questions:

'Mr Mitchel,' said he, 'you will note that Mrs Cortlandt alluded to you as a 'crank who collects gems'. I must admit that I have myself harboured a great curiosity as to your reasons for purchasing jewels, which are valued beyond a mere conservative commercial price. Would you mind explaining why you began your collection?'

'I seldom explain my motives to others, especially when they relate to my more important pursuits in life. But in view of all that has passed between us, I think your curiosity justifiable, and I will gratify it. To begin with, I am a very wealthy man. I inherited great riches, and I have made a fortune myself. Have you any conception of the difficulties which harass a man of means?'

'Perhaps not in minute detail, though I can guess that the lot of the rich is not as free from care as the pauper thinks it is.'

'The point is this: the difficulty with a poor man is to get rich, while with the rich man the greatest trouble is to prevent the increase of his wealth. Some men, of course, make no effort in that direction, and those men are a menace to society. My own idea of the proper use of a fortune is to manage it for the benefit of others, as well as one's self, and especially to prevent its increase.'

'And is it so difficult to do this? Cannot money be spent without limit?'

'Yes; but unlimited evil follows such a course. This is sufficient to indicate to you that I am ever in search of a legitimate means of spending my income, provided that I may do good thereby. If I can do this, and at the same time afford myself pleasure, I claim that I am making the best use of my money. Now I happen to be so constructed, that the most interesting studies to me are social problems, and of these I am most entertained with the causes and environments of crime. Such a problem as the one you brought to me today is of immense attractiveness to me, because the environment is one which is commonly supposed to preclude rather than to invite crime. Yet we have seen that despite the wealth of all concerned, someone has stooped to the commonest of crimes – theft.'

'But what has this to do with your collection of jewels?'

'Everything! Jewels – especially those of great magnitude – seem to be a special cause of crime. A hundred-carat diamond will tempt a man to theft, as surely as the false beacon on a rocky shore entices the mariner to wreck and ruin. All the great jewels of the world have murder and crime woven into their histories. My attention was first called to this by accidentally overhearing a plot in a ballroom to rob the lady of the house of a large ruby which she wore on her breast. I went to her, taking the privilege of an intimate friend, and told her enough to persuade her to sell the stone to me. I fastened it into my scarf, and then sought the presence of the plotters, allowing them to see what had occurred. No words passed between us, but by my act I prevented a crime that night.'

'Then am I to understand that you buy jewels with that end in view?'

'After that night I conceived this idea. If all the great jewels in the world could be collected together, and put in a place of safety, hundreds of crimes would be prevented, even before they had been conceived. Moreover, the search for, and acquirement of these jewels would necessarily afford me abundant opportunity for studying the crimes which are perpetrated in order to gain possession of them. Thus you understand more thoroughly why I am anxious to pursue this problem of the Azteck opal.'

Several hours later Mr Mitchel and Mr Barnes were sitting at a quiet table in the comer of the dining-room at Mr Mitchel's club. On board the yacht Mr Mitchel had acted rather mysteriously. He had been closeted a while with Mr Gray, after which he had had an interview with two or three of the others. Then when Mr Barnes had begun to feel neglected, and tired of waiting alone on deck, Mr Mitchel had come towards him, arm-in-arm with Mr Gray, and the latter said:

'I am very much obliged to you, Mr Barnes, for your services in this affair, and I trust the enclosed cheque will remunerate you for your trouble.'

Mr Barnes, not quite comprehending it all, had attempted to protest, but Mr Mitchel had taken him by the arm, and hurried him off. In the cab which bore them to the club the detective asked for an explanation, but Mr Mitchel only replied:

'I am too hungry to talk now. We will have dinner first.'

The dinner was over at last, and nuts and coffee were before them, when Mr Mitchel took a small parcel from his pocket, and handed it to Mr Barnes, saying:

'It is a beauty, is it not?'

Mr Barnes removed the tissue paper, and a large opal fell on the tablecloth, where it sparkled with a thousand colours under the electric lamps.

'Do you mean that this is—?' cried the detective.

'The Azteck opal, and the finest harlequin I ever saw,' interrupted Mr Mitchel. 'But you wish to know how it came into my possession? Principally so that it may join the collection and cease to be a temptation to this world of wickedness.'

'Then Mr Gray did not steal it?' asked Mr Barnes, with a touch of chagrin in his voice.

'No, Mr Barnes! Mr Gray did not steal it. But you are not to consider yourself very much at fault. Mr Gray tried to steal it, only he failed. That was not your fault, of course. You read his actions aright, but you did not give enough weight to the stories of the others.'

'What important point did I omit from my calculation?'

'I might mention the bare arms which Mrs Gray said she felt round her neck. It was evidently Mr Gray who looked for the opal on the neck of his sister-in-law, but as he did not bare his arms, he would not have done so later.'

'Do you mean that Miss Livingstone was the thief?'

'No! Miss Livingstone being hysterical, she changed her seat without realising it, but that does not make her a thief. Her excitement when with you was due to her suspicions, which, by the way, were correct. But let us return for a moment to the bare arms. That was the clue from which I worked. It was evident to me that the thief was a man, and it was equally plain that in the hurry of the few moments of darkness, no man would have rolled up his sleeves, risking the return of the attendants with lamps, and the consequent discovery of himself in such a singular disarrangement of costume.'

'How do you account for the bare arms?'

'The lady did not tell the truth, that is all. The arms which encircled her neck were not bare. Neither were they unknown to her. She told you that lie to shield the thief. She also told you that her husband wished to sell the Azteck opal to me, but that she had refused. Thus she deftly led you to suspect him. Now, if she wished to shield the thief, yet was willing to accuse her husband, it followed that the husband was not the thief.'

'Very well reasoned, Mr Mitchel. I see now where you are tending, but I shall not get ahead of your story.'

'So much I had deduced, before we went on board the yacht. When I found myself alone with Gray I candidly told him of your suspicions, and your reasons for harbouring them. He was very much disturbed, and pleadingly asked me what I thought. As frankly I told him that I believed that he had tried to take the opal from his wife – we can scarcely call it stealing since the law does not but that I believed he had failed. He then confessed; admitted emptying the lamps, but denied running the boat on the sand-bar. But he assured me that he had not reached his wife's chair when the lamps were brought in. He was, therefore, much astonished at missing the gem. I promised him to find the jewel upon condition that he would sell it to me. To this he most willingly acceded.'

'But how could you be sure that you would recover the opal?'

'Partly by my knowledge of human nature, and partly because of my inherent faith in my own abilities. I sent for Mrs Gray, and noted her attitude of defence, which, however, only satisfied me the more that I was right in my suspicions. I began by asking her if she knew the origin of the superstition that an opal brings bad luck to its owner. She did not, of course, comprehend my tactics, but she added that she "had heard the stupid superstition, but took no interest in such nonsense". I then gravely explained to her that the opal is the engagement stone of the Orient. The lover gives it to his sweetheart, and the belief is that should she deceive him even in the most trifling manner, the opal will lose its brilliancy and become cloudy. I then suddenly asked her if she had ever noted a change in her opal. 'What do you mean to insinuate?' she cried out angrily. 'I mean,' said I, sternly, 'that if an opal has changed colour in accordance with the superstition this one should have done so. I mean that though your husband greatly needs the money which I have offered him you have refused to allow him to sell it, and yet you have permitted another to take it from you tonight. By this act you might have seriously injured if not ruined Mr Gray. Why have you done it?"

'How did she receive it?' asked Mr Barnes, admiring the ingenuity of Mr Mitchel.

'She began to sob, and between her tears she admitted that the opal had been taken by the man I suspected, but she earnestly declared that she had harboured no idea of injuring her husband. Indeed, she was so agitated in speaking upon this point, that I believe that Gray never thoroughly explained to her why he wished to sell the gem. She urged me to recover the opal if possible, and purchase it, so that her husband might be relieved from his pecuniary embarrassment. I then sent for the thief, Mrs Gray told me his name; but would you not like to hear how I had picked him out before we went aboard? I still have that bit of paper upon which I wrote his name, in confirmation of what I say.'

'Of course, I know now that you mean Mr Livingstone, but would like to hear your reasons for suspecting him'.

'From your account Miss Livingstone suspected someone, and this caused her to be so agitated that she was unaware of the fact that she had changed her seat. Women are shrewd in these affairs, and I was confident that the girl had good reason for her conduct. It was evident that the person in her mind was either her brother or her sweetheart. I decided between these two men from your account of your interviews with them. Moore impressed you as being honest, and he told you that one of the ladies suspected him. In this he was mistaken, but his speaking to you of it was not the act of a thief. Mr Livingstone, on the other hand, tried to throw suspicion upon Mr Gray.'

'Of course that was sound reasoning after you had concluded that Mrs Gray was lying. Now tell me how you recovered the jewel?'

'That was easier than I expected. I simply told Mr Livingstone when I got him alone, what I knew, and asked him to hand me the opal. With a perfectly imperturbable manner, understanding that I promised secrecy, he quietly took it from his pocket and gave it to me, saying:

'Women are very poor conspirators. They are too weak."

'What story did you tell Mr Gray?'

'Oh, he would not be likely to enquire too closely into what I should tell him. My cheque was what he most cared for. I told him nothing definitely, but I inferred that his wife had secreted the gem during the darkness, that he might not ask her for it again; and that she had intended to find it again at a future time, just as he had meant to pawn it and then pretend to recover it from the thief by offering a reward.'

'One more question. Why did Mr Livingstone steal it?'

'Ah! The truth about that is another mystery worth probing, and one which I shall make it my business to unravel. I will venture two prophecies. First – Mr Livingstone did not steal it at all. Mrs Gray simply handed it to him in the darkness. There must have been some powerful motive to lead her to such an act; something which she was weighing, and decided impulsively. This brings me to the second point. Livingstone used the word conspirator, which is a clue. You will recall what I told you that this gem is one of a pair of opals, and that with the other, the two would be as interesting as any jewels in the world. I am confident now that Mr Livingstone knows where that other opal is, and that he has been urging Mrs Gray to give or lend him hers, as a means of obtaining the other. If she hoped to do this, it would be easy to understand why she refused to permit the sale of the one she had. This, of course, is guesswork, but I'll promise that if anyone ever owns both it shall be your humble servant, Leroy Mitchel, Jewel Collector.'

DICK DONOVAN

The Problem of Dead Wood Hall

'MYSTERIOUS CASE IN CHESHIRE.' So ran the heading to a paragraph in all the morning papers some years ago, and prominence was
given to the following particulars:

A gentleman, bearing the somewhat curious name of Tuscan
Trankler, resided in a picturesque old mansion, known as Dead
Wood Hall, situated in one of the most beautiful and lonely parts of
Cheshire, not very far from the quaint and old-time village of
Knutsford. Mr Trankler had given a dinner-party at his house, and
amongst the guests was a very well-known county magistrate and
landowner, Mr Manville Charnworth. It appeared that, soon after
the ladies had retired from the table, Mr Charnworth rose and went
into the grounds, saying he wanted a little air. He was smoking a
cigar, and in the enjoyment of perfect health. He had drunk wine,
however, rather freely, as was his wont, but though on exceedingly
good terms with himself and every one else, he was perfectly sober.
An hour passed, but Mr Charnworth had not returned to the table.
Though this did not arouse any alarm, as it was thought that he had
probably joined the ladies, for he was what is called 'a ladies' man',
and preferred the company of females to that of men. A tremendous
sensation, however, was caused when, a little later, it was announced
that Charnworth had been found insensible, lying on his back in a
shrubbery. Medical assistance was at once summoned, and when it
arrived the opinion expressed was that the unfortunate gentleman
had been stricken with apoplexy. For some reason or other, however,
the doctors were led to modify that view, for symptoms were
observed which pointed to what was thought to be a peculiar form of
poisoning, although the poison could not be determined. After a
time, Charnworth recovered consciousness, but was quite unable to
give any information. He seemed to be dazed and confused, and was
evidently suffering great pain. At last his limbs began to swell, and
swelled to an enormous size; his eyes sunk, his cheeks fell in, his lips
turned black, and mortification appeared in the extremities. Everything that could be done for the unfortunate man was done, but
without avail. After six hours' suffering, he died in a paroxysm of

raving madness, during which he had to be held down in the bed by several strong men.

The post-mortem examination, which was necessarily held, revealed the curious fact that the blood in the body had become thin and purplish, with a faint strange odour that could not be identified. All the organs were extremely congested, and the flesh presented every appearance of rapid decomposition. In fact, twelve hours after death putrefaction had taken place. The medical gentlemen who had the case in hand were greatly puzzled, and were at a loss to determine the precise cause of death. The deceased had been a very healthy man, and there was no actual organic disease of any kind. In short, everything pointed to poisoning. It was noted that on the left side of the neck was a tiny scratch, with a slightly livid appearance, such as might have been made by a small sharply pointed instrument. The viscera having been secured for purposes of analysis, the body was hurriedly buried within thirty hours of death.

The result of the analysis was to make clear that the unfortunate gentleman had died through some very powerful and irritant poison being introduced into the blood. That it was a case of blood-poisoning there was hardly room for the shadow of a doubt, but the science of that day was quite unable to say what the poison was, or how it had got into the body. There was no reason – so far as could be ascertained to suspect foul play, and even less reason to suspect suicide. Altogether, therefore, the case was one of profound mystery, and the coroner's jury were compelled to return an open verdict. Such were the details that were made public at the time of Mr Charnworth's death; and from the social position of all the parties, the affair was something more than a nine days' wonder; while in Cheshire itself, it created a profound sensation. But, as no further information was forthcoming, the matter ceased to interest the outside world, and so, as far as the public were concerned, it was relegated to the limbo of forgotten things.

Two years later, Mr Ferdinand Trankler, eldest son of Tuscan Trankler, accompanied a large party of friends for a day's shooting in Mere Forest. He was a young man, about five and twenty years of age; was in the most perfect health, and had scarcely ever had a day's illness in his life. Deservedly popular and beloved, he had a large circle of warm friends, and was about to be married to a charming young lady, a member of an old Cheshire family who were extensive landed proprietors and property owners. His prospects therefore seemed to be unclouded, and his happiness complete.

The shooting-party was divided into three sections, each agreeing to shoot over a different part of the forest, and to meet in the afternoon for refreshments at an appointed rendezvous.

Young Trankler and his companions kept pretty well together for some little time, but ultimately began to spread about a good deal At the appointed hour the friends all met, with the exception of Trankler. He was not there. His absence did not cause any alarm, as it was thought he would soon turn up. He was known to be well acquainted with the forest, and the supposition was he had strayed further afield than the rest. By the time the repast was finished, however, he had not put in an appearance. Then, for the first time, the company began to feel some uneasiness, and vague hints that possibly an accident had happened were thrown out. Hints at last took the form of definite expressions of alarm, and search parties were at once organised to go in search of the absent young man, for only on the hypothesis of some untoward event could his prolonged absence be accounted for, inasmuch as it was not deemed in the least likely that he would show such a lack of courtesy as to go off and leave his friends without a word of explanation. For two hours the search was kept up without any result. Darkness was then closing in, and the now painfully anxious searchers began to feel that they would have to desist until daylight; returned. But at last some of the more energetic and active members of the party came upon Trankler lying on his sides and nearly entirely hidden by masses of half-withered bracken. He was lying near a little stream that meandered through the forest, and near a keeper's shelter that was constructed with logs and thatched with pine boughs. He was stone dead, and his appearance caused his friends to shrink back with horror, for he was not only black in the face, but his body was bloated, and his limbs seemed swollen to twice their natural size.

Amongst the party were two medical men, who, being hastily summoned, proceeded at once to make an examination. They expressed an opinion that the young man had been dead for some time, but they could not account for his death, as there was no wound to be observed. As a matter of fact, his gun was lying near him with both barrels loaded. Moreover, his appearance was not compatible at all with death from a gunshot wound. How then had he died? The consternation amongst those who had known him can well be imagined, and with a sense of suppressed horror, it was whispered that the strange condition of the dead man coincided with that of Mr Manville Charnworth, the county magistrate who had died so mysteriously two years previously.

As soon as it was possible to do so, Ferdinand Trankler's body was removed to Dead Wood Hall, and his people were stricken with profound grief when they realised that the hope and joy of their house was dead. Of course an autopsy had to be performed, owing to the ignorance of the medical men as to the cause of death. And this post-mortem examination disclosed the fact that all the extraordinary appearances which had been noticed in Mr Charnworth's case were present in this one. There was the same purplish coloured blood; the same gangrenous condition of the limbs; but as with Charnworth, so with Trankler, all the organs were healthy. There was no organic disease to account for death. As it was pretty certain, therefore, that death was not due to natural causes, a coroner's inquest was held, and while the medical evidence made it unmistakably clear that young Trankler had been cut down in the flower of his youth and while he was in radiant health by some powerful and potent means which had suddenly destroyed his life, no one had the boldness to suggest what those means were, beyond saying that blood-poisoning of a most violent character had been set up. Now, it was very obvious that blood-poisoning could not have originated without some specific cause, and the most patient investigation was directed to trying to find out the cause, while exhaustive inquiries were made, but at the end of them, the solution of the mystery was as far off as ever, for these investigations had been in the wrong channel, not one scrap of evidence was brought forward which would have justified a definite statement that this or that had been responsible for the young man's death.

It was remembered that when the post-mortem examination of Mr Charnworth took place, a tiny bluish scratch was observed on the left side of the neck. But it was so small, and apparently so unimportant that it was not taken into consideration when attempts were made to solve the problem of 'How did the man die?'. When the doctors examined Mr Trankler's body, they looked to see if there was a similar puncture or scratch, and, to their astonishment, they did find rather a curious mark on the left side of the neck, just under the ear. It was a slight abrasion of the skin, about an inch long as if he had been scratched with a pin, and this abrasion was a faint blue, approximating in colour to the tattoo marks on a sailor's arm. The similarity in this scratch to that which had been observed on Mr Charnworth's body, necessarily gave rise to a good deal of comment amongst the doctors, though they could not arrive at any definite conclusion respecting it. One man went so far as to express an opinion that it was due to an insect or the bite of a snake. But this theory found no supporters, for it was argued that the similar wound on Mr Charnworth could hardly have resulted from an insect or snake bite, for he had died in his friend's garden. Besides, there was no insect or snake in England capable of killing a man as these two men had been killed. That theory, therefore, fell to the ground; and medical science as represented by the local gentlemen, had to confess itself baffled; while the coroner's jury were forced to again return an open verdict.

'There was no evidence to prove how the deceased had come by his death.'

This verdict was considered highly unsatisfactory, but what other could have been returned? There was nothing to support the theory of foul play; on the other hand, no evidence was forthcoming to explain away the mystery which surrounded the deaths of Charnworth and Trankler. The two men had apparently died from precisely the same cause, and under circumstances which were as mysterious as they were startling, but what the cause was, no one seemed able to determine.

Universal sympathy was felt with the friends and relatives of young Trankler, who had perished so unaccountably while in pursuit of pleasure. Had he been taken suddenly ill at home and had died in his bed, even though the same symptoms and morbid appearances had manifested themselves, the mystery would not have been so great. But as Charnworth's end came in his host's garden after a dinner-party, so young Trankler died in a forest while he and his friends were engaged in shooting. There was certainly something truly remarkable that two men, exhibiting all the same post-mortem effects, should have died in such a way; their deaths, in point of time, being separated by a period of two years. On the face of it, it seemed impossible that it could be merely a coincidence. It will be gathered from the foregoing, that in this double tragedy were all the elements of a romance well calculated to stimulate public curiosity to the highest pitch; while the friends and relatives of the two deceased gentlemen were of opinion that the matter ought not to be allowed to drop with the return of the verdict of the coroner's jury. An investigation seemed to be urgently called for. Of course, an investigation of a kind had taken place by the local police, but something more than that was required, so thought the friends. And an application was made to me to go down to Dead Wood Hall; and bring such skill as I possessed to bear on the case, in the hope that the veil of mystery might be drawn aside, and light let in where all was then dark.

Dead Wood Hall was a curious place, with a certain gloominess of aspect which seemed to suggest that it was a fitting scene for a tragedy. It was a large, massive house, heavily timbered in front in a way peculiar to many of the old Cheshire mansions. It stood in extensive grounds, and being situated on a rise commanded a very fine panoramic view which embraced the Derbyshire Hills. How it got its name of Dead Wood Hall no one seemed to know exactly. There was a tradition that it had originally been known as Dark Wood Hall; but the word 'Dark' had been corrupted into 'Dead'. The Tranklers came into possession of the property by purchase, and the family had been the owners of it for something like thirty years.

With great circumstantiality I was told the story of the death of each man, together with the results of the post mortem examination, and the steps that had been taken by the police. On further inquiry I found that the police, in spite of the mystery surrounding the case, were firmly of opinion that the deaths of the two men were, after all, due to natural causes, and that the similarity in the appearance of the bodies after death was a mere coincidence. The superintendent of the county constabulary, who had had charge of the matter, waxed rather warm; for he said that all sorts of ridiculous stories had been set afloat, and absurd theories had been suggested, not one of which would have done credit to the intelligence of an average schoolboy.

'People lose their heads so, and make such fools of themselves in matters of this kind,' he said warmly; 'and of course the police are accused of being stupid, ignorant, and all the rest of it. They seem, in fact, to have a notion that we are endowed with superhuman faculties, and that nothing should baffle us. But, as a matter of fact, it is the doctors who are at fault in this instance. They are confronted with a new disease, about which they are ignorant; and, in order to conceal their want of knowledge, they at once raise the cry of "foul play".'

'Then you are clearly of opinion that Mr Charnworth and Mr Trankler died of a disease,' I remarked.

'Undoubtedly I am.'

'Then how do you explain the rapidity of the death in each case, and the similarity in the appearance of the dead bodies?'

'It isn't for me to explain that at all. That is doctors' work not police work. If the doctors can't explain it, how can I be expected to do so? I only know this, I've put some of my best men on to the job, and they've failed to find anything that would suggest foul play.'

'And that convinces you absolutely that there has been no foul play?'

'Absolutely.'

'I suppose you were personally acquainted with both gentlemen? What sort of man was Mr Charnworth?'

'Oh, well, he was right enough, as such men go. He made a good many blunders as a magistrate; but all magistrates do that. You see, fellows get put on the bench who are no more fit to be magistrates than you are, sir. It's a matter of influence more often as not. Mr Charnworth was no worse and no better than a lot of others I could name.'

'What opinion did you form of his private character?'

'Ah, now, there, there's another matter,' answered the superintendent, in a confidential tone, and with a smile playing about his lips. 'You see, Mr Charnworth was a bachelor.'

'So are thousands of other men,' I answered. 'But bachelorhood is not considered dishonourable in this country.'

'No, perhaps not. But they say as how the reason was that Mr Charnworth didn't get married was because he didn't care for having only one wife.'

'You mean he was fond of ladies generally. A sort of general lover.'

'I should think he was,' said the superintendent, with a twinkle in his eye, which was meant to convey a good deal of meaning. 'I've heard some queer stories about him.'

'What is the nature of the stories?' I asked, thinking that I might get something to guide me.

'Oh, well, I don't attach much importance to them myself,' he said, half-apologetically; 'but the fact is, there was some social scandal talked about Mr Charnworth.'

'What was the nature of the scandal?'

'Mind you,' urged the superintendent, evidently anxious to be freed from any responsibility for the scandal whatever it was, 'I only tell you the story as I heard it. Mr Charnworth liked his little flirtations, no doubt, as we all do; but he was a gentleman and a magistrate, and I have no right to say anything against him that I know nothing about myself.'

'While a gentleman may be a magistrate, a magistrate is not always a gentleman,' I remarked.

'True, true; but Mr Charnworth was. He was a fine specimen of a gentleman, and was very liberal. He did me many kindnesses.'

'Therefore, in your sight, at least, sir, he was without blemish.'

'I don't go as far as that,' replied the superintendent, a little warmly; 'I only want to be just.'

'I give you full credit for that,' I answered; 'but please do tell me about the scandal you spoke of. It is just possible it may afford me a clue.'

'I don't think that it will. However, here is the story. A young lady lived in Knutsford by the name of Downie. She is the daughter of the late George Downie, who for many years carried on the business of a miller. Hester Downie was said to be one of the prettiest girls in Cheshire, or, at any rate, in this part of Cheshire, and rumour has it that she flirted with both Charnworth and Trankler.'

'Is that all that rumour says?' I asked.

'No, there was a good deal more said. But, as I have told you, I know nothing for certain, and so must decline to commit myself to any statement for which there could be no better foundation than common gossip.'

'Does Miss Downie still live in Knutsford?'

'No; she disappeared mysteriously soon after Charnworth's death.'

'And you don't know where she is?'

'No; I have no idea.'

As I did not see that there was much more to be gained from the superintendent I left him, and at once sought a interview with the leading medical man who had made the autopsy of the two bodies. He was a man who was somewhat puffed up with the belief in his own cleverness, but he gave me the impression that, if anything, he was a little below the average country practitioner. He hadn't a single theory to advance to account for the deaths of Charnworth and Trankler. He confessed that he was mystified; that all the appearances were entirely new to him, for neither in his reading nor his practice had he ever heard of a similar case.

'Are you disposed to think, sir, that these two men came to their end by foul play?' I asked.

'No, I am not,' he answered definitely, 'and I said so at the inquest. Foul play means murder, cool and deliberate; and planned and carried out with fiendish cunning. Besides, if it was murder how was the murder committed?'

'*If it was murder?*' I asked significantly. 'I shall hope to answer that question later on.'

'But I am convinced it wasn't murder,' returned the doctor, with a self-confident air. 'If a man is shot, or bludgeoned, or poisoned, there is something to go upon. I scarcely know of a poison that cannot be detected. And not a trace of poison was found in the organs of either man. Science has made tremendous strides of late years, and I doubt if she has much more to teach us in that respect. Anyway, I assert without fear of contradiction that Charnworth and Trankler did not die of poison.'

'What killed them, then?' I asked, bluntly and sharply.

The doctor did not like the question, and there was a roughness in his tone as he answered:

'I'm not prepared to say. If I could have assigned a precise cause of death the coroner's verdict would have been different.'

'Then you admit that the whole affair is a problem which you are incapable of solving?'

'Frankly, I do,' he answered, after a pause. 'There are certain peculiarities in the case that I should like to see cleared up. In fact, in the interests of my profession, I think it is most desirable that the mystery surrounding the death of the unfortunate men should be solved. And I have been trying experiments recently with a view to attaining that end, though without success.'

My interview with this gentleman had not advanced matters, for it only served to show me that the doctors were quite baffled, and I confess that that did not altogether encourage me. Where they had failed, how could I hope to succeed? They had the advantage of seeing the bodies and examining them, and though they found themselves confronted with signs which were in themselves significant, they could not read them. All that I had to go upon was hearsay, and I was asked to solve a mystery which seemed unsolvable. But, as I have so often stated in the course of my chronicles, the seemingly impossible is frequently the most easy to accomplish, where a mind specially trained to deal with complex problems is brought to bear upon it.

In interviewing Mr Tuscan Trankler, I found that he entertained a very decided opinion that there had been foul play, though he admitted that it was difficult in the extreme to suggest even a vague notion of how the deed had been accomplished. If the two men had died together or within a short period of each other, the idea of murder would have seemed more logical. But two years had elapsed, and yet each man had evidently died from precisely same cause. Therefore, if it *was* murder, the same hand that had slain Mr Charnworth slew Mr Trankler. There was no getting away from that; and then of course arose the question of *motive*. Granted that the same hand did the deed, did the same motive prompt in each case? Another aspect of the affair that presented itself to me was that the crime, if crime it was,

was not the work of any ordinary person. There was an originality of conception in it which pointed to the criminal being, in certain respects, a genius. And, moreover, the motive underlying it must have been a very powerful one; possibly, nay probably, due to a sense of some terrible wrong inflicted, and which could only be wiped out with death of the wronger. But this presupposed that each man, though unrelated, had perpetrated the same wrong. Now, it was within the grasp of intelligent reasoning that Charnworth, in his capacity of a county justice, might have given mortal offence to someone, who, cherishing the memory of it, until a mania had been set up, resolved that the magistrate should die. That theory was reasonable when taken singly, but it seemed to lose its reasonableness when connected with young Trankler, unless it was that he had been instrumental in getting somebody convicted. To determine this I made very pointed inquiries, but received the most positive assurances that never in the whole course of his life had he directly or indirectly been instrumental in prosecuting anyone. Therefore, so far as he was concerned, the theory fell to the ground; and if the same person killed both men, the motive prompting in each case was a different one, assuming that Charnworth's death resulted from revenge for a fancied wrong inflicted in the course of his administration of justice.

Although I fully recognised all the difficulties that lay in the way of a rational deduction that would square in with the theory of murder, and of murder committed by one any the same hand, I saw how necessary it was to keep in view the points I have advanced as factors in the problem the had to be worked out, and I adhered to my first impression, and felt tolerably certain that, granted the men had been murdered, they were murdered by the same hand. It may be said that this deduction required no great mental effort. I admit that that is so; but it is strange that nearly all the people in the district were opposed to the theory. Mr Tuscan Trankler spoke very highly of Charnworth. He believed him to be an upright, conscientious man, liberal to a fault with his means, and in his position of magistrate erring on the side of mercy. In his private character he was a *bon vivant*; fond of a good dinner, good wine, and good company. He was much in request at dinner-parties and other social gatherings, for he was accounted a brilliant *raconteur*, possessed of an endless fund of racy jokes and anecdotes. I have already stated that with ladies he was an especial favourite, for he had a singularly suave, winning way, which with most women was irresistible. In age he was more than double that of young Trankler, who was only five and twenty at the time of his death, whereas Charnworth had turned sixty, though I was given to understand that he was a well-preserved, good-looking man, and apparently younger than he really was.

Coming to young Trankler, there was a consensus of opinion that he was an exemplary young man. He had been partly educated at home and partly at the Manchester Grammar School; and, though he had shown a decided talent for engineering, he had not gone in for it seriously, but had dabbled in it as an amateur, for he had ample means and good prospects, and it was his father's desire that he should lead the life of a country gentleman, devote himself to country pursuits, and to improving and keeping together the family estates. To the lady who was to have become his bride, he had been engaged but six months, and had only known her a year. His premature and mysterious death had caused intense grief in both families; and his intended wife had been so seriously affected that her friends had been compelled to take her abroad.

With these facts and particulars before me, I had to set to work and try to solve the problem which was considered unsolvable by most of the people who knew anything about it. But may I be pardoned for saying very positively that, even at this point, I did not consider it so. Its complexity could not be gainsaid; nevertheless, I felt that there were ways and means of arriving at a solution, and I set to work in my own fashion. Firstly, I started on the assumption that both men had been deliberately murdered by the same person. If that was not so, then they had died of some remarkable and unknown disease which had stricken them down under a set of conditions that were closely allied, and the coincidence in that case would be one of the most astounding the world had ever known. Now, if that was correct, a pathological conundrum was propounded which, it was for the medical world to answer, and practically I was placed out of the running, to use a sporting phrase. I found that, with few exceptions – the exceptions being Mr Trankler and his friends – there was an undisguised opinion that what the united local wisdom and skill had failed to accomplish, could not be accomplished by a stranger. As my experience, however, had inured me against that sort of thing, it did not affect me. Local prejudices and jealousies have always to be reckoned with, and it does not do to be thin-skinned. I worked upon my own lines, thought with my own thoughts, and, as an expert in the art of reading human nature, I reasoned from a different set of premises to that employed by the irresponsible chatterers, who cry out 'Impos-

sible!' as soon as the first difficulty presents itself. Marshalling all the
facts of the case so far as I had been able to gather them, I arrived at
the conclusion that the problem could be solved, and, as a preliminary step to that end, I started off to London, much to the astonishment of those who had secured my services. But my reply to the many
queries addressed to me was, 'I hope to find the keynote to the solution in the metropolis'. This reply only increased the astonishment,
but later on I will explain why I took the step, which may seem to the
reader rather an extraordinary one.

After an absence of five days I returned to Cheshire, and I was
then in a position to say, 'Unless a miracle has happened, Charnworth and Trankler were murdered beyond all doubt, and murdered
by the same person in such a cunning, novel and devilish manner,
that even the most astute inquirer might have been pardoned for
being baffled.' Of course there was a strong desire to know my
reasons for the positive statement, but I felt that it was in the interests
of justice itself that I should not allow them to be known at that stage
of the proceedings.

The next important step was to try and find out what had become
of Miss Downie, the Knutsford beauty, with whom Charnworth was
said to have carried on a flirtation. Here, again, I considered secrecy
of great importance.

Hester Downie was about seven and twenty years of age. She was
an orphan, and was believed to have been born in Macclesfield, as her
parents came from there. Her father's calling was that of a miller. He
had settled in Knutsford about fifteen years previous to the period I
am dealing with, and had been dead about five years. Not very much
was known about the family, but it was thought there were other
children living. No very kindly feeling was shown for Hester Downie,
though it was only too obvious that jealousy was at the bottom of it.
Half the young men, it seemed, had lost their heads about her, and all
the girls in the village were consumed with envy and jealousy. It was
said she was 'stuck up', 'above her position', 'a heartless flirt', and so
forth. From those competent to speak, however, she was regarded as
a nice young woman, and admittedly good-looking. For years she
had lived with an old aunt, who bore the reputation of being rather a
sullen sort of woman, and somewhat eccentric. The girl had a little
over fifty pounds a year to live upon, derived from a small property
left to her by her father; and she and her aunt occupied a cottage just
on the outskirts of Knutsford. Hester was considered to be very
exclusive, and did not associate much with the people in Knutsford.

This was sufficient to account for the local bias, and as she often went away from her home for three and four weeks at a time, it was not considered extraordinary when it was known that she had left soon after Trankler's death. Nobody, however, knew where she had gone to; it is right, perhaps, that I should here state that not a soul breathed a syllable of suspicion against her, that either directly or indirectly she could be connected with the deaths of Charnworth or Trankler. The aunt, a widow by the name of Hislop, could not be described as a pleasant or genial woman, either in appearance or manner. I was anxious to ascertain for certain whether there was any truth in the rumour or not that Miss Downie had flirted with Mr Charnworth. If it was true that she did, a clue might be afforded which would lead to the ultimate unravelling of the mystery. I had to approach Mrs Hislop with a good deal of circumspection, for she showed an inclination to resent any inquiries being made into her family matters. She gave me the impression that she was an honest woman, and it was very apparent that she was strongly attached to her niece Hester. Trading on this fact, I managed to draw her out. I said that people in the district were beginning to say unkind things about Hester, and that it would be better for the girl's sake that there should be no mystery associated with her or her movements.

The old lady fired up at this, and declared that she didn't care a jot about what the 'common people' said. Her niece was superior to all of them, and she would 'have the law on anyone who spoke ill of Hester'.

'But there is one thing, Mrs Hislop,' I replied, 'that ought to be set at rest. It is rumoured – in fact, something more than rumoured – that your niece and the late Mr Charnworth were on terms of intimacy, which, to say the least, if it is true, was imprudent for a girl in her position.'

'Them what told you that,' exclaimed the old woman, 'is like the adders the woodmen get in Delamere forest: they're full of poison. Mr Charnworth courted the girl fair and square, and led her to believe he would marry her. But, of course, he had to do the thing in secret. Some folk will talk so, and if it had been known that a gentleman like Mr Charnworth was coming after a girl in Hester's position, all sorts of things would have been said.'

'Did she believe that he was serious in his intentions towards her?'

'Of course she did.'

'Why was the match broken off?'

'Because he died.'

'Then do you mean to tell me seriously, Mrs Hislop, that Mr Charnworth, had he lived, would have married your niece?'

'Yes, I believe he would.'

'Was he the only lover the girl had?'

'Oh dear no. She used to carry on with a man named Job Panton. But, though they were engaged to be married, she didn't like him much, and threw him up for Mr Charnworth.'

'Did she ever flirt with young Mr Trankler?'

'I don't know about flirting; but he called here now and again, and made her some presents. You see, Hester is a superior sort of girl, and I don't wonder at gentlefolk liking her.'

'Just so,' I replied; 'beauty attracts peasant and lord alike. But you will understand that it is to Hester's interest that there should be no concealment – no mystery; and I advise that she return here, for her very presence would tend to silence the tongue of scandal. By the way, where is she?'

'She's staying in Manchester with a relative, a cousin of hers, named Jessie Turner.'

'Is Jessie Turner a married woman?'

'Oh yes: well, that is, she has been married; but she's a widow now, and has two little children. She is very fond of Hester, who often goes to her.'

Having obtained Jessie Turner's address in Manchester, I left Mrs Hislop, feeling somehow as if I had got the key of the problem, and a day or two later I called on Mrs Jessie Turner, who resided in a small house, situated in Tamworth Street, Hulme, Manchester.

She was a young woman, not more than thirty years of age, somewhat coarse, and vulgar-looking in appearance, and with an unpleasant, self-assertive manner. There was a great contrast between her and her cousin, Hester Downie, who was a remarkably attractive and pretty girl, with quite a classical figure, and a childish, winning way, but a painful want of education which made itself very manifest when she spoke; and a harsh, unmusical voice detracted a good deal from her winsomeness, while in everything she did, and almost everything she said, she revealed that vanity was her besetting sin.

I formed my estimate at once of this young woman indeed, of both of them. Hester seemed to me to be shallow, vain, thoughtless, giddy; and her companion, artful, cunning, and heartless.

'I want you, Miss Downie,' I began, 'to tell me truthfully the story of your connection, firstly, with Job Panton; secondly, with Mr Charnworth; thirdly, with Mr Trankler.'

This request caused the girl to fall into a condition of amazement and confusion, for I had not stated what the nature of my business was, and, of course, she was unprepared for the question.

'What should I tell you my business for?' she cried snappishly, and growing very red in the face.

'You are aware,' I remarked, 'that both Mr Charnworth and Mr Trankler are dead?'

'Of course I am.'

'Have you any idea how they came by their death?'

'Not the slightest.'

'Will you be surprised to hear that some very hard things are being said about you?'

'About me!' she exclaimed, in amazement.

'Yes.'

'Why about me?'

'Well, your disappearance from your home, for one thing.'

She threw up her hands and uttered a cry of distress and horror, while sudden paleness took the place of the red flush that had dyed her cheeks. Then she burst into almost hysterical weeping, and sobbed out:

'I declare it's awful. To think that I cannot do anything or go away when I like without all the old cats in the place trying to blacken my character! It's a pity that people won't mind their own business, and not go out of the way to talk about that which doesn't concern them.'

'But, you see, Miss Downie, it's the way of the world,' I answered, with a desire to soothe her; 'one mustn't be too thin-skinned. Human nature is essentially spiteful. However, to return to the subject, you will see, perhaps, the importance of answering my questions. The circumstances of Charnworth's and Trankler's deaths are being closely inquired into, and I am sure you wouldn't like it to be thought that you were withholding information which, in the interest of law and justice, might be valuable.'

'Certainly not,' she replied, suppressing a sob. 'But I have nothing to tell you.'

'But you knew the three men I have mentioned.'

'Of course I did, but Job Panton is an ass. I never could bear him.'

'He was your sweetheart, though, was he not?'

'He used to come fooling about, and declared that he couldn't live without me.'

'Did you never give him encouragement?'

'I suppose every girl makes a fool of herself sometimes.'

'Then you did allow him to sweetheart you?'

'If you like to call it sweethearting you can,' she answered, with a toss of her pretty head. 'I did walk out with him sometimes. But I didn't care much for him. You see, he wasn't my sort at all.'

'In what way?'

'Well, surely I couldn't be expected to marry a gamekeeper, could I?'

'He is a gamekeeper, then?'

'Yes.'

'In whose employ is he?'

'Lord Belmere's.'

'Was he much disappointed when he found that you would have nothing to do with him?'

'I really don't know. I didn't trouble myself about him,' she answered, with a coquettish heartlessness.

'Did you do any sweethearting with Mr Trankler?'

'No, of course not. He used to be very civil to me, and talk to me when he met me.'

'Did you ever walk out with him?'

The question brought the colour back to her face, and her manner grew confused again, 'Once or twice I met him by accident, and he strolled along the road with me – that's all.'

This answer was not a truthful one. Of that I was convinced by her very manner. But I did not betray my mistrust or doubts. I did not think there was any purpose to be served in so doing. So far the object of my visit was accomplished, and as Miss Downie seemed disposed to resent any further questioning, I thought it was advisable to bring the interview to a close; but before doing so, I said:

'I have one more question to ask you, Miss Downie. Permit me to preface it, however, by saying I am afraid that, up to this point, you have failed to appreciate the situation, or grasp the seriousness of the position in which you are placed. Let me, therefore, put it before you in a somewhat more graphic way. Two men – gentlemen of good social position with whom you seem to have been well acquainted, and whose attentions you encouraged – pray do not look at me so angrily as that; I mean what I say. I repeat that you encouraged their attentions, otherwise they would not have gone after you.' Here Miss Downie's nerves gave way again, and she broke into a fit of weeping, and, holding her handkerchief to her eyes, she exclaimed with almost passionate bitterness:

'Well, whatever I did, I was egged on to do it by my cousin, Jessie Turner. She always said I was a fool not to aim at high game.'

'And so you followed her promptings, and really thought that you might have made a match with Mr Charnworth; but, he having died, you turned your thoughts to young Trankler.' She did not reply, but sobbed behind her handkerchief. So I proceeded. 'Now the final question I want to ask you is this: Have you ever had anyone who has made serious love to you but Job Panton?'

'Mr Charnworth made love to me,' she sobbed out.

'He flirted with you,' I suggested.

'No; he made love to me,' she persisted. 'He promised to marry me.'

'And you believed him?'

'Of course I did.'

'Did Trankler promise to marry you?'

'No.'

'Then I must repeat the question, but will add Mr Charnworth's name. Besides him and Panton, is there anyone else in existence who has courted you in the hope that you would become his wife?'

'No – no one,' she mumbled in a broken voice.

As I took my departure I felt that I had gathered up a good many threads, though they wanted arranging, and, so to speak, classifying; that done, they would probably give me the clue I was seeking. One thing was clear, Miss Downie was a weak-headed, giddy, flighty girl, incapable, as it seemed to me, of seriously reflecting on anything. Her cousin was crafty and shallow, and a dangerous companion for Downie, who was sure to be influenced and led by a creature like Jessie Turner. But, let it not be inferred from these remarks that I had any suspicion that either of the two women had in any way been accessory to the crime, for crime I was convinced it was. Trankler and Charnworth had been murdered, but by whom I was not prepared to even hint at at that stage of the proceedings. The two unfortunate gentlemen had, beyond all possibility of doubt, both been attracted by the girl's exceptionally good looks, and they had amused themselves with her. This fact suggested at once the question, was Charnworth in the habit of seeing her before Trankler made her acquaintance? Now, if my theory of the crime was correct, it could be asserted with positive certainty, that Charnworth was the girl's lover before Trankler. Of course it was almost a foregone conclusion that Trankler must have been aware of her existence for along time. The place, be it remembered, was small; she, in her way, was a sort of

local celebrity, and it was hardly likely that young Trankler was ignorant of some of the village gossip in which she figured. But, assuming
that he was, he was well acquainted with Charnworth, who was
looked upon in the neighbourhood as 'a gay dog'. The female con-
quests of such men are often matters of notoriety; though, even if that
was not the case, it was likely enough that Charnworth may have discussed Miss Downie in Trankler's presence. Some men – especially
those of Charnworth's characteristics – are much given to boasting of
their flirtations, and Charnworth may have been rather prow of his
ascendency over the simple village beauty. Of course, all this, it will
be said, was mere theorising. So it was; but it will presently be seen
how it squared in with the general theory of the whole affair, which I
had worked out after much pondering, and a careful weighing and
nice adjustment of all the evidence, such as it was, I had been able to
gather together, and the various parts which were necessary before
the puzzle could be put together.

It was immaterial, however, whether Trankler did or did not know
Hester Downie before or at the same time as Charnworth. A point
that was not difficult to determine was this – he did not make himself
conspicuous as her admirer until after his friend's death, probably not
until some time afterwards. Otherwise, how came it about that the
slayer of Charnworth waited two years before he took the life of
young Trankler? The reader will gather from this remark how my
thoughts ran at that time. Firstly, I was clearly of opinion that both
men had been murdered. Secondly, the murder in each case was the
outcome of jealousy. Thirdly, the murderer must, as a logical
sequence, have been a rejected suitor. This would point necessarily to
Job Panton as the criminal, assuming my information was right that
the girl had not had any other lover. But against that theory this very
strong argument could be used: By what extraordinary and secret
means – means that had baffled all the science of the district – had Job
Panton, who occupied the position of a gamekeeper, been able to do
away with his victims, and bring about death so horrible and so
sudden as to make one shudder to think of it? Herein was displayed a
devilishness of cunning, and a knowledge which it was difficult to
conceive that an ignorant and untravelled man was likely to be in possession of. Logic, deduction, and all the circumstances of the case
were opposed to the idea of Panton being the murderer at the first
blush; and yet, so far as I had gone, I had been irresistibly drawn
towards the conclusion that Panton was either directly or indirectly
responsible for the death of the two gentlemen. But, in order to know

something more of the man whom I suspected, I disguised myself as a travelling showman on the lookout for a good pitch for my show, and I took up my quarters for a day or two at a rustic inn just on the skirts of Knutsford, and known as the Woodman. I had previously ascertained that this inn was a favourite resort of the gamekeepers for miles round about, and Job Panton was to be found there almost nightly.

In a short time I had made his acquaintance. He was a young, big-limbed, powerful man, of a pronounced rustic type. He had the face of a gipsy – swarthy and dark, with keen, small black eyes, and a mass of black curly hair, and in his ears he wore tiny, plain gold rings. Singularly enough his expression was most intelligent; but allied with – as it seemed to me – a certain suggestiveness of latent ferocity. That is to say, I imagined him liable to outbursts of temper and passion, during which he might be capable of anything. As it was, then, he seemed to me subdued, somewhat sullen, and averse to conversation. He smoked heavily, and I soon found that he guzzled beer at a terrible rate. He had received, for a man in his position, a tolerably good education. By that I mean he could write a fair hand, he read well, and had something more than a smattering of arithmetic. I was told also that he was exceedingly skilful with carpenter's tools, although he had had no training that way; he also understood something about plants, while he was considered an authority on the habit, and everything appertaining to game. The same informant thought to still further enlighten me by adding:

'Poor Job bean't the chap he wur a year or more ago. His gal cut un, and that kind a took a hold on un. He doän't say much; but it wur a terrible blow, it wur.'

'How was it his girl cut him?' I asked.

'Well, you see, maaster, it wur this way; she thought hersel' a bit too high for un. Mind you, I baan't a saying as she wur; but when a gel thinks hersel' above a chap, it's no use talking to her.'

'What was the girl's name?'

'They call her Downie. Her father was a miller here in Knutsford, but his gal had too big notions of hersel'; and she chucked poor Job Panton overboard, and they do say as how she took on wi' Measter Charnworth and also wi' Measter Trankler. I doän't know nowt for certain myself, but there wursome rum kind o' talk going about. Leastwise, I know that job took it badly, and he ain't been the same kind o' chap since. But there, what's the use of a breaking one's 'art about a gal? Gals is a queer lot, I tell you. My old grandfaither used to say, "Women folk be curious folk. They be necessary evils, they be, and pleasant enough in their way, but a chap mustn't let 'em get the upper hand. They're like harses, they be, and if you want to manage 'em, you must show 'em you're their measter.'"

The garrulous gentleman who entertained me thus with his views on women, was a tough, sinewy, weather-tanned old codger, who had lived the allotted span according to the psalmist, but who seemed destined to tread the earth for a long time still; for his seventy years had neither bowed nor shrunk him. His chatter was interesting to me because it served to prove what I already suspected, which was that Job Panton had taken his jilting very seriously indeed. Job was by no means a communicative fellow. As a matter of fact, it was difficult to draw him out on any subject; and though I should have liked to have heard his views about Hester Downie, I did not feel warranted in tapping him straight off. I very speedily discovered, however, that his weakness was beer. His capacity for it seemed immeasurable. He soaked himself with it; but when he reached the muddled stage, there was a tendency on his part to be more loquacious, and, taking advantage at last of one of these opportunities, I asked him one night if he had travelled. The question was an exceedingly pertinent one to my theory, and I felt that to a large extent the theory I had worked out depended upon the answers he gave. He turned his beady eyes upon me, and said, with a sort of sardonic grin:

'Yes, I've travelled a bit in my, time, measter. I've been to Manchester often, and I once tramped all the way to Edinburgh. I had to rough it, I tell thee.'

'Yes, I dare say,' I answered. 'But what I mean is, have you ever been abroad? Have you ever been to sea?'

'No, measter, not me.'

'You've been in foreign countries?'

'No. I've never been out of this one. England was good enough for me. But I would like to go away now to Australia, or some of those places.'

Why?'

'Well, measter, I have my own reasons.'

'Doubtless,' I said, 'and no doubt very sound reasons.'

'Never thee mind whether they are, or whether they bean't,' he retorted warmly. 'All I've got to say is, I wouldn't care where I went to if I could only get far enough away from this place. I'm tired of it.'

In the manner of giving his answer, he betrayed the latent fire which I had surmised, and showed that there was a volcanic force of passion underlying his sullen silence, for he spoke with a suppressed force which clearly indicated the intensity of his feelings, and his bright eyes grew brighter with the emotion he felt. I now ventured upon another remark. I intended it to be a test one.

'I heard one of your mates say that you had been jilted. I suppose that's why you hate the place?'

He turned upon me suddenly. His tanned, ruddy face took on a deeper flush of red; his upper teeth closed almost savagely on his nether lip; his chest heaved, and his great, brawny hands clenched with the working of his passion. Then, with one great bang of his ponderous fist, he struck the table until the pots and glasses on it jumped as if they were sentient and frightened; and in a voice thick with smothered passion, he growled, 'Yes, damn her! She's been my ruin.'

'Nonsense!' I said. 'You are a young man and a young man should not talk about being ruined because a girl has jilted him.'

Once more he turned that angry look upon me, and said fiercely:

'Thou knows nowt about it, governor. Thou're a stranger to me; and I doän't allow no strangers to preach to me. So shut up! I'll have nowt more to say to thee.'

There was a peremptoriness, a force of character, and a display of firmness and self-assurance in his tone and manner, which stamped him with a distinct individualism, and made it evident that in his own particular way he was distinct from the class in which his lot was cast. He, further than that, gave me the idea that he was designing and secretive; and given that he had been educated and well trained, he might have made his mark in the world. My interview with him had been instructive, and my opinion that he might prove a very important factor in working out the problem was strengthened; but at that stage of the inquiry I would not have taken upon myself to say, with anything like definiteness, that he was directly responsible for the death of the two gentlemen, whose mysterious ending had caused such a profound sensation. But the reader of this narrative will now see for himself that of all men, so far as one could determine then, who might have been interested in the death of Mr Charnworth and Mr Trankler, Job Panton stood out most conspicuously. His motive for destroying them was one of the most powerful of human passions – namely, jealousy, which in his case was likely to assume a very violent form, inasmuch as there was no evenly balanced judgement, no capability of philosophical reasoning, calculated to restrain the fierce, crude passion of the determined and self-willed man.

A wounded tiger is fiercer and more dangerous than an

unwounded one, and an ignorant and unreasoning man is far more likely to be led to excess by a sense of wrong, than one who is capable of reflecting and moralising. Of course, if I had been the impossible detective of fiction, endowed with the absurd attributes of being able to tell the story of a man's life from the way the tip of his nose was formed, or the number of hairs on his head, or by the shape and size of his teeth, or by the way he held his pipe when smoking, or from the kind of liquor he consumed, or the hundred and one utterly ridiculous and burlesque signs which are so easily read by the detective prig of modern creation, I might have come to a different conclusion with reference to Job Panton. But my work had to be carried out on very different lines, and I had to be guided by certain deductive inferences, aided by an intimate knowledge of human nature, and of the laws which, more or less in every case of crime, govern the criminal.

I have already set forth my unalterable opinion that Charnworth and Trankler had been murdered; and so far as I had proceeded up to this point, I had heard and seen enough to warrant me, in my own humble judgement, in at least suspecting rob Panton of being guilty of the murder. But there was one thing that puzzled me greatly. When I first commenced my inquiries, and was made acquainted with all the extraordinary medical aspects of the case, I argued with myself that if it was murder, it was murder carried out upon very original lines. Some potent, swift and powerful poison must have been suddenly and secretly introduced into the blood of the victim. The bite of a cobra, or of the still more fearful and deadly *Fer de lance* of the West Indies, might have produced symptoms similar to those observed in the two men; but happily our beautiful and quiet woods and gardens of England are not infested with these deadly reptiles, and one had to search for the causes elsewhere. Now everyone knows that the notorious Lucrezia Borgia, and the Marchioness of Brinvilliers, made use of means for accomplishing the death of those whom they were anxious to get out of the way, which were at once effective and secret. These means consisted, amongst others, of introducing into the blood of the intended victim some subtle poison, by the medium of a scratch or puncture. This little and fatal wound could be given by the scratch of a pin, or the sharpened stone of a ring, and in such a way that the victim would be all unconscious of it until the deadly poison so insidiously introduced began to course through his veins, and to sap the props of his life. With these facts in my mind, I asked myself if in the Dead Wood Hall tragedies some similar means had been used; and in order to have competent and authoritative opinion to guide me, I journeyed back to London to consult the eminent chemist and scientist, Professor Lucraft. This gentleman had made a lifelong study of the toxic effect of ptomaines on the human system, and of the various poisons used by savage tribes for tipping their arrows and spears. Enlightened as he was on the subject, he confessed that there were hundreds of these deadly poisons, of which the modern chemist knew absolutely nothing; but he expressed a decided opinion that there were many that would produce all the effects and symptoms observable in the cases of Charnworth and Trankler. And he particularly instanced some of the, herbal extracts used by various tribes of Indians, who wander in the interior of the little known country of Ecuador, and he cited as an authority Mr Hart Thompson, the botanist who travelled from Quito right through Ecuador to the Amazon. This gentleman reported that he found a vegetable poison in use by the natives for poisoning the tips of their arrows and spears of so deadly and virulent a nature, that a scratch even on a panther would bring about the death of the animal within an hour.

Armed with these facts, I returned to Cheshire, and continued my investigations on the assumption that some unknown deadly destroyer of life had been used to put Charnworth and Trankler out of the way. But necessarily I was led to question whether or not it was likely that an untravelled and ignorant man like Job Panton could have known anything about such poisons and their uses. This was a stumbling block; and while I was convinced that Panton had a strong motive for the crime, I was doubtful if he could have been in possession of the means for committing it. At last, in order to try and get evidence on this point, I resolved to search the place in which he lived. He had for along time occupied lodgings in the house of a widow woman in Knutsford, and I subjected his rooms to a thorough and critical search, but without finding a sign of anything calculated to justify my suspicion.

I freely confess that at this stage I began to feel that the problem was a hopeless one, and that I should fail to work it out. My depression, however, did not last long. It was not my habit to acknowledge defeat so long as there were probabilities to guide me, so I began to make inquiries about Panton's relatives, and these inquiries elicited the fact that he had been in the habit of making frequent journeys to Manchester to see an uncle. I soon found that this uncle had been a sailor, and had been one of a small expedition which had travelled through Peru and Ecuador in search of gold. Now, this was a discovery indeed, and the full value of it will be understood when it is taken in connection with the information given to me by Professor Lucraft. Let us see how it works out logically.

Panton's uncle was a sailor and a traveller. He had travelled through Peru, and had been into the interior of Ecuador.

Panton was in the habit of visiting his uncle.

Could the uncle have wandered through Ecuador without hearing something of the marvellous poisons used by the natives?

Having been connected with an exploring expedition, it was reasonable to assume that he was a man of good intelligence, and of an inquiring turn of mind.

Equally probable was it that he had brought home some of the deadly poisons or poisoned implements used by the Indians. Granted that, and what more likely than that he talked of his knowledge and possessions to his nephew? The nephew, brooding on his wrongs, and seeing the means within his grasp of secretly avenging himself on those whom he counted his rivals, obtained the means from his uncle's collection of putting his rivals to death, in a way which to him would seem to be impossible to detect. I had seen enough of Panton to feel sure that he had all the intelligence and cunning necessary for planning and carrying out the deed.

A powerful link in the chain of evidence had now been forged, and I proceeded a step further. After a consultation with the chief inspector of police, who, however, by no means shared my views, I applied for a warrant for Panton's arrest, although I saw that to establish legal proof of his guilt would be extraordinarily difficult, for his uncle at that time was at sea, somewhere in the southern hemisphere. Moreover, the whole case rested upon such a hypothetical basis, that it seemed doubtful whether, even supposing a magistrate would commit, a jury would convict. But I was not daunted; and, having succeeded so far in giving a practical shape to my theory, I did not intend to draw back. So I set to work to endeavour to discover the weapon which had been used for wounding Charnworth and Trankler, so that the poison, might take effect. This, of course, was the crux of the whole affair. The discovery of the medium by which the death-scratch was given would forge almost the last link necessary to ensure a conviction.

Now, in each case there was pretty conclusive evidence that there had been no struggle. This fact justified the belief that the victim was struck silently, and probably unknown to himself. What were the probabilities of that being the case? Assuming that Panton was guilty of the crime, how was it that he, being an inferior, was allowed to come within striking distance of his victims? The most curious thing was that both men had been scratched on the left side of the neck. Charnworth had been killed in his friend's garden on a summer night. Trankler had fallen in midday in the depths of a forest. There was an interval of two years between the death of the one man and the death of the other, yet each had a scratch on the left side of the neck. That could not have been a mere coincidence. It was design.

The next point for consideration was, how did Panton – always assuming that he was the criminal – get access to Mr Trankler's grounds? Firstly, the grounds were extensive, and in connection with a plantation of young fir trees. When Charnworth was found, he was lying behind a clump of rhododendron bushes, and near where the grounds were merged into the plantation, a somewhat dilapidated oak fence separating the two. These details before us make it clear that Panton could have had no difficulty in gaining access to the plantation, and thence to the grounds. But how came it that he was there just at the time that Charnworth was strolling about? It seemed stretching a point very much to suppose that he could have been loafing about on the mere chance of seeing Charnworth. And the only hypothesis that squared in with intelligent reasoning, was that the victim had been lured into the grounds. But this necessarily presupposed a confederate. Close inquiry elicited the fact that Panton was in the habit of going to the house. He knew most of the servants, and frequently accompanied young Trankler on his shooting excursions, and periodically he spent half a day or so in the gun room at the house, in order that he might clean up all the guns, for which he was paid a small sum every month. These circumstances cleared the way of difficulties to a very considerable extent. I was unable, however, to go beyond that, for I could not ascertain the means that had been used to lure Mr Charnworth into the garden – if he had been lured; and I felt sure that he had been. But so much had to remain for the time being a mystery.

Having obtained the warrant to arrest Panton, I proceeded to execute it. He seemed thunderstruck when told that he was arrested on a charge of having been instrumental in bringing about the death of Charnworth and Trankler. For a brief space of time he seemed to collapse, and lose his presence of mind. But suddenly, with an apparent effort, he recovered himself, and said, with a strange smile on his face:

'You've got to prove it, and that you can never do.'

His manner and this remark were hardly compatible with innocence, but I clearly recognised the difficulties of proof. From that moment the fellow assumed a self-assured air, and to those with whom he was brought in contact he would remark:

'I'm as innocent as a lamb, and them as says I done the deed have got to prove it.'

In my endeavour to get further evidence to strengthen my case, I managed to obtain from Job Panton's uncle's brother, who followed the occupation of an engine-minder in a large cotton factory in Oldham, an old chest containing a quantity of lumber. The uncle, on going to sea again, had left this chest in charge of his brother. A careful examination of the contents proved that they consisted of a very miscellaneous collection of odds and ends, including two or three small, carved wooden idols from some savage country; some stone weapons, such as are used by the North American Indians; strings of cowrie shells, a pair of moccasins, feathers of various kinds; a few dried specimens of strange birds; and last, though not least, a small bamboo case containing a dozen tiny sharply pointed darts, feathered at the thick end; while in a stone box, about three inches square, was a viscid thick gummy looking substance of a very dark brown colour, and giving off a sickening and most disagreeable, though faint odour. These things I at once submitted to Professor Lucraft, who expressed an opinion that the gummy substance in the stone box was a vegetable poison, used probably to poison the darts with. He lost no time in experimentalising with this substance, as well as with the darts. With these darts he scratched guinea-pigs, rabbits, a dog, a cat, a hen, and a young pig, and in each case death ensued in periods of time ranging from a quarter of an hour to two hours. By means of a subcutaneous injection into a rabbit of a minute portion of the gummy substance, about the size of a pea, which had been thinned with alcohol, he produced death in exactly seven minutes. A small monkey was next procured, and slightly scratched on the neck with one of the poisoned darts. In a very short time the poor animal exhibited the most distressing symptoms, and in half an hour it was dead, and a post-mortem examination revealed many of the peculiar effect which had been observed. in Charnworth's and Trankler's bodies. Various other exhaustive experiments were carried out, all of which confirmed the deadly nature of these minute poison-darts, which could be puffed through a hollow tube to a great distance, and after some practice, with unerring aim. Analysis of the gummy substance in the box proved it to be a violent vegetable poison; innocuous when swallowed, but singularly active and deadly when introduced direct into the blood.

On the strength of these facts, the magistrate duly committed Job Panton to take his trial at the next assizes, on a charge of murder, although there was not a scrap of evidence forthcoming to prove that he had ever been in possession of any of the darts or the poison; and unless such evidence was forthcoming, it was felt that the case for the prosecution must break down, however clear the mere guilt of the man might seem.

In due course, Panton was put on his trial at Chester, and the principal witness against him was Hester Downie, who was subjected to a very severe cross-examination, which left not a shadow of a doubt that she and Panton had at one time been close sweethearts. But her cousin Jessie Turner proved a tempter of great subtlety. It was made clear that she poisoned the girl's mind against her humble lover. Although it could not be proved, it is highly probable that Jessie Turner was a creature of and in the pay of Mr Charnworth, who seemed to have been very much attracted by him. Hester's connection with Charnworth half maddened Panton, who made frantic appeals to her to be true to him, appeals to which she turned a deaf ear. That Trankler knew her in Charnworth's time was also brought out, and after Charnworth's death she smiled favourably on the young man. On the morning that Trankler's shooting-party went out to Mere Forest, Panton was one of the beaters employed by the party.

So much was proved; so much was made as clear as daylight, and it opened the way for any number of inferences. But the last and most important link was never forthcoming. Panton was defended by an able and unscrupulous counsel, who urged with tremendous force on the notice of the jury, that firstly, not one of the medical witnesses would undertake to swear that the two men had died from the effects of poison similar to that found in the old chest which had belonged to the prisoner's uncle; and secondly, there was not one scrap of evidence tending to prove that Panton had ever been in possession of poisoned darts, or had ever had access to the chest in which they were kept. These two points were also made much of by the learned judge in his summing up. He was at pains to make clear that there was a doubt involved, and that mere inference ought not to be allowed to outweigh the doubt when a human being was on trial for his life. Although circumstantially the evidence very strongly pointed to the probability of the prisoner having killed both men, nevertheless, in the absence of the strong proof which the law demanded, the way was opened for the escape of a suspected man, and it was far better to let the law be cheated of its due, than that an innocent man should suffer. At the same time, the judge went on, two gentlemen had met their deaths in a manner which had baffled medical science, and no one was forthcoming who would undertake to say that they had been killed in the manner suggested by the prosecution, and yet it had been shown that the terrible and powerful poison found in the old chest, and which there was reason to believe had been brought from some part of the little known country near the sources of the mighty Amazon, would produce all the effects which were observed in they bodies of Charnworth and Trankler. The chest, furthermore, in which the poison was discovered, was in the possession of Panton's uncle. Panton had a powerful motive in the shape of consuming jealousy for getting rid of his more favoured rivals; and though he was one of the shooting-party in Mere Forest on the day that Trankler lost his life, no evidence had been produced to prove that he was on the premises of Dead Wood Hall, on the night that Charnworth died. If, in weighing all these points of evidence, the jury were of opinion circumstantial evidence was inadequate, then it was their duty to give the prisoner – whose life was in their hands the benefit of the doubt.

The jury retired, and were absent three long hours, and it became known that they could not agree. Ultimately, they returned into court, and pronounced a verdict of 'not guilty'. In Scotland the verdict must and would have been 'non proven'.

And so Job Panton went free, but an evil odour seemed to cling about him; he was shunned by his former companions, and many a suspicious glance was directed to him, and many a bated murmur was uttered as he passed by, until in a while he went forth beyond the seas, to the far wild west, as some said, and his haunts knew him no more.

The mystery is still a mystery; but how near I came to solving the problem of Dead Wood Hall it is for the reader to judge.

ROBERT W CHAMBERS

The Purple Emperor

Un souvenir heureux est peut-être, sur terre,
Plus vrai que le bonheur. – A De Musset

I.

THE PURPLE Emperor watched me in silence. I cast again, spinning out six feet more of waterproof silk, and, as the line hissed through the air far across the pool, I saw my three flies fall on the water like drifting thistledown. The Purple Emperor sneered.

'You see,' he said, 'I am right. There is not a trout in Brittany that will rise to a tailed fly.'

'They do in America,' I replied.

'Zut! for America!' observed the Purple Emperor.

'And trout take a tailed fly in England,' I insisted sharply.

'Now do I care what things or people do in England?' demanded the Purple Emperor.

'You don't care for anything except yourself and your wriggling caterpillars,' I said, more annoyed than I had yet been.

The Purple Emperor sniffed. His broad, hairless, sunburnt features bore that obstinate expression which always irritated me. Perhaps the manner in which he wore his hat intensified the irritation, for the flapping brim rested on both ears, and the two little velvet ribbons which hung from the silver buckle in front wiggled and fluttered with every trivial breeze. His cunning eyes and sharp-pointed nose were out of all keeping with his fat red face. When he met my eye, he chuckled.

'I know more about insects than any man in Morbihan – or Finistère either, for that matter,' he said.

'The Red Admiral knows as much as you do,' I retorted.

'He doesn't,' replied the Purple Emperor angrily.

'And his collection of butterflies is twice as large as yours,' I added, moving down the stream to a spot directly opposite him.

'It is, is it?' sneered the Purple Emperor. 'Well, let me tell you, Monsieur Darrel, in all his collection he hasn't a specimen, a single specimen, of that magnificent butterfly, *Apatura Iris*, commonly known as the "Purple Emperor".'

'Everybody in Brittany knows that,' I said, casting across the sparkling water; 'but just because you happen to be the only man who ever captured a "Purple Emperor" in Morbihan, it – doesn't follow that you are an authority on sea-trout flies. Why do you say that a Breton sea-trout won't touch a tailed fly?'

'It's so,' he replied.

'Why? There are plenty of mayflies about the stream.'

'Let 'em fly!' snarled the Purple Emperor, 'you won't see a trout touch 'em.'

My arm was aching, but I grasped my split bamboo more firmly, and, half turning, waded out into the stream and began to whip the ripples at the head of the pool. A great green dragonfly came drifting by on the summer breeze and hung a moment above the pool, glittering like an emerald.

'There's a chance! Where is your butterfly net?' I called across the stream.

'What for? That dragonfly? I've got dozens – *Anax Junius*, Drury, characteristic, anal angle of posterior wings, in male, round; thorax marked with...'

'That will do,' I said fiercely. 'Can't I point out an insect in the air without this burst erudition? Can you tell me, in simple everyday French, what this little fly is this one, flitting over the eel grass here beside me? See, it has fallen on the water.'

'Huh!' sneered the Purple Emperor, 'that's a *Linnobia Annulus*.'

'What's that?' I demanded.

Before he could answer there came a heavy splash in the pool, and the fly disappeared.

'He! he! he!' tittered the Purple Emperor. 'Didn't I tell you the fish knew their business? That was a sea-trout. I hope you don't get him.'

He gathered up his butterfly net, collecting box, chloroform bottle, and cyanide jar. Then he rose, swung the box over his shoulder, stuffed the poison bottles into the pockets of his silver-buttoned velvet coat, and lighted his pipe. This latter operation was a demoralising spectacle, for the Purple Emperor, like all Breton peasants, smoked one of those microscopical Breton pipes which requires ten minutes to find, ten minutes to fill, ten minutes to light, and ten seconds to finish. With true Breton stolidity he went through this solemn rite, blew three puffs of smoke into the air, scratched his pointed nose reflectively, and waddled away, calling back an ironical, 'Au revoir, and bad luck to all Yankees!'

I watched him out of sight, thinking sadly of the young girl whose life he made a hell upon earth – Lys Trevec, his niece. She never admitted it, but we all knew what the black-and-blue marks meant on her soft, round arm, and it made me sick to see the look of fear come into her eyes when the Purple Emperor waddled into the café of the Groix Inn.

It was commonly said that he half-starved her. This she denied. Marie Joseph and 'Fine Lelocard had seen him strike her the day after the Pardon of the Birds because she had liberated three bullfinches which he had limed the day before. I asked Lys if this were true, and she refused to speak to me for the rest of the week. There was nothing to do about it. If the Purple Emperor had not been avaricious, I should never have seen Lys at all, but he could not resist the thirty francs a week which I offered him; and Lys posed for me all day long, happy as a linnet in a pink thorn hedge. Nevertheless, the Purple Emperor hated me, and constantly threatened to send Lys back to her dreary flax-spinning. He was suspicious, too, and when he had gulped down the single glass of cider which proves fatal to the sobriety of most Bretons, he would pound the long, discoloured oaken table and roar curses on me, on Yves Terrec, and on the Red Admiral. We were the three objects in the world which he most hated: me, because I was a foreigner, and didn't care a rap for him and his butterflies; and the Red Admiral, because he was a rival entomologist.

He had other reasons for hating Terrec.

The Red Admiral, a little wizened wretch, with a badly adjusted glass eye and a passion for brandy, took his name from a butterfly which predominated in his collection. This butterfly, commonly known to amateurs as the 'Red Admiral', and to entomologists as *Vanessa Atalanta*, had been the occasion of scandal among the entomologists of France and Brittany. For the Red Admiral had taken one of these common insects, dyed it a brilliant yellow by the aid of chemicals, and palmed it off on a credulous collector as a South African species, absolutely unique. The fifty francs which he gained by this rascality were, however, absorbed in a suit for damages brought by the outraged amateur a month later; and when he had sat in the Quimperlé jail for a month, he reappeared in the little village of St Gildas soured, thirsty, and burning for revenge. Of course we named him the Red Admiral, and he accepted the name with suppressed fury.

The Purple Emperor, on the other hand, had gained his imperial title legitimately, for it was an undisputed fact that the only specimen of that beautiful butterfly, *Apatura Iris*, or the Purple Emperor, as it is called by amateurs – the only specimen that had ever been taken in

Finistère or in Morbihan – was captured and brought home alive by Joseph Marie Gloanec, ever afterward to be known as the Purple Emperor.

When the capture of this rare butterfly became known the Red Admiral nearly went crazy. Every day for a week he trotted over to the Groix Inn, where the Purple Emperor lived with his niece, and brought his microscope to bear on the rare newly captured butterfly, in hopes of detecting a fraud. But this specimen was genuine, and he leered through his microscope in vain.

'No chemicals there, Admiral,' grinned the Purple Emperor; and the Red Admiral chattered with rage.

To the scientific world of Brittany and France the capture of an *Apatura Iris* in Morbihan was of great importance. The Museum of Quimper offered to purchase the butterfly, but the Purple Emperor, though a hoarder of gold, was a monomaniac on butterflies, and he jeered at the Curator of the Museum. From all parts of Brittany and France letters of inquiry and congratulation poured in upon him. The French Academy of Sciences awarded him a prize, and the Paris Entomological Society made him an honorary member. Being a Breton peasant, and a more than commonly pig-headed one at that, these honours did not disturb his equanimity; but when the little hamlet of St Gildas elected him mayor, and, as is the custom in Brittany under such circumstances, he left his thatched house to take up an official life in the little Groix Inn, his head became completely turned. To be mayor in a village of nearly one hundred and fifty people! It was an empire! So he became unbearable, drinking himself viciously drunk every night of his life, maltreating his niece, Lys Trevec, like the barbarous old wretch that he was, and driving the Red Admiral nearly frantic with his eternal harping, on the capture of *Apatura Iris*. Of course he refused to tell where he had caught the butterfly. The Red Admiral stalked his footsteps, but in vain.

'He! he! he!' nagged the Purple Emperor, cuddling his chin over a glass of cider; 'I saw you sneaking about the St Gildas spinny yesterday morning. So you think you can find another *Apatura Iris* by running after me? It won't do, Admiral, it won't do, d'ye see?'

The Red Admiral turned yellow with mortification and envy, but the next day he actually took to his bed, for the Purple Emperor had brought home not a butterfly but a live chrysalis, which, if successfully hatched, would become a perfect specimen of the invaluable *Apatura Iris*. This was the last straw. The Red Admiral shut himself up in his little stone cottage, and for weeks now he had been invisible

to everybody except 'Fine Lelocard who carried him a loaf of bread
and a mullet or langouste every morning.

The withdrawal of the Red Admiral from the society of St Gildas
excited first the derision and finally the suspicion of the Purple
Emperor. What deviltry could he be hatching? Was he experimenting
with chemicals again, or was he engaged in some deeper plot, the
object of which was to discredit the Purple Emperor? Roux, the
postman, who carried the mail on foot once a day from Bannalec, a
distance of fifteen miles each way, had brought several suspicious
letters, bearing English stamps, to the Red Admiral, and the next day
the Admiral had been observed at his window grinning up into the
sky and rubbing his hands together. A night or two after this appari-
tion the postman left two packages at the Groix Inn for a moment
while he ran across the way to drink a glass of cider with me. The
Purple Emperor, who was roaming about the café, snooping into
everything that did not concern him, came upon the packages and
examined the postmarks and addresses. One of the packages was
square and heavy, and felt like a book. The other was also square, but
very light, and felt like a pasteboard box. They were both addressed
to the Red Admiral, and they bore English stamps.

When Roux, the postman, came back, the Purple Emperor tried to
pump him, but the poor little postman knew nothing about the contents of the packages, and after he had taken them around the corner
to the cottage of the Red Admiral the Purple Emperor ordered a glass
of cider, and deliberately fuddled himself until Lys came in and tear-
fully supported him to his room. Here he became so abusive and
brutal that Lys called to me, and I went and settled the trouble
without wasting any words. This also the Purple Emperor remembered, and waited his chance to get even with me.

That had happened a week ago, and until today he had not
deigned to speak to me.

Lys had posed for me all the week, and today being Saturday, and
I lazy, we had decided to take a little relaxation, she to visit and
gossip with her little black-eyed friend Yvette in the neighbouring
hamlet of St Julien, and I to try the appetites of the Breton trout with
the contents of my American fly book.

I had thrashed the stream very conscientiously for three hours, but
not a trout had risen to my cast, and I was piqued. I had begun to
believe that there were no trout in the St Gildas stream, and would
probably have given up had I not seen the sea trout snap the little fly
which the Purple Emperor had named so scientifically. That set me

thinking. Probably the Purple Emperor was right, for he certainly was an expert in everything that crawled and wriggled in Brittany. So I matched, from my American fly book, the fly that the sea trout had snapped up, and withdrawing the cast of three, knotted a new leader to the silk and slipped a fly on the loop. It was a queer fly. It was one of those unnameable experiments which fascinate anglers in sporting stores and which generally prove utterly useless. Moreover, it was a tailed fly, but of course I easily remedied that with a stroke of my penknife. Then I was all ready, and I stepped out into the hurrying rapids and cast straight as an arrow to the spot where the sea trout had risen. Lightly as a plume the fly settled on the bosom of the pool; then came a startling splash, a gleam of silver, and the line tightened from the vibrating rod-tip to the shrieking reel. Almost instantly I checked the fish, and as he floundered for a moment, making the water boil along his glittering sides, I sprang to the bank again, for I saw that the fish was a heavy one and I should probably be in for a long run down the stream. The five-ounce rod swept in a splendid circle, quivering under the strain. 'Oh, for a gaff-hook!' I said aloud, for I was now firmly convinced that I had a salmon to deal with, and no sea trout at all.

Then as I stood, bringing every ounce to bear on the sulking fish, a lithe, slender girl came hurriedly along the opposite bank calling out to me by name.

'Why, Lys!' I said, glancing up for a second, 'I thought you were at St Julien with Yvette.'

'Yvette has gone to Bannalec. I went home and found an awful fight going on at the Groix Inn, and I was so frightened that I came to tell you.'

The fish dashed off at that moment, carrying all the line my reel held, and I was compelled to follow him at a jump. Lys, active and graceful as a young deer, in spite of her Pont-Aven *sabots*, followed along the opposite bank until the fish settled in a deep pool, shook the line savagely once or twice, and then relapsed into the sulks.

'Fight at the Groix Inn?' I called across the water. 'What fight?'

'Not exactly fight,' quavered Lys, 'but the Red Admiral has come out of his house at last, and he and my uncle are drinking together and disputing about butterflies. I never saw my uncle so angry, and the Red Admiral is sneering and grinning. Oh, it is almost wicked to see such a face!'

'But Lys,' I said, scarcely able to repress a smile, 'your uncle and the Red Admiral are always quarrelling and drinking.'

'I know oh, dear me! – but this is different, Monsieur Darrel. The Red Admiral has grown old and fierce since he shut himself up three weeks ago, and – oh, dear! I never saw such a look in my uncle's eyes before. He seemed insane with fury. His eyes – I can't speak of it – and then Terrec came in.'

'Oh,' I said more gravely, 'that was unfortunate. What did the Red Admiral say to his son?'

Lys sat down on a rock among the ferns, and gave me a mutinous glance from her blue eyes.

Yves Terrec, loafer, poacher, and son of Louis Jean Terrec, otherwise the Red Admiral, had been kicked out by his father, and had also been forbidden the village by the Purple Emperor, in his majestic capacity of mayor. Twice the young ruffian had returned: once to rifle the bedroom of the Purple Emperor – an unsuccessful enterprise – and another time to rob his own father. He succeeded in the latter attempt, but was never caught, although he was frequently seen roving about the forests and moors with his gun. He openly menaced the Purple Emperor; vowed that he would marry Lys in spite of all gendarmes in Quimperlé; and these same gendarmes he led many a long chase through brier-filled swamps and over miles of yellow gorse.

What he did to the Purple Emperor – what he intended to do – disquieted me but little; but I worried over his threat concerning Lys. During the last three months this had bothered me a great deal; for when Lys came to St Gildas from the convent the first thing she captured was my heart. For a long time I had refused to believe that any tie of blood linked this dainty blue-eyed creature with the Purple Emperor. Although she dressed in the velvet-laced bodice and blue petticoat of Finistère, and wore the bewitching white *coiffe* of St Gildas, it seemed like a pretty masquerade. To me she was as sweet and as gently bred as many a maiden of the noble Faubourg who danced with her cousins at a Louis XV fête champêtre. So when Lys said that Yves Terrec had returned openly to St Gildas, I felt that I had better be there also.

'What did Terrec say, Lys?' I asked, watching the line vibrating above the placid pool.

The wild rose colour crept into her cheeks. 'Oh,' she answered, with a little toss of her chin, 'you know what he always says.'

'That he will carry you away?'

'Yes.'

'In spite of the Purple Emperor, the Red Admiral, and the gendarmes?'

'Yes.'

'And what do you say, Lys?'

'I? Oh, nothing.'

'Then let me say it for you.'

Lys looked at her delicate pointed *sabots*, the *sabots* from Pont-Aven, made to order. They fitted her little foot. They were her only luxury.

'Will you let me answer for you, Lys?' I asked.

'You, Monsieur Darrel?'

'Yes. Will you let me give him his answer?'

'*Mon Dieu*, why should you concern yourself, Monsieur Darrel?'

The fish lay very quiet, but the rod in my hand trembled.

'Because I love you, Lys.'

The wild rose colour in her cheeks deepened; she gave a gentle gasp, then hid her curly head in her hands.

'I love you, Lys.'

'Do you know what you say?' she stammered.

'Yes, I love you.'

She raised her sweet face and looked at me across the pool.

'I love you,' she said, while the tears stood like stars in her eyes. 'Shall I come over the brook to you?'

II.

That night Yves Terrec left the village of St Gildas vowing vengeance against his father, who refused him shelter.

I can see him now, standing in the road, his bare legs rising like pillars of bronze from his straw-stuffed *sabots*, his short velvet jacket torn and soiled by exposure and dissipation, and his eyes, fierce, roving, bloodshot – while the Red Admiral squeaked curses on him, and hobbled away into his little stone cottage.

'I will not forget you!' cried Yves Terrec, and stretched out his hand toward his father with a terrible gesture. Then he whipped his gun to his cheek and took a short step forward, but I caught him by the throat before he could fire, and a second later we were rolling in the dust of Bannalec road. I had to hit him a heavy blow behind the ear before he would let go, and then, rising and shaking myself, I dashed his muzzle-loading fowling piece to bits against a wall, and threw his knife into the river. The Purple Emperor was looking on with a queer light in his eyes. It was plain that he was sorry Terrec had not choked me to death.

'He would have killed his father,' I said, as I passed him, going toward the Groix Inn.

'That's his business,' snarled the Purple Emperor. There was a deadly light in his eyes. For a moment I thought he was going to attack me; but he was merely viciously drunk, so I shoved him out of my way and went to bed, tired and disgusted.

The worst of it was I couldn't sleep, for I feared that the Purple Emperor might begin to abuse Lys. I lay restlessly tossing among the sheets until I could stay there no longer. I did not dress entirely; I merely slipped on a pair of chaussons and *sabots*, a pair of knicker-bockers, a jersey, and a cap. Then, loosely tying a handkerchief about my throat, I went down the worm-eaten stairs and out into the moonlit road. There was a candle flaring in the Purple Emperor's window, but I could not see him.

'He's probably dead drunk,' I thought, and looked up at the window where, three years before, I had first seen Lys.

'Asleep, thank Heaven!' I muttered, and wandered out along the road. Passing the small cottage of the Red Admiral, I saw that it was dark, but the door was open. I stepped inside the hedge to shut it, thinking, in case Yves Terrec should be roving about, his father would lose whatever he had left.

Then after fastening the door with a stone, I wandered on through the dazzling Breton moonlight. A nightingale was singing in a willow swamp below, and from the edge of the mere, among the tall swamp grasses, myriads of frogs chanted a bass chorus.

When I returned, the eastern sky was beginning to lighten, and across the meadows on the cliffs, outlined against the paling horizon, I saw a seaweed gatherer going to his work among the curling break-ers on the coast. His long rake was balanced on his shoulder, and the sea wind carried his song across the meadows to me:

> *St Gildas!*
> *St Gildas!*
> *Pray for us, Shelter us, Us who toil in the sea.*

Passing the shrine at the entrance of the village took off my cap and knelt in prayer to Our Lady of Faöuet; and if I neglected myself in that prayer, surely I believed Our Lady of Faöuet would be kinder to Lys. It is said that the shrine casts white shadows. I looked, but saw only the moonlight. Then very peacefully I went to bed again, and was only awakened by the clank of sabres and the trample of horses in the road below my window.

'Good gracious!' I thought, 'it must be eleven o'clock, for there are the gendarmes from Quimperlé.'

I looked at my watch; it was only half-past eight, and as the gendarmes made their rounds every Thursday at eleven, I wondered what had brought them out so early to St Gildas.

'Of course,' I grumbled, rubbing my eyes, 'they are after Terrec,' and I jumped into my limited bath.

Before I was completely dressed I heard a timid knock, and opening my door, razor in hand, stood astonished and silent. Lys, her blue eyes wide with terror, leaned on the threshold.

'My darling!' I cried, 'what on earth is the matter?' But she only clung to me, panting like a wounded sea gull. At last, when I drew her into the room and raised her face to mine, she spoke in a heart-breaking voice:

'Oh, Dick! they are going to arrest you, but I will die before I believe one word of what they say. No, don't ask me,' and she began to sob desperately.

When I found that something really serious was the matter, I flung on my coat and cap, and, slipping one arm about her waist, went down the stairs and out into the road. Four gendarmes sat on their horses in front of the café door; beyond them, the entire population of St Gildas gaped, ten deep.

'Hello, Durand!' I said to the brigadier, 'what the devil is this I hear about arresting me?'

'It's true, mon ami,' replied Durand with sepulchral sympathy. I looked him over from the tip of his spurred boots to his sulphur-yellow sabre belt, then upward, button by button, to his disconcerted face.

'What for?' I said scornfully. 'Don't try any cheap sleuth work on me! Speak up, man, what's the trouble?'

The Emperor, who sat in the doorway staring at me, started to speak, but thought better of it and got up and went into the house. The gendarmes rolled their eyes mysteriously and looked wise.

'Come, Durand,' I said impatiently, 'what's the charge?'

'Murder,' he said in a faint voice.

'What!' I cried incredulously. 'Nonsense! Do I look like a murderer? Get off your horse, you stupid — and tell me who's murdered.' Durand got down, looking very silly, and came up to me, offering his hand with a propitiatory grin.

'It was the Purple Emperor who denounced you! See, they found your handkerchief at his door:'

'Whose door, for Heaven's sake?' I cried.

'Why, the Red Admiral's!'

'The Red Admiral's? What has he done?'

'Nothing – he's only been murdered.'

I could scarcely believe my senses, although they took me over to the little stone cottage and pointed out the blood-spattered room. But the horror of the thing was that the corpse of the murdered man had disappeared, and there only remained a nauseating lake of blood on the stone floor, in the centre of which lay a human hand. There was no doubt as to whom the hand belonged, for everybody who had ever seen the Red Admiral knew that the shrivelled bit of flesh which lay in the thickening blood was the hand of the Red Admiral. To me it looked like the severed claw of some gigantic bird.

'Well,' I said, 'there's been murder committed. Why don't you do something?'

'What?' asked Durand.

'I don't know. Send for the Commissaire.'

'He's at Quimperlé. I telegraphed.'

'Then send for a doctor, and find out how long this blood has been coagulating.'

'The chemist from Quimperlé is here; he's a doctor.'

'What does he say?'

'He says that he doesn't know.'

'And who are you going to arrest?' I inquired, turning away from the spectacle on the floor.

'I don't know,' said the brigadier solemnly; 'you are denounced by the Purple Emperor, because he found your handkerchief at the door when he went out this morning.'

'Just like a pig-headed Breton!' I exclaimed thoroughly angry. 'Did he not mention Yves Terrec?'

'No.'

'Of course not,' I said. 'He overlooked the fact that Terrec tried to shoot his father last night and that I took away his gun. All that counts for nothing when he finds my handkerchief at the murdered man's door.'

'Come into the café,' said Durand, much disturbed, 'we can talk it over, there. Of course, Monsieur Darrel, I have never had the faintest idea that you were the murderer!'

The four gendarmes and I walked across the the road to the Groix Inn and entered the café. It was crowded with Britons, smoking, drinking, and jabbering in half a dozen dialects, all equally unsatisfactory to a civilised ear; and I pushed through the crowd to where little Max Fortin, the chemist of Quimperlé, stood smoking a vile cigar.

'This is a bad business,' he said, shaking hands and offering me the mate to his cigar, which I politely declined.

'Now, Monsieur Fortin,' I said, 'it appears that the Purple Emperor found my handkerchief near the murdered man's door this morning, and so he concludes' – here I glared at the Purple Emperor – 'that I am the assassin. I will now ask him a question,' and turning on him suddenly, I shouted, 'What were you doing at the Red Admiral's door?'

The Purple Emperor started and turned pale, and I pointed at him triumphantly.

'See what a sudden question will do. Look how embarrassed he is, and yet I do not charge him with murder; and I tell you, gentlemen, that man there knows as well as I do who was the murderer of the Red Admiral!'

'I don't!' bawled the Purple Emperor.

'You do,' I said. 'It was Yves Terrec.'

'I don't believe it,' he said obstinately, dropping his voice.

' Of course not, being pig-headed.'

'I am not pig-headed,' he roared again, 'but I am mayor of St Gildas, and I do not believe that Yves Terrec killed his father.'

'You saw him try to kill him last night?'

The mayor grunted.

'And you saw what I did.'

He grunted again.

'And,' I went on, 'you heard Yves Terrec threaten to kill his father. You heard him curse the Red Admiral and swear to kill him. Now the father is murdered and his body is gone.'

'And your handkerchief?' sneered the Purple Emperor.

'I dropped it of course.

'And the seaweed gatherer who saw you last night lurking about the Red Admiral's cottage,' grinned the Purple Emperor.

I was startled at the man's malice.

'That will do,' I said. 'It is perfectly true that I was walking on the Bannalec road last night, and that I stopped to close the Red Admiral's door, which was ajar, although his light was not burning. After that I went up the road to the Dinez Woods, and then walked over by St Julien, whence I saw the seaweed gatherer on the cliffs. He was near enough for me to hear what he sang. What of that?'

'What did you do then?'

'Then I stopped at the shrine and said a prayer, and then I went to bed and slept until Brigadier Durand's gendarmes awoke me with their clatter.'

'Now, Monsieur Darrel,' said the Purple Emperor, lifting a fat finger and shooting a wicked glance at me. 'Now, Monsieur Darrel, which did you wear last night on your midnight stroll – *sabots* or shoes?'

I thought a moment. 'Shoes – no, *sabots*. I just slipped on my *chaussons* and went out in my *sabots*.'

'Which was it, shoes or *sabots*?' snarled the Purple Emperor.

'Sabots, you fool.'

'Are these your *sabots*? ' he asked, lifting up a wooden shoe with my initials cut on the instep.

'Yes,' I replied.

'Then how did this blood come on the other one?' he shouted, and held up a sabot, the mate to the first, on which a drop of blood had spattered.

'I haven't the least idea,' I said calmly; but my heart was beating very fast and I was furiously angry.

'You blockhead!' I said, controlling my rage, 'I'll make you pay for this when they catch Yves Terrec and convict him. Brigadier Durand, do your duty if you think I am under suspicion. Arrest me, but grant me one favour. Put me in the Red Admiral's cottage, and I'll see whether I can't find some clew that you have overlooked. Of course, I won't disturb anything until the Commissaire arrives. Bah! You all make me very ill.'

'He's hardened,' observed the Purple Emperor, wagging his head.

'What motive had I to kill the Red Admiral?' I asked them all scornfully. And they all cried:

'None! Yves Terrec is the man!'

Passing out the door I swung around and shook my finger at the Purple Emperor.

'Oh, I'll make you dance for this, my friend,' I said; and I followed Brigadier Durand across the street to the cottage of the murdered man.

III.

They took me at my word and placed a gendarme with a bared sabre at the gateway by the hedge.

'Give me your parole,' said poor Durand, 'and I will let you go where you wish.' But I refused, and began prowling about the cottage looking for clews. I found lots of things that some people would have considered most important, such as ashes from the Red Admiral's pipe, footprints in a dusty vegetable bin, bottles smelling of Pouldu cider, and dust – oh lots of dust. I was not an expert, only a stupid, everyday amateur; so I defaced the footprints with my thick shooting boots, and I declined to examine the pipe ashes through a microscope, although the Red Admiral's microscope stood on the table close at hand.

At last I found what I had been looking for, some long wisps of straw, curiously depressed and flattened in the middle, and I was certain I had found the evidence that would settle Yves Terrec for the rest of his life. It was plain as the nose on your face. The straws were sabot straws, flattened where the foot had pressed them, and sticking straight out where they projected beyond the sabot. Now nobody in St Gildas used straw in *sabots* except a fisherman who lived near St Julien, and the straw in his *sabots* was ordinary yellow wheat straw! This straw, or rather these straws, were from the stalks of the red wheat which only grows inland, and which, everybody in St Gildas knew, Yves Terrec wore in his *sabots*. I was perfectly satisfied; and when, three hours later, a hoarse shouting from the Bannalec Road brought me to the window, I was not surprised to see Yves Terrec, bloody, dishevelled, hatless, with his strong arms bound behind him, walking with bent head between two mounted gendarmes. The crowd around him swelled every minute, crying: 'Parricide! parricide! Death to the murderer!' As he passed my window I saw great clots of mud on his dusty *sabots*, from the heels of which projected wisps of red wheat straw. Then I walked back into the Red Admiral's study, determined to find what the microscope would show on the wheat straws. I examined each one very carefully, and then, my eyes aching, I rested my chin on my hand and leaned back in the chair. I had not been as fortunate as some detectives, for there was no evidence that the straws had ever been used in a sabot at all. Furthermore, directly across the hallway stood a carved Breton chest, and now I noticed for the first time that, from beneath the closed lid, dozens of similar red wheat straws projected, bent exactly as mine were bent by the lid.

I yawned in disgust. It was apparent that I was not cut out for a detective, and I bitterly pondered over the difference between clews in real life and clews in a detective story. After a while I rose, walked over to the chest and opened the lid. The interior was wadded with the red wheat straws, and on this wadding lay two curious glass jars, two or three small vials, several empty bottles labelled chloroform, a collecting jar of cyanide of potassium, and a book. In a farther corner of the chest were some letters bearing English stamps, and also the torn coverings of two parcels, all from England, and all directed to the Red Admiral under his proper name of 'Sieur Louis Jean Terrec, St Gildas, par Moëlan, Finistère'.

All these traps I carried over to the desk, shut the lid of the chest, and sat down to read the letters. They were written in commercial French, evidently by an Englishman.

Freely translated, the contents of the first letter were as follows:

LONDON, June 12, 1894.
DEAR MONSIEUR *(sic)*: Your kind favour of the 19th inst received and contents noted. The latest work on the Lepidoptera of England is Blowzer's *How To Catch British Butterflies*, with notes and tables, and an introduction by Sir Thomas Sniffer. The price of this work (in one volume, calf) is £5 or 125 francs of French money. A post-office order will receive our prompt attention. We beg to remain,
Yours, etc,
FRADLEY & TOOMER
470 Regent Square, London, SW.

The next letter was even less interesting. It merely stated that the money had been received and the book would be forwarded. The third engaged my attention, and I shall quote it, the translation being a free one:

DEAR SIR: Your letter of the 1st of July was duly received, and we at once referred it to Mr Fradley himself. Mr Fradley being much interested in your question, sent your letter to Professor Schweineri, of the Berlin Entomological Society, whose note Blowzer refers to on page 630, in his *How To Catch British Butterflies*. We have just received an answer from Professor Schweineri, which we translate into French – (see inclosed slip). Professor Schweineri begs to present to you two jars of cythyl, prepared under his own supervision. We forward the same to you. Trusting that you will find everything satisfactory, we remain,
Yours sincerely,
FRADLEY & TOOMER.
The inclosed slip read as follows:
Messrs. FRADLEY & TOOMER,
GENTLEMEN: Cythaline, a complex hydrocarbon, was first used by Professor Schnoot, of Antwerp, a year ago. I discov-

ered an analogous formula about the same time and named it cythyl.

I have used it with great success everywhere. It is as certain as a magnet. I beg to present you three small jars, and would be pleased to have you forward two of them to your correspondent in St Gildas with my compliments. Blowzer's quotation of me on page 630 of his glorious work, *How To Catch British Butterflies*, is correct.

Yours, etc.

HEINRICH SCHWEINERI, PHD, DD, DS, MS'

When I had finished this letter I folded it up and put it into my pocket with the others. Then I opened Blowzer's valuable work, *How To Catch British Butterflies*, and turned to page 630.

Now, although the Red Admiral could only have acquired the book very recently, and although all the other pages were perfectly clean, this particular page was thumbed black, and heavy pencil marks inclosed a paragraph at the bottom of the page. This the paragraph:

'Professor Schweineri says: "Of the two old methods used by collectors for the capture of the swift-winged, high-flying *Apatura Iris*, or Purple Emperor, the first, which was using a long-handled net, proved successful once in a thousand times; and the second, the placing of bait upon the ground, such as decayed meat, dead cats, rats, etc, was not only disagreeable, even for an enthusiastic collector, but also very uncertain. Once in five hundred times would the splendid butterfly leave the tops of his favourite oak trees to circle about the fetid bait offered. I have found cythyl a perfectly sure bait to draw this beautiful butterfly to the ground, where it can be easily captured. An ounce of cythyl placed in a yellow saucer under an oak tree, will draw to it every *Apatura Iris* within a radius of twenty miles. So, if any collector who possesses a little cythyl, even though it be in a sealed bottle in his pocket – if such a collector does not find a single *Apatura Iris* fluttering close about him within an hour, let him be satisfied that the *Apatura Iris* does not inhabit his country."

When I had finished reading this note I sat for a long while thinking hard. Then I examined the two jars. They were labelled *Cythyl*. One was full, the other *nearly full*. 'The rest must be on the corpse of the Red Admiral,' I thought, 'no matter if it is in a corked bottle... '

I took all the things back to the chest, laid them carefully on the straw, and closed the lid. The gendarme sentinel at the gate saluted me respectfully as I crossed over to the Groix Inn. The inn was surrounded by an excited crowd, and the hallway was choked with gendarmes and peasants. On every side they greeted me cordially, announcing that the real murderer was caught; but I pushed by them without a word and ran upstairs to find Lys. She opened her door when I knocked and threw both arms about my neck. I took her to my breast and kissed her. After a moment I asked her if she would obey me no matter what I commanded, and she said she would, with a proud humility that touched me.

'Then go at once to Yvette in St Julien,' I said. 'Ask her to harness the dog-cart and drive to the convent in Quimperlé. Wait for me there. Will you do this without questioning me, my darling?'

She raised her face to mine. 'Kiss me,' she said innocently; the next moment she had vanished.

I walked deliberately into the Purple Emperor's room and peered into the gauze-covered box which held the chrysalis of *Apatura Iris*. It was as I expected. The chrysalis was empty and transparent, and a great crack ran down the middle of its back, but, on the netting inside the box, a magnificent butterfly slowly waved its burnished purple wings; for the chrysalis had given up its silent tenant, the butterfly symbol of immortality. Then a great fear fell upon me. I know now that it was the fear of the Black Priest, but neither then nor for years after did I know that the Black Priest had ever lived on earth. As I bent over the box I heard a confused murmur outside the house which ended in a furious shout of 'Parricide!' and I heard the gendarmes ride away behind a wagon which rattled sharply on the flinty highway. I went to the window. In the wagon sat Yves Terrec, bound and wild-eyed, two gendarmes at either side of him, and all around the wagon rode mounted gendarmes whose bared sabres scarcely kept the crowd away.

'Parricide!' they howled. 'Let him die!'

I stepped back and opened the gauze-covered box. Very gently but firmly I took the splendid butterfly by its closed fore wings and lifted it unharmed between my thumb and forefinger. Then, holding it concealed behind my back, I went down into the café.

Of all the crowd that had filled it, shouting for the death of Yves Terrec, only three persons remained seated in front of the huge empty fireplace. They were the Brigadier Durand, Max Fortin, the chemist of Quimperlé, and the Purple Emperor. The latter looked abashed when I entered, but I paid no attention to him and walked straight to the chemist.

'Monsieur Fortin,' I said, 'do you know much about hydrocarbons?'

'They are my specialty,' he said astonished.

'Have you ever heard of such thing as cythyl?'

'Schweineri's cythyl? Oh, yes! We use it in perfumery.'

'Good!' I said. 'Has it an odour?'

'No – and yes. One is always aware of its presence, but nobody can affirm it has an odour. It is curious,' he continued, looking at me, 'it is very curious you should have asked me that, for all day I have been imagining I detected the presence of cythyl.'

'Do you imagine so now?' I asked.

'Yes, more than ever.'

I sprang to the front door and tossed out the butterfly. The splendid creature beat the air for a moment, flitted uncertainly hither and thither, and then, to my astonishment, sailed majestically back into the café and alighted on the hearthstone. For a moment I was nonplussed, but when my eyes rested on the Purple Emperor I comprehended in a flash.

'Lift that hearthstone!' I cried to the Brigadier Durand; 'pry it up with your scabbard!'

The Purple Emperor suddenly fell forward in his chair, his face ghastly white, his jaw loose with terror.

'What is cythyl?' I shouted, seizing him by the arm; but he plunged heavily from his chair, face downward on the floor, and at the moment a cry from the chemist made me turn. There stood the Brigadier Durand, one hand supporting the hearthstone, one hand raised in horror. There stood Max Fortin, the chemist, rigid with excitement, and below, in the hollow bed where the hearthstone had rested, lay a crushed mass of bleeding human flesh, from the midst of which stared a cheap glass eye. I seized the Purple Emperor and dragged him to his feet.

'Look!' I cried; 'look at your old friend, the Red Admiral!' but he only smiled in a vacant way, and rolled his head muttering; 'Bait for butterflies! Cythyl! Oh, no, no, no! You can't do it, Admiral, d'ye see. I alone own the Purple Emperor! I alone am the Purple Emperor!'

And the same carriage that bore me to Quimperlé to claim my bride, carried him to Quimper, gagged and bound, a foaming, howling lunatic.

This, then, is the story of the Purple Emperor. I might tell you a pleasanter story if I chose; but concerning the fish that I had hold of, whether it was a salmon, a grilse, or a sea trout, I may not say, because I have promised Lys, and she has promised me, that no power on earth shall wring from our lips the mortifying confession that the fish escaped.

GUY BOOTHBY

The Duchess of Wiltshire's Diamonds

TO THE REFLECTIVE mind the rapidity with which the inhabitants of the world's greatest city seize upon a new name or idea, and familiarise themselves with it, can scarcely prove otherwise than astonishing. As an illustration of my meaning let me take the case of Klimo – the now famous private detective, who has won for himself the right to be considered as great as Lecocq, or even the late lamented Sherlock Holmes.

Up to a certain morning London had never even heard his name, nor had it the remotest notion as to who or what he might be. It was as sublimely ignorant and careless on the subject as the inhabitants of Kamtchatka or Peru. Within twenty-fours hours, however, the whole aspect of the case was changed. The man, woman, or child who had not seen his posters, or heard his name, was counted an ignoramus unworthy of intercourse with human beings.

Princes became familiar with it as their trains bore them to Windsor to luncheon with the Queen; the nobility noticed and commented upon it as they drove about the town; merchants, and business men generally, read it as they made ways by omnibus or underground, to their various shops and counting-houses; street boys called each other by it as a nickname; music hail artists introduced it into their patter, while it was even rumoured that the Stock Exchange itself had paused in the full flood of business to manufacture a riddle on the subject.

That Klimo made his profession pay him well was certain, first from the fact that his advertisements must have cost a good round sum, and, second, because he had taken a mansion in Belverton Street, Park Lane, next door to Porchester House, where, to the dismay of that aristocratic neighbourhood, he advertised that he was prepared to receive and be consulted by his clients. The invitation was responded to with alacrity, and from that day forward, between the hours of twelve and two, the pavement upon the north side of the street was lined with carriages, every one containing some person desirous of testing the great man's skill.

I must here explain that I have narrated all this in order to show the state of affairs in Belverton Street and Park Lane when Simon Carne arrived, or was supposed to arrive, in Kingsland. If my memory serves me correctly, it was on Wednesday, the 3rd of May, that the Earl of Amberley drove to Victoria to meet and welcome the man whose acquaintance he had made in India under such peculiar circumstances, and under the spell of whose fascination he and his family had fallen so completely.

Reaching the station, his lordship descended from his carriage, and made his way to the platform set apart for the reception of the Continental express. He walked with a jaunty air, and seemed to be on the best of terms with himself and the world in general. How little he suspected the existence of the noose into which he was so innocently running his head!

As if out of compliment to his arrival, the train put in an appearance within a few moments of his reaching the platform. He immediately placed himself in such a position that he could make sure of seeing the man he wanted, and waited patiently until he should come in sight. Carne, however, was not among the first batch; indeed, most passengers had passed before his lordship caught sight of him.

One thing was very certain, however great the crush might have been, it would have been difficult to mistake Carne's figure. The man's infirmity and the peculiar beauty of his face rendered him easily recognisable. Possibly, after his long sojourn in India, he found the morning cold, for he wore a long fur coat, the collar of which he had turned up round his ears, thus making a fitting frame for his delicate face. On seeing Lord Amberley he hastened forward to greet him.

'This is most kind and friendly of you,' he said, as he shook the other by the hand. 'A fine day and Lord Amberley to meet me. One could scarcely imagine a better welcome.'

As he spoke, one of his Indian servants approached and salaamed before him. He gave him an order, and received an answer in Hindustani, whereupon he turned again to Lord Amberley.

'You may imagine how anxious I am to see my new dwelling,' he said. 'My servant tells me that my carriage is here, so may I hope that you will drive back with me and see for yourself how I am likely to be lodged?'

'I shall be delighted,' said Lord Amberley, who was longing for the opportunity, and they accordingly went out into the station yard together to discover a brougham, drawn by two magnificent horses, and with Nur Ali, in all the glory of white raiment and crested turban, on the box, waiting to receive them. His lordship dismissed his Victoria, and when Jowur Singh had taken his place beside his fellow servant upon the box, the carriage rolled out of the station yard in the direction of Hyde Park.

'I trust her ladyship is quite well,' said Simon Carne politely, as they turned into Gloucester Place.

'Excellently well, thank you,' replied his lordship. 'She bade me welcome you to England in her name as well as my own, and I was to say that she is looking forward to seeing you.'

'She is most kind, and I shall do myself the honour of calling upon her as soon as circumstances will permit,' answered Carne. 'I beg you will convey my best thanks to her for her thought of me.'

While these polite speeches were passing between them they were rapidly approaching a large hoarding, on which was displayed a poster setting forth the name of the now famous detective, Klimo.

Simon Carne, leaning forward, studied it, and when they had passed, turned to his friend again.

'At Victoria and on all the hoardings we meet I see an enormous placard, bearing the word "Klimo". Pray, what does it mean?'

His lordship laughed.

'You are asking a question which, a month ago, was on the lips of nine out of every ten Londoners. It is only within the last fortnight that we have learned who and what "Klimo" is.'

'And pray what is he?'

'Well, the explanation is very simple. He is neither more nor less than a remarkably astute private detective, who has succeeded in attracting notice in such a way that half London has been induced to patronise him. I have had no dealings with the man myself. But a friend of mine, Lord Orpington, has been the victim of a most audacious burglary, and, the police having failed to solve the mystery, he has called Klimo in. We shall therefore see what he can do before many days are past. But, there, I expect you will soon know more about him than any of us.'

'Indeed! And why?'

'For the simple reason that he has taken number one, Belverton Terrace, the house adjoining your own, and sees his clients there.'

Simon Carne pursed up his lips, and appeared to be considering something.

'I trust he will not prove a nuisance,' he said at last. 'The agents who found me the house should have acquainted me with the fact. Private detectives, on however large a scale, scarcely strike one as the most desirable of neighbours, particularly for a man who is so fond of quiet as myself.' At this moment they were approaching their destination.

As the carriage passed Belverton Street and pulled up, Lord Amberley pointed to a long line of vehicles standing before the detective's door.

'You can see for yourself something of the business he does,' he said. 'Those are the carriages of his clients, and it is probable that twice as many have arrived on foot.'

'I shall certainly speak to the agent on the subject,' said Carne, with a shadow of annoyance upon his face. 'I consider the fact of this man's being so close to me a serious drawback to the house.'

Jowur Singh here descended from the box and opened the door in order that his master and his guest might alight, while portly Ram Gafur, the butler, came down the steps and salaamed before them with Oriental obsequiousness. Carne greeted his domestics with kindly condescension, and then, accompanied by the ex-Viceroy, entered his new abode.

'I think you may congratulate yourself upon having secured one of the most desirable residences in London,' said his lordship ten minutes or so later, when they had explored the principal rooms.

'I am very glad to hear you say so,' said Carne. 'I trust your lordship will remember that you will always be welcome in the house as long as I am its owner.'

'It is very kind of you to say so,' returned Lord Amberley warmly. 'I shall look forward to some months of pleasant intercourse. And now I must be going. Tomorrow, perhaps, if you have nothing better to do, you will give us the pleasure of your company at dinner. Your fame has already gone abroad, and we shall ask one or two nice people to meet you, including my brother and sister-in-law, Lord and Lady Gelpington, Lord and Lady Orpington, and my cousin, the Duchess of Wiltshire, whose interest in china and Indian art, as perhaps you know, is only second to your own. '

'I shall be most glad to come.'

wall between the two houses was disclosed. Through this door Carne passed, drawing it behind him.

In number one, Belverton Terrace, the house occupied by the detective, whose presence in the street Carne seemed to find so objectionable, the entrance thus constructed was covered by the peculiar kind of confessional box in which Klimo invariably sat to receive his clients, the rearmost panels of which opened in the same fashion as those in the wardrobe in the dressing-room. These being pulled aside, he had but to draw them to again after him, take his seat, ring the electric bell to inform his housekeeper that he was ready, and then welcome his clients as quickly as they cared to come.

Punctually at two o'clock the interviews ceased, and Klimo, having reaped an excellent harvest of fees, returned to Porchester House to become Simon Carne once more.

Possibly it was due to the fact that the Earl and Countess of Amberley were brimming over with his praise, or it may have been the rumour that he was worth as many millions as you have fingers upon your hand that did it; one thing, however, was self evident, within twenty-four hours of the noble earl's meeting him at Victoria Station, Simon Carne was the talk, not only of fashionable, but also of unfashionable London.

That his household were, with one exception, natives of India, that he had paid a rental for Porchester House which ran into five figures, that he was the greatest living authority upon china and Indian art generally, and that he had come over to England in search of a wife, were among the smallest of the *canards* set afloat concerning him.

During dinner next evening Carne put forth every effort to please. He was placed on the right hand of his hostess and next to the Duchess of Wiltshire. To the latter he paid particular attention, and to such good purpose that when the ladies returned to the drawing-room afterwards, Her Grace was full of his praises. They had discussed china of all sorts, Carne had promised her a specimen which she had longed for all her life, but had never been able to obtain, and in return she had promised to show him the quaintly carved Indian casket in which the famous necklace, of which he of course, heard, spent most of its time. She would be wearing the jewels in question at her own ball in a week's time, she informed him, and if he would care to see the case when it came from her bankers on that day, she would be only too pleased to show it to him.

As Simon Carne drove home in his luxurious brougham afterwards, he smiled to himself as he thought of the success which was attending his first endeavour. Two of the guests, who were stewards of the Jockey Club, had heard with delight his idea of purchasing a horse, in order to have an interest in the Derby. While another, on hearing that he desired to become the possessor of a yacht, had offered to propose him for the RCYC. To crown it all, however, and much better than all, the Duchess of Wiltshire had promised to show him her famous diamonds.

'But satisfactory as my progress has been hitherto,' he said to himself, 'it is difficult to see how I am to get possession of the stones. From what I have been able to discover, they are only brought from the bank on the day the Duchess intends to wear them, and they are taken back by His Grace the morning following.

'While she has got them on her person it would be manifestly impossible to get them from her. And as, when she takes them off, they are returned to their box and placed in a safe, constructed in the wall of the bedroom adjoining, and which for the occasion is occupied by the butler and one of the under-footmen, the only key being in the possession of the Duke himself, it would be equally foolish to hope to appropriate them. In what manner, therefore, I am to become their possessor passes my comprehension. However, one thing is certain, obtained they must be, and the attempt must be made on the night of the ball if possible. In the meantime I'll set my wits to work upon a plan.'

Next day Simon Carne was the recipient of an invitation to the ball in question, and two days later he called upon the Duchess of Wiltshire, at her residence in Belgrave Square, with a plan prepared. He also took with him the small vase he had promised her four nights before. She received him most graciously, and their talk fell at once into the usual channel. Having examined her collection, and charmed her by means of one or two judicious criticisms, he asked permission to include photographs of certain of her treasures in his forthcoming book, then little by little he skilfully guided the conversation on to the subject of jewels.

'Since we are discussing gems, Mr Carne,' she said, 'perhaps it would interest you to see my famous necklace. By good fortune I have it in the house now, for the reason that an alteration is being made to one of the clasps by my jewellers.'

'I should like to see it immensely,' answered Carne. 'At one time and another I have had the good fortune to examine the jewels of the leading Indian princes, and I should like to be able to say that I have seen the famous Wiltshire necklace.'

'Then you shall certainly have the honour,' she answered with a smile. 'If you will ring that bell I will send for it.'

Carne rang the bell as requested, and when the butler entered he was given the key of the safe and ordered to bring the case to the drawing-room.

'We must not keep it very long,' she observed while the man was absent. 'It is to be returned to the bank in an hour's time.'

'I am indeed fortunate,' Carne replied, and turned to the description of some curious Indian wood carving, of which he was making a special feature in his book. As he explained, he had collected his illustrations from the doors of Indian temples, from the gateways of palaces, from old brass work, and even from carved chairs and boxes he had picked up in all sorts of odd corners. Her Grace was most interested.

'How strange that you should have mentioned it,' she said. 'If carved boxes have any interest for you, it is possible my jewel case itself may be of use to you. As I think I told you during Lady Amberley's dinner, it came from Benares, and has carved upon it the portraits of nearly every god in the Hindu Pantheon.'

'You raise my curiosity to fever heat,' said Carne.

A few moments later the servant returned, bringing with him a wooden box, about sixteen inches long by twelve wide, and eight deep, which he placed upon a table beside his mistress, after which he retired.

'This is the case to which I have just been referring,' said the Duchess, placing her hand on the article in question. 'If you glance at it you will see how exquisitely it is carved.'

Concealing his eagerness with an effort, Simon Carne drew his chair up to the table, and examined the box.

It was with justice she had described it as a work of art. What the wood was of which it was constructed Carne was unable to tell. It was dark and heavy, and, though it was not teak, closely resembled it. It was literally covered with quaint carving and of its kind was an unique work of art.

'It is most curious and beautiful,' said Carne when he had finished his examination. 'In all my experience I can safely say I have never seen its equal. If you will permit me I should very much like to include a description and an illustration of it in my book.'

'Of course you may do so; I shall be only too delighted,' answered Her Grace. 'If it will help you in your work I shall be glad to lend it to you for a few hours, in order that you may have the illustration made.'

This was exactly what Carne had been waiting for, and he accepted the offer with alacrity.

'Very well, then,' she said. 'On the day of my ball, when it will be brought from the bank again, I will take the necklace out and send the case to you. I must make one proviso, however, and that is that you let me have it back the same day.'

'I will certainly promise to do that,' replied Carne.

'And now let us look inside,' said his hostess.

Choosing a key from a bunch she carried in her pocket, she unlocked the casket, and lifted the lid. Accustomed as Carne had all his life been to the sight of gems, what he then saw before him almost took his breath away. The inside of box, both sides and bottom, was quilted with the softest Russia leather, and on this luxurious couch reposed the famous necklace. The fire of the stones when the light caught them was sufficient to dazzle the eyes, so fierce was it.

As Carne could see, every gem was perfect of its kind, and there were no fewer than three hundred of them. The setting was a fine example of the jeweller's art, and last, but not least, the value of the whole affair was fifty thousand pounds, a mere flea-bite to the man who had given it to his wife, but a fortune to any humbler person.

'And now that you have seen my property, what do you think of it?' asked the Duchess as she watched her visitor's face.

'It is very beautiful,' he answered, 'and I do not wonder that you are proud of it. Yes, the diamonds are very fine, but I think it is their abiding place that fascinates me more. Have you any objection to my measuring it?'

'Pray do so, if it is likely to be of any assistance to you,' replied Her Grace.

Carne therefore produced a small ivory rule, ran it over the box, and the figures he thus obtained he jotted down in his pocket-book.

Ten minutes later, when the case had been returned to the safe, he thanked the Duchess for her kindness and took his departure, promising to call in person for the empty case on the morning of the ball.

Reaching home he passed into his study, and, seating himself at his writing table, pulled a sheet of notepaper towards him and began to sketch, as well as he could remember it, the box he had seen. Then he leant back in his chair and closed his eyes.

'I have cracked a good many hard nuts in my time,' he said reflectively, 'but never one that seemed so difficult at first sight as this. As far as I see at present, the case stands as follows: the box will be brought from the bank where it usually reposes to Wiltshire House on the morning of the dance. I shall be allowed to have possession of it, without the stones of course, for a period possibly extending from eleven o'clock in the morning to four or five, at any rate not later than seven in the evening. After the ball the necklace will be returned to it, when it will be locked up in the safe, over which the butler and a footman will mount guard.

'To get into the room during the night is not only too risky, but physically out of the question; while to rob Her Grace of her treasure during the progress of the dance would be equally impossible. The Duke fetches the casket and takes it back to the bank himself, so that to all intents and purposes I am almost as far off the solution as ever.'

Half an hour went by and found him still seated at his desk, staring at the drawing on the paper, then an hour. The traffic of the streets rolled past the house unheeded. Finally Jowur Singh announced his carriage, and, feeling that an idea might come to him with a change of scene, he set off for a drive in the park.

By this time his elegant mail phaeton, with its magnificent horses and Indian servant on the seat behind was as well-known as Her Majesty's state equipage, and attracted almost as much attention. Today, however, the fashionable world noticed that Simon Carne looked preoccupied. He was still working out his problem, but so far without much success. Suddenly something, no one will ever be able to say what, put an idea into his head. The notion was no sooner born in his brain than he left the park and drove quickly home. Ten minutes had scarcely elapsed before he was back in his study again, and had ordered that Wajib Baksh should be sent to him.

When the man he wanted put in an appearance, Carne handed him the paper upon which he had made the drawing of the jewel case.

'This is most wonderful,' he said. And indeed it was as clever a conjuring trick as any he had ever seen.

'Nay, it is very simple,' Wajib Baksh replied. 'The Heaven-born told me that there must be no risk of detection.'

He took the box in his own hands and running his nails down the centre of the quilting, divided the false bottom into two pieces; these he lifted out, revealing the comb lying upon the real bottom beneath.

'The sides, as my lord will see,' said Hiram Singh, taking a step forward, 'are held in their appointed places by these two springs. Thus when the key is turned the springs relax, and the sides are driven by others into their places on the bottom, where the seams in the quilting mask the join. There is but one disadvantage. It is as follows: when the pieces which form the bottom are lifted out in order that my lord may get at whatever lies concealed beneath, the springs must of necessity stand revealed. However, to anyone who knows sufficient of the working of the box to lift out the false bottom, it will be an easy matter to withdraw the springs and conceal them about his person.'

'As you say that is an easy matter,' said Carne, 'and I shall not be likely to forget. Now one other question. Presuming I am in a position to put the real box into your hands for say eight hours, do you think that in that time you can fit it up so that detection will be impossible?'

'Assuredly, my lord,' replied Hiram Singh with conviction. 'There is but the lock and the fitting of the springs to be done. Three hours at most would suffice for that.'

'I am pleased with you,' said Carne. 'As a proof of my satisfaction, when the work is finished you will each receive five hundred rupees. Now you can go.'

According to his promise, ten o'clock on the Friday following found him in his hansom driving towards Belgrave Square. He was a little anxious, though the casual observer would scarcely have been able to tell it. The magnitude of the stake for which he was playing was enough to try the nerve of even such a past master in his profession as Simon Carne.

Arriving at the house he discovered some workmen erecting an awning across the footway in preparation for the ball that was to take place that night. It was not long, however, before he found himself in the boudoir, reminding Her Grace of her promise to permit him an opportunity of making a drawing of the famous jewel case. The Duchess was naturally busy, and within a quarter of an hour he was on his way home with the box placed on the seat of the carriage beside him.

'Now,' he said, as he patted it good-humouredly, 'if only the notion worked out by Hiram Singh and Wajib Baksh holds good, the famous Wiltshire diamonds will become my property before very many hours are passed. By this time tomorrow, I suppose London will be all agog concerning the burglary.'

On reaching his house he left his carriage, and carried the box into the study. Once there he rang his bell and ordered Hiram Singh and Wajib Baksh to be sent to him. When they arrived he showed them the box upon which they were to exercise their ingenuity.

'Bring the tools in here,' he said, 'and do the work under my own eyes. You have but nine hours before you, so you must make the most of them.'

The men went for their implements, and as soon as they were ready set to work. All through the day they were kept hard at it, with the result that by five o'clock the alterations had been effected and the case stood ready. By the time Carne returned from his afternoon drive in the Park it was quite prepared for the part it was to play in his scheme. Having praised the men, he turned them out and locked the door, then went across the room and unlocked a drawer in his writing table. From it he took a flat leather jewel case, which he opened. It contained a necklace of counterfeit diamonds, if anything a little larger than the one he intended to try to obtain. He had purchased it that morning in the Burlington Arcade for the purpose of testing the apparatus his servants had made, and this he now proceeded to do.

Laying it carefully upon the bottom he closed the lid and turned the key. When he opened it again the necklace was gone, and even though he knew the secret he could not for the life of him see where the false bottom began and ended. After that he reset the trap and tossed the necklace carelessly in. To his delight it acted as well as on the previous occasion. He could scarcely contain his satisfaction. His conscience was sufficiently elastic to give him no trouble. To him it was scarcely a robbery he was planning, but an artistic trial of skill, in which he pitted his wits and cunning against the forces of society in general.

At half-past seven he dined, and afterwards smoked a meditative cigar over the evening paper in the billiard room. The invitations to the ball were for ten o'clock, and at nine-thirty he went to his dressing-room.

'Make me tidy as quickly as you can,' he said to Belton when the latter appeared, 'and while you are doing so listen to my final instructions.

'Tonight, as you know, I am endeavouring to secure the Duchess of Wiltshire's necklace. Tomorrow morning all London will resound with the hubbub, and I have been making my plans in such a way as to arrange that Klimo shall be the first person consulted. When the messenger calls, if call he does, see that the old woman next door bids him tell the Duke to come personally at twelve o'clock. Do you understand?'

'Perfectly, sir.'

'Very good. Now give me the jewel case, and let me be off. You need not sit up for me.'

Precisely as the clocks in the neighbourhood were striking ten

Simon Carne reached Belgrave Square, and, as he hoped, found himself the first guest.

His hostess and her husband received him in the anteroom of the drawing-room.

'I come laden with a thousand apologies,' he said as he took Her Grace's hand, and bent over it with that ceremonious politeness which was one of the man's chief characteristics. 'I am most unconscionably early, I know, but I hastened here in order that I might personally return the jewel case you so kindly lent me. I must trust to your generosity to forgive me. The drawings took longer than I expected.'

'Please do not apologise,' answered Her Grace. 'It is very kind of you to have brought the case yourself. I hope the illustrations have proved successful. I shall look forward to seeing them as soon as they are ready. But I am keeping you holding the box. One of my servants will take it to my room.'

She called a footman to her, and bade him take the box and place it upon her dressing-table.

'Before it goes I must let you see that I have not damaged it either externally or internally,' said Carne with a laugh. 'It is such a valuable case that I should never forgive myself if it had even received a scratch during the time it has been in my possession.'

So saying he lifted the lid and allowed her to look inside. To all appearances it was exactly the same as when she had lent it to him earlier in the day.

'You have been most careful,' she said. And then, with an air of banter, she continued: 'If you desire it, I shall be pleased to give you a certificate to that effect.'

They jested in this fashion for a few moments after the servant's departure, during which time Carne promised to call upon her the following morning at o'clock, and to bring with him the illustrations he had made and a queer little piece of china he had had the good fortune to pick up in a dealer's shop the previous afternoon. By this time fashionable London was making its way up the grand staircase, and with its appearance further conversation became impossible.

Shortly after midnight Carne bade his hostess goodnight and slipped away. He was perfectly satisfied with his evening's entertainment, and if the key of the jewel case were not turned before the jewels were placed in it, he was convinced they would become his property. It speaks well for his strength of nerve when I record the fact that on going to bed his slumbers were as peaceful and untroubled as those of a little child.

Breakfast was scarcely over next morning before a hansom drew up at his front door and Lord Amberley alighted. He was ushered into Carne's presence forthwith, and on seeing that the latter was surprised at his early visit, hastened to explain.

'My dear fellow,' he said, as he took possession of the chair the other offered him, 'I have come round to see you on most important business. As I told you last night at the dance, when you so kindly asked me to come and see the steam yacht you have purchased, I had an appointment with Wiltshire at half-past nine this morning. On reaching Belgrave Square, I found the whole house in confusion. Servants were running hither and thither with scared faces, the butler was on the borders of lunacy, the Duchess was well-nigh hysterical in her boudoir, while her husband was in his study vowing vengeance against all the world.'

'You alarm me,' said Carne, lighting a cigarette with a hand that was as steady as a rock. 'What on earth has happened?'

'I think I might safely allow you fifty guesses and then wager a hundred pounds you'd not hit the mark; and yet in a certain measure it concerns you.'

'Concerns me? Good gracious! What have I done to bring all this about?'

'Pray do not look so alarmed,' said Amberley. 'Personally you have done nothing. Indeed, on second thoughts, I don't know that I am right in saying that it concerns you at al. The fact of the matter is, Carne, a burglary took place last night at Wiltshire House, *and the famous necklace has disappeared.*'

'Good heavens! You don't say so?'

'But I *do*. The circumstances of the case are as follows: When my cousin retired to her room last night after the ball, she unclasped the necklace, and, in her husband's presence, placed it carefully in her jewel case, which she locked. That having been done, Wiltshire took the box to the room which contained the safe, and himself placed it there, locking the iron door with his own key. The room was occupied that night, according to custom, by the butler and one of the footmen, both of whom have been in the family since they were boys.

'Next morning, after breakfast, the Duke unlocked the safe and took out the box, intending to convey it to the bank as usual. Before leaving, however, he placed it on his study-table and went upstairs to speak to his wife. He cannot remember exactly how long he was absent, but he feels convinced that he was not gone more than a quarter of an hour at the very utmost.

'Their conversation finished, she accompanied him downstairs, where she saw him take up the case to carry it to his carriage. Before he left the house, however, she said: 'I suppose you have looked to see that the necklace is all right?' 'How could I do so?' was his reply. 'You know you possess the only key that will fit it.'

'She felt in her pockets, but to her surprise the key was not there.'

'If I were a detective I should say that that is a point to be remembered,' said Carne with a smile. 'Pray, where did she find her keys?'

'Upon her dressing-table,' said Amberley. 'Though she has not the slightest recollection of leaving them there.'

'Well, when she had procured the keys, what happened?'

'Why, they opened the box, and, to their astonishment and dismay, *found it empty. The jewels were gone!*'

'Good gracious! What a terrible loss! It seems almost impossible that it can be true. And pray, what did they do?'

'At first they stood staring into the empty box, hardly believing the evidence of their own eyes. Stare how they would, however, they could not bring them back. The jewels had, without doubt, disappeared, but when and where the robbery had taken place it was impossible to say. After that they had up all the servants and questioned them, but the result was what they might have foreseen, no one from the butler to the kitchen maid could throw any light upon the subject. To this minute it remains as great a mystery as when they first discovered it.'

'I am more concerned than I can tell you,' said Carne. 'How thankful I ought to be that I returned the case to Her Grace last night. But in thinking of myself I am forgetting to ask what has brought you to me. If I can be of any assistance I hope you will command me.'

'Well, I'll tell you why I have come,' replied Lord Amberley. 'Naturally, they are most anxious to have the mystery solved and the jewels recovered as soon as possible. Wiltshire wanted to send to Scotland Yard there and then, but his wife and I eventually persuaded him to consult Klimo. As you know, if the police authorities are called in first, he refuses the business altogether. Now, we thought, you are his next door neighbour, you might possibly be able to assist us.

'You may be very sure, my lord, I will do everything that lies in my power. Let us go in and see him at once.'

As he spoke he rose and threw what remained of his cigarette into the fireplace. His visitor having imitated his example, they procured their hats and walked round from Park Lane into Belverton Street to bring up at number one. After they had rung the bell the door was opened to them by the old woman who invariably received the detective's clients.

'Is Mr Klimo at home?' asked Carne. 'And if so, can we see him?'

The old lady was a little deaf, and the question had to be repeated before she could be made to understand what was wanted. As soon, however, as she realised their desire, she informed them that her master was absent from town, but would be back as usual at twelve o'clock to meet his clients.

'What on earth's to be done?' said the Earl, looking at his companion in dismay. 'I am afraid I can't come back again, as I have a most important appointment at that hour.'

'Do you think you could entrust the business to me?' asked Carne. 'If so, I will make a point of seeing him at twelve o'clock, and could call at Wiltshire House afterwards and tell the Duke what I have done.'

'That's very good of you,' replied Amberley. 'If you are sure it would not put you to too much trouble, that would be quite the best thing to be done. '

'I will do it with pleasure,' Carne replied. 'I feel it my duty to help in whatever way I can.'

'You are very kind,' said the other. 'Then, as I understand it, you are to call upon Klimo at twelve o'clock, and afterwards to let my cousins know what you have succeeded in doing. I only hope he will help us to secure the thief. We are having too many of these burglaries just now. I must catch this hansom and be off. Goodbye, and many thanks.'

'Goodbye,' said Carne, and shook him by the hand.

The hansom having rolled away, Carne retraced his steps to his own abode.

'It is really very strange,' he muttered as he walked along, 'how often chance condescends to lend her assistance to my little schemes. The mere fact that His Grace left the box unwatched in his study for a quarter of an hour may serve to throw the police off on quite another scent. I am also glad that they decided to open the case in the house, for if it had gone to the bankers' and had been placed in the strong room unexamined, I should never have been able to get possession of the jewels at all.'

Three hours later he drove to Wiltshire House and saw the Duke. The Duchess was far too much upset by the catastrophe to see anyone.

'This is really most kind of you, Mr Carne,' said His Grace when the other had supplied an elaborate account of his interview with Klimo. 'We are extremely indebted to you. I am sorry he cannot come before ten o'clock tonight, and that he makes this stipulation of my seeing him alone, for I must confess I should like to have had someone else present to ask any questions that might escape me. But if that's his usual hour and custom, well, we must abide by it, that's all. I hope he will do some good, for this is the greatest calamity that has ever befallen me. As I told you just now, it has made my wife quite ill. She is confined to her bedroom and quite hysterical.'

'You do not suspect anyone, I suppose?' inquired Carne.

'Not a soul,' the other answered. 'The thing is such a mystery that we do not know what to think. I feel convinced, however, that my servants are as innocent as I am. Nothing will ever make me think them otherwise. I wish I could catch the fellow, that's all. I'd make him suffer for the trick he's played me.'

Carne offered an appropriate reply, and after a little further conversation upon the subject, bade the irate nobleman goodbye and left the house. From Belgrave Square he drove to one of the clubs of which he had been elected a member, in search of Lord Orpington, with whom he had promised to lunch, and afterwards took him to a shipbuilder's yard near Greenwich, in order to show him the steam yacht he had lately purchased.

It was close upon dinner time before he returned to his own residence. He brought Lord Orpington with him, and they dined in state together. At nine the latter bade him goodbye, and at ten Carne retired to his dressing-room and rang for Belton.

'What have you to report,' he asked, 'with regard to what I bade you do in Belgrave Square?'

'I followed your instructions to the letter,' Belton replied. 'Yesterday morning I wrote to Messrs Horniblow and Jimson, the house agents in Piccadilly, in the name of Colonel Braithwaite, and asked for an order to view the residence to the right of Wiltshire House. I asked that the order might be sent direct to the house, where the Colonel would get it upon his arrival. This letter I posted myself in Basingstoke, as you desired me to do.

'At nine o'clock yesterday morning I dressed myself as much like an elderly army officer as possible, and took a cab to Belgrave Square. The caretaker, an old fellow of close upon seventy years of age, admitted me immediately upon hearing my name, and proposed that he should show me over the house. This, however, I told him was quite unnecessary, backing my speech with a present of half a crown, whereupon he returned to his breakfast perfectly satisfied, while I wandered about the house at my own leisure.

'Reaching the same floor as that upon which is situated the room in which the Duke's safe is kept, I discovered that your supposition was quite correct, and that it would be possible for a man, by opening the window, to make his way along the coping from one house to the other, without being seen. I made certain that there was no one in the bedroom in which the butler slept, and then arranged the long telescope walking-stick you gave me, and fixed one of my boots to it by means of the screw in the end. With this I was able to make a regular succession of footsteps in the dust along the ledge, between one window and the other.

'That done, I went downstairs again, bade the caretaker good morning, and got into my cab. From Belgrave Square I drove to the shop of the pawnbroker whom you told me you had discovered was out of town. His assistant inquired my business, and was anxious to do what he could for me. I told him, however, that I must see his master personally, as it was about the sale of some diamonds I had had left me. I pretended to be annoyed that he was not at home, and muttered to myself, so that the man could hear, something about its meaning a journey to Amsterdam.

'Then I limped out of the shop, paid off my cab, and, walking down a by-street, removed my moustache, and altered my appearance by taking off my great coat and muffler. A few streets further on I purchased a bowler hat in place of the old-fashioned topper I had hitherto been wearing, and then took a cab from Piccadilly and came home.'

'You have fulfilled my instructions admirably,' said Carne. 'And if the business comes off, as I expect it will, you shall receive your usual percentage. Now I must be turned into Klimo and be off to Belgrave Square to put His Grace upon the track of this burglar.'

Before he retired to rest that night Simon Carne took something, wrapped in a red silk handkerchief, from the capacious pocket of the coat Klimo had been wearing a few moments before. Having unrolled the covering, he held up to the light the magnificent necklace which for so many years had been the joy and pride of the ducal house of Wiltshire. The electric light played upon it, and touched it with a thousand different hues.

'Where so many have failed,' he said to himself, as he wrapped it in the handkerchief again and locked it in his safe, 'it is pleasant to be able to congratulate oneself on having succeeded.'

Next morning all London was astonished by the news that the famous Wiltshire diamonds had been stolen, and a few hours later Carne learnt from an evening paper that the detectives who had taken up the case, upon the supposed retirement from it of Klimo, were still completely at fault.

That evening he was to entertain several friends to dinner. They included Lord Amberley, Lord Orpington, and a prominent member of the Privy Council. Lord Amberley arrived late, but filled to overflowing with importance. His friends noticed his state, and questioned him.

'Well, gentlemen,' he answered, as he took up a commanding position upon the drawing-room hearthrug. 'I am in a position to inform you that Klimo has reported upon the case, and the upshot of it is that the Wiltshire Diamond Mystery is a mystery no longer.'

'What do you mean?' asked the others in a chorus.

'I mean that he sent in his report to Wiltshire this afternoon, as arranged. From what he said the other night, after being alone in the room with the empty jewel case and a magnifying glass for two minutes or so, he was in a position to describe the *modus operandi*, and, what is more, to put the police on the scent of the burglar.'

'And how *was* it worked?' asked Carne.

'From the empty house next door,' replied the other. 'On the morning of the burglary a man, purporting to be a retired army officer, called with an order to view, got the caretaker out of the way, clambered along to Wiltshire House by means of the parapet outside, reached the room during the time the servants were at breakfast, opened the safe, and abstracted the jewels.'

'But how did Klimo find all this out?' asked Lord Orpington.

'By his own inimitable cleverness,' replied Lord Amberley. 'At any rate it has been proved that he was correct. The man *did* make his way from next door, and the police have since discovered that an individual answering to the description given, visited a pawnbroker's shop in the city about an hour later, and stated that he had diamonds to sell.' '

'If that is so it turns out to be a very simple mystery after all,' said Lord Orpington as they began their meal.

'Thanks to the ingenuity of the cleverest detective in the world,' remarked Amberley.

'In that case here's a good health to Klimo,' said the Privy Councillor, raising his glass.

'I will join you in that,' said Simon Carne. 'Here's a very good health to Klimo and his connection with the Duchess of Wiltshire's diamonds. May he always be equally successful!'

'Hear, hear to that,' replied his guests.

EW HORNUNG

Gentlemen and Players

OLD RAFFLES MAY or may not have been an exceptional criminal, but as a cricketer I dare swear he was unique. Himself a dangerous bat, a brilliant field, and perhaps the very finest slow bowler of his decade, he took incredibly little interest in the game at large. He never went up to Lord's without his cricket-bag, or showed the slightest interest in the result of a match in which he was not himself engaged. Nor was this mere hateful egotism on his part. He professed to have lost all enthusiasm for the game, and to keep it up only from the very lowest motives.

'Cricket,' said Raffles, 'like everything else, is good enough sport until you discover a better. As a source of excitement it isn't in it with other things you wot of, Bunny, and the involuntary comparison becomes a bore. What's the satisfaction of taking a man's wicket when you want his spoons? Still, if you can bowl a bit your low cunning won't get rusty, and always looking for the weak spot's just the kind of mental exercise one wants. Yes, perhaps there's some affinity between the two things after all. But I'd chuck up cricket tomorrow, Bunny, if it wasn't for the glorious protection it affords a person of my proclivities.'

'How so?' said I. 'It brings you before the public, I should have thought, far more than is either safe or wise.'

'My dear Bunny, that's exactly where you make a mistake. To follow Crime with reasonable impunity you simply *must* have a parallel, ostensible career – the more public the better. The principle is obvious. Mr Peace, of pious memory, disarmed suspicion by acquiring a local reputation for playing the fiddle and taming animals, and it's my profound conviction that Jack the Ripper was a really eminent public man, whose speeches were very likely reported alongside his atrocities. Fill the bill in some prominent part, and you'll never be suspected of doubling it with another of equal prominence. That's why I want you to cultivate journalism, my boy, and sign all you can. And it's the one and only reason why I don't burn my bats for firewood.'

Nevertheless, when he did play there was no keener performer on the field, nor one more anxious to do well for his side. I remember how he went to the nets, before the first match of the season, with his pocket full of sovereigns, which he put on the stumps instead of bails. It was a sight to see the professionals bowling like demons for the hard cash, for whenever a stump was hit a pound was tossed to the bowler and another balanced in its stead, while one man took £3 with a ball that spreadeagled the wicket. Raffles's practice cost him either eight or nine sovereigns; but he had absolutely first class bowling all the time; and he made fifty-seven runs next day.

It became my pleasure to accompany him to all his matches, to watch every ball he bowled, or played, or fielded, and to sit chatting with him in the pavilion when he was doing none of these three things. You might have seen us there, side by side, during the greater part of the Gentlemen's first innings against the Players (who had lost the toss) on the second Monday in July. We were to be seen, but not heard, for Raffles had failed to score, and was uncommonly cross for a player who cared so little for the game. Merely taciturn with me, he was positively rude to more than one member who wanted to know how it had happened, or who ventured to commiserate him on his luck; there he sat, with a straw hat tilted over his nose and a cigarette stuck between lips that curled disagreeably at every advance. I was therefore much surprised when a young fellow of the exquisite type came and squeezed himself in between us, and met with a perfectly civil reception despite the liberty. I did not know the boy by sight, nor did Raffles introduce us; but their conversation proclaimed at once a slightness of acquaintanceship and a license on the lad's part which combined to puzzle me. Mystification reached its height when Raffles was informed that the other's father was anxious to meet him, and he instantly consented to gratify that whim.

'He's in the Ladies' Enclosure. Will you come round now?'

'With pleasure,' says Raffles. 'Keep a place for me, Bunny.'

And they were gone.

'Young Crowley,' said some voice further back. 'Last year's Harrow Eleven.'

'I remember him. Worst man in the team.'

'Keen cricketer, however. Stopped till he was twenty to get his colours. Governor made him. Keen breed. Oh, pretty, sir! Very pretty!'

The game was boring me. I only came to see old Raffles perform. Soon I was looking wistfully for his return, and at length I saw him beckoning me from the palings to the right.

'Want to introduce you to old Amersteth,' he whispered, when I joined him. 'They've a cricket week next month, when this boy Crowley comes of age, and we've both got to go down and play.'

'Both!' I echoed. 'But I'm no cricketer!'

'Shut up,' says Raffles. 'Leave that to me. I've been lying for all I'm worth,' he added sepulchrally as we reached the bottom of the steps. 'I trust to you not to give the show away.'

There was a gleam in his eye that I knew well enough elsewhere, but was unprepared for in those healthy, sane surroundings; and it was with very definite misgivings and surmises that I followed the Zingari blazer through the vast flower-bed of hats and bonnets that bloomed beneath the ladies' awning.

Lord Amersteth was a fine-looking man with a short moustache and a double chin. He received me with much dry courtesy, through which, however, it was not difficult to read a less flattering tale. I was accepted as the inevitable appendage of the invaluable Raffles, with whom I felt deeply incensed as I made my bow.

'I have been bold enough,' said Lord Amersteth, 'to ask one of the Gentlemen of England to come down and play some rustic cricket for us next month. He is kind enough to say that he would have liked nothing better, but for this little fishing expedition of yours, Mr——, Mr——,' and Lord Amersteth succeeded in remembering my name.

It was, of course, the first I had ever heard of that fishing expedition, but I made haste to say that it could easily, and should certainly, be put off. Raffles gleamed approval through his eyelashes. Lord Amersteth bowed and shrugged.

'You're very good, I'm sure,' said he. 'But I understand you're a cricketer yourself?'

'He was one at school,' said Raffles, with infamous readiness.

'Not a real cricketer,' I was stammering meanwhile.

'In the eleven?' said Lord Amersteth.

'I'm afraid not,' said I.

'But only just out of it,' declared Raffles, to my horror.

'Well, well, we can't all play for the Gentlemen,' said Lord Amersteth slyly. 'My son Crowley only just scraped into the eleven at Harrow, and *he's* going to play. I may even come in myself at a pinch; so you won't be the only duffer, if you are one, and I shall be very glad if you will come down and help us too. You shall flog a stream before breakfast and after dinner, if you like.'

'I should be very proud,' I was beginning, as the mere prelude to resolute excuses; but the eye of Raffles opened wide upon me; and I hesitated weakly, to be duly lost.

'Then that's settled,' said Lord Amersteth, with the slightest suspicion of grimness. 'It's to be a little week, you know, when my son comes of age. We play the Free Foresters, the Dorsetshire Gentlemen, and probably some local lot as well. But Mr Raffles will tell you all about it, and Crowley shall write. Another wicket! By Jove, they're all out! Then I rely on you both.' And, with a little nod, Lord Amersteth rose and sidled to the gangway.

Raffles rose also, but I caught the sleeve of his blazer.

'What are you thinking of?' I whispered savagely. 'I was nowhere near the eleven. I'm no sort of cricketer. I shall have to get out of this!'

'Not you,' he whispered back. 'You needn't play, but come you must. If you wait for me after half-past six I'll tell you why.'

But I could guess the reason; and I am ashamed to say that it revolted me much less than did the notion of making a public fool of myself on a cricket-field. My gorge rose at this as it no longer rose at crime, and it was in no tranquil humour that I strolled about the ground while Raffles disappeared in the pavilion. Nor was my annoyance lessened by a little meeting I witnessed between young Crowley and his father, who shrugged as he stopped and stooped to convey some information which made the young man look a little blank. It may have been pure self-consciousness on my part, but I could have sworn that the trouble was their inability to secure the great Raffles without his insignificant friend.

Then the bell rang, and I climbed to the top of the pavilion to watch Raffles bowl. No subtleties are lost up there; and if ever a bowler was full of them, it was AJ Raffles on this day, as, indeed, all the cricket world remembers. One had not to be a cricketer oneself to appreciate his perfect command of pitch and break, his beautifully easy action, which never varied with the varying pace, his great ball on the leg-stump – his dropping head-ball – in a word, the infinite ingenuity of that versatile attack. It was no mere exhibition of athletic prowess, it was an intellectual treat, and one with a special significance in my eyes. I saw the 'affinity between the two things', saw it in that afternoon's tireless warfare against the flower of professional cricket. It was not that Raffles took many wickets for few runs; he was too fine a bowler to mind being hit; and time was short, and the wicket good. What I admired, and what I remember, was the combination of resource and cunning, of patience and precision, of head-work and handiwork, which made every over an artistic whole. It was all so characteristic of that other Raffles whom I alone knew!

'I felt like bowling this afternoon,' he told me later in the hansom. 'With a pitch to help me, I'd have done something big; as it is, three for forty-one, out of the four that fell, isn't so bad for a slow bowler on a plumb wicket against those fellows. But I felt venomous! Nothing riles me more than being asked about for my cricket as though I were a pro' myself.'

'Then why on earth go?'

'To punish them, and – because we shall be jolly hard up, Bunny, before the season's over!'

'Ah!' said I. 'I thought it was that.'

'Of course, it was! It seems they're going to have the very devil of a week of it – balls – dinner parties – swagger house party – general junketings – and obviously a houseful of diamonds as well. Diamonds galore! As a general rule nothing would induce me to abuse my position as a guest. I've never done it, Bunny. But in this case we're engaged like the waiters and the band, and by heaven we'll take our toll! Let's have a quiet dinner somewhere and talk it over.'

'It seems rather a vulgar sort of theft,' I could not help saying; and to this, my single protest, Raffles instantly assented.

'It is a vulgar sort,' said he; 'but I can't help that. We're getting vulgarly hard up again, and there's an end on't. Besides, these people deserve it, and can afford it. And don't you run away with the idea that all will be plain sailing; nothing will be easier than getting some stuff, and nothing harder than avoiding all suspicion, as, of course, we must. We may come away with no more than a good working plan of the premises. Who knows? In any case there's weeks of thinking in it for you and me.'

But with those weeks I will not weary you further than by remarking that the 'thinking', was done entirely by Raffles, who did not always trouble to communicate his thoughts to me. His reticence, however, was no longer an irritant. I began to accept it as a necessary convention of these little enterprises. And, after our last adventure of the kind, more especially after its denouement, my trust in Raffles was much too solid to be shaken by a want of trust in me, which I still believe to have been more the instinct of the criminal than the judgment of the man.

It was on Monday, the tenth of August, that we were due at Milchester Abbey, Dorset; and the beginning of the month found us cruising about that very county, with fly-rods actually in our hands.

The idea was that we should acquire at once a local reputation as decent fishermen, and some knowledge of the countryside, with a view to further and more deliberate operations in the event of an unprofitable week. There was another idea which Raffles kept to himself until he had got me down there. Then one day he produced a cricket-ball in a meadow we were crossing, and threw me catches for an hour together. More hours he spent in bowling to me on the nearest green; and, if I was never a cricketer, at least I came nearer to being one, by the end of that week, than ever before or since.

Incident began early on the Monday. We had sallied forth from a desolate little junction within quite a few miles of Milchester, had been caught in a shower, had run for shelter to a wayside inn. A florid, overdressed man was drinking in the parlour, and I could have sworn it was at the sight of him that Raffles recoiled on the threshold, and afterwards insisted on returning to the station through the rain. He assured me, however, that the odour of stale ale had almost knocked him down. And I had to make what I could of his speculative, downcast eyes and knitted brows.

Milchester Abbey is a grey, quadrangular pile, deep-set in rich woody country, and twinkling with triple rows of quaint windows, every one of which seemed alight as we drove up just in time to dress for dinner. The carriage had whirled us under I know not how many triumphal arches in process of construction, and past the tents and flag-poles of a juicy-looking cricket-field, on which Raffles undertook to bowl up to his reputation. But the chief signs of festival were within, where we found an enormous house-party assembled, including more persons of pomp, majesty, and dominion than I had ever encountered in one room before. I confess I felt overpowered. Our errand and my own presences combined to rob me of an address upon which I have sometimes plumed myself; and I have a grim recollection of my nervous relief when dinner was at last announced. I little knew what an ordeal it was to prove.

I had taken in a much less formidable young lady than might have fallen to my lot. Indeed I began by blessing my good fortune in this respect. Miss Melhuish was merely the rector's daughter, and she had only been asked to make an even number. She informed me of both facts before the soup reached us, and her subsequent conversation was characterised by the same engaging candour. It exposed what was little short of a mania for imparting information. I had simply to listen, to nod, and to be thankful.

When I confessed to knowing very few of those present, even by

sight, my entertaining companion proceeded to tell me who everybody was, beginning on my left and working conscientiously round
to her right. This lasted quite a long time, and really interested me;
but a great deal that followed did not, and, obviously to recapture my
unworthy attention, Miss Melhuish suddenly asked me, in a sensational whisper, whether I could keep a secret.

I said I thought I might, whereupon another question followed, in
still lower and more thrilling accents:

'Are you afraid of burglars?'

Burglars! I was roused at last. The word stabbed me. I repeated it
in horrified query.

'So I've found something to interest you at last!' said Miss Melhuish, in naive triumph. 'Yes – burglars! But don't speak so loud. It's
supposed to be kept a great secret. I really oughtn't to tell you at all!'

'But what is there to tell?' I whispered with satisfactory impatience.

'You promise not to speak of it?'

'Of course!'

'Well, then, there are burglars in the neighbourhood.'

'Have they committed any robberies?'

'Not yet.'

'Then how do you know?'

'They've been seen. In the district. Two well-known London
thieves!'

Two! I looked at Raffles. I had done so often during the evening,
envying him his high spirits, his iron nerve, his buoyant wit, his
perfect ease and self-possession. But now I pitied him; through all my
own terror and consternation, I pitied him as he sat eating and drinking, and laughing and talking, without a cloud of fear or of embarrassment on his handsome, taking, daredevil face. I caught up my
champagne and emptied the glass.

'Who has seen them?' I then asked calmly.

'A detective. They were traced down from town a few days ago.
They are believed to have designs on the Abbey!'

'But why aren't they run in?'

'Exactly what I asked papa on the way here this evening; he says
there is no warrant out against the men at present, and all that can be
done is to watch their movements.'

'Oh! so they are being watched?'

'Yes, by a detective who is down here on purpose. And I heard
Lord Amersteth tell papa that they had been seen this afternoon at
Warbeck Junction!'

The very place where Raffles and I had been caught in the rain! Our stampede from the inn was now explained; on the other hand, I was no longer to be taken by surprise by anything that my companion might have to tell me; and I succeeded in looking her in the face with a smile.

'This is really quite exciting, Miss Melhuish,' said I. 'May I ask how you come to know so much about it?'

'It's papa,' was the confidential reply. 'Lord Amersteth consulted him, and he consulted me. But for goodness' sake don't let it get about! I can't think *what* tempted me to tell you!'

'You may trust me, Miss Melhuish. But – aren't you frightened?'

Miss Melhuish giggled.

'Not a bit! They won't come to the rectory. There's nothing for them there. But look round the table: look at the diamonds: look at old Lady Melrose's necklace alone!'

The Dowager Marchioness of Melrose was one of the few persons whom it had been unnecessary to point out to me. She sat on Lord Amersteth's right, flourishing her ear-trumpet, and drinking champagne with her usual notorious freedom, as dissipated and kindly a dame as the world has ever seen. It was a necklace of diamonds and sapphires that rose and fell about her ample neck.

'They say it's worth five thousand pounds at least,' continued my companion. 'Lady Margaret told me so this morning (that's Lady Margaret next your Mr Raffles, you know); and the old dear *will* wear them every night. Think what a haul they would be! No; we don't feel in immediate danger at the rectory.'

When the ladies rose, Miss Melhuish bound me to fresh vows of secrecy; and left me, I should think, with some remorse for her indiscretion, but more satisfaction at the importance which it had undoubtedly given her in my eyes. The opinion may smack of vanity, though, in reality, the very springs of conversation reside in that same human, universal itch to thrill the auditor. The peculiarity of Miss Melhuish was that she must be thrilling at all costs. And thrilling she had surely been.

I spare you my feelings of the next two hours. I tried hard to get a word with Raffles, but again and again I failed. In the dining-room he and Crowley lit their cigarettes with the same match, and had their heads together all the time. In the drawing-room I had the mortification of hearing him talk interminable nonsense into the ear-trumpet of Lady Melrose, whom he knew in town. Lastly, in the billiard-room, they had a great and lengthy pool, while I sat aloof and chafed more than ever in the company of a very serious Scotchman, who had arrived since dinner, and who would talk of nothing but the recent improvements in instantaneous photography. He had not come to play in the matches (he told me), but to obtain for Lord Amersteth such a series of cricket photographs as had never been taken before; whether as an amateur or a professional photographer I was unable to determine. I remember, however, seeking distraction in little bursts of resolute attention to the conversation of this bore. And so at last the long ordeal ended; glasses were emptied, men said goodnight, and I followed Raffles to his room.

'It's all up!' I gasped, as he turned up the gas and I shut the door. 'We're being watched. We've been followed down from town. There's a detective here on the spot!'

'How do *you* know?' asked Raffles, turning upon me quite sharply, but without the least dismay. And I told him how I knew.

'Of course,' I added, 'it was the fellow we saw in the inn this afternoon.'

'The detective?' said Raffles. 'Do you mean to say you don't know a detective when you see one, Bunny?'

'If that wasn't the fellow, which is?'

Raffles shook his head.

'To think that you've been talking to him for the last hour in the billiard-room and couldn't spot what he was!'

'The Scotch photographer—'

I paused aghast.

'Scotch he is,' said Raffles, 'and photographer he may be. He is also Inspector Mackenzie of Scotland Yard – the very man I sent the message to that night last April. And you couldn't spot who he was in a whole hour! Oh Bunny, Bunny, you were never built for crime!'

'But,' said I, 'if that was Mackenzie, who was the fellow you bolted from at Warbeck?'

'The man he's watching.'

'But he's watching us!'

Raffles looked at me with a pitying eye, and shook his head again before handing me his open cigarette-case.

'I don't know whether smoking's forbidden in one's bedroom, but you'd better take one of these and stand tight, Bunny, because I'm going to say something offensive.'

I helped myself with a laugh.

'Say what you like, my dear fellow, if it really isn't you and I that Mackenzie's after.'

'Well, then, it isn't, and it couldn't be, and nobody but a born Bunny would suppose for a moment that it was! Do you seriously think he would sit there and knowingly watch his man playing pool under his nose? Well, he might; he's a cool hand, Mackenzie; but I'm not cool enough to win a pool under such conditions. At least I don't think I am; it would be interesting to see. The situation wasn't free from strain as it was, though I knew he wasn't thinking of us. Crowley told me all about it after dinner, you see, and then I'd seen one of the men for myself this afternoon. You thought it was a detective who made me turn tail at that inn. I really don't know why I didn't tell you at the time, but it was just the opposite. That loud, red-faced brute is one of the cleverest thieves in London, and I once had a drink with him and our mutual fence. I was an Eastender from tongue to toe at the moment, but you will understand that I don't run unnecessary risks of recognition by a brute like that.'

'He's not alone, I hear.'

'By no means; there's at least one other man with him; and it's suggested that there may be an accomplice here in the house.'

'Did Lord Crowley tell you so?'

'Crowley and the champagne between them. In confidence, of course, just as your girl told you; but even in confidence he never let on about Mackenzie. He told me there was a detective in the background, but that was all. Putting him up as a guest is evidently their big secret, to be kept from the other guests because it might offend them, but more particularly from the servants whom he's here to watch. That's my reading of the situation, Bunny, and you will agree with me that it's infinitely more interesting than we could have imagined it would prove.'

'But infinitely more difficult for us,' said I, with a sigh of pusillanimous relief. 'Our hands are tied for this week, at all events.'

'Not necessarily, my dear Bunny, though I admit that the chances are against us. Yet I'm not so sure of that either. There are all sorts of possibilities in these three-cornered combinations. Set A to watch B, and he won't have an eye left for C. That's the obvious theory, but then Mackenzie's a very big A. I should be sorry to have any boodle about me with that man in the house. Yet it would be great to nip in between A and B and score off them both at once! It would be worth a risk, Bunny, to do that; it would be worth risking something merely to take on old hands like B and his men at their own old game! Eh, Bunny? That would be something like a match. Gentlemen and Players at single wicket, by Jove!'

His eyes were brighter than I had known them for many a day. They shone with the perverted enthusiasm which was roused in him only by the contemplation of some new audacity. He kicked off his shoes and began pacing his room with noiseless rapidity; not since the night of the Old Bohemian dinner to Reuben Rosenthall had Raffles exhibited such excitement in my presence; and I was not sorry at the moment to be reminded of the fiasco to which that banquet had been the prelude.

'My dear AJ,' said I in his very own tone, 'you're far too fond of the uphill game; you will eventually fall a victim to the sporting spirit and nothing else. Take a lesson from our last escape, and fly lower as you value our skins. Study the house as much as you like, but do – not – go and shove your head into Mackenzie's mouth!'

My wealth of metaphor brought him to a standstill, with his cigarette between his fingers and a grin beneath his shining eyes.

'You're quite right, Bunny. I won't. I really won't. Yet – you saw old Lady Melrose's necklace? I've been wanting it for years! But I'm not going to play the fool; honour bright, I'm not; yet – by Jove! – to get to windward of the professors and Mackenzie too! It would be a great game, Bunny, it would be a great game!'

'Well, you mustn't play it this week.'

'No, no, I won't. But I wonder how the professors think of going to work? That's what one wants to know. I wonder if they've really got an accomplice in the house? How I wish I knew their game! But it's all right, Bunny; don't you be jealous; it shall be as you wish.'

And with that assurance I went off to my own room, and so to bed with an incredibly light heart. I had still enough of the honest man in me to welcome the postponement of our actual felonies, to dread their performance, to deplore their necessity: which is merely another way of stating the too patent fact that I was an incomparably weaker man than Raffles, while every whit as wicked.

I had, however, one rather strong point. I possessed the gift of dismissing unpleasant considerations, not intimately connected with the passing moment, entirely from my mind. Through the exercise of this faculty I had lately been living my frivolous life in town with as much ignoble enjoyment as I had derived from it the year before; and similarly, here at Milchester, in the long-dreaded cricket-week, I had after all a quite excellent time.

It is true that there were other factors in this pleasing disappointment. In the first place, *mirabile dictu*, there were one or two even greater duffers than I on the Abbey cricket-field. Indeed, quite early in the week, when it was of most value to me, I gained considerable kudos for a lucky catch; a ball, of which I had merely heard the hum, stuck fast in my hand, which Lord Amersteth himself grasped in public congratulation. This happy accident was not to be undone even by me, and, as nothing succeeds like success, and the constant encouragement of the one great cricketer on the field was in itself an immense stimulus, I actually made a run or two in my very next innings. Miss Melhuish said pretty things to me that night at the great ball in honour of Viscount Crowley's majority; she also told me that was the night on which the robbers would assuredly make their raid, and was full of arch tremors when we sat out in the garden, though the entire premises were illuminated all night long. Meanwhile the quiet Scotchman took countless photographs by day, which he developed by night in a dark room admirably situated in the servants' part of the house; and it is my firm belief that only two of his fellow-guests knew Mr Clephane of Dundee for Inspector Mackenzie of Scotland Yard.

The week was to end with a trumpery match on the Saturday, which two or three of us intended abandoning early in order to return to town that night. The match, however, was never played. In the small hours of the Saturday morning a tragedy took place at Milchester Abbey.

Let me tell of the thing as I saw and heard it. My room opened upon the central gallery, and was not even on the same floor as that on which Raffles – and I think all the other men – were quartered. I had been put, in fact, into the dressing-room of one of the grand suites, and my too near neighbours were old Lady Melrose and my host and hostess. Now, by the Friday evening the actual festivities were at an end, and, for the first time that week, I must have been sound asleep since midnight, when all at once I found myself sitting up breathless. A heavy thud had come against my door, and now I heard hard breathing and the dull stamp of muffled feet.

'I've got ye,' muttered a voice. 'It's no use struggling.'

It was the Scotch detective, and a new fear turned me cold. There was no reply, but the hard breathing grew harder still, and the muffled feet beat the floor to a quicker measure. In sudden panic I sprang out of bed and flung open my door. A light burnt low on the landing, and by it I could see Mackenzie swaying and staggering in a silent tussle with some powerful adversary.

'Hold this man!' he cried, as I appeared. 'Hold the rascal!'

But I stood like a fool until the pair of them backed into me, when, with a deep breath I flung myself on the fellow, whose face I had seen at last. He was one of the footmen who waited at table; and no sooner had I pinned him than the detective loosed his hold.

'Hang on to him,' he cried. 'There's more of 'em below.'

And he went leaping down the stairs, as other doors opened and Lord Amersteth and his son appeared simultaneously in their pyjamas. At that my man ceased struggling; but I was still holding him when Crowley turned up the gas.

'What the devil's all this?' asked Lord Amersteth, blinking. 'Who was that ran downstairs?'

'Mac – Clephane!' said I hastily.

'Aha!' said he, turning to the footman. 'So you're the scoundrel, are you? Well done! Well done! Where was he caught?'

I had no idea.

'Here's Lady Melrose's door open,' said Crowley. 'Lady Melrose! Lady Melrose!'

'You forget she's deaf,' said Lord Amersteth. 'Ah! that'll be her maid.'

An inner door had opened; next instant there was a little shriek, and a white figure gesticulated on the threshold.

'*Ou donc est l'ecrin de Madame la Marquise? La fenetre est ouverte. Il a disparu!*'

'Window open and jewel-case gone, by Jove!' exclaimed Lord Amersteth. '*Mais comment est Madame la Marquise? Est elle bien?*'

'*Oui, milor. Elle dort.*'

'Sleeps through it all,' said my lord. 'She's the only one, then!'

'What made Mackenzie – Clephane – bolt?' young Crowley asked me.

'Said there were more of them below.'

'Why the devil couldn't you tell us so before?' he cried, and went leaping downstairs in his turn.

He was followed by nearly all the cricketers, who now burst upon the scene in a body, only to desert it for the chase. Raffles was one of them, and I would gladly have been another, had not the footman chosen this moment to hurl me from him, and to make a dash in the direction from which they had come. Lord Amersteth had him in an instant; but the fellow fought desperately, and it took the two of us to drag him downstairs, amid a terrified chorus from half-open doors. Eventually we handed him over to two other footmen who appeared with their nightshirts tucked into their trousers, and my host was good enough to compliment me as he led the way outside.

'I thought I heard a shot,' he added. 'Didn't you?'

'I thought I heard three.'

And out we dashed into the darkness.

I remember how the gravel pricked my feet, how the wet grass numbed them as we made for the sound of voices on an outlying lawn. So dark was the night that we were in the cricketers' midst before we saw the shimmer of their pyjamas; and then Lord Amersteth almost trod on Mackenzie as he lay prostrate in the dew.

'Who's this?' he cried. 'What on earth's happened?'

'It's Clephane,' said a man who knelt over him. 'He's got a bullet in him somewhere.'

'Is he alive?'

'Barely.'

'Good God! Where's Crowley?'

'Here I am,' called a breathless voice. 'It's no good, you fellows. There's nothing to show which way they've gone. Here's Raffles; he's chucked it, too.' And they ran up panting.

'Well, we've got one of them, at all events,' muttered Lord Amersteth. 'The next thing is to get this poor fellow indoors. Take his shoulders, somebody. Now his middle. Join hands under him. All together, now; that's the way. Poor fellow! Poor fellow! His name isn't Clephane at all. He's a Scotland Yard detective, down here for these very villains!'

Raffles was the first to express surprise; but he had also been the first to raise the wounded man. Nor had any of them a stronger or more tender hand in the slow procession to the house.

In a little we had the senseless man stretched on a sofa in the library. And there, with ice on his wound and brandy in his throat, his eyes opened and his lips moved.

Lord Amersteth bent down to catch the words.

'Yes, yes,' said he; 'we've got one of them safe and sound. The brute you collared upstairs.' Lord Amersteth bent lower. 'By Jove! Lowered the jewel-case out of the window, did he? And they've got clean away with it! Well, well! I only hope we'll be able to pull this good fellow through. He's off again.'

An hour passed: the sun was rising.

It found a dozen young fellows on the settees in the billiard-room, drinking whiskey and soda-water in their overcoats and pyjamas, and still talking excitedly in one breath. A timetable was being passed from hand to hand: the doctor was still in the library. At last the door opened, and Lord Amersteth put in his head.

'It isn't hopeless,' said he, 'but it's bad enough. There'll be no cricket today.'

Another hour, and most of us were on our way to catch the early train; between us we filled a compartment almost to suffocation. And still we talked all together of the night's event; and still I was a little hero in my way, for having kept my hold of the one ruffian who had been taken; and my gratification was subtle and intense. Raffles watched me under lowered lids. Not a word had we had together; not a word did we have until we had left the others at Paddington, and were skimming through the streets in a hansom with noiseless tires and a tinkling bell.

'Well, Bunny,' said Raffles, 'so the professors have it, eh?'

'Yes,' said I. 'And I'm jolly glad!'

'That poor Mackenzie has a ball in his chest?'

'That you and I have been on the decent side for once.'

He shrugged his shoulders.

'You're hopeless, Bunny, quite hopeless! I take it you wouldn't have refused your share if the boodle had fallen to us? Yet you positively enjoy coming off second best – for the second time running! I confess, however, that the professors' methods were full of interest to me. I, for one, have probably gained as much in experience as I have lost in other things. That lowering the jewel-case out of the window was a very simple and effective expedient; two of them had been waiting below for it for hours.'

'How do you know?' I asked.

'I saw them from my own window, which was just above the dear old lady's. I was fretting for that necklace in particular, when I went up to turn in for our last night – and I happened to look out of my window. In point of fact, I wanted to see whether the one below was open, and whether there was the slightest chance of working the oracle with my sheet for a rope. Of course I took the precaution of turning my light off first, and it was a lucky thing I did. I saw the pros' right down below, and they never saw me. I saw a little tiny luminous disk just for an instant, and then again for an instant a few minutes later. Of course I knew what it was, for I have my own watch-dial daubed with luminous paint; it makes a lantern of sorts when you can get no better. But these fellows were not using theirs as a lantern. They were under the old lady's window. They were watching the time. The whole thing was arranged with their accomplice inside. Set a thief to catch a thief: in a minute I had guessed what the whole thing proved to be.'

'And you did nothing!' I exclaimed.

'On the contrary, I went downstairs and straight into Lady Melrose's room—'

'You did?'

'Without a moment's hesitation. To save her jewels. And I was prepared to yell as much into her ear-trumpet for all the house to hear. But the dear lady is too deaf and too fond of her dinner to wake easily.'

'Well?'

'She didn't stir.'

'And yet you allowed the professors, as you call them, to take her jewels, case and all!'

'All but this,' said Raffles, thrusting his fist into my lap. 'I would have shown it you before, but really, old fellow, your face all day has been worth a fortune to the firm!'

And he opened his fist, to shut it next instant on the bunch of diamonds and of sapphires that I had last seen encircling the neck of Lady Melrose.

BARONESS ORCZY

The Mysterious Death on the Underground Railway

IT WAS all very well for Mr Richard Frobisher (of the *London Mail*) to cut up rough about it. Polly did not altogether blame him.

She liked him all the better for that frank outburst of manlike ill-temper which, after all said and done, was only a very flattering form of masculine jealousy.

Moreover, Polly distinctly felt guilty about the whole thing. She had promised to meet Dickie – that is Mr Richard Frobisher – at two o'clock sharp outside the Palace Theatre, because she wanted to go to a Maud Allan matinee, and because he naturally wished to go with her.

But at two o'clock sharp she was still in Norfolk Street, Strand, inside an ABC shop, sipping cold coffee opposite a grotesque old man who was fiddling with a bit of string.

How could she be expected to remember Maud Allan or the Palace Theatre, or Dickie himself for a matter of that? The man in the corner had begun to talk of that mysterious death on the Underground Railway, and Polly had lost count of time, of place, and circumstance.

She had gone to lunch quite early, for she was looking forward to the matinee at the Palace.

The old scarecrow was sitting in his accustomed place when she came into the ABC shop, but he had made no remark all the time that the young girl was munching her scone and butter. She was just busy thinking how rude he was not even to have said 'Good morning', when an abrupt remark from him caused her to look up.

'Will you be good enough,' he said suddenly, 'to give me a description of the man who sat next to you just now, while you were having your cup of coffee and scone.'

Involuntarily Polly turned her head towards the distant door, through which a man in a light overcoat was even now quickly passing. That man had certainly sat at the next table to hers, when she first sat down to her coffee and scone; he had finished his luncheon – whatever it was – a moment ago, had paid at the desk and gone out. The incident did not appear to Polly as being of the slightest consequence.

Therefore she did not reply to the rude old man, but shrugged her
shoulders, and called to the waitress to bring her bill.

'Do you know if he was tall or short, dark or fair?' continued the
man in the corner, seemingly not the least disconcerted by the young
girl's indifference. 'Can you tell me at all what he was like?'

'Of course I can,' rejoined Polly impatiently, 'but I don't see that
my description of one of the customers of an ABC shop can have the
slightest importance.'

He was silent for a moment, while his nervous fingers fumbled
about in his capacious pockets in search of the inevitable piece of
string. When he had found this necessary 'adjunct to thought', he
viewed the young girl again through his half-closed lids, and added
maliciously:

'But supposing it were of paramount importance that you should
give an accurate description of a man who sat next to you for half an
hour today, how would you proceed?'

'I should say that he was of medium height—'

'Five foot eight, nine, or ten?' he interrupted quietly.

'How can one tell to an inch or two?' rejoined Polly crossly. 'He
was between colours.'

'What's that?' he inquired blandly.

'Neither fair nor dark – his nose—'

'Well, what was his nose like? Will you sketch it?'

'I am not an artist. His nose was fairly straight – his eyes – were
neither dark nor light – his hair had the same striking peculiarity – he
was neither short nor tall – his nose was neither aquiline nor snub…'
he recapitulated sarcastically.

'No,' she retorted; 'he was just ordinary looking.'

'Would you know him again – say tomorrow, and among a
number of other men who were "neither tall nor short, dark nor fair,
aquiline nor snub-nosed", etc?'

'I don't know – I might – he was certainly not striking enough to
be specially remembered.'

'Exactly,' he said, while he leant forward excitedly, for all the
world like a Jack-in-the-box let loose. 'Precisely; and you are a journalist – call yourself one, at least – and it should be part of your business to notice and describe people. I don't mean only the wonderful
personage with the clear Saxon features, the fine blue eyes, the noble
brow and classic face – but the ordinary person – the person who represents ninety out of every hundred of his own kind – the average
Englishman, say, of the middle classes, who is neither very tall nor

very short, who wears a moustache which is neither fair nor dark, but which masks his mouth, and a top hat which hides the shape of his head and brow, a man, in fact, who dresses like hundreds of his fellow-creatures, moves like them, speaks like them, has no peculiarity.

'Try to describe *him*, to recognise him, say a week hence, among his other eighty-nine doubles; worse still, to swear his life away, if he happened to be implicated in some crime, wherein *your* recognition of him would place the halter round his neck.

'Try that, I say, and having utterly failed you will more readily understand how one of the greatest scoundrels unhung is still at large, and why the mystery of the Underground Railway was never cleared up.

'I think it was the only time in my life that I was seriously tempted to give the police the benefit of my own views upon the matter. You see, though I admire the brute for his cleverness, I did not see that his being unpunished could possibly benefit anyone.

'In these days of tubes and motor traction of all kinds, the old-fashioned "best, cheapest, and quickest route to City and West End" is often deserted, and the good old Metropolitan Railway carriages cannot at any time be said to be overcrowded. Anyway, when that particular train steamed into Aldgate at about 4pm on 16 March last, the first-class carriages were all but empty.

'The guard marched up and down the platform looking into all the carriages to see if anyone had left a halfpenny evening paper behind for him, and opening the door of one of the first-class compartments, he noticed a lady sitting in the further corner, with her head turned away towards the window, evidently oblivious of the fact that on this line Aldgate is the terminal station.

'"Where are you for, lady?" he said.

'The lady did not move, and the guard stepped into the carriage, thinking that perhaps the lady was asleep. He touched her arm lightly and looked into her face. In his own poetic language, he was "struck all of a 'eap". In the glassy eyes, the ashen colour of the cheeks, the rigidity of the head, there was the unmistakable look of death.

'Hastily the guard, having carefully locked the carriage door, summoned a couple of porters, and sent one of them off to the police station, and the other in search of the stationmaster.

'Fortunately at this time of day the up platform is not very crowded, all the traffic tending westward in the afternoon. It was only when an inspector and two police constables, accompanied by a

detective in plain clothes and a medical officer, appeared upon the
scene, and stood round a first-class railway compartment, that a few
idlers realised that something unusual had occurred, and crowded
round, eager and curious.

'Thus it was that the later editions of the evening papers, under
the sensational heading, "Mysterious Suicide on the Underground
Railway", had already an account of the extraordinary event. The
medical officer had very soon come to the decision that the guard had
not been mistaken, and that life was indeed extinct.

'The lady was young, and must have been very pretty before the
look of fright and horror had so terribly distorted her features. She
was very elegantly dressed, and the more frivolous papers were able
to give their feminine readers a detailed account of the unfortunate
woman's gown, her shoes, hat and gloves.

'It appears that one of the latter, the one on the right hand, was
partly off, leaving the thumb and wrist bare. That hand held a small
satchel, which the police opened, with a view to the possible identification of the deceased, but which was found to contain only a little
loose silver, some smelling-salts, and a small empty bottle, which was
handed over to the medical officer for purposes of analysis.

'It was the presence of that small bottle which had caused the
report to circulate freely that the mysterious case on the Underground
Railway was one of suicide. Certain it was that neither about the
lady's person, nor in the appearance of the railway carriage, was
there the slightest sign of struggle or even of resistance. Only the look
in the poor woman's eyes spoke of sudden terror, of the rapid vision
of an unexpected and violent death, which probably only lasted an
infinitesimal fraction of a second, but which had left its indelible
mark upon the face, otherwise so placid and so still.

'The body of the deceased was conveyed to the mortuary. So far,
of course, not a soul had been able to identify her, or to throw the
slightest light upon the mystery which hung around her death.

'Against that, quite a crowd of idlers – genuinely interested or not
– obtained admission to view the body, on the pretext of having lost
or mislaid a relative or a friend. At about 8.30pm a young man, very
well dressed, drove up to the station in a hansom, and sent in his card
to the superintendent. It was Mr Hazeldene, shipping agent, of 11
Crown Lane, EC, and number 19 Addison Row, Kensington.

'The young man looked in a pitiable state of mental distress; his
hand clutched nervously a copy of the St *James's Gazette,* which contained the fatal news. He said very little to the superintendent except

that a person who was very dear to him had not returned home that evening.

'He had not felt really anxious until half an hour ago, when suddenly he thought of looking at his paper. The description of the deceased lady, though vague, had terribly alarmed him. He had jumped into a hansom, and now begged permission to view the body, in order that his worst fears might be allayed.

'You know what followed, of course,' continued the man in the corner, 'the grief of the young man was truly pitiable. In the woman lying there in a public mortuary before him, Mr Hazeldene had recognised his wife.

'I am waxing melodramatic,' said the man in the corner, who looked up at Polly with a mild and gentle smile, while his nervous fingers vainly endeavoured to add another knot on the scrappy bit of string with which he was continually playing, 'and I fear that the whole story savours of the penny novelette, but you must admit, and no doubt you remember, that it was an intensely pathetic and truly dramatic moment.

'The unfortunate young husband of the deceased lady was not much worried with questions that night. As a matter of fact, he was not in a fit condition to make any coherent statement. It was at the coroner's inquest on the following day that certain facts came to light, which for the time being seemed to clear up the mystery surrounding Mrs Hazeldene's death, only to plunge that same mystery, later on, into denser gloom than before.

'The first witness at the inquest was, of course, Mr Hazeldene himself. I think everyone's sympathy went out to the young man as he stood before the coroner and tried to throw what light he could upon the mystery. He was well-dressed, as he had been the day before, but he looked terribly ill and worried, and no doubt the fact that he had not shaved gave his face a careworn and neglected air.

'It appears that he and the deceased had been married some six years or so, and that they had always been happy in their married life. They had no children. Mrs Hazeldene seemed to enjoy the best of health till lately, when she had had a slight attack of influenza, in which Dr Arthur Jones had attended her. The doctor was present at this moment, and would no doubt explain to the coroner and the jury whether he thought that Mrs Hazeldene had the slightest tendency to heart disease, which might have had a sudden and fatal ending.

'The coroner was, of course, very considerate to the bereaved husband. He tried by circumlocution to get at the point he wanted, namely, Mrs Hazeldene's mental condition lately. Mr Hazeldene seemed loath to talk about this. No doubt he had been warned as to the existence of the small bottle found in his wife's satchel.

'"It certainly did seem to me at times," he at last reluctantly admitted, "that my wife did not seem quite herself. She used to be very gay and bright, and lately I often saw her in the evening sitting, as if brooding over some matters, which evidently she did not care to communicate to me."

'Still the coroner insisted, and suggested the small bottle.

'"I know, I know," replied the young man, with a short, heavy sigh. "You mean – the question of suicide – I cannot understand it at all – it seems so sudden and so terrible – she certainly had seemed listless and troubled lately – but only at times – and yesterday morning, when I went to business, she appeared quite herself again, and I suggested that we should go to the opera in the evening. She was delighted, I know, and told me she would do some shopping, and pay a few calls in the afternoon."

'"Do you know at all where she intended to go when she got into the Underground Railway?"

'"Well, not with certainty. You see, she may have meant to get out at Baker Street, and go down to Bond Street to do her shopping. Then, again, she sometimes goes to a shop in St Paul's Churchyard, in which case she would take a ticket to Aldersgate Street; but I cannot say."

'"Now, Mr Hazeldene," said the coroner at last very kindly, "will you try to tell me if there was anything in Mrs Hazeldene's life which you know of, and which might in some measure explain the cause of the distressed state of mind, which you yourself had noticed? Did there exist any financial difficulty which might have preyed upon Mrs Hazeldene's mind; was there any friend – to whose intercourse with Mrs Hazeldene – you – er – at any time took exception? In fact," added the coroner, as if thankful that he had got over an unpleasant moment, "can you give me the slightest indication which would tend to confirm the suspicion that the unfortunate lady, in a moment of mental anxiety or derangement, may have wished to take her own life?"

'There was silence in the court for a few moments. Mr Hazeldene seemed to everyone there present to be labouring under some terrible moral doubt. He looked very pale and wretched, and twice attempted to speak before he at last said in scarcely audible tones: "No; there were no financial difficulties of any sort. My wife had an independent fortune of her own – she had no extravagant tastes—"

'"Nor any friend you at any time objected to?" insisted the coroner.

'"Nor any friend, I – at any time objected to," stammered the unfortunate young man, evidently speaking with an effort.

'I was present at the inquest,' resumed the man in the corner, after he had drunk a glass of milk and ordered another, 'and I can assure you that the most obtuse person there plainly realised that Mr Hazeldene was telling a lie. It was pretty plain to the meanest intelligence that the unfortunate lady had not fallen into a state of morbid dejection for nothing, and that perhaps there existed a third person who could throw more light on her strange and sudden death than the unhappy, bereaved young widower.

'That the death was more mysterious even than it had at first appeared became very soon apparent. You read the case at the time, no doubt, and must remember the excitement in the public mind caused by the evidence of the two doctors. Dr Arthur Jones, the lady's usual medical man, who had attended her in a last very slight illness, and who had seen her in a professional capacity fairly recently, declared most emphatically that Mrs Hazeldene suffered from no organic complaint which could possibly have been the cause of sudden death. Moreover, he had assisted Mr Andrew Thornton, the district medical officer, in making a post mortem examination, and together they had come to the conclusion that death was due to the action of prussic acid, which had caused instantaneous failure of the heart, but how the drug had been administered neither he nor his colleague were at present able to state.

'"Do I understand, then, Dr Jones, that the deceased died, poisoned with prussic acid?"

'"Such is my opinion," replied the doctor.

'"Did the bottle found in her satchel contain prussic acid?"

'"It had contained some at one time, certainly."

'"In your opinion, then, the lady caused her own death by taking a dose of that drug?"

'"Pardon me, I never suggested such a thing: the lady died poisoned by the drug, but how the drug was administered we cannot say. By injection of some sort, certainly. The drug certainly was not swallowed; there was not a vestige of it in the stomach."

'"Yes," added the doctor in reply to another question from the coroner, "death had probably followed the injection in this case almost immediately; say within a couple of minutes, or perhaps three. It was quite possible that the body would not have more than one quick and sudden convulsion, perhaps not that; death in such cases is absolutely sudden and crushing."

'I don't think that at the time anyone in the room realised how important the doctor's statement was, a statement, which, by the way, was confirmed in all its details by the district medical officer, who had conducted the post mortem. Mrs Hazeldene had died suddenly from an injection of prussic acid, administered no one knew how or when. She had been travelling in a first-class railway carriage in a busy time of the day. That young and elegant woman must have had singular nerve and coolness to go through the process of a self-inflicted injection of deadly poison in the presence of perhaps two or three other persons.

'Mind you, when I say that no one there realised the importance of the doctors' statements at that moment, I am wrong; there were three persons who fully understood at once the gravity of the situation and the astounding development which the case was beginning to assume.

'Of course, I should have put myself out of the question,' added the weird old man, with that inimitable self-conceit peculiar to himself. 'I guessed then and there in a moment where the police were going wrong, and where they would go on going wrong until the mysterious death on the Underground Railway had sunk into oblivion, together with the other cases which they mismanage from time to time.

'I said there were three persons who understood the gravity of the two doctors' statements – the other two were, firstly, the detective who had originally examined the railway carriage, a young man of energy and plenty of misguided intelligence, the other was Mr Hazeldene.

'At this point the interesting element of the whole story was first introduced into the proceedings, and this was done through the humble channel of Emma Funnel, Mrs Hazeldene's maid, who, as far as was known then, was the last person who had seen the unfortunate lady alive and had spoken to her.

'"Mrs Hazeldene lunched at home," explained Emma, who was shy, and spoke almost in a whisper. "She seemed well and cheerful. She went out at about half-past three, and told me she was going to Spence's, in St Paul's Churchyard, to try on her new tailor-made gown. Mrs Hazeldene had meant to go there in the morning, but was prevented as Mr Errington called."

'"Mr Errington?" asked the coroner casually. "Who is Mr Errington?"'

'But this Emma found difficult to explain. Mr Errington was – Mr Errington, that's all.

'"Mr Errington was a friend of the family. He lived in a flat in the Albert Mansions. He very often came to Addison Row, and generally stayed late."

'Pressed still further with questions, Emma at last stated that latterly Mrs Hazeldene had been to the theatre several times with Mr Errington, and that on those nights the master looked very gloomy, and was very cross.

'Recalled, the young widower was strangely reticent. He gave forth his answers very grudgingly, and the coroner was evidently absolutely satisfied with himself at the marvellous way in which, after a quarter of an hour of firm yet very kind questioning, he had elicited from the witness what information he wanted.

'Mr Errington was a friend of his wife. He was a gentleman of means, and seemed to have a great deal of time at his command. He himself did not particularly care about Mr Errington, but he certainly had never made any observations to his wife on the subject.

'"But who is Mr Errington?" repeated the coroner once more. "What does he do? What is his business or profession?"

'"He has no business or profession."

'"What is his occupation, then?"

'"He has no special occupation. He has ample private means. But he has a great and very absorbing hobby."

'"What is that?"

'"He spends all his time in chemical experiments, and is, I believe, as an amateur, a very distinguished toxicologist."

'Did you ever see Mr Errington, the gentleman so closely connected with the mysterious death on the Underground Railway?' asked the man in the corner as he placed one or two of his little snapshot photos before Miss Polly Burton.

'There he is, to the very life. Fairly good-looking, a pleasant face enough, but ordinary, absolutely ordinary.

'It was this absence of any peculiarity which very nearly, but not quite, placed the halter round Mr Errington's neck.

'But I am going too fast, and you will lose the thread. The public, of course, never heard how it actually came about that Mr Errington, the wealthy bachelor of Albert Mansions, of the Grosvenor, and other young dandies' clubs, one fine day found himself before the magistrates at Bow Street, charged with being concerned in the death of Mary Beatrice Hazeldene, late of number 19, Addison Row.

'I can assure you both press and public were literally flabber-
gasted. You see, Mr Errington was a well-known and very popular
member of a certain smart section of London society. He was a constant visitor at the opera, the racecourse, the Park, and the Carlton,
he had a great many friends, and there was consequently quite a large
attendance at the police court that morning. What had happened was
this: After the very scrappy bits of evidence which came to light at the
inquest, two gentlemen bethought themselves that perhaps they had
some duty to perform towards the State and the public generally.
Accordingly they had come forward offering to throw what light they
could upon the mysterious affair on the Underground Railway.

'The police naturally felt that their information, such as it was,
came rather late in the day, but as it proved of paramount importance, and the two gentlemen, moreover, were of undoubtedly good
position in the world, they were thankful for what they could get, and
acted accordingly; they accordingly brought Mr Errington up before
the magistrate on a charge of murder.

'The accused looked pale and worried when I first caught sight of
him in the court that day, which was not to be wondered at, considering the terrible position in which he found himself. He had been
arrested at Marseilles, where he was preparing to start for Colombo.

'I don't think he realised how terrible his position was until later
in the proceedings, when all the evidence relating to the arrest had
been heard, and Emma Funnel had repeated her statement as to Mr
Errington's call at 19 Addison Row, in the morning, and Mrs
Hazeldene starting off for St Paul's Churchyard at 3.30 in the afternoon. Mr Hazeldene had nothing to add to the statements he had
made at the coroner's inquest. He had last seen his wife alive on the
morning of the fatal day. She had seemed very well and cheerful.

'I think everyone present understood that he was trying to say as
little as possible that could in any way couple his deceased wife's
name with that of the accused.

'And yet, from the servant's evidence, it undoubtedly leaked out
that Mrs Hazeldene, who was young, pretty, and evidently fond of
admiration, had once or twice annoyed her husband by her somewhat open, yet perfectly innocent flirtation with Mr Emington.

'I think everyone was most agreeably impressed by the widower's
moderate and dignified attitude. You will see his photo there, among
this bundle. That is just how he appeared in court. In deep black, of
course, but without any sign of ostentation in his mourning. He had
allowed his beard to grow lately, and wore it closely cut in a point.

'After his evidence, the sensation of the day occurred. A tall, dark-haired man, with the word "City" written metaphorically all over him, had kissed the book, and was waiting to tell the truth, and nothing but the truth.

'He gave his name as Andrew Campbell, head of the firm of Campbell & Co, brokers, of Throgmorton Street.

'In the afternoon of 18 March Mr Campbell, travelling on the Underground Railway, had noticed a very pretty woman in the same carriage as himself. She had asked him if she was in the right train for Aldersgate. Mr Campbell replied in the affirmative, and then buried himself in the Stock Exchange quotations of his evening paper.

'At Gower Street, a gentleman in a tweed suit and bowler hat got into the carriage, and took a seat opposite the lady. She seemed very much astonished at seeing him, but Mr Campbell did not recollect the exact words she said.

'The two talked to one another a good deal, and certainly the lady appeared animated and cheerful. Witness took no notice of them; he was very much engrossed in some calculations, and finally got out at Farringdon Street. He noticed that the man in the tweed suit also got out close behind him, having shaken hands with the lady, and said in a pleasant way: "*Au revoir*! Don't be late tonight." Mr Campbell did not hear the lady's reply, and soon lost sight of the man in the crowd.

'Everyone was on tenterhooks, and eagerly waiting for the palpitating moment when the witness would describe and identify the man who last had seen and spoken to the unfortunate woman, within five minutes probably of her strange and unaccountable death.

'Personally I knew what was coming before the Scotch stockbroker spoke. I could have jotted down the graphic and lifelike description he would give of a probable murderer. It would have fitted equally well the man who sat and had luncheon at this table just now; it would certainly have described five out of every ten young Englishmen you know.

'The individual was of medium height, he wore a moustache which was not very fair nor yet very dark, his hair was between colours. He wore a bowler hat, and a tweed suit – and – and – that was all – Mr Campbell might perhaps know him again, but then again, he might not – he was not paying much attention – the gentleman was sitting on the same side of the carriage as himself – and he had his hat on all the time. He himself was busy with his newspaper – yes – he might know him again – but he really could not say.

'Mr Andrew Campbell's evidence was not worth very much, you

will say. No, it was not in itself, and would not have justified any arrest were it not for the additional statements made by Mr James Verner, manager of Messrs Rodney & Co, colour printers.

'Mr Verner is a personal friend of Mr Andrew Campbell, and it appears that at Farringdon Street, where he was waiting for his train, he saw Mr Campbell get out of a first-class railway carriage. Mr Verner spoke to him for a second, and then, just as the train was moving off, he stepped into the same compartment which had just been vacated by the stockbroker and the man in the tweed suit. He vaguely recollects a lady sitting in the opposite corner to his own, with her face turned away from him, apparently asleep, but he paid no special attention to her. He was like nearly all businessmen when they are travelling – engrossed in his paper. Presently a special quotation interested him; he wished to make a note of it, took out a pencil from his waistcoat pocket, and seeing a clean piece of pasteboard on the floor, he picked it up, and scribbled on it the memorandum, which he wished to keep. He then slipped the card into his pocket-book.'

'It was only two or three days later,' added Mr Verner in the midst of breathless silence, 'that I had occasion to refer to these same notes again.

'In the meanwhile the papers had been full of the mysterious death on the Underground Railway, and the names of those connected with it were pretty familiar to me. It was, therefore, with much astonishment that on looking at the pasteboard which I had casually picked up in the railway carriage I saw the name on it, 'Frank Errington'.

'There was no doubt that the sensation in court was almost unprecedented. Never since the days of the Fenchurch Street mystery, and the trial of Smethurst, had I seen so much excitement. Mind you, I was not excited – I knew by now every detail of that crime as if I had committed it myself. In fact, I could not have done it better, although I have been a student of crime for many years now. Many people there – his friends, mostly – believed that Errington was doomed. I think he thought so, too, for I could see that his face was terribly white, and he now and then passed his tongue over his lips, as if they were parched.

'You see he was in the awful dilemma – a perfectly natural one, by the way – of being absolutely incapable of proving an alibi. The crime – if crime there was – had been committed three weeks ago. A man about town like Mr Frank Errington might remember that he spent certain hours of a special afternoon at his club, or in the Park, but it is very doubtful in nine cases out of ten if he can find a friend who could positively swear as to having seen him there. No! Mr Errington was in a tight corner, and he knew it. You see, there were – besides the evidence – two or three circumstances which did not improve matters for him. His hobby in the direction of toxicology, to begin with. The police had found in his room every description of poisonous substance, including prussic acid.

'Then, again, that journey to Marseilles, the start for Colombo, was, though perfectly innocent, a very unfortunate one. Mr Errington had gone on an aimless voyage, but the public thought that he had fled, terrified at his own crime. Sir Arthur Inglewood, however, here again displayed his marvellous skill on behalf of his client by the masterly way in which he literally turned all the witnesses for the Crown inside out.

'Having first got Mr Andrew to state positively that in the accused he certainly did *not* recognise the man in the tweed suit, the eminent lawyer, after twenty minutes' cross-examination, had so completely upset the stockbroker's equanimity that it is very likely he would not have recognised his own office-boy.

'But through all his flurry and all his annoyance Mr Andrew Campbell remained very sure of one thing; namely, that the lady was alive and cheerful, and talking pleasantly with the man in the tweed suit up to the moment when the latter, having shaken hands with her, left her with a pleasant 'Au revoir! Don't be late tonight'. He had heard neither scream nor struggle, and in his opinion, if the individual in the tweed suit had administered a dose of poison to his companion, it must have been with her own knowledge and free will; and the lady in the train most emphatically neither looked nor spoke like a woman prepared for a sudden and violent death.

'Mr James Verner, against that, swore equally positively that he had stood in full view of the carriage door from the moment that Mr Campbell got out until he himself stepped into the compartment, that there was no one else in that carriage between Farringdon Street and Aldgate, and that the lady, to the best of his belief, had made no movement during the whole of that journey.

'No; Frank Errington was *not* committed for trial on the capital charge,' said the man in the corner with one of his sardonic smiles, 'thanks to the cleverness of Sir Arthur Inglewood, his lawyer. He absolutely denied his identity with the man in the tweed suit, and swore he had not seen Mrs Hazeldene since eleven o'clock in the morning of that fatal day. There was no proof that he had; moreover, according to Mr Campbell's opinion, the man in the tweed suit was in all probability not the murderer. Common sense would not admit that a woman could have a deadly poison injected into her without her knowledge, while chatting pleasantly to her murderer.

'Mr Errington lives abroad now. He is about to marry. I don't think any of his real friends for a moment believed that he committed the dastardly crime. The police think they know better. They do know this much, that it could not have been a case of suicide, that if the man who undoubtedly travelled with Mrs Hazeldene on that fatal afternoon had no crime upon his conscience he would long ago have come forward and thrown what light he could upon the mystery.

'As to who that man was, the police in their blindness have not the faintest doubt. Under the unshakeable belief that Errington is guilty they have spent the last few months in unceasing labour to try and find further and stronger proofs of his guilt. But they won't find them, because there are none. There are no positive proofs against the actual murderer, for he was one of those clever blackguards who think of everything, foresee every eventuality, who know human nature well and can foretell exactly what evidence will be brought against them, and act accordingly.

'This blackguard from the first kept the figure, the personality, of Frank Errington before his mind. Frank Errington was the dust which the scoundrel threw metaphorically in the eyes of the police, and you must admit that he succeeded in blinding them – to the extent even of making them entirely forget the one simple little sentence, overheard by Mr Andrew Campbell, and which was, of course, the clue to the whole thing – the only slip the cunning rogue made – "*Au revoir*! Don't be late tonight." Mrs Hazeldene was going that night to the opera with her husband.

'You are astonished?' he added with a shrug of the shoulders, 'you do not see the tragedy yet, as I have seen it before me all along. The frivolous young wife, the flirtation with the friend? – all a blind, all pretence. I took the trouble which the police should have taken immediately, of finding out something about the finances of the Hazeldene menage. Money is in nine cases out of ten the keynote to a crime.

'I found that the will of Mary Beatrice Hazeldene had been proved by the husband, her sole executor, the estate being sworn at £15,000. I found out, moreover, that Mr Edward Sholto Hazeldene was a poor shipper's clerk when he married the daughter of a wealthy builder in Kensington – and then I made note of the fact that the disconsolate widower had allowed his beard to grow since the death of his wife.

'There's no doubt that he was a clever rogue,' added the strange creature, leaning excitedly over the table, and peering into Polly's face. 'Do you know how that deadly poison was injected into the poor woman's system? By the simplest of all means, one known to every scoundrel in Southern Europe. A ring – yes! a ring, which has a tiny hollow needle capable of holding a sufficient quantity of prussic acid to have killed two persons instead of one. The man in the tweed suit shook hands with his fair companion – probably she hardly felt the prick, not sufficiently in any case to make her utter a scream. And, mind you, the scoundrel had every facility, through his friendship with Mr Errington, of procuring what poison he required, not to mention his friend's visiting card. We cannot gauge how many months ago he began to try and copy Frank Errington in his style of dress, the cut of his moustache, his general appearance, making the change probably so gradual that no one in his own entourage would notice it. He selected for his model a man his own height and build, with the same coloured hair.'

'But there was the terrible risk of being identified by his fellow-traveller in the Underground,' suggested Polly.

'Yes, there certainly was that risk; he chose to take it, and he was wise. He reckoned that several days would in any case elapse before that person, who, by the way, was a business man absorbed in his newspaper, would actually see him again. The great secret of success-ful crime is to study human nature,' added the man in the corner, as he began looking for his hat and coat. 'Edward Hazeldene knew it well.'

'But the ring?'

'He may have bought that when he was on his honeymoon,' he suggested with a grim chuckle; 'the tragedy was not planned in a week, it may have taken years to mature. But you will own that there goes a frightful scoundrel unhung. I have left you his photograph as he was a year ago, and as he is now. You will see he has shaved his beard again; but also his moustache. I fancy he is a friend now of Mr Andrew Campbell.'

He left Miss Polly Burton wondering, not knowing what to believe.

And that is why she missed her appointment with Mr Richard Frobisher (of the *London Mail*) to go and see Maud Allan dance at the Palace Theatre that afternoon.

WILLIAM LE QUEUX

The Secret of the Fox Hunter

IT HAPPENED three winters ago. Having just returned from Stuttgart, where I had spent some weeks at the Marquardt in the guise I so often assumed, that of Monsieur Gustav Dreux, commercial traveller, of Paris, and where I had been engaged in watching the movements of two persons staying in the hotel, a man and a woman, I was glad to be back again in Bloomsbury to enjoy the ease of my armchair and pipe.

I was much gratified that I had concluded a very difficult piece of espionage, and having obtained the information I sought, had been able to place certain facts before my Chief, the Marquess of Macclesfield, which had very materially strengthened his hands in some very delicate diplomatic negotiations with Germany. Perhaps the most exacting position in the whole of British diplomacy is the post of Ambassador at Berlin, for the Germans are at once our foes, as well as our friends, and are at this moment only too ready to pick a quarrel with us from motives of jealousy which may have serious results.

The war cloud was still hovering over Europe; hence a swarm of spies, male and female, were plotting, scheming, and working in secret in our very midst The reader would be amazed if he could but glance at a certain red-bound book, kept under lock and key at the Foreign Office, in which are registered the names, personal descriptions and other facts concerning all the known foreign spies living in London and in other towns in England.

But active as are the agents of our enemies, so also are we active in the opposition camp. Our Empire has such tremendous responsibilities that we cannot now depend upon mere birth, wealth and honest dealing, but must call in shrewdness, tact, subterfuge, and the employment of secret agents in order to combat the plots of those ever seeking to accomplish England's overthrow.

Careful student of international affairs that I was, I knew that trouble was brewing in China. Certain confidential dispatches from our Minister in Pekin had been shown to me by the Marquess, who, on occasion, flattered me by placing implicit trust in me, and from them I gathered that Russia was at work in secret to undermine our influence in the Far East.

I knew that the grave, kindly old statesman was greatly perturbed by the grim shadows that were slowly rising, but when we consulted on the day after my return from Stuttgart, his lordship was of the opinion that at present I had not sufficient ground upon which to institute inquiries.

'For the present, Drew,' he said, 'we must watch and wait. There is war in the air – first at Pekin, and then in Europe. But we must prevent it at all costs. Huntley leaves for Pekin tonight with dispatches in which I have fully explained the line which Sir Henry is to follow. Hold yourself in readiness, for you may have to return to Germany or Russia tomorrow. We cannot afford to remain long in the dark. We must crush any alliance between Petersburg and Berlin.'

'A telegram to my rooms will bring me to your lordship at any moment,' was my answer.

'Ready to go anywhere – eh, Drew?' he smiled; and then, after a further chat, I left Downing Street and returned to Bloomsbury.

Knowing that for at least a week or two I should be free, I left my address with Boyd, and went down to Cotterstock, in Northamptonshire, to stay with my old friend of college days, George Hamilton, who rented a hunting-box and rode with the Fitzwilliam Pack.

I had had a long-standing engagement with him to go down and get a few runs with the hounds, but my constant absence abroad had always prevented it until then. Of course none of my friends knew my real position at the Foreign Office. I was believed to be an attaché.

Personally, I am extremely fond of riding to hounds; therefore, when that night I sat at dinner with George, his wife, and the latter's cousin, Beatrice Graham, I was full of expectation of some good runs. An English country house, with its old oak, old silver and air of solidity, is always delightful to me after the flimsy gimcracks of Continental life. The evening proved a very pleasant one. Never having met Beatrice Graham before, I was much attracted by her striking beauty. She was tall and dark, about twenty-two, with a remarkable figure which was shown to advantage by her dinner-gown of turquoise blue. So well did she talk, so splendidly did she sing Dupont's 'Jeune Fille', and so enthusiastic was she regarding hunting, that, before I had been an hour with her, I found myself thoroughly entranced.

The meet, three days afterwards, was at Wansford, that old-time hunting centre by the Nene, about six miles distant, and as I rode at her side along the road though historic Fotheringay and Nassington, I noticed what a splendid horsewoman she was. Her dark hair was coiled tightly behind, and her bowler hat suited her face admirably while her habit fitted as though it had been moulded to her figure. In her mare's tail was a tiny piece of scarlet silk to warn others that she was a kicker.

At Wansford, opposite the old Haycock, once a hunting inn in the old coaching days, but now Lord Chesham's hunting-box, the gathering was a large one. From the great rambling old house servants carried glasses of sloe gin to all who cared to partake of his lordship's hospitality, while every moment the meet grew larger and the crowd of horses and vehicles more congested.

George had crossed to chat with the Master, Mr George Fitzwilliam, who had just driven up and was still in his overcoat, therefore I found myself alone with my handsome companion, who appeared to be most popular everywhere. Dozens of men and women rode up to her and exchanged greetings, the men more especially, until at last Barnard, the huntsman, drew his hounds together, the word was given, and they went leisurely up the hill to draw the first cover.

The morning was one of those damp cold ones of mid-February; the frost had given and everyone expected a good run, for the scent would be excellent. Riding side by side with my fair companion, we chatted and laughed as we went along, until, on reaching the cover, we drew up with the others and halted while hounds went in.

The first cover was, however, drawn blank, but from the second a fox went away straight for Elton, and soon the hounds were in full cry after him and we followed at a gallop. After a couple of miles more than half the field was left behind, still we kept on, until of a sudden, and without effort, my companion took a high hedge and was cutting across the pastures ere I knew that she had left the road. That she was a straight rider I at once saw, and I must confess that I preferred the gate to the hedge and ditch which she had taken so easily.

Half an hour later the kill took place near Haddon Hall, and of the half dozen in at the death Beatrice Graham was one.

When I rode up, five minutes afterwards, she smiled at me. Her face was a trifle flushed by hard riding, yet her hair was in no way awry, and she declared that she had thoroughly enjoyed that tearing gallop.

Just, however, as we sat watching Barnard cut off the brush, a tall, rather good-looking man rode up, having apparently been left just as

I had. As he approached I noticed that he gave my pretty friend a strange look, almost as of warning, while she on her part, refrained from acknowledging him. It was as though he had made her some secret sign which she had understood.

But there was a further fact that puzzled me greatly.

I had recognised in that well-turned-out hunting man someone whom I had had distinct occasion to recollect. At first I failed to recall the man's identity, but when I did, a few moments later, I sat regarding his retreating figure like one in a dream. The horseman who rode with such military bearing was none other than the renowned spy, one of the cleverest secret agents in the world, Otto Krempelstein, Chief of the German Secret Service.

That my charming little friend knew him was apparent. The slightest quiver in his eyelids and the almost imperceptible curl of his lip had not passed me unnoticed. There was some secret between them, of what nature I, of course, knew not. But all through that day my eyes were ever open to rediscover the man whose ingenuity and cunning had so often been in competition with my own. Twice I saw him again, once riding with a big dark-haired man in pink, on a splendid bay and followed by a groom with a second horse, and on the second occasion, at the edge of Stockbill Wood while we were waiting together he galloped past us, but without the slightest look of recognition.

'I wonder who that man is?' I remarked casually, as soon as he was out of hearing.

'I don't know,' was her prompt reply. 'He's often out with the hounds – a foreigner, I believe. Probably he's one of those who come to England for the hunting season. Since the late Empress of Austria came here to hunt, the Fitzwilliam has always been a favourite pack with the foreigners.'

I saw that she did not intend to admit that she had any knowledge of him. Like all women, she was a clever diplomatist. But he had made a sign to her – a sign of secrecy.

Did Krempelstein recognise me, I wondered? I could not think so, because we had never met face to face. He had once been pointed out to me in the Wilhelmstrasse in Berlin by one of our secret agents who knew him, and his features had ever since been graven on my memory.

That night, when I sat alone with my friend George, I learned from him that Mr Graham, his wife's uncle, had lived a long time on the Continent as manager to a large commercial firm, and that Beatrice had been born in France and had lived there a good many years. I made inquiries regarding the foreigners who were hunting that season with the Fitzwilliam, but he, with an Englishman's prejudice, declared that he knew none of them, and didn't want to know them.

The days passed and we went to several meets together at Apethorpe, at Castor Hanglands, at Laxton Park and other places, but I saw no more of Krempelstein. His distinguished-looking friend, however, I met on several occasions, and discovered that his name was Baron Stern, a wealthy Viennese, who had taken a hunting-box near Stoke Doyle, and had as friend a young man named Percival, who was frequently out with the hounds.

But the discovery there of Krempelstein had thoroughly aroused my curiosity. He had been there for some distinct purpose, without a doubt. Therefore I made inquiry of Kersch, one of our secret agents in Berlin, a man employed in the Ministry of Foreign Affairs, and from him received word that Krempelstein was back in Berlin, and further warning me that something unusual was afoot in England.

This aroused me at once to activity. I knew that Krempelstein and his agents were ever endeavouring to obtain the secrets of our guns, our ships, and our diplomacy with other nations, and I therefore determined that on this occasion he should not succeed. However much I admired Beatrice Graham, I now knew that she had lied to me, and that she was in all probability his associate. So I watched her carefully, and when she went out for a stroll or a ride, as she often did, I followed her.

How far I was justified in this action does not concern me. I had quite unexpectedly alighted upon certain suspicious facts, and was determined to elucidate them. The only stranger she met was Percival. Late one afternoon, just as dusk was deepening into night, she pulled up her mare beneath the bare black trees while crossing Burghley Park, and after a few minutes was joined by the young foreigner, who, having greeted her, chatted for a long time in a low, earnest tone, as though giving her directions. She seemed to remonstrate with him, but at the place I was concealed I was unable to distinguish what was said. I saw him, however, hand her something, and then, raising his hat, he turned his horse and galloped away down the avenue in the opposite direction.

I did not meet her again until. I sat beside her at the dinner-table that night, and then I noticed how pale and anxious she was, entirely changed from her usual sweet, light-hearted self.

She told me that she had ridden into Stamford for exercise, but told me nothing of the clandestine meeting. How I longed to know what the young foreigner had given her. Whatever it was, she kept it a close secret to herself.

More than once I felt impelled to go to her room in her absence and search her cupboards, drawers and travelling trunks. My attitude towards her was that of a man fallen entirely in love, for I had discovered that she was easily flattered by a little attention.

I was searching for some excuse to know Baron Stern, but often for a week he never went to the meets. It was as though he purposely avoided me. He was still at Weldon Lodge, near Stoke Doyle, for George told me that he had met him in Oundle only two days before.

Three whole weeks went by, and I remained just as puzzled as ever. Beatrice Graham was, after all, a most delightful companion, and although she was to me a mystery, yet we had become excellent friends.

One afternoon, just as I entered the drawing-room where she stood alone, she hurriedly tore up a note, and threw the pieces on the great log fire. I noticed one tiny piece about an inch square remained unconsumed, and managed, half an hour later, to get possession of it.

The writing upon it was, I found, in German, four words in all, which, without context, conveyed to me no meaning.

On the following night Mrs Hamilton and Beatrice remained with us in the smoking-room till nearly eleven o'clock, and at midnight I bade my host good night, and ascended the stairs to retire. I had been in my room about half an hour when I heard stealthy footsteps. In an instant the truth flashed upon me. It was Beatrice on her way downstairs.

Quickly I slipped on some things and noiselessly followed my pretty fellow-guest through the drawing-room out across the lawn and into the lane beyond. White mists had risen from the river, and the low roaring of the weir prevented her hearing my footsteps behind her. Fearing lest I should lose her I kept close behind, following her across several grass fields until she came to Southwick Wood, a dark, deserted spot, away from road or habitation.

Her intention was evidently to meet someone, so when, presently, she halted beneath a clump of high black firs, I also took shelter a short distance away.

She sat on a fallen trunk of a tree and waited in patience. Time went on, and so cold was it that I became chilled to the bones. I longed for a pipe, but feared that the smell of tobacco or the light might attract her. Therefore I was compelled to crouch and await the clandestine meeting.

She remained very quiet. Not a dead leaf stirred; not a sound came from her direction. I wondered why she waited in such complete silence.

Nearly two hours passed, when, at last, cramped and half frozen, I raised myself in order to peer into the darkness in her direction.

At first I could see no one, but, on straining my eyes, I saw, to my dismay, that she had fallen from the tree trunk, and was lying motionless in a heap upon the ground.

I called to her, but received no reply. Then rising, I walked to the spot, and in dismay threw myself on my knees and tried to raise her. My hand touched her white cheek. It was as cold as stone.

Next instant I undid her fur cape and bodice, and placed my hand upon her heart. There was no movement.

Beatrice Graham was dead.

The shock of the discovery held me spellbound. But when, a few moments later, I aroused myself to action, a difficult problem presented itself. Should I creep back to my room and say nothing, or should I raise the alarm, and admit that I had been watching her? My first care was to search the unfortunate girl's pocket, but I found nothing save a handkerchief and purse.

Then I walked back, and, regardless of the consequences, gave the alarm.

It is unnecessary here to describe the sensation caused by the discovery, or of how we carried the body back to the house. Suffice it to say that we called the doctor, who could find no mark of violence, or anything to account for death.

And yet she had expired suddenly, without a cry.

One feature, however, puzzled the doctor – namely, that her left hand and arm were much swollen, and had turned almost black, while the spine was curved – a fact which aroused a suspicion of some poison akin to strychnia.

From the very first, I held a theory that she had been secretly poisoned, but with what motive I could not imagine.

A post-mortem examination was made by three doctors on the following day, but, beyond confirming the theory I held, they discovered nothing.

On the day following, a few hours before the inquest, I was recalled to the Foreign Office by telegraph, and that same afternoon sat with the Marquess of Macclesfield in his private room receiving his instructions.

An urgent dispatch from Lord Rockingham, our Ambassador at Petersburg, made it plain that an alliance had been proposed by

Russia to Germany, the effect of which would be to break British power in the Far East. His Excellency knew that the terms of the secret agreement had been settled, and all that remained was its signature. Indeed, it would have already been signed save for opposition in some quarters unknown, and while that opposition existed I might gain time to ascertain the exact terms of the proposed alliance – no light task in Russia, be it said, for police spies exist there in thousands, and my disguise had always to be very carefully thought out whenever I passed the frontier at Wirballen.

The Marquess urged upon me to put all our secret machinery in motion in order to discover the terms of the proposed agreement, and more particularly as regards the extension of Russian influence in Manchuria. 'I know well the enormous difficulties of the inquiry,' his lordship said; 'but recollect, Drew, that in this matter you may be the means of saving the situation in the Far East. If we gain knowledge of the truth, we may be able to act promptly and effectively. If not – well...' and the grey-headed statesman shrugged his shoulders expressively without concluding the sentence.

Full of regret that I was unable to remain at Cotterstock and sift the mystery surrounding Beatrice Graham's death, I left London that night for Berlin, where, on the following evening, I called upon our secret agent, Kersch, who lived in a small but comfortable house at Teltow, one of the suburbs of the German capital. He occupied a responsible position in the German Foreign Office, but, having expensive tastes and a penchant for cards, was not averse to receiving British gold in exchange for the confidential information with which he furnished us from time to time.

I sat with him, discussing the situation for a long time. It was true, he said, that a draft agreement had been prepared and placed before the Tsar and the Kaiser, but it had not yet been signed. He knew nothing of the clauses, however, as they had been prepared in secret by the Minister's own hand, neither could he suggest any means of obtaining knowledge of them.

My impulse was to go on next day to Petersburg. Yet somehow I felt that I might be more successful in Germany than in Russia, so resolved to continue my inquiries.

'By the way,' the German said, 'you wrote me about Krempelstein. He has been absent a great deal lately, but I had no idea he had been to England. Can he be interested in the same matter on which you are now engaged?'

'Is he now in Berlin?' I inquired eagerly.

'I met him at Boxhagen three days ago. He seems extremely active just now.'

'Three days ago!' I echoed. 'You are quite certain of the day?' I asked him this because, if his statement were true, it was proved beyond doubt that the German spy had no hand in the unfortunate girl's death.

'I am quite certain,' was his reply. 'I saw him entering the station on Monday morning.'

At eleven o'clock that same night, I called at the British Embassy and sat for a long time with the Ambassador in his private room. His Excellency told me all he knew regarding the international complication which the Marquess, sitting in Downing Street, had foreseen weeks ago, but could make no suggestion as to my course of action. The war clouds had gathered undoubtedly, and the signing of the agreement between our enemies would cause it at once to burst over Europe. The crisis was one of the most serious in English history.

One fact puzzled us both, just as it puzzled our Chief at home – namely, if the agreement had been seen and approved by both Emperors, why was it not signed? Whatever hitch had occurred, it was more potent than the will of the two most powerful monarchs in Europe.

On my return to the hotel I scribbled a hasty note and sent it by messenger to the house of the Imperial Chancellor's son in Charlottenburg. It was addressed to Miss Maud Baines, the English governess of the Count's children, who, I may as well admit, was in our employ. She was a young, ingenuous and fascinating little woman. She had, at my direction, acted as governess in many of the great families in France, Russia and Germany, and was now in the employ of the Chancellor's son, in order to have an opportunity of keeping a watchful eye on the great statesman himself.

She kept the appointment next morning at an obscure cafe near the Behrenstrasse. She was a neatly dressed, rather petite person, with a face that entirely concealed her keen intelligence and marvellous cunning.

As she sat at the little table with me, I told her in low tones of the object of my visit to Berlin, and sought her aid.

'A serious complication has arisen. I was about to report to you through the Embassy,' was her answer. 'Last night the Chancellor dined with us, and I overheard him discussing the affair with his son as they sat alone smoking after the ladies had left. I listened at the door and heard the Chancellor distinctly say that the draft treaty had been stolen.'

'Stolen!' I gasped. 'By whom?'

'Ah! that's evidently the mystery – a mystery for us to fathom. But the fact that somebody else is in possession of the intentions of Germany and Russia against England, believed to be a secret, is no doubt the reason why the agreement has not been signed.'

'Because it is no longer secret!' I suggested. 'Are you quite certain you've made no mistake?'

'Quite,' was her prompt answer. 'You can surely trust me after the intricate little affairs which I have assisted you in unravelling? When may I return to Gloucester to see my friends?'

'Soon, Miss Baines – as soon as this affair is cleared up. But tell me, does the Chancellor betray any fear of awkward complications when the secret of the proposed plot against England is exposed?'

'Yes. The Prince told his son in confidence that his only fear was of England's retaliation. He explained that, as far as was known, the secret document, after being put before the Tsar and approved, mysteriously disappeared. Every inquiry was being made by the confidential agents of Russia and Germany, and further, he added that even his trusted Krempelstein was utterly nonplussed.'

Mention of Krempelstein brought back to me the recollection of the tragedy in rural England.

'You've done us a great service, Miss Baines,' I said. 'This information is of the highest importance. I shall telegraph in cipher at once to Lord Macclesfield. Do you, by any chance, happen to know a young lady named Graham?' I inquired, recollecting that the deceased woman had lived in Germany for several years.

She responded in the negative, whereupon I drew from my pocket a snapshot photograph, which I had taken of one of the meets of hounds at Wansford, and handing it to her inquired if she recognised any of the persons in it.

Having carefully examined it, she pointed to Baron Stern, whom I had taken in the act of lighting a cigarette, and exclaimed: 'Why! that's Colonel Davidoff, who was secretary to Prince Obolenski when I was in his service. Do you know him?'

'No,' I answered. 'But he has been hunting in England as Baron Stern, of Vienna. This man is his friend,' I added, indicating Percival.

'And that's undoubtedly a man whom you know well by repute – Moore, Chief of the Russian Secret Service in England. He came to Prince Obolenski's once, when he was in Petersburg, and the Princess told me who he was.'

Unfortunately, I had not been able to include Beatrice in the group, therefore I had only her description to place before the clever young woman, who had, on so many occasions, gained knowledge of secrets where I and my agents had failed. Her part was always a difficult one to play, but she was well paid, was a marvellous linguist, and for patience and cunning was unequalled.

I described her as minutely as I could, but still she had no knowledge of her. She remained thoughtful a long time, and then observed:

'You have said that she apparently knew Moore? He has, I know recently been back in Petersburg, therefore they may have met there. She may be known. Why not seek for traces of her in Russia?'

It seemed something of a wild-goose chase, yet with the whole affair shrouded in mystery and tragedy as it was, I was glad to adopt any suggestion that might lead to a solution of the enigma. The reticence of Mrs Hamilton regarding her cousin, and the apparent secret association of the dead girl with those two notorious spies, had formed a problem which puzzled me almost to the point of madness.

The English governess told me where in Petersburg I should be likely to find either of the two Russian agents, Davidoff or Moore, who had been posing in England for some unknown purpose as hunting men of means; therefore I left by the night mail for the Russian capital. I put up at a small, and not over-clean hotel, in preference to the Europe, and, compelled to carefully conceal my identity, I at once set about making inquiries in various quarters, whether the two men had returned to Russia. They had, and had both had long interviews, two days before, with General Zouboff, Chief of the Secret Service, and with the Russian Foreign Minister.

At the Embassy, and in various English quarters, I sought trace of the woman whose death was such a profound mystery, but all in vain. At last I suddenly thought of another source of information as yet untried – namely, the register of the English Charity in Petersburg, and on searching it, I found, to my complete satisfaction, that about six weeks before Beatrice Graham applied to the administration, and was granted money to take her back to England. She was the daughter, it was registered, of a Mr Charles Graham, the English manager of a cotton mill in Moscow, who had been killed by an accident, and had left her penniless. For some months she had tried to earn her own living, in a costumier's shop in the Newski, and, not knowing Russian sufficiently well, had been discharged. Before her father's death she had been engaged to marry a young Englishman, whose name was not given, but who was said to be tutor to the children of General Vraski, Governor-General of Warsaw.

The information was interesting, but carried me no further, therefore I set myself to watch the two men who had travelled from England to consult the Tsar's chief adviser. Aided by two Russians, who were in British pay, I shadowed them day and night for six days, until, one evening, I followed Davidoff down to the railway station, where he took a ticket for the frontier. Without baggage I followed him, for his movements were of a man who was escaping from the country. He passed out across the frontier, and went on to Vienna and then direct to Paris, where he put up at the Hotel Terminus, Gare St Lazare. Until our arrival at the hotel he had never detected that I was following him, but on the second day in Paris we came face to face in the large central hail, used as a reading room. He glanced at me quickly, but whether he recognised me as the companion of Beatrice Graham in the hunting field I have no idea. All I know is that his movements were extremely suspicious, and that I invoked the aid of all three of our Secret Agents in Paris to keep watch on him, just as had been done in Petersburg.

On the fourth night of our arrival in the French capital I returned to the hotel about midnight, having dined at the Cafe Americain with Greville, the naval attaché at the Embassy. In washing my hands prior to turning in, I received a nasty scratch on my left wrist from a pin which a careless laundress had left in the towel. There was a little blood, but I tied my handkerchief around it, and, tired outs lay down and was soon asleep.

Half an hour afterwards, however, I was aroused by an excruciating pain over my whole heft side, a strange twitching of the muscles of my face and hands, and a contraction of the throat which prevented me from breathing or crying out.

I tried to press the electric bell for assistance, but could not. My whole body seemed entirely paralysed. Then the ghastly truth flashed upon me, causing me to break out into a cold sweat.

That pin had been placed there purposely. I had been poisoned and in the same manner as Beatrice Graham!

I recollect that my heart seemed to stop, and my nails clenched themselves in the palms in agony. Then next moment I knew no more.

When I recovered consciousness, Ted Greville, together with a tall, black-bearded man named Delisle, who was in the confidential department of the Quai d'Orsay and who often furnished us with information – at a very high figure, be it said – were standing by my bedside, while a French doctor was leaning over the foot rail watching me.

'Thank heaven you're better, old chap!' Greville exclaimed. 'They thought you were dead. You've had a narrow squeak. How did it happen?'

'That pin!' I cried, pointing to the towel.

'What pin?' he asked.

'Mind! don't touch the towel,' I cried. 'There's a pin in it – a pin that's poisoned! That Russian evidently came here in my absence and very cunningly laid a death-trap for me.'

'You mean Davidoff,' chimed in the Frenchman. 'When, monsieur, the doctor has left the room I can tell you something in confidence.'

The doctor' discreetly withdrew, and then our spy said, 'Davidoff has turned traitor to his own country. I have discovered that the reason of his visit here is because he has in his possession the original draft of a proposed secret agreement between Russia and Germany against England, and is negotiating for its sale to us for one hundred thousand francs. He had a secret interview with our Chief last night at his private house in the Avenue des Champs Elysees.'

'Then it is he who stole it, after it had the Tsar's approval!' I cried, starting up in bed, aroused at once to action by the information. 'Has he disposed of it to France?'

'Not yet. It is still in his possession.'

'And he is here?'

'No. He has hidden himself in lodgings in the Rue Lafayette, number 247, until the Foreign Minister decides whether he shall buy the document.'

'And the name by which he is known there?'

'He is passing as a Greek named Geunadios.'

'Keep a strict watch on him. He must not escape,' I said. 'He has endeavoured to murder me.'

'A watch is being kept,' was the Frenchman's answer, as, exhausted, I sank again upon the pillow.

Just before midnight I entered the traitor's room in the Rue Lafayette, and when he saw me he fell back with blanched face and trembling hands.

'No doubt my presence here surprises you,' I said, 'but I may as well at once state my reason for coming here. I want a certain document which concerns Germany and your own country – the document which you have stolen to sell to France.'

'What do you mean, m'sieur?' he asked, with an attempted hauteur.

'My meaning is simple. I require that document, otherwise I shall give you into the hands of the police for attempted murder. The Paris police will detain you until the police of Petersburg apply for your extradition as a traitor. You know what that means – Schusselburg.'

Mention of that terrible island fortress, dreaded by every Russian, caused him to quiver. He looked me straight in the face, and saw determination written there, yet he was unyielding, and refused for a long time to give the precious document into my hands. I referred to his stay at Stoke Doyle, and spoke of his friendship with the spy Moore, so that he should know that I was aware of the truth, until at last he suggested a bargain with me, namely, that in exchange for the draft agreement against England I should preserve silence and permit him to return to Russia.

To this course I acceded, and then the fellow took from a secret cavity of his travelling bag a long official envelope, which contained the innocent-looking paper, which would, if signed, have destroyed England's prestige in the Far East. He handed it to me, the document for which he hoped to obtain one hundred thousand francs, and in return I gave him his liberty to go back to Russia unmolested.

Our parting was the reverse of cordial, for undoubtedly he had placed in my towel the pin which had been steeped in some subtle and deadly poison, and then escaped from the hotel, in the knowledge that I must sooner or later become scratched and fall a victim.

I had had a very narrow escape it was true, but I did not think so much of my good fortune in regaining my life as the rapid delivery of the all-important document into Lord Macclesfield's hands, which I effected at noon next day.

My life had been at stake, for I afterwards found that a second man had been his accomplice, but happily I had succeeded in obtaining possession of the actual document, the result being that England acted so promptly and vigourously that the situation was saved, and the way was, as you know, opened for the Anglo-Japanese Treaty, which, to the discomfiture of Germany, was effected a few months later.

Nearly two years have gone by since then, and it was only the other day, by mere accident, that I made a further discovery which explained the death of the unfortunate Beatrice Graham.

A young infantry lieutenant, named Bellingham, having passed in Russian, had some four years before entered our Secret Service, and been employed in Russia on certain missions. A few days ago, on his return to London, after performing a perilous piece of espionage on the Russo-German frontier, he called upon me in Bloomsbury, and in course of conversation, mentioned that about two years ago, in order to get access to certain documents relating to the Russian mobilisation scheme for her western frontier, he acted as tutor to the sons of the Governor-General of Warsaw.

In an instant a strange conjecture flashed across my mind.

'Am I correct in assuming that you knew a young English lady in Russia named Graham – Beatrice Graham?'

He looked me straight in the face, open-mouthed in astonishment, yet I saw that a cloud of sadness overshadowed him instantly.

'Yes,' he said. 'I knew her. Our meeting resulted in a terrible tragedy. Owing to the position I hold I have been compelled to keep the details to myself – although it is the tragedy of my life.'

'How? Tell me,' I urged sympathetically.

'Ah!' he sighed, 'it is a strange story. We met in Petersburg, where she was employed in a shop in the Newski. I loved her, and we became engaged. Withholding nothing from her I told her who I was and the reason I was in the service of the Governor-General. At once, instead of despising me as a spy, she became enthusiastic as an Englishwoman, and declared her readiness to assist me. She was looking forward to our marriage, and saw that if I could effect a big coup my position would at once be improved, and we could then be united.'

He broke off, and remained silent for a few moments, looking blankly down into the grey London street. Then he said, 'I explained to her the suspicion that Germany and Russia were conspiring in the Far East, and told her that a draft treaty was probably in existence, and that it was a document of supreme importance to British interests. Judge my utter surprise when, a week later, she came to me with the actual document which she said she had managed to secure from the private cabinet of Prince Korolkoff, director of the private Chancellerie of the Emperor, to whose house she had gone on a commission to the Princess. Truly she had acted with a boldness and cleverness that were amazing. Knowing the supreme importance of that document, I urged her to leave Russia at once, and conceal herself with friends in England, taking care always that the draft treaty never left her possession. This plan she adopted, first, however, placing herself under the protection of the English charity, thus allaying any suspicions that the police might entertain.

'Poor Beatrice went to stay with her cousin, a lady named Hamilton, in Northamptonshire, but the instant the document was missed the Secret Services of Germany and Russia were at once agog, and the whole machinery was set in, motion, with the result that two Russian agents – an Englishman named Moore, and a Russian named David-off – as well as Krempelstein, chief of the German Service, had suspicions, and followed her to England with the purpose of obtaining repossession of the precious document. For some weeks they plotted in vain, although both the German and the Englishman succeeded in getting on friendly terms with her.

'She telegraphed to me, asking how she should dispose of the document, fearing to keep it long in her possession, but not being aware of the desperate character of the game, I replied that there was nothing to be feared. I was wrong,' he cried, bitterly. 'I did not recognise the vital importance of the information; I did not know that Empires were at stake. The man Davidoff, who posed as a wealthy Austrian Baron, had by some means discovered that she always carried the precious draft concealed in the bodice of her dress, therefore he had recourse to a dastardly ruse. From what I have since discovered he one day succeeded in concealing in the fur of her cape a pin impregnated with a certain deadly arrow poison unknown to toxicologists. Then he caused to be dispatched from London a telegram purporting to come from me, urging her to meet me in secret at a certain spot on that same night. In eager expectation the poor girl went forth to meet me, believing I had returned unexpectedly from Russia, but in putting on her cape, she tore her finger with the poisoned pin. While waiting for me the fatal paralysis seized her, and she expired, after which Davidoff crept up, secured the missing document and escaped. His anxiety to get hold of it was to sell it at a high price to a foreign country, nevertheless he was compelled first to return to Russia and report. No one knew that he actually held the draft, for to Krempelstein, as well as to Moore, my poor love's death was believed to be due to natural causes, while Davidoff, on his part, took care so to arrange matters, that his presence at the spot where poor Beatrice expired could never be proved. The spies therefore left England reluctantly after the tragedy, believing that the document, if ever possessed by my unfortunate love, had passed out of her possession into unknown hands.'

'And what of the assassin Davidoff now?' I inquired.

'I have avenged her death,' answered Bellingham with set teeth. 'I gave information to General Zouboff of the traitor's attempted sale of the draft treaty to France, with the result that the court martial has condemned him to incarceration for life in the cells below the lake at Schusselburg.'

CLIFFORD ASHDOWN

The Submarine Boat

TRIC-TRAC! tric-trac! went the black and white discs as the players moved them over the backgammon board in expressive justification of the French term for the game. Tric-trac! They are indeed a nation of poets, reflected Mr Pringle. Was not Teuf-teuf! for the motorcar a veritable inspiration? And as he smoked, the not unmusical clatter of the enormous wooden discs filled the atmosphere.

In these days of cookery not entirely based upon air-tights – to use the expressive Americanism for tinned meats – it is no longer necessary for the man who wishes to dine, as distinguished from the mere feeding animal, to furtively seek some restaurant in remote Soho, jealously guarding its secret from his fellows. But Mr Pringle, in his favourite study of human nature, was an occasional visitor to the 'Poissoniere' in Gerrard Street, and, the better to pursue his researches, had always denied familiarity with the foreign tongues he heard around him. The restaurant was distinctly close – indeed, some might have called it stuffy – and Pringle, though near a ventilator, thoughtfully provided by the management, was fast being lulled into drowsiness, when a man who had taken his seat with a companion at the next table leaned across the intervening gulf and addressed him.

'*Nous ne vous derangeons pas, monsieur?*'

Pringle, with a smile of fatuous uncomprehending, bowed, but said never a word.

'*Cochon d'Anglais, n'entendez-vous pas?*'

'I'm afraid I do not understand,' returned Pringle, shaking his head hopelessly, but still smiling.

'*Canaille! Faut-il que je vous tire le nez?*' persisted the Frenchman, as, apparently still sceptical of Pringle's assurance, he added threats to abuse.

'I have known the English gentleman a long time, and without a doubt he does not understand French,' testified the waiter who had now come forward for orders. Satisfied by this corroboration of Pringle's innocence, the Frenchman bowed and smiled sweetly to him, and, ordering a bottle of Clos de Vougeot, commenced an earnest conversation with his neighbour.

By the time this little incident had closed, Pringle's drowsiness had given place to an intense feeling of curiosity. For what purpose could the Frenchman have been so insistent in disbelieving his expressed ignorance of the language? Why, too, had he striven to make Pringle betray himself by resenting the insults showered upon him? In a Parisian restaurant, as he knew, far more trivial affronts had ended in meetings in the Bois de Boulogne. Besides, *cochon* was an actionable term of opprobrium in France. The Frenchman and his companion had seated themselves at the only vacant table, also it was in a corner; Pringle, at the next, was the single person within earshot, and the Frenchman's extraordinary behaviour could only be due to a consuming thirst for privacy. Settling himself in an easy position, Pringle closed his eyes, and while appearing to resume his slumber, strained every nerve to discern the lightest word that passed at the next table. Dressed in the choicest mode of Piccadilly, the Frenchman bore himself with all the intolerable self-consciousness of the Boulevardier; but there was no trace of good-natured levity in the dark aquiline features, and the evil glint of the eyes recalled visions of an operatic Mephistopheles. His guest was unmistakably an Englishman of the bank-clerk type, who contributed his share of the conversation in halting Anglo-French, punctuated by nervous laughter as, with agonising pains, he dredged his memory for elusive colloquialisms.

Freely translated, this was what Pringle heard:

'So your people have really decided to take up the submarine, after all? '

'Yes; I am working out the details of some drawings in small-scale.'

'But are they from headquarters?'

'Certainly! Duly initialled and passed by the chief constructor.'

'And you are making—'

'Full working drawings.'

'There will be no code or other secret about them?'

'What I am doing can be understood by any naval architect.'

'Ah, an English one!'

'The measurements of course, are English, but they are easily convertible.'

'You could do that?'

'Too dangerous! Suppose a copy in metric scale were found in my possession! Besides, any draughtsman could reduce them in an hour or two.'

'And when can you let me have it?'

'In about two weeks.'

'Impossible! I shall not be here.'

'Unless something happens to let me get on with it quickly, I don't see how I can do it even then. I am never sufficiently free from interruption to take tracings; there are far too many eyes upon me. The only chance I have is to spoil the thing as soon as I have the salient points worked out on it, and after I have pretended to destroy it, smuggle it home; then I shall have to take elaborate notes every day and work out the details from them in the evening. It is simply impossible for me to attempt to take a finished drawing out of the yard, and, as it is, I don't quite see my way to getting the spoilt one out – they look so sharply after spoilt drawings.'

'Two weeks you say, then?'

'Yes; and I shall have to sit up most nights copying the day's work from my notes to do it.'

'Listen! In a week I must attend at the Ministry of Marine in Paris, but our military attaché is my friend. I can trust him; he shall come down to you.'

'What, at Chatham? Do you wish to ruin me?' A smile from the Frenchman. 'No; it must be in London, where no one knows me.'

'Admirable! My friend will be better able to meet you.'

'Very well, as soon as I am ready I will telegraph to you.'

'Might not the address of the embassy be remarked by the telegraph officials? Your English post-office is charmingly unsuspicious, but we must not risk anything.'

'Ah, perhaps so. Well, I will come up to London and telegraph to you from here. But your representative will he be prepared for it?'

'I will warn him to expect it in fourteen days.' He made an entry in his pocket-book. 'How will you sign the message?'

'Gustave Zédé,' suggested the Englishman, sniggering for the first and only time.

'Too suggestive. Sign yourself "Pauline", and simply add the time.'

'"Pauline",' then. Where shall the rendezvous be?'

'The most public place we can find.'

'Public?'

'Certainly. Some place where everyone will be too much occupied with his own affairs to notice you. What say you to your Nelson's column? There you can wait in a way we shall agree upon.'

'It would be a difficult thing for me to wear a disguise.'

'All disguises are clumsy unless one is an expert. Listen! You shall be gazing at the statue with one hand in your breast – so.'

'Yes; and I might hold a "Baedeker" in my other hand.'

'Admirable, my friend! You have the true spirit of an artist,' sneered the Frenchman.

'Your representative will advance and say to me, "Pauline", and the exchange can be made without another word.'

'Exchange?'

'I presume your Government is prepared to pay me handsomely for the very heavy risks I am running in this matter,' said the Englishman stiffly.

'Pardon, my friend! How imbecile of me! I am authorised to offer you ten thousand francs.'

A pause, during which the Englishman made a calculation on the back of an envelope.

'That is four hundred pounds,' he remarked, tearing the envelope into carefully minute fragments. 'Far too little for such a risk.'

'Permit me to remind you, my friend, that you came in search of me, or rather of those I represent. You have something to sell? Good! But it is customary for the merchant to display his wares first.'

'I pledge myself to give you copies of the working drawings made for the use of the artificers themselves. I have already met you oftener than is prudent. As I say, you offer too little.'

'Should the drawings prove useless to us, we should, of course, return them to your Admiralty, explaining how they came into our possession.' There was an unpleasant smile beneath the Frenchman's waxed moustache as he spoke. 'What sum do you ask?'

'Five hundred pounds in small notes – say, five pounds each.'

'That is – what do you say? Ah, twelve thousand five hundred francs! Impossible! My limit is twelve thousand.'

To this the Englishman at length gave an ungracious consent, and after some adroit compliments beneath which the other sought to bury his implied threat, the pair rose from the table. Either by accident or design, the Frenchman stumbled over the feet of Pringle, who, with his long legs stretching out from under the table, his head bowed and his lips parted, appeared in a profound slumber. Opening his eyes slowly, he feigned a lifelike yawn, stretched his arms, and gazed lazily around, to the entire satisfaction of the Frenchman, who, in the act of parting with his companion, was watching him from the door.

Calling for some coffee, Pringle lighted a cigarette, and reflected with a glow of indignant patriotism upon the sordid transaction he had become privy to. It is seldom that public servants are in this country found ready to betray their trust – with all honour be it recorded of them! But there ever exists the possibility of some under-paid official succumbing to the temptation at the command of the less scrupulous representatives of foreign powers, whose actions in this respect are always ignored officially by their superiors. To Pringle's somewhat cynical imagination, the sordid huckstering of a dockyard draughtsman with a French naval attaché appealed as corroboration of Walpole's famous principle, and as he walked homewards to Fur-nival's Inn, he determined, if possible, to turn his discovery to the mutual advantage of his country and himself – especially the latter.

During the next few days Pringle elaborated a plan of taking up a residence at Chatham, only to reject it as he had done many previous ones. Indeed, so many difficulties presented themselves to every single course of action, that the tenth day after found him strolling down Bond Street in the morning without having taken any further step in the matter. With his characteristic fastidious neatness in personal matters, he was bound for the Piccadilly establishment of the chief and, for West-Enders, the only firm of hatters in London.

'Breton Street, do you noh?' said a voice suddenly. And Pringle, turning found himself accosted by a swarthy foreigner.

'Bruton Street, *n'est-ce pas?*' Pringle suggested.

'*Mais oui*, Brrruten Street, monsieur!' was the reply in faint echo of the English syllables.

'*Le voila! à droite*,' was Pringle's glib direction. Politely raising his hat in response to the other's salute, he was about to resume his walk when he noticed that the Frenchman had been joined by a compan-ion, who appeared to have been making similar inquiries. The latter started and uttered a slight exclamation on meeting Pringle's eye. The recognition was mutual – it was the French attaché! As he hurried down Bond Street, Pringle realised with acutest annoyance that his deception at the restaurant had been unavailing, while he must now abandon all hope of a counter-plot for the honour of his country, to say nothing of his own profit. The port-wine mark on his right cheek was far too conspicuous for the attaché not to recognise him by it, and he regretted his neglect to remove it as soon as he had decided to follow up the affair. Forgetful of all beside, he walked on into Pic-cadilly, and it was not until he found himself more than halfway back to his chambers that he remembered the purpose for which he had set out; but matters of greater moment now claimed his attention, and he endeavoured by the brisk exercise to work off some of the chagrin with which he was consumed. Only as he reached the Inn and turned into the gateway did it occur to him that he had been culpably careless in thus going straight homeward. What if he had been followed? Never in his life had he shown such disregard of ordinary precautions. Glancing back, he just caught a glimpse of a figure which seemed to whip behind the corner of the gateway. He retraced his steps and looked out into Holborn. There, in the very act of retreat, and still but a few feet from the gate, was the attaché himself. Cursing the persistence of his own folly, Pringle dived through the arch again, and determined that the Frenchman should discover no more that day he turned nimbly to the left and ran up his own stairway before the pursuer could have time to re-enter the Inn.

The most galling reflection was his absolute impotence in the matter. Through lack of the most elementary foresight he had been fairly run to earth, and could see no way of ridding himself of this unwelcome attention. To transfer his domicile, to tear himself up by the roots as it were, was out of the question; and as he glanced around him, from the soft carpets and luxurious chairs to the warm, distempered walls with their old prints above the dado of dwarf bookcases, he felt that the pang of severance from the refined associations of his chambers would be too acute. Besides, he would inevitably be tracked elsewhere. He would gain nothing by the transfer. One thing at least was absolutely certain – the trouble which the Frenchman was taking to watch him showed the importance he attached to Pringle's discovery. But this again only increased his disgust with the ill-luck which had met him at the very outset. After all, he had done nothing illegal, however contrary it might be to the code of ethics, so that if it pleased them the entire French legation might continue to watch him till the Day of Judgment, and, consoling himself with this reflection, he philosophically dismissed the matter from his mind.

It was nearly six when he again left the Inn for Pagani's, the Great Portland Street restaurant which he much affected; instead of proceeding due west, he crossed Holborn intending to bear round by way of the Strand and Regent Street, and so get up an appetite. In Staple Inn he paused a moment in the further archway. The little square, always reposeful amid the stress and turmoil of its environment, seemed doubly so this evening, its eighteenth-century calm so welcome after the raucous thoroughfare. An approaching footfall echoed noisily, and as Pringle moved from the shadow of the narrow wall the newcomer hesitated and stopped, and then made the circuit of the square, scanning the doorways as if in search of a name. The action was not unnatural, and twenty-four hours earlier Pringle would have thought nothing of it, but after the events of the morning he endowed it with a personal interest, and, walking on, he ascended the steps into Southampton Buildings and stopped by a hoarding. As he looked back he was rewarded by the sight of a man stealthily emerging from the archway and making his way up the steps, only to halt as he suddenly came abreast of Pringle. Although his face was unfamiliar, Pringle could only conclude that the man was following him, and all doubt was removed when, having walked along the street and turning about at the entrance to Chancery Lane, he saw the spy had resumed the chase and was now but a few yards back. Pringle, as a philosopher, felt more inclined to laughter than resentment at this ludicrous espionage. In a spirit of mischief, he pursued his way to the Strand at a tortoise-like crawl, halting as if doubtful of his way at every corner, and staring into every shop whose lights still invited customers. Once or twice he even doubled back, and passing quite close to the man, had several opportunities of examining him. He was quite unobtrusive, even respectable-looking; there was nothing of the foreigner about him, and Pringle shrewdly conjectured that the attaché, wearied of sentry-go, had turned it over to some English servant on whom he could rely.

Thus shepherded, Pringle arrived at the restaurant, from which he only emerged after a stay maliciously prolonged over each item of the menu, followed by the smoking of no fewer than three cigars of a brand specially lauded by the proprietor. With a measure of humanity diluting his malice, he was about to offer the infallibly exhausted sentinel some refreshment when he came out, but as the man was invisible, Pringle started for home, taking much the same route as before, and calmly debating whether or no the cigars he had just sampled would be a wise investment; nor until he had reached Southampton Buildings and the sight of the hoarding recalled the spy's discomfiture, did he think of looking back to see if he were still followed. All but the main thoroughfares were by this time deserted, and although he shot a keen glance up and down Chancery Lane, now clear of all but the most casual traffic, not a soul was anywhere near him. By a curious psychological process Pringle felt inclined to resent the man's absence. He had begun to regard him almost in the light of a bodyguard, the private escort of some eminent politician. Besides, the whole incident was pregnant with possibilities appealing to his keenly intellectual sense of humour, and as he passed the hoarding, he peered into its shadow with the half-admitted hope that his attendant might be lurking in the depths. Later on he recalled how, as he glanced upwards, a man's figure passed like a shadow from a ladder to an upper platform of the scaffold. The vision, fleeting and insubstantial, had gone almost before his retina had received it, but the momentary halt was to prove his salvation. Even as he turned to walk on, a cataract of planks, amid scaffold-poles and a chaos of loose bricks, crashed on the spot he was about to traverse; a stray beam, more erratic in its descent, caught his hat, and, telescoping it, glanced off his shoulder, bearing him to the ground, where he lay dazed by the sudden uproar and half-choked by the cloud of dust. Rapid and disconcerting as was the event, he remembered afterwards a dim and spectral shape approaching through the gloom. In a dreamy kind of way he connected it with that other shadow-figure he had seen high up on the scaffold, and as it bent over him he recognised the now familiar features of the spy. But other figures replaced the first, and, when helped to his feet, he made futile search for it amid the circle of faces gathered round him. He judged it an hallucination. By the time he had undergone a tentative dust-down, he was sufficiently collected to acknowledge the sympathetic congratulations of the crowd and to decline the homeward escort of a constable.

In the privacy of his chambers, his ideas began to clarify. Events arranged themselves in logical sequence, and the spectres assumed more tangible form. A single question dwarfed all others. He asked himself, 'Was the cataclysm such an accident as it appeared?' And as he surveyed the battered ruins of his hat, he began to realise how nearly had he been the victim of a murderous vendetta!

When he arose the next morning, he scarcely needed the dilapidated hat to remind him of the events of yesterday. Normally a sound and dreamless sleeper, his rest had been a series of short snatches of slumber interposed between longer spells of rumination. While he marvelled at the intensity of malice which he could no longer doubt pursued him – a vindictiveness more natural to a mediaeval Italian state than to this present-day metropolis – he bitterly regretted the fatal curiosity which had brought him to such an extremity. By no means deficient in the grosser forms of physical courage, his sense that in the game which was being played his adversaries, as unscrupulous as they were crafty, held all the cards, and above all, that their espionage effectually prevented him filling the gaps in the plot which he had as yet only half-discovered, was especially galling to his active and somewhat neurotic temperament. Until yesterday he had almost decided to drop the affair of the Restaurant Poissoniere but now, after what he firmly believed to be a deliberate attempt to assassinate him, he realised the desperate situation of a duellist with his back to a wall – having scarce room to parry, he felt the prick of his antagonist's rapier deliberately goading him to an incautious thrust. Was he regarded as the possessor of a dangerous secret? Then it behoved him to strike, and that without delay.

Now that he was about to attack, a disguise was essential; and reflecting how lamentably he had failed through the absence of one hitherto, he removed the port-wine mark from his right cheek with his customary spirit-lotion, and blackened his fair hair with a few smart applications of a preparation from his bureau. It was with a determination to shun any obscure streets or alleys, and especially all buildings in course of erection, that he started out after his usual light breakfast. At first he was doubtful whether he was being followed or not, but after a few experimental turns and doublings he was unable to single out any regular attendant of his walk; either his disguise had proved effectual, or his enemies imagined that the attempt of last night had been less innocent in its results.

Somewhat soothed by this discovery, Pringle had gravitated towards the Strand and was nearing Charing Cross, when he observed a man cross from the station to the opposite corner carrying a brown paper roll. With his thoughts running in the one direction, Pringle in a flash recognised the dockyard draughtsman. Could he be even now on his way to keep the appointment at Nelson's Column? Had he been warned of Pringle's discovery, and so expedited his treacherous task? And thus reflecting, Pringle determined at all hazards to follow him. The draughtsman made straight for the telegraph office. It was now the busiest time of the morning, most of the little desks were occupied by more or less glib message-writers, and the draughtsman had found a single vacancy at the far end when Pringle followed him in and reached over his shoulder to withdraw a form from the rack in front of him. Grabbing three or four, Pringle neatly spilled them upon the desk, and with an abject apology hastily gathered them up together with the form the draughtsman was employed upon. More apologies, and Pringle, seizing a suddenly vacant desk, affected to compose a telegram of his own. The draughtsman's message had been short, and (to Pringle) exceptionally sweet, consisting as it did of the three words – 'Four-thirty, Pauline'. The address Pringle had not attempted to read – he knew that already. The moment the other left Pringle took up a sheaf of forms, and, as if they had been the sole reason of his visit, hurried out of the office and took a hansom back to Furnival's Inn.

Here his first care was to fold some newspapers into a brown-paper parcel resembling the one carried by the draughtsman as nearly as he remembered it, and having cut a number of squares of stiff tissue paper, he stuffed an envelope with them and pondered over a cigarette the most difficult stage of his campaign. Twice had the draughtsman seen him. Once at the restaurant, in his official guise as the sham literary agent, with smooth face, fair hair, and the fugitive port-wine mark staining his right cheek; again that morning, with blackened hair and unblemished face. True, he might have forgotten the stranger at the restaurant; on the other hand, he might not – and Pringle was then (as always) steadfastly averse to leaving anything to chance. Besides, in view of this sudden journey to London, it was very likely that he had received warning of Pringle's discovery. Lastly, it was more than probable that the spy was still on duty, even though he had failed to recognise Pringle that morning. The matter was clinched by a single glance at the Venetian mirror above the mantel, which reflected a feature he had overlooked – his now blackened hair. Nothing remained for him but to assume a disguise which should impose on both the spy and the draughtsman, and after some thought he decided to make up as a Frenchman of the South, and to pose as a servant of the French embassy. Reminiscent of the immortal Tartarin, his ready bureau furnished him with a stiff black moustache and some specially stout horsehair to typify the stubbly beard of that hero. When, at almost a quarter to four, he descended into the Inn with the parcel in his hand, a Baedeker and the envelope of tissues in his pocket, a cab was just setting down, and impulsively he chartered it as far as Exeter Hall. Concealed in the cab, he imagined he would the more readily escape observation, and by the time he alighted, flattered himself that any pursuit had been baffled. As he discharged the cab, however, he noticed a hansom draw up a few paces in the rear, whilst a man got out and began to saunter westward behind him. His suspicions alert, although the man was certainly a stranger, Pringle at once put him to the test by entering Romano's and ordering a small whisky. After a decent delay, he emerged, and his pulse quickened when he saw a couple of doors off the same man staring into a shop window! Pringle walked a few yards back, and then crossed to the opposite side of the street, but although he dodged at infinite peril through a string of omnibuses, he was unable to shake off his satellite, who, with unswerving persistence, occupied the most limited horizon whenever he looked back.

For almost the first time in his life, Pringle began to despair. The complacent regard of his own precautions had proved but a fool's paradise. Despite his elaborate disguise, he must have been plainly recognisable to his enemies, and he began to ask himself whether it was not useless to struggle further. As he paced slowly on, an indefinable depression stole over him. He thought of the heavy price so nearly exacted for his interposition. Resentment surged over him at the memory, and his hand clenched on the parcel. The contact furnished the very stimulus he required. The instrument of settling such a score was in his hands, and rejecting his timorous doubts, he strode on, determined to make one bold and final stroke for vengeance. The shadows had lengthened appreciably, and the quarter chiming from near St Martin's warned him that there was no time to lose; the spy must be got rid of at any cost. Already could he see the estuary of the Strand, with the Square widening beyond; on his right loomed the tunnel of the Lowther Arcade, with its vista of juvenile delights. The sight was an inspiration. Darting in, he turned off sharp to the left into an artist's repository, with a double entrance to the Strand and the Arcade, and, softly closing the door, peeped through the palettes and frames which hung upon the glass. Hardly had they ceased swinging to his movement when he had the satisfaction of seeing the spy, the scent already cold, rush furiously up the Arcade, his course marked by falling toys and the cries of the outraged stall-keepers. Turning, Pringle made the purchase of a sketching-block, the first thing handy, and then passed through the door which gave on the Strand. At the post office he stopped to survey the scene. A single policeman stood by the eastward base of the column, and the people scattered round seemed but ordinary wayfarers, but just across the maze of traffic was a spectacle of intense interest to him. At the quadrant of the Grand Hotel, patrolling aimlessly in front of the shops, at which he seemed too perturbed to stare for more than a few seconds at a time, the draughtsman kept palpitating vigil until the clock should strike the half-hour of his treason. True to the Frenchman's advice, he sought safety in a crowd, avoiding the desert of the square until the last moment.

It wanted two minutes to the half-hour when Pringle opened his Baedeker, and thrusting one hand into his breast, examined the statue and coil of rope erected to the glory of our greatest hero. 'Pauline!' said a voice, with the musical inflection unattainable by any but a Frenchman. Beside him stood a slight, neatly dressed young man, with close-cropped hair, and a moustache and imperial, who cast a significant look at the parcel. Pringle immediately held it towards him, and the dark gentleman producing an envelope from his breast-pocket, the exchange was effected in silence. With bows and a raising of hats they parted, while Big Ben boomed on his eight bells.

The attaché's representative had disappeared some minutes beyond the westernmost lion before the draughtsman appeared from the opposite direction, his uncertain steps intermitted by frequent halts and nervous backward glances. With his back to the National Gallery he produced a Baedeker and commenced to stare up at the monument, withdrawing his eyes every now and then to cast a shame-faced look to right and left. In his agitation the draughtsman had omitted the hand-in-the-breast attitude, and even as Pringle advanced to his side and murmured 'Pauline,' his legs (almost stronger than his will) seemed to be urging him to a flight from the field of dishonour. With tremulous eagerness he thrust a brown paper parcel into Pringle's hands, and, snatching the envelope of tissue slips, rushed across the road and disappeared in the bar of the Grand Hotel.

Pringle turned to go, but was confronted by a revolver, and as his eye traversed the barrel and met that of its owner, he recognised the Frenchman to whom he had just sold the bundle of newspapers. Dodging the weapon, he tried to spring into the open, but a restraining grip on each elbow held him in the angle of the plinth, and turning ever so little Pringle found himself in custody of the man whom he had last seen in full cry up the Lowther Arcade. No constable was anywhere near, and even casual passengers walked unheeding by the nook, so quiet was the progress of this little drama. Lowering his revolver, the dark gentleman picked up the parcel which had fallen from Pringle in the struggle. He opened it with delicacy, partially withdrew some sheets of tracing paper, which he intently examined, and then placed the whole in an inner pocket, and giving a sign to the spy to loose his grasp, he spoke for the first time.

'May I suggest, sir,' he said in excellent English with the slightest foreign accent, 'may I suggest that in future you do not meddle with what cannot possibly concern you? These documents have been bought and sold, and although you have been good enough to act as intermediary in the transaction, I can assure you we were under no necessity of calling on you for your help.' Here his tone hardened, and, speaking with less calmness, the accent became more noticeable. 'I discovered your impertinence in selling me a parcel of worthless papers very shortly after I left you. Had you succeeded in the attempt you appear to have planned so carefully, it is possible you might have

lived long enough to regret it – perhaps not! I wish you good day, sir.'
He bowed, as did his companion, and Pringle, walking on, turned up
by the corner of the Union Club.

Dent's clock marked twenty minutes to five, and Pringle reflected
how much had been compressed into the last quarter of an hour.
True, he had not prevented the sale of his country's secrets; on the
other hand – he pressed the packet which held the envelope of notes.
Hailing a cab, he was about to step in, when, looking back, at the
nook between the lions he saw a confused movement about the spot.
The two men he had just left were struggling with a third, who, bran-
dishing a handful of something white, was endeavouring, with
varying success, to plant his fist on divers areas of their persons. He
was the draughtsman. A small crowd, which momentarily increased,
surrounded them, and as Pringle climbed into the hansom two policemen were seen to penetrate the ring and impartially lay hands upon
the three combatants.

ARNOLD BENNETT

A Solution of the Algiers Mystery

'AND THE launch?'

'I am unaware of the precise technical term, sir, but the launch awaits you. Perhaps I should have said it is alongside.'

The reliable Lecky hated the sea; and when his master's excursions became marine, he always squinted more formidably and suddenly than usual, and added to his reliability a certain quality of ironic bitterness.

'My overcoat, please,' said Cecil Thorold, who was in evening dress.

The apartment, large and low, was paneled with bird's-eye maple; divans ran along the walls, and above the divans orange curtains were drawn; the floor was hidden by the skins of wild African animals; in one corner was a Steinway piano, with the score of 'The Orchid' open on the music-stand; in another lay a large, flat bowl filled with blossoms that do not bloom in England; the illumination, soft and yellow, came from behind the cornice of the room, being reflected therefrom downwards by the cream-coloured ceiling. Only by a faintly-heard tremor of some gigantic but repressed force, and by a very slight unsteadiness on the part of the floor, could you have guessed that you were aboard a steam-yacht and not in a large, luxurious house.

Lecky, having arrayed the millionaire in overcoat, muffler, crush-hat, and white gloves, drew aside a portière and followed him up a flight of stairs. They stood on deck, surrounded by the mild but treacherous Algerian night. From the white double funnels a thin smoke oozed. On the white bridge, the second mate, a spectral figure, was testing the engine-room signals, and the sharp noise of the bell seemed to desecrate the mysterious silence of the bay; but there was no other sign of life; the waiting launch was completely hidden under the high bows of the Claribel. In distant regions of the deck, glimmering beams came oddly up from below, throwing into relief some part of a boat on its davits or a section of a mast.

Cecil looked about him, at the serried lights of the Boulevard Carnot, and the riding lanterns of the vessels in the harbour. Away to the left on the hill, a few gleams showed Mustapha Supérieure, where the great English hotels are; and ten miles further east, the lighthouse on Cape Matifou flashed its eternal message to the Mediterranean. He was on the verge of feeling poetic.

'Suppose anything happens while you are at this dance, sir?'

Lecky jerked his thumb in the direction of a small steamer which lay moored scarcely a cable's-length away, under the eastern jetty. 'Suppose—?' He jerked his thumb again in exactly the same direction. His tone was still pessimistic and cynical.

'You had better fire our beautiful brass cannon,' Cecil replied. 'Have it fired three times. I shall hear it well enough up at Mustapha.'

He descended carefully into the launch, and was whisked puffingly over the dark surface of the bay to the landing-stage, where he summoned a fiacre.

'Hotel St James,' he instructed the driver.

And the driver smiled joyously; everyone who went to the Hotel St James was rich and lordly, and paid well, because the hill was long and steep and so hard on the poor Algerian horses.

II.

Every hotel up at Mustapha Supérieure has the finest view, the finest hygienic installation, and the finest cooking in Algeria; in other words, each is better than all the others. Hence the Hotel St James could not be called 'first among equals', since there are no equals, and one must be content to describe it as first among the unequalled. First it undoubtedly was – and perhaps will be again. Although it was new, it had what one visitor termed 'that indefinable thing – cachet'. It was frequented by the best people – namely, the richest people, the idlest people, the most arrogant people, the most bored people, the most titled people – that came to the southern shores of the Mediterranean in search of what they would never find – an escape from themselves. It was a vast building, planned on a scale of spaciousness only possible in a district where commercial crises have depressed the value of land, and it stood in the midst of a vast garden of oranges, lemons, and medlars. Every room – and there were three storeys and two hundred rooms – faced south: this was charged for in the bill. The public rooms, Oriental in character, were immense and complete. They included a dining-room, a drawing-room, a reading-room, a smoking-room, a billiard-room, a bridge-room, a ping-pong-room, a concert-room (with resident orchestra), and a room where Aissouias, negroes, and other curiosities from the native town might perform before select parties. Thus it was entirely self-sufficient, and lacked nothing which is necessary to the proper existence of the best people. On Thursday nights, throughout the season, there was a five-franc dance in the concert-hall. You paid five francs, and ate and drank as much as you could while standing up at the supper-tables arrayed in the dining-room.

On a certain Thursday night in early January, this Anglo-Saxon microcosm, set so haughtily in a French colony between the Mediterranean and the Djujura Mountains (with the Sahara behind), was at its most brilliant. The hotel was crammed, the prices were high, and everybody was supremely conscious of doing the correct thing. The dance had begun somewhat earlier than usual, because the eagerness of the younger guests could not be restrained. And the orchestra seemed gayer, and the electric lights brighter, and the toilettes more resplendent that night. Of course, guests came in from the other hotels. Indeed, they came in to such an extent that to dance in the ballroom was an affair of compromise and ingenuity. And the other rooms were occupied, too. The bridge players recked not of Terpsichore, the cheerful sound of ping-pong came regularly from the ping-pong-room; the retired Indian judge was giving points as usual in the billiard-room; and in the reading room the steadfast intellectuals were studying the *World* and the *Paris New York Herald*.

And all was English and American, pure Anglo-Saxon in thought and speech and gesture – save the manager of the hotel, who was Italian, the waiters, who were anything, and the wonderful concierge, who was everything.

As Cecil passed through the imposing suite of public rooms, he saw in the reading-room – posted so that no arrival could escape her eye – the elegant form of Mrs Macalister, and, by way of a wild, impulsive freak, he stopped and talked to her, and ultimately sat down by her side.

Mrs Macalister was one of those Englishwomen that are to be found only in large and fashionable hotels. Everything about her was mysterious, except the fact that she was in search of a second husband. She was tall, pretty, dashing, daring, well-dressed, well-informed, and, perhaps thirty-four. But no one had known her husband or her family, and no one knew her county, or the origin of her income, or how she got herself into the best cliques in the hotel. She had the air of being the merriest person in Algiers; really, she was one of the saddest, for the reason that every day left her older, and harder, and less likely to hook – well, to hook a millionaire. She had met Cecil Thorold at the dance of the previous week, and had clung to him so artfully that the coteries talked of it for three days, as Cecil well knew. And tonight he thought he might, as well as not, give Mrs Macalister an hour's excitement of the chase, and the coteries another three days' employment.

So he sat down beside her, and they talked.

First she asked him whether he slept on his yacht or in the hotel; and he replied, sometimes in the hotel and sometimes on the yacht. Then she asked him where his bedroom was, and he said it was on the second floor, and she settled that it must be three doors from her own. Then they discussed bridge, the Fiscal Inquiry, the weather, dancing, food, the responsibilities of great wealth, Algerian railway-travelling, Cannes, gambling, Mr Morley's *Life of Gladstone*, and the extraordinary success of the hotel. Thus, quite inevitably, they reached the subject of the Algiers Mystery. During the season, at any rate, no two guests in the hotel ever talked small-talk for more than ten minutes without reaching the subject of the Algiers Mystery.

For the hotel had itself been the scene of the Algiers Mystery, and the Algiers Mystery was at once the simplest, the most charming, and the most perplexing mystery in the world. One morning, the first of April in the previous year, an honest John Bull of a guest had come down to the hotel-office, and laying a five-pound note before the head clerk, had exclaimed: 'I found that lying on my dressing-table. It isn't mine. It looks good enough, but I expect it's someone's joke.' Seven other people that day confessed that they had found five-pound notes in their rooms, or pieces of paper that resembled five-pound notes. They compared these notes, and then the eight went off in a body down to an agency in the Boulevard de la République, and without the least demur the notes were changed for gold. On the second of April, twelve more people found five-pound notes in their rooms, now prominent on the bed, now secreted – as, for instance, under a candlestick. Cecil himself had been a recipient. Watches were set, but with no result whatever. In a week nearly seven hundred pounds had been distributed amongst the guests by the generous, invisible ghosts. It was magnificent, and it was very soon in every newspaper in England and America. Some of the guests did not 'care' for it; thought it 'queer', and 'uncanny', and not 'nice', and these left. But the majority cared for it very much indeed, and remained till the utmost limit of the Season.

The rainfall of notes had not recommenced so far, in the present Season. Nevertheless, the hotel had been thoroughly well patronised from November onwards, and there was scarcely a guest but who went to sleep at night hoping to descry a fiver in the morning.

'Advertisement!' said some perspicacious individuals. Of course, the explanation was an obvious one. But the manager had indignantly and honestly denied all knowledge of the business, and, moreover, not a single guest had caught a single note in the act of settling down. Further, the hotel changed hands and that manager left. The mystery, therefore, remained, a delightful topic always at hand for discussion.

After having chatted, Cecil Thorold and Mrs Macalister danced – two dances. And the hotel began audibly to wonder that Cecil could be such a fool. When, at midnight, he retired to bed, many mothers of daughters and daughters of mothers were justifiably angry, and consoled themselves by saying that he had disappeared in order to hide the shame which must have suddenly overtaken him. As for Mrs Macalister, she was radiant.

Safely in his room, Cecil locked and wedged the door, and opened the window and looked out from the balcony at the starry night. He could hear cats playing on the roof. He smiled when he thought of the things Mrs Macalister had said, and of the ardour of her glances. Then he felt sorry for her. Perhaps it was the whisky-and-soda which he had just drunk that momentarily warmed his heart towards the lonely creature. Only one item of her artless gossip had interested him – a statement that the new Italian manager had been ill in bed all day.

He emptied his pockets, and, standing on a chair, he put his pocket-book on the top of the wardrobe, where no Algerian marauder would think of looking for it; his revolver he tucked under his pillow. In three minutes he was asleep.

III.

He was awakened by a vigourous pulling and shaking of his arm; and he, who usually woke wide at the least noise, came to his senses with difficulty. He looked up. The electric light had been turned on.

'There's a ghost in my room, Mr Thorold! You'll forgive me – but I'm so—'

It was Mrs Macalister, dishevelled and in white, who stood over him.

'This is really a bit too thick,' he thought vaguely and sleepily, regretting his impulsive flirtation of the previous evening. Then he collected himself and said sternly, severely, that if Mrs Macalister would retire to the corridor, he would follow in a moment; he added that she might leave the door open if she felt afraid. Mrs Macalister retired, sobbing, and Cecil arose. He went first to consult his watch; it was gone – a chronometer worth a couple of hundred pounds. He whistled, climbed on to a chair, and discovered that his pocket-book was no longer in a place of safety on the top of the wardrobe; it had contained something over five hundred pounds in a highly negotiable form. Picking up his overcoat, which lay on the floor, he found that the fur lining – a millionaire's fancy, which had cost him nearly a hundred and fifty pounds – had been cut away, and was no more to be seen. Even the revolver had departed from under his pillow!

'Well!' he murmured, 'this is decidedly the grand manner.'

Quite suddenly it occurred to him, as he noticed a peculiar taste in his mouth, that the whisky-and-soda had contained more than whisky-and-soda – he had been drugged! He tried to recall the face of the waiter who had served him. Eyeing the window and the door, he argued that the thief had entered by the former and departed by the latter. 'But the pocket-book!' he mused. 'I must have been watched!'

Mrs Macalister, stripped now of all dash and all daring, could be heard in the corridor.

'Can she… ?' He speculated for a moment, and then decided positively in the negative. Mrs Macalister could have no design on anything but a bachelor's freedom.

He assumed his dressing-gown and slippers and went to her. The corridor was in darkness, but she stood in the light of his doorway.

'Now,' he said, 'this ghost of yours, dear lady!'

'You must go first,' she whimpered. 'I daren't. It was white…. but with a black face. It was at the window.'

Cecil, getting a candle, obeyed. And having penetrated alone into the lady's chamber, he perceived, to begin with, that a pane had been pushed out of the window by the old, noiseless device of a sheet of treacled paper, and then, examining the window more closely, he saw that, outside, a silk ladder depended from the roof and trailed in the balcony.

'Come in without fear,' he said to the trembling widow. 'It must have been someone with more appetite than a ghost that you saw. Perhaps an Arab.'

She came in, femininely trusting to him; and between them they ascertained that she had lost a watch, sixteen rings, an opal necklace, and some money. Mrs Macalister would not say how much money. 'My resources are slight,' she remarked, 'I was expecting remittances.'

Cecil thought: 'This is not merely in the grand manner. If it fulfils it promise, it will prove to be one of the greatest things of the age.'

He asked her to keep cool, not to be afraid, and to dress herself. Then he returned to his room and dressed as quickly as he could. The hotel was absolutely quiet, but out of the depths below came the sound of a clock striking four. When, adequately but not æsthetically attired, he opened his door again, another door near by also opened, and Cecil saw a man's head.

'I say,' drawled the man's head, 'excuse me, but have you noticed anything?'

'Why? What?'

'Well, I've been robbed!'

The Englishman laughed awkwardly, apologetically, as though ashamed to have to confess that he had been victimised.

'Much?' Cecil inquired.

'Two hundred or so. No joke, you know.'

'So have I been robbed,' said Cecil. 'Let us go downstairs. Got a candle? These corridors are usually lighted all night.'

'Perhaps our thief has been at the switches,' said the Englishman.

'Say our thieves,' Cecil corrected.

'You think there was more than one?'

'I think there were more than half a dozen,' Cecil replied.

The Englishman was dressed, and the two descended together, candles in hand, forgetting the lone lady. But the lone lady had no intention of being forgotten, and she came after them, almost screaming. They had not reached the ground floor before three other doors had opened and three other victims proclaimed themselves.

Cecil led the way through the splendid saloons, now so ghostly in their elegance, which only three hours before had been the illuminated scene of such polite revelry. Ere he reached the entrance-hall, where a solitary jet was burning, the assistant-concierge (one of those officials who seem never to sleep) advanced towards him, demanding in his broken English what was the matter.

'There have been thieves in the hotel,' said Cecil. 'Waken the concierge.'

From that point, events succeeded each other in a sort of complex rapidity. Mrs Macalister fainted at the door of the billiard-room and was laid out on a billiard-table, with a white ball between her shoulders. The head concierge was not in his narrow bed in the alcove by the main entrance, and he could not be found. Nor could the Italian manager be found (though he was supposed to be ill in bed), nor the

Italian manager's wife. Two stablemen were searched out from somewhere; also a cook. And then the Englishman who had lost two
hundred or so went forth into the Algerian night to bring a gendarme
from the post in the Rue d'Isly.

Cecil Thorold contented himself with talking to people as, in ones
and twos, and in various stages of incorrectness, they came into the
public rooms, now brilliantly lighted. All who came had been robbed.
What surprised him was the slowness of the hotel to wake up. There
were two hundred and twenty guests in the place. Of these, in a
quarter of an hour, perhaps fifteen had risen. The remainder were
apparently oblivious of the fact that something very extraordinary,
and something probably very interesting to them personally, had
occurred and was occurring.

'Why! It's a conspiracy, sir. It's a conspiracy, that's what it is!'
decided the Indian judge.

'Gang is a shorter word,' Cecil observed, and a young girl in a
macintosh giggled.

Sleepy employees now began to appear, and the rumour ran that
six waiters and a chambermaid were missing. Mrs Macalister rallied
from the billiard table and came into the drawing-room, where most
of the company had gathered. Cecil yawned (the influence of the drug
was still upon him) as she approached him and weakly spoke. He
answered absently; he was engaged in watching the demeanour of
these idlers on the face of the earth – how incapable they seemed of
any initiative, and yet with what magnificent Britannic phlegm they
endured the strange situation! The talking was neither loud nor
impassioned.

Then the low, distant sound of a cannon was heard. Once, twice,
thrice.

Silence ensued.

'Heavens!' sighed Mrs Macalister, swaying towards Cecil. 'What
can that be?'

He avoided her, hurried out of the room, and snatched somebody
else's hat from the hat-racks in the hall. But just as he was turning the
handle of the main door of the hotel, the Englishman who had lost
two hundred or so returned out of the Algerian night with an inspector of police. The latter courteously requested Cecil not to leave the
building, as he must open the inquiry (*ouvrir l'enquête*) at once. Cecil
was obliged, regretfully, to comply.

The inspector of police then commenced his labours. He telephoned (no one had thought of the telephone) for assistance and

asked the Central Bureau to watch the railway station, the port, and the stage coaches. He acquired the names and addresses of *tout le monde*. He made catalogues of articles. He locked all the servants in the ping-pong-room. He took down narratives, beginning with Cecil's. And while the functionary was engaged with Mrs Macalister, Cecil quietly but firmly disappeared.

After his departure, the affair loomed larger and larger in mere magnitude, but nothing that came to light altered its leading characteristics. A wholesale robbery had been planned with the most minute care and knowledge, and executed with the most daring skill. Some ten persons – the manager and his wife, a chambermaid, six waiters, and the concierge – seemed to have been concerned in the enterprise, excluding Mrs Macalister's Arab and no doubt other assistants. (The guests suddenly remembered how superior the concierge and the waiters had been to the ordinary concierge and waiter!) At a quarter past five o'clock the police had ascertained that a hundred rooms had been entered, and horrified guests were still descending! The occupants of many rooms, however, made no response to a summons to awake. These, it was discovered afterwards, had either, like Cecil, received a sedative unawares, or they had been neatly gagged and bound. In the result, the list of missing valuables comprised nearly two hundred watches, eight hundred rings, a hundred and fifty other articles of jewellery, several thousand pounds' worth of furs, three thousand pounds in coin, and twenty-one thousand pounds in banknotes and other forms of currency. One lady, a doctor's wife, said she had been robbed of eight hundred pounds in Bank of England notes, but her story obtained little credit; other tales of enormous loss, chiefly by women, were also taken with salt. When the dawn began, at about six o'clock, an official examination of the facade of the hotel indicated that nearly every room had been invaded by the balconied window, either from the roof or from the ground. But the stone flags of the terrace, and the beautifully asphalted pathways of the garden disclosed no trace of the plunderers.

'I guess your British habit of sleeping with the window open don't cut much ice today, anyhow!' said an American from Indianapolis to the company.

That morning no omnibus from the hotel arrived at the station to catch the six-thirty train which takes two days to ramble to Tunis and to Biskra. And all the liveried porters talked together in excited Swiss-German.

*

IV.

'My compliments to Captain Black,' said Cecil Thorold, 'and repeat to him that all I want him to do is to keep her in sight. He needn't overhaul her too much.'

'Precisely, sir.' Lecky bowed; he was pale.

'And you had better lie down.'

'I thank you, sir, but I find a recumbent position inconvenient. Perpetual motion seems more agreeable.'

Cecil was back in the large, low room panelled with bird's-eye maple. Below him the power of two thousand horses drove through the nocturnal Mediterranean swell his Claribel of a thousand tons. Thirty men were awake and active on board her, and twenty slept in the vast, clean forecastle, with electric lights blazing six inches above their noses. He lit a cigarette, and going to the piano, struck a few chords from 'The Orchid'; but since the music would not remain on the stand, he abandoned that attempt and lay down on a divan to think.

He had reached the harbour, from the hotel, in twenty minutes, partly on foot at racing speed, and partly in an Arab cart, also at racing speed. The Claribel's launch awaited him, and in another five minutes the launch was slung to her davits, and the Claribel under way. He learnt that the small and sinister vessel, the Perroquet Vert (of Oran), which he and his men had been watching for several days, had slipped unostentatiously between the southern and eastern jetties, had stopped for a few minutes to hold converse with a boat that had put off from the neighbourhood of Lower Mustapha, and had then pointed her head north-west, as though for some port in the province of Oran or in Morocco.

And in the rings of cigarette smoke which he made, Cecil seemed now to see clearly the whole business. He had never relaxed his interest in the affair of the five-pound notes. He had vaguely suspected it to be part of some large scheme; he had presumed, on slight grounds, a connection between the Perroquet Vert and the Italian manager of the hotel. Nay, more, he had felt sure that some great stroke was about to be accomplished. But of precise knowledge, of satisfactory theory, of definite expectation, he had had none – until Mrs Macalister, that unconscious and man-hunting agent of Destiny, had fortunately wakened him in the nick of time. Had it not been for his flirtation of the previous evening, he might still be asleep in his bed at the hotel... He perceived the entire plan. The five-pound notes had been mysteriously scattered, certainly to advertise the hotel, but only to advertise it for a particular and colossal end, to fill it full and over-flowing with fat victims. The situation had been thoroughly studied in all its details, and the task had been divided and allotted to various brains. Every room must have been examined, watched, and sepa-rately plotted against; the habits and idiosyncrasy of every victim must have been individually weighed and considered. Nothing, no trifle, could have been forgotten. And then some supreme intelligence had drawn the threads together and woven them swiftly into the pattern of a single night, almost a single hour!... And the loot (Cecil could estimate it pretty accurately) had been transported down the hill to Mustapha Inférieure, tossed into a boat, and so to the Perro-quet Vert. And the Perroquet Vert, with loot and looters on board, was bound, probably, for one of those obscure and infamous ports of Oran or Morocco – Tenez, Mostaganem, Beni Sar, Melilla, or the city of Oran, or Tangier itself! He knew something of the Spanish and Maltese dens of Oran and Tangier, the clearing-houses for stolen goods of two continents, and the impregnable refuge of scores of ingenious villains.

And when he reflected upon the grandeur and immensity of the scheme, so simple in its essence, and so leisurely in its achievement, like most grand schemes; when he reflected upon the imagination which had been necessary even to conceive it, and the generalship which had been necessary to its successful conclusion, he murmured admiringly:

'The man who thought of that and did it may be a scoundrel; but he is also an artist, and a great one!'

And just because he, Cecil Thorold, was a millionaire, and pos-sessed a hundred-thousand-pound toy, which could do nineteen knots an hour, and cost fifteen hundred pounds a month to run, he was about to defeat that great artist and nullify that great scheme, and incidentally to retrieve his watch, his revolver, his fur, and his five hundred pounds. He had only to follow, and to warn one of the French torpedo-boats which are always patrolling the coast between Algiers and Oran, and the bubble would burst!

He sighed for the doomed artist; and he wondered what that vic-timised crowd of European loungers, who lounged sadly round the Mediterranean in winter, and sadly round northern Europe in summer, had done in their languid and luxurious lives that they should be saved, after all, from the pillage to which the great artist in theft had subjected them!

Then Lecky re-entered the state room.

'We shall have a difficulty in keeping the Perroquet Vert in sight, sir.'

'What!' exclaimed Cecil. 'That tub! That coffin! You don't mean she can do twenty knots?'

'Exactly, sir. Coffin! It – I mean she – is sinking.'

Cecil ran on deck. Dawn was breaking over Matifou, and a faint, cold, grey light touched here and there the heaving sea. His captain spoke and pointed. Ahead, right ahead, less than a mile away, the Perroquet Vert was sinking by the stern, and even as they gazed at her, a little boat detached itself from her side in the haze of the morning mist; and she sank, disappeared, vanished amid a cloud of escaping steam. They were four miles north-east of Cape Caxine. Two miles further westward, a big Dominion liner, bound direct for Algiers from the New World, was approaching and had observed the catastrophe – for she altered her course. In a few minutes, the Claribel picked up the boat of the Perroquet Vert. It contained three Arabs.

The tale told by the Arabs (two of them were brothers, and all three came from Oran) fully sustained Cecil Thorold's theory of the spoliation of the hotel. Naturally they pretended at first to an entire innocence concerning the schemes of those who had charge of the Perroquet Vert. The two brothers, who were black with coal-dust when rescued, swore that they had been physically forced to work in the stokehold; but ultimately all three had to admit a knowledge of things which was decidedly incriminating, and all three got three years' imprisonment. The only part of the Algiers mystery which remained a mystery was the cause of the sinking of the Perroquet Vert. Whether she was thoroughly unseaworthy (she had been picked up cheap at Melilla), or whether someone (not on board) had deliberately arranged her destruction, perhaps to satisfy a Moorish vengeance, was not ascertained. The three Arabs could only be persuaded to say that there had been eleven Europeans and seven natives on the ship, and that they alone, by the mercy of Allah, had escaped from the swift catastrophe.

The hotel underwent an acute crisis, from which, however, it is emerging. For over a week a number of the pillaged guests discussed a diving enterprise of salvage. But the estimates were too high, and it came to nothing. So they all, Cecil included, began to get used to the idea of possessing irrecoverable property to the value of forty thousand pounds in the Mediterranean. A superb business in telegraphed remittances was done for several days. The fifteen beings who had accompanied the Perroquet Vert to the bottom were scarcely thought of, for it was almost universally agreed that the way of transgressors is, and ought to be, hard.

JACQUES FUTRELLE

The Problem of Cell 13

PRACTICALLY ALL those letters remaining in the alphabet after Augustus SFX Van Dusen was named were afterward acquired by that gentleman in the course of a brilliant scientific career, and, being honourably acquired, were tacked on to the other end. His name, therefore, taken with all that belonged it, was a wonderfully imposing structure. He was a PhD, an LLD, an FRS, an MD, and an MDS. He was also some other things – just what he himself couldn't say – through recognition of his ability by various foreign educational and scientific institutions.

In appearance he was no less striking than in nomenclature. He was slender with the droop of the student in his thin shoulders and the pallor of a close, sedentary life on his clean-shaven face. His eyes wore a perceptual, forbidding squint – the squint of a man who studies little things – and when they could be seen at all through his thick spectacles, were mere slits of watery blue. But above his eyes was his most striking feature. This was a tall, broad brow, almost abnormal in height and width, crowned by a heavy shock of bushy, yellow hair. All these things conspired to give him a peculiar, almost grotesque, personality.

Professor Van Dusen was remotely German. For generations his ancestors had been noted in the sciences; he was the logical result, the mastermind. First and above all he was a logician. At least thirty-five years of the half century or so of his existence had been devoted exclusively to providing that two and two always equal four, except in unusual cases, where they equalled three or five, as the case may be. He stood broadly on the general propositions that all things that start must go somewhere, and was able to bring the concentrated mental force of his forefathers to bear on a given problem. Incidentally it may be remarked that Professor Van Dusen wore a number 8 hat.

The world at large had heard vaguely of Professor Van Dusen as The Thinking Machine. It was a newspaper catchphrase applied to him at the time of a remarkable exhibition at chess; he had demonstrated then that a stranger to the game might, by the force of inevitable logic, defeat a champion who had devoted a lifetime to its study. The Thinking Machine! Perhaps that more nearly described him than all his honorary initials, for he had spent week after week, month after month, in the seclusion of his small laboratory from which had gone forth thoughts that staggered scientific associates and deeply stirred the world at large.

It was only occasionally that The Thinking Machine had visitors, and these were usually men who, themselves high in the sciences, dropped in to argue a point and perhaps convince themselves. Two of these men, Dr Charles Ransome and Alfred Fielding, called one evening to discuss some theory which is not of consequence here.

'Such a thing is impossible,' declared Dr Ransome emphatically, in the course of the conversation.

'Nothing is impossible,' declared The Thinking Machine with equal emphasis. He always spoke petulantly. 'The mind is master of all things. When science fully recognises that fact a great advance will have been made.'

'How about the airship?' asked Dr Ransome.

'That's not impossible at all,' asserted The Thinking Machine 'it will be invented some time. I'd do it myself, but I'm busy.'

Dr Ransome laughed tolerantly.

'I've heard you say such things before,' he said. 'But they mean nothing. Mind may be master of matter, but it hasn't yet found away to apply itself. There are some things that can't be thought out of existence, or rather which would not yield to any amount of thinking.'

'What, for instance?' demanded The Thinking Machine.

Dr Ransome was thoughtful for a moment as he smoked.

'Well, say prison walls,' he replied. 'No man can think himself out of a cell. If he could, there would be no prisoners.'

'A man can so apply his brain and ingenuity that he can leave a cell, which is the same thing,' snapped The Thinking Machine.

Dr Ransome was slightly amused.

'Let's suppose a case,' he said, after a moment. 'Take a cell where prisoners under sentence of death are confined – men who are desperate and, maddened by fear, would take any chance to escape – suppose you were locked in such a cell. Could you escape?'

'Certainly,' declared The Thinking Machine.

'Of course,' said Mr Fielding, who entered the conversation for the first time, 'you might wreck the cell with an explosive – but inside, a prisoner, you couldn't have that.'

'There would be nothing of that kind,' said The Thinking

Machine. 'You might treat me precisely as you treated prisoners under sentence of death, and I would leave the cell.'

'Not unless you entered it with tools prepared to get out,' said Dr Ransome.

The Thinking Machine was visibly annoyed and his blue eyes snapped.

'Lock me in any cell in any prison anywhere at any time, wearing only what is necessary, and I'll escape in a week,' he declared, sharply. Dr Ransome sat up straight in his chair, interested. Mr Fielding lighted a new cigar.

'You mean you could actually think yourself out?' asked Dr Ransome.

'I would get out' was the response.

'Are you serious?'

'Certainly I an serious.'

Dr Ransome and Mr Fielding were silent for a long time.

'Would you be willing to try it?' asked Mr Fielding, finally.

'Certainly,' said Professor Van Dusen, and there was a trace of irony in his voice. 'I have done more asinine things than that to convince other men of less important truths.'

The tone was offensive and there was an undercurrent strongly resembling anger on both sides. Of course it was an absurd thing, but Professor Van Dusen reiterated his willingness to undertake the escape and it was decided on.

'To begin now,' added Dr Ransome.

'I'd prefer that it begin tomorrow,' said The Thinking Machine, 'because—'

'No, now,' said Mr Fielding, flatly. 'You are arrested, figuratively speaking, of course, without any warning locked in a cell with no chance to communicate with friends, and left there with identically the same care and attention that would be given to a man under sentence of death. Are you willing?'

'All right, now, then,' said The Thinking Machine, and he arose.

'Say, the death cell in Chisholm Prison.'

'The death cell in Chisholm Prison.'

'And what will you wear?'

'As little as possible,' said The Thinking Machine. Shoes, stockings, trousers and a shirt.'

'You will permit yourself to be searched, of course?'

'I am to be treated precisely as all prisoners are treated,' said The Thinking Machine. 'No more attention and no less.'

There were some preliminaries to be arranged in the matter of obtaining permission for the test, but all these were influential men and everything was done satisfactorily by telephone, albeit the prison commissioners, to whom the experiment was explained on purely scientific grounds, were sadly bewildered. Professor Van Dusen would be the most distinguished prisoner they had ever entertained.

When The Thinking Machine had donned those things which he was to wear during his incarceration, he called the little old woman who was his housekeeper, cook and maidservant all in one.

'Martha,' he said, 'it is now twenty-seven minutes past nine o'clock. I am going away. One week from tonight, at half past nine, these gentlemen and one, possibly two, others will take supper with me here. Remember Dr Ransome is very fond of artichokes.'

The three men were driven to Chisholm Prison, where the warden was awaiting them, having been informed of the matter by telephone. He understood merely that the eminent Professor Van Dusen was to be his prisoner, if he could keep him, for one week; that he had committed no crime, but that he was to be treated as all other prisoners were treated.

'Search him,' instructed Dr Ransome.

The Thinking Machine was searched. Nothing was found on him; the pockets of the trousers were empty; the white, stiff-bosomed shirt had no pocket. The shoes and stockings were removed, examined, then replaced. As he watched all these preliminaries, and noted the pitiful, childlike physical weakness of the man – the colourless face, and the thin, white hands – Dr Ransome almost regretted his part in the affair.

'Are you sure you want to do this?' he asked. 'Would you be convinced if I did not?' inquired The Thinking Machine in turn.

'No.'

'All right. I'll do it.'

What sympathy Dr Ransome had was dissipated by the tone. It nettled him, and he resolved to see the experiment to the end; it would be a stinging reproof to egotism.

'It will be impossible for him to communicate with anyone outside?' he asked.

'Absolutely impossible,' replied the warden. 'He will not be permitted writing materials of any sort.'

'And your jailers, would they deliver a message from him?'

'Not one word, directly or indirectly,' said the warden. 'You may rest assured of that. They will report anything he might say or turn over to me, anything he might give them.'

'That seems entirely satisfactory,' said Mr Fielding, who was frankly interested in the problem.

'Of course, in the event he fails,' said Dr Ransome, 'and asks for his liberty, you understand you are to set him free?'

'I understand,' replied the warden.

The Thinking Machine stood listening, but had nothing to say until all this was ended, then: 'I should like to make three small requests. You may grant them or not, as you wish.'

'No special favours, now,' warned Mr Fielding.

'I am asking none,' was the stiff response. I should like to have some tooth powder – buy it yourself to see that it is tooth powder – and I should like to have one five-dollar and two ten-dollar bills.'

Dr Ransome, Mr Fielding and the warden exchanged astonished glances. They were not surprised at the request for tooth powder, but were at the request for money.

'Is there any man with whom our friend would come in contact that he could bribe with twenty-five dollars?'

'Not for twenty-five hundred dollars,' was the positive reply.

'And what is the third request?' asked Dr Ransome.

'I should like to have my shoes polished.'

Again the astonished glances were exchanged. This last request was the height of absurdity, so they agreed to it. These things all being attended to, The Thinking Machine was led back into the prison from which he had undertaken to escape.

'Here is Cell 13,' said the warden, stopping three doors down the steel corridor. 'This is where we keep condemned murderers. No one can leave it without my permission; and no one in it can communicate with the outside. I'll stake my reputation on that. It's only three doors back of my office and I can readily hear any unusual noise.'

'Will this cell do, gentleman?' asked The Thinking Machine. There was a touch of irony in his voice.

'Admirably,' was the reply.

The heavy steel door was thrown open, there was a great scurrying and scampering of tiny feet, and The Thinking Machine passed into the gloom of the cell. Then the door was closed and double locked by the warden.

'What is that noise in there?' asked Dr Ransome, through the bars.

'Rats – dozens of them,' replied The Thinking Machine, tersely.

The three men, with final good nights, were turning away when The Thinking Machine called:

'What time is it exactly, Warden?'

'Eleven-seventeen,' replied the warden.

'Thanks. I will join you gentlemen in your office at half past eight o'clock one week from tonight,' said The Thinking Machine.

'And if you do not?'

'There is no "if" about it.'

Chisolm Prison was a great, spreading structure of granite, four stories in all, which stood in the centre of acres of open space. It was surrounded by a wall of solid masonry eighteen feet high, and so smoothly finished inside and out as to offer no foothold to a climber, no matter how expert. Atop of this fence, as a further precaution, was a five foot fence of steel rods, each terminating in a keen point. This fence in itself marked an absolute deadline between freedom and imprisonment, for, even if a man escaped from his cell, it would seem impossible for him to pass the wall.

The yard, which on all sides of the prison building was twenty-five feet wide, that being the distance from the building to the wall, was by day an exercises ground for those prisoners to whom was granted the boon of occasional semi-liberty. But that was not for those in Cell 13. At all times of the day there were armed guards in the yard, four of them, one patrolling each side of the prison building.

By night the yard was almost as brilliantly lighted as by day. On each of the four sides was a great arc light which rose above the prison wall and gave to the guards a clear sight. The lights, too, brightly illuminated the spiked top of the wall. The wires which fed the arc lights ran up the side of the prison building on insulators and from the top story led out to the poles supporting the arc lights. All these things were seen and comprehended by The Thinking Machine, who was only enabled to see out his closely barred cell window by standing on his bed. This was on the morning following his incarceration. He gathered, too, that the river lay over there beyond the wall somewhere, because he heard faintly the pulsation of a motor boat and high up in the air he saw a river bird. From that same direction came the shouts of boys at play and the occasional crack of a batted ball. He knew then that between the prison wall and the river was an open space, a playground.

Chisolm prison was regarded as absolutely safe. No man had ever escaped from it. The Thinking Machine, from his perch on the bed, seeing what he saw, could readily understand why. The walls of the cell, though built he judged twenty years before, were perfectly solid, and the window bars of new iron had not a shadow of rust on them.

The window itself, even with the bars out, would be a difficult mode of egress because it was small.

Yet, seeing these things, The Thinking Machine was not discouraged. Instead, he thoughtfully squinted at the great arc light – there was bright sunlight now – and traced with his eyes the wire which led from it to the building. That electric wire, he reasoned, must come down the side of the building not a great distance from his cell. That might be worth knowing.

Cell 13 was on the same floor with the offices of the prison – that is, not in the basement, nor yet upstairs. There were only four steps up to the office floor, therefore the level of the floor must be only three or four feet above the ground. He couldn't see the ground directly beneath his window, but he could see it further out toward the wall. It would be an easy drop from the window. Well and good.

Then The Thinking Machine fell to remembering how he had come to the cell. First, there was the outside guards booth, a part of the wall. There were two heavily barred gates there, both of steel. At this gate was one man always on guard. He admitted persons to the prison after much clanking of keys and locks, and let them out when ordered to do so. The warden's office was in the prison building, and in order to reach that official from the prison yard one had to pass a gate of solid steel with only a peephole in it. Then coming from that inner office to Cell 13, where he was now, one must pass a heavy wooden door and two steel doors into the corridors of the prison; and always there was the double-locked door of Cell 13 to reckon with.

There were then, The Thinking Machine recalled, seven doors to be overcome before one could pass from Cell 13 into the outer world, a free man. But against this was the fact that he was rarely interrupted. A jailer appeared at his cell door at six in the morning with a breakfast of prison fare; he would come again at noon, and again at six in the afternoon. At nine o'clock at night would come the inspection tour. That would be all.

'It's admirably arranged, this prison system,' was the mental tribute paid by The Thinking Machine. 'I'll have to study it a little when I get out. I had no idea there was such great care exercised in the prisons.

There was nothing, positively nothing, in his cell, except his iron bed, so firmly put together that no man could tear it to pieces save with sledges or a file. He had neither of these. There was not even a chair, or a small table, or a bit of crockery. Nothing! The jailer stood by when he ate, then took away the wooden spoon and bowl which he had used.

One by one these things sank into the brain of The Thinking Machine. When the last possibility had been considered he began an examination of his cell. From the roof, down the walls on all sides, he examined the stones and the cement between them. He stamped over the floor carefully time after time, but it was cement, perfectly solid. After the examination he sat on the edge of the iron bed and was lost in thought for a long time. For Professor Augustus SFX Van Dusen, The Thinking Machine, had something to think about.

He was disturbed by a rat, which ran across his foot, then scampered away into a dark corner of the cell, frightened at its own daring. After a while The Thinking Machine, squinting steadily into the darkness of the corner where the rat had gone, was able to make out in the gloom many little beady eyes staring at him. He counted six pair, and there were perhaps others; he didn't see very well.

Then The Thinking Machine, from his seat on the bed, noticed for the first time the bottom of his cell door. There was an opening there of two inches between the steel bar and the floor. Still looking steadily at the opening, The Thinking Machine backed suddenly into the corner where he had seen the beady eyes. There was a great scampering of tiny feet, several squeaks of frightened rodents, and then silence.

None of the rats had gone out the door, yet there were none in the cell. Therefore there must be another way out of the cell, however small. The Thinking Machine, in hands and knees, started a search for the spot, feeling in the darkness with his long, slender fingers.

At last his search was rewarded. He came upon a small opening in the floor, level with the cement. It was perfectly round and somewhat larger than a silver dollar. This was the way the rats had gone. He put his fingers deep into the opening; it seemed to be a disused drainage pipe and was dry and dusty.

Having satisfied himself on this point, he sat on the bed again for an hour, then made another inspection of his surroundings through the small cell window. One of the outside guards stood directly opposite, beside the wall, and happened to be looking at the window of Cell 13 when the head of The Thinking Machine appeared. But the scientist didn't notice the guard.

Noon came and the jailer appeared with the prison dinner of repulsively plain food. At home The Thinking Machine merely ate to live; here he took what was offered without comment. Occasionally he spoke to the jailer who stood outside the door watching him.

'Any improvements made here in the last few years?' he asked.

'Nothing particularly,' replied the jailer. 'New wall was built four years ago.'

'Anything done to the prison proper?'

'Painted the woodwork outside, and I believe about seven years ago a new system of plumbing was put in.'

'Ah!' said the prisoner. 'How far is the river over there?'

'About three hundred feet. The boys have a baseball ground between the wall and the river.'

The Thinking Machine had nothing further to say just then, but when the jailer was ready to go he asked for some water.

'I get very thirsty here,' he explained. 'Would it be possible for you to leave a little water in a bowl for me?'

'I'll ask the warden,' replied the jailer, and he went away.

Half an hour later he returned with water in a small earthen bowl.

'The warden says you may keep this bowl,' he informed the prisoner. 'But you must show it to me when I ask for it. If it is broken, it will be the last.'

'Thank you,' said The Thinking Machine. 'I shan't break it.'

The jailer went on about his duties. For just the fraction of a second it seemed that The Thinking Machine wanted to ask a question, but he didn't.

Two hours later this same jailer, in passing the door of Cell number 13, heard a noise inside and stopped. The Thinking Machine was down on his hands and knees in a corner of the cell, and from that same corner came several frightened squeaks. The jailer looked on interestedly.

'Ah, I've got you,' he heard the prisoner say.

'Got what?' he asked, sharply.

'One of these rats,' was the reply. See?' And between the scientist's long fingers the jailer saw a small grey rat struggling. The prisoner brought it over to the light and looked at it closely.

'It's a water rat,' he said.

'Ain't you got anything better to do than catch rats?' asked the jailer.

'It's disgraceful that they should be here at all,' was the irritated reply. 'Take this one away and kill it. There are dozens more where it came from.'

The jailer took the wriggling, squirmy rodent and flung it down on the floor violently. It gave one squeak and lay still. Later he reported the incident to the warden, who only smiled.

Still later that afternoon the outside armed guard on the Cell 13 side of the prison looked up again at the window and saw the prisoner looking out. He saw a hand raised to the barred window and then something white fluttered to the ground, directly under the window of Cell 13. It was a little roll of linen, evidently of white shirting material, and tied around it was a five dollar bill. 'The guard looked up at the window again, but the face had disappeared.

With a grim smile he took the little linen roll and the five-dollar bill to the wardens office. There together they deciphered something which was written on it in a queer sort of ink, frequently blurred. On the outside was this:

'Finder of this please deliver to Dr Charles Ransome.'

'Ah.' said the warden, with a chuckle, 'plan of escape number one has gone wrong.' Then, as an afterthought: 'But why did he address it to Dr Ransome?'

'And where did he get the pen and ink to write with?' asked the guard.

The warden looked at the guard and the guard looked at the warden. There was no apparent solution of that mystery. The warden studied the writing carefully, then shook his head.

'Well, let's see what he was going to say to Dr Ransome,' he said at length, still puzzled, and he unrolled the inner piece of linen.

'Well, if that – what – what do you think of that?' he asked dazed.

The guard took the bit of linen and read this:

'Epa cseot d'net niiy awe htto n'si sih. T.'

The warden spent an hour wondering what sort of cipher it was, and half an hour wondering why his prisoner should attempt to communicate with Dr Ransome, who was the cause of his being there. After this the warden devoted some thought to the question of where the prisoner got writing materials, and what sort of writing materials he had. With the idea of illuminating this point, he examined the linen again. It was a torn part of a white shirt and had ragged edges.

Now it was possible to account for the linen, but what the prisoner had used to write with was another matter. The warden knew it would have been impossible for him to have either pen or pencil, and, besides, neither pen nor pencil had been used in this writing. What then? The warden decided to investigate personally. The Thinking Machine was his prisoner; he had orders to hold his prisoners; if this one sought to escape by sending cipher messages to persons outside, he would stop it, as he would have stopped it in the case of any other prisoner.

The warden went back to Cell 13 and found The Thinking Machine on his hands and knees on the floor, engaged in nothing more alarming than catching rats. The prisoner heard the warden's step and turned to him quickly.

'It's disgraceful,' he snapped, 'these rats. There are scores of them.'

'Other men have been able to stand them,' said the warden. 'Here is another shirt for you – let me have the one you have on'

'Why?' demanded The Thinking Machine, quickly. His tone was hardly natural, his manner suggested actual perturbation.

'You have attempted to communicate with Dr Ransome,' said the warden severely. 'As my prisoner, it is my duty to put a stop to it'

The Thinking Machine was silent for a moment.

'All right,' he said, finally. 'Do your duty.'

The warden smiled grimly. The prisoner arose from the floor and removed the white shirt, putting on instead a striped convict shirt the warden had bought. The warden took the white shirt eagerly, and then and there compared the pieces of linen on which was written the cipher with certain torn places in the shirt. The Thinking Machine looked on curiously.

'The guard brought you those, then?' he asked.

'He certainly did,' relied the warden triumphantly. 'And that ends your first attempt to escape.'

The Thinking Machine watched the warden as he, by comparison, established to his own satisfaction that only two pieces of linen had been torn from the white shirt.

'What did you write this with?' demanded the warden.

'I should think it part of your duty to find out,' said The Thinking Machine, irritably.

The warden started to say some harsh things, then restrained himself and made a minute search of the cell and of the prisoner instead. He found absolutely nothing; not even a match or toothpick which might have been used for a pen. The same mystery surrounded the fluid with which the cipher had been written. Although the warden left Cell 13 visibly annoyed, he took the torn shirt in triumph.

'Well, writing notes on a shirt won't get him out, that's certain,' he told himself with some complacency. He put the linen scraps into his desk to await developments. 'If that man escapes from that cell I'll – hang it – I'll resign.'

On the third day of his incarceration The Thinking Machine openly attempted to bribe his way out. The jailer had brought his dinner and was leaning against the barred door, waiting, when The Thinking Machine began the conversation.

'The drainage pipes of the prison lead to the river, don't they?' he asked.

'Yes,' said the jailer.

'I suppose they are very small.'

'Too small to crawl through, if that's what your thinking about,' was the grinning response.

There was a silence until The Thinking Machine finished his meal. Then:

'You know I'm not a criminal, don't you?'

'Yes.'

'And that I've a perfect right to be freed if I demand it?'

'Yes.'

'Well, I came here believing I could make my escape,' said the prisoner, and his squint eyes studied the face of the jailer. 'Would you consider a financial reward for aiding me to escape?'

The jailer, who happened to be an honest man, looked at the slender, weak figure of the prisoner, at the large head with its mass of yellow hair, and was almost sorry.

'I guess prisons like these were not built for the likes of you to get out of,' he said at last.

'But would you consider a proposition to help me get out?' the prisoner insisted, almost beseechingly.

'No,' said the jailer, shortly.

'Five hundred dollars,' urged The Thinking Machine. 'I am not a criminal.'

'No,' said the jailer.

'A thousand?'

'No,' again said the jailer, and he started away hurriedly to escape further temptation. Then he turned back. 'If you should give me ten thousand dollars I couldn't get you out. You'd have to pass through seven doors, and I only have the keys to two.'

Then he told the warden all about it.

'Plan number two fails,' said the warden, smiling grimly. 'First a cipher, then bribery.'

When the jailer was on his way to Cell 13 at six o'clock, again bearing food to The Thinking Machine, he paused, startled by the unmistakable scrape, scrape of steel versus steel. It stopped at the sound of his steps, then craftily the jailer, who was beyond the prisoners range of vision, resumed his trampling, the sound being apparently that of a man going away from Cell 13. As a matter of fact he was in the same spot.

After a moment there came again the steady scrape, scrape, and the jailer crept cautiously on tiptoes to the door and peered between the bars. The Thinking Machine was standing in the iron bed working at the bars of the little window. He was using a file, judging from the backward and forward swing of his arms.

Cautiously the jailer crept back to the office, summoned the warden in person, and they returned to Cell 13 on tiptoes. The steady scrape was still audible. The warden listened to satisfy himself and then suddenly appeared at the door.

'Well?' he demanded, and there was a smile on his face.

The Thinking Machine glanced back from his perch on the bed and leaped suddenly to the floor, making frantic efforts to hide something. The warden went in, with hand extended.

'Give it up,' he said.

'No,' said the prisoner, sharply.

'Come, give it up,' urged the warden. 'I don't want to have to search you again.'

'No,' repeated the prisoner.

'What was it – a file?' asked the warden.

The Thinking Machine was silent and stood squinting at the warden with something very nearly approaching disappointment on his face – nearly, but not quite. The warden was almost sympathetic.

'Plan number three fails, eh?' he asked, good-naturedly. 'Too bad, isn't it?'

The prisoner didn't say.

'Search him.' instructed the warden.

The jailer searched the prisoner carefully. At last, artfully concealed in the waistband of the trousers, he found a piece of steel about two inches long, with one side curved like a half moon.

'Ah,' said the warden, as he received it from the jailer. 'From your shoe heel,' and he smiled pleasantly.

The jailer continued his search and on the other side of the trousers waistband found another piece of steel identical with the first. The edges showed where they had been worn against the bars of the window.

'You couldn't saw through those bars with these,' said the warden.

'I could have,' said The Thinking Machine firmly.

'In six months, perhaps,' said the warden, good-naturedly.

The warden shook his head slowly as he gazed into the slightly flushed face of his prisoner.

'Ready to give up?' he asked.

'I haven't started yet,' was the prompt reply.

Then came another exhaustive search of the cell. Carefully the two men went over it, finally turning out the bed and searching that. Nothing. The warden in person climbed upon the bed and examined the bars of the window where the prisoner had been sawing. When he looked he was amused.

'Just made it a little bright by hard rubbing,' he said to the prisoner, who stood looking on with a somewhat crestfallen air. The warden grasped the iron bars in his strong hands and tried to shake them. They were immovable, set firmly in the solid granite. He examined each in turn and found them all satisfactory. Finally he climbed down from the bed.

'Give it up, Professor,' he advised.

The Thinking Machine shook his head and the warden and jailer passed on again. As they disappeared down the corridor The Thinking Machine sat on the edge of the bed with his head in his hands.

'He's crazy to try and get out of that cell,' commented the jailer.

'Of course he can't get out,' said the warden. 'But he's clever. I would like to know what he wrote that cipher with.'

It was four o'clock next morning when an awful, heart-racking shriek of terror resounded through the great prison. It came from a cell, somewhere about the centre, and its tone told a tale of horror, agony, terrible fear. The warden heard and with three of his men rushed into the long corridor leading to Cell 13.

As they ran there came again that awful cry. It died away in a sort of a wail. The white faces of prisoners appeared at cell doors upstairs and down, staring out wonderingly, frightened.

'It's that fool in Cell 13,' grumbled the warden.

He stopped and stared in as one of the jailers flashed a lantern. 'That fool in Cell 13' lay comfortably on his cot, flat on his back with his mouth open, snoring. Even as they looked there came again the piercing cry, from somewhere above. The wardens face blanched a little as he started up the stairs. There on the top floor he found a man in Cell 43, directly above Cell 13, but two floors higher, cowering in the corner of his cell.

'What's the matter?' demanded the warden.

'Thank god you've come,' exclaimed the prisoner, and he cast himself against the bars of his cell.

'What is it?' demanded the warden again.

He threw open the door and went in. The prisoner dropped on his knees and clasped the warden about the body. His face was white with terror, his eyes were widely distended, and he was shuddering. His hands, icy cold, clutched at the warden's.

'Take me out of this cell, please take me out,' he pleaded.

'What's the matter with you, anyhow?' insisted the warden, impatiently.

'I've heard something – something,' said the prisoner, and his eyes roved nervously around the cell.

'What did you hear?'

'I – I can't tell you,' stammered the prisoner. Then in a sudden burst of terror: 'Take me out of this cell – put me anywhere – but take me out of here.'

The warden and the three jailers exchanged glances.

'Who is this fellow? What's he accused of?' asked the warden.

'Joseph Ballard,' said one of the jailers. 'He's accused of throwing acid in a woman's face. She died from it.'

'But they can't prove it,' gasped the prisoner. 'They can't prove it. Please put me in some other cell.'

He was still clinging to the warden, and that official threw his arms off roughly. Then for a time he stood looking at the cowering wretch, who seemed possessed of all the wild, unreasoning terror of a child.

'Look here, Ballard,' said the warden, finally, 'if you heard anything, I want to know what it was. Now tell me.'

'I can't, I can't,' was the reply. He was sobbing.

'Where did it come from?'

'I don't know. Everywhere – nowhere. I just heard it.'

'What was it – a voice?'

'Please don't make me answer,' pleaded the prisoner.

'You must answer,' said the warden, sharply.

'It was a voice – but – but it wasn't human,' was the sobbing reply.

'Voice, but not human?' repeated the warden, puzzled.

'It sounded muffled and – and far away – and ghostly,' explained the man.

'Did it come from inside or outside the prison?'

'It didn't seem to come from anywhere – it was just here, here, everywhere. I heard it. I heard it.'

For an hour the warden tried to get the story, but Ballard had become suddenly obstinate and would say nothing – only pleaded to be placed in another cell, or to have one of the jailers remain near him until daylight. These requests were gruffly refused.

'And see here,' said the warden, in conclusion, 'if there's any more of this screaming I'll put you in a padded cell.'

Then the warden went his way, a sadly puzzled man. Ballard sat at his cell door until daylight, his face, drawn and white with terror, pressed against the bars, and looked out into the prison with wide, staring eyes.

That day, the fourth since the incarceration of The Thinking Machine, was enlivened considerably by the volunteer prisoner, who spent most of his time at the little window of his cell. He began proceedings by throwing another piece of linen down to the guard, who picked it up dutifully and took it to the warden. On it was written:

'Only three days more.'

The warden was in no way surprised at what he read; he understood that The Thinking Machine meant only three days more of his imprisonment, and he regarded the note as a boast. But how was the thing written? Where had The Thinking Machine found the new piece of linen? Where? How? He carefully examined the linen. It was white, of fine texture, shirting material. He took the shirt which he had taken and carefully fitted the two original pieces of the linen to the torn places. The third pieces was entirely superfluous; it didn't fit anywhere, and yet it was unmistakably the same goods.

'And where – where does he get anything to write with?' demanded the warden of the world at large.

Still later on the fourth day The Thinking Machine, through the window of his cell, spoke to the armed guard outside.

'What day of the month is it?' he asked.

'The fifteenth,' was the answer.

The Thinking Machine made a mental astronomical calculation and satisfied himself that the moon would not rise until after nine o'clock that night. Then he asked another question:

'Who attends to those arc lights?'

'Man from the company.'

'You have no electricians in the building?'

'No.'

'I should think you could save money if you had your own man.'

'None of my business,' relied the guard.

The guard noticed The Thinking Machine at the cell window frequently during that day, but always the face seemed listless and there was a certain wistfulness in the squint eyes behind the glasses. After a while he accepted the presence of the leonine head as a matter of course. He had seen other prisoners do the same thing; it was the longing for the outside world.

That afternoon, just before the day guard was relieved, the head appeared at the window again, and The Thinking Machine's hand held something out between the bars. It fluttered to the ground and the guard picked it up. It was five-dollar bill.

'That's for you' called the prisoner.

As usual, the guard took it to the warden. The gentleman looked at it suspiciously; he looked at everything that came from Cell 13 with suspicion.

'He said it was for me,' explained the guard.

'It's a sort of tip, I suppose,' said the warden. 'I see no particular reason why you shouldn't accept—'

Suddenly he stopped. He had remembered that The Thinking Machine had gone into Cell 13 with one five-dollar bill and two ten-dollar bills; twenty-five dollars in all. Now a five-dollar bill had been tied around the first pieces of linen that came from the cell. The warden still had it, and to convince himself he took it out and looked at it. It was five dollars; yet here was another five dollars, and The Thinking Machine had only had ten-dollar bills.

'Perhaps somebody changed one of the bills for him,' he thought at last, with a sigh of relief.

But then and there he made up his mind. He would search Cell 13 as a cell was never searched in this world. When a man could write at will, and change money, and do other wholly inexplicable things, there was something radically wrong with his prison. He planned to enter the cell at night – three o'clock would be an excellent time. The Thinking Machine must do all the weird things he did sometime. Night seemed the most reasonable.

Thus it happened that the warden stealthily descended upon Cell 13 that night at three o'clock. He paused at the door and listened. There was no sound save the steady, regular breathing of the prisoner. The keys unfastened the double locks with scarcely a clank, and the warden entered, locking the door behind him. Suddenly he flashed his dark lantern in the face of the recumbent figure.

If the warden had planned to startle The Thinking Machine he was mistaken, for that individual merely opened his eyes quietly, reached for his glasses and inquired, in a most matter-of-fact tone: 'Who is it?'

It would be useless to describe the search that the warden made. It was minute. Not one inch of the cell or the bed was overlooked. He found the round hole in the floor, and with a flash of inspiration thrust his fingers into it. After a moment of fumbling there he drew up something and looked at it in the light of his lantern.

'Ugh!' he exclaimed.

The thing he had taken out was a rat – a dead rat. His inspiration fled as a mist before the sun. But he continued the search. The Thinking Machine, without a word, arose and kicked the rat out of the cell into the corridor.

The warden climbed on the bed and tried the steel bars in the tiny window. They were perfectly rigid; every bar of the door was the same.

Then the warden searched the prisoners clothing, beginning at the shoes. Nothing hidden in them! Then the trousers waistband. Still nothing! Then the pockets of the trousers. From one side he drew out some paper money and examined it.

'Five one-dollar bills,' he gasped.

'That's right,' said the prisoner.

'But the – you had two tens and a five – what the – how do you do it?'

'That's my business,' said The Thinking Machine.

'Did any of my men change this money for you – on your word of honour?'

The Thinking Machine paused just a fraction of a second.

'No,' he said.

'Well, do you make it?' asked the warden. He was prepared to believe anything.

'That's my business,' again said the prisoner.

The warden glared at the eminent scientist fiercely. He felt – he knew – that this man was making a fool out of him, yet he didn't know how. If he were a real prisoner he would get the truth – but, then, perhaps, these inexplicable things which had happened would not have been brought before him so sharply. Neither of the men spoke for a long time, then suddenly the warden turned fiercely and left the cell, slamming the door behind him. He didn't dare speak then.

He glanced at the clock. It was ten minutes to four. He had hardly settled himself in bed when again came the heartbreaking shriek through the prison. With a few muttered words, which, while not elegant, were highly expressive, he relit his lantern and rushed through the prison again to the cell on the upper floor.

Again Ballard was crushing himself against the steel door, shrieking, shrieking at the top of his voice. He stopped only when the
warden flashed his lamp in the cell.

'Take me out, take me out,' he screamed. 'I did it, I did it, I killed
her. Take it away.'

'Take what away?' asked the warden.

'I threw the acid in her face – I did it – I confess. Take me out of
here.'

Ballard's condition was pitiable; it was only an act of mercy to let
him out into the corridor. There he crouched in a corner, like an
animal at bay, and clasped his hands to his ears. It took half an hour
to calm him sufficiently to speak. Then he told incoherently what had
happened. On the night before at four o'clock he had heard a voice –
a sepulchral voice, muffled and wailing in tone.

'What did it say?' asked the warden, curiously.

'Acid – acid – acid!' gasped the prisoner. 'It accused me. Acid! I
threw the acid, and the woman died. Oh!' It was a long, shuddering
wail of terror.

'Acid?' echoed the warden, puzzled. The case was beyond him.

'Acid. That's all I heard – that one word, repeated several times.
There were other things too, but I didn't hear them.'

'That was last night, eh?' asked the warden. 'What happened
tonight – what frightened you just now?'

'It was the same thing,' gasped the prisoner. 'Acid – acid – acid!'
He covered his face with his hands and sat shivering. 'It was acid I
used on her, but I didn't mean to kill her. I just head the words. It was
something accusing me – accusing me.' He mumbled, and was silent.

'Did you hear anything else?'

'Yes – but I could understand – only a little bit – just a word or
two.'

'Well, what was it?'

'I heard 'acid' three times, then I heard a long, moaning sound,
then – then – I heard 'Number 8 hat.' I heard that twice.'

'Number 8 hat,' repeated the warden. 'What the devil – number 8
hat? Accusing voices of conscience have never talked about number 8
hats, so far as I ever heard.'

'He's insane,' said one of the jailers, with an air of finality.

'I believe you,' said the warden. 'He must be. He probably heard
something and got frightened. He's trembling now. Number 8 hat!
What the—'

When the fifth day of The Thinking Machine's imprisonment

rolled around the warden was wearing a hunted look. He was anxious for the end of the thing. He could not help but feel that his distinguished prisoner had been amusing himself. And if this were so, The Thinking Machine had lost none of his sense of humour. For on this fifth day he flung down another linen note to the outside guard, bearing the words: 'Only two days more.' Also he flung down half a dollar.

Now the warden knew – he knew – that the man in Cell 13 didn't have any half dollars – he couldn't have any half dollars, no more than he could have pen and ink and linen, and yet he did have them. It was a condition, not a theory; that is one reason why the warden was wearing a hunted look.

That ghastly, uncanny thing, too, about 'Acid' and 'Number 8 hat' clung to him tenaciously. They didn't mean anything, of course, merely the ravings of an insane murderer who had been driven by fear to confess his crime, still there were so many things that 'didn't mean anything' happening in the prison now since The Thinking Machine was there.

On the sixth day the warden received a card stating that Dr Ransome and Mr Fielding would be at Chisholm Prison on the following evening, Thursday, and in the event of Professor Van Dusen had not yet escaped – and they presumed he had not because they had not heard from him – they would meet him there.

'In the event he had not yet escaped!' The warden smiled grimly. Escaped!

The Thinking Machine enlivened this day for the warden with three notes. They were on the usual linen and bore generally on the appointment at half past eight o'clock Thursday night, which appointment the scientist had made at the time of his imprisonment.

On the afternoon of the seventh day the warden passed Cell 13 and glanced in. The Thinking Machine was lying on the iron bed, apparently sleeping lightly. The cell appeared precisely as it always did from a casual glance. The warden would swear that no man was going to leave it between that hour – it was then four o'clock – and half past eight o'clock that evening.

On his way back past the cell the warden heard the steady breathing again, and coming close to the door looked in. He wouldn't have done so if The Thinking Machine had been looking, but now – well, it was different.

A ray of light came through the high window and fell on the face of the sleeping man. It occurred to the warden for the first time that his prisoner appeared haggard and weary. Just then The Thinking Machine stirred slightly and the warden hurried on up the corridor guiltily. That evening after six o'clock he saw the jailer.

'Everything all right in Cell 13?' he asked.

'Yes sir,' replied the jailer. 'He didn't eat much, though.'

It was with a feeling of having done his duty that the warden received Dr Ransome and Mr Fielding shortly after seven o'clock. He intended to show them the linen notes and lay before them the full story of his woes, which was a long one. But before this came to pass the guard from the river side of the prison yard entered the office.

'The arc light in my side of the yard won't light,' he informed the warden.

'Confound it, that man's a hoodoo,' thundered the official. 'Everything has happened since he's been here.'

The guard went back to his post in the darkness, and the warden phoned to the electric light company.

'This is Chisholm Prison,' he said through the phone. 'Send three or four men down here quick, to fix an arc light.'

The reply was evidently satisfactory, for the warden hung up the receiver and passed out into the yard. While Dr Ransome and Mr Fielding sat waiting, the guard at the outer gate came in with a special-delivery letter. Dr Ransome happened to notice the address, and, when the guard went out, looked at the letter more closely.

'By George!' he exclaimed.

'What is it?' asked Mr Fielding.

Silently the doctor offered the letter. Mr Fielding examined it closely.

'Coincidence,' he said. 'It must be.'

It was nearly eight o'clock when the warden returned to his office. The electricians had arrived in a wagon, and were now at work. The warden pressed the buzz-button communicating with the man at the outer gate in the wall.

'How many electricians came in?' he asked, over the short phone. 'Four? Three workmen in jumpers and overalls and the manager? Frock coat and silk hat? All right. Be certain that only four go out. That's all.'

He turned to Dr Ransome and Mr Fielding.

'We have to be careful here – particularly,' and there was broad sarcasm in his tone, 'since we have scientists locked up.'

The warden picked up the special delivery letter carelessly, and then began to open it.

'When I read this I want to tell you gentlemen something about how – Great Caesar!' he ended, suddenly, as he glanced at the letter. He sat with mouth open, motionless, from astonishment.

'What is it?' asked Mr Fielding.

'A special delivery letter from Cell 13,' gasped the warden. ' An invitation to supper.'

'What?' and the two others arose, unanimously.

The warden sat dazed, staring at the letter for a moment, then called sharply to a guard outside the corridor.

'Run down to Cell 13 and see if that man's in there.'

The guard went as directed, while Dr Ransome and Mr Fielding examined the letter.

'It's Van Dusen's handwriting; there's no question of that,' said Dr Ransome. 'I've seen too much of it.'

Just then the buzz on the telephone from the outer gate sounded, and the warden, in a semi-trance, picked up the receiver.

'Hello! Two reporters, eh? Let 'em come in.' He turned suddenly to the doctor and Mr Fielding. 'Why; the man can't be out. He must be in his cell.'

Just at that moment the guard returned.

'He's still in his cell, sir,' he reported, 'I saw him. He's lying down.'

'There, I told you so,' said the warden, and he breathed freely again. 'But how did he mail that letter?'

There was a rap on the steel door which led from the jail yard into the warden's office.

'It's the reporters,' said the warden. 'Let them in,' he instructed the guard; then to the other two gentlemen: 'Don't say anything about this before them, because I'd never hear the last of it.'

The door opened, and the two men from the front gate entered.

'Good-evening, gentlemen,' said one. That was Hutchinson Hatch; the warden knew him well.

'Well?' demanded the other, irritably. 'I'm here.'

That was The Thinking Machine.

He squinted belligerently at the warden, who sat with mouth agape. For the moment that official had nothing to say. Dr Ransome and Mr Fielding were amazed, but they didn't know what the warden knew. They were only amazed; he was paralysed. Hutchinson Hatch, the reporter, took in the scene with greedy eyes.

'How – how – how did you do it?' gasped the warden, finally.

'Come back to the cell,' said The Thinking Machine, in the irritated voice which his scientific associates knew so well.

The warden, still in a condition bordering on trance, led the way.

'Flash your light in there,' directed The Thinking Machine.

The warden did so. There was nothing unusual in the appearance of the cell, and there – there on the bed lay the figure of The Thinking Machine. Certainly! There was the yellow hair! Again the warden looked at the man beside him and wondered at the strangeness of his own dreams.

With trembling hands he unlocked the cell door and The Thinking Machine passed inside.

'See here,' he said.

He kicked at the steel bars in the bottom of the cell door and three of them were pushed out of place. A fourth broke off and rolled away in the corridor.

'And here, too,' directed the erstwhile prisoner as he stood on the bed to reach the small window. He swept his hand across the opening and every bar came out.

'What's this in bed?' demanded the warden, who was slowly recovering.

'A wig,' was the reply. 'Turn down the cover.'

The warden did so. Beneath it lay a large coil of strong rope, thirty feet or more, a dagger, three files, ten feet of electric wire, a thin, powerful pair of steel pliers, a small track hammer with its handle, and – a derringer pistol.

'How did you do it?' demanded the warden.

'You gentlemen have an engagement to supper with me at half past nine o'clock,' said The Thinking Machine. 'Come on, or we shall be late.'

'But how did you do it?' insisted the warden.

'Don't ever think you can hold any man who can use his brain,' said The Thinking Machine. 'Come on; we shall be late.'

It was an impatient supper party in the rooms of Professor Van Dusen and a somewhat silent one. The guests were Dr Ransome, Alfred Fielding, the warden, and Hutchinson Hatch, reporter. The meal was served to the minute, in accordance with Professor Van Dusen's instructions of one week before; Dr Ransome found the artichokes delicious. At last supper was finished and The Thinking Machine turned on Dr Ransome and squinted at him fiercely.

'Do you believe it now?' he demanded.

'I do,' replied Dr Ransome.

'Do you admit that it was a fair test?'

'I do.'

With the others, particularly the warden, he was waiting anxiously for the explanation.

'Suppose you tell us how—' began Mr Fielding.

'Yes, tell us how,' said the warden.

The Thinking Machine readjusted his glasses, took a couple of preparatory squints at his audience, and began his story. He told it from the beginning logically; and no man ever talked to more interested listeners.

'My agreement was,' he began, 'to go into a cell, carrying nothing except what was necessary to wear, and to leave that cell within a week. I had never seen Chisholm Prison. When I went into the cell I asked for tooth powder, two ten, and one five-dollar bills, and also to have my shoes blacked. Even if these requests had been refused it would not have mattered seriously. But you agreed to them.

'I knew there would be nothing in the cell which you thought I might use to advantage. So when the warden locked the door on me I was apparently helpless, unless I could turn three seemingly innocent things to use. They were things which would have been permitted any prisoner under sentence of death, were they not, warden?'

'Tooth powder and polished shoes, yes, but not money,' replied the warden.

'Anything is dangerous in the hands of a man who knows how to use it,' went on The Thinking Machine. 'I did nothing that first night but sleep and chase rats.' he glared at the warden. 'When the subject was broached I knew I could do nothing that night, so suggested the next day. You gentleman thought I wanted time to arrange an escape with outside assistance, but this was not true. I knew I could communicate with whom I pleased, when I pleased.'

The warden stared at him a moment, then went on smoking solemnly.

'I was aroused next morning at six o'clock by the jailer with my breakfast,' continued the scientist. 'He told me dinner was at twelve and supper at six. Between these times, I gathered, I would be pretty much to myself. So immediately after breakfast I examined my outside surroundings from my cell window. One look told me it would be useless to try to scale the wall, even should I decide to leave my cell by the window, for my purpose was to leave not only the cell, but the prison. Of course, I could have gone over the wall, but it would have taken me longer to lay my plans that way. Therefore, for the moment, I dismissed all idea of that.

'From this first observation I knew the river was on that side of the prison, and that there was also a playground there. Subsequently these surmises were verified by a keeper. I knew then one important thing – that anyone might approach the prison wall from that side if necessary without attracting any particular attention. That was well to remember. I remembered it.

'But the outside thing which most attracted my attention was the feed wire to the arc light which ran within a few feet – probably three or four – of my cell window. I knew that would be valuable in the event I found it necessary to cut off that arc light.'

'Oh, you shut it off tonight, then?' asked the warden.

'Having learned all I could from the window,' resumes The Thinking Machine, without heeding the interruption, 'I considered the idea of escaping through the prison proper. I recalled just how I had come into the cell, which I knew would be the only way. Seven doors lay between me and the outside. So, also for the time being, I gave up the idea of escaping that way. And I couldn't go through the solid granite walls of the cell.'

The Thinking Machine paused for a moment and Dr Ransome lighted a new cigar. For several minutes there was silence, then the scientific jailbreaker went on:

'While I was thinking about these things a rat ran across my foot. It suggested a new line of thought. There were at least half a dozen rats in the cell – I could see their beady eyes. Yet I had noticed none come under the cell door. I frightened them purposely and watched the cell door to see if they went out that way. They did not, but they were gone. Obviously they went another way. Another way meant another opening.

'I searched for this opening and found it. It was an old drain pipe, long unused and partly choked with dirt and dust. But this was the way the rats had come. They came from somewhere. Where? Drain pipes usually lead outside prison grounds. This one probably led to the river, or near it. The rats must therefore come from that direction. If they came a part of the way, I reasoned they came all the way, because it was extremely unlikely that a solid iron or lead pipe would have any hole in it except at the exit.

'When the jailer came with my luncheon he told me two important things, although he didn't know it. One was that a new system of plumbing had been put in the prison seven years ago; another that the river was only three hundred feet away. Then I knew positively that the pipe was a part of the old system; I knew, too, that it slanted generally toward the river. But did the pipe end on the water or on land?

'This was the next question to be decided. I decided it by catching several of the rats in the cell. My jailer was surprised to see me engaged in this work. I examined at least a dozen of them. They were perfectly dry; they had come through the pipe, and, most important of all, they were not house rats, but field rats. The other end of the pipe was on land, then, outside the prison walls. So far, so good.

'Then, I knew that if I worked freely from this point I must attract the warden's attention in another direction. You see, by telling the warden that I had come to escape you made the test more severe, because I had to trick him by false scents.'

The warden looked up with a sad expression in his eyes.

'The first thing was to make him think I was trying to communicate with you, Dr Ransome. So I wrote a note on a piece of linen I tore from my shirt, addressed it to Dr Ransome, tied a five-dollar bill around it and threw it out the window. I knew the guard would take it to the warden, but I rather hoped the warden would send it as addressed. Have you the first linen note, warden?'

The warden produced the cipher.

'What does it mean, anyhow?' he asked.

'Read it backward, beginning with the 'T' signature and disregard the division into words,' instructed The Thinking Machine.

The warden did so. 'T-h-i-s, this,' he spelled, studied it for a moment, then read it off, grinning:

'This is not the way I intend to escape.

'Well, now what do you think o' that? he demanded, still grinning.

'I knew that would attract your attention, just as it did,' said The Thinking Machine, 'and if you really found out what it was it would be a sort of gentle rebuke.'

'What did you write it with?' asked Dr Ransome, after he had examined the linen and passed it to Mr Fielding.

'This,' said the erstwhile prisoner, and he extended his foot. On it was the shoe he had worn in prison, though the polish was gone – scraped off clean. 'The shoe blacking, moistened with water, was my ink; the metal tip of the shoe lace made a fairly good pen.'

The warden looked up and suddenly burst into a laugh, half of relief, half of amusement.

'You're a wonder,' he said, admiringly. 'Go on.'

'That precipitated a search of my cell by the warden, as I had intended,' continued The Thinking Machine. 'I was anxious to get the warden in the habit of searching my cell, so that finally, constantly finding nothing, he would get disgusted and quit. This at last happened, practically.'

The warden blushed.

'He then took my white shirt away and gave me a prison shirt. He was satisfied that those two pieces of the shirt were all that was missing. But while he was searching my cell I had another pieces of that same shirt, about nine inches square, rolled up into a small ball in my mouth.'

'Nine inches of that shirt?' demanded the warden. 'Where did it come from?'

'The bosoms of all stiff white shirts are of triple thickness,' was the explanation. 'I tore out the inside thickness, leaving the bosom only two thicknesses. I knew you wouldn't see it. So much for that.'

There was a little pause, and the warden looked from one to another of the men with a sheepish grin.

'Having disposed of the warden for a while by giving him something else to think about, I took my first serious step toward freedom,' said Professor Van Dusen. 'I knew, within reason, that the pipe led somewhere to the playground outside; I knew a great many boys played there; I knew the rats came into my cell from out there. Could I communicate with someone outside with these things at hand?

'First was necessary, I saw, a long and fairly reliable thread, so – but here,' he pulled up his trousers legs and showed that the tops of both stockings, of fine, strong lisle, were gone. 'I untravelled those – after I got them started it wasn't difficult – and I had easily a quarter of a mile of thread that I could depend on.

'Then on half of my remaining linen I wrote, laboriously enough I assure you, a letter explaining my situation to this gentleman here,' and he indicated Hutchinson Hatch. 'I knew he would assist me – for the value of the newspaper story. I tied firmly to this linen letter a ten-dollar bill – there is no surer way of attracting the eye of anyone – and wrote on the linen: 'finder of this deliver to Hutchinson Hatch, *Daily American*, who will give another ten dollars for the information.'

The next thing was to get this note outside on that playground where a boy might find it. There were two ways, but I chose the best. I took one of the rats – I became adept at catching then – tied the linen and money firmly to one leg, fastened my lisle thread to another, and turned him loose in the drain pipe. I reasoned that the natural fright of the rodent would make him run until he was outside the pipe and then out on earth he would probably stop to gnaw off the linen and money.

'From the moment the rat disappeared into that dusty pipe I became anxious. I was taking so many chances. The rat might gnaw the string, of which I held one end; other rats might gnaw at it; the rat might run out of the pipe and leave the linen and money where they would never be found; a thousand other things might have happened. So began some nervous hours, but the fact that the rat ran on until only a few feet of the string remained in my cell made me think he was outside the pipe. I had carefully instructed Mr Hatch what to do in case the note reached him. The question was: Would it reach him?

'This done, I could only wait and make other plans in case this one failed. I openly attempted to bribe my jailer, and I learned from him that he held the keys to only two of seven doors between me and freedom. Then I did something else to make the warden nervous. I took the steel supports out of the heels of my shoes and made a pretence of sawing the bars of my cell window. The warden raised a pretty row about that. He developed, too, the habit of shaking the bars of my cell window to see if they were solid. They were – *then*.'

Again the warden grinned. He had ceased being astonished.

'With this one plan I had done all I could and could only wait to see what happened,' the scientist went on. 'I couldn't know whether my note had been delivered or even found, or whether the mouse had gnawed it up. And I didn't dare to draw back through the pipe the one slender thread which connected me with the outside.

'When I went to bed that night I didn't sleep, for fear there would come the slight signal twitch at the thread which was to tell me that Mr Hatch had received the note. At half past three o'clock, I judge, I felt this twitch, and no prisoner actually under sentence of death ever welcomed a thing more heartily.'

The Thinking Machine stopped and turned to the reporter.

'You'd better explain just what you did,' he said.

'The linen note was brought to me by a small boy who had been playing baseball,' said Mr Hatch. 'I immediately saw a big story in it, so I gave the boy another ten dollars, and got several spools of silk, some twine, and a roll of light, pliable wire. The Professor's note suggested that I have the finder of the note show me just where it was picked up, and told me to make my search from there, beginning at two o'clock in the morning. If I found the other end of the thread, I was to twitch it gently three times, then a fourth.

'I began the search with a small-bulb electric light. It was an hour and twenty minutes before I found the end of the drain pipe, half hidden in the weeds. The pipe was very large there, say twelve inches across. Then I found the end of the lisle thread, twitched it as directed and immediately I got an answering twitch.

'Then I fastened the silk to this and Professor Van Dusen began to pull it into his cell. I nearly had heart disease for fear the string would break. To the end of the silk I fastened the twine, and when that had been pulled in I tied on the wire. Then that was drawn into the pipe and we had a substantial line, which rats couldn't gnaw, from the mouth of the drain into the cell.'

The Thinking Machine raised his hand and Hatch stopped.

'All this was done in absolute silence,' said the scientist. 'but when the wire reached my hand I could have shouted. Then we tried another experiment, which Mr Hatch was prepared for. I tested the pipe as a speaking tube. Neither of us could hear very clearly, but I dared not speak loud for fear of attracting attention in the prison. At last I made him understand what I wanted immediately. He seemed to have great difficulty in understanding when I asked for nitric acid, and I repeated the word "acid" several times.

'Then I heard a shriek from a cell above me. I knew instantly that someone had overheard, and when I heard you coming, Mr Warden, I feigned sleep. If you had entered my cell at that moment the whole plan of escape would have ended there. But you passed on. That was the nearest I ever came to being caught.

'Having established this improvised trolley it is easy to see how I got things into the cell and made them disappear at will. I merely dropped them back into the pipe. You, Mr Warden, could not have reached the connecting wire with your fingers; they are too large. My fingers, you see, are longer and more slender. In addition I guarded the top of that pipe with a rat – you remember how.'

'I remember,' said the warden, with a grimace.

'I thought that if anyone were tempted to investigate that hole the rat would dampen his ardour. Mr Hatch could not send me anything useful through the pipe until next night, although he did send me change for ten dollars as a test, so I proceeded with other parts of my plan. Then I evolved the method of escape I finally employed.

'In order to carry this out successfully it was necessary for the guard in the yard to get accustomed to seeing me at the cell window. I arranged this by dropping linen notes to him, boastful in tone, to make the warden believe, if possible, one of his assistants was communicating with the outside for me. I would stand at my window for hours gazing out, so the guard could see me, and occasionally I spoke to him. In that way I learned the prison had no electricians of its own, but was dependent upon the lighting company should anything go wrong.

'That cleared the way to freedom perfectly. Early in the evening of the last day of my imprisonment, when it was dark, I planned to cut the feed wire which was only a few feet from my window, reaching it with an acid tipped wire I had. That would make that side of the prison perfectly dark while the electricians were searching for the break. That would also bring Mr Hatch into the prison yard.'

'There was only one more thing to do before I actually began the work of setting myself free. This was to arrange final details with Mr Hatch through our speaking tube. I did this within half an hour after the warden left my cell on the fourth night of my imprisonment. Mr Hatch again had serious difficulty in understanding me, and I repeated the word "acid" to him several times, and later on the words: "Number 8 hat" – that's my size – and these were the things which made the prisoner upstairs confess to murder, so one of the jailers told me the next day. The prisoner had heard our voices, confused of course, through the pipe, which also went to his cell. The cell directly over me was not occupied, hence no one else heard.

'Of course the actual work of cutting the steel bars out of the window and door was comparatively easy with nitric acid, which I got through the pipe in tin bottles, but it took time. Hour after hour on the fifth and sixth and seventh days the guard below was looking at me as I worked on the bars of the window with the acid on a piece of wire. I used the tooth powder to prevent the acid spreading. I looked away abstractly as I worked and each minute the acid cut deeper into the metal. I noticed that the jailers always tried the door by shaking the upper part, never the lower bars, therefore I cut the lower bars, leaving them hanging in place by thin strips of metal. But that was a bit of daredeviltry. I could not have gone away so easily.'

The Thinking Machine sat silent for several minutes.

'I think that makes everything clear,' he went on. 'Whatever points I have not explained were merely to confuse the warden and jailers. These things in my bed I brought in to please Mr Hatch, who wanted to improve the story. Of course, the wig was necessary in my plan. The special delivery letter I wrote and directed in my cell with Mr Hatch's fountain pen, then sent it out to him and he mailed it. That's all, I think.'

'But your actually leaving the prison grounds and then coming in through the outer gate to my office?' asked the warden.

'Perfectly simple,' said the scientist. 'I cut the electric light wire with acid, as I said, when the current was off. Therefore when the current was turned on the arc didn't light. I knew it would take some time to find out what was the matter and make repairs. When the guard went to report to you the yard was dark, I crept out the window – it was a tight fit, too – replaced the bars by standing on a narrow ledge and remained in shadow until the force of electricians arrived. Mr Hatch was one of them.

'When I saw him I spoke and he handed me a cap, a jumper and overalls, which I put on within ten feet of you, Mr Warden, while you were in the yard. Later Mr Hatch called me, presumably as a workman, and together we went out the gate to get something out of the wagon. The gate guard let us pass out readily as two workmen who had just passed in. We changed our clothing and reappeared, asking to see you. We saw you. That's all.'

There was a silence for several minutes. Dr Ransome was first to speak.

'Wonderful!' he exclaimed. 'Perfectly amazing.'

'How did Mr Hatch happen to come in with the electricians?' asked Mr Fielding.

'His father is manager of the company,' relied The Thinking Machine.

'But what if there had been no Mr Hatch outside to help?'

'Every prisoner has one friend outside who would help him escape if he could.'

'Suppose – just suppose – there had been no old plumbing system there?' asked the warden, curiously.

'There were two other ways out,' said The Thinking Machine, enigmatically.

Ten minutes later the telephone bell rang. It was a request for the warden.

'Light all right, eh?' the warden asked, through the phone. 'Good. Wire cut beside Cell 13? Yes, I know. One electrician too many? What's that? Two came out?'

The warden turned to the others with a puzzled expression.

'He only let in four electricians, he has let out two and says there are three left.'

'I was the odd one,' said The Thinking Machine.

'Oh,' said the warden. 'I see.' Then through the phone: 'Let the fifth man go. He's all right.'

MAURICE LEBLANC

The Mysterious Railway Passenger

I HAD sent my motorcar to Rouen by road on the previous day I was to meet it by train, and go on to some friends, who have a house on the Seine

A few minutes before we left Paris my compartment was invaded by seven gentlemen, five of whom were smoking. Short though the journey by the fast train be, I did not relish the prospect of taking it in such company, the more so as the old-fashioned carriage had no corridor. I therefore collected my overcoat, my newspapers, and my railway guide, and sought refuge in one of the neighbouring compartments.

It was occupied by a lady. At the sight of me, she made a movement of vexation which did not escape my notice, and leaned towards a gentleman standing on the footboard – her husband, no doubt, who had come to see her off. The gentleman took stock of me, and the examination seemed to conclude to my advantage; for he whispered to his wife and smiled, giving her the look with which we reassure a frightened child. She smiled in her turn, and cast a friendly glance in my direction, as though she suddenly realised that I was one of those well-bred men with whom a woman can remain locked up for an hour or two in a little box six feet square without having anything to fear.

Her husband said to her:

'You must not mind, darling; but I have an important appointment, and I must not wait.'

He kissed her affectionately, and went away. His wife blew him some discreet little kisses through the window, and waved her handkerchief.

Then the guard's whistle sounded, and the train started.

At that moment, and in spite of the warning shouts of the railway officials, the door opened, and a man burst into our carriage. My travelling companion, who was standing up and arranging her things in the rack, uttered a cry of terror, and dropped down upon the seat.

I am no coward – far from it; but I confess that these sudden incursions at the last minute are always annoying. They seem so ambiguous, so unnatural. There must be something behind them, else...

The appearance of the newcomer, however, and his bearing were such as to correct the bad impression produced by the manner of his entrance. He was neatly, almost smartly, dressed; his tie was in good taste, his gloves clean; he had a powerful face... But, speaking of his face, where on earth had I seen it before? For I had seen it: of that there was no possible doubt; or at least, to be accurate, I found within myself that sort of recollection which is left by the sight of an oft-seen portrait of which one has never beheld the original. And at the same time I felt the uselessness of any effort of memory that I might exert, so inconsistent and vague was that recollection.

But when my eyes reverted to the lady I sat astounded at the pallor and disorder of her features. She was staring at her neighbour – he was seated on the same side of the carriage – with an expression of genuine affright, and I saw one of her hands steal trembling towards a little travelling-bag that lay on the cushion a few inches from her lap. She ended by taking hold of it, and nervously drew it to her.

Our eyes met, and I read in hers so great an amount of uneasiness and anxiety that I could not help saying:

'I hope you are not unwell, madame... Would you like me to open the window?'

She made no reply, but, with a timid gesture, called my attention to the individual beside her. I smiled as her husband had done, shrugged my shoulders, and explained to her by signs that she had nothing to fear, that I was there, and that, besides, the gentleman in question seemed quite harmless.

Just then he turned towards us, contemplated us, one after the other, from head to foot, and then huddled himself into his corner, and made no further movement.

A silence ensued; but the lady, as though she had summoned up all her energies to perform an act of despair, said to me, in a hardly audible voice:

'You know he is in our train.'

'Who?'

'Why, he... he himself... I assure you.'

'Whom do you mean?'

'Arsène Lupin!'

She had not removed her eyes from the passenger, and it was at him rather than at me that she flung the syllables of that alarming name.

He pulled his hat down upon his nose. Was this to conceal his agitation, or was he merely preparing to go to sleep?

I objected.

'Arsène Lupin was sentenced yesterday, in his absence, to twenty years' penal servitude. It is not likely that he would commit the imprudence of showing himself in public today. Besides, the newspapers have discovered that he has been spending the winter in Turkey ever since his famous escape from the Sante.'

'He is in this train,' repeated the lady, with the ever more marked intention of being overheard by our companion. 'My husband is a deputy prison-governor, and the station-inspector himself told us that they were looking for Arsène Lupin.'

'That is no reason why... '

'He was seen at the booking-office. He took a ticket for Rouen.'

'It would have been easy to lay hands upon him.'

'He disappeared. The ticket-collector at the door of the waiting-room did not see him; but they thought that he must have gone round by the suburban platforms and stepped into the express that leaves ten minutes after us.'

'In that case, they will have caught him there.'

'And supposing that, at the last moment, he jumped out of that express and entered this, our own train... as he probably... as he most certainly did?'

'In that case they will catch him here; for the porters and the police cannot have failed to see him going from one train to the other, and, when we reach Rouen, they will net him finely.'

'Him? Never! He will find some means of escaping again.'

'In that case I wish him a good journey.'

'But think of all that he may do in the mean time!'

'What?'

'How can I tell? One must be prepared for anything.'

She was greatly agitated; and, in point of fact, the situation, to a certain degree, warranted her nervous state of excitement. Almost in spite of myself, I said:

'There are such things as curious coincidences, it is true... But calm yourself. Admitting that Arsène Lupin is in one of these carriages, he is sure to keep quiet, and, rather than bring fresh trouble upon himself, he will have no other idea than that of avoiding the danger that threatens him.'

My words failed to reassure her. However she said no more, fearing, no doubt, lest I should think her troublesome.

As for myself, I opened my newspapers and read the reports of Arsène Lupin's trial. They contained nothing that was not already known, and they interested me but slightly. Moreover, I was tired, I had had a poor night, I felt my eye-lids growing heavy, and my head began to nod.

'But surely, sir, you are not going to sleep?'

The lady snatched my paper from my hands, and looked at me with indignation.

'Certainly not,' I replied. 'I have no wish to.'

'It would be most imprudent,' she said.

'Most,' I repeated.

And I struggled hard, fixing my eyes on the landscape, on the clouds that streaked the sky. And soon all this became confused in space, the image of the excited lady and the drowsy man was obliterated in my mind, and I was filled with the great, deep silence of sleep.

It was soon made agreeable by light and incoherent dreams, in which a being who played the part and bore the name of Arsène Lupin occupied a certain place. He turned and shifted on the horizon, his back laden with valuables, clambering over walls and stripping country-houses of their contents.

But the outline of this being, who had ceased to be Arsène Lupin, grew more distinct. He came towards me, grew bigger and bigger, leaped into the carriage with incredible agility, and fell full upon my chest.

A sharp pain… a piercing scream… I awoke. The man, my fellow-traveller, with one knee on my chest, was clutching my throat.

I saw this very dimly, for my eyes were shot with blood. I also saw the lady in a corner writhing in a violent fit of hysterics. I did not even attempt to resist. I should not have had the strength for it had I wished to: my temples were throbbing, I choked … my throat rattled… Another minute… and I should have been suffocated.

The man must have felt this. He loosened his grip. Without leaving hold of me, with his right hand he stretched a rope, in which he had prepared a slipknot, and, with a quick turn, tied my wrists together. In a moment I was bound, gagged – rendered motionless and helpless.

And he performed this task in the most natural manner in the world, with an ease that revealed the knowledge of a master, of an expert in theft and crime. Not a word, not a fevered movement. Sheer coolness and audacity. And there lay I on the seat, roped up like a mummy – I, Arsène Lupin!

It was really ridiculous. And notwithstanding the seriousness of the circumstances I could not but appreciate and almost enjoy the irony of the situation. Arsène Lupin 'done' like a novice, stripped like the first-comer! For of course the scoundrel relieved me of my pocket-book and purse! Arsène Lupin victimised in his turn – duped and beaten! What an adventure!

There remained the lady. He took no notice of her at all. He contented himself with picking up the wrist-bag that lay on the floor, and extracting the jewels, the purse, the gold and silver knickknacks which it contained. The lady opened her eyes, shuddered with fright, took off her rings and handed them to the man as though she wished to spare him any superfluous exertion. He took the rings, and looked at her: she fainted away.

Then, calm and silent as before, without troubling about us further, he resumed his seat, lit a cigarette, and abandoned himself to a careful scrutiny of the treasures which he had captured, the inspection of which seemed to satisfy him completely.

I was much less satisfied. I am not speaking of the twelve thousand francs of which I had been unduly plundered: this was a loss which I accepted only for the time; I had no doubt that those twelve thousand francs would return to my possession after a short interval, together with the exceedingly important papers which my pocket-book contained: plans, estimates, specifications, addresses, lists of correspondents, letters of a coin-promising character. But, for the moment, a more immediate and serious care was worrying me: what was to happen next?

As may be readily imagined, the excitement caused by my passing through the Gare Saint-Lazare had not escaped me. As I was going to stay with friends who knew me by the name of Guillaume Berlat, and to whom my resemblance to Arsène Lupin was the occasion of many a friendly jest, I had not been able to disguise myself after my wont, and my presence had been discovered. Moreover, a man, doubtless Arsène Lupin, had been seen to rush from the express into the fast train. Hence it was inevitable and fated that the commissary of police at Rouen, warned by telegram, would await the arrival of the train, assisted by a decent number of constables, question any suspicious passengers, and proceed to make a minute inspection of the carriages.

All this I had foreseen, and had not felt greatly excited about it; for I was certain that the Rouen police would display no greater perspicacity than the Paris police, and that I should have been able to pass unperceived: was it not sufficient for me, at the wicket, carelessly to show my deputy's card, collector at Saint-Lazare with every confidence? But how things had changed since then! I was no longer free. It was impossible to attempt one of my usual moves. In one of the carriages the commissary would discover the Sieur Arsène Lupin, whom a propitious fate was sending to him bound hand and foot, gentle as a lamb, packed up complete. He had only to accept delivery, just as you receive a parcel addressed to you at a railway station, a hamper of game, or a basket of vegetables and fruit.

And to avoid this annoying catastrophe, what could I do, entangled as I was in my bonds?

The train was speeding towards Rouen, the next and the only stopping-place; it rushed through Vernon, through Saint-Pierre…

I was puzzled also by another problem in which I was not so directly interested, but the solution of which aroused my professional curiosity: What were my fellow-traveller's intentions?

If I had been alone he would have had ample time to alight quite calmly at Rouen. But the lady? As soon as the carriage door was opened the lady, meek and quiet as she sat at present, would scream, and throw herself about, and cry for help!

Hence my astonishment. Why did he not reduce her to the same state of powerlessness as myself, which would have given him time to disappear before his twofold misdeed was discovered?

He was still smoking, his eyes fixed on the view outside, which a hesitating rain was beginning to streak with long, slanting lines. Once, however, he turned round, took up my railway guide, and consulted it.

As for the lady, she made every effort to continue fainting, so as to quiet her enemy. But a fit of coughing, produced by the smoke, gave the lie to her pretended swoon.

Myself, I was very uncomfortable, and had pains all over my body. And I thought… I planned.

Pont-de-l'Arche… Oissel… The train was hurrying on, glad, drunk with speed… Saint-Etienne…

At that moment the man rose and took two steps towards us, to which the lady hastened to reply with a new scream and a genuine fainting fit.

But what could his object be? He lowered the window on our side. The rain was now falling in torrents, and he made a movement of annoyance at having neither umbrella nor overcoat. He looked up at the rack: the lady's *en-tout-cas* was there; he took it. He also took my overcoat and put it on.

We were crossing the Seine. He turned up his trousers, and then, leaning out of the window, raised the outer latch.

Did he mean to fling himself on the permanent way? At the rate at which we were going it would have been certain death. We plunged into the tunnel pierced under the Cote Sainte-Catherine. The man opened the door, and, with one foot, felt for the step. What madness! The darkness, the smoke, the din – all combined to give a fantastic appearance to any such attempt. But suddenly the train slowed up, the Westinghouse brakes counteracted the movement of the wheels. In a minute the pace from fast became normal, and decreased still more. Without a doubt there was a gang at work repairing this part of the tunnel; this would necessitate a slower passage of the trains for some days perhaps, and the man knew it.

He had only, therefore, to put his other foot on the step, climb down to the footboard, and walk away quietly, not without first closing the door, and throwing back the latch.

He had scarcely disappeared when the smoke showed whiter in the daylight. We emerged into a valley. One more tunnel, and we should be at Rouen.

The lady at once recovered her wits, and her first care was to bewail the loss of her jewels. I gave her a beseeching glance. She understood, and relieved me of the gag which was stifling me. She wanted also to unfasten my bonds, but I stopped her.

'No, no; the police must see everything as it was. I want them to be fully informed as regards that blackguard's actions.'

'Shall I pull the alarm-signal?'

'Too late. You should have thought of that while he was attacking me.'

'But he would have killed me! Ah, sir, didn't I tell you that he was travelling by this train? I knew him at once, by his portrait. And now he's taken my jewels!'

'They'll catch him, have no fear.'

'Catch Arsène Lupin! Never.'

'It all depends on you, madam. Listen. When we arrive be at the window, call out, make a noise. The police and porters will come up. Tell them what you have seen in a few words: the assault of which I was the victim, and the flight of Arsène Lupin. Give his description: a soft hat, an umbrella – yours – a grey frock-overcoat... '

'Yours,' she said.

'Mine? No, his own. I didn't have one.'

'I thought that he had none either when he got in.'

'He must have had… unless it was a coat which someone left behind in the rack. In any case, he had it when he got out, and that is the essential thing… A grey frock-overcoat, remember… Oh, I was forgetting… tell them your name to start with. Your husband's functions will stimulate the zeal of all those men.'

We were arriving. She was already leaning out of the window. I resumed, in a louder, almost imperious voice, so that my words should sink into her brain:

'Give my name also, Guillaume Berlat. If necessary, say you know me… That will save time… we must hurry on the preliminary inquiries… the important thing is to catch Arsène Lupin… with your jewels… You quite understand, don't you? Guillaume Berlat, a friend of your husband's.'

'Quite… Guillaume Berlat.'

She was already calling out and gesticulating. Before the train had come to a standstill a gentleman climbed in, followed by a number of other men. The critical hour was at hand.

Breathlessly the lady exclaimed:

'Arsène Lupin… he attacked us… he has stolen my jewels… I am Madame Renaud… my husband is a deputy prison-governor… Ah, here's my brother, Georges Andelle, manager of the Credit Rouennais… What I want to say is… '

She kissed a young man who had just come up, and who exchanged greetings with the commissary. She continued, weeping:

'Yes, Arsène Lupin… He flew at this gentleman's throat in his sleep… Monsieur Berlat, a friend of my husband's.'

'But where is Arsène Lupin?'

'He jumped out of the train in the tunnel, after we had crossed the Seine.'

'Are you sure it was he?'

'Certain. I recognised him at once. Besides, he was seen at the Gare Saint-Lazare. He was wearing a soft hat… '

'No; a hard felt hat, like this,' said the commissary, pointing to my hat.

'A soft hat, I assure you,' repeated Madame Renaud, 'and a grey frock-overcoat.'

'Yes,' muttered the commissary; 'the telegram mentions a grey frock-overcoat with a black velvet collar.'

'A black velvet collar, that's it!' exclaimed Madame Renaud, triumphantly.

I breathed again. What a good, excellent friend I had found in her!

Meanwhile the policemen had released me from my bonds. I bit my lips violently till the blood flowed. Bent in two, with my handkerchief to my mouth, as seems proper to a man who has long been sitting in a constrained position, and who bears on his face the bloodstained marks of the gag, I said to the commissary, in a feeble voice:

'Sir, it was Arsène Lupin, there is no doubt of it... You can catch him if you hurry... I think I may be of some use to you...'

The coach, which was needed for the inspection by the police, was slipped. The remainder of the train went on towards Le Havre. We were taken to the stationmaster's office through a crowd of onlookers who filled the platform.

Just then I felt a hesitation. I must make some excuse to absent myself, find my motorcar, and be off. It was dangerous to wait. If anything happened, if a telegram came from Paris, I was lost.

Yes; but what about my robber? Left to my own resources, in a district with which I was not very well acquainted, I could never hope to come up with him.

'Bah!' I said to myself. 'Let us risk it, and stay. It's a difficult hand to win, but a very amusing one to play, and the stakes are worth the trouble.'

And as we were being asked provisionally to repeat our depositions, I exclaimed: 'Mr Commissary, Arsène Lupin is getting a start of us. My motor is waiting for me in the yard. If you will do me the pleasure to accept a seat in it, we will try...'

The commissary gave a knowing smile.

'It's not a bad idea... such a good idea, in fact, that it's already being carried out.'

'Oh!'

'Yes; two of my officers started on bicycles... some time ago.'

'But where to?'

'To the entrance to the tunnel. There they will pick up the clews and the evidence, and follow the track of Arsène Lupin.'

I could not help shrugging my shoulders.

'Your two officers will pick up no clews and no evidence.'

'Really!'

'Arsène Lupin will have arranged that no one should see him leave the tunnel. He will have taken the nearest road, and from there...'

'From there made for Rouen, where we shall catch him.'

'He will not go to Rouen.'

'In that case, he will remain in the neighbourhood, where we shall be even more certain...'

'He will not remain in the neighbourhood.'

'Oh! Then where will he hide himself?'

I took out my watch.

'At this moment Arsène Lupin is hanging about the station at Darnetal. At ten-fifty – that is to say, in twenty-two minutes from now – he will take the train which leaves Rouen from the Gare du Nord for Amiens.'

'Do you think so? And how do you know?'

'Oh, it's very simple. In the carriage Arsène Lupin consulted my railway guide. What for? To see if there was another line near the place where he disappeared, a station on that line, and a train which stopped at that station. I have just looked at the guide myself, and learned what I wanted to know.'

'Upon my word, sir,' said the commissary, 'you possess marvellous powers of deduction. What an expert you must be!'

Dragged on by my certainty, I had blundered by displaying too much cleverness. He looked at me in astonishment, and I saw that a suspicion flickered through his mind. Only just, it is true; for the photographs despatched in every direction were so unlike, represented an Arsène Lupin so different from the one that stood before him, that he could not possibly recognise the original in me. Nevertheless, he was troubled, restless, perplexed.

There was a brief silence. A certain ambiguity and doubt seemed to interrupt our words. A shudder of anxiety passed through me.

Was luck about to turn against me? Mastering myself, I began to laugh.

'Ah well, there's nothing to sharpen one's wits like the loss of a pocket-book and the desire to find it again. And it seems to me that, if you will give me two of your men, the three of us might, perhaps... '

'Oh, please, Mr Commissary,' exclaimed Madame Renaud, 'do what Monsieur Berlat suggests.'

My kind friend's intervention turned the scale. Uttered by her, the wife of an influential person, the name of Berlat became mine in reality, and conferred upon me an identity which no suspicion could touch. The commissary rose.

'Believe me, Monsieur Berlat, I shall be only too pleased to see you succeed. I am as anxious as yourself to have Arsène Lupin arrested.'

He accompanied me to my car. He introduced two of his men to me: Honore Massol and Gaston Delivet. They took their seats. I placed myself at the wheel. My chauffeur started the engine. A few seconds later we had left the station. I was saved.

I confess that as we dashed in my powerful 35hp Moreau-Lepton along the boulevards that skirt the old Norman city I was not without a certain sense of pride. The engine hummed harmoniously. The trees sped behind us to right and left. And now, free and out of danger, I had nothing to do but to settle my own little private affairs with the co-operation of two worthy representatives of the law. Arsène Lupin was going in search of Arsène Lupin!

Ye humble mainstays of the social order of things, Gaston Delivet and Honore Massol, how precious was your assistance to me! Where should I have been without you? But for you, at how many cross-roads should I have taken the wrong turning! But for you, Arsène Lupin would have gone astray and the other escaped!

But all was not over yet. Far from it. I had first to capture the fellow and next to take possession, myself, of the papers of which he had robbed me. At no cost must my two satellites be allowed to catch a sight of those documents, much less lay hands upon them. To make us of them and yet act independently of them was what I wanted to do; and it was no easy matter.

We reached Darnetal three minutes after the train had left. I had the consolation of learning that a man in a grey frock-overcoat with a black velvet collar had got into a second-class carriage with a ticket for Amiens. There was no doubt about it: my first appearance as a detective was a promising one.

Delivet said:

'The train is an express, and does not stop before Monterolier-Buchy, in nineteen minutes from now. If we are not there before Arsène Lupin he can go on towards Amiens, branch off to Cleres, and, from there, make for Dieppe or Paris.'

'How far is Monterolier?'

'Fourteen miles and a half.'

'Fourteen miles and a half in nineteen minutes... We shall be there before he is.'

It was a stirring race. Never had my trusty Moreau-Lepton responded to my impatience with greater ardour and regularity. It seemed to me as though I communicated my wishes to her directly, without the intermediary of levers or handles. She shared my desires. She approved of my determination. She understood my animosity against that blackguard Arsène Lupin. The scoundrel! The sneak! Should I get the best of him? Or would he once more baffle authority, that authority of which I was the incarnation?

'Right!' cried Delivet... 'Left! ... Straight ahead!... '

We skimmed the ground. The milestones looked like little timid animals that fled at our approach.

And suddenly at the turn of a road a cloud of smoke – the north express!

For half a mile it was a struggle side by side – an unequal struggle, of which the issue was certain – we beat the train by twenty lengths.

In three seconds we were on the platform in front of the second class. The doors were flung open. A few people stepped out. My thief was not among them. We examined the carriages. No Arsène Lupin.

'By Jove!' I exclaimed, 'he must have recognised me in the motor while we were going alongside of him, and jumped!'

The guard of the train confirmed my supposition. He had seen a man scrambling down the embankment at two hundred yards from the station.

'There he is!... Look!... At the level crossing!'

I darted in pursuit, followed by my two satellites, or, rather, by one of them; for the other, Massol, turned out to be an uncommonly fast sprinter, gifted with both speed and staying power. In a few seconds the distance between him and the fugitive was greatly diminished. The man saw him, jumped a hedge, and scampered off towards a slope, which he climbed. We saw him, farther still, entering a little wood.

When we reached the wood we found Massol waiting for us. He had thought it no use to go on, lest he should lose us.

'You were quite right, my dear fellow,' I said. 'After a run like this our friend must be exhausted. We've got him.'

I examined the skirts of the wood while thinking how I could best proceed alone to arrest the fugitive, in order myself to effect certain recoveries which the law, no doubt, would only have allowed after a number of disagreeable inquiries. Then I returned to my companions.

'Look here, it's very easy. You, Massol, take up your position on the left. You, Delivet, on the right. From there you can watch the whole rear of the wood, and he can't leave it unseen by you except by this hollow, where I shall stand. If he does not come out, I'll go in and force him back towards one or the other of you. You have nothing to do, therefore, but wait. Oh, I was forgetting: in case of alarm, I'll fire a shot.'

Massol and Delivet moved off, each to his own side. As soon as they were out of sight I made my way into the wood with infinite precautions, so as to be neither seen nor heard. It consisted of close thickets, contrived for the shooting, and intersected by very narrow paths, in which it was only possible to walk by stooping, as though in a leafy tunnel.

One of these ended in a glade, where the damp grass showed the marks of footsteps. I followed them, taking care to steal through the underwood. They led me to the bottom of a little mound, crowned by a tumble-down lath-and-plaster hovel.

'He must be there,' I thought. 'He has selected a good post of observation.'

I crawled close up to the building. A slight sound warned me of his presence, and, in fact, I caught sight of him through an opening; with his back turned towards me.

Two bounds brought me upon him. He tried to point the revolver which he held in his hand. I did not give him time, but pulled him to the ground in such a way that his two arms were twisted and caught under him, while I held him pinned down with my knee upon his chest.

'Listen to me, old chap,' I whispered in his ear. 'I am Arsène Lupin. You've got to give me back, this minute and without any fuss, my pocket-book and the lady's wrist-bag... in return for which I'll save you from the clutches of the police and enrol you among my friends. Which is it to be: yes or no?'

'Yes,' he muttered.

'That's right. Your plan of this morning was cleverly thought out. We shall be good friends.'

I got up. He fumbled in his pocket, fetched out a great knife, and tried to strike me with it.

'You ass!' I cried.

With one hand I parried the attack. With the other I caught him a violent blow on the carotid artery, the blow which is known as 'the carotid hook'. He fell back stunned.

In my pocket-book I found my papers and banknotes. I took his own out of curiosity. On an envelope addressed to him I read his name: Pierre Onfrey.

I gave a start. Pierre Onfrey, the perpetrator of the murder in the Rue Lafontaine at Auteuil! Pierre Onfrey, the man who had cut the throats of Madame Delbois and her two daughters. I bent over him. Yes, that was the face which, in the railway-carriage, had aroused in me the memory of features which I had seen before.

But time was passing. I placed two hundred-franc notes in an envelope, with a visiting-card bearing these words:

'Arsène Lupin to his worthy assistants, Honore Massol and

Gaston Delivet, with his best thanks.'

I laid this where it could be seen, in the middle of the room. Beside it I placed Madame Renaud's wrist-bag. Why should it not be restored to the kind friend who had rescued me? I confess, however, that I took from it everything that seemed in any way interesting, leaving only a tortoise-shell comb, a stick of lip-salve, and an empty purse. Business is business, when all is said and done! And, besides, her husband followed such a disreputable occupation!...

There remained the man. He was beginning to move. What was I to do? I was not qualified either to save or to condemn him.

I took away his weapons, and fired my revolver in the air.

'That will bring the two others,' I thought. 'He must find a way out of his own difficulties. Let fate take its course.'

And I went down the hollow road at a run.

Twenty minutes later a crossroad which I had noticed during our pursuit brought me back to my car.

At four o'clock I telegraphed to my friends from Rouen that an unexpected incident compelled me to put off my visit. Between ourselves, I greatly fear that, in view of what they must now have learned, I shall be obliged to postpone it indefinitely. It will be a cruel disappointment for them!

At six o'clock I returned to Paris by L'Isle-Adam, Enghien, and the Porte Bineau.

I gathered from the evening papers that the police had at last succeeded in capturing Pierre Onfrey.

The next morning – why should we despise the advantages of intelligent advertisement? – the *Echo de France* contained the following sensational paragraph:

'Yesterday, near Buchy, after a number of incidents, Arsène Lupin effected the arrest of Pierre Onfrey. The Auteuil murderer had robbed a lady of the name of Renaud, the wife of the deputy prison-governor, in the train between Paris and Le Havre. Arsène Lupin has restored to Madame Renaud the wrist-bag which contained her jewels, and has generously rewarded the two detectives who assisted him in the matter of this dramatic arrest.'

WILLIAM J LOCKE

A Christmas Mystery:
The Story of Three Wise Men

THREE MEN who had gained great fame and honour throughout the world met unexpectedly in front of the bookstall at Paddington Station. Like most of the great ones of the earth they were personally acquainted, and they exchanged surprised greetings.

Sir Angus McCurdie, the eminent physicist, scowled at the two others beneath his heavy black eyebrows.

'I'm going to a Godforsaken place in Cornwall called Trehenna,' said he.

'That's odd; so am I,' croaked Professor Biggleswade. He was a little, untidy man with round spectacles, a fringe of greyish beard and a weak, rasping voice, and he knew more of Assyriology than any man, living or dead. A flippant pupil once remarked that the Professor's face was furnished with a Babylonic cuneiform in lieu of features.

'People called Deverill, at Foullis Castle?' asked Sir Angus.

'Yes,' replied Professor Biggleswade.

'How curious! I am going to the Deverills, too,' said the third man.

This man was the Right Honourable Viscount Doyne, the renowned Empire Builder and Administrator, around whose solitary and remote life popular imagination had woven many legends. He looked at the world through tired grey eyes, and the heavy, drooping, blonde moustache seemed tired too, and had dragged down the tired face into deep furrows. He was smoking a long black cigar.

'I suppose we may as well travel down together,' said Sir Angus, not very cordially.

Lord Doyne said courteously: 'I have a reserved carriage. The railway company is always good enough to place one at my disposal. It would give me great pleasure if you would share it.'

The invitation was accepted, and the three men crossed the busy, crowded platform to take their seats in the great express train. A porter, laden with an incredible load of paraphernalia, trying to make his way through the press, happened to jostle Sir Angus McCurdie. He rubbed his shoulder fretfully.

'Why the whole land should be turned into a bear garden on account of this exploded superstition of Christmas is one of the anomalies of modern civilisation. Look at this insensate welter of fools travelling in wild herds to disgusting places merely because it's Christmas!'

'You seem to be travelling yourself, McCurdie,' said Lord Doyne.

'Yes – and why the devil I'm doing it, I've not the faintest notion,' replied Sir Angus. 'It's going to be a beast of a journey,' he remarked some moments later, as the train carried them slowly out of the station. 'The whole country is under snow – and as far as I can understand we have to change twice and wind up with a twenty-mile motor drive.'

He was an iron-faced, beetle-browed, stern man; and this morning he did not seem to be in the best of tempers. Finding his companions inclined to be sympathetic, he continued his lamentation.

'And merely because it's Christmas I've had to shut up my laboratory and give my young fools a holiday – just when I was in the midst of a most important series of experiments.'

Professor Biggleswade, who had heard vaguely of and rather looked down upon such new-fangled toys as radium and thorium and helium and argon – for the latest astonishing developments in the theory of radioactivity had brought Sir Angus McCurdie his world-wide fame – said somewhat ironically: 'If the experiments were so important, why didn't you lock yourself up with your test-tubes and electric batteries and finish them alone?'

'Man!' said McCurdie, bending across the carriage, and speaking with a curious intensity of voice, 'd'ye know I'd give a hundred pounds to be able to answer that question?'

'What do you mean?' asked the Professor, startled.

'I should like to know why I'm sitting in this damned train and going to visit a couple of addle-headed society people whom I'm scarcely acquainted with, when I might be at home in my own good company furthering the progress of science.'

'I myself,' said the Professor, 'am not acquainted with them at all.'

It was Sir Angus McCurdie's turn to look surprised.

'Then why are you spending Christmas with them?'

'I reviewed a ridiculous blank-verse tragedy written by Deverill on the Death of Sennacherib. Historically it was puerile. I said so in no measured terms. He wrote a letter claiming to be a poet and not an archaeologist I replied that the day had passed when poets could with impunity commit the abominable crime of distorting history. He retorted with some futile argument, and we went on exchanging letters, until his invitation and my acceptance concluded the correspondence.'

McCurdie, still bending his black brows on him, asked him why he had not declined. The Professor screwed up his face till it looked more like a cuneiform than ever. He, too, found the question difficult to answer, but he showed a bold front.

'I felt it my duty,' said he, 'to teach that preposterous ignoramus something worth knowing about Sennacherib. Besides, I am a bachelor and would sooner spend Christmas, as to whose irritating and meaningless annoyance I cordially agree with you, among strangers than with my married sisters' numerous and nerve-racking families.'

Sir Angus McCurdie, the hard, metallic apostle of radioactivity, glanced for a moment out of the window at the grey, frost-bitten fields. Then he said:

'I'm a widower. My wife died many years ago and, thank God, we had no children. I generally spend Christmas alone.'

He looked out of the window again. Professor Biggleswade suddenly remembered the popular story of the great scientist's antecedents, and reflected that as McCurdie had once run, a barefoot urchin, through the Glasgow mud, he was likely to have little kith or kin. He himself envied McCurdie. He was always praying to be delivered from his sisters and nephews and nieces, whose embarrassing demands no calculated coldness could repress.

'Children are the root of all evil,' said he. 'Happy the man who has his quiver empty.'

Sir Angus McCurdie did not reply at once; when he spoke again it was with reference to their prospective host.

'I met Deverill,' said he, 'at the Royal Society's Soirée this year. One of my assistants was demonstrating a peculiar property of thorium and Deverill seemed interested. I asked him to come to my laboratory the next day, and found he didn't know a damned thing about anything. That's all the acquaintance I have with him.'

Lord Doyne, the great administrator, who had been wearily turning over the pages of an illustrated weekly chiefly filled with flamboyant photographs of obscure actresses, took his gold glasses from his nose and the black cigar from his lips, and addressed his companions.

'I've been considerably interested in your conversation,' said he, 'and as you've been frank, I'll be frank too. I knew Mrs Deverill's mother, Lady Carstairs, very well years ago, and of course Mrs Deverill when she was a child. Deverill I came across once in Persia – he had been sent on a diplomatic mission to Teheran. As for our being invited on such slight acquaintance, little Mrs Deverill has the reputation of being the only really successful celebrity hunter in England. She inherited the faculty from her mother, who entertained the whole world. We're sure to find archbishops, and eminent actors, and illustrious divorcées asked to meet us. That's one thing. But why I, who loathe country-house parties and children and Christmas as much as Biggleswade, am going down there today, I can no more explain than you can. It's a devilish odd coincidence.'

The three men looked at one another. Suddenly McCurdie shivered and drew his fur coat around him. 'I'll thank you,' said he, 'to shut that window.'

'It is shut,' said Doyne.

'It's just uncanny,' said McCurdie, looking from one to the other.

'What?' asked Doyne.

'Nothing, if you didn't feel it.'

'There did seem to be a sudden draught,' said Professor Biggleswade. 'But as both window and door are shut, it could only be imaginary.'

'It wasn't imaginary,' muttered McCurdie.

Then he laughed harshly. 'My father and mother came from Cromarty,' he said with apparent irrelevance.

'That's the Highlands,' said the Professor.

'Ay,' said McCurdie.

Lord Doyne said nothing, but tugged at his moustache and looked out of the window as the frozen meadows and bits of river and willows raced past. A dead silence fell on them. McCurdie broke it with another laugh and took a whisky-flask from his handbag.

'Have a nip?'

'Thanks, no,' said the Professor. 'I have to keep to a strict dietary, and I only drink hot milk and water – and of that sparingly. I have some in a thermos bottle.'

Lord Doyne also declining the whisky, McCurdie swallowed a dram and declared himself to be better. The Professor took from his bag a foreign review in which a German sciolist had dared to question his interpretation of a Hittite inscription. Over the man's ineptitude he fell asleep and snored loudly.

To escape from his immediate neighbourhood McCurdie went to the other end of the seat and faced Lord Doyne, who had resumed his gold glasses and his listless contemplation of obscure actresses. McCurdie lit a pipe, Doyne another black cigar. The train thundered on.

Presently they all lunched together in the restaurant car. The windows steamed, but here and there through a wiped patch of pane a white world was revealed. The snow was falling. As they passed through Westbury, McCurdie looked mechanically for the famous white horse carved into the chalk of the down; but it was not visible beneath the thick covering of snow.

'It'll be just like this all the way to Gehenna – Trehenna, I mean,' said McCurdie.

Doyne nodded. He had done his life's work amid all extreme fiercenesses of heat and cold, in burning droughts, in simooms and in icy wildernesses, and a ray or two more of the pale sun or a flake or two more of the gentle snow of England mattered to him but little. But Biggleswade rubbed the pane with his table-napkin and gazed apprehensively at the prospect.

'If only this wretched train would stop,' said he, 'I would go back again.'

And he thought how comfortable it would be to sneak home again to his books and thus elude not only the Deverills, but the Christmas jollities of his sisters' families, who would think him miles away. But the train was timed not to stop till Plymouth, two hundred and thirty-five miles from London, and thither was he being relentlessly carried. Then he quarrelled with his food, which brought a certain consolation.

The train did stop, however, before Plymouth – indeed, before Exeter. An accident on the line had dislocated the traffic. The express was held up for an hour, and when it was permitted to proceed, instead of thundering on, it went cautiously, subject to continual stoppings. It arrived at Plymouth two hours late. The travellers learned that they had missed the connection on which they had counted and that they could not reach Trehenna till nearly ten o'clock. After weary waiting at Plymouth they took their seats in the little, cold local train that was to carry them another stage on their journey. Hot-water cans put in at Plymouth mitigated to some extent the iciness of the compartment. But that only lasted a comparatively short time, for soon they were set down at a desolate, shelterless wayside junction, dumped in the midst of a hilly snow-covered waste, where they went through another weary wait for another dismal local train that was to carry them to Trehenna. And in this train there were no hot-water cans, so that the compartment was as cold as death. McCurdie fretted and shook his fist in the direction of Trehenna.

'And when we get there we have still a twenty miles' motor drive to Foullis Castle. It's a fool name and we're fools to be going there.'

'I shall die of bronchitis,' wailed Professor Biggleswade.

'A man dies when it is appointed for him to die,' said Lord Doyne, in his tired way; and he went on smoking long black cigars.

'It's not the dying that worries me,' said McCurdie. 'That's a mere mechanical process which every organic being from a king to a cauliflower has to pass through. It's the being forced against my will and my reason to come on this accursed journey, which something tells me will become more and more accursed as we go on, that is driving me to distraction.'

'What will be, will be,' said Doyne.

'I can't see where the comfort of that reflection comes in,' said Biggleswade.

'And yet you've travelled in the East,' said Doyne. 'I suppose you know the Valley of the Tigris as well as any man living.'

'Yes,' said the Professor. 'I can say I dug my way from Tekrit to Baghdad and left not a stone unexamined.'

'Perhaps, after all,' Doyne remarked, 'that's not quite the way to know the East.'

'I never wanted to know the modern East,' returned the Professor. 'What is there in it of interest compared with the mighty civilisations that have gone before?'

McCurdie took a pull from his flask.

'I'm glad I thought of having a refill at Plymouth,' said he.

At last, after many stops at little lonely stations, they arrived at Trehenna. The guard opened the door and they stepped out on to the snow-covered platform. An oil-lamp hung from the tiny penthouse roof that, structurally, was Trehenna Station. They looked around at the silent gloom of white undulating moorland, and it seemed a place where no man lived and only ghosts could have a bleak and unsheltered being. A porter came up and helped the guard with the luggage. Then they realised that the station was built on a small embankment, for, looking over the railing, they saw below the two great lamps of a motorcar. A fur-clad chauffeur met them at the bottom of the stairs. He clapped his hands together and informed them cheerily that he had been waiting for four hours. It was the bitterest winter in these parts within the memory of man, said he, and he himself had not seen snow there for five years. Then he settled the three travellers in the great roomy touring-car covered with a Cape-cart hood, wrapped them up in many rugs and started.

After a few moments, the huddling together of their bodies – for, the Professor being a spare man, there was room for them all on the back seat – the pile of rugs, the serviceable and all but air-tight hood, induced a pleasant warmth and a pleasant drowsiness. Where they were being driven they knew not. The perfectly upholstered seat eased their limbs, the easy swinging motion of the car soothed their spirits. They felt that already they had reached the luxuriously appointed home which, after all, they knew awaited them. McCurdie no longer railed, Professor Biggleswade forgot the dangers of bronchitis, and Lord Doyne twisted the stump of a black cigar between his lips without any desire to relight it. A tiny electric lamp inside the hood made the darkness of the world to right and left and in front of the talc windows still darker. McCurdie and Biggleswade fell into a doze. Lord Doyne chewed the end of his cigar. The car sped on through an unseen wilderness.

Suddenly there was a horrid jolt and a lurch and a leap and a rebound, and then the car stood still, quivering like a ship that has been struck by a heavy sea. The three men were pitched and tossed and thrown sprawling over one another on to the bottom of the car. Biggleswade screamed. McCurdie cursed. Doyne scrambled from the confusion of rugs and limbs and, tearing open the side of the Cape-cart hood, jumped out. The chauffeur had also just leaped from his seat. It was pitch dark save for the great shaft of light down the snowy road cast by the headlamps. The snow had ceased falling.

'What's gone wrong?'

'It sounds like the axle,' said the chauffeur ruefully.

He unshipped a lamp and examined the car, which had wedged itself against a great drift of snow on the off side. Meanwhile McCurdie and Biggleswade had alighted.

'Yes, it's the axle,' said the chauffeur.

'Then we're done,' remarked Doyne.

'I'm afraid so, my lord.'

'What's the matter? Can't we get on?' asked Biggleswade in his querulous voice.

McCurdie laughed. 'How can we get on with a broken axle? The thing's as useless as a man with a broken back. Gad, I was right. I said it was going to be an infernal journey.'

The little Professor wrung his hands. 'But what's to be done?' he cried.

'Tramp it,' said Lord Doyne, lighting a fresh cigar.

'It's ten miles,' said the chauffeur.

'It would be the death of me,' the Professor wailed.

'I utterly refuse to walk ten miles through a Polar waste with a gouty foot,' McCurdie declared wrathfully.

The chauffeur offered a solution of the difficulty. He would set out alone for Foullis Castle – five miles farther on was an inn where he could obtain a horse and trap – and would return for the three gentlemen with another car. In the meanwhile they could take shelter in a little house which they had just passed, some half-mile up the road. This was agreed to. The chauffeur went on cheerily enough with a lamp, and the three travellers with another lamp started off in the opposite direction. As far as they could see they were in a long, desolate valley, a sort of No Man's Land, deathly silent. The eastern sky had cleared somewhat, and they faced a loose rack through which one pale star was dimly visible.

'I'm a man of science,' said McCurdie as they trudged through the snow, 'and I dismiss the supernatural as contrary to reason; but I have Highland blood in my veins that plays me exasperating tricks. My reason tells me that this place is only a commonplace moor, yet it seems like a Valley of Bones haunted by malignant spirits who have lured us here to our destruction. There's something guiding us now. It's just uncanny.'

'Why on earth did we ever come?' croaked Biggleswade.

Lord Doyne answered: 'The Koran says, "Nothing can befall us but what God hath destined for us". So why worry?'

'Because I'm not a Mohammedan,' retorted Biggleswade.

'You might be worse,' said Doyne.

Presently the dim outline of the little house grew perceptible. A faint light shone from the window. It stood unfenced by any kind of hedge or railing a few feet away from the road in a little hollow beneath some rising ground. As far as they could discern in the darkness when they drew near, the house was a mean, dilapidated hovel. A guttering candle stood on the inner sill of the small window and afforded a vague view into a mean interior. Doyne help up the lamp so that its rays fell full on the door. As he did so, an exclamation broke from his lips and he hurried forward, followed by the others. A man's body lay huddled together on the snow by the threshold. He was dressed like a peasant, in old corduroy trousers and rough coat, and a handkerchief was knotted round his neck. In his hand he grasped the neck of a broken bottle. Doyne set the lamp on the ground and the three bent down together over the man. Close by the neck lay the rest of the broken bottle, whose contents had evidently run out into the snow.

'Drunk?' asked Biggleswade.

Doyne felt the man and laid his hand on his heart.

'No,' said he, 'dead.'

McCurdie leaped to his full height. 'I told you the place was uncanny!' he cried. 'It's fey.' Then he hammered wildly at the door.

There was no response. He hammered again till it rattled. This time a faint prolonged sound like the wailing of a sea-creature was heard from within the house. McCurdie turned round, his teeth chattering.

'Did ye hear that, Doyne?'

'Perhaps it's a dog,' said the Professor.

Lord Doyne, the man of action, pushed them aside and tried the door-handle. It yielded, the door stood open, and the gust of cold wind entering the house extinguished the candle within. They entered and found themselves in a miserable stone-paved kitchen, furnished with poverty-stricken meagreness – a wooden chair or two, a dirty table, some broken crockery, old cooking utensils, a fly-blown missionary society almanac, and a fireless grate. Doyne set the lamp on the table.

'We must bring him in,' said he.

They returned to the threshold, and as they were bending over to grip the dead man the same sound filled the air, but this time louder, more intense, a cry of great agony. The sweat dripped from McCurdie's forehead. They lifted the dead man and brought him into the room, and after laying him on a dirty strip of carpet they did their best to straighten the stiff limbs. Biggleswade put on the table a bundle which he had picked up outside. It contained some poor provisions – a loaf, a piece of fat bacon, and a paper of tea. As far as they could guess (and, as they learned later, they guessed rightly), the man was the master of the house, who, coming home blind drunk from some distant inn, had fallen at his own threshold and got frozen to death. As they could not unclasp his fingers from the broken bottle-necks they had to let him clutch it as a dead warrior clutches the hilt of his broken sword.

Then suddenly the whole place was rent with another and yet another long, soul-piercing moan of anguish.

'There's a second room,' said Doyne, pointing to a door. 'The sound comes from there.'

He opened the door, peeped in, and then, returning for the lamp, disappeared, leaving McCurdie and Biggleswade in the pitch darkness, with the dead man on the floor.

'For Heaven's sake, give me a drop of whisky,' aid the Professor, 'or I shall faint.'

Presently the door opened and Lord Doyne appeared in the shaft of light. He beckoned to his companions.

'It is a woman in childbirth,' he said in his even, tired voice. 'We must aid her. She appears unconscious. Does either of you know anything about such things?'

They shook their heads, and the three looked at each other in dismay. Masters of knowledge that had won them world-fame and honour, they stood helpless, abashed before this, the commonest phenomenon of nature.

'My wife had no child,' said McCurdie.

'I've avoided women all my life,' said Biggleswade.

'And I've been too busy to think of them. God forgive me,' said Doyne.

The history of the next two hours was one that none of the three men ever cared to touch upon. They did things blindly, instinctively, as men do when they come face to face with the elemental. A fire was made, they knew not how, water drawn they knew not whence, and a kettle boiled. Doyne, accustomed to command, directed. The others obeyed. At his suggestion they hastened to the wreck of the car and came staggering back beneath rugs and travelling bags which could supply clean linen and needful things, for amid the poverty of the house they could find nothing fit for human touch or use. Early they saw that the woman's strength was failing, and that she could not live. And there, in that nameless hovel, with death on the hearthstone and death and life hovering over the pitiful bed, the three great men went through the pain and the horror and squalor of birth, and they knew that they had never yet stood before so great a mystery.

With the first wail of the newly born infant a last convulsive shudder passed through the frame of the unconscious mother. Then three or four short gasps for breath, and the spirit passed away. She was dead. Professor Biggleswade threw a corner of the sheet over her face, for he could not bear to see it.

They washed and dried the child as any crone of a midwife would have done, and dipped a small sponge which had always remained unused in a cut-glass bottle in Doyne's dressing-bag in the hot milk and water of Biggleswade's thermos bottle and put it to his lips; and then they wrapped him up warm in some of their own woollen under-garments, and took him into the kitchen and placed him on a bed made of their fur coats in front of the fire. As the last piece of fuel was exhausted they took one of the wooden chairs and broke it up and cast it into the blaze. And then they raised the dead man from the strip of carpet and carried him into the bedroom and laid him rever-ently by side of his dead wife, after which they left the dead in the darkness and returned to the living. And the three grave men stood over the wisp of flesh that had been born a male into the world. Then, their task being accomplished, reaction came, and even Doyne, who had seen death in many lands, turned faint. But the others, losing control of their nerves, shook like men stricken with palsy.

Suddenly McCurdie cried in a high-pitched voice: 'My God! Don't you feel it?' and clutched Doyne by the arm. An expression of terror appeared on his iron features. 'There! It's here with us.'

Little Professor Biggleswade sat on a corner of the table and wiped his forehead.

'I heard it. I felt it. It was like the beating of wings.'

'It's the fourth time,' said McCurdie. 'The first time was just before I accepted the Deverills' invitation. The second in the railway carriage this afternoon. The third on the way here. This is the fourth.'

Biggleswade plucked nervously at the fringe of whisker under his jaws and said faintly, 'It's the fourth time up to now. I thought it was fancy.'

'I have felt it too,' said Doyne. 'It is the Angel of Death.' And he pointed to the room where the dead man and woman lay.

'For God's sake let us get away from this,' cried Biggleswade.

'And leave the child to die, like the others?' said Doyne.

'We must see it through,' said McCurdie.

A silence fell upon them as they sat round in the blaze with the new-born babe wrapped in its odd swaddling clothes asleep on the pile of fur coats, and it lasted until Sir Angus McCurdie looked at his watch.

'Good Lord,' said he, 'it's twelve o'clock.'

'Christmas morning,' said Biggleswade.

'A strange Christmas,' mused Doyne.

McCurdie put up his hand. 'There it is again! The beating of wings.' And they listened like men spellbound. McCurdie kept his hand uplifted, and gazed over their heads at the wall, and his gaze was that of a man in a trance, and he spoke:

'Unto us a child is born, unto us a son is given—'

Doyne sprang from his chair, which fell behind him with a crash.

'Man – what the devil are you saying?'

Then McCurdie rose and met Biggleswade's eyes staring at him through the great round spectacles, and Biggleswade turned and met the eyes of Doyne. A pulsation like the beating of wings stirred the air.

The three wise men shivered with a queer exaltation. Something strange, mystical, dynamic had happened. It was as if scales had fallen from their eyes and they saw with a new vision. They stood together humbly, divested of all their greatness, touching one another in the instinctive fashion of children, as if seeking mutual protection, and they looked, with one accord, irresistibly compelled, at the child.

At last McCurdie unbent his black brows and said hoarsely:

'It was not the Angel of Death, Doyne, but another Messenger that drew us here.'

The tiredness seemed to pass away from the great administrator's face, and he nodded his head with the calm of a man who has come to the quiet heart of a perplexing mystery.

'It's true,' he murmured. 'Unto us a child is born, unto us a son is given. Unto the three of us.'

Biggleswade took off his great round spectacles and wiped them.

'Gaspar, Melchior, Balthazar. But where are the gold, frankincense and myrrh?'

'In our hearts, man,' said McCurdie.

The babe cried and stretched its tiny limbs.

Instinctively they all knelt down together to, discover, if possible, and administer ignorantly to its wants. The scene had the appearance of an adoration.

Then these three wise, lonely, childless men who, in furtherance of their own greatness, had cut themselves adrift from the sweet and simple things of life and from the kindly ways of their brethren, and had grown old in unhappy and profitless wisdom, knew that an inscrutable Providence had led them, as it had led three Wise Men of old, on a Christmas morning long ago, to a nativity which should give them a new wisdom, a new link with humanity, a new spiritual outlook, a new hope.

And, when their watch was ended, they wrapped up the babe with precious care, and carried him with them, an inalienable joy and possession, into the great world.

GK CHESTERTON

The Wrong Shape

CERTAIN OF the great roads going north out of London continue far into the country, a sort of attenuated and interrupted spectre of a street, with great gaps in the building, but preserving the line.

Here will be a group of shops, followed by a fenced field or paddock, and then a famous public house, and then perhaps a market garden or a nursery garden, and then one large private house, and then another field and another inn, and so on. If anyone walks along one of these roads he will pass a house which will probably catch his eye, though he may not be able to explain its attraction.

It is a long, low house, running parallel with the road, painted mostly white and pale green, with a veranda and sun-blinds, and porches capped with those quaint sort of cupolas like wooden umbrellas that one sees in some old-fashioned houses. In fact, it is an old-fashioned house, very English and very suburban in the good old wealthy Clapham sense. And yet the house has a look of having been built chiefly for the hot weather. Looking at its white paint and sun-blinds one thinks vaguely of pugarees and even of palm trees. I cannot trace the feeling to its root; perhaps the place was built by an Anglo-Indian.

Anyone passing this house, I say, would be namelessly fascinated by it; would feel that it was a place about which some story was to be told. And he would have been right, as you shall shortly hear. For this is the story – the story of the strange things that did really happen in it in the Whitsuntide of the year 18—:

Anyone passing the house on the Thursday before Whit Sunday at about 4.30pm would have seen the front door open, and Father Brown, of the small church of St Mungo, come out smoking a large pipe in company with a very tall French friend of his called Flambeau, who was smoking a very small cigarette. These persons may or may not be of interest to the reader, but the truth is that they were not the only interesting things that were displayed when the front door of the white-and-green house was opened. There are further peculiarities about this house, which must be described to start with, not only that the reader may understand this tragic tale, but also that he may realise what it was that the opening of the door revealed.

The whole house was built upon the plan of a T, but a T with a very long cross piece and a very short tail piece. The long cross piece was the frontage that ran along in face of the street, with the front door in the middle; it was two stories high, and contained nearly all the important rooms. The short tail piece, which ran out at the back immediately opposite the front door, was one story high, and consisted only of two long rooms, the one leading into the other. The first of these two rooms was the study in which the celebrated Mr Quinton wrote his wild Oriental poems and romances. The farther room was a glass conservatory full of tropical blossoms of quite unique and almost monstrous beauty, and on such afternoons as these glowing with gorgeous sunlight. Thus when the hall door was open, many a passer-by literally stopped to stare and gasp; for he looked down a perspective of rich apartments to something really like a transformation scene in a fairy play: purple clouds and golden suns and crimson stars that were at once scorchingly vivid and yet transparent and far away.

Leonard Quinton, the poet, had himself most carefully arranged this effect; and it is doubtful whether he so perfectly expressed his personality in any of his poems. For he was a man who drank and bathed in colours, who indulged his lust for colour somewhat to the neglect of form – even of good form. This it was that had turned his genius so wholly to eastern art and imagery; to those bewildering carpets or blinding embroideries in which all the colours seem fallen into a fortunate chaos, having nothing to typify or to teach. He had attempted, not perhaps with complete artistic success, but with acknowledged imagination and invention, to compose epics and love stories reflecting the riot of violent and even cruel colour; tales of tropical heavens of burning gold or blood-red copper; of eastern heroes who rode with twelve-turbaned mitres upon elephants painted purple or peacock green; of gigantic jewels that a hundred negroes could not carry, but which burned with ancient and strange-hued fires.

In short (to put the matter from the more common point of view), he dealt much in eastern heavens, rather worse than most western hells; in eastern monarchs, whom we might possibly call maniacs; and in eastern jewels which a Bond Street jeweller (if the hundred staggering negroes brought them into his shop) might possibly not regard as genuine. Quinton was a genius, if a morbid one; and even his morbidity appeared more in his life than in his work. In temperament he was weak and waspish, and his health had suffered heavily from oriental experiments with opium. His wife – a handsome, hard-working, and, indeed, overworked woman objected to the opium, but objected much more to a live Indian hermit in white and yellow robes, whom her husband insisted on entertaining for months together, a Virgil to guide his spirit through the heavens and the hells of the east.

It was out of this artistic household that Father Brown and his friend stepped on to the doorstep; and to judge from their faces, they stepped out of it with much relief. Flambeau had known Quinton in wild student days in Paris, and they had renewed the acquaintance for a weekend; but apart from Flambeau's more responsible developments of late, he did not get on well with the poet now. Choking oneself with opium and writing little erotic verses on vellum was not his notion of how a gentleman should go to the devil. As the two paused on the doorstep, before taking a turn in the garden, the front garden gate was thrown open with violence, and a young man with a billycock hat on the back of his head tumbled up the steps in his eagerness. He was a dissipated-looking youth with a gorgeous red necktie all awry, as if he had slept in it, and he kept fidgeting and lashing about with one of those little jointed canes.

'I say,' he said breathlessly, 'I want to see old Quinton. I must see him. Has he gone?'

'Mr Quinton is in, I believe,' said Father Brown, cleaning his pipe, 'but I do not know if you can see him. The doctor is with him at present.'

The young man, who seemed not to be perfectly sober, stumbled into the hall; and at the same moment the doctor came out of Quinton's study, shutting the door and beginning to put on his gloves.

'See Mr Quinton?' said the doctor coolly. 'No, I'm afraid you can't. In fact, you mustn't on any account. Nobody must see him; I've just given him his sleeping draught.'

'No, but look here, old chap,' said the youth in the red tie, trying affectionately to capture the doctor by the lapels of his coat. 'Look here. I'm simply sewn up, I tell you. I—'

'It's no good, Mr Atkinson,' said the doctor, forcing him to fall back; 'when you can alter the effects of a drug I'll alter my decision,' and, settling on his hat, he stepped out into the sunlight with the other two. He was a bull-necked, good-tempered little man with a small moustache, inexpressibly ordinary, yet giving an impression of capacity.

The young man in the billycock, who did not seem to be gifted with any tact in dealing with people beyond the general idea of clutching hold of their coats, stood outside the door, as dazed as if he had been thrown out bodily, and silently watched the other three walk away together through the garden.

'That was a sound, spanking lie I told just now,' remarked the medical man, laughing. 'In point of fact, poor Quinton doesn't have his sleeping draught for nearly half an hour. But I'm not going to have him bothered with that little beast, who only wants to borrow money that he wouldn't pay back if he could. He's a dirty little scamp, though he is Mrs Quinton's brother, and she's as fine a woman as ever walked.'

'Yes,' said Father Brown. 'She's a good woman.'

'So I propose to hang about the garden till the creature has cleared off,' went on the doctor, 'and then I'll go in to Quinton with the medicine. Atkinson can't get in, because I locked the door.'

'In that case, Dr Harris,' said Flambeau, 'we might as well walk round at the back by the end of the conservatory. There's no entrance to it that way, but it's worth seeing, even from the outside.'

'Yes, and I might get a squint at my patient,' laughed the doctor, 'for he prefers to lie on an ottoman right at the end of the conservatory amid all those blood-red poinsettias; it would give me the creeps. But what are you doing?'

Father Brown had stopped for a moment, and picked up out of the long grass, where it had almost been wholly hidden, a queer, crooked Oriental knife, inlaid exquisitely in coloured stones and metals.

'What is this?' asked Father Brown, regarding it with some disfavour.

'Oh, Quinton's, I suppose,' said Dr Harris carelessly; 'he has all sorts of Chinese knickknacks about the place. Or perhaps it belongs to that mild Hindoo of his whom he keeps on a string.'

'What Hindoo?' asked Father Brown, still staring at the dagger in his hand.

'Oh, some Indian conjuror,' said the doctor lightly; 'a fraud, of course.'

'You don't believe in magic?' asked Father Brown, without looking up.

'Oh crikey, magic!' said the doctor.

'It's very beautiful,' said the priest in a low, dreaming voice; 'the colours are very beautiful. But it's the wrong shape.'

'What for?' asked Flambeau, staring.

'For anything. It's the wrong shape in the abstract. Don't you ever feel that about Eastern art? The colours are intoxicatingly lovely; but the shapes are mean and bad – deliberately mean and bad. I have seen wicked things in a Turkey carpet.'

'*Mon Dieu!*' cried Flambeau, laughing.

'They are letters and symbols in a language I don't know; but I know they stand for evil words,' went on the priest, his voice growing lower and lower. 'The lines go wrong on purpose – like serpents doubling to escape.'

'What the devil are you talking about?' said the doctor with a loud laugh.

Flambeau spoke quietly to him in answer. 'The Father sometimes gets this mystic's cloud on him,' he said; 'but I give you fair warning that I have never known him to have it except when there was some evil quite near.'

'Oh, rats!' said the scientist.

'Why, look at it,' cried Father Brown, holding out the crooked knife at arm's length, as if it were some glittering snake.

'Don't you see it is the wrong shape? Don't you see that it has no hearty and plain purpose? It does not point like a spear. It does not sweep like a scythe. It does not look like a weapon. It looks like an instrument of torture.'

'Well, as you don't seem to like it,' said the jolly Harris, 'it had better be taken back to its owner. Haven't we come to the end of this confounded conservatory yet? This house is the wrong shape, if you like.'

'You don't understand,' said Father Brown, shaking his head. 'The shape of this house is quaint – it is even laughable. But there is nothing wrong about it.'

As they spoke they came round the curve of glass that ended the conservatory, an uninterrupted curve, for there was neither door nor window by which to enter at that end. The glass, however, was clear, and the sun still bright, though beginning to set; and they could see not only the flamboyant blossoms inside, but the frail figure of the poet in a brown velvet coat lying languidly on the sofa, having, apparently, fallen half asleep over a book. He was a pale, slight man, with loose, chestnut hair and a fringe of beard that was the paradox of his face, for the beard made him look less manly. These traits were well known to all three of them; but even had it not been so, it may be doubted whether they would have looked at Quinton just then. Their eyes were riveted on another object.

Exactly in their path, immediately outside the round end of the glass building, was standing a tall man, whose drapery fell to his feet in faultless white, and whose bare, brown skull, face, and neck gleamed in the setting sun like splendid bronze. He was looking through the glass at the sleeper, more motionless than a mountain.

'Who is that?' cried Father Brown, stepping back with a hissing intake of his breath.

'Oh, it is only that Hindoo humbug,' growled Harris; 'but I don't know what the deuce he's doing here.'

'It looks like hypnotism,' said Flambeau, biting his black moustache.

'Why are you unmedical fellows always talking bosh about hypnotism?' cried the doctor. 'It looks a deal more like burglary.'

'Well, we will speak to it, at any rate,' said Flambeau, who was always for action. One long stride took him to the place where the Indian stood. Bowing from his great height, which overtopped even the Oriental's, he said with placid impudence:

'Good evening, sir. Do you want anything?'

Quite slowly, like a great ship turning into a harbour, the great yellow face turned, and looked at last over its white shoulder. They were startled to see that its yellow eyelids were quite sealed, as in sleep. 'Thank you,' said the face in excellent English. 'I want nothing.' Then, half opening the lids, so as to show a slit of opalescent eyeball, he repeated, 'I want nothing.' Then he opened his eyes wide with a startling stare, said, 'I want nothing,' and went rustling away into the rapidly darkening garden.

'The Christian is more modest,' muttered Father Brown; 'he wants something.'

'What on earth was he doing?' asked Flambeau, knitting his black brows and lowering his voice.

'I should like to talk to you later,' said Father Brown.

The sunlight was still a reality, but it was the red light of evening, and the bulk of the garden trees and bushes grew blacker and blacker against it. They turned round the end of the conservatory, and walked in silence down the other side to get round to the front door. As they went they seemed to wake something, as one startles a bird, in the deeper corner between the study and the main building; and again they saw the white-robed fakir slide out of the shadow, and slip round towards the front door. To their surprise, however, he had not been alone. They found themselves abruptly pulled up and forced to banish their bewilderment by the appearance of Mrs Quinton, with her heavy golden hair and square pale face, advancing on them out of the twilight. She looked a little stern, but was entirely courteous.

'Good evening, Dr Harris,' was all she said.

'Good evening, Mrs Quinton,' said the little doctor heartily. 'I am just going to give your husband his sleeping draught.'

'Yes,' she said in a clear voice. 'I think it is quite time.'

And she smiled at them, and went sweeping into the house.

'That woman's over-driven,' said Father Brown; 'that's the kind of woman that does her duty for twenty years, and then does something dreadful.'

The little doctor looked at him for the first time with an eye of interest. 'Did you ever study medicine?' he asked.

'You have to know something of the mind as well as the body,' answered the priest; 'we have to know something of the body as well as the mind.'

'Well,' said the doctor, 'I think I'll go and give Quinton his stuff.'

They had turned the corner of the front facade, and were approaching the front doorway. As they turned into it they saw the man in the white robe for the third time. He came so straight towards the front door that it seemed quite incredible that he had not just come out of the study opposite to it. Yet they knew that the study door was locked.

Father Brown and Flambeau, however, kept this weird contradiction to themselves, and Dr Harris was not a man to waste his thoughts on the impossible. He permitted the omnipresent Asiatic to make his exit, and then stepped briskly into the hall. There he found a figure which he had already forgotten. The inane Atkinson was still hanging about, humming and poking things with his knobby cane. The doctor's face had a spasm of disgust and decision, and he whispered rapidly to his companion: 'I must lock the door again, or this rat will get in. But I shall be out again in two minutes.'

He rapidly unlocked the door and locked it again behind him, just balking a blundering charge from the young man in the billycock. The young man threw himself impatiently on a hall chair. Flambeau looked at a Persian illumination on the wall; Father Brown, who seemed in a sort of daze, dully eyed the door.

In about four minutes the door was opened again. Atkinson was quicker this time. He sprang forward, held the door open for an instant, and called out: 'Oh, I say, Quinton, I want—'

From the other end of the study came the clear voice of Quinton, in something between a yawn and a yell of weary laughter.

'Oh, I know what you want. Take it, and leave me in peace. I'm writing a song about peacocks.'

Before the door closed half a sovereign came flying through the aperture; and Atkinson, stumbling forward, caught it with singular dexterity.

'So that's settled,' said the doctor, and, locking the door savagely, he led the way out into the garden.

'Poor Leonard can get a little peace now,' he added to Father Brown; 'he's locked in all by himself for an hour or two.'

'Yes,' answered the priest; 'and his voice sounded jolly enough when we left him.' Then he looked gravely round the garden, and saw the loose figure of Atkinson standing and jingling the half-sovereign in his pocket, and beyond, in the purple twilight, the figure of the Indian sitting bolt upright upon a bank of grass with his face turned towards the setting sun. Then he said abruptly: 'Where is Mrs Quinton!'

'She has gone up to her room,' said the doctor. 'That is her shadow on the blind.'

Father Brown looked up, and frowningly scrutinised a dark outline at the gas-lit window.

'Yes,' he said, 'that is her shadow,' and he walked a yard or two and threw himself upon a garden seat.

Flambeau sat down beside him; but the doctor was one of those energetic people who live naturally on their legs. He walked away, smoking, into the twilight, and the two friends were left together.

'My father,' said Flambeau in French, 'what is the matter with you?'

Father Brown was silent and motionless for half a minute, then he said: 'Superstition is irreligious, but there is something in the air of this place. I think it's that Indian – at least, partly.'

He sank into silence, and watched the distant outline of the Indian, who still sat rigid as if in prayer. At first sight he seemed motionless, but as Father Brown watched him he saw that the man swayed ever so slightly with a rhythmic movement, just as the dark treetops swayed ever so slightly in the wind that was creeping up the dim garden paths and shuffling the fallen leaves a little.

The landscape was growing rapidly dark, as if for a storm, but they could still see all the figures in their various places.

Atkinson was leaning against a tree with a listless face; Quinton's wife was still at her window; the doctor had gone strolling round the end of the conservatory; they could see his cigar like a will-o'-the-wisp; and the fakir still sat rigid and yet rocking, while the trees above him began to rock and almost to roar. Storm was certainly coming.

'When that Indian spoke to us,' went on Brown in a conversational undertone, 'I had a sort of vision, a vision of him and all his universe. Yet he only said the same thing three times. When first he said "I want nothing", it meant only that he was impenetrable, that Asia does not give itself away. Then he said again, "I want nothing", and I knew that he meant that he was sufficient to himself, like a cosmos, that he needed no God, neither admitted any sins. And when he said the third time, "I want nothing", he said it with blazing eyes. And I knew that he meant literally what he said; that nothing was his desire and his home; that he was weary for nothing as for wine; that annihilation, the mere destruction of everything or anything—'

Two drops of rain fell; and for some reason Flambeau started and looked up, as if they had stung him. And the same instant the doctor down by the end of the conservatory began running towards them, calling out something as he ran.

As he came among them like a bombshell, the restless Atkinson happened to be taking a turn nearer to the house front; and the doctor clutched him by the collar in a convulsive grip. 'Foul play!' he cried; 'what have you been doing to him, you dog?'

The priest had sprung erect, and had the voice of steel of a soldier in command.

'No fighting,' he cried coolly. 'We are enough to hold anyone we want to. What is the matter, doctor?'

'Things are not right with Quinton,' said the doctor, quite white. 'I could just see him through the glass, and I don't like the way he's lying. It's not as I left him, anyhow.'

'Let us go in to him,' said Father Brown shortly. 'You can leave Mr Atkinson alone. I have had him in sight since we heard Quinton's voice.'

'I will stop here and watch him,' said Flambeau hurriedly. 'You go in and see.'

The doctor and the priest flew to the study door, unlocked it, and fell into the room. In doing so they nearly fell over the large mahogany table in the centre at which the poet usually wrote; for the place was lit only by a small fire kept for the invalid. In the middle of this table lay a single sheet of paper, evidently left there on purpose. The doctor snatched it up, glanced at it, handed it to Father Brown, and crying, 'Good God, look at that!' plunged toward the glass room beyond, where the terrible tropic flowers still seemed to keep a crimson memory of the sunset.

Father Brown read the words three times before he put down the paper. The words were: 'I die by my own hand; yet I die murdered!'

They were in the quite inimitable, not to say illegible, handwriting of Leonard Quinton.

Then Father Brown, still keeping the paper in his hand, strode towards the conservatory, only to meet his medical friend coming back with a face of assurance and collapse.

'He's done it,' said Harris.

They went together through the gorgeous unnatural beauty of cactus and azalea and found Leonard Quinton, poet and romancer, with his head hanging downward off his ottoman and his red curls sweeping the ground. Into his left side was thrust the queer dagger that they had picked up in the garden, and his limp hand still rested on the hilt.

Outside the storm had come at one stride, like the night in Coleridge, and garden and glass roof were darkened with driving rain. Father Brown seemed to be studying the paper more than the corpse; he held it close to his eyes; and seemed trying to read it in the twilight. Then he held it up against the faint light, and, as he did so, lightning stared at them for an instant so white that the paper looked black against it.

Darkness full of thunder followed, and after the thunder Father Brown's voice said out of the dark: 'Doctor, this paper is the wrong shape.'

'What do you mean?' asked Doctor Harris, with a frowning stare.

'It isn't square,' answered Brown. 'It has a sort of edge snipped off at the corner. What does it mean?'

'How the deuce should I know?' growled the doctor. 'Shall we move this poor chap, do you think? He's quite dead.'

'No,' answered the priest; 'we must leave him as he lies and send for the police.' But he was still scrutinising the paper.

As they went back through the study he stopped by the table and picked up a small pair of nail scissors. 'Ah,' he said, with a sort of relief, 'this is what he did it with. But yet—' And he knitted his brows.

'Oh, stop fooling with that scrap of paper,' said the doctor emphatically. 'It was a fad of his. He had hundreds of them. He cut all his paper like that,' as he pointed to a stack of sermon paper still unused on another and smaller table. Father Brown went up to it and held up a sheet. It was the same irregular shape.

'Quite so,' he said. 'And here I see the corners that were snipped off.' And to the indignation of his colleague he began to count them.

'That's all right,' he said, with an apologetic smile.

'Twenty-three sheets cut and twenty-two corners cut off them. And as I see you are impatient we will rejoin the others.'

'Who is to tell his wife?' asked Dr Harris. 'Will you go and tell her now, while I send a servant for the police?'

'As you will,' said Father Brown indifferently. And he went out to the hall door.

Here also he found a drama, though of a more grotesque sort.

It showed nothing less than his big friend Flambeau in an attitude to which he had long been unaccustomed, while upon the pathway at the bottom of the steps was sprawling with his boots in the air the amiable Atkinson, his billycock hat and walking cane sent flying in opposite directions along the path. Atkinson had at length wearied of Flambeau's almost paternal custody, and had endeavoured to knock him down, which was by no means a smooth game to play with the *Roi des Apaches*, even after that monarch's abdication.

Flambeau was about to leap upon his enemy and secure him once more, when the priest patted him easily on the shoulder.

'Make it up with Mr Atkinson, my friend,' he said. 'Beg a mutual pardon and say "Good night". We need not detain him any longer.' Then, as Atkinson rose somewhat doubtfully and gathered his hat and stick and went towards the garden gate, Father Brown said in a more serious voice: 'Where is that Indian?'

They all three (for the doctor had joined them) turned involuntarily towards the dim grassy bank amid the tossing trees purple with twilight, where they had last seen the brown man swaying in his strange prayers. The Indian was gone.

'Confound him,' cried the doctor, stamping furiously. 'Now I know that it was that fakir that did it.'

'I thought you didn't believe in magic,' said Father Brown quietly.

'No more I did,' said the doctor, rolling his eyes. 'I only know that I loathed that yellow devil when I thought he was a sham wizard. And I shall loathe him more if I come to think he was a real one.'

'Well, his having escaped is nothing,' said Flambeau. 'For we could have proved nothing and done nothing against him. One hardly goes to the parish constable with a story of suicide imposed by witchcraft or auto-suggestion.'

Meanwhile Father Brown had made his way into the house, and now went to break the news to the wife of the dead man.

When he came out again he looked a little pale and tragic, but what passed between them in that interview was never known, even when all was known.

Flambeau, who was talking quietly with the doctor, was surprised to see his friend reappear so soon at his elbow; but Brown took no notice, and merely drew the doctor apart. 'You have sent for the police, haven't you?' he asked.

'Yes,' answered Harris. 'They ought to be here in ten minutes.'

'Will you do me a favour?' said the priest quietly. 'The truth is, I make a collection of these curious stories, which often contain, as in the case of our Hindoo friend, elements which can hardly be put into a police report. Now, I want you to write out a report of this case for my private use. Yours is a clever trade,' he said, looking the doctor gravely and steadily in the face. 'I sometimes think that you know some details of this matter which you have not thought fit to mention. Mine is a confidential trade like yours, and I will treat anything you write for me in strict confidence. But write the whole.'

The doctor, who had been listening thoughtfully with his head a little on one side, looked the priest in the face for an instant, and said: 'All right,' and went into the study, closing the door behind him.

'Flambeau,' said Father Brown, 'there is a long seat there under the veranda, where we can smoke out of the rain. You are my only friend in the world, and I want to talk to you. Or, perhaps, be silent with you.'

They established themselves comfortably in the veranda seat; Father Brown, against his common habit, accepted a good cigar and smoked it steadily in silence, while the rain shrieked and rattled on the roof of the veranda.

'My friend,' he said at length, 'this is a very queer case, a very queer case.'

'I should think it was,' said Flambeau, with something like a shudder.

'You call it queer, and I call it queer,' said the other, 'and yet we mean quite opposite things. The modern mind always mixes up two different ideas: mystery in the sense of what is marvellous, and mystery in the sense of what is complicated. That is half its difficulty about miracles. A miracle is startling; but it is simple. It is simple because it is a miracle. It is power coming directly from God (or the devil) instead of indirectly through nature or human wills. Now, you mean that this business is marvellous because it is miraculous, because it is witchcraft worked by a wicked Indian. Understand, I do not say that it was not spiritual or diabolic. Heaven and hell only know by what surrounding influences strange sins come into the lives of men.

But for the present my point is this: If it was pure magic, as you think, then it is marvellous; but it is not mysterious – that is, it is not complicated. The quality of a miracle is mysterious, but its manner is simple. Now, the manner of this business has been the reverse of simple.'

The storm that had slackened for a little seemed to be swelling again, and there came heavy movements as of faint thunder. Father Brown let fall the ash of his cigar and went on:

'There has been in this incident,' he said, 'a twisted, ugly, complex quality that does not belong to the straight bolts either of heaven or hell. As one knows the crooked track of a snail, I know the crooked track of a man.'

The white lightning opened its enormous eye in one wink, the sky shut up again, and the priest went on:

'Of all these crooked things, the crookedest was the shape of that piece of paper. It was crookeder than the dagger that killed him.'

'You mean the paper on which Quinton confessed his suicide,' said Flambeau.

'I mean the paper on which Quinton wrote, "I die by my own hand",' answered Father Brown. 'The shape of that paper, my friend, was the wrong shape; the wrong shape, if ever I have seen it in this wicked world.'

'It only had a corner snipped off,' said Flambeau, 'and I understand that all Quinton's paper was cut that way.'

'It was a very odd way,' said the other, 'and a very bad way, to my taste and fancy. Look here, Flambeau, this Quinton – God receive his soul! – was perhaps a bit of a cur in some ways, but he really was an artist, with the pencil as well as the pen. His handwriting, though hard to read, was bold and beautiful. I can't prove what I say; I can't prove anything. But I tell you with the full force of conviction that he could never have cut that mean little piece off a sheet of paper. If he had wanted to cut down paper for some purpose of fitting in, or binding up, or what not, he would have made quite a different slash with the scissors. Do you remember the shape? It was a mean shape. It was a wrong shape. Like this. Don't you remember?'

And he waved his burning cigar before him in the darkness, making irregular squares so rapidly that Flambeau really seemed to see them as fiery hieroglyphics upon the darkness – hieroglyphics such as his friend had spoken of, which are indecipherable, yet can have no good meaning.

'But,' said Flambeau, as the priest put his cigar in his mouth again and leaned back, staring at the roof, 'suppose somebody else did use the scissors. Why should somebody else, cutting pieces off his sermon paper, make Quinton commit suicide?'

Father Brown was leaning back and staring at the roof. He took his cigar out of his mouth and said: 'Quinton never did commit suicide.'

Flambeau stared at him. 'Why, confound it all,' he cried, 'then why did he confess to suicide?'

The priest leant forward again, settled his elbows on his knees, looked at the ground, and said, in a low, distinct voice:

'He never did confess to suicide.'

Flambeau laid his cigar down. 'You mean,' he said, 'that the writing was forged?'

'No,' said Father Brown. 'Quinton wrote it all right.'

'Well, there you are,' said the aggravated Flambeau; 'Quinton wrote, "I die by my own hand", with his own hand on a plain piece of paper.'

'Of the wrong shape,' said the priest calmly.

'Oh, the shape be damned!' cried Flambeau. 'What has the shape to do with it?'

'There were twenty-three snipped papers,' resumed Brown unmoved, 'and only twenty-two pieces snipped off. Therefore one of the pieces had been destroyed, probably that from the written paper. Does that suggest anything to you?'

A light dawned on Flambeau's face, and he said: 'There was something else written by Quinton, some other words. "They will tell you I die by my own hand", or "Do not believe that—".'

'Hotter, as the children say,' said his friend. 'But the piece was hardly half an inch across; there was no room for one word, let alone five. Can you think of anything hardly bigger than a comma which the man with hell in his heart had to tear away as a testimony against him?'

'I can think of nothing,' said Flambeau at last.

'What about quotation marks?' said the priest, and flung his cigar far into the darkness like a shooting star.

All words had left the other man's mouth, and Father Brown said, like one going back to fundamentals:

'Leonard Quinton was a romancer, and was writing an Oriental romance about wizardry and hypnotism. He—'

At this moment the door opened briskly behind them, and the doctor came out with his hat on. He put a long envelope into the priest's hands.

'That's the document you wanted,' he said, 'and I must be getting home. Good night.'

'Good night,' said Father Brown, as the doctor walked briskly to the gate. He had left the front door open, so that a shaft of gaslight fell upon them. In the light of this Brown opened the envelope and read the following words:

DEAR FATHER BROWN, – Vicisti Galilee. Otherwise, damn your eyes, which are very penetrating ones. Can it be possible that there is something in all that stuff of yours after all?

I am a man who has ever since boyhood believed in Nature and in all natural functions and instincts, whether men called them moral or immoral. Long before I became a doctor, when I was a schoolboy keeping mice and spiders, I believed that to be a good animal is the best thing in the world. But just now I am shaken; I have believed in Nature; but it seems as if Nature could betray a man. Can there be anything in your bosh? I am really getting morbid.

I loved Quinton's wife. What was there wrong in that? Nature told me to, and it's love that makes the world go round. I also thought quite sincerely that she would be happier with a clean animal like me than with that tormenting little lunatic. What was there wrong in that? I was only facing facts, like a man of science. She would have been happier.

According to my own creed I was quite free to kill Quinton, which was the best thing for everybody, even himself. But as a healthy animal I had no notion of killing myself. I resolved, therefore, that I would never do it until I saw a chance that would leave me scot free. I saw that chance this morning.

I have been three times, all told, into Quinton's study today.

The first time I went in he would talk about nothing but the weird tale, called 'The Cure of a Saint', which he was writing, which was all about how some Indian hermit made an English colonel kill himself by thinking about him. He showed me the last sheets, and even read me the last paragraph, which was something like this:

'The conqueror of the Punjab, a mere yellow skeleton, but still gigantic, managed to lift himself on his elbow and gasp in his nephew's ear: "I die by my own hand, yet I die murdered!" It so

happened by one chance out of a hundred, that those last words were written at the top of a new sheet of paper. I left the room, and went out into the garden intoxicated with a frightful opportunity.

We walked round the house; and two more things happened in my favour. You suspected an Indian, and you found a dagger which the Indian might most probably use. Taking the opportunity to stuff it in my pocket I went back to Quinton's study, locked the door, and gave him his sleeping draught. He was against answering Atkinson at all, but I urged him to call out and quiet the fellow, because I wanted a clear proof that Quinton was alive when I left the room for the second time. Quinton lay down in the conservatory, and I came through the study. I am a quick man with my hands, and in a minute and a half I had done what I wanted to do. I had emptied all the first part of Quinton's romance into the fireplace, where it burnt to ashes. Then I saw that the quotation marks wouldn't do, so I snipped them off, and to make it seem likelier, snipped the whole quire to match. Then I came out with the knowledge that Quinton's confession of suicide lay on the front table, while Quinton lay alive but asleep in the conservatory beyond.

The last act was a desperate one; you can guess it: I pretended to have seen Quinton dead and rushed to his room. I delayed you with the paper, and, being a quick man with my hands, killed Quinton while you were looking at his confession of suicide. He was half-asleep, being drugged, and I put his own hand on the knife and drove it into his body. The knife was of so queer a shape that no one but an operator could have calculated the angle that would reach his heart. I wonder if you noticed this.

When I had done it, the extraordinary thing happened. Nature deserted me. I felt ill. I felt just as if I had done something wrong. I think my brain is breaking up; I feel some sort of desperate pleasure in thinking I have told the thing to somebody; that I shall not have to be alone with it if I marry and have children. What is the matter with me? ... Madness... or can one have remorse, just as if one were in Byron's poems! I cannot write any more.
James Erskine Harris.

Father Brown carefully folded up the letter, and put it in his breast pocket just as there came a loud peal at the gate bell, and the wet waterproofs of several policemen gleamed in the road outside.

ERNEST BRAMAH

The Tragedy at Brookbend Cottage

'MAX,' SAID Mr Carlyle, when Parkinson had closed the door behind him, 'this is Lieutenant Hollyer, whom you consented to see.'

'To hear,' corrected Carrados, smiling straight into the healthy and rather embarrassed face of the stranger before him. 'Mr Hollyer knows of my disability?'

'Mr Carlyle told me,' said the young man, 'but, as a matter of fact, I had heard of you before, Mr Carrados, from one of our men. It was in connection with the foundering of the Ivan Saratov.'

Carrados wagged his head in good-humoured resignation.

'And the owners were sworn to inviolable secrecy!' he exclaimed. 'Well, it is inevitable, I suppose. Not another scuttling case, Mr Hollyer?'

'No, mine is quite a private matter,' replied the lieutenant. 'My sister, Mrs Creake – but Mr Carlyle would tell you better than I can. He knows all about it.'

'No, no; Carlyle is a professional. Let me have it in the rough, Mr Hollyer. My ears are my eyes, you know.'

'Very well, sir. I can tell you what there is to tell, right enough, but I feel that when all's said and done it must sound very little to another, although it seems important to me.'

'We have occasionally found trifles of significance ourselves,' said Carrados encouragingly. 'Don't let that deter you.'

This was the essence of Lieutenant Hollyer's narrative:

'I have a sister, Millicent, who is married to a man called Creake. She is about twenty-eight now and he is at least fifteen years older. Neither my mother (who has since died) nor I cared very much about Creake. We had nothing particular against him, except, perhaps, the moderate disparity of age, but none of us appeared to have anything in common. He was a dark, taciturn man, and his moody silence froze up conversation. As a result, of course, we didn't see much of each other.'

'This, you must understand, was four or five years ago, Max,' interposed Mr Carlyle officiously.

Carrados maintained an uncompromising silence. Mr Carlyle

blew his nose and contrived to impart a hurt significance into the operation. Then Lieutenant Hollyer continued:

'Millicent married Creake after a very short engagement. It was a frightfully subdued wedding – more like a funeral to me. The man professed to have no relations and apparently he had scarcely any friends or business acquaintances. He was an agent for something or other and had an office off Holborn. I suppose he made a living out of it then, although we knew practically nothing of his private affairs, but I gather that it has been going down since, and I suspect that for the past few years they have been getting along almost entirely on Millicent's little income. You would like the particulars of that?'

'Please,' assented Carrados.

'When our father died about seven years ago, he left three thousand pounds. It was invested in Canadian stock and brought in a little over a hundred a year. By his will my mother was to have the income of that for life and on her death it was to pass to Millicent, subject to the payment of a lump sum of five hundred pounds to me. But my father privately suggested to me that if I should have no particular use for the money at the time, he would propose my letting Millicent have the income of it until I did want it, as she would not be particularly well off. You see, Mr Carrados, a great deal more had been spent on my education and advancement than on her; I had my pay, and, of course, I could look out for myself better than a girl could.'

'Quite so,' agreed Carrados.

'Therefore I did nothing about that,' continued the lieutenant. 'Three years ago I was over again but I did not see much of them. They were living in lodgings. That was the only time since the marriage that I have seen them until last week. In the meanwhile our mother died and Millicent had been receiving her income. She wrote me several letters at the time. Otherwise we did not correspond much, but about a year ago she sent me their new address – Brookbend Cottage, Mulling Common – a house that they had taken. When I got two months' leave I invited myself there as a matter of course, fully expecting to stay most of my time with them, but I made an excuse to get away after a week. The place was dismal and unendurable, the whole life and atmosphere indescribably depressing.' He looked round with an instinct of caution, leaned forward earnestly, and dropped his voice. 'Mr Carrados, it is my absolute conviction that Creake is only waiting for a favourable opportunity to murder Millicent.'

'Go on,' said Carrados quietly. 'A week of the depressing surroundings of Brookbend Cottage would not alone convince you of that, Mr Hollyer.'

'I am not so sure,' declared Hollyer doubtfully. 'There was a feeling of suspicion and – before me – polite hatred that would have gone a good way towards it. All the same there was something more definite. Millicent told me this the day after I went there. There is no doubt that a few months ago Creake deliberately planned to poison her with some weed-killer. She told me the circumstances in a rather distressed moment, but afterwards she refused to speak of it again – even weakly denied it – and, as a matter of fact, it was with the greatest difficulty that I could get her at any time to talk about her husband or his affairs. The gist of it was that she had the strongest suspicion that Creake doctored a bottle of stout which he expected she would drink for her supper when she was alone. The weed-killer, properly labelled, but also in a beer bottle, was kept with other miscellaneous liquids in the same cupboard as the beer but on a high shelf. When he found that it had miscarried he poured away the mixture, washed out the bottle and put in the dregs from another. There is no doubt in my mind that if he had come back and found Millicent dead or dying he would have contrived it to appear that she had made a mistake in the dark and drunk some of the poison before she found out.'

'Yes,' assented Carrados. 'The open way; the safe way.'

'You must understand that they live in a very small style, Mr Carrados, and Millicent is almost entirely in the man's power. The only servant they have is a woman who comes in for a few hours every day. The house is lonely and secluded. Creake is sometimes away for days and nights at a time, and Millicent, either through pride or indifference, seems to have dropped off all her old friends and have made no others. He might poison her, bury the body in the garden, and be a thousand miles away before anyone began even to inquire about her. What am I to do, Mr Carrados?'

'He is less likely to try poison than some other means now,' pondered Carrados. 'That having failed, his wife will always be on her guard. He may know, or at least suspect, that others know. No... The common-sense precaution would be for your sister to leave the man, Mr Hollyer. She will not?'

'No,' admitted Hollyer, 'she will not. I at once urged that.' The young man struggled with some hesitation for a moment and then blurted out: 'The fact is, Mr Carrados, I don't understand Millicent. She is not the girl she was. She hates Creake and treats him with a silent contempt that eats into their lives like acid, and yet she is so jealous of him that she will let nothing short of death part them. It is a horrible life they lead. I stood it for a week and I must say, much as I dislike my brother-in-law, that he has something to put up with. If only he got into a passion like a man and killed her it wouldn't be altogether incomprehensible.'

'That does not concern us,' said Carrados. 'In a game of this kind one has to take sides and we have taken ours. It remains for us to see that our side wins. You mentioned jealousy, Mr Hollyer. Have you any idea whether Mrs Creake has real ground for it?'

'I should have told you that,' replied Lieutenant Hollyer.

'I happened to strike up with a newspaper man whose office is in the same block as Creake's. When I mentioned the name he grinned. 'Creake,' he said, 'oh, he's the man with the romantic typist, isn't he?' 'Well he's my brother-in-law,' I replied. 'What about the typist?' Then the chap shut up like a knife. 'No, no,' he said, 'I didn't know he was married. I don't want to get mixed up in anything of that sort. I only said that he had a typist. Well, what of that? So have we; so has everyone.' There was nothing more to be got out of him, but the remark and the grin meant – well, about as usual, Mr Carrados.'

Carrados turned to his friend.

'I suppose you know all about the typist by now, Louis?'

'We have had her under efficient observation, Max,' replied Mr Carlyle, with severe dignity.

'Is she unmarried?'

'Yes; so far as ordinary repute goes, she is.'

'That is all that is essential for a moment. Mr Hollyer opens up three excellent reasons why this man might wish to dispose of his wife. If we accept the suggestion of poisoning – though we have only a jealous woman's suspicion for it – we add to the wish the determination. Well, we will go forward on that. Have you got a photograph of Mr Creake?'

The lieutenant took out his pocket book.

'Mr Carlyle asked me for one. Here is the best I could get.'

Carrados rang the bell.

'This, Parkinson,' he said, when the man appeared, 'is a photograph of a Mr— What first name by the way?'

'Austin,' put in Hollyer, who was following everything with a boyish mixture of excitement and subdued importance.

'—of a Mr Austin Creake. I may require you to recognise him.'

Parkinson glanced at the print and returned it to his master's hand.

'May I inquire if it is a recent photograph of the gentleman, sir?' he asked.

'About six years ago,' said the lieutenant, taking in this new actor in the drama with frank curiosity. 'But he is very little changed.'

'Thank you, sir. I will endeavour to remember Mr Creake, sir.'

Lieutenant Hollyer stood up as Parkinson left the room. The interview seemed to be at an end.

'Oh, there's one other matter,' he remarked. 'I am afraid that I did rather an unfortunate thing while I was at Brookbend. It seemed to me that as all Millicent's money would probably pass into Creake's hands sooner or later I might as well have my five hundred pounds, if only to help her with afterwards. So I broached the subject and said that I should like to have it now as I had an opportunity for investing.'

'And you think?'

'It may possibly influence Creake to act sooner than he otherwise might have done. He may have got possession of the principal even and find it very awkward to replace it.'

'So much the better. If your sister is going to be murdered it may as well be done next week as next year as far as I am concerned. Excuse my brutality, Mr Hollyer, but this is simply a case to me and I regard it strategically. Now Mr Carlyle's organisation can look after Mrs Creake for a few weeks, but it cannot look after her for ever. By increasing the immediate risk we diminish the permanent risk.'

'I see,' agreed Hollyer. 'I'm awfully uneasy but I'm entirely in your hands.'

'Then we will give Mr Creake every inducement and every opportunity to get to work. Where are you staying now?'

'Just now with some friends at St Albans.'

'That is too far.' The inscrutable eyes retained their tranquil depth but a new quality of quickening interest in the voice made Mr Carlyle forget the weight and burden of his ruffled dignity. 'Give me a few minutes, please. The cigarettes are behind you, Mr Hollyer.' The blind man walked to the window and seemed to look over the cypress-shaded lawn. The lieutenant lit a cigarette and Mr Carlyle picked up *Punch*. Then Carrados turned round again.

'You are prepared to put your own arrangements aside?' he demanded of his visitor.

'Certainly.'

'Very well. I want you to go down now – straight from here – to Brookbend Cottage. Tell your sister that your leave is unexpectedly cut short and that you sail tomorrow.'

'The Martian?'

'No, no; the Martian doesn't sail. Look up the movements on your way there and pick out a boat that does. Say you are transferred. Add that you expect to be away only two or three months and that you really want the five hundred pounds by the time of your return. Don't stay in the house long, please.'

'I understand, sir.'

'St Albans is too far. Make your excuse and get away from there today. Put up somewhere in town, where you will be in reach of the telephone. Let Mr Carlyle and myself know where you are. Keep out of Creake's way. I don't want actually to tie you down to the house, but we may require your services. We will let you know at the first sign of anything doing and if there is nothing to be done we must release you.'

'I don't mind that. Is there nothing more that I can do now?'

'Nothing. In going to Mr Carlyle you have done the best thing possible; you have put your sister into the care of the shrewdest man in London.' Whereat the object of this quite unexpected eulogy found himself becoming covered with modest confusion.

'Well, Max?' remarked Mr Carlyle tentatively when they were alone.

'Well, Louis?'

'Of course it wasn't worth while rubbing it in before young Hollyer, but, as a matter of fact, every single man carries the life of any other man – only one, mind you – in his hands, do what you will.'

'Provided he doesn't bungle,' acquiesced Carrados.

'Quite so.'

'And also that he is absolutely reckless of the consequences.'

'Of course.'

'Two rather large provisos. Creake is obviously susceptible to both. Have you seen him?'

'No. As I told you, I put a man on to report his habits in town. Then, two days ago, as the case seemed to promise some interest – for he certainly is deeply involved with the typist, Max, and the thing might take a sensational turn at any time – I went down to Mulling Common myself. Although the house is lonely it is on the electric tram route. You know the sort of market garden rurality that about a dozen miles out of London offers – alternate bricks and cabbages. It was easy enough to get to know about Creake locally. He mixes with no one there, goes into town at irregular times but generally every day, and is reputed to be devilish hard to get money out of. Finally I made the acquaintance of an old fellow who used to do a day's gardening at Brookbend occasionally. He has a cottage and a garden of his own with a greenhouse, and the business cost me the price of a pound of tomatoes.'

'Was it – a profitable investment?'

'As tomatoes, yes; as information, no. The old fellow had the fatal disadvantage from our point of view of labouring under a grievance. A few weeks ago Creake told him that he would not require him again as he was going to do his own gardening in future.'

'That is something, Louis.'

'If only Creake was going to poison his wife with hyoscyamine and bury her, instead of blowing her up with a dynamite cartridge and claiming that it came in among the coal.'

'True, true. Still—'

'However, the chatty old soul had a simple explanation for everything that Creake did. Creake was mad. He had even seen him flying a kite in his garden where it was bound to get wrecked among the trees. A lad of ten would have known better, he declared. And certainly the kite did get wrecked, for I saw it hanging over the road myself. But that a sane man should spend his time "playing with a toy" was beyond him.'

'A good many men have been flying kites of various kinds lately,' said Carrados. 'Is he interested in aviation?'

'I dare say. He appears to have some knowledge of scientific subjects. Now what do you want me to do, Max?'

'Will you do it?'

'Implicitly – subject to the usual reservations.'

'Keep your man on Creake in town and let me have his reports after you have seen them. Lunch with me here now.

'Phone up to your office that you are detained on unpleasant business and then give the deserving Parkinson an afternoon off by looking after me while we take a motor run round Mulling Common. If we have time we might go on to Brighton, feed at the Ship, and come back in the cool.'

'Amiable and thrice lucky mortal,' sighed Mr Carlyle, his glance wandering round the room.

But, as it happened, Brighton did not figure in that day's itinerary. It had been Carrados's intention merely to pass Brookbend Cottage on this occasion, relying on his highly developed faculties, aided by Mr Carlyle's description, to inform him of the surroundings. A hundred yards before they reached the house he had given an order to his chauffeur to drop into the lowest speed and they were leisurely drawing past when a discovery by Mr Carlyle modified their plans.

'By Jupiter!' that gentleman suddenly exclaimed; 'there's a board up, Max. The place is to be let.' Carrados picked up the tube again. A couple of sentences passed and the car stopped by the roadside, a score of paces past the limit of the garden. Mr Carlyle took out his notebook and wrote down the address of a firm of house agents.

'You might raise the bonnet and have a look at the engines, Harris,' said Carrados. 'We want to be occupied here for a few minutes.'

'This is sudden; Hollyer knew nothing of their leaving,' remarked Mr Carlyle.

'Probably not for three months yet. All the same, Louis, we will go on to the agents and get a card to view whether we use it today or not.'

A thick hedge, in its summer dress, effectively screening the house beyond from public view, lay between the garden and the road. Above the hedge showed an occasional shrub; at the corner nearest to the car a chestnut flourished. The wooden gate, once white, which they had passed, was grimed and rickety. The road itself was still the unpretentious country lane that the advent of the electric car had found it. When Carrados had taken in these details there seemed little else to notice. He was on the point of giving Harris the order to go on when his ear caught a trivial sound.

'Someone is coming out of the house, Louis,' he warned his friend. 'It may be Hollyer, but he ought to have gone by this time.'

'I don't hear anyone,' replied the other, but as he spoke a door banged noisily and Mr Carlyle slipped into another seat and ensconced himself behind a copy of *The Globe*.

'Creake himself,' he whispered across the car, as a man appeared at the gate. 'Hollyer was right; he is hardly changed. Waiting for a car, I suppose.'

But a car very soon swung past them from the direction in which Mr Creake was looking and it did not interest him. For a minute or two longer he continued to look expectantly along the road. Then he walked slowly up the drive back to the house.

'We will give him five or ten minutes,' decided Carrados. 'Harris is behaving very naturally.'

Before even the shorter period had run out they were repaid. A telegraph-boy cycled leisurely along the road, and, leaving his machine at the gate, went up to the cottage. Evidently there was no reply, for in less than a minute he was trundling past them back again.

Round the bend an approaching tram clanged its bell noisily, and, quickened by the warning sound, Mr Creake again appeared, this time with a small portmanteau in his hand. With a backward glance he hurried on towards the next stopping-place, and, boarding the car as it slackened down, he was carried out of their knowledge.

'Very convenient of Mr Creake,' remarked Carrados, with quiet satisfaction. 'We will now get the order and go over the house in his absence. It might be useful to have a look at the wire as well.'

'It might, Max,' acquiesced Mr Carlyle, a little dryly. 'But if it is, as it probably is, in Creake's pocket, how do you propose to get it?'

'By going to the post office, Louis,'

'Quite so. Have you ever tried to see a copy of a telegram addressed to someone else?'

'I don't think I have ever had occasion yet,' admitted Carrados. 'Have you?'

'In one or two cases I have perhaps been an accessory to the act. It is generally a matter either of extreme delicacy or considerable expenditure.'

'Then for Hollyer's sake we will hope for the former here.' And Mr Carlyle smiled darkly and hinted that he was content to wait for a friendly revenge.

A little later, having left the car at the beginning of the straggling High Street, the two men called at the village post office. They had already visited the house agent and obtained an order to view Brookbend Cottage, declining with some difficulty the clerk's persistent offer to accompany them. The reason was soon forthcoming. 'As a matter of fact,' explained the young man, 'the present tenant is under our notice to leave.'

'Unsatisfactory, eh?' said Carrados encouragingly.

'He's a corker,' admitted the clerk, responding to the friendly tone. 'Fifteen months and not a dot of rent have we had. That's why I should have liked—'

'We will make every allowance,' replied Carrados.

The post office occupied one side of a stationer's shop. It was not without some inward trepidation that Mr Carlyle found himself committed to the adventure. Carrados, on the other hand, was the personification of bland unconcern.

'You have just sent a telegram to Brookbend Cottage,' he said to the young lady behind the brasswork lattice. 'We think it may have come inaccurately and should like a repeat.' He took out his purse. 'What is the fee?'

The request evidently was not a common one. 'Oh,' said the girl uncertainly, 'wait a minute, please.' She turned to a pile of telegram duplicates behind the desk and ran a doubtful finger along the upper sheets. 'I think this is all right. You want it repeated?'

'Please.' Just a tinge of questioning surprise gave point to the courteous tone.

'It will be fourpence. If there is an error the amount will be refunded.'

Carrados put down his coin and received his change.

'Will it take long?' he inquired carelessly, as he pulled on his glove.

'You will most likely get it within a quarter of an hour,' she replied.

'Now you've done it,' commented Mr Carlyle, as they walked back to their car. 'How do you propose to get that telegram, Max?'

'Ask for it,' was the laconic explanation.

And, stripping the artifice of any elaboration, he simply asked for it and got it. The car, posted at a convenient bend in the road, gave him a warning note as the telegraph-boy approached. Then Carrados took up a convincing attitude with his hand on the gate while Mr Carlyle lent himself to the semblance of a departing friend. That was the inevitable impression when the boy rode up.

'Creake, Brookbend Cottage?' inquired Carrados, holding out his hand, and without a second thought the boy gave him the envelope and rode away on the assurance that there would be no reply.

'Some day, my friend,' remarked Mr Carlyle, looking nervously towards the unseen house, 'your ingenuity will get you into a tight corner.'

'Then my ingenuity must get me out again,' was the retort. 'Let us have our "view" now. The telegram can wait.'

An untidy workwoman took their order and left them standing at the door. Presently a lady whom they both knew to be Mrs Creake appeared.

'You wish to see over the house?' she said, in a voice that was utterly devoid of any interest. Then, without waiting for a reply, she turned to the nearest door and threw it open.

'This is the drawing-room,' she said, standing aside.

They walked into a sparsely furnished, damp-smelling room and made a pretence of looking round, while Mrs Creake remained silent and aloof.

'The dining-room,' she continued, crossing the narrow hall and opening another door.

Mr Carlyle ventured a genial commonplace in the hope of inducing conversation. The result was not encouraging. Doubtless they would have gone through the house under the same frigid guidance had not Carrados been at fault in a way that Mr Carlyle had never known him fail before. In crossing the hall he stumbled over a mat and almost fell.

'Pardon my clumsiness,' he said to the lady. 'I am, unfortunately, quite blind. But,' he added, with a smile, to turn off the mishap, 'even a blind man must have a house.'

The man who had eyes was surprised to see a flood of colour rush into Mrs Creake's face.

'Blind!' she exclaimed, 'oh, I beg your pardon. Why did you not tell me? You might have fallen.'

'I generally manage fairly well,' he replied. 'But, of course, in a strange house—'

She put her hand on his arm very lightly.

'You must let me guide you, just a little,' she said.

The house, without being large, was full of passages and inconvenient turnings. Carrados asked an occasional question and found Mrs Creake quite amiable without effusion. Mr Carlyle followed them from room to room in the hope, though scarcely the expectation, of learning something that might be useful.

'This is the last one. It is the largest bedroom,' said their guide. Only two of the upper rooms were fully furnished and Mr Carlyle at once saw, as Carrados knew without seeing, that this was the one which the Creakes occupied.

'A very pleasant outlook,' declared Mr Carlyle.

'Oh, I suppose so,' admitted the lady vaguely. The room, in fact, looked over the leafy garden and the road beyond. It had a French window opening on to a small balcony, and to this, under the strange influence that always attracted him to light, Carrados walked.

'I expect that there is a certain amount of repair needed?' he said, after standing there a moment.

'I am afraid there would be,' she confessed.

'I ask because there is a sheet of metal on the floor here,' he continued. 'Now that, in an old house, spells dry rot to the wary observer.'

'My husband said that the rain, which comes in a little under the window, was rotting the boards there,' she replied. 'He put that down recently. I had not noticed anything myself.'

It was the first time she had mentioned her husband; Mr Carlyle pricked up his ears.

'Ah, that is a less serious matter,' said Carrados. 'May I step out on to the balcony?'

'Oh yes, if you like to.' Then, as he appeared to be fumbling at the catch, 'Let me open it for you.'

But the window was already open, and Carrados, facing the various points of the compass, took in the bearings.

'A sunny, sheltered corner,' he remarked. 'An ideal spot for a deck-chair and a book.'

She shrugged her shoulders half contemptuously.

'I dare say,' she replied, 'but I never use it.'

'Sometimes, surely,' he persisted mildly. 'It would be my favourite retreat. But then—'

'I was going to say that I had never even been out on it, but that would not be quite true. It has two uses for me, both equally romantic; I occasionally shake a duster from it, and when my husband returns late without his latchkey he wakes me up and I come out here and drop him mine.'

Further revelation of Mr Creake's nocturnal habits was cut off, greatly to Mr Carlyle's annoyance, by a cough of unmistakable significance from the foot of the stairs. They had heard a trade cart drive up to the gate, a knock at the door, and the heavy-footed woman tramp along the hall.

'Excuse me a minute, please,' said Mrs Creake.

'Louis,' said Carrados, in a sharp whisper, the moment they were alone, 'stand against the door.'

With extreme plausibility Mr Carlyle began to admire a picture so situated that while he was there it was impossible to open the door more than a few inches. From that position he observed his confederate go through the curious procedure of kneeling down on the bedroom floor and for a full minute pressing his ear to the sheet of metal that had already engaged his attention. Then he rose to his feet, nodded, dusted his trousers, and Mr Carlyle moved to a less equivocal position.

'What a beautiful rose-tree grows up your balcony,' remarked Carrados, stepping into the room as Mrs Creake returned. 'I suppose you are very fond of gardening?'

'I detest it,' she replied.

'But this Glorie, so carefully trained—?'

'Is it?' she replied. 'I think my husband was nailing it up recently.'

By some strange fatality Carrados's most aimless remarks seemed to involve the absent Mr Creake. 'Do you care to see the garden?'

The garden proved to be extensive and neglected. Behind the house was chiefly orchard. In front, some semblance of order had been kept up; here it was lawn and shrubbery, cut across by the drive they had walked along. Two things interested Carrados: the soil at the foot of the balcony, which he declared on examination to be particularly suitable for roses, and the fine chestnut-tree in the corner by the road.

As they walked back to the car Mr Carlyle lamented that they had learned so little of Creake's movements.

'Perhaps the telegram will tell us something,' suggested Carrados. 'Read it, Louis.'

Mr Carlyle cut open the envelope, glanced at the enclosure, and in spite of his disappointment could not restrain a chuckle.

'My poor Max,' he explained, 'you have put yourself to an amount of ingenious trouble for nothing. Creake is evidently taking a few days' holiday and prudently availed himself of the Meteorological Office forecast before going. Listen: 'Immediate prospect for London warm and settled. Further outlook cooler but fine.' Well, well; I did get a pound of tomatoes for my fourpence.'

'You certainly scored there, Louis,' admitted Carrados, with humorous appreciation. 'I wonder,' he added speculatively, 'whether it is Creake's peculiar taste usually to spend his weekend holiday in London.'

'Eh?' exclaimed Mr Carlyle, looking at the words again, 'by gad, that's rum, Max. They go to Weston-super-Mare. Why on earth should he want to know about London?'

'I can make a guess, but before we are satisfied I must come here again. Take another look at that kite, Louis. Are there a few yards of string hanging loose from it?'

'Yes, there are.'

'Rather thick string – unusually thick for the purpose?'

'Yes; but how do you know?'

As they drove home again Carrados explained, and Mr Carlyle sat aghast, saying incredulously: 'Good God, Max, is it possible?'

An hour later he was satisfied that it was possible. In reply to his inquiry someone in his office telephoned him the information that 'they' had left Paddington by the four-thirty for Weston.

It was more than a week after his introduction to Carrados that Lieutenant Hollyer had a summons to present himself at The Turrets

again. He found Mr Carlyle already there and the two friends awaiting his arrival.

'I stayed in all day after hearing from you this morning, Mr Carrados,' he said, shaking hands. 'When I got your second message I was
all ready to walk straight out of the house. That's how I did it in the
time. I hope everything is all right?'

'Excellent,' replied Carrados. 'You'd better have something
before we start. We probably have a long and perhaps an exciting
night before us.'

'And certainly a wet one,' assented the lieutenant. 'It was thundering over Mulling way as I came along.'

'That is why you are here,' said his host. 'We are waiting for a
certain message before we start, and in the meantime you may as well
understand what we expect to happen. As you saw, there is a thun-
derstorm coming on. The Meteorological Office morning forecast
predicted it for the whole of London if the conditions remained. That
was why I kept you in readiness. Within an hour it is now inevitable
that we shall experience a deluge. Here and there damage will be
done to trees and buildings; here and there a person will probably be
struck and killed.'

'Yes.'

'It is Mr Creake's intention that his wife should be among the
victims.'

'I don't exactly follow,' said Hollyer, looking from one man to the
other. 'I quite admit that Creake would be immensely relieved if such
a thing did happen, but the chance is surely an absurdly remote one.'

'Yet unless we intervene it is precisely what a coroner's jury will
decide has happened. Do you know whether your brother-in-law has
any practical knowledge of electricity, Mr Hollyer?'

'I cannot say. He was so reserved, and we really knew little of
him—'

'Yet in 1896 an Austin Creake contributed an article on "Alter-
nating Currents" to the American Scientific World. That would argue
a fairly intimate acquaintanceship.'

'But do you mean that he is going to direct a flash of lightning?'

'Only into the minds of the doctor who conducts the post-
mortem, and the coroner. This storm, the opportunity of which he
had been awaiting for weeks, is merely the cloak to his act. The
weapon which he has planned to use – scarcely less powerful than
lightning but much more tractable – is the high voltage current of
electricity that flows along the tram wire at his gate.'

'Oh!' exclaimed Lieutenant Hollyer, as the sudden revelation struck him.

'Some time between eleven o'clock tonight – about the hour when your sister goes to bed – and one-thirty in the morning – the time up to which he can rely on the current – Creake will throw a stone up to the balcony window. Most of his preparation has long been made; it only remains for him to connect up a short length to the window handle and a longer one at the other end to tap the live wire. That done, he will wake his wife in the way I have said. The moment she moves the catch of the window – and he has carefully filed its parts to ensure perfect contact – she will be electrocuted as effectually as if she sat in the executioner's chair in Sing Sing prison.'

'But what are we doing here!' exclaimed Hollyer, starting to his feet, pale and horrified. 'It is past ten now and anything may happen.'

'Quite natural, Mr Hollyer,' said Carrados reassuringly, 'but you need have no anxiety. Creake is being watched, the house is being watched, and your sister is as safe as if she slept tonight in Windsor Castle. Be assured that whatever happens he will not be allowed to complete his scheme; but it is desirable to let him implicate himself to the fullest limit. Your brother-in-law, Mr Hollyer, is a man with a peculiar capacity for taking pains.'

'He is a damned cold-blooded scoundrel!' exclaimed the young officer fiercely. 'When I think of Millicent five years ago—'

'Well, for that matter, an enlightened nation has decided that electrocution is the most humane way of removing its superfluous citizens,' suggested Carrados mildly. 'He is certainly an ingenious-minded gentleman. It is his misfortune that in Mr Carlyle he was fated to be opposed by an even subtler brain—'

'No, no! Really, Max!' protested the embarrassed gentleman.

'Mr Hollyer will be able to judge for himself when I tell him that it was Mr Carlyle who first drew attention to the significance of the abandoned kite,' insisted Carrados firmly. 'Then, of course, its object became plain to me – as indeed to anyone. For ten minutes, perhaps, a wire must be carried from the overhead line to the chestnut-tree. Creake has everything in his favour, but it is just within possibility that the driver of an inopportune train might notice the appendage. What of that? Why, for more than a week he has seen a derelict kite with its yards of trailing string hanging in the tree. A very calculating mind, Mr Hollyer. It would be interesting to know what line of action Mr Creake has mapped out for himself afterwards. I expect he has half-a-dozen artistic little touches up his sleeve. Possibly he would

merely singe his wife's hair, burn her feet with a red-hot poker, shiver
the glass of the French window, and be content with that to let well
alone. You see, lightning is so varied in its effects that whatever he
did or did not do would be right. He is in the impregnable positionof
the body showing all the symptoms of death by lightning shock and
nothing else but lightning to account for it – a dilated eye, heart con-
tracted in systole, bloodless lungs shrunk to a third the normal
weight, and all the rest of it. When he has removed a few outward
traces of his work Creake might quite safely "discover" his dead wife
and rush off for the nearest doctor. Or he may have decided to
arrange a convincing alibi, and creep away, leaving the discovery to
another. We shall never know; he will make no confession.'

'I wish it was well over,' admitted Hollyer. 'I'm not particularly
jumpy, but this gives me a touch of the creeps.'

'Three more hours at the worst, Lieutenant,' said Carrados cheerfully. 'Ah-ha, something is coming through now.'

He went to the telephone and received a message from one
quarter; then made another connection and talked for a few minutes
with someone else.

'Everything working smoothly,' he remarked between times over
his shoulder. 'Your sister has gone to bed, Mr Hollyer.'

Then he turned to the house telephone and distributed his orders.

'So we,' he concluded, 'must get up.'

By the time they were ready a large closed motor car was waiting.
The lieutenant thought he recognised Parkinson in the well-swathed
form beside the driver, but there was no temptation to linger for a
second on the steps. Already the stinging rain had lashed the drive
into the semblance of a frothy estuary; all round the lightning jagged
its course through the incessant tremulous glow of more distant lightning, while the thunder only ceased its muttering to turn at close
quarters and crackle viciously.

'One of the few things I regret missing,' remarked Carrados tranquilly, 'but I hear a good deal of colour in it.'

The car slushed its way down to the gate, lurched a little heavily
across the dip into the road, and, steadying as it came upon the
straight, began to hum contentedly along the deserted highway.

'We are not going direct?' suddenly inquired Hollyer, after they
had travelled perhaps half-a-dozen miles. The night was bewildering
enough but he had the sailor's gift for location.

'No; through Hunscott Green and then by a field-path to the
orchard at the back,' replied Carrados. 'Keep a sharp look out for the

man with the lantern about here, Harris,' he called through the tube.

'Something flashing just ahead, sir,' came the reply, and the car slowed down and stopped.

Carrados dropped the near window as a man in glistening waterproof stepped from the shelter of a lych-gate and approached.

'Inspector Beedel, sir,' said the stranger, looking into the car.

'Quite right, Inspector,' said Carrados. 'Get in.'

'I have a man with me, sir.'

'We can find room for him as well.'

'We are very wet.'

'So shall we all be soon.'

The lieutenant changed his seat and the two burly forms took places side by side. In less than five minutes the car stopped again, this time in a grassy country lane.

'Now we have to face it,' announced Carrados. 'The inspector will show us the way.'

The car slid round and disappeared into the night, while Beedel led the party to a stile in the hedge. A couple of fields brought them to the Brookbend boundary. There a figure stood out of the black foliage, exchanged a few words with their guide and piloted them along the shadows of the orchard to the back door of the house.

'You will find a broken pane near the catch of the scullery window,' said the blind man. 'Right, sir,' replied the inspector. 'I have it. Now who goes through?'

'Mr Hollyer will open the door for us. I'm afraid you must take off your boots and all wet things, Lieutenant. I We cannot risk a single spot inside.'

They waited until the back door opened, then each one divested himself in a similar manner and passed into the kitchen, where the remains of a fire still burned. The man from the orchard gathered together the discarded garments and disappeared again.

Carrados turned to the lieutenant.

'A rather delicate job for you now, Mr Hollyer. I want you to go up to your sister, wake her, and get her into another room with as little fuss as possible. Tell her as much as you think fit and let her understand that her very life depends on absolute stillness when she is alone. Don't be unduly hurried, but not a glimmer of a light, please.'

Then minutes passed by the measure of the battered old alarum on the dresser shelf before the young man returned.

'I've had rather a time of it,' he reported, with a nervous laugh, 'but I think it will be all right now. She is in the spare room.'

'Then we will take our places. You and Parkinson come with me to the bedroom. Inspector, you have your own arrangements. Mr Carlyle will be with you.'

They dispersed silently about the house, Hollyer glanced apprehensively at the door of the spare room as they passed it, but within all was as quiet as the grave. Their room lay at the other end of the passage.

'You may as well take your place in the bed now, Hollyer,' directed Carrados when they were inside and the door closed. 'Keep well down among the clothes. Creake has to get up on the balcony, you know, and he will probably peep through the window, but he dare come no farther. Then when he begins to throw up stones slip on this dressing-gown of your sister's. I'll tell you what to do after.'

The next sixty minutes drew out into the longest hour that the lieutenant had ever known. Occasionally he heard a whisper pass between the two men who stood behind the window curtains, but he could see nothing. Then Carrados threw a guarded remark in his direction.

'He is in the garden now.'

Something scraped slightly against the outer wall. But the night was full of wilder sounds, and in the house the furniture and the boards creaked and sprung between the yawling of the wind among the chimneys, the rattle of the thunder and the pelting of the rain. It was a time to quicken the steadiest pulse, and when the crucial moment came, when a pebble suddenly rang against the pane with a sound that the tense waiting magnified into a shivering crash, Hollyer leaped from the bed on the instant.

'Easy, easy,' warned Carrados feelingly. 'We will wait for another knock.' He passed something across. 'Here is a rubber glove. I have cut the wire but you had better put it on. Stand just for a moment at the window, move the catch so that it can blow open a little, and drop immediately. Now.'

Another stone had rattled against the glass. For Hollyer to go through his part was the work merely of seconds, and with a few touches Carrados spread the dressing-gown to more effective disguise about the extended form. But an unforeseen and in the circumstances rather horrible interval followed, for Creake, in accordance with some detail of his never-revealed plan, continued to shower missile after missile against the panes until even the unimpressionable Parkinson shivered.

'The last act,' whispered Carrados, a moment after the throwing had ceased. 'He has gone round to the back. Keep as you are. We take cover now.' He pressed behind the arras of an extemporised wardrobe, and the spirit of emptiness and desolation seemed once more to reign over the lonely house.

From half-a-dozen places of concealment ears were straining to catch the first guiding sound. He moved very stealthily, burdened, perhaps, by some strange scruple in the presence of the tragedy that he had not feared to contrive, paused for a moment at the bedroom door, then opened it very quietly, and in the fickle light read the consummation of his hopes.

'At last!' they heard the sharp whisper drawn from his relief. 'At last!'

He took another step and two shadows seemed to fall upon him from behind, one on either side. With primitive instinct a cry of terror and surprise escaped him as he made a desperate movement to wrench himself free, and for a short second he almost succeeded in dragging one hand into a pocket. Then his wrists slowly came together and the handcuffs closed.

'I am Inspector Beedel,' said the man on his right side. 'You are charged with the attempted murder of your wife, Millicent Creake.'

'You are mad,' retorted the miserable creature, falling into a desperate calmness. 'She has been struck by lightning.'

'No, you blackguard, she hasn't,' wrathfully exclaimed his brother-in-law, jumping up. 'Would you like to see her?'

'I also have to warn you,' continued the inspector impassively, 'that anything you say may be used as evidence against you.'

A startled cry from the farthest end of the passage arrested their attention.

'Mr Carrados,' called Hollyer, 'oh, come at once.'

At the open door of the other bedroom stood the lieutenant, his eyes still turned towards something in the room beyond, a little empty bottle in his hand.

'Dead!' he exclaimed tragically, with a sob, 'with this beside her. Dead just when she would have been free of the brute.'

The blind man passed into the room, sniffed the air, and laid a gentle hand on the pulseless heart.

'Yes,' he replied. 'That, Hollyer, does not always appeal to the woman, strange to say.'

R AUSTIN FREEMAN

The Case of the White Footprints

'WELL,' SAID my friend Foxton, pursuing a familiar and apparently inexhaustible topic, 'I'd sooner have your job than my own.'

'I've no doubt you would,' was my unsympathetic reply. 'I never met a man who wouldn't. We all tend to consider other men's jobs in terms of their advantages and our own in terms of their drawbacks. It is human nature.'

'Oh, it's all very well for you to be so beastly philosophical,' retorted Foxton. 'You wouldn't be if you were in my place. Here, in Margate, it's measles, chickenpox and scarlatina all the summer, and bronchitis, colds and rheumatism an the winter. A deadly monotony. Whereas you and Thorndyke sit there in your chambers and let your clients feed you up with the raw material of romance. Why, your life is a sort of everlasting Adelphi drama.'

'You exaggerate, Foxton,' said I. 'We, like you, have our routine work, only it is never heard of outside the Law Courts; and you, like every other doctor, must run up against mystery and romance from time to time.'

Foxton shook his head as he held out his hand for my cup. 'I don't,' said be. 'My practice yields nothing but an endless round of dull routine.'

And then, as if in commentary on this last statement, the housemaid burst into the room and, with hardly dissembled agitation, exclaimed: 'If you please, sir, the page from Beddingfield's Boardinghouse says that a lady has been found dead in her bed and would you go round there immediately.'

'Very well, Jane,' said Foxton, and as the maid retired, he deliberately helped himself to another fried egg and, looking across the table at me, exclaimed: 'Isn't that always the way? Come immediately – now – this very instant, although the patient may have been considering for a day or two whether he'll send for you or not. But directly he decides you must spring out of bed, or jump up from your breakfast, and run.'

'That's quite true,' I agreed; 'but this really does seem to be an urgent case.'

'What's the urgency?' demanded Foxton. 'The woman is already dead. Anyone would think she was in imminent danger of coming to life again and that my instant arrival the only thing that could prevent such a catastrophe.'

'You've only a third-hand statement that she is dead,' said I. 'It is just possible that she isn't; and even if she is, as you will have to give evidence at the inquest, you do want the police to get there first and turn out the room before you've made your inspection.'

'Gad!' exclaimed Foxton. 'I hadn't thought of that. Yes. You're right. I'll hop round at once.'

He swallowed the remainder of the egg at a single gulp rose from the table. Then he paused and stood for a few moments looking down at me irresolutely.

'I wonder, Jervis,' he said, 'if you would mind coming round with me. You know all the medico-legal ropes, and I don't. What do you say?'

I agreed instantly, having, in fact, been restrained only by delicacy from making the suggestion myself; and when I had fetched from my room my pocket camera and telescopic tripod, we set forth together without further delay.

Beddingfield's Boarding-house was but a few minutes walk from Foxton's residence, being situated near the middle of Ethelred Road, Cliftonville, a quiet, suburban street which abounded in similar establishments, many of which, I noticed, were undergoing a spring-cleaning and renovation to prepare them for the approaching season.

'That's the house,' said Foxton, 'where that woman is standing at the front door. Look at the boarders, collected at the dining-room window. There's a rare commotion in that house, I'll warrant.'

Here, arriving at the house, he ran up the steps and accosted in sympathetic tones the elderly woman who stood by the open street door.

'What a dreadful thing this is, Mrs Beddingfield! Terrible! Most distressing for you!'

'Ah, you're right, Dr Foxton,' she replied. 'It's an awful affair. Shocking. So bad for business, too. I do hope, and trust there won't be any scandal.'

'I'm sure I hope not,' said Foxton. 'There shan't be if I can help it. And as my friend Dr Jervis, who is staying with me for a few days, is a lawyer as well as a doctor, we shall have the best advice. When was the affair discovered?'

'Just before I sent for you, Dr Foxton. The maid, noticed that Mrs

Toussaint – that is the poor creature's name – had not taken in her hot water, so she knocked at the door. As she couldn't get any answer, she tried the door and found it bolted on the inside, and then she came and told me. I went up and knocked loudly, and then, as I couldn't get any reply, I told our boy, James, to force the door open with a case-opener, which he did quite easily as the bolt was only a small one. Then I went in, all of a tremble, for I had a presentiment that there was something wrong; and there she was lying stone dead, with a most 'orrible stare on her face and an empty bottle in her hand.'

'A bottle, eh!' said Foxton.

'Yes. She'd made away with herself, poor thing; and all on account of some silly love affair – and it was hardly even that.'

'Ah,' said Foxton. 'The usual thing. You must tell us about that later. Now we'd better go up and see the patient – at least the – er – perhaps you'll show us the room, Mrs Beddingfield.'

The landlady turned and preceded us up the stairs to the first-floor back, where she paused, and softly opening a door, peered nervously into the room. As we stepped past her and entered, she seemed inclined to follow, but, at a significant glance from me, Foxton persuasively ejected her and closed the door. Then we stood silent for a while and looked about us.

In the aspect of the room there was something strangely incongruous with the tragedy that had been enacted within its walls; a mingling of the commonplace and the terrible that almost amounted to anticlimax. Through the wide-open window the bright spring sunshine streamed in on the garish wallpaper and cheap furniture; from the street below, the periodic shouts of a man selling 'sole and mackro!' broke into the brisk staccato of a barrel-organ and both sounds mingled with a raucous voice close at hand, cheerfully trolling a popular song, and accounted for by a linen-clad elbow that bobbed in front of the window and evidently appertained to a housepainter on an adjacent ladder.

It was all very commonplace and familiar and discordantly out of character with the stark figure that lay on the bed like a waxen effigy symbolic of tragedy. Here was none of that gracious somnolence in which death often presents itself with a suggestion of eternal repose. This woman was dead; horribly, aggressively dead. The thin, sallow face was rigid as stone, the dark eyes stared into infinite space with a horrid fixity that was quite disturbing to look on. And yet the posture of the corpse was not uneasy, being, in fact, rather curiously symmetrical, with both arms outside the bedclothes and both hands closed, the right grasping, as Mrs Beddingfield had said, an empty bottle.

'Well,' said Foxton, as he stood looking down on the dead woman, 'it seems a pretty clear case. She appears to have laid herself out and kept hold of the bottle so that there should be no mistake. How long do you suppose this woman has been dead, Jervis?'

I felt the rigid limbs and tested the temperature of the body surface.

'Not less than six hours,' I replied. 'Probably more. I should say that she died about two o'clock this morning.'

'And that is about all we can say,' said Foxton, 'until the post-mortem has been made. Everything looks quite straightforward. No signs of a struggle or marks of violence. That blood on the mouth is probably due to her biting her lip when she drank from the bottle. Yes; here's a little cut on the inside of the lip, corresponding to the upper incisors. By the way, I wonder if there is anything left in the bottle.'

As he spoke, he drew the small, unlabelled, green glass phial from the closed hand – out of which it slipped quite easily – and held it up to the light.

'Yes,' he exclaimed, 'there's more than a drachm left; quite enough for an analysis. But I don't recognise the smell. Do you?'

I sniffed at the bottle and was aware of a faint unfamiliar vegetable odour.

'No,' I answered. 'It appears to be a watery solution of some kind, but I can't give it a name. Where is the cork?'

'I haven't seen it,' he replied. 'Probably it is on the floor somewhere.'

We both stooped to look for the missing cork and presently found it in the shadow, under the little bedside table. But, in the course of that brief search, I found something else, which had indeed been lying in full view all the time – a wax match. Now a wax match is a perfectly innocent and very commonplace object, but yet the presence of this one gave me pause. In the first place, women do not, as a rule, use wax matches, though there was not much in that. What was more to the point was that the candlestick by the bedside contained a box of safety matches, and that, as the burnt remains of one lay in the tray, it appeared to have been used to light the candle. Then why the wax match?

While I was turning over this problem Foxton had corked the bottle, wrapped it carefully in a piece of paper which he took from the dressing-table and bestowed it in his pocket.

'Well, Jervis,' said he, 'I think we've seen everything. The analysis and the post-mortem will complete the case. Shall we go down and hear what Mrs Beddingfield has to say?'

But that wax match, slight as was its significance, taken alone, had presented itself to me as the last of a succession of phenomena each of which was susceptible of a sinister interpretation; and the cumulative effect of these slight suggestions began to impress me somewhat strongly.

'One moment, Foxton,' said I. 'Don't let us take anything for granted. We are here to collect evidence, and we must go warily. There is such a thing as homicidal poisoning, you know.'

'Yes, of course,' he replied, 'but there is nothing to suggest it in this case; at least, I see nothing. Do you?'

'Nothing very positive,' said I; 'but there are some facts that seem to call for consideration. Let us go over what we have seen. In the first place, there is a distinct discrepancy in the appearance of the body. The general easy, symmetrical posture, like that of a figure on a tomb, suggests the effect of a slow, painless poison. But look at the face. There is nothing reposeful about that. It is very strongly suggestive of pain or terror or both.'

'Yes,' said Foxton, 'that is so. But you can't draw any satisfactory conclusions from the facial expression of dead bodies. Why, men who have been hanged, or even, stabbed, often look as peaceful as babes.'

'Still,' I said, 'it is a fact to be noted. Then there is that cut on the lip. It may have been produced in the way you suggest; but it may equally well he the result of pressure on the mouth.'

Foxton made no comment on this beyond a slight shrug of the shoulders, and I continued:

'Then there is the state of the hand. It was closed, but, it did not really grasp the object it contained. You drew the bottle out without any resistance. It simply lay in the closed hand. But that is not a normal state of affairs. As you know, when a person dies grasping any object, either the hand relaxes and lets it drop, or the muscular action passes into cadaveric spasm and grasps the object firmly. And lastly, there is this wax match. Where did it come from? The dead woman apparently lit her candle with a safety match from the box. It is a small matter, but it wants explaining.'

Foxton raised his eyebrows protestingly. 'You're like all specialists, Jervis,' said he. 'You see your speciality in everything. And while you are straining these flimsy suggestions to turn a simple suicide into murder, you ignore the really conclusive fact that the door was bolted and had to be broken open before anyone could get in.'

'You are not forgetting, I suppose,' said I, 'that the window was wide open and that there were housepainters about and possibly a ladder left standing against the house.'

'As to the ladder,' said Foxton, 'that is a pure assumption; but we can easily settle the question by asking that fellow out there if it was or was not left standing last night.'

Simultaneously we moved towards the window; but halfway we both stopped short. For the question of the ladder had in a moment become negligible. Staring up at us from the dull red linoleum which covered the floor were the impressions of a pair of bare feet, imprinted in white paint with the distinctness of a woodcut. There was no need to ask if they had been made by the dead woman: they were unmistakably the feet of a man, and large feet at that. Nor could there be any doubt as to whence those feet had come. Beginning with startling distinctness under the window, the tracks shed rapidly in intensity until they reached the carpeted portion of the room, where they vanished abruptly; and only by the closest scrutiny was it possible to detect the faint traces of the retiring tracks.

Foxton and I stood for some moments gazing in, silence at the sinister white shapes; then we looked at one another.

'You've saved me from a most horrible blunder, Jervis,' said Foxton. 'Ladder or no ladder, that fellow came in at the window; and he came in last night, for I saw them painting these windowsills yesterday afternoon. Which side did he come from, I wonder?'

We moved to the window and looked out on the sill. A set of distinct, though smeared impressions on the new paint gave unneeded confirmation and showed that the intruder had approached from the left side, close to which was a cast-iron stack-pipe, now covered with fresh green paint.

'So,' said Foxton, 'the presence or absence of the ladder is of no significance. The man got into the window somehow, and that's all that matters.'

'On the contrary,' said I, 'the point may be of considerable importance in identification. It isn't everyone who could climb up a stack-pipe, whereas most people could make shift to climb a ladder, even if it were guarded by a plank. But the fact that the man took off his boots and socks suggests that he came up by the pipe. If he had merely aimed at silencing his footfalls, he would probably have removed his boots only.'

From the window we turned to examine more closely the foot-prints on the floor, and while I took a series of measurements with my spring tape Foxton entered them in my notebook.

'Doesn't it strike you as rather odd, Jervis,' said he, 'that neither of the little toes has made any mark?'

'It does indeed,' I replied. 'The appearances suggest that the little toes were absent, but I have never met with such a condition. Have you?'

'Never. Of course one is acquainted with the supernumerary toe deformity, but I have never heard of congenitally deficient little toes.'

Once more we scrutinised the footprints, and even examined those on the windowsill, obscurely marked on the fresh paint; but, exquisitely distinct as were those on the linoleum, showing every wrinkle and minute skin-marking, not the faintest hint of a little toe was to be seen on either foot.

'It's very extraordinary,' said Foxton. 'He has certainly lost his little toes, if he ever had any. They couldn't have failed to make some mark. But it's a queer affair. Quite a windfall for the police, by the way; I mean for purposes of identification.'

'Yes,' I agreed, 'and having regard to the importance of the foot-prints, I think it would be wise to get a photograph of them.'

'Oh, the police will see to that,' said Foxton. 'Besides, we haven't got a camera, unless you thought of using that little toy snapshotter of yours.'

As Foxton was no photographer I did not trouble him that my camera, though small, had been specially made for scientific purposes.

'Any photograph is better than none,' I said, and with this I opened the tripod and set it over one of the most distinct of the foot-prints, screwed the camera to the gooseneck, carefully framed the footprint in the finder and adjusted the focus, finally making the exposure by means of an antinous release. This process I repeated four times, twice on a right footprint and twice on a left.

'Well,' Foxton remarked, 'with all those photographs the police ought to be able to pick up the scent.'

'Yes, they've got something to go on; but they'll have to catch their hare before they can cook him. He won't be walking about barefooted, you know.'

'No. It's a poor clue in that respect. And now we may as well be off as we've seen all there is to see. I think we won't have much to say to Mrs Beddingfield. This is a police case, and the less I'm mixed up in it the better it will be for my practice.'

I was faintly amused at Foxton's caution when considered by the light of his utterances at the breakfast-table. Apparently his appetite for mystery and romance was easily satisfied. But that was no affair of mine. I waited on the doorstep while he said a few – probably evasive – words to the landlady and then, as we started off together in the direction of the police station, I began to turn over in my mind the salient features of the case. For some time we walked on in silence, and must have been pursuing a parallel train of thought for, when he at length spoke, he almost put my reflections into words.

'You know, Jervis,' said he, 'there ought to be a clue in those footprints. I realise that you can't tell how many toes a man has by looking at his booted feet. But those unusual footprints ought to give an expert a hint as to what sort of man to look for. Don't they convey any hint to you?'

I felt that Foxton was right; that if my brilliant colleague, Thorndyke, had been in my place he would have extracted from those footprints some leading fact that would have given the police a start along some definite line of inquiry; and that belief, coupled with Foxton's challenge, put me on my mettle.

'They offer no particular suggestions to me at this moment,' said I, 'but I think that, if we consider them systematically, we may be able to draw some useful deductions.'

'Very well,' said Foxton, 'then let us consider them systematically. Fire away. I should like to hear how you work these things out.'

Foxton's frankly spectatorial attitude was a little disconcerting, especially as it seemed to commit me to a result that I was by no means confident of attaining. I therefore began a little diffidently.

'We are assuming that both the feet that made those prints were from some cause devoid of little toes. That assumption – which is almost certainly correct – we treat as a fact, and, taking it as our starting point, the first step in the inquiry is to find some explanation of it. Now there are three possibilities, and only three: deformity, injury, and disease. The toes may have been absent from birth, they may have been lost as a result of mechanical injury, or they may have been lost by disease. Let us take those possibilities in order.

'Deformity we exclude since such a malformation is unknown to us.

'Mechanical injury seems to be excluded by the fact that the two little toes are on opposite sides of the body and could not conceivably be affected by any violence which left the intervening feet uninjured. This seems to narrow the possibilities down to disease; and the question that arises is, What diseases are there which might result in the loss of both little toes?'

I looked inquiringly at Foxton, but he merely nodded encouragingly. His rôle was that of listener.

'Well,' I pursued, 'the loss of both toes seems to exclude local disease, just as it excluded local injury; and as to general diseases, I can think only of three which might produce this condition – Raynaud's disease, ergotism, and frost-bite.'

'You don't call frost-bite a general disease, do you?' objected Foxton.

'For our present purpose, I do. The effects are local, but the cause – low external temperature – affects the whole body and is a general cause. Well, now, taking the diseases in order. I think we can exclude Raynaud's disease. It does, it is true, occasionally cause the fingers or toes to die and drop off, and the little toes would be especially liable to be affected as being most remote from the heart. But in such a severe case the other toes would be affected. They would be shrivelled and tapered, whereas, if you remember, the toes of these feet were quite plump and full, to judge by the large impressions they made. So I think we may safely reject Raynaud's disease. There remain ergotism and frost-bite; and the choice between them is just a question of relative frequency. Frost-bite is more common; therefore frost-bite is more probable.'

'Do they tend equally to affect the little toes?' asked Foxton.

'As a matter of probability, yes. The poison of ergot acting from within, and intense cold acting from without, contract the small blood-vessels and arrest, the circulation. The feet, being the most distant parts of the body from the heart, are the first to feel the effects; and the little toes, which are the most distant parts of the feet, are the most susceptible of all.'

Foxton reflected awhile, and then remarked: 'This is all very well, Jervis, but I don't see that you are much forwarder. This man has lost both his little toes and on your showing, the probabilities are that the loss was due either to chronic ergot poisoning or to frost-bite, with a balance of probability in favour of frost-bite. That's all. No proof, no verification, just the law of probability applied to a particular case, which is always unsatisfactory. He may have lost his toes in some totally different way. But even if the probabilities work out correctly, I don't see what use your conclusions would be to the police. They wouldn't tell them what sort of man to look for.'

There was a good deal of truth in Foxton's objection. A man who has suffered from ergotism or frost-bite is not externally different from any other man. Still, we had not exhausted the case, as I ventured to point out.

'Don't be premature, Foxton,' said I. 'Let us pursue our argument a little farther. We have established a probability that this unknown man has suffered either from ergotism or frost-bite. That, as you say, is of no use by itself; but supposing we can show that these conditions tend to affect a particular class of persons, we shall have established a fact that will indicate a line of investigation. And I think we can. Let us take the case of ergotism first.

'Now how is chronic ergot poisoning caused? Not by the medicinal use of the drug, but, by the consumption of the diseased rye in which ergot occurs. It is therefore peculiar to countries in which rye is used extensively as food. Those countries, broadly speaking, are the countries of North-Eastern Europe, and especially Russia and Poland.

'Then take the case of frost-bite. Obviously, the most likely person to get frost-bitten is the inhabitant of a country with a cold climate. The most rigourous climates inhabited by white people are North America and North-Eastern Europe, especially Russia and Poland. So you see, the areas associated with ergotism and frost-bite overlap to some extent. In fact they do more thin overlap; for a person even slightly affected by ergot would be specially liable to frost-bite, owing to the impaired circulation. The conclusion is that, racially, in both ergotism and frost-bite, the balance of probability is in favour of a Russian, a Pole, or a Scandinavian.

'Then in the case of frost-bite there is the occupation factor. What class of men tend most to become frost-bitten? Well, beyond all doubt, the greatest sufferers from frost-bite are sailors, especially those on sailing ships, and, naturally, on ships trading to Arctic and sub-Arctic countries. But the bulk of such sailing ships are those engaged in the Baltic and Archangel trade; and the crews of those ships are almost exclusively Scandinavians, Finns, Russians and Poles. So that, again, the probabilities point to a native of North-Eastern Europe, and, taken as a whole, by the overlapping of factors, to a Russian, a Pole, or a Scandinavian.'

Foxton smiled sardonically. 'Very ingenious, Jervis,' said he. 'Most ingenious. As an academic statement of probabilities, quite excellent. But for practical purposes absolutely useless. However, here we are at the police-station. I'll just run in and give them the facts and then go on to the coroner's office.'

'I suppose I'd better not come in with you?' I said.

'Well, no,' he replied. 'You see, you have no official connection with the case, and they mightn't like it. You'd better go and amuse yourself while I get the morning's visits done. We can talk things over at lunch.'

With this he disappeared into the police-station, and I turned away with a smile of grim amusement. Experience is apt to make us a trifle uncharitable, and experience had taught me that those who are the most scornful of academic reasoning are often not above retailing it with some reticence as to its original authorship. I had a shrewd suspicion that Foxton was at this very moment disgorging my despised 'academic statement of probabilities' to an admiring police-inspector.

My way towards the sea lay through Ethelred Road, and I had traversed about half its length and was approaching the house of the tragedy when I observed Mrs Beddingfield at the bay window. Evidently she recognised me, for a few moments later she appeared in outdoor clothes on the doorstep and advanced to meet me.

'Have you seen the police?' she asked, as we met.

I replied that Dr Foxton was even now at the police-station.

'Ah!' she said, 'it's a dreadful affair; most unfortunate, too, just at the beginning of the season. A scandal is absolute ruin to a boarding-house. What do you think of the case? Will it be possible to hush it up? Dr Foxton said you were a lawyer, I think, Dr Jervis?'

'Yes, I am a lawyer, but really I know nothing of the circumstances of this case. Did I understand that there had been something in the nature of a love affair?'

'Yes – at least – well, perhaps I oughtn't to have said that. But hadn't I better tell you the whole story? – that is, if I am not taking up too much of your time.'

'I should be interested to hear what led to the disaster,' said I.

'Then,' she said, 'I will tell you all about it. Will you come indoors, or shall I walk a little way with you?'

As I suspected that the police were at that moment on their way to the house, I chose the latter alternative and led her away seawards at a pretty brisk pace.

'Was this poor lady a widow?' I asked, as we started up the street.

'No, she wasn't,' replied Mrs Beddingfield, 'and that was the trouble. Her husband was abroad – at least, he had been, and he was just coming home. A pretty homecoming it will be for him, poor man. He is an officer in the Civil Police at Sierra Leone, but he hasn't been there long. He went there for his health.'

'What! To Sierra Leone!' I exclaimed, for the 'White Man's Grave' seemed a queer health resort.

'Yes. You see, Mr Toussaint is a French Canadian, and it seems that he has always been somewhat of a rolling stone. For some time he was in the Klondyke, but he suffered so much from the cold that he had to come away. It injured his health very severely; I don't quite know in what way, but I do know that he was quite a cripple for a time. When he got better he looked out for a post in a warm climate and eventually obtained the appointment of Inspector of Civil Police at Sierra Leone. That was about ten months ago, and when he sailed for Africa his wife came to stay with me, and has been here ever since.'

'And this love affair that you spoke of?'

'Yes, but I oughtn't to have called it that. Let me explain what happened. About three months ago a Swedish gentleman – a Mr Bergson – came to stay here, and he seemed to be very much smitten with Mrs Toussaint.'

'And she?'

'Oh, she liked him well enough. He is a tall, good-looking man – though for that matter he is no taller than her husband, nor any better-looking. Both men are over six feet. But there was no harm so far as she was concerned, excepting that she didn't see the position quite soon enough. She wasn't very discreet, in fact I thought it necessary to give her a little advice. However, Mr Bergson left here and went to live at Ramsgate to superintend the unloading of the ice-ships (he came from Sweden in one), and I thought the trouble was at an end. But it wasn't, for he took to coming over to see Mrs Toussaint, and of course I couldn't have that. So at last I had to tell him that he mustn't come to the house again. It was very unfortunate, for on that occasion I think he had been "tasting", as they say in Scotland. He wasn't drunk, but he was excitable and noisy, and when I told him he mustn't come again he made such a disturbance that two of the gentlemen boarders – Mr Wardale and Mr Macauley – had to interfere. And then he was most insulting to them, especially to Mr Macauley, who is a coloured gentleman; called him a "buck nigger" and all sorts of offensive names.'

'And how did the coloured gentleman take it?'

'Not very well, I am sorry to say, considering that he is a gentleman – a law student with chambers in the Temple. In fact, his language was so objectionable that Mr Wardale insisted on my giving him notice on the spot. But I managed to get him taken in next door but one; you see, Mr Wardale had been a Commissioner at, Sierra Leone – it was through him that Mr Toussaint got his appointment – so I suppose he was rather on his dignity with coloured people.'

'And was that the last you heard of Mr Bergson?'

'He never came here again, but he wrote several times to Mrs Toussaint, asking her to meet him. At last, only a few days ago, she wrote to him and told him that the acquaintance must cease.'

'And has it ceased?'

'As far as I know, it has.'

'Then, Mrs Beddingfield,' said I, 'what makes you connect the affair with-with what has happened?'

'Well, you see,' she explained, 'there is the husband. He was coming home, and is probably in England already.'

'Indeed!' said I.

'Yes,' she continued. 'He went up into the bush to arrest some natives belonging to one of these gangs of murderers – Leopard Societies, I think they are called – and he got seriously wounded. He wrote to his wife from hospital saying that he would be sent home as soon as he was fit to travel, and about ten days ago she got a letter from him saying that he was coming by the next ship.

'I noticed that she seemed very nervous and upset when she got the letters from hospital, and still more so when the last letter came. Of course, I don't know what he said to her in those letters. It may be that he had heard something about Mr Bergson, and threatened to take some action. Of course, I can't say. I only know that she was very nervous and restless, and when we saw in the paper four days ago that the ship he would be coming by had arrived in Liverpool she seemed dreadfully upset. And she got worse and worse until – well, until last night.'

'Has anything been heard of the husband since the ship arrived?' I asked.

'Nothing whatever,' replied Mrs Beddingfield, with a meaning look at me which I had no difficulty in interpreting. 'No letter, no telegram, not a word. And you see, if he hadn't come by that ship he would almost certainly have sent a letter to her. He must have arrived in England, but why hasn't he turned up, or at least sent a wire? What is he doing? Why is be staying away? Can he have heard something? And what does he mean to do? That's what kept the poor thing on wires, and that, I feel certain, is what drove her to make away with herself.'

It was not my business to contest Mrs Beddingfield's erroneous deductions. I was seeking information – it seemed that I had nearly exhausted the present source. But one point required amplifying.

'To return to Mr Bergson, Mrs Beddingfield,' said I. 'Do I understand that he is a seafaring man?'

'He was,' she replied. 'At present he is settled at Ramsgate as manager of a company in the ice trade, but formerly he was a sailor. I have heard him say that he was one, of the crew of an exploring ship that went in search of the North Pole and that he was locked up in the ice for months and months. I should have thought he would have had enough of ice after that.'

With this view I expressed warm agreement, and having now obtained all the information that appeared to be available I proceeded to bring the interview to an end.

'Well, Mrs Beddingfield,' I said, 'it is a rather mysterious affair. Perhaps more light may be thrown on it at the inquest. Meanwhile, I should think that it will be wise of you to keep your own counsel as far as outsiders are concerned.'

The remainder of the morning I spent pacing the smooth stretch of sand that lies to the east of the jetty, and reflecting on the evidence that I had acquired in respect of this singular crime. Evidently there was no lack of clues in this case. On the contrary, there were two quite obvious lines of inquiry, for both the Swede and the missing husband presented the characters of the hypothetical murderer. Both had been exposed to the conditions which tend to produce frost-bite; one of them had probably been a consumer of rye meal, and both might be said to have a motive – though, to be sure, it was a very insufficient one – for committing the crime. Still in both cases the evidence was merely speculative; it suggested a line of investigation but it did nothing more.

When I met Foxton at lunch I was sensible of a curious change in his manner. His previous expansiveness had given place to marked reticence and a certain official secretiveness.

'I don't think, you know, Jervis,' he said, when I opened the subject, 'that we had better discuss this affair. You see, I am the principal witness, and while the case is sub judice – well, in fact the police don't want the case talked about.'

'But surely I am a witness, too, and an expert witness, moreover—'

'That isn't the view of the police. They look on you as more or less of an amateur, and as you have no official connection with the case, I don't think they propose to subpoena you. Superintendent Platt, who is in charge of the case, wasn't very pleased at my having taken you to the house. Said it was quite irregular. Oh, and by the way, he says you must hand over those photographs.'

'But isn't Platt going to have the footprints photographed on his own account?' I objected.

'Of course he is. He is going to have a set of proper photographs taken by an expert photographer – he was mightily amused when he heard about your little snapshot affair. Oh, you can trust Platt. He is a great man. He has had a course of instruction at the Fingerprint Department in London.'

'I don't see how that is going to help him, as there aren't any fingerprints in this case.'

This was a mere fly-cast on my part, but Foxton rose at once at the rather clumsy bait.

'Oh, aren't there?' he exclaimed. 'You didn't happen to spot them, but they were there. Platt has got the prints of a complete right hand. This is in strict confidence, you know,' he added, with somewhat belated caution.

Foxton's sudden reticence restrained me from uttering the obvious comment on the superintendent's achievement. I returned to the subject of the photographs.

'Supposing I decline to hand over my film?' said I.

'But I hope you won't – and in fact you mustn't. I am officially connected with the case, and I've got to live with these people. As the police-surgeon, I am responsible for the medical evidence, and Platt expects me to get those photographs from you. Obviously you can't keep them. It would be most irregular.'

It was useless to argue. Evidently the police did not want me to be introduced into the case, and after all the superintendent was within his rights, if he chose to regard me, as a private individual and to demand the surrender of the film.

Nevertheless I was loth to give up the photographs, at least until I had carefully studied them. The, case was within my own speciality of practice, and was a strange and interesting one. Moreover, it appeared to be in unskilful hands, judging from the fingerprint episode, and then experience had taught me to treasure up small scraps of chance evidence, since one never knew when one might be drawn into a case in a professional capacity. In effect, I decided not to give up the photographs, though that decision committed me to a ruse that I was not very willing to adopt. I would rather have acted quite straightforwardly.

'Well if you insist, Foxton,' I said, 'I will hand over the film or, if you like, I will destroy it in your presence.'

'I think Platt would rather have the film uninjured,' said Foxton. 'Then he'll know, you know,' he added, with a sly grin.

In my heart, I thanked Foxton for that grin. It made my own guileful proceedings so much easier; for a suspicious man invites you to get the better of him if you can.

After lunch I went up to my room, locked the door and took the little camera from my pocket. Having fully wound up the film, I extracted it, wrapped it up carefully and bestowed it in my inside breast-pocket. Then I inserted a fresh film, and going to the open window, took four successive snapshots of the sky. This done, I closed the camera, slipped it into my pocket and went downstairs. Foxton was in the hall, brushing his hat, as I descended, and at once renewed his demand.

'About those photographs, Jervis,' said he; 'I shall be looking in at the police-station presently, so if you wouldn't mind—'

'To be sure,' said I. 'I will give you the film now if you like.'

Taking the camera from my pocket, I solemnly wound up the remainder of the film, extracted it, stuck down the loose end with ostentatious care, and handed it to him.

'Better not expose it to the light,' I said, going the whole hog of deception, 'or you may fog the exposures.'

Foxton took the spool from me as if it were hot – he was not a photographer – and thrust it into his handbag. He was still thanking me quite profusely when the front-door bell rang. The visitor who stood revealed when Foxton opened door was a small, spare gentleman with a complexion of peculiar brown-papery quality that suggests long residence the tropics. He stepped in briskly and introduced him and his business without preamble.

'My name is Wardale – boarder at Beddingfield's. I called with reference to the tragic event which—'

Here Foxton interposed in his frostiest official tone. 'I am afraid, Mr Wardale, I can't give you any information about the case at present.'

'I saw you two gentlemen at the house this morning' Mr Wardale continued, but Foxton again cut him short.

'You did. We were there – or at least, I was – as representative of the Law, and while the case is sub judice—'

'It isn't yet,' interrupted Wardale.

'Well, I can't enter into any discussion of it—'

'I am not asking you to,' said Wardale a little impatiently. 'But I understand that one of you is Dr Jervis.'

'I am,' said I.

'I must really warn you—' Foxton began again; but Mr Wardale interrupted testily: 'My dear sir, I am a lawyer and a magistrate and understand perfectly well what is and what is not permissible. I have come simply to make a professional engagement with Dr Jervis.'

'In what way can I be of service to you,' I asked.

'I will tell you,' said Mr Wardale. 'This poor lady, whose death has occurred in so mysterious a manner, was the wife of a man who was, like myself, a servant of the Government of Sierra Leone. I was the friend of both of them, and in the absence of the husband I should like to have the inquiry into the circumstances of this lady's death watched by a competent lawyer with the necessary special knowledge of medical evidence. Will you or your colleague, Dr Thorndyke, undertake to watch the case for me?'

Of course I was willing to undertake the case and said so.

'Then,' said Mr Wardale, 'I will instruct my solicitor to write to you and formally retain you in the case. Here is my card. You will find my name in the Colonial Office List, and you know my address here.'

He handed me his card, wished us both good afternoon, and then, with a stiff little bow, turned and took his departure.

'I think I had better run up to town and confer with Thorndyke,' said I. 'How do the trains run?'

'There is a good train in about three-quarters of an hour,' replied Foxton.

'Then I will go by it, but I shall come down again tomorrow or the next day, and probably Thorndyke will come down with me.'

'Very well,' said Foxton. 'Bring him in to lunch or dinner, but I can't put him up, I am afraid.'

'It would be better not,' said I. 'Your friend Platt wouldn't like it. He won't want Thorndyke – or me either for that matter. And what about those photographs, Thorndyke will want them, you know.'

'He can't have them,' said Foxton doggedly, 'unless Platt is willing to hand them back; which I don't suppose he will be.'

I had private reasons for thinking otherwise, but I kept them to myself; and as Foxton went forth on his afternoon round, I returned upstairs to pack my suitcase and write the telegram to Thorndyke informing him of my movements.

It was only a quarter past five when I let myself into our chambers in King's Bench Walk. To my relief I found my colleague at home and our laboratory assistant, Polton, in the act of laying tea, for two.

'I gather,' said Thorndyke, as we shook hands, 'that my learned brother brings grist to the mill?'

'Yes,' I replied. 'Nominally a watching brief, but I think you will agree with me that it is a case for independent investigation.'

'Will there be anything in my line, sir?' inquired Polton, who was always agog at the word 'investigation'.

'There is a film to be developed. Four exposures of white footprints on a dark ground.'

'Ah!' said Polton, 'you'll want good strong negatives, and they ought to be enlarged if they are from the little camera. Can you give me the dimensions?'

I wrote out the measurements from my notebook and handed him the paper together with the spool of film, with which he retired gleefully to the laboratory.

'And now, Jervis,' said Thorndyke, 'while Polton is operating on the film and we are discussing our tea, let us have a sketch of the case.'

I gave him more than a sketch, for the events were recent and I had carefully sorted out the facts during my journey to town, making rough notes, which I now consulted. To my rather lengthy recital he listened in his usual attentive manner, without any comment, excepting in regard to my manoeuvre to retain possession of the exposed film.

'It's almost a pity you didn't refuse,' said he. 'They could hardly have enforced their demand, and my feeling is that it is more convenient as well as more dignified to avoid direct deception unless one is driven to it. But perhaps you considered that you were.'

As a matter of fact I had at the time, but I had since come to Thorndyke's opinion. My little manoeuvre was going to be a source of inconvenience presently.

'Well,' said Thorndyke, when I had finished my recital, 'I think we may take it that the police theory is, in the main, your own theory derived from Foxton.'

'I think so, excepting that I learned from Foxton that Superintendent Platt has obtained the complete fingerprints of a right hand.'

Thorndyke raised his eyebrows. 'Fingerprints!' he exclaimed. 'Why, the fellow must be a mere simpleton. But there,' he added, 'everybody – police, lawyers, judges, even Galton himself – seems to lose every vestige of common sense as soon as the subject of fingerprints is raised. But it would be interesting to know how he got them and what they are like. We must try to find that out. However, to return to your case, since your theory and the police theory are probably the same, we may as well consider the value of your inferences.

'At present we are dealing with the case in the abstract. Our data are largely assumptions, and our inferences are largely derived from an application of the mathematical laws of probability. Thus we assume that a murder has been committed, whereas it may turn out to have been suicide. We assume the murder to have been committed by the person who made the footprints, and we assume that that person has no little toes, whereas he may have retracted little toes which do not touch the ground and so leave no impression. Assuming the little toes to be absent, we account for their absence by considering known causes in the order of their probability. Excluding – quite properly, I think – Raynaud's disease, we arrive at frost-bite and ergotism.

'But two persons, both of whom are of a stature corresponding to the size of the footprints, may have had a motive though a very inadequate one – for committing the crime, and both have been exposed to the conditions which tend to produce frost-bite, while one of them has probably, been exposed to the conditions which tend to produce ergotism. The laws of probability point to both of these two men; and the chances in favour of the Swede being the murderer rather than the Canadian would be represented by the common factor – frost-bite – multiplied by the additional factor, ergotism. But this is purely speculative at present. There is no evidence that either man has ever been frost-bitten or has ever eaten spurred rye. Nevertheless, it is a perfectly sound method at this stage. It indicates a line of investigation. If it should transpire that either man has suffered from frost-bite or ergotism, a definite advance would have been made. But here is Polton with a couple of finished prints. How on earth did you manage it in the time, Polton?'

'Why, you see, sir, I just dried the film with spirit,' replied Polton. 'It saved a lot of time. I will let you have a pair of enlargements in about a quarter of an hour.'

Handing us the two wet prints, each stuck on a glass plate, he retired to the laboratory, and Thorndyke and I proceeded to scrutinise the photographs with the aid of our pocket lenses. The promised enlargements were really hardly necessary excepting for the purpose of comparative measurements, for the image of the white footprint, fully two inches long, was so microscopically sharp that, with the assistance of the lens, the minutest detail could be clearly seen.

'There is certainly not a vestige of little toe,' remarked Thorndyke, 'and the plump appearance of the other toes supports your rejection of Raynaud's disease. Does the character of the footprint convey any other suggestion to you, Jervis?'

'It gives me the impression that the man had been accustomed to go barefooted in early life and had only taken to boots comparatively recently. The position of the great toe suggests this, and the presence of a number of small scars on the toes and ball of the foot seems to confirm it. A person walking barefoot would sustain innumerable small wounds from treading on small, sharp objects.'

Thorndyke looked dissatisfied. 'I agree with you,' he said, 'as to the suggestion offered by the undeformed state of the great toes; but those little pits do not convey to me the impression of scars produced as you suggest. Still, you may be right.'

Here our conversation was interrupted by a knock on the outer oak. Thorndyke stepped out through the lobby and I heard him answer it. A moment or so later he re-entered, accompanied by a short, brown-faced gentleman whom I instantly recognised as Mr Wardale.

'I must have come up by the same train as you,' he remarked, as we shook hands, 'and to a certain extent, I suspect, on the same errand. I thought I would like to put our arrangement on a business footing, as I am a stranger to both of you.'

'What do you want us to do?' asked Thorndyke.

'I want you to watch the case, and, if necessary, to look into the facts independently.'

'Can you give us any information that may help us?'

Mr Wardale reflected. 'I don't think I can,' he said at length. 'I have no facts that you have not, and any surmises of mine might be misleading. I had rather you kept an open mind. But perhaps we might go into the question of costs.'

This, of course, was somewhat difficult, but Thorndyke contrived to indicate the probable liabilities involved, to Mr Wardale's satisfaction.

'There is one other little matter,' said Wardale, as he rose to depart. 'I have got a suitcase here which Mrs Beddingfield lent me to bring some things up to town. It is one that Mr Macauley left behind when he went away from the boarding-house. Mrs Beddingfield suggested that I might leave it at his chambers when I had finished with it; but I don't know his address, excepting that it is somewhere in the Temple, and I don't want to meet the fellow if he should happen to have come up to town.'

'Is it empty?' asked Thorndyke.

'Excepting for a suit of pyjamas and a pair of shocking old slippers.' He opened the suitcase as he spoke and exhibited its contents with a grin.

'Characteristic of a negro, isn't it? Pink silk pyjamas and slippers about three sizes too small.'

'Very well,' said Thorndyke. 'I will get my man to find out the address and leave it there.'

As Mr Wardale went out, Polton entered with the enlarged photographs, which showed the footprints the natural size. Thorndyke handed them to me, and as I sat down to examine them he followed his assistant to the laboratory. He returned in a few minutes, and after a brief inspection of the photographs, remarked:

'They show us nothing more than we have seen, though they may be useful later. So your stock of facts is all we have to go on at present. Are you going home tonight?'

'Yes, I shall go back to Margate tomorrow.'

'Then, as I have to call at Scotland Yard, we may as well walk to Charing Cross together.'

As we walked down the Strand we gossiped on general topics, but before we separated at Charing Cross, Thorndyke reverted to the case.

'Let me know the date of the inquest,' said he, 'and try to find out what the poison was – if it was really a poison.'

'The liquid that was left in the bottle seemed to be a watery solution of some kind,' said I, 'as I think I mentioned.'

'Yes,' said Thorndyke. 'Possibly a watery infusion of strophanthus.'

'Why strophanthus?' I asked.

'Why not?' demanded Thorndyke. And with this and an inscrutable smile, he turned and walked down Whitehall.

Three days later I found myself at Margate – sitting beside Thorndyke in a room adjoining the Town Hall, in which the inquest on the death of Mrs Toussaint was to be held. Already the coroner was in his chair, the jury were in their seats and the witnesses assembled in a group of chairs apart. These included Foxton, a stranger who sat by him – presumably the other medical witness – Mrs Beddingfield, Mr Wardale, the police superintendent and a well-dressed coloured man, whom I correctly assumed to be Mr Macauley.

As I sat by my-rather sphinx-like colleague my mind recurred for the hundredth time to his extraordinary powers of mental synthesis.

That parting remark of his as to the possible nature of the poison had brought home to me in a flash the fact that he already had a definite theory of this crime, and that his theory was not mine nor that of the police. True, the poison might not be strophanthus, after all, but that would not alter the position. He had a theory of the crime, but yet he was in possession of no facts excepting those with which I had supplied him. Therefore those facts contained the material for a theory, whereas I had deduced from them nothing but the bald, ambiguous mathematical probabilities.

The first witness called was naturally Dr Foxton, who described the circumstances already known to me. He further stated that he had been present at the autopsy, that he had found on the throat and limbs of the deceased bruises that suggested a struggle and violent restraint. The immediate cause of death was heart failure, but whether that failure was due to shock, terror, or the action of a poison he could not positively say.

The next witness was a Dr Prescott, an expert pathologist and toxicologist. He had made the autopsy and agreed with Dr Foxton as to the cause of death. He had examined the liquid contained in the bottle taken from the hand of the deceased and found it to be a watery infusion or decoction of strophanthus seeds. He had analysed the fluid contained in the stomach and found it to consist largely of the same infusion.

'Is infusion of strophanthus seeds used in medicine?' the coroner asked.

'No,' was the reply. 'The tincture is the form in which strophanthus is administered unless it is given in the form of strophanthine.'

'Do you consider that the strophanthus caused or contributed to death?'

'It is difficult to say,' replied Dr Prescott. 'Strophanthus is a heart poison, and there was a very large poisonous dose. But very little had been absorbed, and the appearances were not inconsistent with death from shock.'

'Could death have been self-produced by the voluntary taking of the poison?' asked the coroner.

'I should say, decidedly not. Dr Foxton's evidence shows that the bottle was almost certainly placed in the hands of the deceased after death, and this is in complete agreement with the enormous dose and small absorption.'

'Would you say that appearances point to suicidal or homicidal poisoning?'

'I should say that they point to homicidal poisoning, but that death was probably due mainly to shock.'

This concluded the expert's evidence. It was followed by that of Mrs Beddingfield, which brought out nothing new to me but the fact that a trunk had been broken open and a small attaché-case belonging to the deceased abstracted and taken away.

'Do you know what the deceased kept in that case?' the coroner asked.

'I have seen her put her husband's letters into it. She had quite a number of them. I don't know what else she kept in it except, of course, her chequebook.'

'Had she any considerable balance at the bank?'

'I believe she had. Her husband used to send most of his pay home and she used to pay it in and leave it with the bank. She might have two or three hundred pounds to her credit.'

As Mrs Beddingfield concluded Mr Wardale was called, and he was followed by Mr Macauley. The evidence of both was quite brief and concerned entirely with the disturbance made by Bergson, whose absence from the court I had already noted.

The last witness was the police superintendent, and he, as I had expected, was decidedly reticent. He did refer to the footprints, but, like Foxton – who presumably had his instructions – he abstained from describing their peculiarities. Nor did he say anything about fingerprints. As to the identity of the criminal, that had to be further inquired into. Suspicion had at first fastened upon Bergson, but it had since transpired that the Swede sailed from Ramsgate on an ice-ship two days before the occurrence of the tragedy. Then suspicion had pointed to the husband, who was known to have landed at Liverpool four days before the death of his wife and who had mysteriously disappeared. But he (the superintendent) had only that morning received a telegram from the Liverpool police informing him that the body of Toussaint had been found floating in the Mersey, and that it bore a number of wounds of an apparently homicidal character. Apparently he had been murdered and his corpse thrown into the river.

'This is very terrible,' said the coroner. 'Does this second murder throw any light on the case which we are investigating?'

'I think it does,' replied the officer, without any great conviction, however; 'but it is not advisable to go into details.'

'Quite so,' agreed the coroner. 'Most inexpedient. But are we to understand that you have a clue to the perpetrator of this crime – assuming a crime to have been committed?'

'Yes,' replied Platt. 'We have several important clues.'

'And do they point to any particular individual?'

The superintendent hesitated. 'Well…' he began with some embarrassment, but the coroner interrupted him: 'Perhaps the question is indiscreet. We mustn't hamper the police, gentlemen, and the point is not really material to our inquiry. You would rather we waived that question Superintendent?'

'If you please, sir,' was the emphatic reply.

'Have any cheques from the deceased woman's cheque book been presented at the bank?'

'Not since her death. I inquired at the bank only this morning.'

This concluded the evidence, and after a brief but capable summing-up by the coroner, the jury returned a verdict of 'Wilful murder against some person unknown'.

As the proceedings terminated, Thorndyke rose and turned round, and then to my surprise I perceived Superintendent Miller, of the Criminal Investigation Department, who had come in unperceived by me and was sitting immediately behind us.

'I have followed your instructions, sir,' said he, addressing Thorndyke, 'but before we take any definite action I should like to have a few words with you.'

He led the way to an adjoining room and, as we entered we were followed by Superintendent Platt and Dr Foxton.

'Now, Doctor,' said Miller, carefully closing the door, 'I have carried out your suggestions. Mr Macauley is being detained, but before we commit ourselves to an arrest we must have something to go upon. I shall want you to make out a prima facie case.'

'Very well,' said Thorndyke, laying upon the table the small green suitcase that was his almost invariable companion.

'I've seen that prima facie case before,' Miller remarked with a grin, as Thorndyke unlocked it and drew out a large envelope. 'Now, what have you got there?'

As Thorndyke extracted from the envelope Polton's enlargements of my small photographs, Platt's eyes appeared to bulge, while Foxton gave me a quick glance of reproach.

'These,' said Thorndyke, 'are the full-sized photographs of the footprints of the suspected murderer. Superintendent Platt can probably verify them.'

Rather reluctantly Platt produced from his pocket a pair of whole-plate photographs, which he laid beside the enlargements.

'Yes,' said Miller, after comparing them, 'they are the same footprints. But you say, Doctor, that they are Macauley's footprints. Now, what evidence have you?'

Thorndyke again had recourse to the green case, from which he produced two copper plates mounted on wood and coated with printing ink.

'I propose,' said he, lifting the plates out of their protecting frame, 'that we take prints of Macauley's feet and compare them with the photographs.'

'Yes,' said Platt. 'And then there are the fingerprints that we've got. We can test those, too.'

'You don't want fingerprints if you've got a set of toeprints,' objected Miller.

'With regard to those fingerprints, said Thorndyke. 'May I ask if they were obtained from the bottle?'

'They were,' Platt admitted.

'And were there any other fingerprints?'

'No,' replied Platt. 'These were the only ones.'

As he spoke he laid on the table a photograph showing the prints of the thumb and fingers of a right hand.

Thorndyke glanced at the photograph and, turning to Miller, said: 'I suggest that those are Dr Foxton's fingerprints.'

'Impossible!' exclaimed Platt, and then suddenly fell silent.

'We can soon see,' said Thorndyke, producing from the case a pad of white paper. 'If Dr Foxton will lay the fingertips of his right hand first on this inked plate and then on the paper, we can compare the prints with' the photograph.'

Foxton placed his fingers on the blackened plate and then pressed them on the paper pad, leaving on the latter four beautifully clear, black fingerprints. These Superintendent Platt scrutinised eagerly, and as his glance travelled from the prints to the photographs he broke into a sheepish grin.

'Sold again!' he muttered. 'They are the same prints.'

'Well,' said Miller, in a tone of disgust, 'you must have been a mug not to have thought of that when you knew that Dr Foxton had handled the bottle.'

'The fact, however, is important,' said Thorndyke. 'The absence of any fingerprints but Dr Foxton's not only suggests that the murderer took the precaution to wear gloves, but especially it proves that the bottle was not handled by the deceased during life. A suicide's hands will usually be pretty moist and would leave conspicuous, if not very clear, impressions.'

'Yes,' agreed Miller, 'that is quite true. But with regard to these footprints. We can't compel this man to let us examine his feet without arresting him. Don't think, Dr Thorndyke, that I suspect you of guessing. I've known you too long for that. You've got your facts all right, I don't doubt, but you must let us have enough to justify our arrest.'

Thorndyke's answer was to plunge once more into the inexhaustible green case, from which he now produced two objects wrapped in tissue-paper. The paper being removed, there was revealed what looked like a model of an excessively shabby Pair of brown shoes.

'These,' said Thorndyke, exhibiting the 'models' to Superintendent Miller – who viewed them with an undisguised grin—'are plaster casts of the interiors of a pair of slippers – very old and much too tight-belonging to Mr Macauley. His name was written inside them. The casts have been waxed and painted with raw umber, which has been lightly rubbed off, thus accentuating the prominences and depressions. You will notice that the impressions of the toes on the soles and of the 'knuckles' on the uppers appear as prominences; in fact we have in these casts a sketchy reproduction of the actual feet.

'Now, first as to dimensions. Dr Jervis's measurements of the footprints give us ten inches and three-quarters as, the extreme length and four inches and five-eighths as the extreme width at the heads of the metatarsus. On these casts, as you see, the extreme length is ten inches and five-eighths – the loss of one-eighth being accounted for by the curve of the sole – and the extreme width is four inches and a quarter – three-eighths being accounted for by the lateral compression of a tight slipper. The agreement of the dimensions is remarkable, considering the unusual size. And now as to the peculiarities of the feet.

'You notice that each toe has made a perfectly distinct impression on the sole, excepting the little toe; of which there is no trace in either cast. And, turning to the uppers, you notice that the knuckles of the toes appear quite distinct and prominent – again excepting the little toes, which have made no impression at all. Thus it is not a case of retracted little toes, for they would appear as an extra prominence. Then, looking at the feet as a whole, it is evident that the little toes are absent; there is a distinct hollow, where there should be a prominence.'

'M'yes,' said Miller dubiously, 'it's all very neat. But isn't it just a bit speculative?'

'Oh, come, Miller,' protested Thorndyke; 'just consider the facts. Here is a suspected murderer known to have feet of an unusual size and presenting a very rare deformity; and they are the feet of a man who had actually lived in the same house as the murdered woman and who, at the date of the crime, was living only two doors away. What more would you have?'

'Well, there is the question of motive,' objected Miller.

'That hardly belongs to a prima facie case,' said Thorndyke, 'But even if it did, is there not ample matter for suspicion? Remember who the murdered woman was, what her husband was, and who this Sierra Leone gentleman is.'

'Yes, yes; that's true,' said Miller somewhat hastily, either perceiving the drift of Thorndyke's argument (which I did not), or being unwilling to admit that he was still in the dark. 'Yes, we'll have the fellow in and get his actual footprints.'

He went to the door and, putting his head out, made some sign, which was almost immediately followed by a trampling of feet, and Macauley entered the room, followed by two large plainclothes policemen. The negro was evidently alarmed, for he looked about him with the wild expression of a hunted animal. But his manner was aggressive and truculent.

'Why am I being interfered with in this impertinent manner?' he demanded in the deep buzzing voice characteristic of the male negro.

'We want to have a look at your feet, Mr Macauley,' said Miller. 'Will you kindly take off your shoes and socks?'

'No,' roared Macauley. 'I'll see you damned first!'

'Then,' said Miller, 'I arrest you on a charge of having murdered—'

The rest of the sentence was drowned in a sudden uproar. The tall, powerful negro, bellowing like an angry bull, had whipped out a large, strangely-shaped knife and charged furiously at the Superintendent. But the two plainclothes men had been watching him from behind and now sprang upon him, each seizing an arm. Two sharp, metallic clicks in quick succession, a thunderous crash and an ear-splitting yell, and the formidable barbarian lay prostrate on the floor with one massive constable sitting astride his chest and the other seated on his knees.

'Now's your chance, Doctor,' said Miller. 'I'll get his shoes and socks off.'

As Thorndyke re-inked his plates, Miller and the local superintendent expertly removed the smart patent shoes and the green silk socks from the feet of the writhing, bellowing negro. Then Thorndyke rapidly and skilfully applied the inked plates to the soles of the feet – which I steadied for the purpose-and followed up with a dextrous pressure of the paper pad, first to one foot and then – having torn off the printed sheet-to the other. In spite of the difficulties occasioned by Macauley's struggles, each sheet presented a perfectly clear and sharp print of the sole of the foot, even the ridge-patterns of the toes and ball of the foot being quite distinct. Thorndyke laid each of the new prints on the table beside the corresponding large photograph, and invited the two superintendents to compare them.

'Yes,' said Miller – and Superintendent Platt nodded his acquiescence – 'there can't be a shadow of a doubt. The ink-prints and the photographs are identical, to every line and skin-marking. You've made out your case, Doctor, as you always do.'

'So you see,' said Thorndyke, as we smoked our evening pipes on the old stone pier, 'your method was a perfectly sound one, only you didn't apply it properly. Like too many mathematicians, you started on your calculations before you had secured your data. If you had applied the simple laws of probability to the real data, they would have pointed straight to Macauley.'

'How do you suppose he lost his little toes?' I asked.

'I don't suppose at all. Obviously it was a clear case of double ainhum.'

'Ainhum!' I exclaimed with a sudden flash of recollection.

'Yes; that was what you overlooked, you compared the probabilities of three diseases either of which only very rarely causes the loss of even one little toe and infinitely rarely causes the loss of both, and none of which conditions is confined to any definite class of persons; and you ignored ainhum, a disease which attacks almost exclusively the little toe, causing it to drop off, and quite commonly destroys both little toes – a disease, moreover, which is confined to the black-skinned races. In European practice ainhum is unknown, but in Africa, and to a less extent in India, it is quite common.

'If you were to assemble all the men in the world who have lost both little toes more than nine-tenths of them would be suffering from ainhum; so that, by the laws of probability, your footprints were, by nine chances to one, those of a man who had suffered from ainhum, and therefore a black-skinned man. But as soon as you had established a black man as the probable criminal, you opened up a new field of corroborative evidence. There was a black man on the spot. That man was a native of Sierra Leone and almost certainly a

man of importance there. But the victim's husband had deadly
enemies in the native secret societies of Sierra Leone. The letters of
the husband to the wife probably contained matter incriminating
certain natives of Sierra Leone. The evidence became cumulative, you
see. Taken as a whole, it pointed plainly to Macauley, apart from the
new fact of the murder of Toussaint in Liverpool, a city with a considerable floating population of West Africans.'

'And I gather from your reference to the African poison, strophanthus, that you fixed on Macauley at once when I gave you my
sketch of the case?'

'Yes; especially when I saw your photographs of the footprints
with the absent little toes and those characteristic chigger-scars on the
toes that remained. But it was sheer luck that enabled me to fit the
keystone into its place and turn mere probability into virtual certainty. I could have embraced the magician Wardale when he brought
us the magic slippers. Still, it isn't an absolute certainty, even now,
though I expect it will be by tomorrow.'

And Thorndyke was right. That very evening the police entered
Macauley's chambers in Tanfield Court, where they discovered the
dead woman's attaché-case. It still contained Toussaint's letters to his
wife, and one of those letters mentioned by name, as members of a
dangerous secret society, several prominent Sierra Leone men, including the accused, David Macauley.

SELECT BIBLIOGRAPHY

Melvyn Barnes, *Murder in Print, A Guide to Two Centuries of Crime Fiction* (1986)

Jacques Barzun and Wendell Hertig Taylor, *A Catalogue of Crime* (1971)

TJ Binyon, *Murder Will Out: The Detective in Fiction* (1983)

Michael Cox (ed), *Victorian Tales of Mystery & Detection*(1992)

Hugh Green (ed), *The Rivals of Sherlock Holmes* (1970)

— *More Rivals of Sherlock Holmes* (1971)

— *The Crooked Counties: Further Rivals of Sherlock Holmes* (1973)

Howard Haycraft, *Murder for Pleasure: The Life and Times of the Detective Story* (1942, 1951)

— *The Art of the Mystery Story* (1946)

Allen J Hubin, *Crime Fiction IV: A Comprehensive Bibliography 1749-2000, Volume 4*. CD-ROM (2001)

HRF Keating (ed), *Whodunit? A Guide to Crime, Suspense and Spy Fiction* (1982)

Murphy, Bruce F, *The Encyclopedia of Murder and Mystery* (1999)

Ian Ousby, *Bloodhounds of Heaven: the Detective in English Fiction from Godwin to Doyle* (1976)

Otto Penzler, Chris Steinbrunner and Marvin Lachman (eds), *Detectionary: a Biographical Dictionary of Leading Characters in Detective and Mystery Fiction* (1977)

Chris Steinbrunner and Otto Penzler (eds), *Encyclopedia of Mystery and Detection* (1976)

Julian Symonds, *Bloody Murder: From the Detective Story to the Crime Novel* (1972, revised 1985)

Websites

Crimeculture.com
http://www.crimeculture.com

Michael E Grost,*A Guide to Classic Mystery and Detection*
http://members.aol.com/mg4273/classics.htm

Jess Nevins, *Fantastic Victoriana*
http://www.geocities.com/jessnevins/vicintro.html

The Sherlock Holmes Society of London
http://www.sherlock-holmes.org.uk

THE TEN COMMANDMENTS OF DETECTIVE FICTION

As put forward by Ronald Knox in 1929.

1. The criminal must be mentioned in the early part of the story, but must not be anyone whose thoughts the reader has been allowed to follow.

2. All supernatural or prenatural agencies are ruled out as a matter of course.

3. Not more than one secret room or passage is allowable.

4. No hitherto undiscovered poisons may be used, nor any appliance which will need a long and scientific explanation at the end.

5. No Chinaman must figure in the story.

6. No accident must ever help the detective, nor must he have an unaccountable intuition which proves to be right.

7. The detective himself must not commit the crime.

8. The detective is bound to declare any clues upon which he may happen to light.

9. The stupid friend of the detective, the Watson, must not conceal from the reader any thoughts which pass through his mind; his intelligence must be slightly, but very slightly, below that of the average reader.

10. Twin brothers, and doubles generally, must not appear unless we have been duly prepared for them.

Biographical note: Monsignor Knox (1888-1959) was an author, theologian, and dignitary of the Roman Catholic Church, best known for his translation of the Bible. He also wrote detective novels, the best of them being *Still Dead* (1934).

For information on other books published by The Do-Not Press (including ground-breaking crime fiction by authors such as Ken Bruen, Mark Timlin and Bill James) please visit our website:

www.thedonotpress.com